PENGUIN ENGLISH LIBRARY

GULLIVER'S TRAVELS

JONATHAN SWIFT

Michael Foot, Member of Parliament for Ebbw Vale, was for many years a political columnist and editor of *Tribune*, of which he is now the managing director.

Peter Dixon is a lecturer in English at Queen Mary College, University of London and author of a critical study of Pope's Satires.

John Chalker is a lecturer in English at University College, London.

Jonathan Swift

GULLIVER'S TRAVELS

EDITED BY
PETER DIXON AND
JOHN CHALKER
WITH AN INTRODUCTION
BY MICHAEL FOOT
*

PENGUIN BOOKS

Penguin Books Ltd, Harmondsworth, Middlesex, England
Penguin Books, 625 Madison Avenue, New York, New York 10022, U.S.A.
Penguin Books Australia Ltd, Ringwood, Victoria, Australia
Penguin Books Canada Ltd, 2801 John Street,
Markham, Ontario, Canada L3R 1B4
Penguin Books (N.Z.) Ltd, 182–190 Wairau Road, Auckland 10, New Zealand

—

First published in 1726
Published in Penguin English Library 1967
Reprinted 1968, 1970, 1971, 1972, 1973, 1974, 1975 (twice), 1976, 1977 (twice)

—

Introduction copyright © Michael Foot, 1967
All rights reserved

—

Made and printed in Great Britain
by Richard Clay (The Chaucer Press), Ltd,
Bungay, Suffolk
Set in Monotype Garamond

Contents

TRAVELS INTO SEVERAL REMOTE NATIONS
OF THE WORLD. IN FOUR PARTS.
BY LEMUEL GULLIVER.

Introduction

Gulliver's Travels, like most of the other great books of the world, has been freshly interpreted from age to age. Cherished alongside *Robinson Crusoe* as a children's book, it has, quite unlike *Crusoe*, been the subject of furious debate among historians, philosophers and literary critics. Many of its pages are devoted to direct political satire, but we may safely guess that not one in ten thousand of its appreciative readers is aware of even the most patent particular references. Writers claiming to do no more than appraise its philosophical content have been driven to paroxysms of denunciation. Somehow the foremost exponent of lucidity in the English language has left as his chief legacy a grotesque enigma.

The author protests at the outset that 'the style is very plain and simple'. And so it is. In accordance with his custom, Swift read large chunks aloud to his servants, to make sure that every sentence attained his rigorous standard of simplicity. It is possible, with much enjoyment, to skate over the surface, most of it as smooth as ice, without noticing the dark chasms underneath, and this no doubt is what children do with their expurgated editions. But no one can deceive himself for long. Gentleness, playfulness, irony, finely poised argument and lacerating invectives are so carefully enfolded one within another that it is evident Jonathan Swift created the endless mystery on purpose.

Part One, *A Voyage to Lilliput*, is the fantasy about the giant in the land of midgets told in such unchallengeable, precise, matter-of-fact terms that it has become a household word and idea in every civilized tongue throughout the world. Yet through this section in particular runs a long, weaving stream of topical innuendo about the forgotten politics of the reign of Queen Anne. Part Two, *A Voyage to Brobdingnag*, is Lilliput in reverse, but it also offers some of Swift's fiercest assaults upon the behaviour of his fellow countrymen and the nearest effort he ever made to describe his own notion of an ideal State. Part Three, *A Voyage to Laputa, etc.* is evidently directed against the scientists and philosophers of his own age, but how up to date these gentlemen appear; no less so at least than Beachcomber's Dr Strabismus of Utrecht or characters from Spike Milligan's Goon Show. Part Four, *A Voyage to the Houyhnhms,* has been regarded as a vile or corrective satire on human nature itself, but any attempt to compress its meaning into a sentence becomes an absurdity. In the country of the Houyhnhnms, the ground trembles beneath our feet; a storm beats about our heads; terrifying shafts of light and darkness are thrown backwards across the rest of the book, into every corner of the human mind.

The reader, then, must be warned from the start: *Gulliver's Travels* is a perpetual unfinished argument, one from which flatly contradictory morals have been and still can be extracted. Perhaps one service which a 1967 introduction can do is to indicate how the controversy has proceeded over the past two and a half centuries and what temporary and insecure resting place has now been reached. And let no reader be deterred by the experts from forming his own judgement. On this subject, some of the most eminent authorities have made the most eminent asses of themselves, a development which Swift foresaw and invited. He says in the last chapter that he hopes he may pronounce himself 'an author perfectly blameless, against whom the tribe of answerers, considerers, observers, reflecters, detecters, remarkers, will never be able to find matter for exercising their talents'. By which, of course, he meant the opposite. One of the fascinations of *Gulliver's Travels* is that, although every phrase seems immediately comprehensible, the whole subject matter is endlessly complex.

When the book was published, anonymously, on 28 October 1726, success was instantaneous. One report said that ten thousand copies were sold in three weeks. Immediate translations were made into French and Dutch, weekly journals started printing pirated extracts, and Swift's friends in London competed with one another in dispatching glowing reports to the author in Dublin. Dr John Arbuthnot, the closest friend of all, wrote:

I will make over all my profits to you for the property of Gullivers Travels; which, I believe, will have as great a run as John Bunyan. Gulliver is a happy man, that, at his age [Swift was 59], can write such a merry book.

Alexander Pope and John Gay wrote jointly: 'From the highest to the lowest it is universally read, from the cabinet council to the nursery.' Thus soon was the volume accepted as a classic simultaneously from the cradle to the corridors of power. The old Duchess of Marlborough, once the victim of Swift's harshest abuse, was said to be 'in raptures at it; she says she can dream of nothing else since she read it'. And Swift's own fears were set at rest. He had told Pope a year before that publication would have to wait until 'a printer shall be found brave enough to venture his ears'; in those days authors at odds with the authorities risked the pillory or imprisonment as well as mere poverty. He had warned the publisher, to whom the manuscript was deviously delivered, that some parts of what he had written 'may be thought in one or two places to be a little satirical'. But all was well. No hint of a prosecution, such as had often threatened Swift before in his pamphleteering career, was heard. 'It has passed Lords and Common's *nemine contradicente*; and the whole town, men, women and children are full of it,' was Pope's reassurance. One of the few expressions of protest at the time, heralding what was to follow later, came, curiously, from a member of Swift's intimate circle, Lord Bolingbroke; 'he is the person', continued Pope, 'who least approves it, blaming it as a design of evil consequence to depreciate human nature'. But this might have been no more than a joke at Bolingbroke's expense, comparable with that told of the old gentleman who, when lent the book, was alleged to have gone immediately to his map to search for Lilliput, or of the Bishop who said it was 'full of improbable lies, and, for his part, he hardly believed a word of it'. Pope, the Roman Catholic, and Swift, the militant Church of England or Church of Ireland man, needed no excuse to poke fun at Bolingbroke, and his deistical or even atheistical deviations from the Christian faith. 'A merry book' by a man gay-spirited and greatly loved as well as feared; that was the general view of Swift's contemporaries. Stomachs were stronger in the reigns of Queen Anne and George I.

Fifty years later in his *Lives of the English Poets* Dr Johnson gravely recalled the publication of the already famous volume:

a production so new and strange that it filled the reader with a mingled emotion of merriment and amazement. It was received with such avidity, that the price of the first edition was raised before the second could be made; it was read by high and low, the learned and illiterate. Criticism was for a while lost in wonder; no rules of judgement were applied to a book written in open defiance of truth and regularity.

Thereafter, Johnson applied his own rules. Boswell tells how the assault upon Swift was renewed on all available occasions, despite his own valiant efforts to withstand the deluge of nonsense. Johnson thought that Swift's political writings were inferior to Addison's, that his most brilliant pamphlet, *The Conduct of the Allies*, was a mere bundle of facts, that *Gulliver's Travels* might be assigned to its proper place thus: 'When once you have thought of the big men and little men, it is very easy to do all the rest.' A good Johnsonian joke, maybe, but it still leaves us wondering whether he ever got past the first two books and the disappearance of the big men and the little men.

More insidiously effective, however, than the criticism of Swift's talents was the denigration of his demeanour and character. A man of muddy complexion, of sour and severe countenance, deficient in both wit and humour, one 'who stubbornly resisted any tendency to laughter', was Johnson's summary. The beloved friend of Arbuthnot and Pope, the drinking companion of Addison and Steele, recedes, and a grim twisted specimen begins to take his place. Dr Johnson even recalls, with some relish and too faint repudiation, the false tale that Pope entrusted to his executors a defamatory Life of Swift which he had prepared in advance as an instrument of vengeance to be drawn from its scabbard if provocation arose; the implication being, presumably, that Swift might have savaged Pope or at least that Pope considered him capable of it. The historical evidence is different. Never in our literary annals has there existed between two prominent figures a purer friendship and one so untinged by the slightest strain of jealousy or envy as that which prevailed between Pope and Swift. All Pope's superabundant venom subsided in the presence of Swift, and Swift's devotion, in particular it could be said, never wavered or weakened to the end of his days. Yet the tale-bearers spread lies about Swift's disloyalties, his eccentricities, his furies, his diseased nature, his madness. 'The merry book' was quite forgotten; it had become something sinister. Indeed, the strangest fate overtook Swift's general reputation. When he died in 1745, he had already, in the words of a recent critic, Professor Ricardo Quintana,

ceased to be understood by the eighteenth century. . . . No English writer of corresponding stature has been repudiated so persistently and so fiercely by immediately succeeding generations.

How the change occurred, from the first exultation that the human mind had produced a delight and marvel to such frantic fear or hate, is not easy to discern. Some responsibility may rest with the ineffectualness of Swift's early biographers who purveyed silly gossip about him with ponderous assiduity. But the heaviest burden of guilt must rest on Dr Johnson.

True, ever-growing multitudes of readers continued to read Swift despite Johnson's condemnation of his manners and his morals. True, some years later, a few stray voices were raised openly in his defence – William Godwin, William Cobbett, William Hazlitt. But these were literary no less than political outcasts, quite beyond the pale of the early nineteenth-century literary Establishment; rabid apologists for, if not actual advocates of, revolution after the French style. Defence from that quarter damned Swift more than ever.

Then, in the early decades of the nineteenth century, an additional offence committed by the miscreant was added to the charge sheet, if it had ever been absent. Swift's politics – the truth can be concealed no longer – left much to be desired. He himself had made the confession in playful verse:

> He was an Honest Man, I'll swear –
> Why, Sir, I differ from you there.
> For, I have heard another Story
> He was a most confounded Tory.

The ugly fact did not deter a fellow Tory, Sir Walter Scott, who produced a life and collected works of Swift in 1814. But he, be it noted, could not swallow *Gulliver's Travels*.

Severe, unjust and degrading as this satire is [he wrote], it was hailed with malignant triumph by those whose disappointed hopes had thrown them into the same state of gloomy misanthropy which it argues in its author.

If this was how Swift was to be defended by his political friends, what could he expect from his enemies? Francis Jeffrey, in his *Edinburgh Review* article on Scott's book, made a momentary effort to distinguish between the literary achievement and the character, and then launched into a brilliant libel in which the victim might have been a composite Tory figure of Jeffrey's own age. Macaulay, in 1833, went much farther. He conjured up in one ferocious sentence a vision hard to dispel:

the apostate politician, the ribald priest, the perjured lover, a heart burning with hatred against the whole human race, a mind richly stored with images from the dunghill and the lazar house.

The portrait of the monster was now widely accepted, and, in 1851, Thackeray unloosed an invective which, even when its more flamboyant passages are dismissed as hysterical, leaves no doubt about what had become the settled verdict of Victorian opinion.

Dr Johnson, wrote Thackeray (it was always safe to ride into battle behind that shield),

could not give the Dean that honest hand of his; the stout old man puts it into his breast, and moves off from him. . . . As fierce a beak and talon as ever struck, as strong as ever beat, belonged to Swift. . . . One can gaze, and not without awe and pity, at the lonely eagle chained behind bars. . . . The 'saeva indignatio' of which he spoke as lacerating his heart, and which he dares to inscribe on his tombstone – as if the wretch who lay under that stone waiting God's Judgement had a right to be angry – breaks out from him in a thousand pages of his writing, and tears and rends him . . .

Thus the prelude on Swift's character has prepared the way for the cool appraisal of his book.

Mr Dean has no softness, and enters the nursery with the tread and gaiety of an ogre. . . . Our great satirist was of the opinion that conjugal love was inadvisable, and illustrated the theory by his own practice and example – God help him – which made him about the most wretched being in God's world. . . . As for the humour and conduct of this famous fable, I suppose there is no person who reads but must admire; as for the moral, I think it horrible, shameful, unmanly, blasphemous; and giant and great as this Dean is, I say we should hoot him. . . . It [the fourth book of *Gulliver*] is Yahoo language: a monster, gibbering shrieks and gnashing imprecations against mankind – tearing down all shreds of modesty, past all sense of manliness and shame; filthy in word, filthy in thought, furious, raging, obscene.

And thus – but there is much more of it – in the name of everything the nineteenth century considered holy, Thackeray anticipated the Day of Judgement. The merry book had become a work of the devil.

A few decades later, some lesser figures than Macaulay and Thackeray struggled to retrieve the century's critical reputation. A series of writers attempted the serious work of biography previously neglected and the more they assembled facts in their proper context the more the picture of Swift, the ogre, began to dissolve. Leslie Stephen in his volume (1882) and Churton Collins in his (1893) surveyed the work already done in rectifying glaring injustices, but, even so, both quailed before the later sections of *Gulliver's Travels*. Leslie Stephen called them 'painful and repulsive' and 'a ghastly caricature'.

Readers who wish to indulge in a harmless play of fancy will do well to omit the last two voyages; for the strain of misanthropy which breathes in them is simply oppressive. They are probably the sources from which the popular impression of Swift's character is often derived. It is important therefore to remember that they were wrung from him in later years, after a life tormented by constant disappointment and disease.

Churton Collins's reactions were similar.

It [*Gulliver's Travels*, he wrote,] has no moral, no social, no philosophical purpose. It was the mere ebullition of cynicism and misanthropy. A savage *jeu d'esprit*. And as such wise men will regard it. . . . At no period distinguished by generosity of sentiment, by humanity, by decency, could such satire have been universally applauded. Yet so it was. The men and women of those times appear to have seen nothing objectionable in an apologue which would scarcely have passed without protest in the Rome of Petronius.

So even strong Swift defenders seemed unable to repel the

weight of the attack. Augustine Birrell, reviewing Churton Collins's biography in the 1890s, could write:

It is a question not of morality, but of decency, whether it is becoming to sit in the same room with the works of this divine. ... Thackeray's criticism is severe, but is it not just? Are we to stand by and hear our nature libelled, and our purest affections beslimed, without a word of protest?

Somehow *Gulliver* could not be treated as a book at all: it was unfit for human consumption.

Twenty-five years later, to his credit, Birrell had recovered a sense of proportion. Partly he had been studying Swift's new biographers, although these, as we have seen, were still on the defensive about *Gulliver*. Partly he attributed the conversion to a warm-hearted lecture in defence of Swift, as the enemy of injustice and oppression, delivered by Charles Whibley at Cambridge in 1917. But, more obviously, he himself had been reading – and writing a life of – William Hazlitt, and Hazlitt could have saved all concerned a century of trouble and defamation. For in the year 1818 – exactly a century before Whibley's apologia – Hazlitt had delivered a lecture which both replied to Dr Johnson and leaped forward to adopt a modern view of *Gulliver's Travels*. Little notice was taken of it at the time, except by an unknown John Keats, then twenty-two years old. Leslie Stephen and Churton Collins, disinterring Hazlitt's case as if they had made some recondite discoveries, both acknowledged its force, but found it too extreme for acceptance. It must be pardonable to quote a part of the passage at length and to marvel that Hazlitt, Macaulay, Thackeray and the rest were supposedly talking about the same man and the same book.

Whether the excellence of *Gulliver's Travels* is in the conception or the execution, is of little consequence; the power is somewhere, and it is a power that has moved the world. The power is not that of big words and vaunting common places. Swift left these to those who wanted them; and has done what his acuteness and intensity of mind alone could enable any one to conceive or to perform. His object was to strip empty pride and grandeur of the imposing air which external circumstances throw around them; and for this purpose he has cheated the imagination of the illusions which the prejudices of sense and of the world put upon it, by reducing every thing to the abstract predicament of size. He enlarges or diminishes the scale, as he wishes to shew the insignificance or the grossness of our overweening self-love. That he has done this with mathematical precision, with complete presence of mind and perfect keeping, in a manner that comes equally home to the understanding of the man and of the child, does not take away from the merit of the work or the genius of the author. He has taken a new view of human nature, such as a being of a higher sphere might take of it; he has torn the scales from off his moral vision; he has tried an experiment upon human life, and sifted its pretensions from the alloy of circumstances; he has measured it with a rule, has weighed it in a balance, and found it, for the most part, wanting and worthless – in substance and in shew. Nothing solid, nothing valuable is left in his system but virtue and wisdom. What a libel is this upon mankind! What a convincing proof of misanthropy! What presumption and what *malice prepense*, to shew men what they are, and to teach them what they ought to be! What a mortifying stroke aimed at national glory, is that unlucky incident of Gulliver's wading across the channel and carrying off the whole fleet of Blefuscu! After that, we have only to consider which of the contending parties was in the right. What a shock to personal vanity is given in the account of Gulliver's nurse Glumdalclitch! Still, notwithstanding the disparagement of her personal charms, her good-nature remains the same amiable quality as before. I cannot see the harm, the misanthropy, the immoral and degrading tendency of this. The moral lesson is as fine as the intellectual exhibition is amusing. It is an attempt to tear off the mask of imposture from the world; and nothing but imposture has a right to complain of it.

There! Swift, one feels, would have cheered. At last someone had understood. In the next paragraph, Hazlitt, at the distance of a century, took it upon himself to forgive Swift for having been a Tory, and Swift, if he had read this encomium, would surely have repaid the compliment and forgiven Hazlitt for a lifetime's dedication to his rebel faith. Across the gulf of time and politics, there was a kinship between their spirits, and the common strand runs through *Gulliver's Travels*. Others on the Left in the English political tradition detected the same strand of sympathy while Swift's seemingly more natural political allies were turning aside in horror. In Hazlitt's time there were a few, although none spoke as explicitly as he. Leigh Hunt named his own weekly journal *The Examiner*, after the one Swift had used as his sling and pebbles to overthrow the Duke of Marlborough. William Cobbett at the age of fourteen paid threepence for a copy of *A Tale of a Tub* and prized it as his dearest possession; it is well-nigh certain that he was an almost equally avid student of *Gulliver*. William Godwin, the mentor of Shelley, of Hazlitt himself, and of the long, honourable theme of English anarchism, found in the book 'a more profound insight into the true principles of political justice than in any preceding or contemporary author'! And coming to our own century, to the period of the so-called Whibley revaluation, it is curious that Birrell did not take into account an essay by H. W. Nevinson far more telling than Whibley's and written some years earlier. Nevinson, the rebel and the intimate friend of rebels, like Hazlitt, recognized Swift as one of the same tribe. The rebel streak was not the whole of Swift, but it was part of him.

It was not [wrote Nevinson] any spirit of hatred or cruelty but an intensely personal sympathy with suffering, that tore his heart and kindled that furnace of indignation against the stupid, the hateful and the cruel to whom most suffering is due; and it was a furnace in which he himself was consumed. Writing while he was still a youth in *A Tale of a Tub*, he composed a terrible sentence, in which all his rage and pity and ironical bareness of style seem foretold: 'Last week,' he says, 'I saw a woman flayed, and you will hardly believe how much it altered her person for the worse.'

How has it ever been possible to think that the man who wrote those words lacked a heart, and could anyone but the author of *Gulliver* have written them?

The man and the book; the two become inextricable, however open to objection such a method of judgement may be. It is peculiarly difficult to discuss Swift's writings, insists F. R. Leavis, without shifting the focus of discussion to the kind of man that Swift was.

For instance, one may (it appears), having offered to discuss the nature and import of Swift's satire find oneself countering imputations of misanthropy with the argument that Swift earned the love of Pope, Arbuthnot, Gay, several other men and two women; this should not be found necessary by the literary critic.

Yet it is doubtful whether Dr Leavis abides by his own rule. Having reached the conclusion that Swift's greatness 'is no matter of moral grandeur or human centrality; our sense is merely a sense of great force', he adds: 'And this force, as we feel it, is conditioned by frustration and constriction: the channels of life have been blocked and perverted.' The man-monster peeps out again, and before proceeding farther it must be discovered how valid the apparition may be. Was *Gulliver's Travels*, or at least the Voyage to the Houyhnhnms, the product of a perverted, diseased mind? Was Swift a gloomy misanthrope who never laughed, a tormented hater of all men and, more particularly, all women, consumed at last in the furnace of his own fury? Did he, in short, go mad? 'The odds are', we have recently been told on the medical authority of Mr Malcolm Muggeridge, a delighted and delightful admirer of Swift, 'that the illness which finally struck him down was G.P.I., doubtless due to syphilis, contracted when he was young and addicted to what he called low company.' Maybe literary critics should not be concerned with such trifles. But, if the author did in truth go mad, it would be hard to deny that some support is given to the Johnson, even the Thackeray, view of the book.

Swift, it must be acknowledged, has offered much testimony against himself. Someone called him justly an inverted hypocrite because he often seemed to paint himself in undeservedly harsh colours. 'I shall be like that tree, I shall die at the top,' he said, and the prophecy has been quoted a hundred times, out of context, as a key to his personality. 'Principally I hate and detest that animal called man . . .' runs another half sentence. He bequeathed his small fortune to found an asylum in Dublin and wrote the famous lines on his own death:

> He gave the little wealth he had,
> To build a House for Fools and Mad.
> And shew'd by one Satyric Touch,
> No nation needed it so much.

Have we not here intimations of his sympathy for those who suffered his own fate? He resented his enforced exile in Ireland and talked of dying 'in a rage, like a poisoned rat in a hole'. There is, alas, plentiful evidence from various witnesses of the scarcely endurable pains and miseries which bore him to the grave. Is all this, then, – plus the horrific passages of *Gulliver's Travels* – not enough to clinch the case?

It is not, and nothing like it. Absolute certainty, one way or another, is necessarily not available, but most of the evidence that does exist strongly suggests that Swift did *not* go mad, and that the story of an appalling end compounded of rage, violence and fatuity was a myth adopted and disseminated by Dr Johnson. This is no place to scrutinize the known facts in detail, but that has been done by one of Britain's most distinguished brain neurologists, Sir Walter Russell Brain, now Lord Brain, and by Professor Irvin Ehrenpreis in his book *The Personality of Jonathan Swift*. There seems to be no reason to dissent, or rather no means of escape, from Dr Ehrenpreis's conclusion:

Swift, from birth to death, was insane by no medical definition. He was no more eccentric or neurotic than Pope or Johnson, and probably less so. The tradition of his madness has been rejected for forty years by every qualified scholar who has bothered to look into the question.

As for the verses on his own death now cited as an illustration of Swift's awareness of his own fate, no claim could be more ludicrous. They were written some thirteen years before his death, long before the first time when the most virulent of his enemies has thought to suggest that he showed signs of insanity. To argue, even to hint, that they reveal a premonition of madness is to wrench four from the 486 most cheerful lines Swift ever wrote. It might indeed be the shortest cure for those who still talk of Swift's madness – better even than Lord Brain's diagnoses or Dr Ehrenpreis's scholarship – to compel them to read the verses on the Death of Dr Swift right through. They have some claim to be the gayest poem in the English language.

What in any case has this interminable two-and-a-half-century-old debate about the last few years of Swift's life to do with *Gulliver*? 'A man's life', wrote Hazlitt in another connexion, 'is his whole life, not the last glimmering snuff of the candle.' If Swift had gone mad in the last years, here would have been a sufficient retort. For *Gulliver's Travels* was published about twenty years before Swift's death; it was mostly written earlier still; the especially offensive voyage to the Houyhnhnms, the scholars reckon, was not the last part of the book to be compiled. It is just not true, as even the appreciative Leslie Stephen had inferred, that the last chapters were the outpouring of 'a diseased condition of his mind, perhaps of actual mental decay'. When he finished the book Swift was fifty-eight years old, still fully active, in complete possession of his faculties. If what he produced then, by far the most ambitious literary achievement of his life, was morbid and demonic, then the whole man was morbid and demonic.

And such is often still the claim which must now be considered.

Yet, before proceeding, the vigilant may observe that even an attempted answer to one teasing, personal question has been omitted. What of the perjured, syphilitic lover? Is nothing to be said of the treacherous or impotent suitor of Stella and Vanessa, not to mention two more shadowy beauties, Varina and Betty Jones, and not to forget Mr Muggeridge's low company? Alas, these mysteries must remain mysteries. Swift, for all his devotion to truth, could be defensive and secretive. He insisted upon his independence and privacy, even to his lifelong companion, Stella. The nearest we can come to intimacy with him is through his letters to her ('diurnal trifles', as Dr Johnson called them), and yet these cover only a few years of his life and all but the most oblique reference to Vanessa is excluded from them. The enigma of Swift's love life is so enticing and tantalizing that the endless effort to unravel it is bound to go on. In my belief the best and most comprehensive theory which at least fits the known facts and does not, like the syphilis theory, defy them, is provided by Denis Johnston in his *In Search of Swift*. But this and all other theories, supported with whatever scholarship, are far removed from anything which can be called proof. That, almost certainly, we shall never have. *Gulliver's Travels* must be judged without the aid of Stella's secret.

Thackeray talked as if it were Swift's treatment of the divine Stella which stirred him to his highest pitch of fury: surely a combined piece of impertinence and vanity, if ever there was one, since he, like the rest of us, did not know the intimate details of Swift's relationship with the apparently uncomplaining Stella and since we are obviously intended to admire the gallantry with which Thackeray rushes to her aid. But Stella or Vanessa or anyone else, male or female, whom Swift is alleged to have used badly, serves the same purpose – to feed the insensate hostility which he beyond all other great writers seems to provoke. His enemies can catch him either way: either he wrote *Gulliver* because he was mad, or *Gulliver* is there to prove how mad he was. Some of his more recent and reputable critics can admit his qualities, as if they were making a grudging confession, or accuse him of vices which seem the exact opposite of those which could ever be attributed to him. George Orwell, for example, accepts that Swift was 'a diseased writer' and that he solved his dilemmas by blowing everything to pieces in the only way open to him, that is, by going mad, and then cudgels his brain to discover how a man with 'a world view which only just passes the test of sanity' can still have such appeal to so many, himself included. He offers no sufficient answer, and given the diseased mind as the unalterable factor in the situation, the failure is not surprising; men do not gather grapes of thorns and figs of thistles. Aldous Huxley is even more startling. He accused Swift of being an incurable sentimentalist and romantic, one who resented the world of reality and would never dare face it. And Dr Leavis concludes that 'he certainly does not impress us as a mind in possession of its experience'. These, from three such powerful and independent minds, seem the oddest conclusions. Surely the author of *Gulliver*, whatever else he was doing, was consciously compressing his whole life into one book and stripping aside all sentimental impurities.

George Orwell's essay, however, offers some useful signposts to other conclusions. 'Why is it,' he asks, 'that we don't mind being called Yahoos although firmly convinced that we are not Yahoos?' His own reply is unconvincing, and perhaps a better one is that Swift does *not* call us Yahoos; Lemuel Gulliver does, but he is not Swift. Orwell also remarks, as others have done, how dreary is the ideal world of the Houyhnhnms. 'Swift did his best for the Houyhnhnms,' says Dr Leavis, 'and they may have all the reason, but the Yahoos have all the life.' This undeniable effect of the last book in *Gulliver* is commonly attributed to the failure of all writers to produce a tolerable ideal. All Utopias are too dull to be lived in; the perfection, the immobility, become suffocating. But suppose Swift knew that as well as, or better than, we. Suppose he intended the ideal world to be dreary, its inhabitants too good to be true. Suppose he wanted those who might rise above that brutish Yahoo level to be quite endearing creatures, despite their assortment of obvious defects. Suppose it was his purpose to expose the insufficiency and the insipidity of the Augustan virtues of Reason, Truth and Nature which the Houyhnhnms allegedly exemplify. Suppose the Houyhnhnms are not the heroes and heroines of the book. Suppose (and a fair hint of it is given in the last chapter of the *Voyage to the Houyhnhnms*) it is the wise and humane and 'least corrupted' Brobdingnagians and their kind-hearted king who represent Swift's positive standard for erring man. Suppose in short that *Gulliver's Travels* is not the work of some indefinable demon operating in the decaying carcase of the famous Dean of St Patrick's but the deliberate contrivance of his intense, luminous, compassionate mind.

The view crudely summarized in these suppositions is expounded at length with something approaching Swiftian grace and lucidity in the book *Jonathan Swift and the Age of Compromise* by Miss Kathleen Williams. It is fortified in the conclusions reached by Professor Irvin Ehrenpreis in *The Personality of Jonathan Swift* and the three-volume Life on which he is now engaged.

Swift [insists Miss Williams] refuses to simplify; as a moral being and a political being man is a complex creature, and only a process of compromise can produce in any sphere a state of things which will do justice to his complexity.

She makes a startling comparison between Swift and Montaigne, and at first thought any alleged common characteristics between the two may seem absurd. How can the meandering ruminations of Montaigne be likened to Swift's fierce polemical thrust? But she notes how Montaigne must have been one of Swift's favourites; 'your old prating friend' was Boling-broke's taunt.

Both search among ideas, rather than assert ideas [writes Miss Williams], feeling their way among a multiplicity of conflicting and assertive doctrines . . . but for Swift the search is a thing of urgency, and he cannot exist calmly in the life of suspense.

It is tempting to lift one quotation after another from her book, especially as she sees the *Voyage of the Houyhnhnms* as summing up all Swift's writing, the most complete expression of his moral, political and social outlook. But since her views are complex to match Swift's, quotations impair the complete effect. One may be given, since it offers a fresh approach to the perpetually changing interpretation of *Gulliver's Travels*:

Our first impression, in Swift's work [she writes], is of the elusive brilliance of the attack; a glancing, dazzling mind appears to be concerned solely with the presentation of absurdity or of evil, shifting its point of view constantly the better to perform its task. But as we grow accustomed to his ways of thinking and feeling we become aware that at the heart of Swift's work are unity and con-sistency, and we see that the attack is also a defence, that tools of destruction are being employed for a positive and constructive purpose. The inventiveness and resourcefulness of his satiric method is seen as arising directly out of the necessities of his mind and of his age: the changing complications of his irony are the necessary expression of an untiring devotion to the few certainties that life affords. For all his elusiveness and indirection, his readiness to compromise or change his ground, few writers have been more essentially consistent than Swift, but for him consistency could be sustained only by such methods as these. Balance in the state or in the individual mind could be kept only by an agile shifting of weights.

It may be added that there is nothing accidental in Miss Williams's return to the estimate Swift's contemporaries made of him, for her method is to discover and describe the exact context in which he wrote.

Swift, then, as a militant Montaigne! One can almost hear the snort of derision from Dr Johnson or Dr Leavis. Pope, Gay, Arbuthnot and Bolingbroke might have found it easier to recognize the likeness. They knew how sane he was and how cheerful he could be, and did he not write to them about *Gulliver* and say:

I desire you and all my friends will take a special care that my dis-affection to the world may not be imputed to my age. . . . I tell you after all, that I do not hate mankind: it is *vous autres* who hate them, because you would have them reasonable animals, and are angry for being disappointed.

Swift's scepticism never went so far as Montaigne's. His pessimism about man and his sinful nature and the possibilities of improvement by human effort stayed close to that of ortho-dox Christianity. But it did not reach the depths of black despair which is supposed to have issued in his madness, nor did it prevent him from declaiming, denouncing, preach-ing and exhorting with all his skill and might, occupations which certainly would have been senseless if man's condition were incurable. No one indeed has ever lashed the brutalities and bestialities which men inflict upon one another with a greater intensity. He loathed cruelty. He was enraged by the attempts of one nation to impose its will on another which we call imperialism. He exposed, as never before or since, the crimes committed in the name of a strutting, shouting patriot-ism. He had a horror of state tyranny and, as George Orwell has underlined, an uncanny presentiment of totalitarianism and all the torture it would brand on body and mind. Above all, he hated war and the barbarisms it let loose. War, for him, embraced all other forms of agony and wickedness. *Gulliver's Travels* is still the most powerful of pacifist pamphlets. And, of course, it is these aspects of his iconoclasm which have won for him persistent allegiance on the Left. Yet the truth remains that his general tone was conservative; that he eagerly resisted innovations; that he revered the past and seemed only to envisage or approve a static society; that the climax of his book is an attack on the deadly sin of pride, a sermon which established church and state are always inclined to applaud since it helps to induce obedience. Humble revolutionaries rarely change anything.

Yes, the hard impeachment cannot be denied: the fellow *was* a Tory. Yet we may join with Hazlitt in his handsome act of forgiveness; for, first, it is only charitable to remember that in those far-off days the Tories were the peace party and, second, the Left is offered a priceless compensation. No one can read *Gulliver's Travels* without at some point feeling a whip across his own back; no single sinner escapes. But it is arrogant, self-satisfied, savage, corrupt and corrupting *power* which comes off worst. It is not surprising that Hazlitt, Cobbett, Leigh Hunt and Godwin, in the midst of another great war when spies and informers were at work in the interests of exorbitant authority, in the age of the press gang and Peterloo, treasured *Gulliver's Travels* as a seditious tract. It spoke the truth at that hour called high treason. It sounded the trumpet of anarchistic revolt when others who did so were being dispatched to Botany Bay. It assailed the Establishment, Whig and Tory (what Cobbett called 'The Thing'), and reduced the whole pretentious bunch to their proper stature. Small wonder that stout patriots like Dr Johnson, Sir Walter Scott, Macaulay and the rest, found the meat too strong for them. But they might, in their various epochs, have hit upon a more creditable retort than merely to call the man mad. Not even we today, in the twentieth century, regard a hatred of slavery, oppression and war as infallible signs of insanity.

*

Swift's philosophy, whatever it may be, forms only one part of *Gulliver's Travels*. The book is stuffed with personal, literary and political allusions. On every page there are more or less abstruse references which had a special meaning for the readers of Swift's own age. Many of these references are explained in the Notes at the end of this edition, but some of the major ones perhaps require some comment here. In the first book, Lilliput and its diminutive political figures represent England, Blefuscu is France, Flimnap, the Treasurer, is Swift's old enemy, Sir Robert Walpole, whereas Gulliver, for the most part, is Swift's old friend, Bolingbroke, who made the Peace of Utrecht with the French and then was shamefully exiled by an ungrateful nation. The well-known scene where Gulliver puts out the fire in the Emperor's palace by pissing on it was once thought to portray Swift's service to the English Church when he wrote *A Tale of a Tub*. That book was devoted to the Church's cause but in such a style that Queen Anne was scandalized and vowed ever after to refuse its author a bishopric. Recently, however, the interpretation has changed. It is now argued, more plausibly, that the incident represents the stopping of the terrible war against France by unavoidable methods, however deplorable. And this one example indicates the continuous debate which the detailed interpretation of *Gulliver* involves. It is a specialized, fascinating indoor sport, requiring not merely a knowledge of all the twists and turns in English (and Irish) politics in the first quarter of the eighteenth century but also a proof of which particular sections of this knowledge were available to Swift at each stage in the proceedings. Second only to chess, it is the best game I know. Variations are infinite; there is always something new to learn. But, as with chess too, participation is possible at quite different levels. *Gulliver* can be enjoyed by those who know nothing of openings and gambits. It is not necessary to be at home in the political and social merry-go-round of Queen Anne, to know at first hand that distant world of treason and war, of intrigue and apostasy, of power-crazed soldiers and sinewy politicians. It is enough to have watched courts and court favourites at work in twentieth-century London, to have marked the conduct of men and women in the age of Passchendaele and Stalin's trials, of Auschwitz and Hiroshima.

Some references may remain obscure. Modern readers may pause to wonder why Swift should have digressed so extra-vagantly to introduce the doctors who invent imaginary cures for imaginary diseases; the lawyers who record all the decisions formerly made against common justice in order that they may be applied again; the ministers who achieve high office by a furious zeal in public assemblies against the corruptions of the court; the young noblemen who consume their vigour and contract odious diseases among lewd females in their youth but yet retain the authority to ensure which laws should be enacted, repealed or not altered without their consent; the mem-bers of the House of Commons who are so violently bent to serve the nation in that assembly, despite the great trouble and expense, often to the ruin of their families. But such lapses are rare. The whole maze may be explored, the whole panorama may be surveyed, without a guide. Soon even the amateur Swiftian scholar will be conducting his own researches and making his own discoveries.

For example, I invite attention to be directed to Chapter III of the *Voyage to Laputa*. The merit of the Voyage, by the way, has sometimes been shamefully depreciated, the bad fashion being set by Dr Arbuthnot, who, despite his love for Swift, possibly found the attack on the medical profession too near the bone. Anyhow, Laputa contains many varied treasures, including the two best sentences ever written in the whole literature of comedy which I now inscribe here, or rather roll round my tongue, without purpose or apology:

He had been eight years upon a project for extracting sunbeams out of cucumbers, which were to be put into vials hermetically sealed, and let out to warm the air in raw inclement summers. He told me, he did not doubt in eight years more, that he should be able to supply the Governor's gardens with sunshine at a reasonable rate; but he complained that his stock was low, and entreated me to give him something as an encouragement to ingenuity, especially since this had been a very dear season for cucumbers.

Could the man who wrote that really be a humourless monster? Certainly he has left behind him a trail of crazy speculation. For me, ever since, cucumbers have become a more glamorous vegetable, English summers can be borne, and I can never inquire the price without a rapid calculation of the Governor's chances of getting his sunshine. At least, in this age of plastics, those vials should be cheaper. But now consider the theme even more serious and topical than the cost of living, dealt with in Chapter III. If the story of the king and his ingenious scientists, who invented an all-conquering contraption which could only be used at the price of blasting all Laputa to kingdom come, is not a prophecy of the H-bomb, I will eat my academic hat and surrender my literary critic's cloak altogether.

MICHAEL FOOT

Selected Bibliography

CASE, A. E., *Four Essays on 'Gulliver's Travels'* (Princeton University Press: Oxford University Press, 1947).

EDDY, W. A., *'Gulliver's Travels': A Critical Study* (Peter Smith, Mass., 1923).

EHRENPREIS, I., *Swift: the Man, his Works and the Age: Volume I: Mr Swift and his Contemporaries* (Methuen, 1962). Volumes II and III are in progress.

FOSTER, M. P., (ed.) *A Casebook on Gulliver amoung the Houyhnhnms* (Thomas Y. Crowell Co., N.Y., 1961).

QUINTANA, R., *The Mind and Art of Jonathan Swift* (Methuen, 2nd edn, 1953).

TUVESON, E., (ed.) *Swift: A Collection of Critical Essays* (Prentiss-Hall Inc., N.J., 1964).

VOIGHT, M., *Swift and the Twentieth Century* (Wayne State University Press, Detroit, 1964).

WILLIAMS, K., *Jonathan Swift and the Age of Compromise* (Constable, 1959).

A Note on the Text

THE textual history of *Gulliver's Travels*, like almost every-thing else about the book, is far from straightforward. In August 1726 'Richard Sympson' offered the first instalment of the manuscript to a London publisher, Benjamin Motte, who reacted with gratifying speed (the two volumes of *Travels* appeared on 28 October), but also with alarming disrespect for the author's intentions. Swift was understandably indig-nant when he discovered the many liberties which Motte had taken. The satire on the legal profession, on the House of Hanover, on the treatment of the Irish, had been damped down, or simply omitted, and Motte had inserted a eulogy of Queen Anne in order to counterbalance the devastating attack on 'a *First* or *Chief Minister of State*' (Part IV, Chapter 6). At Swift's direction his friend Charles Ford wrote to the publisher in January 1727, requesting that the paragraph about Queen Anne be withdrawn, complaining of the 'many gross Errors of the Press', and listing fifty of them. In his 'corrected' edition (May 1727), Motte made most of the required minor improvements, and introduced a few plausible emendations of his own; the corrupted passages, however, remained corrupt.

Meanwhile Ford entered the corrections, together with several new readings, in at least two copies of the first edition; he also inserted the passages which Motte had omitted, and restored those he had tampered with. One of these carefully prepared copies (probably that now in the Forster Collection, South Kensington) formed the basis of the *Gulliver's Travels* which was published in Dublin, as Volume III of Swift's *Works*, by George Faulkner. (This edition is dated 1735; it appeared, in fact, in November 1734.) Although Swift professed indifference to the whole of Faulkner's venture, he took this opportunity to revise and retouch the text, making numerous stylistic improvements, and deleting two short passages towards the end of Part IV. The prefatory Letter from Gulliver to Sympson, which publicly rebukes Motte for having mangled the text, may well have been specially prepared for the new edition, in spite of its being dated 1727. Yet the author's wishes were still not entirely respected. On a few occasions Faulkner preferred the mild reading of Motte to the more acid correction of Ford's copy, and like Motte he omitted, presumably from motives of political prudence, the account of the Lindalinian rebellion (Part III, Chapter 3). Moreover, Swift would not have concerned himself with small details of style and presentation, which were then, much more than today, at the printer's discretion. So that while Faulkner gave back to Swift's topical satire most of its original cutting edge, he imposed on the whole work a degree of formality and consistency which Swift's manuscript is unlikely to have possessed.

Motte's 1726 text, for all its glaring deficiencies, is relatively free from this kind of editorial sophistication, and has therefore been accepted as the starting-point for the present edition. I have incorporated into it all the minor corrections supplied by Ford, except those few about which Swift himself seems to have had second thoughts in 1734; all Ford's major restorations, as they appear in the Forster Library copy, but again with Swift's 1734 repolishings; and, finally, those new readings in Faulkner's edition for which Swift may be presumed to be responsible. Four emendations have been adopted from Motte's 1727 edition, and one from a later Faulkner edition. Two small emendations have been made in order to avoid a chronological discrepancy at the end of Part III, and a geographical one at the end of Part IV. The punctuation follows, as closely as is practicable, that of 1726. Typography and spelling have been modernized, but archaic words, such as *hautboys*, *sprites*, *uncapable*, have been retained.

Queen Mary College, London   PETER DIXON

TRAVELS INTO
SEVERAL REMOTE NATIONS
OF THE WORLD
IN FOUR PARTS
BY LEMUEL GULLIVER

Title-page of the First Edition, 1726

TRAVELS

INTO SEVERAL

Remote Nations

OF THE

WORLD.

IN FOUR PARTS.

By *LEMUEL GULLIVER*,
first a Surgeon, and then a Captain
of several SHIPS.

VOL. I.

LONDON:

Printed for Benj. Motte, *at the Middle*
Temple-Gate *in* Fleet-street.
M, DCC, XXVI.

A Letter from Capt. Gulliver, to his Cousin Sympson [1]

I HOPE you will be ready to own publicly, whenever you shall be called to it, that by your great and frequent urgency you prevailed on me to publish a very loose and uncorrect account of my travels; with direction to hire some young gentlemen of either University to put them in order, and correct the style, as my cousin Dampier [2] did by my advice, in his book called *A Voyage round the World*. But I do not remember I gave you power to consent, that anything should be omitted, and much less that anything should be inserted: therefore, as to the latter, I do here renounce everything of that kind; particularly a paragraph about her Majesty the late Queen Anne, [3] of most pious and glorious memory; although I did reverence and esteem her more than any of human species. But you, or your interpolator, ought to have considered, that as it was not my inclination, so was it not decent to praise any animal of our composition before my master Houyhnhnm: and besides, the fact was altogether false; for to my knowledge, being in England during some part of her Majesty's reign, she did govern by a chief Minister; nay, even by two successively; the first whereof was the Lord of Godolphin, [4] and the second the Lord of Oxford; [5] so that you have made me *say the thing that was not*. Likewise, in the account of the Academy of Projectors, and several passages of my discourse to my master Houyhnhnm, you have either omitted some material circumstances, or minced or changed them in such a manner, that I do hardly know mine own work. [6] When I formerly hinted to you something of this in a letter, you were pleased to answer, that you were afraid of giving offence; that people in power were very watchful over the press, and apt not only to interpret, but to punish everything which looked like an *innuendo* (as I think you called it). But pray, how could that which I spoke so many years ago, and at above five thousand leagues distance, in another reign, be applied to any of the Yahoos who now are said to govern the herd; especially at a time when I little thought on or feared the unhappiness of living under them? Have not I the most reason to complain, when I see these very Yahoos carried by Houyhnhnms in a vehicle, as if these were brutes, and those the rational creatures? And, indeed, to avoid so monstrous and detestable a sight, was one principal motive of my retirement hither.

Thus much I thought proper to tell you in relation to yourself, and to the trust I reposed in you.

I do in the next place complain of my own great want of judgment, in being prevailed upon by the entreaties and false reasonings of you and some others, very much against mine own opinion, to suffer my Travels to be published. Pray bring to your mind how often I desired you to consider, when you insisted on the motive of *public good*, that the Yahoos were a species of animals utterly incapable of amendment by precepts or examples: and so it hath proved; for instead of seeing a full stop put to all abuses and corruptions, at least in this little island, as I had reason to expect: behold, after above six months' warning, I cannot learn that my book hath produced one single effect according to mine intentions: I desired you would let me know by a letter, when party and faction were extinguished; judges learned and upright; pleaders honest and modest, with some tincture of common sense; and Smithfield[7] blazing with pyramids of law-books; the young nobility's education entirely changed; the physicians banished; the female Yahoos abounding in virtue, honour, truth and good sense; Courts and levees of great Ministers thoroughly weeded and swept; wit, merit and learning rewarded; all disgracers of the press in prose and verse, condemned to eat nothing but their own cotton,[8] and quench their thirst with their own ink. These, and a thousand other reformations, I firmly counted upon by your encouragement; as indeed they were plainly deducible from the precepts delivered in my book. And, it must be owned, that seven months were a sufficient time to correct every vice and folly to which Yahoos are subject; if their natures had been capable of the least disposition to virtue or wisdom: yet so far have you been from answering mine expectation in any of your letters, that on the contrary you are loading our carrier every week with Libels, and Keys,[9] and Reflections, and Memoirs, and Second Parts; wherein I see myself accused of reflecting upon great states-folk; of degrading human nature (for so they have still the confidence to style it), and of abusing the female sex. I find likewise, that the writers of those bundles are not agreed among themselves; for some of them will not allow me to be author of mine own Travels; and others make me author of books to which I am wholly a stranger.[10]

I find likewise, that your printer hath been so careless as to confound the times,[11] and mistake the dates of my several voyages and returns; neither assigning the true year, or the true month, or day of the month: and I hear the original manuscript is all destroyed, since the publication of my book. Neither have I any copy left; however, I have sent you some corrections, which you may insert, if ever there should be a second edition: and yet I cannot stand to them, but shall leave that matter to my judicious and candid readers, to adjust it as they please.

I hear some of our sea-Yahoos find fault with my sea-language, as not proper in many parts, nor now in use. I cannot help it. In my first voyages, while I was young, I was instructed by the oldest mariners, and learned to speak as they did. But I have since found that the sea-Yahoos are apt, like the land ones, to become new-fangled in their words; which the latter change every year; insomuch, as I remember upon each return to mine own country, their old dialect was so altered, that I could hardly understand the new. And I observe, when any Yahoo comes from London out of curiosity to visit me at mine own house, we neither of us are able to deliver our conceptions in a manner intelligible to the other.

If the censure of Yahoos could any way affect me, I should have great reason to complain, that some of them are so bold as to think my book of Travels a mere fiction out of mine own brain; and have gone so far as to drop hints, that the Houyhnhnms and Yahoos have no more existence than the inhabitants of Utopia.

Indeed I must confess, that as to the people of Lilliput, Brobdingrag (for so the word should have been spelt, and not erroneously 'Brobdingnag'), and Laputa; I have never yet heard of any Yahoo so presumptuous as to dispute their being, or the facts I have related concerning them; because the truth immediately strikes every reader with conviction. And, is there less probability in my account of the Houyhnhnms or Yahoos, when it is manifest as to the latter, there are so many thousands even in this city, who only differ from their brother brutes in Houyhnhnmland, because they use a sort of a *jabber*, and do not go naked? I wrote for their amendment, and not their approbation. The united praise of the whole race would be of less consequence to me, than the neighing of those two degenerate Houyhnhnms I keep in my stable; because, from these, degenerate as they are, I still improve in some virtues, without any mixture of vice.

Do these miserable animals presume to think that I am so far degenerated as to defend my veracity? Yahoo as I am, it is well known through all Houyhnhnmland, that by the instructions and example of my illustrious master, I was able in the compass of two years (although I confess with the utmost difficulty) to remove that infernal habit of lying, shuffling, deceiving, and equivocating, so deeply rooted in the very souls of all my species; especially the Europeans.

I have other complaints to make upon this vexatious occasion; but I forbear troubling myself or you any further. I must freely confess, that since my last return, some corruptions of my Yahoo nature have revived in me by conversing with a few of your species, and particularly those of mine own family, by an unavoidable necessity; else I should never have attempted so absurd a project as that of reforming the Yahoo race in this kingdom; but, I have now done with all such visionary schemes for ever.

April 2, 1727.

The Publisher to the Reader

THE author of these Travels, Mr Lemuel Gulliver, is my ancient and intimate friend; there is likewise some relation between us by the mother's side. About three years ago, Mr Gulliver, growing weary of the concourse of curious people coming to him at his house in Redriff,¹ made a small purchase of land, with a convenient house, near Newark in Nottinghamshire, his native country; where he now lives retired, yet in good esteem among his neighbours.

Although Mr Gulliver were born in Nottinghamshire, where his father dwelt, yet I have heard him say, his family came from Oxfordshire; to confirm which, I have observed in the churchyard at Banbury, in that county, several tombs and monuments of the Gullivers.

Before he quitted Redriff, he left the custody of the following papers in my hands, with the liberty to dispose of them as I should think fit. I have carefully perused them three times: the style is very plain and simple; and the only fault I find is, that the author, after the manner of travellers, is a little too circumstantial. There is an air of truth apparent through the whole; and indeed the author was so distinguished for his veracity, that it became a sort of proverb among his neighbours at Redriff, when anyone affirmed a thing, to say, it was as true as if Mr Gulliver had spoke it.

By the advice of several worthy persons, to whom, with the author's permission, I communicated these papers, I now venture to send them into the world, hoping they may be, at least, for some time, a better entertainment to our young noblemen, than the common scribbles of politics and party.

This volume would have been at least twice as large, if I had not made bold to strike out innumerable passages relating to the winds and tides, as well as to the variations and bearings in the several voyages; together with the minute descriptions of the management of the ship in storms, in the style of sailors: likewise the account of the longitudes and latitudes; wherein I have reason to apprehend that Mr Gulliver may be a little dissatisfied: but I was resolved to fit the work as much as possible to the general capacity of readers. However, if my own ignorance in sea-affairs shall have led me to commit some mistakes, I alone am answerable for them: and if any traveller hath a curiosity to see the whole work at large, as it came from the hand of the author, I shall be ready to gratify him.

As for any further particulars relating to the author, the reader will receive satisfaction from the first pages of the book.

RICHARD SYMPSON.

The Contents

PART III

A VOYAGE TO LAPUTA, BALNIBARBI,
GLUBBDUBDRIB, LUGGNAGG, AND
JAPAN

PART IV

A VOYAGE TO THE COUNTRY OF THE
HOUYHNHNMS

CHAP. 1. The author sets out as captain of a ship. His men conspire against him, confine him a long time to his cabin, set him on shore in an unknown land. He travels up into the country. The Yahoos a strange

CONTENTS

TRAVELS · PART I

A VOYAGE TO LILLIPUT

*

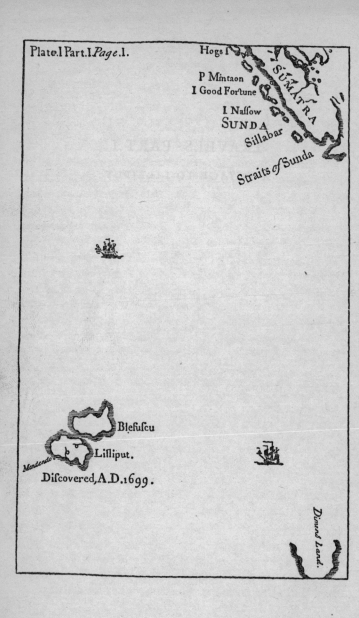

Plate.I Part.I *Page*.I.

Hogs I

SUMATRA

P Mintaon
I Good Fortune

I Nassow
SUNDA
Sillabar

Straits *of* Sunda

Blefuscu

Mendendo

Lilliput.

Discovered, A.D. 1699.

Dimens Land.

CHAPTER I

The author giveth some account of himself and family, his first inducements to travel. He is shipwrecked, and swims for his life, gets safe on shore in the country of Lilliput, is made a prisoner, and carried up the country.

My father had a small estate in Nottinghamshire; I was the third of five sons. He sent me to Emanuel College in Cambridge, at fourteen years old,[1] where I resided three years, and applied myself close to my studies: but the charge of maintaining me (although I had a very scanty allowance) being too great for a narrow fortune, I was bound apprentice to Mr James Bates, an eminent surgeon in London, with whom I continued four years; and my father now and then sending me small sums of money, I laid them out in learning navigation, and other parts of the mathematics, useful to those who intend to travel, as I always believed it would be some time or other my fortune to do. When I left Mr Bates, I went down to my father; where, by the assistance of him and my uncle John, and some other relations, I got forty pounds, and a promise of thirty pounds a year to maintain me at Leyden:[2] there I studied physic[3] two years and seven months, knowing it would be useful in long voyages.

Soon after my return from Leyden, I was recommended by my good master Mr Bates, to be surgeon to the *Swallow*, Captain Abraham Pannell commander; with whom I continued three years and a half, making a voyage or two into the Levant, and some other parts. When I came back, I resolved to settle in London, to which Mr Bates, my master, encouraged me, and by him I was recommended to several patients. I took part of a small house in the Old Jury;[4] and being advised to alter my condition, I married Mrs Mary Burton,[5] second daughter to Mr Edmond Burton hosier in Newgate Street, with whom I received four hundred pounds for a portion.

But, my good master Bates dying in two years after, and I having few friends, my business began to fail; for my conscience would not suffer me to imitate the bad practice of too many among my brethren. Having therefore consulted with my wife, and some of my acquaintance, I determined to go again to sea. I was surgeon successively in two ships, and made several voyages, for six years, to the East and West Indies, by which I got some addition to my fortune. My hours of leisure I spent in reading the best authors ancient and modern, being always provided with a good number of books; and when I was ashore, in observing the manners and dispositions of the people, as well as learning their language, wherein I had a great facility by the strength of my memory.

The last of these voyages not proving very fortunate, I grew weary of the sea, and intended to stay at home with my wife and family. I removed from the Old Jury to Fetter Lane, and from thence to Wapping, hoping to get business among the sailors; but it would not turn to account. After three years' expectation that things would mend, I accepted an advantageous offer from Captain William Prichard, master of the *Antelope*, who was making a voyage to the South Sea. We set sail from Bristol, May 4th, 1699, and our voyage at first was very prosperous.

It would not be proper, for some reasons, to trouble the reader with the particulars of our adventures in those seas: let it suffice to inform him, that in our passage from thence to the East Indies, we were driven by a violent storm to the north-west of Van Diemen's Land.[6] By an observation, we found ourselves in the latitude of 30 degrees 2 minutes south. Twelve of our crew were dead by immoderate labour, and ill food, the rest were in a very weak condition. On the fifth of November, which was the beginning of summer in those parts, the weather being very hazy, the seamen spied a rock, within half a cable's length of the ship; but the wind was so strong, that we were driven directly upon it, and immediately split. Six of the crew, of whom I was one, having let down the boat into the sea, made a shift to get clear of the ship, and the rock. We rowed by my computation about three leagues, till we were able to work no longer, being already spent with labour while we were in the ship. We therefore trusted ourselves to the mercy of the waves, and in about half an hour the boat was overset by a sudden flurry from the north. What became of my companions in the boat, as well as of those who escaped on the rock, or were left in the vessel, I cannot tell; but conclude they were all lost. For my own part, I swam as Fortune directed me, and was pushed forward by wind and tide. I often let my legs drop, and could feel no bottom: but when I was almost gone, and able to struggle no longer, I found myself within my depth; and by this time the storm was much abated. The declivity was so small, that I walked near a mile before I got to the shore, which I conjectured was about eight o'clock in the evening. I then advanced forward near half a mile, but could not discover any sign of houses or inhabitants; at least I was in so weak a condition, that I did not observe them. I was extremely tired, and with that, and the heat of the weather, and about half a pint of brandy that I drank as I left the ship, I found myself much inclined to sleep. I lay down on the grass, which was very short and soft, where I slept sounder than ever I remember to have done in my life, and as I reckoned, above nine hours; for when I awaked, it was just daylight. I attempted to rise, but was not able to stir: for as I happened to lie on my back, I found my arms and legs were strongly fastened on each side to the ground; and my hair, which was long and thick, tied down in the same manner. I likewise felt several slender ligatures across my body, from my armpits to my thighs. I could only look upwards, the sun began to grow hot, and the light offended mine eyes. I heard a confused noise about me, but in the posture I lay, could see nothing except the sky. In a little time I felt something alive moving on my left leg, which advancing gently forward over my breast, came almost up to my chin; when bending mine eyes downwards as much as I could, I perceived it to be a human creature not six inches high,[7] with a bow and arrow in his hands, and a quiver at his back. In the meantime, I felt at least forty more of the same kind (as I conjectured) following the first. I was in the utmost astonishment, and roared so loud, that they all ran back in a fright; and some of them, as I was afterwards told, were hurt with the falls they got by leaping from my sides upon the ground. However, they soon returned, and one of them, who ventured so far as to get a full sight of my face, lifting up his hands and eyes by way of admiration,[8] cried out in a shrill, but distinct voice, *Hekinah degul*:[9] the others repeated the same words several times, but I then knew not what they meant. I lay all this while, as the reader may believe, in great uneasiness: at length, struggling to get loose, I had the fortune to break the strings, and wrench out the pegs that fastened my left arm to the ground; for, by lifting it up to my face, I discovered the methods they had taken to bind me; and, at the same time, with a violent pull, which gave me excessive pain, I a little loosened the strings that tied down my hair on the left side, so that I was just able to turn my head about two inches. But the creatures ran off a second time, before I could seize them; whereupon there was a great shout in a very shrill accent, and after it ceased, I heard one of them cry aloud, *Tolgo phonac*; when in an instant I felt above an hundred arrows discharged on my left hand, which pricked me like so many needles; and besides, they shot another flight into the air, as we do bombs in Europe, whereof many, I suppose, fell on my body (though I felt them not), and some on my face, which I immediately covered with my left hand. When this shower of arrows was over, I fell a groaning with grief and pain, and then striving again to get loose, they discharged another volley larger than the first, and some of them attempted with spears to stick me in the sides; but, by good luck, I had on me a buff jerkin, which they could not pierce. I thought it the most prudent method to lie still, and my design was to continue so till night, when, my left hand being already loose, I could easily free myself: and as for the inhabitants, I had reason to believe I might be a match for the greatest armies they could bring against me, if they were all of the same size with him that I saw. But Fortune disposed otherwise of me. When the people observed I was quiet, they discharged no more arrows: but, by the noise increasing, I knew their numbers were greater; and about four yards from me, over-against my right ear, I heard a knocking for above an hour, like people at work; when, turning my head that way, as well as the pegs and strings would permit me, I saw a stage erected about a foot and a half from the ground, capable of holding four of the inhabitants, with two or three ladders to mount it: from whence one of them, who seemed to be a person of quality, made me a long speech, whereof I understood not one syllable. But I should have mentioned, that before the principal person began his oration, he cried out three times *Langro dehul san* (these words and the former were afterwards repeated and explained to me): whereupon immediately about fifty of the inhabitants came, and cut the strings that fastened the left side of my head, which gave me the liberty of turning it to the right, and of observing the person and gesture of him who was to speak. He appeared to be of a middle age, and taller than any of the other three who attended him, whereof one was a page who held up his train, and seemed to be somewhat longer than my middle finger; the other two stood one on each side to support him. He acted every part of an orator, and I could observe many periods of threatenings, and others of promises, pity and kindness. I answered in a few words, but in the most submissive manner, lifting up my left hand and both mine eyes to the sun, as calling him for a witness; and being almost famished with hunger, having not eaten a morsel for some hours before I left the ship, I found the demands of nature so strong upon me, that I could not forbear showing my impatience (perhaps against the strict rules of decency) by putting my finger frequently on my mouth, to signify that I wanted food. The *Hurgo* (for so they call a great lord, as I afterwards learnt) understood me very well. He descended from the stage, and commanded that several ladders should be applied to my sides, on which above an hundred of the inhabitants mounted, and walked towards my mouth, laden with baskets full of meat, which had been provided and sent thither by the King's orders upon the first intelligence he received of me. I observed there was the flesh of several animals, but could not distinguish them by the taste. There were shoulders, legs and loins, shaped like those of mutton, and very well dressed, but smaller than the wings of a lark. I ate them by two or three at a mouthful, and took three loaves at a time, about the bigness of musket bullets. They supplied me as fast as they could, showing a thousand marks of wonder and astonishment at my bulk and appetite. I then made another sign that I wanted drink. They found by my eating that a small quantity would not suffice me; and being a most ingenious people, they slung up with great dexterity one of their largest hogsheads, then rolled it towards my hand, and beat out the top; I drank it off at a draught, which I might well do, for it hardly held half a pint, and tasted like a small wine of Burgundy, but much more delicious. They brought me a second hogshead, which I drank in the same manner, and made signs for more, but they had none to give me. When I had performed these wonders, they shouted for joy, and danced upon my breast, repeating several times as they did at first, *Hekinah degul*. They made me a sign that I should throw down the two hogsheads, but first warned the people below to stand out of the way, crying aloud, *Borach mivola*, and when they saw the vessels in the air, there was an universal shout of *Hekinah degul*. I confess I was often tempted, while they were passing backwards and forwards on my body, to seize forty or fifty of the first that came in my reach, and dash them against the ground. But the remembrance of what I had felt, which probably might not be the worst they could do, and the promise of honour I made them, for so I interpreted my submissive behaviour, soon drove out those imaginations.[10] Besides, I now considered myself as bound by the laws of hospitality to a people who had treated me with so much expense and magnificence. However, in my thoughts I could not sufficiently wonder at the intrepidity of these diminutive mortals, who durst venture to mount and walk on my body, while one of my hands was at liberty, without trembling at the very sight of so prodigious a creature as I must appear to them. After some time, when they observed that I made no more demands for meat, there appeared before me a person of high rank from his Imperial Majesty. His Excellency having mounted on the small of my right leg, advanced forwards up to my face, with about a dozen of his retinue. And producing his credentials under the Signet Royal, which he applied close to mine eyes, spoke about ten minutes, without any signs of anger, but with a kind of determinate resolution; often pointing forwards, which, as I afterwards found, was towards the capital city, about half a mile distant, whither it was agreed by his Majesty in council that I must be conveyed. I answered in few words, but to no purpose, and made a sign with my hand that was loose, putting it to the other (but over his Excellency's head, for fear of hurting him or his train) and then to my own head and body, to signify that I desired my liberty. It appeared that he understood me well enough, for he shook his head by way of disapprobation, and held his hand in a posture to show that I must be carried as a prisoner. However, he made other signs to let me understand that I should have meat and drink enough, and very good treatment. Whereupon I once more thought of attempting to break my bonds, but again, when I felt the smart of their arrows upon my face and hands, which were all in blisters, and many of the darts still sticking in them, and observing likewise that the number of my enemies increased, I gave tokens to let them know that they might do with me what they pleased. Upon this, the *Hurgo* and his train withdrew with much civility and cheerful countenances. Soon after I heard a general shout, with frequent repetitions of the words, *Peplom selan*, and I felt great numbers of the people on my left side relaxing the cords to such a degree, that I was able to turn upon my right, and to ease myself with making water; which I very plentifully did, to the great astonishment of the people, who conjecturing by my motions what I was going to do, immediately opened to the right and left on that side, to avoid the torrent which fell with such noise and violence from me. But before this, they had daubed my face and both my hands with a sort of ointment very pleasant to the smell, which in a few minutes removed all the smart of their arrows. These circumstances, added to the refreshment I had received by their victuals and drink, which were very nourishing, disposed me to sleep. I slept about eight hours, as I was afterwards assured; and it was no wonder, for the physicians, by the Emperor's order, had mingled a sleepy potion in the hogsheads of wine.

It seems that upon the first moment I was discovered sleeping on the ground after my landing, the Emperor had early notice of it by an express, and determined in council that I should be tied in the manner I have related (which was done in the night while I slept), that plenty of meat and drink should be sent me, and a machine prepared to carry me to the capital city.

This resolution perhaps may appear very bold and dangerous, and I am confident would not be imitated by any prince in Europe on the like occasion; however, in my opinion it was extremely prudent as well as generous. For supposing these people had endeavoured to kill me with their spears and arrows while I was asleep, I should certainly have awaked with the first sense of smart, which might so far have roused my rage and strength, as to enable me to break the strings wherewith I was tied; after which, as they were not able to make resistance, so they could expect no mercy.

These people are most excellent mathematicians, and arrived to a great perfection in mechanics by the countenance and encouragement of the Emperor, who is a renowned patron of learning. This prince hath several machines fixed on wheels for the carriage of trees and other great weights. He often buildeth his largest men-of-war, whereof some are nine foot long, in the woods where the timber grows, and has them carried on these engines [11] three or four hundred yards to the sea. Five hundred carpenters and engineers were immediately set at work to prepare the greatest engine they had. It was a frame of wood raised three inches from the ground, about seven foot long and four wide, moving upon twenty-two wheels. The shout I heard was upon the arrival of this engine, which it seems set out in four hours after my landing. It was brought parallel to me as I lay. But the principal difficulty was to raise and place me in this vehicle. Eighty poles, each of one foot high, were erected for this purpose, and very strong cords of the bigness of pack-thread were fastened by hooks to many bandages, which the workmen had girt round my neck, my hands, my body, and my legs. Nine hundred of the strongest men were employed to draw up these cords by many pulleys fastened on the poles, and thus in less than three hours, I was raised and slung into the engine, and there tied fast. All this I was told, for while the whole operation was performing, I lay in a profound sleep, by the force of that soporiferous medicine infused into my liquor. Fifteen hundred of the Emperor's largest horses, each about four inches and a half high, were employed to draw me towards the metropolis, which, as I said, was half a mile distant.

About four hours after we began our journey, I awaked by a very ridiculous accident; for the carriage being stopped a while to adjust something that was out of order, two or three of the young natives had the curiosity to see how I looked when I was asleep; they climbed up into the engine, and advancing very softly to my face, one of them, an officer in the Guards, put the sharp end of his half-pike a good way up into my left nostril, which tickled my nose like a straw, and made me sneeze violently: whereupon they stole off unperceived, and it was three weeks before I knew the cause of my awaking so suddenly. We made a long march the remaining part of that day, and rested at night with five hundred guards on each side of me, half with torches, and half with bows and arrows, ready to shoot me if I should offer to stir. The next morning at sunrise we continued our march, and arrived within two hundred yards of the city gates about noon. The Emperor and all his Court came out to meet us, but his great officers would by no means suffer his Majesty to endanger his person by mounting on my body.

At the place where the carriage stopped, there stood an ancient temple,[12] esteemed to be the largest in the whole kingdom, which having been polluted some years before by an unnatural murder, was, according to the zeal of those people, looked upon as profane, and therefore had been applied to common uses, and all the ornaments and furniture carried away. In this edifice it was determined I should lodge. The great gate fronting to the north was about four foot high, and almost two foot wide, through which I could easily creep. On each side of the gate was a small window not above six inches from the ground: into that on the left side, the King's smiths conveyed fourscore and eleven chains, like those that hang to a lady's watch in Europe, and almost as large, which were locked to my left leg with six and thirty padlocks. Over against this temple, on t'other side of the great highway, at twenty foot distance, there was a turret at least five foot high. Here the Emperor ascended with many principal lords of his Court, to have an opportunity of viewing me, as I was told, for I could not see them. It was reckoned that above an hundred thousand inhabitants came out of the town upon the same errand; and in spite of my guards, I believe there could not be fewer than ten thousand, at several times, who mounted upon my body by the help of ladders. But a proclamation was soon issued to forbid it upon pain of death. When the workmen found it was impossible for me to break loose, they cut all the strings that bound me; whereupon I rose up with as melancholy a disposition as ever I had in my life. But the noise and astonishment of the people at seeing me rise and walk are not to be expressed. The chains that held my left leg were about two yards long, and gave me not only the liberty of walking backwards and forwards in a semicircle; but being fixed within four inches of the gate, allowed me to creep in, and lie at my full length in the temple.

CHAPTER 2

The Emperor of Lilliput, attended by several of the nobility, comes to see the author in his confinement. The Emperor's person and habit described. Learned men appointed to teach the author their language. He gains favour by his mild disposition. His pockets are searched, and his sword and pistols taken from him.

WHEN I found myself on my feet, I looked about me, and must confess I never beheld a more entertaining prospect. The country round appeared like a continued garden, and the inclosed fields, which were generally forty foot square, resembled so many beds of flowers. These fields were intermingled with woods of half a stang,[13] and the tallest trees, as I could judge, appeared to be seven foot high. I viewed the town on my left hand, which looked like the painted scene of a city in a theatre.

I had been for some hours extremely pressed by the necessities of nature; which was no wonder, it being almost two days since I had last disburthened myself. I was under great difficulties between urgency and shame. The best expedient I could think on, was to creep into my house, which I accordingly did; and shutting the gate after me, I went as far as the length of my chain would suffer, and discharged my body of that uneasy load. But this was the only time I was ever guilty of so uncleanly an action; for which I cannot but hope the candid reader will give some allowance, after he hath maturely and impartially considered my case, and the distress I was in. From this time my constant practice was, as soon as I rose, to perform that business in open air, at the full extent of my chain, and due care was taken every morning before company came, that the offensive matter should be carried off in wheelbarrows by two servants appointed for that purpose. I would not have dwelt so long upon a circumstance, that perhaps at first sight may appear not very momentous, if I had not thought it necessary to justify my character in point of cleanliness to the world; which I am told some of my maligners have been pleased, upon this and other occasions, to call in question.

When this adventure was at an end, I came back out of my house, having occasion for fresh air. The Emperor[14] was already descended from the tower, and advancing on horseback towards me, which had like to have cost him dear; for the beast, although very well trained, yet wholly unused to such a sight, which appeared as if a mountain moved before him, reared up on his hinder feet: but that prince, who is an excellent horseman, kept his seat, till his attendants ran in, and held the bridle, while his Majesty had time to dismount. When he alighted, he surveyed me round with great admiration, but kept beyond the length of my chain. He ordered his cooks and butlers, who were already prepared, to give me victuals and drink, which they pushed forward in a sort of vehicles upon wheels till I could reach them. I took these vehicles, and soon emptied them all; twenty of them were filled with meat, and ten with liquor; each of the former afforded me two or three good mouthfuls, and I emptied the liquor of ten vessels, which was contained in earthen vials, into one vehicle, drinking it off at a draught, and so I did with the rest. The Empress, and young Princes of the Blood, of both sexes, attended by many ladies, sat at some distance in their chairs; but upon the accident that happened to the Emperor's horse, they alighted, and came near his person, which I am now going to describe. He is taller by almost the breadth of my nail, than any of his Court, which alone is enough to strike an awe into the beholders. His features are strong and masculine, with an Austrian lip and arched nose, his complexion olive, his countenance erect, his body and limbs well proportioned, all his motions graceful, and his deportment majestic. He was then past his prime, being twenty-eight years and three quarters old, of which he had reigned about seven, in great felicity, and generally victorious. For the better convenience of beholding him, I lay on my side, so that my face was parallel to his, and he stood but three yards off: however, I have had him since many times in my hand, and therefore cannot be deceived in the description. His dress was very plain and simple, the fashion of it between the Asiatic and the European; but he had on his head a light helmet of gold, adorned with jewels, and a plume on the crest. He held his sword drawn in his hand, to defend himself, if I should happen to break loose; it was almost three inches long, the hilt and scabbard were gold enriched with diamonds. His voice was shrill, but very clear and articulate, and I could distinctly hear it when I stood up. The ladies and courtiers were all most magnificently clad, so that the spot they stood upon seemed to resemble a petticoat spread on the ground, embroidered with figures of gold and silver. His Imperial Majesty spoke often to me, and I returned answers, but neither of us could understand a syllable. There were several of his priests and lawyers present (as I conjectured by their habits) who were commanded to address themselves to me, and I spoke to them in as many languages as I had the least smattering of, which were High and Low Dutch,[15] Latin, French, Spanish, Italian, and Lingua Franca; but all to no purpose. After about two hours the Court retired, and I was left with a strong guard, to prevent the impertinence, and probably the malice of the rabble, who were very impatient to crowd about me as near as they durst, and some of them had the impudence to shoot their arrows at me as I sat on the ground by the door of my house, whereof one very narrowly missed my left eye. But the colonel ordered six of the ringleaders to be seized, and thought no punishment so proper as to deliver them bound into my hands, which some of his soldiers accordingly did, pushing them forwards with the butt-ends of their pikes into my reach; I took them all in my right hand, put five of them into my coat-pocket, and as to the sixth, I made a countenance as if I would eat him alive. The poor man squalled terribly, and the colonel and his officers were in much pain, especially when they saw me take out my penknife: but I soon put them out of fear; for, looking mildly, and immediately cutting the strings he was bound with, I set him gently on the ground, and away he ran; I treated the rest in the same manner, taking them one by one out of my pocket, and I observed both the soldiers and people were highly obliged at this mark of my clemency, which was represented very much to my advantage at Court.

Towards night I got with some difficulty into my house, where I lay on the ground, and continued to do so about a fortnight; during which time the Emperor gave orders to have a bed prepared for me. Six hundred beds[16] of the common measure were brought in carriages, and worked up in my house; an hundred and fifty of their beds sewn together made up the breadth and length, and these were four double, which however kept me but very indifferently from the hardness of the floor, that was of smooth stone. By the same computation they provided me with sheets, blankets, and coverlets, tolerable enough for one who had been so long inured to hardships as I.

As the news of my arrival spread through the kingdom, it brought prodigious numbers of rich, idle, and curious people to see me; so that the villages were almost emptied, and great neglect of tillage and household affairs must have ensued, if his Imperial Majesty had not provided by several proclamations and orders of state against this inconveniency. He directed that those, who had already beheld me, should return home, and not presume to come within fifty yards of my house without licence from Court; whereby the Secretaries of State got considerable fees.

In the meantime, the Emperor held frequent councils to debate what course should be taken with me; and I was afterwards assured by a particular friend, a person of great quality, who was as much in the *secret* as any, that the Court was under many difficulties concerning me. They apprehended my breaking loose, that my diet would be very expensive, and might cause a famine. Sometimes they determined to starve me, or at least to shoot me in the face and hands with poisoned arrows, which would soon dispatch me: but again they considered, that the stench of so large a carcass might produce a plague in the metropolis, and probably spread through the whole kingdom. In the midst of these consultations, several officers of the army went to the door of the great council-chamber; and two of them being admitted, gave an account of my behaviour to the six criminals above-mentioned, which made so favourable an impression in the breast of his Majesty and the whole Board in my behalf, that an Imperial Commission was issued out, obliging all the villages nine hundred yards round the city, to deliver in every morning six beeves,[17] forty sheep, and other victuals for my sustenance; together with a proportionable quantity of bread, and wine, and other liquors: for the due payment of which, his Majesty gave assignments upon his Treasury. For this Prince lives chiefly upon his own demesnes, seldom except upon great occasions raising any subsidies upon his subjects, who are bound to attend him in his wars at their own expense. An establishment was also made of six hundred persons to be my domestics, who had board-wages allowed for their maintenance, and tents built for them very conveniently on each side of my door. It was likewise ordered, that three hundred tailors should make me a suit of clothes after the fashion of the country: that six of his Majesty's greatest scholars should be employed to instruct me in their language: and, lastly, that the Emperor's horses, and those of the nobility and troops of guards, should be exercised in my sight, to accustom themselves to me. All these orders were duly put in execution, and in about three weeks I made a great progress in learning their language; during which time, the Emperor frequently honoured me with his visits, and was pleased to assist my masters in teaching me. We began already to converse together in some sort; and the first words I learnt were to express my desire that he would please to give me my liberty, which I every day repeated on my knees. His answer, as I could apprehend, was, that this must be a work of time, not to be thought on without the advice of his Council, and that first I must *lumos kelmin pesso desmar lon emposo*; that is, swear a peace with him and his kingdom. However, that I should be used with all kindness, and he advised me to acquire by my patience, and discreet behaviour, the good opinion of himself and his subjects. He desired I would not take it ill, if he gave orders to certain proper officers to search me;[18] for probably I might carry about me several weapons, which must needs be dangerous things, if they answered the bulk of so prodigious a person. I said, his Majesty should be satisfied, for I was ready to strip myself, and turn up my pockets before him. This I delivered part in words, and part in signs. He replied, that by the laws of the kingdom I must be searched by two of his officers; that he knew this could not be done without my consent and assistance; that he had so good an opinion of my generosity and justice, as to trust their persons in my hands: that whatever they took from me should be returned when I left the country, or paid for at the rate which I would set upon them. I took up the two officers in my hands, put them first into my coat-pockets, and then into every other pocket about me, except my two fobs, and another secret pocket which I had no mind should be searched, wherein I had some little necessaries of no consequence to any but myself. In one of my fobs there was a silver watch, and in the other a small quantity of gold in a purse. These gentlemen, having pen, ink and paper about them, made an exact inventory of everything they saw; and when they had done, desired I would set them down, that they might deliver it to the Emperor. This inventory I afterwards translated into English, and is word for word as follows.

IMPRIMIS, In the right coat-pocket of the Great Man-Mountain (for so I interpret the words *Quinbus Flestrin*) after the strictest search, we found only one great piece of coarse cloth, large enough to be a foot-cloth for your Majesty's chief room of state. In the left pocket, we saw a huge silver chest, with a cover of the same metal, which we the searchers were not able to lift. We desired it should be opened, and one of us stepping into it, found himself up to the mid leg in a sort of dust, some part whereof flying up to our faces, set us both a sneezing for several times together. In his right waistcoat-pocket, we found a prodigious bundle of white thin substances, folded one over another, about the bigness of three men, tied with a strong cable, and marked with black figures; which we humbly conceive to be writings, every letter almost half as large as the palm of our hands. In the left, there was a sort of engine, from the back of which were extended twenty long poles, resembling the palisados before your Majesty's Court; wherewith we conjecture the Man-Mountain combs his head, for we did not always trouble him with questions, because we found it a great difficulty to make him understand us. In the large pocket on the right side of his middle cover (so

I translate the word *ranfu-lo*, by which they meant my breeches), we saw a hollow pillar of iron, about the length of a man, fastened to a strong piece of timber, larger than the pillar; and upon one side of the pillar were huge pieces of iron sticking out, cut into strange figures, which we know not what to make of. In the left pocket, another engine of the same kind. In the smaller pocket on the right side, were several round flat pieces of white and red metal, of different bulk; some of the white, which seemed to be silver, were so large and heavy, that my comrade and I could hardly lift them. In the left pocket were two black pillars irregularly shaped: we could not, without difficulty, reach the top of them as we stood at the bottom of his pocket. One of them was covered, and seemed all of a piece: but at the upper end of the other, there appeared a white round substance, about twice the bigness of our heads. Within each of these was enclosed a prodigious plate of steel; which, by our orders, we obliged him to show us, because we apprehended they might be dangerous engines. He took them out of their cases, and told us, that in his own country his practice was to shave his beard with one of these, and to cut his meat with the other. There were two pockets which we could not enter: these he called his fobs; they were two large slits cut into the top of his middle cover, but squeezed close by the pressure of his belly. Out of the right fob hung a great silver chain, with a wonderful kind of engine at the bottom. We directed him to draw out whatever was at the end of that chain; which appeared to be a globe, half silver, and half of some transparent metal: for on the transparent side we saw certain strange figures circularly drawn, and thought we could touch them, till we found our fingers stopped with that lucid substance. He put this engine to our ears, which made an incessant noise like that of a watermill. And we conjecture it is either some unknown animal, or the god that he worships: but we are more inclined to the latter opinion, because he assured us (if we understood him right, for he expressed himself very imperfectly), that he seldom did anything without consulting it. He called it his oracle, and said it pointed out the time for every action of his life. From the left fob he took out a net almost large enough for a fisherman, but contrived to open and shut like a purse, and served him for the same use: we found therein several massy pieces of yellow metal, which if they be of real gold, must be of immense value.

Having thus, in obedience to your Majesty's commands, diligently searched all his pockets, we observed a girdle about his waist made of the hide of some prodigious animal; from which, on the left side, hung a sword of the length of five men; and on the right, a bag or pouch divided into two cells, each cell capable of holding three of your Majesty's subjects. In one of these cells were several globes or balls of a most ponderous metal, about the bigness of our heads, and required a strong hand to lift them: the other cell contained a heap of certain black grains, but of no great bulk or weight, for we could hold above fifty of them in the palms of our hands.

This is an exact inventory of what we found about the body of the Man-Mountain, who used us with great civility, and due respect to your Majesty's Commission. Signed and sealed on the fourth day of the eighty-ninth moon of your Majesty's auspicious reign.

Clefven Frelock, Marsi Frelock.

When this inventory was read over to the Emperor, he directed me to deliver up the several particulars. He first called for my scimitar, which I took out, scabbard and all. In the meantime he ordered three thousand of his choicest troops (who then attended him) to surround me at a distance, with their bows and arrows just ready to discharge: but I did not observe it, for mine eyes were wholly fixed upon his Majesty. He then desired me to draw my scimitar, which, although it had got some rust by the seawater, was in most parts exceeding bright. I did so, and immediately all the troops gave a shout between terror and surprise; for the sun shone clear, and the reflection dazzled their eyes as I waved the scimitar to and fro in my hand. His Majesty, who is a most magnanimous prince, was less daunted than I could expect; he ordered me to return it into the scabbard, and cast it on the ground as gently as I could, about six foot from the end of my chain. The next thing he demanded was one of the hollow iron pillars, by which he meant my pocket-pistols. I drew it out, and at his desire, as well as I could, expressed to him the use of it; and charging it only with powder, which by the closeness of my pouch happened to scape wetting in the sea (an inconvenience that all prudent mariners take special care to provide against), I first cautioned the Emperor not to be afraid, and then I let it off in the air. The astonishment here was much greater than at the sight of my scimitar. Hundreds fell down as if they had been struck dead; and even the Emperor, although he stood his ground, could not recover himself in some time. I delivered up both my pistols in the same manner as I had done my scimitar, and then my pouch of powder and bullets; begging him that the former might be kept from fire, for it would kindle with the smallest spark, and blow up his imperial palace into the air. I likewise delivered up my watch, which the Emperor was very curious to see, and commanded two of his tallest Yeomen of the Guards to bear it on a pole upon their shoulders, as draymen in England do a barrel of ale. He was amazed at the continual noise it made, and the motion of the minute-hand, which he could easily discern; for their sight is much more acute than ours: he asked the opinions of his learned men about him, which were various and remote, as the reader may well imagine without my repeating; although indeed I could not very perfectly understand them. I then gave up my silver and copper money, my purse with nine large pieces of gold, and some smaller ones; my knife and razor, my comb and silver snuff-box, my handkerchief and journal book. My scimitar, pistols, and pouch, were conveyed in carriages to his Majesty's stores; but the rest of my goods were returned me.

I had, as I before observed, one private pocket which escaped their search, wherein there was a pair of spectacles (which I sometimes use for the weakness of mine eyes), a pocket perspective,[19] and several other little conveniences; which being of no consequence to the Emperor, I did not think myself bound in honour to discover, and I apprehended they might be lost or spoiled if I ventured them out of my possession.

CHAPTER 3

The author diverts the Emperor and his nobility of both sexes in a very uncommon manner. The diversions of the Court of Lilliput described. The author hath his liberty granted him upon certain conditions.

My gentleness and good behaviour had gained so far on the Emperor and his Court, and indeed upon the army and people in general, that I began to conceive hopes of getting my liberty in a short time. I took all possible methods to cultivate this favourable disposition. The natives came by degrees to be less apprehensive of any danger from me. I would sometimes lie down, and let five or six of them dance on my hand. And at last the boys and girls would venture to come and play at hide and seek in my hair. I had now made a good progress in understanding and speaking their language. The Emperor had a mind one day to entertain me with several of the country shows, wherein they exceed all nations I have known, both for dexterity and magnificence. I was diverted with none so much as that of the rope-dancers, performed upon a slender white thread, extended about two foot, and twelve inches from the ground. Upon which I shall desire liberty, with the reader's patience, to enlarge a little.

This diversion is only practised by those persons who are candidates for great employments, and high favour, at Court. They are trained in this art from their youth, and are not always of noble birth, or liberal education. When a great office is vacant either by death or disgrace (which often happens) five or six of those candidates petition the Emperor to entertain his Majesty and the Court with a dance on the rope, and whoever jumps the highest without falling, succeeds in the office. Very often the chief Ministers themselves are commanded to show their skill, and to convince the Emperor that they have not lost their faculty. Flimnap,[20] the Treasurer, is allowed to cut a caper on the strait rope, at least an inch higher than any other lord in the whole Empire. I have seen him do the summerset[21] several times together upon a trencher fixed on the rope, which is no thicker than a common pack-thread in England. My friend Reldresal,[22] Principal Secretary for Private Affairs, is, in my opinion, if I am not partial, the second after the Treasurer; the rest of the great officers are much upon a par.

These diversions are often attended with fatal accidents, whereof great numbers are on record. I myself have seen two or three candidates break a limb. But the danger is much greater when the Ministers themselves are commanded to show their dexterity; for by contending to excel themselves and their fellows, they strain so far, that there is hardly one of them who hath not received a fall, and some of them two or three. I was assured that a year or two before my arrival, Flimnap would have infallibly broke his neck, if one of the *King's cushions*,[23] that accidentally lay on the ground, had not weakened the force of his fall.

There is likewise another diversion, which is only shown before the Emperor and Empress, and first Minister, upon particular occasions. The Emperor lays on a table three fine silken threads[24] of six inches long. One is blue, the other red, and the third green. These threads are proposed as prizes for those persons whom the Emperor hath a mind to distinguish by a peculiar mark of his favour. The ceremony is performed in his Majesty's great chamber of state, where the candidates are to undergo a trial of dexterity very different from the former, and such as I have not observed the least resemblance of in any other country of the old or the new world. The Emperor holds a stick in his hands, both ends parallel to the horizon, while the candidates, advancing one by one, sometimes leap over the stick, sometimes creep under it backwards and forwards several times, according as the stick is advanced or depressed. Sometimes the Emperor holds one end of the stick, and his first Minister the other; sometimes the Minister has it entirely to himself. Whoever performs his part with most agility, and holds out the longest in *leaping* and *creeping*, is rewarded with the blue-coloured silk; the red is given to the next, and the green to the third, which they all wear girt twice round about the middle; and you see few great persons about this Court who are not adorned with one of these girdles.

The horses of the army, and those of the royal stables, having been daily led before me, were no longer shy, but would come up to my very feet without starting. The riders would leap them over my hand as I held it on the ground, and one of the Emperor's huntsmen, upon a large courser, took my foot, shoe and all; which was indeed a prodigious leap. I had the good fortune to divert the Emperor one day after a very extraordinary manner. I desired he would order several sticks of two foot high, and the thickness of an ordinary cane, to be brought me; whereupon his Majesty commanded the Master of his Woods to give directions accordingly, and the next morning six woodmen arrived with as many carriages, drawn by eight horses to each. I took nine of these sticks, and fixing them firmly in the ground in a quadrangular figure, two foot and a half square, I took four other sticks, and tied them parallel at each corner, about two foot from the ground; then

I fastened my handkerchief to the nine sticks that stood erect, and extended it on all sides till it was as tight as the top of a drum; and the four parallel sticks, rising about five inches higher than the handkerchief, served as ledges on each side. When I had finished my work, I desired the Emperor to let a troop of his best horse, twenty-four in number, come and exercise upon this plain. His Majesty approved of the proposal, and I took them up one by one in my hands, ready mounted and armed, with the proper officers to exercise them. As soon as they got into order, they divided into two parties, performed mock skirmishes, discharged blunt arrows, drew their swords, fled and pursued, attacked and retired, and in short discovered the best military discipline I ever beheld. The parallel sticks secured them and their horses from falling over the stage; and the Emperor was so much delighted, that he ordered this entertainment to be repeated several days, and once was pleased to be lifted up, and give the word of command; and, with great difficulty, persuaded even the Empress herself to let me hold her in her close chair25 within two yards of the stage, from whence she was able to take a full view of the whole performance. It was my good fortune that no ill accident happened in these entertainments, only once a fiery horse that belonged to one of the captains pawing with his hoof struck a hole in my handkerchief, and his foot slipping, he overthrew his rider and himself; but I immediately relieved them both, and covering the hole with one hand, I set down the troop with the other, in the same manner as I took them up. The horse that fell was strained in the left shoulder, but the rider got no hurt, and I repaired my handkerchief as well as I could; however, I would not trust to the strength of it any more in such dangerous enterprises.

About two or three days before I was set at liberty, as I was entertaining the Court with these kinds of feats, there arrived an express to inform his Majesty, that some of his subjects, riding near the place where I was first taken up, had seen a great black substance lying on the ground, very oddly shaped, extending its edges round as wide as his Majesty's bed-chamber, and rising up in the middle as high as a man; that it was no living creature, as they at first apprehended, for it lay on the grass without motion, and some of them had walked round it several times; that by mounting upon each others' shoulders, they had got to the top, which was flat and even, and stamping upon it they found it was hollow within; that they humbly conceived it might be something belonging to the Man-Mountain, and if his Majesty pleased, they would undertake to bring it with only five horses. I presently[26] knew what they meant, and was glad at heart to receive this intelligence. It seems upon my first reaching the shore after our shipwreck, I was in such confusion, that before I came to the place where I went to sleep, my hat, which I had fastened with a string to my head while I was rowing, and had stuck on all the time I was swimming, fell off after I came to land; the string, as I conjecture, breaking by some accident which I never observed, but thought my hat had been lost at sea. I entreated his Imperial Majesty to give orders it might be brought to me as soon as possible, describing to him the use and the nature of it: and the next day the waggoners arrived with it, but not in a very good condition; they had bored two holes in the brim, within an inch and a half of the edge, and fastened two hooks in the holes; these hooks were tied by a long cord to the harness, and thus my hat was dragged along for above half an English mile: but the ground in that country being extremely smooth and level, it received less damage than I expected.

Two days after this adventure, the Emperor having ordered that part of his army which quarters in and about his metro-polis to be in a readiness, took a fancy of diverting himself in a very singular manner. He desired I would stand like a colossus,[27] with my legs as far asunder as I conveniently could. He then commanded his General (who was an old experienced leader, and a great patron of mine) to draw up the troops in close order, and march them under me, the foot by twenty-four in a breast, and the horse by sixteen, with drums beating, colours flying, and pikes advanced. This body consisted of three thousand foot, and a thousand horse. His Majesty gave orders, upon pain of death, that every soldier in his march should observe the strictest decency with regard to my person; which, however, could not prevent some of the younger officers from turning up their eyes as they passed under me. And, to confess the truth, my breeches were at that time in so ill a condition, that they afforded some opportunities for laughter and admiration.

I had sent so many memorials and petitions for my liberty, that his Majesty at length mentioned the matter, first in the Cabinet, and then in a full council; where it was opposed by none, except Skyresh Bolgolam,[28] who was pleased, without any provocation, to be my mortal enemy. But it was carried against him by the whole Board, and confirmed by the Emperor. That Minister was *Galbet*, or Admiral of the Realm, very much in his master's confidence, and a person well versed in affairs, but of a morose and sour complexion. However, he was at length persuaded to comply; but prevailed that the articles and conditions upon which I should be set free, and to which I must swear, should be drawn up by himself. These articles were brought to me by Skyresh Bolgolam in person, attended by two Under-Secretaries, and several persons of distinction. After they were read, I was demanded to swear to the performance of them; first in the manner of my own country, and afterwards in the method prescribed by their laws; which was to hold my right foot in my left hand, to place the middle finger of my right hand on the crown of my head, and my thumb on the tip of my right ear. But, because the reader may perhaps be curious to have some idea of the style and manner of expression peculiar to that people, as well as to know the articles upon which I recovered my liberty, I have made a translation of the whole instrument word for word, as near as I was able, which I here offer to the public.

GOLBASTO MOMAREN EVLAME GURDILO SHEFIN MULLY ULLY GUE, most mighty Emperor of Lilliput, Delight and Terror of the Universe, whose dominions extend five thousand blustrugs (about twelve miles in circumference), to the extremities of the globe; Monarch of all Monarchs, taller than the sons of men; whose feet press down to the centre, and whose head strikes against the sun: at whose nod the princes of the earth shake their knees; pleasant as the spring, comfortable as the summer, fruitful as autumn, dreadful as winter. His most sublime Majesty proposeth to the Man-Mountain, lately arrived to our celestial dominions, the following articles, which by a solemn oath he shall be obliged to perform.

First, The Man-Mountain shall not depart from our dominions, without our licence under our great seal.

2nd, He shall not presume to come into our metropolis, without our express order; at which time the inhabitants shall have two hours warning to keep within their doors.

3rd, The said Man-Mountain shall confine his walks to our principal high roads, and not offer to walk or lie down in a meadow or field of corn.

4th, As he walks the said roads, he shall take the utmost care not to trample upon the bodies of any of our loving subjects, their horses, or carriages, nor take any of our said subjects into his hands, without their own consent.

5th, If an express require extraordinary dispatch, the Man-Mountain shall be obliged to carry in his pocket the messenger and horse a six days' journey once in every moon, and return the said messenger back (if so required) safe to our Imperial Presence.

6th, He shall be our ally against our enemies in the island of

Blefuscu, and do his utmost to destroy their fleet, which is now preparing to invade us.

7th, That the said Man-Mountain shall, at his times of leisure, be aiding and assisting to our workmen, in helping to raise certain great stones, towards covering the wall of the principal park, and other our royal buildings.

8th, That the said Man-Mountain shall, in two moons' time, deliver in an exact survey of the circumference of our dominions by a computation of his own paces round the coast.

Lastly, That upon his solemn oath to observe all the above articles, the said Man-Mountain shall have a daily allowance of meat and drink sufficient for the support of 1728 of our subjects, with free access to our Royal Person, and other marks of our favour. Given at our palace at Belfaborac the twelfth day of the ninety-first moon of our reign.

I swore and subscribed to these articles with great cheerfulness and content, although some of them were not so honourable as I could have wished; which proceeded wholly from the malice of Skyresh Bolgolam the High Admiral: whereupon my chains were immediately unlocked, and I was at full liberty; the Emperor himself in person did me the honour to be by at the whole ceremony. I made my acknowledgements by prostrating myself at his Majesty's feet: but he commanded me to rise; and after many gracious expressions, which, to avoid the censure of vanity, I shall not repeat, he added, that he hoped I should prove a useful servant, and well deserve all the favours he had already conferred upon me, or might do for the future.

The reader may please to observe, that in the last article for the recovery of my liberty, the Emperor stipulates to allow me a quantity of meat and drink sufficient for the support of 1728 Lilliputians. Some time after, asking a friend at Court how they came to fix on that determinate number, he told me, that his Majesty's mathematicians, having taken the height of my body by the help of a quadrant, and finding it to exceed theirs in the proportion of twelve to one, they concluded from the similarity of their bodies, that mine must contain at least 1728 of theirs, and consequently would require as much food as was necessary to support that number of Lilliputians. By which, the reader may conceive an idea of the ingenuity of that people, as well as the prudent and exact economy of so great a prince.

CHAPTER 4

Mildendo, the metropolis of Lilliput, described, together with the Emperor's palace. A conversation between the author and a principal Secretary, concerning the affairs of that Empire; the author's offers to serve the Emperor in his wars.

THE first request I made after I had obtained my liberty, was, that I might have licence to see Mildendo, the metropolis; which the Emperor easily granted me, but with a special charge to do no hurt, either to the inhabitants, or their houses. The people had notice by proclamation of my design to visit the town. The wall which encompassed it is two foot and an half high, and at least eleven inches broad, so that a coach and horses may be driven very safely round it; and it is flanked with strong towers at ten foot distance. I stepped over the great western gate, and passed very gently and sideling[29] through the two principal streets, only in my short waistcoat, for fear of damaging the roofs and eaves of the houses with the skirts of my coat. I walked with the utmost circumspection, to avoid treading on any stragglers, who might remain in the streets, although the orders were very strict, that all people should keep in their houses, at their own peril. The garret windows and tops of houses were so crowded with spectators, that I thought in all my travels I had not seen a more populous place. The city is an exact square, each side of the wall being five hundred foot long. The two great streets, which run cross [30] and divide it into four quarters, are five foot wide. The lanes and alleys, which I could not enter, but only viewed them as I passed, are from twelve to eighteen inches. The town is capable of holding five hundred thousand souls. The houses are from three to five stories. The shops and markets well provided.

The Emperor's palace is in the centre of the city, where the two great streets meet. It is enclosed by a wall of two foot high, and twenty foot distant from the buildings. I had his Majesty's permission to step over this wall; and the space being so wide between that and the palace, I could easily view it on every side. The outward court is a square of forty foot, and includes two other courts: in the inmost are the royal apartments, which I was very desirous to see, but found it extremely difficult; for the great gates, from one square into another, were but eighteen inches high, and seven inches wide. Now the buildings of the outer court were at least five foot high, and it was impossible for me to stride over them, without infinite damage to the pile, though the walls were strongly built of hewn stone, and four inches thick. At the same time the Emperor had a great desire that I should see the magnificence of his palace; but this I was not able to do till three days after, which I spent in cutting down with my knife some of the largest trees in the royal park, about an hundred yards distant from the city. Of these trees I made two stools, each about three foot high, and strong enough to bear my weight. The people having received notice a second time, I went again through the city to the palace, with my two stools in my hands. When I came to the side of the outer court, I stood upon one stool, and took the other in my hand: this I lifted over the roof, and gently set it down on the space between the first and second court, which was eight foot wide. I then stepped over the buildings very conveniently from one stool to the other, and drew up the first after me with a hooked stick. By this contrivance I got into the inmost court; and lying down upon my side, I applied my face to the windows of the middle stories, which were left open on purpose, and discovered the most splendid apartments that can be imagined. There I saw the Empress, and the young Princes in their several lodgings, with their chief attendants about them. Her Imperial Majesty was pleased to smile very graciously upon me, and gave me out of the window her hand to kiss.

But I shall not anticipate the reader with farther descriptions of this kind, because I reserve them for a greater work, which is now almost ready for the press, containing a general description of this Empire, from its first erection, through a long series of princes, with a particular account of their wars and politics, laws, learning, and religion; their plants and animals, their peculiar manners and customs, with other matters very curious and useful; my chief design at present being only to relate such events and transactions as happened to the public, or to myself, during a residence of about nine months in that Empire.

One morning, about a fortnight after I had obtained my liberty, Reldresal, Principal Secretary (as they style him) of Private Affairs, came to my house, attended only by one servant. He ordered his coach to wait at a distance, and desired I would give him an hour's audience; which I readily consented to, on account of his quality, and personal merits, as well as of the many good offices he had done me during my solicitations at Court. I offered to lie down, that he might the more conveniently reach my ear; but he chose rather to let me hold him in my hand during our conversation. He began with compliments on my liberty, said he might pretend to some merit in it; but, however, added, that if it had not been for the present situation of things at Court, perhaps I might not have obtained it so soon. For, *said he*, as flourishing a condition as we appear to be in to foreigners, we labour under two mighty evils; a violent faction at home, and the danger of an invasion by a most potent enemy from abroad. As to the first, you are to understand, that for above seventy moons past, there have been two struggling parties in this Empire, under the names of *Tramecksan* and *Slamecksan*,[31] from the high and low heels on their shoes, by which they distinguish themselves. It is alleged indeed, that the high heels are most agreeable to our ancient constitution: but however this be, his Majesty hath determined to make use of only low heels in the administration of the government, and all offices in the gift of the Crown, as you cannot but observe; and particularly, that his Majesty's imperial heels are lower at least by a *drurr* than any of his Court (*drurr* is a measure about the fourteenth part of an inch). The animosities between these two parties run so high, that they will neither eat nor drink, nor talk with each other. We compute the *Tramecksan*, or High-Heels, to exceed us in number; but the power is wholly on our side. We apprehend his Imperial Highness, the heir to the Crown,[32] to have some tendency towards the High-Heels; at least we can plainly discover one of his heels higher than the other, which gives him a hobble in his gait. Now, in the midst of these intestine disquiets, we are threatened with an invasion from the island of Blefuscu,[33] which is the other great Empire of the universe, almost as large and powerful as this of his Majesty. For as to what we have heard you affirm, that there are other kingdoms and states in the world, inhabited by human creatures as large as yourself, our philosophers are in much doubt, and would rather conjecture that you dropped from the moon, or one of the stars; because it is certain, that an hundred mortals of your bulk would, in a short time, destroy all the fruits and cattle of his Majesty's dominions. Besides, our histories of six thousand moons make no mention of any other regions, than the two great Empires of Lilliput and Blefuscu. Which two mighty powers have, as I was going to tell you, been engaged in a most obstinate war[34] for six and thirty moons past. It began upon the following occasion. It is allowed on all hands, that the primitive way of breaking eggs before we eat them, was upon the larger end:[35] but his present Majesty's grandfather,[36] while he was a boy, going to eat an egg, and breaking it according to the ancient practice, happened to cut one of his fingers. Whereupon the Emperor his father published an edict, commanding all his subjects, upon great penalties, to break the smaller end of their eggs. The people so highly resented this law, that our Histories tell us there have been six rebellions raised on that account; wherein one Emperor lost his life, and another his crown.[37] These civil commotions were constantly fomented by the monarchs of Blefuscu; and when they were quelled, the exiles always fled for refuge to that Empire. It is computed, that eleven thousand persons have, at several times, suffered death, rather than submit to break their eggs at the smaller end. Many hundred large volumes have been published upon this controversy: but the books of the Big-Endians have been long forbidden, and the whole party rendered incapable by law[38] of holding employments. During the course of these troubles, the Emperors of Blefuscu did frequently expostulate by their ambassadors, accusing us of making a schism in religion, by offending against a fundamental doctrine of our great prophet Lustrog, in the fifty-fourth chapter of the *Brundecral* (which is their Alcoran). This, however, is thought to be a mere strain upon the text: for the words are these; *That all true believers shall break their eggs at the convenient end*: and which is the convenient end, seems, in my humble opinion, to be left to every man's conscience, or at least in the power of the chief magistrate to determine. Now the Big-Endian exiles have found so much credit in the Emperor of Blefuscu's Court, and so much private assistance and encouragement from their party here at home, that a bloody war hath been carried on between the two Empires for six and thirty moons with various success; during which time we have lost forty capital ships, and a much greater number of smaller vessels, together with thirty thousand of our best seamen and soldiers; and the damage received by the enemy is reckoned to be somewhat greater than ours. However, they have now equipped a numerous fleet, and are just preparing to make a descent upon us; and his Imperial Majesty, placing great confidence in your valour and strength, hath commanded me to lay this account of his affairs before you.

I desired the Secretary to present my humble duty to the Emperor, and to let him know, that I thought it would not become me, who was a foreigner, to interfere with parties; but I was ready, with the hazard of my life, to defend his person and state against all invaders.

CHAPTER 5

The author by an extraordinary stratagem prevents an invasion. A high title of honour is conferred upon him. Ambassadors arrive from the Emperor of Blefuscu, and sue for peace. The Empress's apartment on fire by an accident; the author instrumental in saving the rest of the palace.

THE Empire of Blefuscu is an island situated to the north-north-east side of Lilliput, from whence it is parted only by a channel of eight hundred yards wide. I had not yet seen it, and upon this notice of an intended invasion, I avoided appearing on that side of the coast, for fear of being discovered by some of the enemy's ships, who had received no intelligence of me, all intercourse between the two Empires having been strictly forbidden during the war, upon pain of death, and an embargo laid by our Emperor upon all vessels whatsoever. I communicated to his Majesty a project I had formed of seizing the enemy's whole fleet; which, as our scouts assured us, lay at anchor in the harbour ready to sail with the first fair wind. I consulted the most experienced seamen upon the depth of the channel, which they had often plumbed, who told me, that in the middle at high water it was seventy *glumgluffs* deep, which is about six foot of European measure; and the rest of it fifty *glumgluffs* at most. I walked to the north-east coast over against Blefuscu; where, lying down behind a hillock, I took out my small pocket perspective-glass, and viewed the enemy's fleet at anchor, consisting of about fifty men-of-war, and a great number of transports: I then came back to my house, and gave order (for which I had a warrant) for a great quantity of the strongest cable and bars of iron. The cable was about as thick as pack-thread, and the bars of the length and size of a knitting-needle. I trebled the cable to make it stronger, and for the same reason I twisted three of the iron bars together, bending the extremities into a hook. Having thus fixed fifty hooks to as many cables, I went back to the north-east coast, and putting off my coat, shoes, and stockings, walked into the sea in my leathern jerkin, about half an hour before high water. I waded with what haste I could, and swam in the middle about thirty yards till I felt ground; I arrived at the fleet in less than half an hour. The enemy was so frighted when they saw me, that they leaped out of their ships, and swam to shore, where there could not be fewer than thirty thousand souls. I then took my tackling, and fastening a hook to the hole at the prow of each, I tied all the cords together at the end. While I was thus employed, the enemy discharged several thousand arrows, many of which stuck in my hands and face; and besides the excessive smart, gave me much disturbance in my work. My greatest apprehension was for mine eyes, which I should have infallibly lost, if I had not suddenly thought of an expedient. I kept among other little necessaries a pair of spectacles in a private pocket, which, as I observed before, had scaped the Emperor's searchers. These I took out and fastened as strongly as I could upon my nose, and thus armed went on boldly with my work in spite of the enemy's arrows, many of which struck against the glasses of my spectacles, but without any other effect, further than a little to discompose them. I had now fastened all the hooks, and taking the knot in my hand, began to pull; but not a ship would stir, for they were all too fast held by their anchors, so that the boldest part of my enterprise remained. I therefore let go the cord, and leaving the hooks fixed to the ships, I resolutely cut with my knife the cables that fastened the anchors, receiving above two hundred shots in my face and hands; then I took up the knotted end of the cables to which my hooks were tied, and with great ease drew fifty of the enemy's largest men-of-war after me.

The Blefuscudians, who had not the least imagination of what I intended, were at first confounded with astonishment. They had seen me cut the cables, and thought my design was only to let the ships run adrift, or fall foul on each other: but when they perceived the whole fleet moving in order, and saw me pulling at the end, they set up such a scream of grief and despair, that it is almost impossible to describe or conceive. When I had got out of danger, I stopped a while to pick out the arrows that stuck in my hands and face, and rubbed on some of the same ointment that was given me at my first arrival, as I have formerly mentioned. I then took off my spectacles, and waiting about an hour till the tide was a little fallen, I waded through the middle with my cargo, and arrived safe at the royal port of Lilliput.

The Emperor and his whole Court stood on the shore expecting the issue of this great adventure. They saw the ships move forward in a large half-moon, but could not discern me, who was up to my breast in water. When I advanced to the middle of the channel, they were yet more in pain, because I was under water to my neck. The Emperor concluded me to be drowned, and that the enemy's fleet was approaching in a hostile manner: but he was soon eased of his fears, for the channel growing shallower every step I made, I came in a short time within hearing, and holding up the end of the cable by which the fleet was fastened, I cried in a loud voice, *Long live the most puissant Emperor of Lilliput!* This great prince received me at my landing with all possible encomiums, and created me a *Nardac* upon the spot, which is the highest title of honour among them.

His Majesty desired I would take some other opportunity of bringing all the rest of his enemy's ships into his ports. And so unmeasureable is the ambition of princes, that he seemed to think of nothing less than reducing the whole Empire of Blefuscu into a province, and governing it by a Viceroy; of destroying the Big-Endian exiles, and compelling that people to break the smaller end of their eggs, by which he would remain sole monarch of the whole world. But I endeavoured to divert him from this design, by many arguments drawn from the topics of policy as well as justice: and I plainly protested, that I would never be an instrument of bringing a free and brave people into slavery.[39] And when the matter was debated in Council, the wisest part of the Ministry were of my opinion.

This open bold declaration of mine was so opposite to the schemes and politics of his Imperial Majesty, that he could never forgive me; he mentioned it in a very artful manner at Council, where I was told that some of the wisest appeared, at least, by their silence, to be of my opinion; but others, who were my secret enemies, could not forbear some expressions, which by a side-wind reflected on me. And from this time began an intrigue between his Majesty and a junto of Ministers[40] maliciously bent against me, which broke out in less than two months, and had like to have ended in my utter destruction. Of so little weight are the greatest services to princes, when put into the balance with a refusal to gratify their passions.

About three weeks after this exploit, there arrived a solemn embassy from Blefuscu, with humble offers of a peace;[41] which was soon concluded upon conditions very advantageous to our Emperor, wherewith I shall not trouble the reader. There were six ambassadors, with a train of about five hundred persons, and their entry was very magnificent, suitable to the grandeur of their master, and the importance of their business. When their Treaty was finished, wherein I did them several good offices by the credit I now had, or at least appeared to have at Court, their Excellencies, who were privately told how much I had been their friend, made me a visit in form. They began with many compliments upon my valour and generosity, invited me to that kingdom in the Emperor their master's name, and desired me to show them some proofs of my prodigious strength, of which they had heard so many wonders; wherein I readily obliged them, but shall not interrupt the reader with the particulars.

When I had for some time entertained their Excellencies to their infinite satisfaction and surprise, I desired they would do me the honour to present my most humble respects to the Emperor their master, the renown of whose virtues had so justly filled the whole world with admiration, and whose royal person I resolved to attend before I returned to my own country: accordingly, the next time I had the honour to see our Emperor, I desired his general licence to wait on the Blefuscudian monarch, which he was pleased to grant me, as I could plainly perceive, in a very cold manner; but could not guess the reason, till I had a whisper from a certain person, that Flimnap and Bolgolam had represented my intercourse with those ambassadors as a mark of disaffection, from which I am sure my heart was wholly free. And this was the first time I began to conceive some imperfect idea of Courts and Ministers.

It is to be observed, that these ambassadors spoke to me by an interpreter, the languages of both Empires differing as much from each other as any two in Europe, and each nation priding itself upon the antiquity, beauty, and energy of their own tongues, with an avowed contempt for that of their neighbour; yet our Emperor, standing upon the advantage he had got by the seizure of their fleet, obliged them to deliver their credentials, and make their speech, in the Lilliputian tongue. And it must be confessed, that from the great intercourse of trade and commerce between both realms, from the continual reception of exiles, which is mutual among them, and from the custom in each Empire to send their young nobility and richer gentry to the other, in order to polish themselves, by seeing the world, and understanding men and manners, there are few persons of distinction, or merchants, or seamen, who dwell in the maritime parts, but what can hold conversation in both tongues; as I found some weeks after, when I went to pay my respects to the Emperor of Blefuscu, which in the midst of great misfortunes, through the malice of my enemies, proved a very happy adventure to me, as I shall relate in its proper place.

The reader may remember, that when I signed those articles upon which I recovered my liberty, there were some which I disliked upon account of their being too servile, neither could anything but an extreme necessity have forced me to submit. But being now a *Nardac*, of the highest rank in that Empire, such offices were looked upon as below my dignity, and the Emperor (to do him justice) never once mentioned them to me. However, it was not long before I had an opportunity of doing his Majesty, at least, as I then thought, a most signal service. I was alarmed at midnight with the cries of many hundred people at my door; by which being suddenly awaked, I was in some kind of terror. I heard the word *burglum* repeated incessantly: several of the Emperor's Court, making their way through the crowd, entreated me to come immediately to the palace, where her Imperial Majesty's apartment was on fire, by the carelessness of a Maid of Honour, who fell asleep while she was reading a romance. I got up in an instant; and orders being given to clear the way before me, and it being likewise a moonshine night, I made a shift to get to the palace without trampling on any of the people. I found they had already applied ladders to the walls of the apartment, and were well provided with buckets, but the water was at some distance. These buckets were about the size of a large thimble, and the poor people supplied me with them as fast as they could; but the flame was so violent, that they did little good. I might easily have stifled it with my coat, which I unfortunately left behind me for haste, and came away only in my leathern jerkin. The case seemed wholly desperate and deplorable, and this magnificent palace would have infallibly been burnt down to the ground, if, by a presence of mind, unusual to me, I had not suddenly thought of an expedient. I had the evening before drank plentifully of a most delicious wine, called *glimigrim* (the Blefuscudians call it *flunec*, but ours is esteemed the better sort), which is very diuretic. By the luckiest chance in the world, I had not discharged myself of any part of it. The heat I had contracted by coming very near the flames, and by my labouring to quench them, made the wine begin to operate by urine; which I voided in such a quantity, and applied so well to the proper places, that in three minutes the fire was wholly extinguished,[42] and the rest of that noble pile, which had cost so many ages in erecting, preserved from destruction.

It was now daylight, and I returned to my house, without waiting to congratulate with the Emperor; because, although I had done a very eminent piece of service, yet I could not tell how his Majesty might resent the manner by which I had performed it: for, by the fundamental laws of the realm, it is capital in any person, of what quality soever, to make water within the precincts of the palace. But I was a little comforted by a message from his Majesty, that he would give orders to the Grand Justiciary for passing my pardon in form; which, however, I could not obtain. And I was privately assured, that the Empress, conceiving the greatest abhorrence of what I had done, removed to the most distant side of the court, firmly resolved that those buildings should never be repaired for her use; and, in the presence of her chief confidants, could not forbear vowing revenge.

CHAPTER 6

Of the inhabitants of Lilliput; their learning, laws, and customs, the manner of educating their children. The author's way of living in that country. His vindication of a great Lady.

ALTHOUGH I intend to leave the description of this Empire to a particular treatise, yet in the meantime I am content to gratify the curious reader with some general ideas. As the common size of the natives is somewhat under six inches, so there is an exact proportion in all other animals, as well as plants and trees: for instance, the tallest horses and oxen are between four and five inches in height, the sheep an inch and a half, more or less; their geese about the bigness of a sparrow, and so the several gradations downwards, till you come to the smallest, which, to my sight, were almost invisible; but Nature hath adapted the eyes of the Lilliputians to all objects proper for their view: they see with great exactness, but at no great distance. And to show the sharpness of their sight towards objects that are near, I have been much pleased with observing a cook pulling a lark, which was not so large as a common fly; and a young girl threading an invisible needle with invisible silk. Their tallest trees are about seven foot high; I mean some of those in the great royal park, the tops whereof I could but just reach with my fist clinched.[43] The other vegetables[44] are in the same proportion; but this I leave to the reader's imagination.

I shall say but little at present of their learning, which for many ages hath flourished in all its branches among them: but their manner of writing is very peculiar, being neither from the left to the right, like the Europeans; nor from the right to the left, like the Arabians; nor from up to down, like the Chinese; nor from down to up, like the Cascagians;[45] but aslant from one corner of the paper to the other, like our ladies in England.

They bury their dead with their heads directly downwards, because they hold an opinion that in eleven thousand moons they are all to rise again, in which period the earth (which they conceive to be flat) will turn upside down, and by this means they shall, at their resurrection, be found ready standing on their feet. The learned among them confess the absurdity of this doctrine, but the practice still continues, in compliance to the vulgar.

There are some laws and customs in this Empire very peculiar, and if they were not so directly contrary to those of my own dear country, I should be tempted to say a little in their justification. It is only to be wished, that they were as well executed. The first I shall mention, relateth to informers. All crimes against the state are punished here with the utmost severity; but if the person accused make his innocence plainly to appear upon his trial, the accuser is immediately put to an ignominious death; and out of his goods or lands, the innocent person is quadruply recompensed for the loss of his time, for the danger he underwent, for the hardship of his imprisonment, and for all the charges he hath been at in making his defence. Or, if that fund be deficient, it is largely supplied by the Crown. The Emperor doth also confer on him some public mark of his favour, and proclamation is made of his innocence through the whole city.

They look upon fraud as a greater crime than theft, and therefore seldom fail to punish it with death; for they allege, that care and vigilance, with a very common understanding, may preserve a man's goods from thieves, but honesty hath no fence [46] against superior cunning: and since it is necessary that there should be a perpetual intercourse of buying and selling, and dealing upon credit, where fraud is permitted or connived at, or hath no law to punish it, the honest dealer is always undone, and the knave gets the advantage. I remember when I was once interceding with the King for a criminal who had wronged his master of a great sum of money, which he had received by order, and ran away with; and happening to tell his Majesty, by way of extenuation, that it was only a breach of trust; the Emperor thought it monstrous in me to offer, as a defence, the greatest aggravation of the crime: and truly, I had little to say in return, farther than the common answer, that different nations had different customs; for, I confess, I was heartily ashamed.

Although we usually call reward and punishment the two hinges upon which all government turns, yet I could never observe this maxim to be put in practice by any nation except that of Lilliput. Whoever can there bring sufficient proof that he hath strictly observed the laws of his country for seventy-three moons, hath a claim to certain privileges, according to his quality and condition of life, with a proportionable sum of money out of a fund appropriated for that use: he likewise acquires the title of *Snilpall*, or *Legal*, which is added to his name, but doth not descend to his posterity. And these people thought it a prodigious defect of policy among us, when I told them that our laws were enforced only by penalties without any mention of reward. It is upon this account that the image of Justice, in their courts of judicature, is formed with six eyes, two before, as many behind, and on each side one, to signify circumspection; with a bag of gold open in her right hand, and a sword sheathed in her left, to show she is more disposed to reward than to punish.

In choosing persons for all employments, they have more regard to good morals than to great abilities; for, since government is necessary to mankind, they believe that the common size of human understandings is fitted to some station or other, and that Providence never intended to make the management of public affairs a mystery,[47] to be comprehended only by a few persons of sublime genius, of which there seldom are three born in an age: but, they suppose truth, justice, temperance, and the like, to be in every man's power; the practice of which virtues, assisted by experience and a good intention, would qualify any man for the service of his country, except where a course of study is required. But they thought the want of moral virtues was so far from being supplied by superior endowments of the mind, that employments could never be put into such dangerous hands as those of persons so qualified; and at least, that the mistakes committed by ignorance in a virtuous disposition, would never be of such fatal consequence to the public weal, as the practices of a man whose inclinations led him to be corrupt, and had great abilities to manage, and multiply, and defend his corruptions.

In like manner, the disbelief of a Divine Providence renders a man uncapable of holding any public station; for since kings avow themselves to be the deputies of Providence, the Lilliputians think nothing can be more absurd than for a prince to employ such men as disown the authority under which he acteth.

In relating these and the following laws, I would only be understood to mean the original institutions, and not the most scandalous corruptions into which these people are fallen by the degenerate nature of man. For as to that infamous practice of acquiring great employments by dancing on the ropes, or badges of favour and distinction by leaping over sticks, and creeping under them, the reader is to observe, that they were first introduced by the grandfather of the Emperor now reigning, and grew to the present height by the gradual increase of party and faction.

Ingratitude is among them a capital crime, as we read it to have been in some other countries; for they reason thus, that whoever makes ill returns to his benefactor, must needs be a common enemy to the rest of mankind, from whom he hath received no obligation, and therefore such a man is not fit to live.

Their notions relating to the duties of parents and children differ extremely from ours. For, since the conjunction of male and female is founded upon the great Law of Nature, in order to propagate and continue the species, the Lilliputians will needs have it, that men and women are joined together like other animals, by the motives of concupiscence; and that their tenderness towards their young, proceedeth from the like natural principle: for which reason they will never allow, that a child is under any obligation to his father for begetting him, or to his mother for bringing him into the world; which, considering the miseries of human life, was neither a benefit in itself, nor intended so by his parents, whose thoughts in their love-encounters were otherwise employed. Upon these, and the like reasonings, their opinion is, that parents are the last of all others to be trusted with the education of their own children: and therefore they have in every town public nurseries, where all parents, except cottagers and labourers, are obliged to send their infants of both sexes to be reared and educated when they come to the age of twenty moons, at which time they are supposed to have some rudiments of docility. These schools are of several kinds, suited to different qualities, and to both sexes. They have certain professors well skilled in preparing children for such a condition of life as befits the rank of their parents, and their own capacities as well as inclinations. I shall first say something of the male nurseries, and then of the female.

The nurseries for males of noble or eminent birth are provided with grave and learned professors,[48] and their several deputies. The clothes and food of the children are plain and simple. They are bred up in the principles of honour, justice, courage, modesty, clemency, religion, and love of their country; they are always employed in some business, except in the times of eating and sleeping, which are very short, and two hours for diversions, consisting of bodily exercises. They are dressed by men till four years of age, and then are obliged to dress themselves, although their quality be ever so great; and the women attendants, who are aged proportionably to ours at fifty, perform only the most menial offices.

They are never suffered to converse with servants, but go together in small or greater numbers to take their diversions, and always in the presence of a professor, or one of his deputies; whereby they avoid those early bad impressions of folly and vice to which our children are subject. Their parents are suffered to see them only twice a year; the visit is not to last above an hour. They are allowed to kiss the child at meeting and parting; but a professor, who always standeth by on those occasions, will not suffer them to whisper, or use any fondling expressions, or bring any presents of toys, sweetmeats, and the like.

The pension from each family for the education and entertainment of a child, upon failure of due payment, is levied by the Emperor's officers.

The nurseries for children of ordinary gentlemen, merchants, traders, and handicrafts, are managed proportionally after the same manner; only those designed for trades are put out apprentices at seven years old, whereas those of persons of quality continue in their nurseries till fifteen, which answers to one and twenty with us: but the confinement is gradually lessened for the last three years.

In the female nurseries, the young girls of quality are educated much like the males, only they are dressed by orderly servants of their own sex, but always in the presence of a professor or deputy, till they come to dress themselves, which is at five years old. And if it be found that these nurses ever presume to entertain the girls with frightful or foolish stories, or the common follies practised by chambermaids among us, they are publicly whipped thrice about the city, imprisoned for a year, and banished for life to the most desolate parts of the country. Thus the young ladies there are as much ashamed of being cowards and fools as the men, and despise all personal ornaments beyond decency and cleanliness: neither did I perceive any difference in their education, made by their difference of sex, only that the exercises of the females were not altogether so robust, and that some rules were given them relating to domestic life, and a smaller compass of learning was enjoined them: for their maxim is, that among people of quality, a wife should be always a reasonable and agreeable companion, because she cannot always be young. When the girls are twelve years old, which among them is the marriageable age, their parents or guardians take them home, with great expressions of gratitude to the professors, and seldom without tears of the young lady and her companions.

In the nurseries of females of the meaner sort, the children are instructed in all kinds of works proper for their sex, and their several degrees: those intended for apprentices are dismissed at seven years old, the rest are kept to eleven.

The meaner families who have children at these nurseries are obliged, besides their annual pension, which is as low as possible, to return to the steward of the nursery a small monthly share of their gettings, to be a portion for the child; and therefore all parents are limited in their expenses by the law. For the Lilliputians think nothing can be more unjust, than that people, in subservience to their own appetites, should bring children into the world, and leave the burthen of supporting them on the public. As to persons of quality, they give security to appropriate a certain sum for each child, suitable to their condition; and these funds are always managed with good husbandry, and the most exact justice.

The cottagers and labourers keep their children at home, their business being only to till and cultivate the earth, and therefore their education is of little consequence to the public; but the old and diseased among them are supported by hospitals: for begging is a trade unknown in this Empire.

And here it may perhaps divert the curious reader, to give some account of my domestic,[49] and my manner of living in this country, during a residence of nine months and thirteen days. Having a head mechanically turned, and being likewise forced by necessity, I had made for myself a table and chair convenient enough, out of the largest trees in the royal park. Two hundred sempstresses were employed to make me shirts, and linen for my bed and table, all of the strongest and coarsest kind they could get; which, however, they were forced to quilt together in several folds, for the thickest was some degrees finer than lawn. Their linen is usually three inches wide, and three foot make a piece. The sempstresses took my measure as I lay on the ground, one standing at my neck, and another at my mid leg, with a strong cord extended, that each held by the end, while the third measured the length of the cord with a rule of an inch long. Then they measured my right thumb, and desired no more; for by a mathematical computation, that twice round the thumb is once round the wrist, and so on to the neck and the waist, and by the help of my old shirt, which I displayed on the ground before them for a pattern, they fitted me exactly. Three hundred tailors were employed in the same manner to make me clothes; but they had another contrivance for taking my measure. I kneeled down, and they raised a ladder from the ground to my neck; upon this ladder one of them mounted, and let fall a plumb-line from my collar to the floor, which just answered the length of my coat; but my waist and arms I measured myself. When my clothes were finished, which was done in my house (for the largest of theirs would not have been able to hold them), they looked like the patchwork made by the ladies in England, only that mine were all of a colour.

I had three hundred cooks to dress my victuals, in little convenient huts built about my house, where they and their families lived, and prepared me two dishes apiece. I took up twenty waiters in my hand, and placed them on the table; an hundred more attended below on the ground, some with dishes of meat, and some with barrels of wine, and other liquors, slung on their shoulders; all which the waiters above drew up as I wanted, in a very ingenious manner, by certain cords, as we draw the bucket up a well in Europe. A dish of their meat was a good mouthful, and a barrel of their liquor a reasonable draught. Their mutton yields to ours, but their beef is excellent. I have had a sirloin so large, that I have been forced to make three bits of it; but this is rare. My servants were astonished to see me eat it bones and all, as in our country we do the leg of a lark. Their geese and turkeys I usually ate at a mouthful, and I must confess they far exceed ours. Of their smaller fowl I could take up twenty or thirty at the end of my knife.

One day his Imperial Majesty, being informed of my way of living, desired that himself, and his Royal Consort, with the young Princes of the Blood of both sexes, might have the happiness (as he was pleased to call it) of dining with me. They came accordingly, and I placed 'em upon chairs of state on my table, just over-against me, with their guards about them. Flimnap the Lord High Treasurer attended there likewise, with his white staff;[50] and I observed he often looked on me with a sour countenance, which I would not seem to regard, but ate more than usual, in honour to my dear country, as well as to fill the Court with admiration. I have some private reasons to believe, that this visit from his Majesty gave Flimnap an opportunity of doing me ill offices to his master. That Minister had always been my secret enemy, although he outwardly caressed me more than was usual to the moroseness of his nature. He represented to the Emperor the low condition of his Treasury; that he was forced to take up money at great discount; that Exchequer bills would not circulate under nine per cent below par; that I had cost his Majesty above a million and a half of *sprugs* (their greatest gold coin, about the bigness of a spangle); and upon the whole, that it would be advisable in the Emperor to take the first fair occasion of dismissing me.

I am here obliged to vindicate the reputation of an excellent Lady,[51] who was an innocent sufferer upon my account. The Treasurer took a fancy to be jealous of his wife, from the malice of some evil tongues, who informed him that her Grace had taken a violent affection for my person, and the Court-scandal ran for some time, that she once came privately to my lodging. This I solemnly declare to be a most infamous false-hood, without any grounds, farther than that her Grace was pleased to treat me with all innocent marks of freedom and friendship. I own she came often to my house, but always publicly, nor ever without three more in the coach, who were usually her sister, and young daughter, and some particular acquaintance; but this was common to many other ladies of the Court. And I still appeal to my servants round, whether they at any time saw a coach at my door without knowing what persons were in it. On those occasions, when a servant had given me notice, my custom was to go immediately to the door; and after paying my respects, to take up the coach and two horses very carefully in my hands (for if there were six horses, the postillion always unharnessed four), and place them on a table, where I had fixed a moveable rim quite round, of five inches high, to prevent accidents. And I have often had four coaches and horses at once on my table full of company, while I sat in my chair leaning my face towards them; and when I was engaged with one set, the coachmen would gently drive the others round my table. I have passed many an after-noon very agreeably in these conversations. But I defy the Treasurer, or his two informers (I will name them, and let 'em make their best of it), Clustril and Drunlo, to prove that any person ever came to me *incognito*, except the Secretary Reld-resal, who was sent by express command of his Imperial Majesty, as I have before related. I should not have dwelt so long upon this particular, if it had not been a point wherein the reputation of a great Lady is so nearly concerned, to say nothing of my own; though I had the honour to be a *Nardac*, which the Treasurer himself is not, for all the world knows he is only a *Clumglum*, a title inferior by one degree, as that of a marquis is to a duke in England; yet I allow he preceded me in right of his post. These false informations, which I afterwards came to the knowledge of, by an accident not proper to mention, made the Treasurer show his Lady for some time an ill countenance, and me a worse; for although he were at last undeceived and reconciled to her, yet I lost all credit with him, and found my interest decline very fast with the Emperor himself, who was indeed too much governed by that favourite.

CHAPTER 7

The author being informed of a design to accuse him of high treason, makes his escape to Blefuscu. His reception there.

BEFORE I proceed to give an account of my leaving this kingdom, it may be proper to inform the reader of a private intrigue which had been for two months forming against me.

I had been hitherto all my life a stranger to Courts, for which I was unqualified by the meanness of my condition. I had indeed heard and read enough of the dispositions of great princes and ministers; but never expected to have found such terrible effects of them in so remote a country, governed, as I thought, by very different maxims from those in Europe.

When I was just preparing to pay my attendance on the Emperor of Blefuscu, a considerable person at Court (to whom I had been very serviceable at a time when he lay under the highest displeasure of his Imperial Majesty) came to my house very privately at night in a close chair, and without sending his name, desired admittance: the chairmen were dismissed; I put the chair, with his Lordship in it, into my coat-pocket; and giving orders to a trusty servant to say I was indisposed and gone to sleep, I fastened the door of my house, placed the chair on the table, according to my usual custom, and sat down by it. After the common salutations were over, observing his Lordship's countenance full of concern, and enquiring into the reason, he desired I would hear him with patience in a matter that highly concerned my honour and my life. His speech was to the following effect, for I took notes of it as soon as he left me.

You are to know, said he, that several Committees of Council have been lately called in the most private manner on your account: and it is but two days since his Majesty came to a full resolution.

You are very sensible that Skyresh Bolgolam (*Galbet*, or High Admiral) hath been your mortal enemy almost ever since your arrival. His original reasons I know not, but his hatred is much increased since your great success against Blefuscu, by which his glory, as Admiral, is obscured. This Lord, in conjunction with Flimnap the High Treasurer, whose enmity against you is notorious on account of his Lady, Limtoc the General, Lalcon the Chamberlain, and Balmuff the Grand Justiciary, have prepared articles of impeachment against you, for treason, and other capital crimes.

This preface made me so impatient, being conscious of my own merits and innocence, that I was going to interrupt; when he entreated me to be silent; and thus proceeded.

Out of gratitude for the favours you have done me, I procured information of the whole proceedings, and a copy of the articles, wherein I venture my head for your service.

Articles [52] *of Impeachment against* Quinbus Flestrin (*the* Man-Mountain).

ARTICLE I.

Whereas, by a statute made in the reign of his Imperial Majesty Calin Deffar Plune, it is enacted, That whoever shall make water within the precincts of the royal palace, shall be liable to the pains and penalties of high treason: notwithstanding, the said Quinbus Flestrin, in open breach of the said law, under colour of extinguishing the fire kindled in the apartment of his Majesty's most dear Imperial Consort, did maliciously, traitorously, and devilishly, by discharge of his urine, put out the said fire kindled in the said apartment, lying and being within the precincts of the said royal palace, against the statute in that case provided, etc., against the duty, etc.

ARTICLE II.

That the said Quinbus Flestrin, having brought the imperial fleet of Blefuscu into the royal port, and being afterwards commanded by his Imperial Majesty to seize all the other ships of the said Empire of Blefuscu, and reduce that Empire to a province, to be governed by a Viceroy from hence, and to destroy and put to death not only all the Big-Endian exiles, but likewise all the people of that Empire who would not immediately forsake the Big-Endian heresy: he, the said Flestrin, like a false traitor against his most Auspicious, Serene, Imperial Majesty, did petition to be excused from the said service, upon pretence of unwillingness to force the consciences, or destroy the liberties and lives of an innocent people.

ARTICLE III.

That, whereas certain ambassadors arrived from the Court of Blefuscu to sue for peace in his Majesty's Court: he the said Flestrin did, like a false traitor, aid, abet, comfort, and divert the said ambassadors, although he knew them to be servants to a Prince who was lately an open enemy to his Imperial Majesty, and in open war against his said Majesty.

ARTICLE IV.

That the said Quinbus Flestrin, contrary to the duty of a faithful subject, is now preparing to make a voyage to the Court and Empire of Blefuscu, for which he hath received only verbal licence from his Imperial Majesty; and under colour of the said licence, doth falsely and traitorously intend to take the said voyage, and thereby to aid, comfort, and abet the Emperor of Blefuscu, so late an enemy, and in open war with his Imperial Majesty aforesaid.

There are some other articles, but these are the most important, of which I have read you an abstract.

In the several debates upon this impeachment, it must be confessed that his Majesty gave many marks of his great *lenity*, often urging the services you had done him, and endeavouring to extenuate your crimes. The Treasurer and Admiral insisted that you should be put to the most painful and ignominious death, by setting fire on your house at night, and the General was to attend with twenty thousand men armed with poisoned arrows to shoot you on the face and hands. Some of your servants were to have private orders to strew a poisonous juice on your shirts and sheets, which would soon make you tear your own flesh, and die in the utmost torture. The General came into the same opinion, so that for a long time there was a majority against you. But his Majesty resolving, if possible, to spare your life, at last brought off the Chamberlain.

Upon this incident, Reldresal, Principal Secretary for Private Affairs, who always approved himself your true friend, was commanded by the Emperor to deliver his opinion, which he accordingly did; and therein justified the good thoughts you have of him. He allowed your crimes to be great, but that still there was room for mercy, the most commendable virtue in a prince, and for which his Majesty was so justly celebrated. He said, the friendship between you and him was so well known to the world, that perhaps the most honourable Board might think him partial: however, in obedience to the command he had received, he would freely offer his sentiments. That if his Majesty, in consideration of your services, and pursuant to his own merciful disposition, would please to spare your life, and only give order to put out both your eyes,[53] he humbly conceived, that by this expedient justice might in some measure be satisfied, and all the world would applaud the *lenity* of the Emperor, as well as the fair and generous proceedings of those who have the honour to be his counsellors. That the loss of your eyes would be no impediment to your bodily strength, by which you might still be useful to his Majesty. That blindness is an addition to courage, by concealing dangers from us; that the fear you had for your eyes, was the greatest difficulty in bringing over the enemy's fleet, and it would be sufficient for you to see by the eyes of the Ministers, since the greatest princes do no more.

This proposal was received with the utmost disapprobation by the whole Board. Bolgolam, the Admiral, could not preserve his temper; but rising up in fury, said, he wondered how the Secretary durst presume to give his opinion for preserving the life of a traitor: that the services you had performed were, by all true reasons of state, the great aggravation of your crimes; that you, who were able to extinguish the fire, by discharge of urine in her Majesty's apartment (which he mentioned with horror), might, at another time, raise an inundation by the same means, to drown the whole palace; and the same strength which enabled you to bring over the enemy's fleet, might serve, upon the first discontent, to carry it back: that he had good reasons to think you were a Big-Endian in your heart; and as treason begins in the heart before it appears in overt acts, so he accused you as a traitor on that account, and therefore insisted you should be put to death.

The Treasurer was of the same opinion; he showed to what straits his Majesty's revenue was reduced by the charge of maintaining you, which would soon grow insupportable: that the Secretary's expedient of putting out your eyes was so far from being a remedy against this evil, that it would probably increase it, as it is manifest from the common practice of blinding some kind of fowl, after which they fed the faster, and grew sooner fat: that his sacred Majesty, and the Council, who are your judges, were in their own consciences fully convinced of your guilt, which was a sufficient argument to condemn you to death, without the *formal proofs* [54] *required by the strict letter of the law.*

But his Imperial Majesty, fully determined against capital punishment, was graciously pleased to say, that since the Council thought the loss of your eyes too easy a censure, some other may be inflicted hereafter. And your friend the Secretary humbly desiring to be heard again, in answer to what the Treasurer had objected concerning the great charge his Majesty was at in maintaining you, said, that his Excellency, who had the sole disposal of the Emperor's revenue, might easily provide against this evil, by gradually lessening your establishment; by which, for want of sufficient food, you would grow weak and faint, and lose your appetite, and consequently decay and consume in a few months; neither would the stench of your carcass be then so dangerous, when it should become more than half diminished; and immediately upon your death, five or six thousand of his Majesty's subjects might, in two or three days, cut your flesh from your bones, take it away by cart-loads, and bury it in distant parts to prevent infection, leaving the skeleton as a monument of admiration to posterity.

Thus by the great friendship of the Secretary, the whole affair was compromised. It was strictly enjoined, that the project of starving you by degrees should be kept a secret, but the sentence of putting out your eyes was entered on the books; none dissenting except Bolgolam the Admiral, who being a creature of the Empress, was perpetually instigated by her Majesty to insist upon your death, she having borne perpetual malice against you, on account of that infamous and illegal method you took to extinguish the fire in her apartment.

In three days your friend the Secretary will be directed to come to your house, and read before you the articles of impeachment; and then to signify the great *lenity* and favour of his Majesty and Council, whereby you are only condemned to the loss of your eyes, which his Majesty doth not question you will gratefully and humbly submit to; and twenty of his Majesty's surgeons will attend, in order to see the operation well performed, by discharging very sharp-pointed arrows into the balls of your eyes, as you lie on the ground.

I leave to your prudence what measures you will take; and to avoid suspicion, I must immediately return in as private a manner as I came.

His Lordship did so, and I remained alone, under many doubts and perplexities of mind.

It was a custom introduced by this Prince and his Ministry (very different, as I have been assured, from the practices of former times), that after the Court had decreed any cruel execution, either to gratify the monarch's resentment, or the malice of a favourite, the Emperor always made a speech to his whole Council, expressing his *great lenity and tenderness, as qualities known and confessed by all the world.* This speech was immediately published through the kingdom; nor did anything terrify the people so much as those encomiums [55] on his Majesty's mercy; because it was observed, that the more these praises were enlarged and insisted on, the more *inhuman* was the punishment, and the *sufferer more innocent.* Yet, as to myself, I must confess, having never been designed for a courtier either by my birth or education, I was so ill a judge of things, that I could not discover the *lenity* and favour of this sentence, but conceived it (perhaps erroneously) rather to be rigorous than gentle. I sometimes thought of standing my trial, for although I could not deny the facts alleged in the several articles, yet I hoped they would admit of some extenuations. But having in my life perused many state trials, which I ever observed to terminate as the judges thought fit to direct, I durst not rely on so dangerous a decision, in so critical a juncture, and against such powerful enemies. Once I was strongly bent upon resistance, for while I had liberty, the whole strength of that Empire could hardly subdue me, and I might easily with stones pelt the metropolis to pieces; but I soon rejected that project with horror, by remembering the oath I had made to the Emperor, the favours I received from him, and the high title of *Nardac* he conferred upon me. Neither had I so soon learned the gratitude of courtiers, to persuade myself that his Majesty's *present severities acquitted me of all past obligations*.

At last I fixed upon a resolution, for which it is probable I may incur some censure, and not unjustly; for I confess I owe the preserving mine eyes, and consequently my liberty, to my own great rashness and want of experience: because if I had then known the nature of princes and ministers, which I have since observed in many other courts, and their methods of treating criminals less obnoxious than myself, I should with great alacrity and readiness have submitted to so *easy* a punishment. But hurried on by the precipitancy of youth, and having his Imperial Majesty's licence to pay my attendance upon the Emperor of Blefuscu, I took this opportunity, before the three days were elapsed, to send a letter to my friend the Secretary, signifying my resolution of setting out that morning for Blefuscu pursuant to the leave I had got; and without waiting for an answer, I went to that side of the island where our fleet lay. I seized a large man-of-war, tied a cable to the prow, and lifting up the anchors, I stripped myself, put my clothes (together with my coverlet, which I carried under my arm) into the vessel, and drawing it after me between wading and swimming, arrived at the royal port of Blefuscu, where the people had long expected me; they lent me two guides to direct me to the capital city, which is of the same name. I held them in my hands till I came within two hundred yards of the gate, and desired them to signify my arrival to one of the Secretaries, and let him know, I there waited his Majesty's commands. I had an answer in about an hour, that his Majesty, attended by the Royal Family, and great officers of the Court, was coming out to receive me. I advanced a hundred yards. The Emperor, and his train, alighted from their horses, the Empress and ladies from their coaches, and I did not perceive they were in any fright or concern. I lay on the ground to kiss his Majesty's and the Empress's hand. I told his Majesty that I was come according to my promise, and with the licence of the Emperor my master, to have the honour of seeing so mighty a monarch, and to offer him any service in my power, consistent with my duty to my own prince; not mentioning a word of my disgrace, because I had hitherto no regular information of it, and might suppose myself wholly ignorant of any such design; neither could I reasonably conceive that the Emperor would discover [56] the secret while I was out of his power: wherein, however, it soon appeared I was deceived.

I shall not trouble the reader with the particular account of my reception at this Court, which was suitable to the generosity of so great a prince; nor of the difficulties I was in for want of a house and bed, being forced to lie on the ground, wrapped up in my coverlet.

CHAPTER 8

The author, by a lucky accident, finds means to leave Blefuscu; and, after some difficulties, returns safe to his native country.

THREE days after my arrival, walking out of curiosity to the north-east coast of the island, I observed, about half a league off, in the sea, somewhat that looked like a boat overturned. I pulled off my shoes and stockings, and wading two or three hundred yards, I found the object to approach nearer by force of the tide, and then plainly saw it to be a real boat, which I supposed might, by some tempest, have been driven from a ship; whereupon I returned immediately towards the city, and desired his Imperial Majesty to lend me twenty of the tallest vessels he had left after the loss of his fleet, and three thousand seamen under the command of his Vice-Admiral. This fleet sailed round, while I went back the shortest way to the coast where I first discovered the boat; I found the tide had driven it still nearer. The seamen were all provided with cordage, which I had beforehand twisted to a sufficient strength. When the ships came up, I stripped myself, and waded till I came within an hundred yards of the boat, after which I was forced to swim till I got up to it. The seamen threw me the end of the cord, which I fastened to a hole in the fore-part of the boat, and the other end to a man-of-war: but I found all my labour to little purpose; for being out of my depth, I was not able to work. In this necessity, I was forced to swim behind, and push the boat forwards as often as I could, with one of my hands; and the tide favouring me, I advanced so far, that I could just hold up my chin and feel the ground. I rested two or three minutes, and then gave the boat another shove, and so on till the sea was no higher than my armpits; and now the most laborious part being over, I took out my other cables, which were stowed in one of the ships, and fastening them first to the boat, and then to nine of the vessels which attended me; the wind being favourable, the seamen towed, and I shoved till we arrived within forty yards of the shore, and waiting till the tide was out, I got dry to the boat, and by the assistance of two thousand men, with ropes and engines, I made a shift to turn it on its bottom, and found it was but little damaged.

I shall not trouble the reader with the difficulties I was under by the help of certain paddles, which cost me ten days making, to get my boat to the royal port of Blefuscu, where a mighty concourse of people appeared upon my arrival, full of wonder at the sight of so prodigious a vessel. I told the Emperor, that my good fortune had thrown this boat in my way, to carry me to some place from whence I might return into my native country, and begged his Majesty's orders for getting materials to fit it up, together with his licence to depart; which, after some kind expostulations, he was pleased to grant.

I did very much wonder, in all this time, not to have heard of an express relating to me from our Emperor to the Court of Blefuscu. But I was afterwards given privately to understand, that his Imperial Majesty, never imagining I had the least notice of his designs, believed I was only gone to Blefuscu in performance of my promise, according to the licence he had given me, which was well known at our Court, and would return in a few days when that ceremony was ended. But he was at last in pain at my long absence; and, after consulting with the Treasurer, and the rest of that Cabal, a person of quality was dispatched [57] with the copy of the articles against me. This envoy had instructions to represent to the monarch of Blefuscu the great *lenity* of his master, who was content to punish me no further than with the loss of mine eyes; that I had fled from justice, and if I did not return in two hours, I should be deprived of my title of *Nardac*, and declared a traitor. The envoy further added, that in order to maintain the peace and amity between both Empires, his master expected, that his brother of Blefuscu would give orders to have me sent back to Lilliput, bound hand and foot, to be punished as a traitor.

The Emperor of Blefuscu, having taken three days to consult, returned an answer consisting of many civilities and excuses. He said, that as for sending me bound, his brother knew it was impossible; that although I had deprived him of his fleet, yet he owed great obligations to me for many good offices I had done him in making the peace. That however both their Majesties would soon be made easy; for I had found a prodigious vessel on the shore, able to carry me on the sea, which he had given order to fit up with my own assistance and direction, and he hoped in a few weeks both Empires would be freed from so insupportable an incumbrance.

With this answer the envoy returned to Lilliput, and the Monarch of Blefuscu related to me all that had passed, offering me at the same time (but under the strictest confidence) his gracious protection, if I would continue in his service; wherein although I believed him sincere, yet I resolved never more to put any confidence in princes or ministers, where I could possibly avoid it; and therefore, with all due acknowledgements for his favourable intentions, I humbly begged to be excused. I told him, that since Fortune, whether good or evil, had thrown a vessel in my way, I was resolved to venture myself in the ocean, rather than be an occasion of difference between two such mighty monarchs. Neither did I find the Emperor at all displeased; and I discovered by a certain accident, that he was very glad of my resolution,[58] and so were most of his Ministers.

These considerations moved me to hasten my departure somewhat sooner than I intended; to which the Court, impatient to have me gone, very readily contributed. Five hundred workmen were employed to make two sails to my boat, according to my directions, by quilting thirteen fold of their strongest linen together. I was at the pains of making ropes and cables, by twisting ten, twenty or thirty of the thickest and strongest of theirs. A great stone that I happened to find, after a long search by the seashore, served me for an anchor. I had the tallow of three hundred cows for greasing my boat, and other uses. I was at incredible pains in cutting down some of the largest timber-trees for oars and masts, wherein I was, however, much assisted by his Majesty's ship-carpenters, who helped me in smoothing them, after I had done the rough work.

In about a month, when all was prepared, I sent to receive his Majesty's commands, and to take my leave. The Emperor and Royal Family came out of the palace; I lay down on my face to kiss his hand, which he very graciously gave me; so did the Empress, and young Princes of the Blood. His Majesty presented me with fifty purses of two hundred *sprugs* apiece, together with his picture at full length, which I put immediately into one of my gloves, to keep it from being hurt.

The ceremonies at my departure were too many to trouble the reader with at this time.

I stored the boat with the carcasses of an hundred oxen, and three hundred sheep, with bread and drink proportionable, and as much meat ready dressed as four hundred cooks could provide. I took with me six cows and two bulls alive, with as many ewes and rams, intending to carry them into my own country, and propagate the breed. And to feed them on board, I had a good bundle of hay, and a bag of corn. I would gladly have taken a dozen of the natives, but this was a thing the Emperor would by no means permit; and besides a diligent search into my pockets, his Majesty engaged my honour not to carry away any of his subjects, although with their own consent and desire.

Having thus prepared all things as well as I was able, I set sail on the twenty-fourth day of September, 1701, at six in the morning; and when I had gone about four leagues to the northward, the wind being at south-east, at six in the evening, I descried a small island about half a league to the north-west. I advanced forward, and cast anchor on the lee-side of the island, which seemed to be uninhabited. I then took some refreshment, and went to my rest. I slept well, and as I conjecture at least six hours, for I found the day broke in two hours after I awaked. It was a clear night. I ate my breakfast before the sun was up; and heaving anchor, the wind being favourable, I steered the same course that I had done the day before, wherein I was directed by my pocket-compass. My intention was to reach, if possible, one of those islands, which I had reason to believe lay to the north-east of Van Diemen's Land. I discovered nothing all that day; but upon the next, about three in the afternoon, when I had by my computation made twenty-four leagues from Blefuscu, I descried a sail steering to the south-east; my course was due east. I hailed her, but could get no answer; yet I found I gained upon her, for the wind slackened. I made all the sail I could, and in half an hour she spied me, then hung out her ancient,[59] and discharged a gun. It is not easy to express the joy I was in upon the unexpected hope of once more seeing my beloved country, and the dear pledges I had left in it. The ship slackened her sails, and I came up with her between five and six in the evening, September 26; but my heart leapt within me to see her English colours. I put my cows and sheep into my coat-pockets, and got on board with all my little cargo of provisions. The vessel was an English merchantman, returning from Japan by the North and South Seas;[60] the captain, Mr John Biddel of Deptford, a very civil man, and an excellent sailor. We were now in the latitude of 30 degrees south; there were about fifty men in the ship; and here I met an old comrade of mine, one Peter Williams, who gave me a good character to the captain. This gentleman treated me with kindness, and desired I would let him know what place I came from last, and whither I was bound; which I did in few words, but he thought I was raving, and that the dangers I underwent had disturbed my head; whereupon I took my black cattle and sheep out of my pocket, which, after great astonishment, clearly convinced him of my veracity. I then showed him the gold given me by the Emperor of Blefuscu, together with his Majesty's picture at full length, and some other rarities of that country. I gave him two purses of two hundred *sprugs* each, and promised, when we arrived in England, to make him a present of a cow and a sheep big with young.

I shall not trouble the reader with a particular account of this voyage, which was very prosperous for the most part. We arrived in the Downs on the 13th of April, 1702. I had only one misfortune, that the rats on board carried away one of my sheep; I found her bones in a hole, picked clean from the flesh. The rest of my cattle I got safe on shore, and set them a grazing in a bowling-green at Greenwich, where the fineness of the grass made them feed very heartily, though I had always feared the contrary: neither could I possibly have preserved them in so long a voyage, if the captain had not allowed me some of his best biscuit, which, rubbed to powder, and mingled with water, was their constant food. The short time I continued in England, I made a considerable profit by showing my cattle to many persons of quality, and others: and before I began my second voyage, I sold them for six hundred pounds. Since my last return, I find the breed is considerably increased, especially the sheep; which I hope will prove much to the advantage of the woollen manufacture, by the fineness of the fleeces.

I stayed but two months with my wife and family; for my insatiable desire of seeing foreign countries would suffer me to continue no longer. I left fifteen hundred pounds with my wife, and fixed her in a good house at Redriff. My remaining stock I carried with me, part in money, and part in goods, in hopes to improve my fortunes. My eldest uncle John had left me an estate in land, near Epping, of about thirty pounds a year; and I had a long lease of the Black Bull in Fetter Lane, which yielded me as much more: so that I was not in any danger of leaving my family upon the parish. My son Johnny, named so after his uncle, was at the grammar school, and a towardly [61] child. My daughter Betty (who is now well married, and has children) was then at her needlework. I took leave of my wife, and boy and girl, with tears on both sides, and went on board the *Adventure*, a merchant-ship of three hundred tons, bound for Surat, Captain John Nicholas of Liverpool, commander. But my account of this voyage must be referred to the second part of my Travels.

THE END OF THE FIRST PART.

TRAVELS · PART II

A VOYAGE TO BROBDINGNAG

*

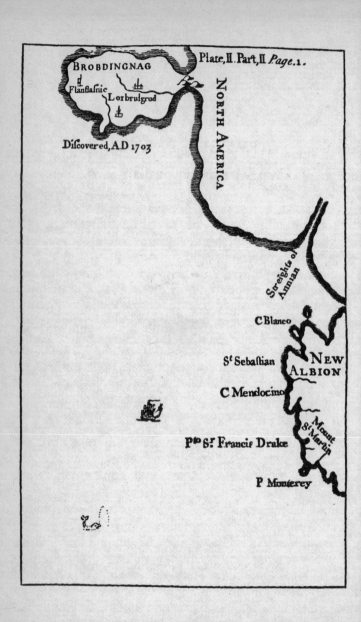

Plate. II. Part. II. *Page. 1.*

BROBDINGNAG

Flanflasnic

Lorbrulgrud

Discovered, A D 1703

NORTH AMERICA

Streights of Annian

C Blanco

St Sebastian

C Mendocino

NEW ALBION

Mount St Martin

Pto Sr Francis Drake

P Monterey

CHAPTER I

A great storm described. The long-boat sent to fetch water, the author goes with it to discover the country. He is left on shore, is seized by one of the natives, and carried to a farmer's house. His reception there, with several accidents that happened there. A description of the inhabitants.

HAVING been condemned by Nature and Fortune to an active and restless life, in two months after my return I again left my native country, and took shipping in the Downs on the 20th day of June, 1702, in the *Adventure*, Capt. John Nicholas, a Cornish man, commander, bound for Surat. We had a very prosperous gale[1] till we arrived at the Cape of Good Hope, where we landed for fresh water, but discovering a leak we unshipped our goods, and wintered there; for the captain falling sick of an ague, we could not leave the Cape till the end of March. We then set sail, and had a good voyage till we passed the Straits of Madagascar; but having got northward of that island, and to about five degrees south latitude, the winds, which in those seas are observed to blow a constant equal gale between the north and west from the beginning of December to the beginning of May, on the 19th of April began to blow with much greater violence, and more westerly than usual, continuing so for twenty days together, during which time we were driven a little to the east of the Molucca Islands, and about three degrees northward of the Line, as our captain found by an observation he took the 2nd of May, at which time the wind ceased, and it was a perfect calm, whereat I was not a little rejoiced. But he, being a man well experienced in the navigation of those seas, bid us all prepare against a storm, which accordingly happened the day following: for a southern wind, called the southern *monsoon*, began to set in.

Finding it was like to overblow,[2] we took in our spritsail, and stood by to hand the fore-sail; but making foul weather, we looked the guns were all fast, and handed the mizen. The ship lay very broad off, so we thought it better spooning before the sea, than trying or hulling. We reefed the fore-sail and set him, we hauled aft the fore-sheet; the helm was hard a-weather. The ship wore bravely. We belayed the fore-down-haul; but the sail was split, and we hauled down the yard, and got the sail into the ship, and unbound all the things clear of it. It was a very fierce storm; the sea broke strange and dangerous. We hauled off upon the lanyard of the whipstaff, and helped the man at helm. We would not get down our topmast, but let all stand, because she scudded before the sea very well, and we knew that the topmast being aloft, the ship was the wholesomer, and made better way through the sea, seeing we had sea-room. When the storm was over, we set fore-sail and mainsail, and brought the ship to. Then we set the mizen, main-topsail and the fore-topsail. Our course was east-north-east, the wind was at south-west. We got the starboard tacks aboard, we cast off our weather-braces and lifts; we set in the lee-braces, and hauled forward by the weather-bowlings, and hauled them tight, and belayed them, and hauled over the mizen tack to windward, and kept her full and by as near as she would lie.

During this storm, which was followed by a strong wind west-south-west, we were carried by my computation about five hundred leagues to the east, so that the oldest sailor on board could not tell in what part of the world we were. Our provisions held out well, our ship was staunch, and our crew all in good health; but we lay in the utmost distress for water. We thought it best to hold on the same course rather than turn more northerly, which might have brought us to the north-west parts of Great Tartary,[3] and into the frozen sea.[4]

On the 16th day of June, 1703, a boy on the topmast discovered land. On the 17th we came in full view of a great island or continent (for we knew not whether),[5] on the south side whereof was a small neck of land jutting out into the sea, and a creek too shallow to hold a ship of above one hundred tons. We cast anchor within a league of this creek, and our captain sent a dozen of his men well armed in the long-boat, with vessels for water if any could be found. I desired his leave to go with them, that I might see the country, and make what discoveries I could. When we came to land we saw no river or spring, nor any sign of inhabitants. Our men therefore wandered on the shore to find out some fresh water near the sea, and I walked alone about a mile on the other side, where I observed the country all barren and rocky. I now began to be weary, and seeing nothing to entertain my curiosity, I returned gently down towards the creek; and the sea being full in my view, I saw our men already got into the boat, and rowing for life to the ship. I was going to hollow after them, although it had been to little purpose, when I observed a huge creature walking after them in the sea, as fast as he could: he waded not much deeper than his knees, and took prodigious strides: but our men had the start of him half a league, and the sea thereabouts being full of sharp-pointed rocks, the monster was not able to overtake the boat. This I was afterwards told, for I durst not stay to see the issue of that adventure; but ran as fast as I could the way I first went; and then climbed up a steep hill, which gave me some prospect of the country. I found it fully cultivated; but that which first surprised me was the length of the grass, which in those grounds that seemed to be kept for hay, was above twenty foot high.

I fell into a high road, for so I took it to be, though it served to the inhabitants only as a footpath through a field of barley. Here I walked on for some time, but could see little on either side, it being now near harvest, and the corn rising at least forty foot. I was an hour walking to the end of this field, which was fenced in with a hedge of at least one hundred and twenty foot high, and the trees so lofty that I could make no computation of their altitude. There was a stile to pass from this field into the next. It had four steps, and a stone to cross over when you came to the uppermost. It was impossible for me to climb this stile, because every step was six foot high, and the upper stone above twenty. I was endeavouring to find some gap in the hedge, when I discovered one of the inhabitants in the next field advancing towards the stile, of the same size with him whom I saw in the sea pursuing our boat. He appeared as tall as an ordinary spire-steeple, and took about ten yards at every stride, as near as I could guess. I was struck with the utmost fear and astonishment, and ran to hide myself in the corn, from whence I saw him at the top of the stile, looking back into the next field on the right hand, and heard him call in a voice many degrees louder than a speaking-trumpet; but the noise was so high in the air, that at first I certainly thought it was thunder. Whereupon seven monsters like himself came towards him with reaping-hooks in their hands, each hook about the largeness of six scythes. These people were not so well clad as the first, whose servants or labourers they seemed to be. For, upon some words he spoke, they went to reap the corn in the field where I lay. I kept from them at as great a distance as I could, but was forced to move with extreme difficulty, for the stalks of the corn were sometimes not above a foot distant, so that I could hardly squeeze my body betwixt them. However, I made a shift to go forward till I came to a part of the field where the corn had been laid by the rain and wind. Here it was impossible for me to advance a step: for the stalks were so interwoven that I could not creep through, and the beards of the fallen ears so strong and pointed that they pierced through my clothes into my flesh. At the same time I heard the reapers not above an hundred yards behind me. Being quite dispirited with toil, and wholly overcome by grief and despair, I lay down between two ridges, and heartily wished I might there end my days. I bemoaned my desolate widow, and fatherless children. I lamented my own folly and wilfulness in attempting a second voyage against the advice of all my friends and relations. In this terrible agitation of mind I could not forbear thinking of Lilliput, whose inhabitants looked upon me as the greatest prodigy that ever appeared in the world: where I was able to draw an imperial fleet in my hand, and perform those other actions which will be recorded for ever in the chronicles of that Empire, while posterity shall hardly believe them, although attested by millions. I reflected what a mortification it must prove to me to appear as inconsiderable in this nation as one single Lilliputian would be among us. But this I conceived was to be the least of my misfortunes: for, as human creatures are observed to be more savage and cruel in proportion to their bulk, what could I expect but to be a morsel in the mouth of the first among these enormous barbarians who should happen to seize me? Undoubtedly philosophers are in the right when they tell us, that nothing is great or little otherwise than by comparison.[6] It might have pleased Fortune to let the Lilliputians find some nation, where the people were as diminutive with respect to them, as they were to me. And who knows but that even this prodigious race of mortals might be equally overmatched in some distant part of the world, whereof we have yet no discovery?

Scared and confounded as I was, I could not forbear going on with these reflections, when one of the reapers approaching within ten yards of the ridge where I lay, made me apprehend that with the next step I should be squashed to death under his foot, or cut in two with his reaping-hook. And therefore when he was again about to move, I screamed as loud as fear could make me. Whereupon the huge creature trod short, and looking round about under him for some time, at last espied me as I lay on the ground. He considered a while with the caution of one who endeavours to lay hold on a small dangerous animal in such a manner that it shall not be able either to scratch or to bite him, as I myself have sometimes done with a weasel in England. At length he ventured to take me up behind by the middle between his forefinger and thumb, and brought me within three yards of his eyes, that he might behold my shape more perfectly. I guessed his meaning, and my good fortune gave me so much presence of mind, that I resolved not to struggle in the least as he held me in the air above sixty foot from the ground, although he grievously pinched my sides, for fear I should slip through his fingers. All I ventured was to raise mine eyes towards the sun, and place my hands together in a supplicating posture, and to speak some words in an humble melancholy tone, suitable to the condition I then was in. For I apprehended every moment that he would dash me against the ground, as we usually do any little hateful animal which we have a mind to destroy. But my good star would have it, that he appeared pleased with my voice and gestures, and began to look upon me as a curiosity, much wondering to hear me pronounce articulate words, although he could not understand them. In the meantime I was not able to forbear groaning and shedding tears, and turning my head towards my sides; letting him know, as well as I could, how cruelly I was hurt by the pressure of his thumb and finger. He seemed to apprehend my meaning; for, lifting up the lappet of his coat, he put me gently into it, and immediately ran along with me to his master, who was a substantial farmer, and the same person I had first seen in the field.

The farmer having (as I supposed by their talk) received such an account of me as his servant could give him, took a piece of a small straw, about the size of a walking-staff, and therewith lifted up the lappets of my coat; which it seems he thought to be some kind of covering that nature had given me. He blew my hairs aside to take a better view of my face. He called his hinds[7] about him, and asked them (as I afterwards learned) whether they had ever seen in the fields any little creature that resembled me. He then placed me softly on the ground upon all four, but I got immediately up, and walked slowly backwards and forwards, to let those people see I had no intent to run away. They all sat down in a circle about me, the better to observe my motions. I pulled off my hat, and made a low bow towards the farmer. I fell on my knees, and lifted up my hands and eyes, and spoke several words as loud as I could: I took a purse of gold out of my pocket, and humbly presented it to him. He received in on the palm of his hand, then applied it close to his eye, to see what it was, and afterwards turned it several times with the point of a pin (which he took out of his sleeve), but could make nothing of it. Whereupon I made a sign that he should place his hand on the ground. I then took the purse, and opening it, poured all the gold into his palm. There were six Spanish pieces of four pistoles each, besides twenty or thirty smaller coins. I saw him wet the tip of his little finger upon his tongue, and take up one of my largest pieces, and then another, but he seemed to be wholly ignorant what they were. He made me a sign to put them again into my purse, and the purse again into my pocket, which after offering to him several times, I thought it best to do.

The farmer by this time was convinced I must be a rational creature. He spoke often to me, but the sound of his voice pierced my ears like that of a watermill, yet his words were articulate enough. I answered as loud as I could in several languages, and he often laid his ear within two yards of me, but all in vain, for we were wholly unintelligible to each other. He then sent his servants to their work, and taking his handkerchief out of his pocket, he doubled and spread it on his left hand, which he placed flat on the ground with the palm upwards, making me a sign to step into it, as I could easily do, for it was not above a foot in thickness. I thought it my part to obey; and for fear of falling, laid myself at full length upon the handkerchief, with the remainder of which he lapped me up to the head for further security, and in this manner carried me home to his house. There he called his wife, and showed me to her; but she screamed and ran back as women in England do at the sight of a toad or a spider.

However, when she had a while seen my behaviour, and how well I observed the signs her husband made, she was soon reconciled, and by degrees grew extremely tender of me.

It was about twelve at noon, and a servant brought in dinner. It was only one substantial dish of meat (fit for the plain condition of an husbandman) in a dish of about four and twenty foot diameter. The company were the farmer and his wife, three children, and an old grandmother: when they were sat down, the farmer placed me at some distance from him on the table, which was thirty foot high from the floor. I was in a terrible fright, and kept as far as I could from the edge for fear of falling. The wife minced a bit of meat, then crumbled some bread on a trencher, and placed it before me. I made her a low bow, took out my knife and fork, and fell to eat, which gave them exceeding delight. The mistress sent her maid for a small dram-cup, which held about two gallons, and filled it with drink; I took up the vessel with much difficulty in both hands, and in a most respectful manner drank to her ladyship's health, expressing the words as loud as I could in English, which made the company laugh so heartily, that I was almost deafened with the noise. This liquor tasted like a small cider, and was not unpleasant. Then the master made me a sign to come to his trencher side; but as I walked on the table, being in great surprise all the time, as the indulgent reader will easily conceive and excuse, I happened to stumble against a crust, and fell flat on my face, but received no hurt. I got up immediately, and observing the good people to be in much concern, I took my hat (which I held under my arm out of good manners) and waving it over my head, made three huzzas, to show I had got no mischief by the fall. But advancing forwards toward my master (as I shall henceforth call him) his youngest son who sat next him, an arch boy of about ten years old, took me up by the legs, and held me so high in the air, that I trembled every limb; but his father snatched me from him, and at the same time gave him such a box on the left ear, as would have felled an European troop of horse to the earth, ordering him to be taken from the table. But, being afraid the boy might owe me a spite, and well remembering how mischievous all children among us naturally are to sparrows, rabbits, young kittens, and puppy dogs, I fell on my knees, and pointing to the boy, made my master understand, as well as I could, that I desired his son might be pardoned. The father complied, and the lad took his seat again; whereupon I went to him and kissed his hand, which my master took, and made him stroke me gently with it.

In the midst of dinner my mistress's favourite cat leapt into her lap. I heard a noise behind me like that of a dozen stocking-weavers at work; and turning my head I found it proceeded from the purring of this animal, who seemed to be three times larger than an ox, as I computed by the view of her head, and one of her paws, while her mistress was feeding and stroking her. The fierceness of this creature's countenance altogether discomposed me; though I stood at the farther end of the table, above fifty foot off, and although my mistress held her fast for fear she might give a spring, and seize me in her talons. But it happened there was no danger; for the cat took not the least notice of me when my master placed me within three yards of her. And as I have been always told, and found true by experience in my travels, that flying, or discovering fear before a fierce animal, is a certain way to make it pursue or attack you, so I resolved in this dangerous juncture to show no manner of concern. I walked with intrepidity five or six times before the very head of the cat, and came within half a yard of her; whereupon she drew herself back, as if she were more afraid of me: I had less apprehension concerning the dogs, whereof three or four came into the room, as it is usual in farmers' houses; one of which was a mastiff equal in bulk to four elephants, and a greyhound somewhat taller than the mastiff, but not so large.

When dinner was almost done, the nurse came in with a

child of a year old in her arms, who immediately spied me, and
began a squall that you might have heard from London
Bridge to Chelsea, after the usual oratory of infants, to get me
for a plaything. The mother out of pure indulgence took me
up, and put me towards the child, who presently seized me by
the middle, and got my head in his mouth, where I roared so
loud that the urchin was frighted, and let me drop, and I
should infallibly have broke my neck if the mother had not
held her apron under me. The nurse to quiet her babe made
use of a rattle, which was a kind of hollow vessel filled with
great stones, and fastened by a cable to the child's waist: but
all in vain, so that she was forced to apply the last remedy by
giving it suck. I must confess no object ever disgusted me so
much as the sight of her monstrous breast, which I cannot tell
what to compare with, so as to give the curious reader an idea
of its bulk, shape and colour. It stood prominent six foot, and
could not be less than sixteen in circumference. The nipple
was about half the bigness of my head, and the hue both of
that and the dug so varified with spots, pimples and freckles,
that nothing could appear more nauseous: for I had a near
sight of her, she sitting down the more conveniently to give
suck, and I standing on the table. This made me reflect upon
the fair skins of our English ladies, who appear so beautiful to
us, only because they are of our own size, and their defects not
to be seen but through a magnifying glass, where we find by
experiment that the smoothest and whitest skins look rough
and coarse, and ill coloured.

I remember when I was at Lilliput, the complexions of those
diminutive people appeared to me the fairest in the world; and
talking upon this subject with a person of learning there, who
was an intimate friend of mine, he said that my face appeared
much fairer and smoother when he looked on me from the
ground, than it did upon a nearer view when I took him up in
my hand, and brought him close, which he confessed was at
first a very shocking sight. He said, he could discover great

holes in my skin, that the stumps of my beard were ten times stronger than the bristles of a boar, and my complexion made up of several colours altogether disagreeable: although I must beg leave to say for myself, that I am as fair as most of my sex and country, and very little sunburnt by all my travels. On the other side, discoursing of the ladies in that Emperor's Court, he used to tell me, one had freckles, another too wide a mouth, a third too large a nose, nothing of which I was able to distinguish. I confess this reflection was obvious enough; which, however, I could not forbear, lest the reader might think those vast creatures were actually deformed: for I must do them justice to say they are a comely race of people; and particularly the features of my master's countenance, although he were but a farmer, when I beheld him from the height of sixty foot, appeared very well proportioned.

When dinner was done, my master went out to his labourers, and as I could discover by his voice and gesture, gave his wife a strict charge to take care of me. I was very much tired and disposed to sleep, which my mistress perceiving, she put me on her own bed, and covered me with a clean white handkerchief, but larger and coarser than the mainsail of a man-of-war.

I slept about two hours, and dreamed I was at home with my wife and children, which aggravated my sorrows when I awaked and found myself alone in a vast room, between two and three hundred foot wide, and above two hundred high, lying in a bed twenty yards wide. My mistress was gone about her household affairs, and had locked me in. The bed was eight yards from the floor. Some natural necessities required me to get down; I durst not presume to call, and if I had, it would have been in vain with such a voice as mine at so great a distance from the room where I lay to the kitchen where the family kept. While I was under these circumstances, two rats crept up the curtains, and ran smelling backwards and forwards on the bed. One of them came up almost to my face, whereupon I rose in a fright, and drew out my hanger to defend myself. These horrible animals had the boldness to attack me on both sides, and one of them held his fore-feet at my collar; but I had the good fortune to rip up his belly before he could do me any mischief. He fell down at my feet, and the other, seeing the fate of his comrade, made his escape, but not without one good wound on the back, which I gave him as he fled, and made the blood run trickling from him. After this exploit I walked gently to and fro on the bed, to recover my breath and loss of spirits. These creatures were of the size of a large mastiff, but infinitely more nimble and fierce, so that if I had taken off my belt before I went to sleep, I must have infallibly been torn to pieces and devoured. I measured the tail of the dead rat, and found it to be two yards long wanting an inch; but it went against my stomach to drag the carcass off the bed, where it lay still bleeding; I observed it had yet some life, but with a strong slash cross the neck I thoroughly dispatched it.

Soon after my mistress came into the room, who seeing me all bloody, ran and took me up in her hand. I pointed to the dead rat, smiling and making other signs to show I was not hurt, whereat she was extremely rejoiced, calling the maid to take up the dead rat with a pair of tongs, and throw it out of the window. Then she set me on a table, where I showed her my hanger all bloody, and wiping it on the lappet of my coat, returned it to the scabbard. I was pressed to do more than one thing, which another could not do for me, and therefore endeavoured to make my mistress understand that I desired to be set down on the floor; which after she had done, my bashfulness would not suffer me to express myself farther than by pointing to the door, and bowing several times. The good woman with much difficulty at last perceived what I would be at, and taking me up again in her hand, walked into the garden where she set me down. I went on one side about two hundred yards, and beckoning to her not to look or to follow me, I hid myself between two leaves of sorrel, and there discharged the necessities of nature.

I hope the gentle reader will excuse me for dwelling on these and the like particulars, which however insignificant they may appear to grovelling vulgar minds, yet will certainly help a philosopher to enlarge his thoughts and imagination, and apply them to the benefit of public as well as private life, which was my sole design in presenting this and other accounts of my travels to the world; wherein I have been chiefly studious of truth, without affecting any ornaments of learning or of style. But the whole scene of this voyage made so strong an impression on my mind, and is so deeply fixed in my memory, that in committing it to paper I did not omit one material circumstance: however, upon a strict review, I blotted out several passages of less moment which were in my first copy, for fear of being censured as tedious and trifling, whereof travellers are often, perhaps not without justice, accused.

CHAPTER 2

A description of the farmer's daughter. The author carried to a market-town, and then to the metropolis. The particulars of his journey.

MY mistress had a daughter of nine years old, a child of forward parts for her age, very dexterous at her needle, and skilful in dressing her baby.[8] Her mother and she contrived to fit up the baby's cradle for me against night: the cradle was put into a small drawer of a cabinet, and the drawer placed upon a hanging shelf for fear of the rats. This was my bed all the time I stayed with those people, though made more convenient by degrees, as I began to learn their language, and make my wants known. This young girl was so handy, that after I had once or twice pulled off my clothes before her, she was able to dress and undress me, although I never gave her that trouble when she would let me do either myself. She made me seven shirts, and some other linen, of as fine cloth as could be got, which indeed was coarser than sackcloth; and these she constantly washed for me with her own hands. She was likewise my school-mistress to teach me the language: when I pointed to anything, she told me the name of it in her own tongue, so that in a few days I was able to call for whatever I had a mind to. She was very good-natured, and not above forty foot high, being little for her age. She gave me the name of *Grildrig*, which the family took up, and afterwards the whole kingdom. The word imports what the Latins call *nanunculus*, the Italians *homunceletino*, and the English *manikin*. To her I chiefly owe my preservation in that country: we never parted while I was there; I called her my *glumdalclitch*, or 'little nurse': and I should be guilty of great ingratitude if I omitted this honourable mention of her care and affection towards me, which I heartily wish it lay in my power to requite as she deserves, instead of being the innocent but unhappy instrument of her disgrace, as I have too much reason to fear.

It now began to be known and talked of in the neighbourhood, that my master had found a strange animal in the fields, about the bigness of a *splacknuck*, but exactly shaped in every part like a human creature; which it likewise imitated in all its actions; seemed to speak in a little language of its own, had already learned several words of theirs, went erect upon two legs, was tame and gentle, would come when it was called, do whatever it was bid, had the finest limbs in the world, and a complexion fairer than a nobleman's daughter of three years old. Another farmer who lived hard by, and was a particular friend of my master, came on a visit on purpose to enquire into the truth of this story. I was immediately produced, and placed upon a table, where I walked as I was commanded, drew my hanger, put it up again, made my reverence [9] to my master's guest, asked him in his own language how he did, and told him he was welcome, just as my little nurse had instructed me. This man, who was old and dim-sighted, put on his spectacles to behold me better, at which I could not forbear laughing very heartily, for his eyes appeared like the full moon shining into a chamber at two windows. Our people, who discovered the cause of my mirth, bore me company in laughing, at which the old fellow was fool enough to be angry and out of countenance. He had the character of a great miser, and to my misfortune he well deserved it by the cursed advice he gave my master to show me as a sight upon a market-day in the next town, which was half an hour's riding, about two and twenty miles from our house. I guessed there was some mischief contriving, when I observed my master and his friend whispering long together, sometimes pointing at me; and my fears made me fancy that I overheard and understood some of their words. But, the next morning Glumdalclitch my little nurse told me the whole matter, which she had cunningly picked out from her mother. The poor girl laid me on her bosom, and fell a weeping with shame and grief. She apprehended some mischief would happen to me from rude vulgar folks, who might squeeze me to death or break one of my limbs by taking me in their hands. She had also observed how modest I was in my nature, how nicely I regarded my honour, and what an indignity I should conceive it to be exposed for money as a public spectacle[10] to the meanest of the people. She said, her papa and mamma had promised that Grildrig should be hers, but now she found they meant to serve her as they did last year, when they pretended to give her a lamb, and yet, as soon as it was fat, sold it to a butcher. For my own part, I may truly affirm that I was less concerned than my nurse. I had a strong hope, which never left me, that I should one day recover my liberty; and as to the ignominy of being carried about for a monster, I considered myself to be a perfect stranger in the country, and that such a misfortune could never be charged upon me as a reproach if ever I should return to England; since the King of Great Britain himself, in my condition, must have undergone the same distress.

My master, pursuant to the advice of his friend, carried me in a box the next market-day to the neighbouring town, and took along with him his little daughter my nurse upon a pillion behind me. The box was close on every side, with a little door for me to go in and out, and a few gimlet-holes to let in air. The girl had been so careful to put the quilt of her baby's bed into it, for me to lie down on. However, I was terribly shaken and discomposed in this journey, though it were but of half an hour. For the horse went about forty foot at every step, and trotted so high, that the agitation was equal to the rising and falling of a ship in a great storm, but much more frequent: our journey was somewhat further than from London to St Albans. My master alighted at an inn which he used to frequent; and after consulting a while with the inn-keeper, and making some necessary preparations, he hired the *Grultrud*, or Crier, to give notice through the town of a strange creature to be seen at the Sign of the Green Eagle, not so big as a *splacknuck* (an animal in that country very finely shaped, about six foot long) and in every part of the body resembling an human creature, could speak several words, and perform an hundred diverting tricks.

I was placed upon a table in the largest room of the inn, which might be near three hundred foot square. My little nurse stood on a low stool close to the table, to take care of me, and direct what I should do. My master, to avoid a crowd, would suffer only thirty people at a time to see me. I walked about on the table as the girl commanded; she asked me questions as far as she knew my understanding of the language reached, and I answered them as loud as I could. I turned about several times to the company, paid my humble respects, said they were welcome, and used some other speeches I had been taught. I took up a thimble filled with liquor, which Glumdalclitch had given me for a cup, and drank their health. I drew out my hanger, and flourished with it after the manner of fencers in England. My nurse gave me part of a straw, which I exercised as a pike, having learned the art in my youth. I was that day shown to twelve sets of company, and as often forced to go over again with the same fopperies, till I was half dead with weariness and vexation. For those who had seen me made such wonderful reports, that the people were ready to break down the doors to come in. My master for his own interest would not suffer anyone to touch me except my nurse; and, to prevent danger, benches were set round the table at such a distance as put me out of everybody's reach. However, an unlucky school-boy aimed a hazel nut directly at my head, which very narrowly missed me; otherwise, it came with so much violence that it would have infallibly knocked out my brains, for it was almost as large as a small pumpion:[11] but I had the satisfaction to see the young rogue well beaten, and turned out of the room.

My master gave public notice, that he would show me again the next market-day, and in the meantime he prepared a more convenient vehicle for me, which he had reason enough to do; for I was so tired with my first journey, and with entertaining company for eight hours together, that I could hardly stand upon my legs, or speak a word. It was at least three days before I recovered my strength; and that I might have no rest at home, all the neighbouring gentlemen from an hundred miles round, hearing of my fame, came to see me at my master's own house. There could not be fewer than thirty persons with their wives and children (for the country is very populous); and my master demanded the rate of a full room whenever he showed me at home, although it were only to a single family. So that for some time I had but little ease every day of the week (except Wednesday, which is their Sabbath) although I were not carried to the town.

My master, finding how profitable I was like to be, resolved to carry me to the most considerable cities of the kingdom. Having therefore provided himself with all things necessary for a long journey, and settled his affairs at home, he took leave of his wife, and upon the 17th of August, 1703, about two months after my arrival, we set out for the metropolis, situated near the middle of that Empire, and about three thousand miles distance from our house: my master made his daughter Glumdalclitch ride behind him. She carried me on her lap in a box tied about her waist. The girl had lined it on all sides with the softest cloth she could get, well quilted underneath, furnished it with her baby's bed, provided me with linen and other necessaries, and made everything as convenient as she could. We had no other company but a boy of the house, who rode after us with the luggage.

My master's design was to show me in all the towns by the way, and to step out of the road for fifty or an hundred miles, to any village or person of quality's house where he might expect custom. We made easy journeys of not above seven or eight score miles a day: for Glumdalclitch, on purpose to spare me, complained she was tired with the trotting of the horse. She often took me out of my box at my own desire, to give me air, and show me the country, but always held me fast by leading-strings. We passed over five or six rivers many degrees broader and deeper than the Nile or the Ganges; and there was hardly a rivulet so small as the Thames at London Bridge. We were ten weeks in our journey, and I was shown in eighteen large towns, besides many villages and private families.

On the 26th day of October, we arrived at the metropolis, called in their language *Lorbrulgrud*, or *Pride of the Universe*. My master took a lodging in the principal street of the city, not far from the royal palace, and put out bills in the usual form, containing an exact description of my person and parts. He hired a large room between three and four hundred foot wide. He provided a table sixty foot in diameter, upon which I was to act my part, and palisadoed it round three foot from the edge, and as many high, to prevent my falling over. I was shown ten times a day to the wonder and satisfaction of all people. I could now speak the language tolerably well, and perfectly understood every word that was spoken to me. Besides, I had learnt their alphabet, and could make a shift to explain a sentence here and there; for Glumdalclitch had been my instructor while we were at home, and at leisure hours during our journey. She carried a little book in her pocket, not much larger than a Sanson's *Atlas*;[12] it was a common treatise for the use of young girls, giving a short account of their religion; out of this she taught me my letters, and interpreted the words.

CHAPTER 3

The author sent for to Court. The Queen buys him of his master the farmer, and presents him to the King. He disputes with his Majesty's great scholars. An apartment at Court provided for the author. He is in high favour with the Queen. He stands up for the honour of his own country. His quarrels with the Queen's dwarf.

THE frequent labours I underwent every day made in a few weeks a very considerable change in my health: the more my master got by me, the more unsatiable he grew. I had quite lost my stomach, and was almost reduced to a skeleton. The farmer observed it, and concluding I soon must die, resolved to make as good a hand of me as he could. While he was thus reasoning and resolving with himself, a *Slardral*, or Gentleman Usher, came from Court, commanding my master to bring me immediately thither for the diversion of the Queen and her ladies. Some of the latter had already been to see me, and reported strange things of my beauty, behaviour, and good sense. Her Majesty and those who attended her were beyond measure delighted with my demeanour. I fell on my knees, and begged the honour of kissing her imperial foot; but this gracious Princess held out her little finger towards me (after I was set on a table) which I embraced in both my arms, and put the tip of it, with the utmost respect, to my lips. She made me some general questions about my country and my travels, which I answered as distinctly and in as few words as I could. She asked whether I would be content to live at Court. I bowed down to the board of the table, and humbly answered that I was my master's slave, but if I were at my own disposal, I should be proud to devote my life to her Majesty's service. She then asked my master whether he were willing to sell me at a good price. He, who apprehended I could not live a month, was ready enough to part with me, and demanded a thousand pieces of gold, which were ordered him on the spot, each piece being about the bigness of eight hundred moidores; but, allowing for the proportion of all things between that country and Europe, and the high price of gold among them, was hardly so great a sum as a thousand guineas would be in England. I then said to the Queen, since I was now her Majesty's most humble creature and vassal, I must beg the favour, that Glumdalclitch, who had always tended me with so much care and kindness, and understood to do it so well, might be admitted into her service, and continue to be my nurse and instructor. Her Majesty agreed to my petition, and easily got the farmer's consent, who was glad enough to have his daughter preferred at Court: and the poor girl herself was not able to hide her joy: my late master withdrew, bidding me farewell, and saying he had left me in a good service; to which I replied not a word, only making him a slight bow.

The Queen observed my coldness, and when the farmer was gone out of the apartment, asked me the reason. I made bold to tell her Majesty that I owed no other obligation to my late master, than his not dashing out the brains of a poor harmless creature found by chance in his field; which obligation was amply recompensed by the gain he had made in showing me through half the kingdom, and the price he had now sold me for. That the life I had since led was laborious enough to kill an animal of ten times my strength. That my health was much impaired by the continual drudgery of entertaining the rabble every hour of the day, and that if my master had not thought my life in danger, her Majesty perhaps would not have got so cheap a bargain. But as I was out of all fear of being ill treated under the protection of so great and good an Empress, the Ornament of Nature, the Darling of the World, the Delight of her Subjects, the Phoenix of the Creation; so, I hoped my late master's apprehensions would appear to be groundless, for I already found my spirits to revive by the Influence of her most August Presence.

This was the sum of my speech, delivered with great improprieties and hesitation; the latter part was altogether framed in the style peculiar to that people, whereof I learned some phrases from Glumdalclitch, while she was carrying me to Court.

The Queen, giving great allowance for my defectiveness in speaking, was however surprised at so much wit and good sense in so diminutive an animal. She took me in her own hand, and carried me to the King, who was then retired to his cabinet. His Majesty, a prince of much gravity, and austere countenance, not well observing my shape at first view, asked the Queen after a cold manner, how long it was since she grew fond of a *splacknuck*; for such it seems he took me to be, as I lay upon my breast in her Majesty's right hand. But this Princess, who hath an infinite deal of wit and humour, set me gently on my feet upon the scrutore,[13] and commanded me to give his Majesty an account of myself, which I did in a very few words; and Glumdalclitch, who attended at the cabinet door, and could not endure I should be out of her sight, being admitted, confirmed all that had passed from my arrival at her father's house.

The King, although he be as learned a person as any in his dominions, and had been educated in the study of philosophy,[14] and particularly mathematics; yet when he observed my shape exactly, and saw me walk erect, before I began to speak, conceived I might be a piece of clock-work (which is in that country arrived to a very great perfection), contrived by some ingenious artist. But, when he heard my voice, and found what I delivered to be regular and rational, he could not conceal his astonishment. He was by no means satisfied with the relation I gave him of the manner I came into his kingdom, but thought it a story concerted between Glumdalclitch and her father, who had taught me a set of words to make me sell at a higher price. Upon this imagination he put several other questions to me, and still received rational answers, no otherwise defective than by a foreign accent, and an imperfect knowledge in the language, with some rustic phrases which I had learned at the farmer's house, and did not suit the polite style of a Court.

His Majesty sent for three great scholars who were then in their weekly waiting[15] (according to the custom in that country). These gentlemen, after they had a while examined my shape with much nicety, were of different opinions concerning me. They all agreed that I could not be produced according to the regular Laws of Nature, because I was not framed with a capacity of preserving my life, either by swiftness, or climbing of trees, or digging holes in the earth. They observed by my teeth, which they viewed with great exactness, that I was a carnivorous animal; yet most quadrupeds being an overmatch for me, and field mice, with some others, too nimble, they could not imagine how I should be able to support myself, unless I fed upon snails and other insects, which they offered by many learned arguments to evince that I could not possibly do. One of them seemed to think that I might be an embryo, or abortive birth. But this opinion was rejected by the other two, who observed my limbs to be perfect and finished, and that I had lived several years, as it was manifested from my beard, the stumps whereof they plainly discovered through a magnifying glass. They would not allow me to be a dwarf, because my littleness was beyond all degrees of comparison; for the Queen's favourite dwarf, the smallest ever known in that kingdom, was near thirty foot high. After much debate, they concluded unanimously that I was only *relplum scalcath*, which is interpreted literally, *lusus naturæ*;[16] a determination exactly agreeable to the modern philosophy of Europe, whose professors, disdaining the old evasion of *occult causes*, whereby the followers of Aristotle endeavour in vain to disguise their ignorance, have invented this wonderful solution of all difficulties, to the unspeakable advancement of human knowledge.

After this decisive conclusion, I entreated to be heard a word or two. I applied myself to the King, and assured his Majesty that I came from a country which abounded with several millions of both sexes, and of my own stature; where the animals, trees, and houses were all in proportion, and where by consequence I might be as able to defend myself, and to find sustenance, as any of his Majesty's subjects could do here; which I took for a full answer to those gentlemen's arguments. To this they only replied with a smile of contempt, saying, that the farmer had instructed me very well in my lesson. The King, who had a much better understanding, dismissing his learned men, sent for the farmer, who by good fortune was not yet gone out of town: having therefore first examined him privately, and then confronted him with me and the young girl, his Majesty began to think that what we told him might possibly be true. He desired the Queen to order that a particular care should be taken of me, and was of opinion, that Glumdalclitch should still continue in her office of tending me, because he observed we had a great affection for each other. A convenient apartment was provided for her at Court; she had a sort of governess appointed to take care of her education, a maid to dress her, and two other servants for menial offices; but the care of me was wholly appropriated to herself. The Queen commanded her own cabinet-maker to contrive a box that might serve me for a bed-chamber, after the model that Glumdalclitch and I should agree upon. This man was a most ingenious artist,[17] and according to my directions, in three weeks finished for me a wooden chamber of sixteen foot square, and twelve high, with sash-windows, a door, and two closets, like a London bed-chamber. The board that made the ceiling was to be lifted up and down by two hinges, to put in a bed ready furnished by her Majesty's upholsterer, which Glumdalclitch took out every day to air, made it with her own hands, and letting it down at night, locked up the roof over me. A nice workman, who was famous for little curiosities, undertook to make me two chairs, with backs and frames, of a substance not unlike ivory, and two tables, with a cabinet to put my things in. The room was quilted on all sides, as well as the floor and the ceiling, to prevent any accident from the carelessness of those who carried me, and to break the force of a jolt when I went in a coach. I desired a lock for my door to prevent rats and mice from coming in: the smith after several attempts made the smallest that was ever seen among them; for I have known a larger at the gate of a gentleman's house in England. I made a shift to keep the key in a pocket of my own, fearing Glumdalclitch might lose it. The Queen likewise ordered the thinnest silks that could be gotten, to make me clothes, not much thicker than an English blanket, very cumbersome till I was accustomed to them. They were after the fashion of the kingdom, partly resembling the Persian, and partly the Chinese; and are a very grave decent habit.

The Queen became so fond of my company, that she could not dine without me. I had a table placed upon the same at which her Majesty ate, just at her left elbow, and a chair to sit on. Glumdalclitch stood upon a stool on the floor, near my table, to assist and take care of me. I had an entire set of silver dishes and plates, and other necessaries, which, in proportion to those of the Queen, were not much bigger than what I have

seen in a London toy-shop, for the furniture of a baby-house:
these my little nurse kept in her pocket, in a silver box, and
gave me at meals as I wanted them, always cleaning them herself. No person dined with the Queen but the two Princesses
Royal, the elder sixteen years old, and the younger at that time
thirteen and a month. Her Majesty used to put a bit of meat
upon one of my dishes, out of which I carved for myself; and
her diversion was to see me eat in miniature. For the Queen
(who had indeed but a weak stomach) took up at one mouthful as much as a dozen English farmers could eat at a meal,
which to me was for some time a very nauseous sight. She
would craunch the wing of a lark, bones and all, between her
teeth, although it were nine times as large as that of a full-
grown turkey; and put a bit of bread in her mouth, as big as
two twelve-penny loaves. She drank out of a golden cup,
above a hogshead at a draught. Her knives were twice as
long as a scythe set straight upon the handle. The spoons,
forks, and other instruments were all in the same proportion. I remember when Glumdalclitch carried me out
of curiosity to see some of the tables at Court, where ten or
a dozen of these enormous knives and forks were lifted up
together, I thought I had never till then beheld so terrible a
sight.

It is the custom that every Wednesday (which as I have before observed, was their Sabbath), the King and Queen, with
the royal issue of both sexes, dine together in the apartment of
his Majesty, to whom I was now become a great favourite; and
at these times my little chair and table were placed at his left
hand before one of the salt-cellars. This Prince took a pleasure
in conversing with me, enquiring into the manners, religion,
laws, government, and learning of Europe, wherein I gave
him the best account I was able. His apprehension was so clear,
and his judgment so exact, that he made very wise reflections
and observations upon all I said. But, I confess, that after I had
been a little too copious in talking of my own beloved country,

of our trade, and wars by sea and land, of our schisms in religion, and parties in the state, the prejudices of his education prevailed so far, that he could not forbear taking me up in his right hand, and stroking me gently with the other, after an hearty fit of laughing, asked me whether I were a Whig or a Tory. Then turning to his first Minister, who waited behind him with a white staff, near as tall as the mainmast of the *Royal Sovereign*,[18] he observed how contemptible a thing was human grandeur, which could be mimicked by such diminutive insects as I: And yet, said he, I dare engage, these creatures have their titles and distinctions of honour; they contrive little nests and burrows, that they call houses and cities; they make a figure in dress and equipage; they love, they fight, they dispute, they cheat, they betray. And thus he continued on, while my colour came and went several times, with indignation to hear our noble country, the Mistress of Arts and Arms, the Scourge of France, the Arbitress of Europe, the Seat of Virtue, Piety, Honour and Truth, the Pride and Envy of the World, so contemptuously treated.

But, as I was not in a condition to resent injuries, so, upon mature thoughts, I began to doubt whether I were injured or no. For, after having been accustomed several months to the sight and converse of this people, and observed every object upon which I cast mine eyes to be of proportionable magnitude, the horror I had first conceived from their bulk and aspect was so far worn off, that if I had then beheld a company of English Lords and Ladies in their finery and birthday clothes,[19] acting their several parts in the most courtly manner of strutting, and bowing and prating; to say the truth, I should have been strongly tempted to laugh as much at them as this King and his grandees did at me. Neither indeed could I forbear smiling at myself, when the Queen used to place me upon her hand towards a looking-glass, by which both our persons appeared before me in full view together; and there could nothing be more ridiculous than the comparison: so that I really began to imagine myself dwindled many degrees below my usual size.

Nothing angered and mortified me so much as the Queen's dwarf, who being of the lowest stature that was ever in that country (for I verily think he was not full thirty foot high) became so insolent at seeing a creature so much beneath him, that he would always affect to swagger and look big as he passed by me in the Queen's antechamber, while I was standing on some table talking with the Lords or Ladies of the Court, and he seldom failed of a smart word or two upon my littleness; against which I could only revenge myself by calling him *Brother*, challenging him to wrestle, and such repartees as are usual in the mouths of *Court pages*. One day at dinner this malicious little cub was so nettled with something I had said to him, that raising himself upon the frame of her Majesty's chair, he took me up by the middle, as I was sitting down, not thinking any harm, and let me drop into a large silver bowl of cream, and then ran away as fast as he could. I fell over head and ears, and if I had not been a good swimmer, it might have gone very hard with me; for Glumdalclitch in that instant happened to be at the other end of the room, and the Queen was in such a fright that she wanted presence of mind to assist me. But my little nurse ran to my relief, and took me out, after I had swallowed above a quart of cream. I was put to bed; however I received no other damage than the loss of a suit of clothes, which was utterly spoiled. The dwarf was soundly whipped, and as a further punishment, forced to drink up the bowl of cream, into which he had thrown me; neither was he ever restored to favour: for, soon after the Queen bestowed him to a lady of high quality, so that I saw him no more, to my very great satisfaction; for I could not tell to what extremities such a malicious urchin might have carried his resentment.

He had before served me a scurvy trick, which set the Queen a laughing, although at the same time she were heartily vexed, and would have immediately cashiered him, if I had not been so generous as to intercede. Her Majesty had taken a marrow-bone upon her plate, and after knocking out the marrow, placed the bone again in the dish erect as it stood before; the dwarf watching his opportunity, while Glumdalclitch was gone to the sideboard, mounted the stool that she stood on to take care of me at meals, took me up in both hands, and squeezing my legs together, wedged them into the marrow-bone above my waist, where I stuck for some time, and made a very ridiculous figure. I believe it was near a minute before anyone knew what was become of me, for I thought it below me to cry out. But, as princes seldom get their meat hot, my legs were not scalded, only my stockings and breeches in a sad condition. The dwarf at my entreaty had no other punishment than a sound whipping.

I was frequently rallied by the Queen upon account of my fearfulness, and she used to ask me whether the people of my country were as great cowards as myself. The occasion was this. The kingdom is much pestered with flies in summer, and these odious insects, each of them as big as a Dunstable lark,[20] hardly gave me any rest while I sat at dinner, with their continual humming and buzzing about mine ears. They would sometimes alight upon my victuals, and leave their loathsome excrement or spawn behind, which to me was very visible, though not to the natives of that country, whose large optics were not so acute as mine in viewing smaller objects. Sometimes they would fix upon my nose or forehead, where they stung me to the quick, smelling very offensively, and I could easily trace that viscous matter, which our naturalists tell us enables those creatures to walk with their feet upwards upon a ceiling. I had much ado to defend myself against these detestable animals, and could not forbear starting when they came on my face. It was the common practice of the dwarf to catch a number of these insects in his hand as schoolboys do among us, and let them out suddenly under my nose on purpose to frighten me, and divert the Queen. My remedy was to cut them in pieces with my knife as they flew in the air, wherein my dexterity was much admired.

I remember one morning when Glumdalclitch had set me in my box upon a window, as she usually did in fair days to give me air (for I durst not venture to let the box be hung on a nail out of the window, as we do with cages in England) after I had lifted up one of my sashes, and sat down at my table to eat a piece of sweet cake for my breakfast, above twenty wasps, allured by the smell, came flying into the room, humming louder than the drones of as many bagpipes. Some of them seized my cake, and carried it piecemeal away, others flew about my head and face, confounding me with the noise, and putting me in the utmost terror of their stings. However I had the courage to rise and draw my hanger, and attack them in the air. I dispatched four of them, but the rest got away, and I presently shut my window. These insects were as large as partridges; I took out their stings, found them an inch and a half long, and as sharp as needles. I carefully preserved them all, and having since shown them with some other curiosities in several parts of Europe, upon my return to England I gave three of them to Gresham College,[21] and kept the fourth for myself.

CHAPTER 4

The country described. A proposal for correcting modern maps. The King's palace, and some account of the metropolis. The author's way of travelling. The chief temple described.

I NOW intend to give the reader a short description of this country, as far as I travelled in it, which was not above two thousand miles round Lorbrulgrud the metropolis. For the Queen, whom I always attended, never went further when she accompanied the King in his progresses, and there stayed till his Majesty returned from viewing his frontiers. The whole extent of this Prince's dominions reacheth about six thousand miles in length, and from three to five in breadth. From whence I cannot but conclude that our geographers of Europe are in a great error, by supposing nothing but sea between Japan and California; for it was ever my opinion, that there must be a balance of earth to counterpoise the great continent of Tartary; and therefore they ought to correct their maps and charts, by joining this vast tract of land to the north-west parts of America, wherein I shall be ready to lend them my assistance.

The kingdom is a peninsula, terminated to the north-east by a ridge of mountains thirty miles high, which are altogether impassable by reason of the volcanoes upon the tops. Neither do the most learned know what sort of mortals inhabit beyond those mountains, or whether they be inhabited at all. On the three other sides it is bounded by the ocean. There is not one seaport in the whole kingdom, and those parts of the coasts into which the rivers issue are so full of pointed rocks, and the sea generally so rough, that there is no venturing with the smallest of their boats, so that these people are wholly excluded from any commerce with the rest of the world. But the large rivers are full of vessels, and abound with excellent fish, for they seldom get any from the sea, because the sea-fish are of the same size with those in Europe, and consequently not worth catching; whereby it is manifest, that Nature in the production of plants and animals of so extraordinary a bulk is wholly confined to this continent, of which I leave the reasons to be determined by philosophers. However, now and then they take a whale that happens to be dashed against the rocks, which the common people feed on heartily. These whales I have known so large that a man could hardly carry one upon his shoulders; and sometimes for curiosity they are brought in hampers to Lorbrulgrud: I saw one of them in a dish at the King's table, which passed for a rarity, but I did not observe he was fond of it; for I think indeed the bigness disgusted him, although I have seen one somewhat larger in Greenland.

The country is well inhabited, for it contains fifty-one cities, near an hundred walled towns, and a great number of villages. To satisfy my curious reader, it may be sufficient to describe Lorbrulgrud. This city stands upon almost two equal parts on each side the river that passes through. It contains above eighty thousand houses. It is in length three *glonglungs* (which make about fifty-four English miles) and two and a half in breadth, as I measured it myself in the royal map made by the King's order, which was laid on the ground on purpose for me, and extended an hundred feet; I paced the diameter and circumference several times barefoot, and computing by the scale, measured it pretty exactly.

The King's palace is no regular edifice, but an heap of buildings about seven miles round: the chief rooms are generally two hundred and forty foot high, and broad and long in proportion. A coach was allowed to Glumdalclitch and me, wherein her governess frequently took her out to see the town, or go among the shops; and I was always of the party, carried in my box; although the girl at my own desire would often take me out, and hold me in her hand, that I might more conveniently view the houses and the people as we passed along the streets. I reckoned our coach to be about a square of Westminster Hall,[22] but not altogether so high; however, I cannot be very exact. One day the governess ordered our coachman to stop at several shops, where the beggars, watching their opportunity, crowded to the sides of the coach, and gave me the most horrible spectacles that ever an European eye beheld. There was a woman with a cancer in her breast, swelled to a monstrous size, full of holes, in two or three of which I could have easily crept, and covered my whole body. There was a fellow with a wen in his neck, larger than five woolpacks, and another with a couple of wooden legs, each about twenty foot high. But, the most hateful sight of all was the lice crawling on their clothes. I could see distinctly the limbs of these vermin with my naked eye, much better than those of an European louse through a microscope, and their snouts with which they rooted like swine. They were the first I had ever beheld, and I should have been curious enough to dissect one of them, if I had proper instruments (which I unluckily left behind me in the ship) although indeed the sight was so nauseous, that it perfectly turned my stomach.

Beside the large box in which I was usually carried, the Queen ordered a smaller one to be made for me, of about twelve foot square, and ten high, for the convenience of travelling, because the other was somewhat too large for Glumdalclitch's lap, and cumbersome in the coach; it was made by the same artist, whom I directed in the whole contrivance. This travelling closet was an exact square with a window in the middle of three of the squares, and each window was latticed with iron wire on the outside, to prevent accidents in long journeys. On the fourth side, which had no window, two strong staples were fixed, through which the person that carried me, when I had a mind to be on horseback, put in a leathern belt, and buckled it about his waist. This was always the office of some grave trusty servant in whom I could confide, whether I attended the King and Queen in their progresses, or were disposed to see the gardens, or pay a visit to some great Lady or Minister of State in the Court, when Glumdalclitch happened to be out of order: for I soon began to be known and esteemed among the greatest officers, I suppose more upon account of their Majesties' favour, than any merit of my own. In journeys, when I was weary of the coach, a servant on horseback would buckle my box, and place it on a cushion before him; and there I had a full prospect of the country on three sides from my three windows. I had in this closet a field-bed and a hammock hung from the ceiling, two chairs and a table, neatly screwed to the floor, to prevent being tossed about by the agitation of the horse or the coach. And having been long used to sea-voyages, those motions, although sometimes very violent, did not much discompose me.

Whenever I had a mind to see the town, it was always in my travelling-closet, which Glumdalclitch held in her lap in a kind of open sedan, after the fashion of the country, borne by four men, and attended by two others in the Queen's livery. The people, who had often heard of me, were very curious to crowd about the sedan, and the girl was complaisant enough to make the bearers stop, and to take me in her hand that I might be more conveniently seen.

I was very desirous to see the chief temple, and particularly the tower belonging to it, which is reckoned the highest in the kingdom. Accordingly one day my nurse carried me thither, but I may truly say I came back disappointed; for the height is not above three thousand foot, reckoning from the ground to the highest pinnacle top; which allowing for the difference between the size of those people, and us in Europe, is no great matter for admiration, nor at all equal in proportion (if I rightly remember) to Salisbury steeple. But, not to detract from a nation to which during my life I shall acknowledge myself extremely obliged, it must be allowed that whatever this famous tower wants in height is amply made up in beauty and strength. For the walls are near an hundred foot thick, built of hewn stone, whereof each is about forty foot square, and adorned on all sides with statues of gods and Emperors cut in marble larger than the life, placed in their several niches. I measured a little finger which had fallen down from one of these statues, and lay unperceived among some rubbish, and found it exactly four foot and an inch in length. Glumdalclitch wrapped it up in a handkerchief, and carried it home in her pocket to keep among other trinkets, of which the girl was very fond, as children at her age usually are.

The King's kitchen is indeed a noble building, vaulted at top, and about six hundred foot high. The great oven is not so wide by ten paces as the cupola at St Paul's: for I measured the latter on purpose after my return. But if I should describe the kitchen-grate, the prodigious pots and kettles, the joints of meat turning on the spits, with many other particulars, perhaps I should be hardly believed; at least a severe critic would be apt to think I enlarged a little, as travellers are often suspected to do. To avoid which censure, I fear I have run too much into the other extreme; and that if this treatise should happen to be translated into the language of Brobdingnag (which is the general name of that kingdom), and transmitted thither, the King and his people would have reason to complain that I had done them an injury by a false and diminutive representation.

His Majesty seldom keeps above six hundred horses in his stables: they are generally from fifty-four to sixty foot high. But, when he goes abroad on solemn days, he is attended for state by a militia guard of five hundred horse, which indeed I thought was the most splendid sight that could be ever beheld, till I saw part of his army in battalia,²³ whereof I shall find another occasion to speak.

CHAPTER 5

Several adventures that happened to the author. The execution of a criminal. The author shows his skill in navigation.

I SHOULD have lived happy enough in that country, if my littleness had not exposed me to several ridiculous and troublesome accidents; some of which I shall venture to relate. Glumdalclitch often carried me into the gardens of the Court in my smaller box, and would sometimes take me out of it and hold me in her hand, or set me down to walk. I remember, before the dwarf left the Queen, he followed us one day into those gardens, and my nurse having set me down, he and I being close together, near some dwarf apple-trees, I must needs show my wit by a silly allusion between him and the trees, which happens to hold in their language as it doth in ours. Whereupon, the malicious rogue, watching his opportunity, when I was walking under one of them, shook it directly over my head, by which a dozen apples, each of them near as large as a Bristol barrel,[24] came tumbling about my ears; one of them hit me on the back as I chanced to stoop, and knocked me down flat on my face, but I received no other hurt, and the dwarf was pardoned at my desire, because I had given the provocation.

Another day Glumdalclitch left me on a smooth grass-plot to divert myself while she walked at some distance with her governess. In the meantime there suddenly fell such a violent shower of hail, that I was immediately by the force of it struck to the ground: and when I was down, the hailstones gave me such cruel bangs all over the body, as if I had been pelted with tennis-balls; however I made a shift to creep on all four, and shelter myself by lying flat on my face on the lee-side of a border of lemon thyme, but so bruised from head to foot that I could not go abroad in ten days. Neither is this at all to be wondered at, because Nature in that country observing the same proportion through all her operations, a hailstone is near eighteen hundred times as large as one in Europe, which I can assert upon experience, having been so curious to weigh and measure them.

But, a more dangerous accident happened to me in the same garden, when my little nurse, believing she had put me in a secure place, which I often entreated her to do, that I might enjoy my own thoughts, and having left my box at home to avoid the trouble of carrying it, went to another part of the gardens with her governess and some ladies of her acquaintance. While she was absent and out of hearing, a small white spaniel belonging to one of the chief gardeners, having got by accident into the garden, happened to range near the place where I lay. The dog, following the scent, came directly up, and taking me in his mouth, ran straight to his master, wagging his tail, and set me gently on the ground. By good fortune he had been so well taught, that I was carried between his teeth without the least hurt, or even tearing my clothes. But, the poor gardener, who knew me well, and had a great kindness for me, was in a terrible fright. He gently took me up in both his hands, and asked me how I did; but I was so amazed and out of breath, that I could not speak a word. In a few minutes I came to myself, and he carried me safe to my little nurse, who by this time had returned to the place where she left me, and was in cruel agonies when I did not appear, nor answer when she called: she severely reprimanded the gardener on account of his dog. But, the thing was hushed up, and never known at Court; for the girl was afraid of the Queen's anger, and truly as to myself, I thought it would not be for my reputation that such a story should go about.

This accident absolutely determined Glumdalclitch never to trust me abroad for the future out of her sight. I had been long afraid of this resolution, and therefore concealed from her some little unlucky adventures that happened in those times when I was left by myself. Once a kite hovering over the garden made a stoop[25] at me, and if I had not resolutely drawn my hanger, and run under a thick espalier, he would have certainly carried me away in his talons. Another time walking to the top of a fresh mole-hill, I fell to my neck in the hole through which that animal had cast up the earth, and coined some lie not worth remembering, to excuse myself for spoiling my clothes. I likewise broke my right shin against the shell of a snail, which I happened to stumble over, as I was walking alone, and thinking on poor England.

I cannot tell whether I were more pleased or mortified to observe in those solitary walks, that the smaller birds did not appear to be at all afraid of me, but would hop about within a yard distance, looking for worms and other food with as much indifference and security as if no creature at all were near them. I remember, a thrush had the confidence to snatch out of my hand with his bill, a piece of cake that Glumdalclitch had just given me for my breakfast. When I attempted to catch any of these birds, they would boldly turn against me, endeavouring to pick my fingers, which I durst not venture within their reach; and then they would hop back unconcerned to hunt for worms or snails, as they did before. But, one day I took a thick cudgel, and threw it with all my strength so luckily at a linnet, that I knocked him down, and seizing him by the neck with both my hands, ran with him in triumph to my nurse. However, the bird, who had only been stunned, recovering himself, gave me so many boxes with his wings on both sides of my head and body, though I held him at arm's length, and was out of the reach of his claws, that I was twenty times thinking to let him go. But I was soon relieved by one of our servants, who wrung off the bird's neck, and I had him next day for dinner by the Queen's command. This linnet, as near as I can remember, seemed to be somewhat larger than an English swan.

The Maids of Honour often invited Glumdalclitch to their apartments, and desired she would bring me along with her, on purpose to have the pleasure of seeing and touching me. They would often strip me naked from top to toe, and lay me at full length in their bosoms; wherewith I was much disgusted; because, to say the truth, a very offensive smell came from their skins; which I do not mention or intend to the disadvantage of those excellent ladies, for whom I have all manner of respect; but I conceive that my sense was more acute in proportion to my littleness, and that those illustrious persons were no more disagreeable to their lovers, or to each other, than people of the same quality are with us in England. And, after all, I found their natural smell was much more supportable than when they used perfumes, under which I immediately swooned away. I cannot forget that an intimate friend of mine in Lilliput took the freedom in a warm day, when I had used a good deal of exercise, to complain of a strong smell about me, although I am as little faulty that way as most of my sex: but I suppose his faculty of smelling was as nice with regard to me, as mine was to that of this people. Upon this point, I cannot forbear doing justice to the Queen my mistress, and Glumdalclitch my nurse, whose persons were as sweet as those of any lady in England.

That which gave me most uneasiness among these Maids of Honour, when my nurse carried me to visit them, was to see them use me without any manner of ceremony, like a creature who had no sort of consequence. For, they would strip themselves to the skin, and put on their smocks in my presence, while I was placed on their toilet directly before their naked bodies, which, I am sure, to me was very far from being a tempting sight, or from giving me any other emotions than those of horror and disgust. Their skins appeared so coarse and uneven, so variously coloured, when I saw them near, with a mole here and there as broad as a trencher, and hairs hanging from it thicker than pack-threads; to say nothing further concerning the rest of their persons. Neither did they at all scruple while I was by to discharge what they had drunk, to the quantity of at least two hogsheads, in a vessel that held above three tuns. The handsomest among these Maids of Honour, a pleasant frolicsome girl of sixteen, would sometimes set me astride upon one of her nipples, with many other tricks, wherein the reader will excuse me for not being over particular. But, I was so much displeased, that I entreated Glumdalclitch to contrive some excuse for not seeing that young lady any more.

One day, a young gentleman, who was nephew to my nurse's governess, came and pressed them both to see an execution. It was of a man who had murdered one of that gentleman's intimate acquaintance. Glumdalclitch was prevailed on to be of the company, very much against her inclination, for she was naturally tender-hearted: and, as for myself, although I abhorred such kind of spectacles,[26] yet my curiosity tempted me to see something that I thought must be extraordinary. The malefactor was fixed in a chair upon a scaffold erected for the purpose, and his head cut off at one blow with a sword of about forty foot long. The veins and arteries spouted up such a prodigious quantity of blood, and so high in the air, that the great *jet d'eau* at Versailles was not equal for the time it lasted; and the head when it fell on the scaffold floor, gave such a bounce as made me start, although I were at least an English mile distant.

The Queen, who often used to hear me talk of my sea-voyages, and took all occasions to divert me when I was melancholy, asked me whether I understood how to handle a sail or an oar, and whether a little exercise of rowing might not be convenient for my health. I answered, that I understood both very well. For although my proper employment had been to be surgeon or doctor to the ship, yet often, upon a pinch, I was forced to work like a common mariner. But, I could not see how this could be done in their country, where the smallest wherry was equal to a first rate man-of-war among us, and such a boat as I could manage would never live in any of their rivers: her Majesty said, if I would contrive a boat, her own joiner should make it, and she would provide a place for me to sail in. The fellow was an ingenious workman, and by my instructions in ten days finished a pleasure-boat with all its tackling, able conveniently to hold eight Europeans. When it was finished, the Queen was so delighted, that she ran with it in her lap to the King, who ordered it to be put in a cistern full of water, with me in it, by way of trial, where I could not manage my two sculls or little oars for want of room. But, the Queen had before contrived another project. She ordered the joiner to make a wooden trough of three hundred foot long, fifty broad, and eight deep; which being well pitched to prevent leaking, was placed on the floor along the wall, in an outer room of the palace. It had a cock near the bottom to let out the water when it began to grow stale, and two servants could easily fill it in half an hour. Here I often used to row for my own diversion, as well as that of the Queen and her ladies, who thought themselves agreeably entertained with my skill and agility. Sometimes I would put up my sail, and then my business was only to steer, while the ladies gave me a gale with their fans; and when they were weary, some of the pages would blow my sail forward with their breath, while I showed my art by steering starboard or larboard as I pleased. When I had done, Glumdalclitch always carried back my boat into her closet, and hung it on a nail to dry.

In this exercise I once met an accident which had like to have cost me my life. For, one of the pages having put my boat into the trough, the governess who attended Glumdalclitch very officiously[27] lifted me up to place me in the boat, but I happened to slip through her fingers, and should have infallibly fallen down forty foot upon the floor, if by the luckiest chance in the world, I had not been stopped by a corking-pin that stuck in the good gentlewoman's stomacher; the head of the pin passed between my shirt and the waistband of my breeches, and thus I was held by the middle in the air till Glumdalclitch ran to my relief.

Another time, one of the servants, whose office it was to fill my trough every third day with fresh water, was so careless to let a huge frog (not perceiving it) slip out of his pail. The frog lay concealed till I was put into my boat, but then seeing a resting-place, climbed up, and made it lean so much on one side, that I was forced to balance it with all my weight on the other, to prevent overturning. When the frog was got in, it hopped at once half the length of the boat, and then over my head, backwards and forwards, daubing my face and clothes with its odious slime. The largeness of its features made it appear the most deformed animal that can be conceived. However, I desired Glumdalclitch to let me deal with it alone. I banged it a good while with one of my sculls, and at last forced it to leap out of the boat.

But, the greatest danger I ever underwent in that kingdom was from a monkey, who belonged to one of the Clerks of the Kitchen. Glumdalclitch had locked me up in her closet, while she went somewhere upon business or a visit. The weather being very warm, the closet window was left open, as well as the windows and the door of my bigger box, in which I usually lived, because of its largeness and conveniency. As I sat quietly meditating at my table, I heard something bounce in at the closet window, and skip about from one side to the other; whereat, although I were much alarmed, yet I ventured to look out, but not stirring from my seat; and then I saw this frolicsome animal, frisking and leaping up and down, till at last he came to my box, which he seemed to view with great pleasure and curiosity, peeping in at the door and every window. I retreated to the farther corner of my room, or box, but the monkey, looking in at every side, put me into such a fright, that I wanted presence of mind to conceal myself under the bed, as I might easily have done. After some time spent in peeping, grinning, and chattering, he at last espied me, and reaching one of his paws in at the door, as a cat does when she plays with a mouse, although I often shifted place to avoid him, he at length seized the lappet of my coat (which being made of that country silk, was very thick and strong) and dragged me out. He took me up in his right forefoot, and held me as a nurse doth a child she is going to suckle, just as I have seen the same sort of creature do with a kitten in Europe: and when I offered to struggle, he squeezed me so hard, that I thought it more prudent to submit. I have good reason to believe that he took me for a young one of his own species, by his often stroking my face very gently with his other paw. In these diversions he was interrupted by a noise at the closet door, as if somebody were opening it; whereupon he suddenly leaped up to the window at which he had come in, and thence upon the leads and gutters, walking upon three legs, and holding me in the fourth, till he clambered up to a roof that was next to ours. I heard Glumdalclitch give a shriek at the moment he was carrying me out. The poor girl was almost distracted: that quarter of the palace was all in an uproar; the servants ran for ladders; the monkey was seen by hundreds in the Court, sitting upon the ridge of a building, holding me like a baby in one of his fore-paws, and feeding me with the other, by cramming into my mouth some victuals he had squeezed out of the bag on one side of his chaps, and patting me when I would not eat; whereat many of the rabble below could not forbear laughing; neither do I think they justly ought to be blamed, for without question the sight was ridiculous enough to everybody but myself. Some of the people threw up stones, hoping to drive the monkey down; but this was strictly forbidden, or else very probably my brains had been dashed out.

The ladders were now applied, and mounted by several men, which the monkey observing, and finding himself almost encompassed, not being able to make speed enough with his three legs, let me drop on a ridge-tile, and made his escape. Here I sat for some time five hundred yards from the ground, expecting every moment to be blown down by the wind, or to fall by my own giddiness, and come tumbling over and over from the ridge to the eaves. But an honest lad, one of my nurse's footmen, climbed up, and putting me into his breeches pocket, brought me down safe.

I was almost choked with the filthy stuff the monkey had crammed down my throat; but, my dear little nurse picked it out of my mouth with a small needle, and then I fell a vomiting, which gave me great relief. Yet I was so weak and bruised in the sides with the squeezes given me by this odious animal, that I was forced to keep my bed a fortnight. The King, Queen and all the Court sent every day to enquire after my health, and her Majesty made me several visits during my sickness. The monkey was killed, and an order made that no such animal should be kept about the palace.

When I attended the King after my recovery, to return him

thanks for his favours, he was pleased to rally me a good deal upon this adventure. He asked me what my thoughts and speculations were while I lay in the monkey's paw, how I liked the victuals he gave me, his manner of feeding, and whether the fresh air on the roof had sharpened my stomach. He desired to know what I would have done upon such an occasion in my own country. I told his Majesty, that in Europe we had no monkeys, except such as were brought for curiosities from other places, and so small, that I could deal with a dozen of them together, if they presumed to attack me. And as for that monstrous animal with whom I was so lately engaged (it was indeed as large as an elephant), if my fears had suffered me to think so far as to make use of my hanger (looking fiercely and clapping my hand upon the hilt as I spoke) when he poked his paw into my chamber, perhaps I should have given him such a wound, as would have made him glad to withdraw it with more haste than he put it in. This I delivered in a firm tone, like a person who was jealous lest his courage should be called in question. However, my speech produced nothing else besides a loud laughter, which all the respect due to his Majesty from those about him could not make them contain. This made me reflect how vain an attempt it is for a man to endeavour doing himself honour among those who are out of all degree of equality or comparison with him. And yet I have seen the moral of my own behaviour very frequent in England since my return, where a little contemptible varlet, without the least title to birth, person, wit, or common sense, shall presume to look with importance, and put himself upon a foot with the greatest persons of the kingdom.

I was every day furnishing the Court with some ridiculous story; and Glumdalclitch, although she loved me to excess, yet was arch enough to inform the Queen, whenever I committed any folly that she thought would be diverting to her Majesty. The girl, who had been out of order, was carried by her governess to take the air about an hour's distance, or thirty miles from town. They alighted out of the coach near a small footpath in a field, and Glumdalclitch setting down my travelling-box, I went out of it to walk. There was a cow-dung in the path, and I must needs try my activity by attempting to leap over it. I took a run, but unfortunately jumped short, and found myself just in the middle up to my knees. I waded through with some difficulty, and one of the footmen wiped me as clean as he could with his handkerchief; for I was filthily bemired, and my nurse confined me to my box till we returned home; where the Queen was soon informed of what had passed, and the footmen spread it about the Court, so that all the mirth, for some days, was at my expense.

CHAPTER 6

Several contrivances of the author to please the King and Queen. He shows his skill in music. The King inquires into the state of Europe, which the author relates to him. The King's observations thereon.

I USED to attend the King's levee[28] once or twice a week, and had often seen him under the barber's hand, which indeed was at first very terrible to behold. For, the razor was almost twice as long as an ordinary scythe. His Majesty according to the custom of the country was only shaved twice a week. I once prevailed on the barber to give me some of the suds or lather, out of which I picked forty or fifty of the strongest stumps of hair. I then took a piece of fine wood, and cut it like the back of a comb, making several holes in it at equal distance with as small a needle as I could get from Glumdalclitch. I fixed in the stumps so artificially, scraping and sloping them with my knife towards the points, that I made a very tolerable comb; which was a seasonable supply, my own being so much broken in the teeth, that it was almost useless: neither did I know any artist in that country so nice and exact, as would undertake to make me another.

And this puts me in mind of an amusement wherein I spent many of my leisure hours. I desired the Queen's woman to save for me the combings of her Majesty's hair, whereof in time I got a good quantity, and consulting with my friend the cabinet-maker, who had received general orders to do little jobs for me, I directed him to make two chair-frames, no larger than those I had in my box, and then to bore little holes with a fine awl round those parts where I designed the backs and seats; through these holes I wove the strongest hairs I could pick out, just after the manner of cane-chairs in England. When they were finished, I made a present of them to her Majesty, who kept them in her cabinet, and used to show them for curiosities, as indeed they were the wonder of everyone who beheld them. The Queen would have had me sit upon one of these chairs, but I absolutely refused to obey her, protesting I would rather die a thousand deaths than place a dishonourable part of my body on those precious hairs that once adorned her Majesty's head. Of these hairs (as I had always a mechanical genius) I likewise made a neat little purse about five foot long, with her Majesty's name deciphered in gold letters, which I gave to Glumdalclitch, by the Queen's consent. To say the truth, it was more for show than use, being not of strength to bear the weight of the larger coins, and therefore she kept nothing in it, but some little toys that girls are fond of.

The King, who delighted in music, had frequent consorts[29] at Court, to which I was sometimes carried, and set in my box on a table to hear them: but, the noise was so great, that I could hardly distinguish the tunes. I am confident that all the drums and trumpets of a royal army, beating and sounding together just at your ears, could not equal it. My practice was to have my box removed from the places where the performers sat, as far as I could, then to shut the doors and windows of it, and draw the window-curtains; after which I found their music not disagreeable.

I had learned in my youth to play a little upon the spinet. Glumdalclitch kept one in her chamber, and a master attended twice a week to teach her: I call it a spinet, because it somewhat resembled that instrument, and was played upon in the same manner. A fancy came into my head that I would entertain the King and Queen with an English tune upon this instrument. But this appeared extremely difficult: for, the spinet was near sixty foot long, each key being almost a foot wide, so that, with my arms extended, I could not reach to above five keys, and to press them down required a good smart stroke with my fist, which would be too great a labour, and to no purpose. The method I contrived was this. I prepared two round sticks about the bigness of common cudgels; they were thicker at one end than the other, and I covered the thicker ends with a piece of a mouse's skin, that by rapping on them, I might neither damage the tops of the keys, nor interrupt the sound. Before the spinet a bench was placed about four foot below the keys, and I was put upon the bench. I ran sideling upon it that way and this, as fast as I could, banging the proper keys with my two sticks, and made a shift to play a jig to the great satisfaction of both their Majesties: but it was the most violent exercise I ever underwent, and yet I could not strike above sixteen keys, nor, consequently, play the bass and treble together, as other artists do; which was a great disadvantage to my performance.

The King, who as I before observed, was a Prince of excellent understanding, would frequently order that I should be brought in my box, and set upon the table in his closet. He would then command me to bring one of my chairs out of the box, and sit down within three yards distance upon the top of the cabinet, which brought me almost to a level with his face. In this manner I had several conversations with him. I one day took the freedom to tell his Majesty, that the contempt he discovered towards Europe, and the rest of the world, did not seem answerable to those excellent qualities of mind, that he was master of. That reason did not extend itself with the bulk of the body: on the contrary, we observed in our country that the tallest persons were usually least provided with it. That among other animals, bees and ants had the reputation of more industry, art and sagacity than many of the larger kinds. And that, as inconsiderable as he took me to be, I hoped I might live to do his Majesty some signal service. The King heard me with attention, and began to conceive a much better opinion of me than he had ever before. He desired I would give him as exact an account of the government of England as I possibly could; because, as fond as princes commonly are of their own customs (for so he conjectured of other monarchs by my former discourses), he should be glad to hear of anything that might deserve imitation.

Imagine with thyself, courteous reader, how often I then wished for the tongue of Demosthenes or Cicero, that might have enabled me to celebrate the praises of my own dear native country in a style equal to its merits and felicity.

I began my discourse by informing his Majesty that our dominions consisted of two islands, which composed three mighty kingdoms under one sovereign, besides our plantations [30] in America. I dwelt long upon the fertility of our soil, and the temperature of our climate. I then spoke at large upon the constitution of an English Parliament, partly made up of an illustrious body called the House of Peers, persons of the noblest blood, and of the most ancient and ample patrimonies. I described that extraordinary care always taken of their education in arts and arms, to qualify them for being counsellors born to the King and kingdom, to have a share in the legislature, to be members of the highest court of judicature from whence there could be no appeal; and to be champions always ready for the defence of their prince and country by their valour, conduct and fidelity. That these were the ornament and bulwark of the kingdom, worthy followers of their most renowned ancestors, whose honour had been the reward of their virtue, from which their posterity were never once known to degenerate. To these were joined several holy persons, as part of that assembly, under the title of Bishops, whose peculiar business it is, to take care of religion, and of those who instruct the people therein. These were searched and sought out through the whole nation, by the Prince and his wisest counsellors, among such of the priesthood, as were most deservedly distinguished by the sanctity of their lives, and the depth of their erudition; who were indeed the spiritual fathers of the clergy and the people.

That the other part of the Parliament consisted of an assembly called the House of Commons, who were all principal gentlemen, *freely* picked and culled out by the people themselves, for their great abilities, and love of their country, to represent the wisdom of the whole nation. And these two bodies make up the most august assembly in Europe, to whom, in conjunction with the Prince, the whole legislature is committed.

I then descended to the Courts of Justice, over which the Judges, those venerable sages and interpreters of the law, presided, for determining the disputed rights and properties of men, as well as for the punishment of vice, and protection of innocence. I mentioned the prudent management of our Treasury, the valour and achievements of our forces by sea and land. I computed the number of our people, by reckoning how many millions there might be of each religious sect, or political party among us. I did not omit even our sports and pastimes, or any other particular which I thought might redound to the honour of my country. And, I finished all with a brief historical account of affairs and events in England for about an hundred years past.

This conversation was not ended under five audiences, each of several hours, and the King heard the whole with great attention, frequently taking notes of what I spoke, as well as memorandums of what questions he intended to ask me.

When I had put an end to these long discourses, his Majesty in a sixth audience, consulting his notes, proposed many doubts, queries, and objections, upon every article. He asked, what methods were used to cultivate the minds and bodies of our young nobility, and in what kind of business they commonly spent the first and teachable part of their lives. What course was taken to supply that assembly when any noble family became extinct. What qualifications were necessary in those who are to be created new Lords: whether the humour of the Prince, a sum of money to a Court lady, or a Prime Minister, or a design of strengthening a party opposite to the public interest, ever happened to be motives in those advancements. What share of knowledge these Lords had in the laws of their country, and how they came by it, so as to enable them to decide the properties of their fellow-subjects in the last resort. Whether they were always so free from avarice, partialities, or want, that a bribe, or some other sinister view, could have no place among them. Whether those holy Lords I spoke of were constantly promoted to that rank upon account of their knowledge in religious matters, and the sanctity of their lives; had never been compliers with the times while they were common priests, or slavish prostitute chaplains[31] to some nobleman, whose opinions they continued servilely to follow after they were admitted into that assembly.

He then desired to know what arts were practised in electing those whom I called Commoners. Whether, a stranger with a strong purse might not influence the vulgar voters to choose him before their own landlord, or the most considerable gentleman in the neighbourhood. How it came to pass, that people were so violently bent upon getting into this assembly, which I allowed to be a great trouble and expense, often to the ruin of their families, without any salary or pension: because this appeared such an exalted strain of virtue and public spirit, that his Majesty seemed to doubt it might possibly not be always sincere: and he desired to know whether such zealous gentlemen could have any views of refunding themselves for the charges and trouble they were at, by sacrificing the public good to the designs of a weak and vicious prince in conjunction with a corrupted ministry. He multiplied his questions, and sifted me thoroughly upon every part of this head, proposing numberless enquiries and objections, which I think it not prudent or convenient to repeat.

Upon what I said in relation to our Courts of Justice, his Majesty desired to be satisfied in several points: and, this I was the better able to do, having been formerly almost ruined by a long suit in Chancery, which was decreed for me with costs. He asked, what time was usually spent in determining between right and wrong, and what degree of expense. Whether advocates and orators had liberty to plead in causes manifestly known to be unjust, vexatious, or oppressive. Whether party in religion or politics were observed to be of any weight in the scale of justice. Whether those pleading orators were persons educated in the general knowledge of equity, or only in provincial, national, and other local customs. Whether they or their Judges had any part in penning those laws which they assumed the liberty of interpreting and glossing upon at their pleasure. Whether they had ever at different times pleaded for and against the same cause, and cited precedents to prove contrary opinions. Whether they were a rich or a poor corporation. Whether they received any pecuniary reward for pleading or delivering their opinions. And particularly whether they were ever admitted as members in the lower senate.

He fell next upon the management of our Treasury; and said, he thought my memory had failed me, because I computed our taxes at about five or six millions a year, and when I came to mention the issues, he found they sometimes amounted to more than double;[32] for, the notes he had taken were very particular in this point, because he hoped, as he told me, that the knowledge of our conduct might be useful to him, and he could not be deceived in his calculations. But, if what I told him were true, he was still at a loss how a kingdom could run out of its estate like a private person. He asked me, who were our creditors? and, where we found money to pay them? He wondered to hear me talk of such chargeable and extensive wars; that, certainly we must be a quarrelsome people, or live among very bad neighbours, and that our generals must needs be richer than our kings.[33] He asked what business we had out of our own islands, unless upon the score of trade or treaty, or to defend the coasts with our fleet. Above all, he was amazed to hear me talk of a mercenary standing army[34] in the midst of peace, and among a free people. He said, if we were governed by our own consent in the persons of our representatives, he could not imagine of whom we were afraid, or against whom we were to fight, and would hear my opinion, whether a private man's house might not better be defended by himself, his children, and family, than by half-a-dozen rascals picked up at a venture in the streets, for small wages, who might get an hundred times more by cutting their throats.

He laughed at my odd kind of arithmetic (as he was pleased to call it) in reckoning the numbers of our people by a computation drawn from the several sects among us in religion and politics. He said, he knew no reason, why those who entertain opinions prejudicial to the public should be obliged to change, or should not be obliged to conceal them.[35] And as it was tyranny in any government to require the first, so it was weakness not to enforce the second: for, a man may be allowed to keep poisons in his closet, but not to vend them about as cordials.

He observed, that among the diversions of our nobility and gentry, I had mentioned gaming. He desired to know at what age this entertainment was usually taken up, and when it was laid down. How much of their time it employed; whether it ever went so high as to affect their fortunes. Whether mean vicious people by their dexterity in that art might not arrive at great riches, and sometimes keep our very nobles in dependence, as well as habituate them to vile companions, wholly take them from the improvement of their minds, and force them by the losses they received, to learn and practise that infamous dexterity upon others.

He was perfectly astonished with the historical account I gave him of our affairs during the last century, protesting it was only an heap of conspiracies, rebellions, murders, massacres, revolutions, banishments, and very worst effects that avarice, faction, hypocrisy, perfidiousness, cruelty, rage, madness, hatred, envy, lust, malice, and ambition could produce. His Majesty in another audience was at the pains to recapitulate the sum of all I had spoken, compared the questions he made with the answers I had given; then taking me into his hands, and stroking me gently, delivered himself in these words, which I shall never forget, nor the manner he spoke them in. My little friend Grildrig; you have made a most admirable panegyric upon your country. You have clearly proved that ignorance, idleness, and vice are the proper ingredients for qualifying a legislator. That laws are best explained, interpreted, and applied by those whose interest and abilities lie in perverting, confounding, and eluding them. I observe among you some lines of an institution, which in its original might have been tolerable, but these half erased, and the rest wholly blurred and blotted by corruptions. It doth not appear from all you have said, how any one perfection is required towards the procurement of any one station among you, much less that men are ennobled on account of their virtue, that priests are advanced for their piety or learning, soldiers for their conduct or valour, judges for their integrity, senators for the love of their country, or counsellors for their wisdom. As for yourself (continued the King) who have spent the greatest part of your life in travelling, I am well disposed to hope you may hitherto have escaped many vices of your country. But, by what I have gathered from your own relation, and the answers I have with much pains wringed and extorted from you, I cannot but conclude the bulk of your natives, to be the most pernicious race of little odious vermin that Nature ever suffered to crawl upon the surface of the earth.

CHAPTER 7

The author's love of his country. He makes a proposal of much advantage to the King, which is rejected. The King's great ignorance in politics. The learning of that country very imperfect and confined. Their laws, and military affairs, and parties in the state.

NOTHING but an extreme love of truth could have hindered me from concealing this part of my story. It was in vain to discover my resentments, which were always turned into ridicule; and I was forced to rest with patience while my noble and most beloved country was so injuriously treated. I am heartily sorry as any of my readers can possibly be, that such an occasion was given: but this Prince happened to be so curious and inquisitive upon every particular, that it could not consist either with gratitude or good manners to refuse giving him what satisfaction I was able. Yet thus much I may be allowed to say in my own vindication, that I artfully eluded many of his questions, and gave to every point a more favourable turn by many degrees than the strictness of truth would allow. For, I have always borne that laudable partiality to my own country, which Dionysius Halicarnassensis[36] with so much justice recommends to an historian. I would hide the frailties and deformities of my political mother, and place her virtues and beauties in the most advantageous light. This was my sincere endeavour in those many discourses I had with that mighty monarch, although it unfortunately failed of success.

But, great allowances should be given to a King who lives wholly secluded from the rest of the world, and must therefore be altogether unacquainted with the manners and customs that most prevail in other nations: the want of which knowledge will ever produce many *prejudices*, and a certain *narrowness of thinking*, from which we and the politer countries of Europe are wholly exempted. And it would be hard indeed, if so remote a Prince's notions of virtue and vice were to be offered as a standard for all mankind.

To confirm what I have now said, and further to show the miserable effects of a *confined education*, I shall here insert a passage which will hardly obtain belief. In hopes to ingratiate myself farther into his Majesty's favour, I told him of an invention discovered between three and four hundred years ago, to make a certain powder, into an heap of which the smallest spark of fire falling, would kindle the whole in a moment, although it were as big as a mountain, and make it all fly up in the air together, with a noise and agitation greater than thunder. That, a proper quantity of this powder rammed into an hollow tube of brass or iron, according to its bigness, would drive a ball of iron or lead with such violence and speed as nothing was able to sustain its force. That the largest balls thus discharged, would not only destroy whole ranks of an army at once, but batter the strongest walls to the ground, sink down ships with a thousand men in each, to the bottom of the sea; and when linked together by a chain, would cut through masts and rigging, divide hundreds of bodies in the middle, and lay all waste before them. That we often put this powder into large hollow balls of iron, and discharged them by an engine into some city we were besieging, which would rip up the pavements, tear the houses to pieces, burst and throw splinters on every side, dashing out the brains of all who came near. That I knew the ingredients very well, which were cheap, and common; I understood the manner of compounding them, and could direct his workmen how to make those tubes of a size proportionable to all other things in his Majesty's kingdom, and the largest need not be above two hundred foot long; twenty or thirty of which tubes, charged with the proper quantity of powder and balls, would batter down the walls of the strongest town in his dominions in a few hours, or destroy the whole metropolis, if ever it should pretend to dispute his absolute commands. This I humbly offered to his Majesty as a small tribute of acknowledgement in return of so many marks that I had received of his royal favour and protection.

The King was struck with horror at the description I had given of those terrible engines, and the proposal I had made. He was amazed how so impotent and grovelling an insect as I (these were his expressions) could entertain such inhuman ideas, and in so familiar a manner as to appear wholly unmoved at all the scenes of blood and desolation, which I had painted as the common effects of those destructive machines, whereof he said, some evil genius, enemy to mankind, must have been the first contriver. As for himself, he protested, that although few things delighted him so much as new discoveries in art or in nature, yet he would rather lose half his kingdom than be privy to such a secret, which he commanded me, as I valued my life, never to mention any more.

A strange effect of *narrow principles* and *short views*! that a Prince possessed of every quality which procures veneration, love, and esteem; of strong parts, great wisdom and profound learning, endued with admirable talents for government, and almost adored by his subjects, should from a *nice unnecessary scruple*, whereof in Europe we can have no conception, let slip an opportunity put into his hands, that would have made him absolute master of the lives, the liberties, and the fortunes of his people. Neither do I say this with the least intention to detract from the many virtues of that excellent King, whose character I am sensible will on this account be very much lessened in the opinion of an English reader: but I take this defect among them to have risen from their ignorance, by not having hitherto reduced *politics* into a *science*, as the more acute wits of Europe have done. For, I remember very well, in a discourse one day with the King, when I happened to say there were several thousand books among us written upon the *Art of Government*, it gave him (directly contrary to my intention) a very mean opinion of our understandings. He professed both to abominate and despise all *mystery, refinement*, and *intrigue*, either in a prince or a minister. He could not tell what I meant by *Secrets of State*, where an enemy or some rival nation were not in the case. He confined the knowledge of governing within very *narrow bounds*; to common sense and reason, to justice and lenity, to the speedy determination of civil and criminal causes; with some other obvious topics which are not worth considering. And, he gave it for his opinion, that whoever could make two ears of corn, or two blades of grass to grow upon a spot of ground where only one grew before, would deserve better of mankind, and do more essential service to his country, than the whole race of politicians put together.

The learning of this people is very defective, consisting only in morality, history, poetry and mathematics, wherein they must be allowed to excel. But, the last of these is wholly applied to what may be useful in life, to the improvement of agriculture and all mechanical arts; so that among us it would be little esteemed. And as to ideas, entities, abstractions and transcendentals,[37] I could never drive the least conception into their heads.

No law of that country must exceed in words the number of letters in their alphabet, which consists only of two and twenty. But indeed, few of them extend even to that length. They are expressed in the most plain and simple terms, wherein those people are not mercurial enough to discover above one interpretation. And to write a comment upon any law is a capital crime. As to the decision of civil causes, or proceedings against criminals, their precedents are so few, that they have little reason to boast of any extraordinary skill in either.

They have had the art of printing, as well as the Chinese, time out of mind. But their libraries are not very large; for that of the King's, which is reckoned the largest, doth not amount to above a thousand volumes, placed in a gallery of twelve hundred foot long, from whence I had liberty to borrow what books I pleased. The Queen's joiner had contrived in one of Glumdalclitch's rooms a kind of wooden machine five and twenty foot high, formed like a standing ladder; the steps were each fifty foot long: it was indeed a moveable pair of stairs, the lowest end placed at ten foot distance from the wall of the chamber. The book I had a mind to read was put up leaning against the wall. I first mounted to the upper step of the ladder, and turning my face towards the book, began at the top of the page, and so walking to the right and left about eight or ten paces according to the length of the lines, till I had gotten a little below the level of mine eyes, and then descending gradually till I came to the bottom: after which I mounted again, and began the other page in the same manner, and so turned over the leaf, which I could easily do with both my hands, for it was as thick and stiff as a pasteboard, and in the largest folios not above eighteen or twenty foot long.

Their style is clear,[38] masculine, and smooth, but not florid, for they avoid nothing more than multiplying unnecessary words, or using various expressions. I have perused many of their books, especially those in history and morality. Among the latter I was much diverted with a little old treatise, which always lay in Glumdalclitch's bedchamber, and belonged to her governess, a grave elderly gentlewoman, who dealt in writings of morality and devotion. The book treats of the weakness of human kind, and is in little esteem except among the women and the vulgar. However, I was curious to see what an author of that country could say upon such a subject.

This writer went through all the usual topics of European moralists, showing how diminutive, contemptible, and helpless an animal was man in his own nature; how unable to defend himself from the inclemencies of the air, or the fury of wild beasts. How much he was excelled by one creature in strength, by another in speed, by a third in foresight, by a fourth in industry. He added, that Nature was degenerated [39] in these latter declining ages of the world, and could now produce only small abortive births in comparison of those in ancient times. He said it was very reasonable to think, not only that the species of men were originally much larger, but also that there must have been giants in former ages, which, as it is asserted by history and tradition, so it hath been confirmed by huge bones and skulls casually dug up in several parts of the kingdom, far exceeding the common dwindled race of man in our days. He argued, that the very Laws of Nature absolutely required we should have been made, in the beginning, of a size more large and robust, not so liable to destruction from every little accident of a tile falling from an house, or a stone cast from the hand of a boy, or of being drowned in a little brook. From this way of reasoning the author drew several moral applications useful in the conduct of life, but needless here to repeat. For my own part, I could not avoid reflecting, how universally this talent was spread of drawing lectures in morality, or indeed rather matter of discontent and repining, from the quarrels we raise with Nature. And, I believe upon a strict enquiry, those quarrels might be shown as ill-grounded among us, as they are among that people.

As to their military affairs, they boast that the King's army consists of an hundred and seventy-six thousand foot, and thirty-two thousand horse: if that may be called an army [40] which is made up of tradesmen in the several cities, and farmers in the country, whose commanders are only the nobility and gentry without pay or reward. They are indeed perfect enough in their exercises, and under very good discipline, wherein I saw no great merit; for how should it be otherwise, where every farmer is under the command of his own landlord, and every citizen under that of the principal men in his own city, chosen after the manner of Venice by ballot?

I have often seen the militia of Lorbrulgrud drawn out to exercise in a great field near the city, of twenty miles square. They were in all not above twenty-five thousand foot, and six thousand horse; but it was impossible for me to compute their number, considering the space of ground they took up. A cavalier mounted on a large steed might be about ninety foot high. I have seen this whole body of horse upon the word of command draw their swords at once, and brandish them in the air. Imagination can figure nothing so grand, so surprising and so astonishing. It looked as if ten thousand flashes of lightning were darting at the same time from every quarter of the sky.

I was curious to know how this Prince, to whose dominions there is no access from any other country, came to think of armies, or to teach his people the practice of military discipline. But I was soon informed, both by conversation, and reading their histories. For, in the course of many ages they have been troubled with the same disease to which the whole race of mankind is subject; the nobility often contending for power, the people for liberty, and the King for absolute dominion. All which, however happily tempered by the laws of that kingdom, have been sometimes violated by each of the three parties; and have more than once occasioned civil wars, the last whereof was happily put an end to by this Prince's grandfather in a general composition; and the militia then settled with common consent hath been ever since kept in the strictest duty.

CHAPTER 8

The King and Queen make a progress to the frontiers. The author attends them. The manner in which he leaves the country very particularly related. He returns to England.

I HAD always a strong impulse that I should sometime recover my liberty, though it were impossible to conjecture by what means, or to form any project with the least hope of succeeding. The ship in which I sailed was the first ever known to be driven within sight of that coast, and the King had given strict orders, that if at any time another appeared, it should be taken ashore, and with all its crew and passengers brought in a tumbril to Lorbrulgrud. He was strongly bent to get me a woman of my own size, by whom I might propagate the breed: but I think I should rather have died than undergone the disgrace of leaving a posterity to be kept in cages like tame canary birds, and perhaps in time sold about the kingdom to persons of quality for curiosities. I was indeed treated with much kindness; I was the favourite of a great King and Queen, and the delight of the whole Court, but it was upon such a foot as ill became the dignity of human kind. I could never forget those domestic pledges I had left behind me. I wanted to be among people with whom I could converse upon even terms, and walk about the streets and fields without fear of being trod to death like a frog or a young puppy. But, my deliverance came sooner than I expected, and in a manner not very common: the whole story and circumstances of which I shall faithfully relate.

I had now been two years in this country; and about the beginning of the third, Glumdalclitch and I attended the King and Queen in a progress to the south coast of the kingdom. I was carried as usual in my travelling-box, which, as I have already described, was a very convenient closet of twelve foot wide. I had ordered a hammock to be fixed by silken ropes from the four corners at the top, to break the jolts, when a servant carried me before him on horseback, as I sometimes desired, and would often sleep in my hammock while we were upon the road. On the roof of my closet, set not directly over the middle of the hammock, I ordered the joiner to cut out a hole of a foot square to give me air in hot weather as I slept, which hole I shut at pleasure with a board that drew backwards and forwards through a groove.

When we came to our journey's end, the King thought proper to pass a few days at a palace he hath near Flanflasnic, a city within eighteen English miles of the seaside. Glumdalclitch and I were much fatigued; I had gotten a small cold, but the poor girl was so ill as to be confined to her chamber. I longed to see the ocean, which must be the only scene of my escape, if ever it should happen. I pretended to be worse than I really was, and desired leave to take the fresh air of the sea, with a page whom I was very fond of, and who had sometimes been trusted with me. I shall never forget with what unwillingness Glumdalclitch consented, nor the strict charge she gave the page to be careful of me, bursting at the same time into a flood of tears, as if she had some foreboding of what was to happen. The boy took me out in my box about half an hour's walk from the palace towards the rocks on the seashore. I ordered him to set me down, and lifting up one of my sashes, cast many a wistful melancholy look towards the sea. I found myself not very well, and told the page that I had a mind to take a nap in my hammock, which I hoped would do me good. I got in, and the boy shut the window close down to keep out the cold. I soon fell asleep, and all I can conjecture is, that while I slept, the page, thinking no danger could happen, went among the rocks to look for birds' eggs, having before observed him from my window searching about, and picking up one or two in the clefts. Be that as it will, I found myself suddenly awaked with a violent pull upon the ring which was fastened at the top of my box for the conveniency of carriage. I felt the box raised very high in the air, and then borne forward with prodigious speed. The first jolt had like to have shaken me out of my hammock, but afterwards the motion was easy enough. I called out several times as loud as I could raise my voice, but all to no purpose. I looked towards my windows, and could see nothing but the clouds and sky. I heard a noise just over my head like the clapping of wings, and then began to perceive the woeful condition I was in; that some eagle had got the ring of my box in his beak, with an intent to let it fall on a rock like a tortoise in a shell, and then pick out my body and devour it. For the sagacity and smell of this bird enable him to discover his quarry at a great distance, though better concealed than I could be within a two-inch board.

In a little time I observed the noise and flutter of wings to increase very fast, and my box was tossed up and down like a signpost in a windy day. I heard several bangs or buffets, as I thought, given to the eagle (for such I am certain it must have been that held the ring of my box in his beak) and then all on a sudden felt myself falling perpendicularly down for above a minute, but with such incredible swiftness that I almost lost my breath. My fall was stopped by a terrible squash, that sounded louder to mine ears than the cataract of Niagara; after which I was quite in the dark for another minute, and then my box began to rise so high that I could see light from the tops of my windows. I now perceived that I was fallen into the sea. My box, by the weight of my body, the goods that were in, and the broad plates of iron fixed for strength at the four corners of the top and bottom, floated about five foot deep in water. I did then, and do now suppose that the eagle which flew away with my box was pursued by two or three others, and forced to let me drop while he was defending himself against the rest, who hoped to share in the prey. The plates of iron fastened at the bottom of the box (for those were the strongest) preserved the balance while it fell, and hindered it from being broken on the surface of the water. Every joint of it was well grooved, and the door did not move on hinges, but up and down like a sash, which kept my closet so tight that very little water came in. I got with much difficulty out of my hammock, having first ventured to draw back the slip-board on the roof already mentioned, contrived on purpose to let in air, for want of which I found myself almost stifled.

How often did I then wish myself with my dear Glumdalclitch, from whom one single hour had so far divided me! And I may say with truth, that in the midst of my own misfortunes I could not forbear lamenting my poor nurse, the grief she would suffer for my loss, the displeasure of the Queen, and the ruin of her fortune. Perhaps many travellers have not been under greater difficulties and distress than I was at this juncture, expecting every moment to see my box dashed in pieces, or at least overset by the first violent blast, or a rising wave. A breach in one single pane of glass would have been immediate death: nor could anything have preserved the windows but the strong lattice wires placed on the outside against accidents in travelling. I saw the water ooze in at several crannies, although the leaks were not considerable, and I endeavoured to stop them as well as I could. I was not able to lift up the roof of my closet, which otherwise I certainly should have done, and sat on the top of it, where I might at least preserve myself from being shut up, as I may call it, in the hold. Or, if I escaped these dangers for a day or two, what could I expect but a miserable death of cold and hunger! I was four hours under these circumstances, expecting and indeed wishing every moment to be my last.

I have already told the reader, that there were two strong staples fixed upon the side of my box which had no window, and into which the servant who used to carry me on horseback would put a leathern belt, and buckle it about his waist. Being in this disconsolate state, I heard or at least thought I heard some kind of grating noise on that side of my box where the staples were fixed, and soon after I began to fancy that the box was pulled, or towed along in the sea; for I now and then felt a sort of tugging which made the waves rise near the tops of my windows, leaving me almost in the dark. This gave me some faint hopes of relief, although I were not able to imagine how it could be brought about. I ventured to unscrew one of my chairs, which were always fastened to the floor; and having made a hard shift to screw it down again directly under the slipping-board that I had lately opened, I mounted on the chair, and putting my mouth as near as I could to the hole, I called for help in a loud voice, and in all the languages I understood. I then fastened my handkerchief to a stick I usually carried, and thrusting it up the hole, waved it several times in the air, that if any boat or ship were near, the seamen might conjecture some unhappy mortal to be shut up in the box.

I found no effect from all I could do, but plainly perceived my closet to be moved along; and in the space of an hour, or better, that side of the box where the staples were, and had no window, struck against something that was hard. I apprehended it to be a rock, and found myself tossed more than ever. I plainly heard a noise upon the cover of my closet, like that of a cable, and the grating of it as it passed through the ring. I then found myself hoisted up by degrees at least three foot higher than I was before. Whereupon, I again thrust up my stick and handkerchief, calling for help till I was almost hoarse. In return to which, I heard a great shout repeated three times, giving me such transports of joy as are not to be conceived but by those who feel them. I now heard a trampling over my head, and somebody calling through the hole with a loud voice in the English tongue: *If there be anybody below let them speak*. I answered, I was an Englishman, drawn by ill fortune into the greatest calamity that ever any creature underwent, and begged, by all that was moving, to be delivered out of the dungeon I was in. The voice replied, I was safe, for my box was fastened to their ship; and the carpenter should immediately come, and saw an hole in the cover, large enough to pull me out. I answered, that was needless, and would take up too much time, for there was no more to be done, but let one of the crew put his finger into the ring, and take the box out of the sea into the ship, and so into the captain's cabin. Some of them upon hearing me talk so wildly thought I was mad; others laughed; for indeed it never came into my head that I was now got among people of my own stature and strength. The carpenter came, and in a few minutes sawed a passage about four foot square, then let down a small ladder, upon which I mounted, and from thence was taken into the ship in a very weak condition.

The sailors were all in amazement, and asked me a thousand questions, which I had no inclination to answer. I was equally confounded at the sight of so many pygmies, for such I took them to be, after having so long accustomed mine eyes to the monstrous objects I had left. But the captain, Mr Thomas Wilcocks, an honest worthy Shropshire man, observing I was ready to faint, took me into his cabin, gave me a cordial to comfort me, and made me *turn in* upon his own bed, advising me to take a little rest, of which I had great need. Before I went to sleep I gave him to understand that I had some valuable furniture in my box, too good to be lost; a fine hammock, an handsome field-bed, two chairs, a table and a cabinet: that my closet was hung on all sides, or rather quilted, with silk and cotton: that if he would let one of the crew bring my closet into his cabin, I would open it before him, and show him my goods. The captain, hearing me utter these absurdities, concluded I was raving: however (I suppose to pacify me), he promised to give order as I desired, and going upon deck, sent some of his men down into my closet, from whence (as I afterwards found) they drew up all my goods, and stripped off the quilting; but the chairs, cabinet and bedstead, being screwed to the floor, were much damaged by the ignorance of the seamen, who tore them up by force. Then they knocked off some of the boards for the use of the ship, and when they had got all they had a mind for, let the hulk drop into the sea, which, by reason of many breaches made in the bottom and sides, sunk *to rights*. And indeed I was glad not to have been a spectator of the havoc they made; because I am confident it would have sensibly touched me, by bringing former passages into my mind, which I had rather forget.

I slept some hours, but perpetually disturbed with dreams of the place I had left, and the dangers I had escaped. However, upon waking I found myself much recovered. It was now about eight o'clock at night, and the captain ordered supper immediately, thinking I had already fasted too long. He entertained me with great kindness, observing me not to look wildly, or talk inconsistently; and when we were left alone, desired I would give him a relation of my travels, and by what accident I came to be set adrift in that monstrous wooden chest. He said, that about twelve o'clock at noon, as he was looking through his glass, he spied it at a distance, and thought it was a sail, which he had a mind to make, being not much out of his course, in hopes of buying some biscuit, his own beginning to fall short. That, upon coming nearer, and finding his error, he sent out his long-boat to discover what I was; that his men came back in a fright, swearing they had seen a swimming house. That he laughed at their folly, and went himself in the boat, ordering his men to take a strong cable along with them. That the weather being calm, he rowed round me several times, observed my windows, and the wire lattices that defended them. That he discovered two staples upon one side, which was all of boards, without any passage for light. He then commanded his men to row up to that side, and fastening a cable to one of the staples, ordered his men to tow my chest (as he called it) towards the ship. When it was there, he gave directions to fasten another cable to the ring fixed in the cover, and to raise up my chest with pulleys, which all the sailors were not able to do above two or three foot. He said, they saw my stick and handkerchief thrust out of the hole, and concluded that some unhappy man must be shut up in the cavity. I asked whether he or the crew had seen any prodigious birds in the air about the time he first discovered me. To which he answered, that discoursing this matter with the sailors while I was asleep, one of them said he had *observed* three eagles flying towards the north, but remarked nothing of their being larger than the usual size, which I suppose must be imputed to the great height they were at: and he could not guess the reason of my question. I then asked the captain how far he reckoned we might be from land; he said, by the best computation he could make, we were at least an hundred leagues. I assured him, that he must be mistaken by almost half, for I had not left the country from whence I came above two hours before I dropped into the sea. Whereupon he began again to think that my brain was disturbed, of which he gave me a hint, and advised me to go to bed in a cabin he had provided. I assured him I was well refreshed with his good entertainment and company, and as much in my senses as ever I was in my life. He then grew serious, and desired to ask me freely whether I were not troubled in mind by the consciousness of some enormous crime, for which I was punished at the command of some prince, by exposing me in that chest, as great criminals in other countries have been forced to sea in a leaky vessel without provisions: for, although he should be sorry to have taken so ill a man into his ship, yet he would engage his word to set me safe on shore in the first port where we arrived. He added, that his suspicions were much increased by some very absurd speeches I had delivered at first to the sailors, and afterwards to himself, in relation to my closet or chest, as well as by my odd looks and behaviour while I was at supper.

I begged his patience to hear me tell my story, which I

faithfully did from the last time I left England to the moment
he first discovered me. And, as truth always forceth its way
into rational minds, so this honest worthy gentleman, who
had some tincture of learning, and very good sense, was immediately convinced of my candour and veracity. But, further
to confirm all I had said, I entreated him to give order that
my cabinet should be brought, of which I kept the key in my
pocket (for he had already informed me how the seamen disposed of my closet); I opened it in his presence, and showed
him the small collection of rarities I made in the country from
whence I had been so strangely delivered. There was the comb
I had contrived out of the stumps of the King's beard, and
another of the same materials, but fixed into a paring of her
Majesty's thumb-nail, which served for the back. There was
a collection of needles and pins from a foot to half a yard long.
Four wasp-stings, like joiners' tacks: some combings of the
Queen's hair: a gold ring which one day she made me a
present of in a most obliging manner, taking it from her little
finger, and throwing it over my head like a collar. I desired
the captain would please to accept this ring in return of his
civilities, which he absolutely refused. I showed him a corn
that I had cut off with my own hand from a Maid of Honour's
toe; it was about the bigness of a Kentish pippin, and grown
so hard, that when I returned to England, I got it hollowed
into a cup and set in silver. Lastly, I desired him to see the
breeches I had then on, which were made of a mouse's skin.

I could force nothing on him but a footman's tooth, which
I observed him to examine with great curiosity, and found he
had a fancy for it. He received it with abundance of thanks,
more than such a trifle could deserve. It was drawn by an un-
skilful surgeon in a mistake from one of Glumdalclitch's
men, who was afflicted with the toothache, but it was as
sound as any in his head. I got it cleaned, and put it into my
cabinet. It was about a foot long, and four inches in diameter.

The captain was very well satisfied with this plain relation I had given him; and said, he hoped when we returned to England, I would oblige the world by putting it in paper, and making it public. My answer was, that I thought we were already overstocked with books of travels: that nothing could now pass which was not extraordinary, wherein I doubted some authors less consulted truth than their own vanity or interest, or the diversion of ignorant readers. That my story could contain little besides common events, without those ornamental descriptions of strange plants, trees, birds, and other animals, or the barbarous customs and idolatry of savage people, with which most writers abound. However, I thanked him for his good opinion, and promised to take the matter into my thoughts.

He said he wondered at one thing very much, which was to hear me speak so loud, asking me whether the King or Queen of that country were thick of hearing. I told him it was what I had been used to for above two years past, and that I admired as much at the voices of him and his men, who seemed to me only to whisper, and yet I could hear them well enough. But, when I spoke in that country, it was like a man talking in the street to another looking out from the top of a steeple, unless when I was placed on a table, or held in any person's hand. I told him I had likewise observed another thing, that when I first got into the ship, and the sailors stood all about me, I thought they were the most little contemptible creatures I had ever beheld. For, indeed, while I was in that Prince's country, I could never endure to look in a glass after mine eyes had been accustomed to such prodigious objects, because the comparison gave me so despicable a conceit of myself. The captain said, that while we were at supper, he observed me to look at everything with a sort of wonder, and that I often seemed hardly able to contain my laughter, which he knew not well how to take, but imputed it to some disorder in my brain. I answered, it was very true, and I wondered how I could forbear, when I saw his dishes of the size of a silver threepence,

a leg of pork hardly a mouthful, a cup not so big as a nutshell:
and so I went on, describing the rest of his household-stuff
and provisions after the same manner. For although the
Queen had ordered a little equipage of all things necessary for
me while I was in her service, yet my ideas were wholly taken
up with what I saw on every side of me, and I winked at my
own littleness as people do at their own faults. The captain
understood my raillery very well, and merrily replied with the
old English proverb, that he doubted mine eyes were bigger
than my belly, for he did not observe my stomach so good,
although I had fasted all day; and continuing in his mirth,
protested he would have gladly given an hundred pounds to
have seen my closet in the eagle's bill, and afterwards in its
fall from so great an height into the sea; which would certainly have been a most astonishing object, worthy to have the
description of it transmitted to future ages: and the comparison of Phaethon [41] was so obvious, that he could not forbear applying it, although I did not much admire the conceit.

The captain, having been at Tonquin, [42] was in his return to
England driven north-eastward to the latitude of 44 degrees,
and of longitude 143. But meeting a trade wind two days after
I came on board him, we sailed southward a long time, and
coasting New Holland [43] kept our course west-south-west,
and then south-south-west till we doubled the Cape of Good
Hope. Our voyage was very prosperous, but I shall not trouble
the reader with a journal of it. The captain called in at one or
two ports and sent in his long-boat for provisions and fresh
water, but I never went out of the ship till we came into the
Downs, which was on the 3rd day of June, 1706, about nine
months after my escape. I offered to leave my goods in security
for payment of my freight; but the captain protested he would
not receive one farthing. We took kind leave of each other,
and I made him promise he would come to see me at my house
in Redriff. I hired a horse and guide for five shillings, which I
borrowed of the captain.

As I was on the road, observing the littleness of the houses, the trees, the cattle and the people, I began to think myself in Lilliput. I was afraid of trampling on every traveller I met, and often called aloud to have them stand out of the way, so that I had like to have gotten one or two broken heads for my impertinence.

When I came to my own house, for which I was forced to enquire, one of the servants opening the door, I bent down to go in (like a goose under a gate) for fear of striking my head. My wife ran out to embrace me, but I stooped lower than her knees, thinking she could otherwise never be able to reach my mouth. My daughter kneeled to ask me blessing, but I could not see her till she arose, having been so long used to stand with my head and eyes erect to above sixty foot; and then I went to take her up with one hand, by the waist. I looked down upon the servants and one or two friends who were in the house, as if they had been pygmies, and I a giant. I told my wife she had been too thrifty, for I found she had starved herself and her daughter to nothing. In short, I behaved myself so unaccountably, that they were all of the captain's opinion when he first saw me, and concluded I had lost my wits. This I mention as an instance of the great power of habit and prejudice.

In a little time I and my family and friends came to a right understanding: but my wife protested I should never go to sea any more; although my evil destiny so ordered that she had not power to hinder me, as the reader may know hereafter. In the meantime I here conclude the second part of my unfortunate Voyages.

THE END OF THE SECOND PART.

As I was on the road, observing the littleness of the houses, the trees, the cattle and the people, I began to think myself in Lilliput. I was afraid of trampling on every traveller I met, and often called aloud to have them stand out of the way; so that I had like to have gotten one or two broken heads for my impertinence.

When I came to my own house, for which I was forced to enquire, one of the servants opening the door, I bent down to go in (like a goose under a gate) for fear of striking my head. My wife ran out to embrace me, but I stooped lower than her knees, thinking she could otherwise never be able to reach my mouth. My daughter kneeled to ask my blessing, but I could not see her till she arose, having been so long used to stand with my head and eyes erect to above sixty foot; and then I went to take her up with one hand by the waist. I looked down upon the servants and one or two friends who were in the house, as if they had been pygmies, and I a giant. I told my wife she had been too thrifty, for I found she had starved herself and her daughter to nothing. In short, I behaved myself so unaccountably, that they were all of the captain's opinion when he first saw me; and concluded I had lost my wits. This I mention as an instance of the great power of habit and prejudice.

In a little time I and my family and friends came to a right understanding; but my wife protested I should never go to sea any more; although, her evil destiny so ordered, that she had not power to hinder me, as the reader may know hereafter. In the meantime I here conclude the second part of my unfortunate voyages.

THE END OF THE SECOND PART.

TRAVELS · PART III

A VOYAGE TO LAPUTA, BALNIBARBI, GLUBBDUBDRIB, LUGGNAGG AND JAPAN

*

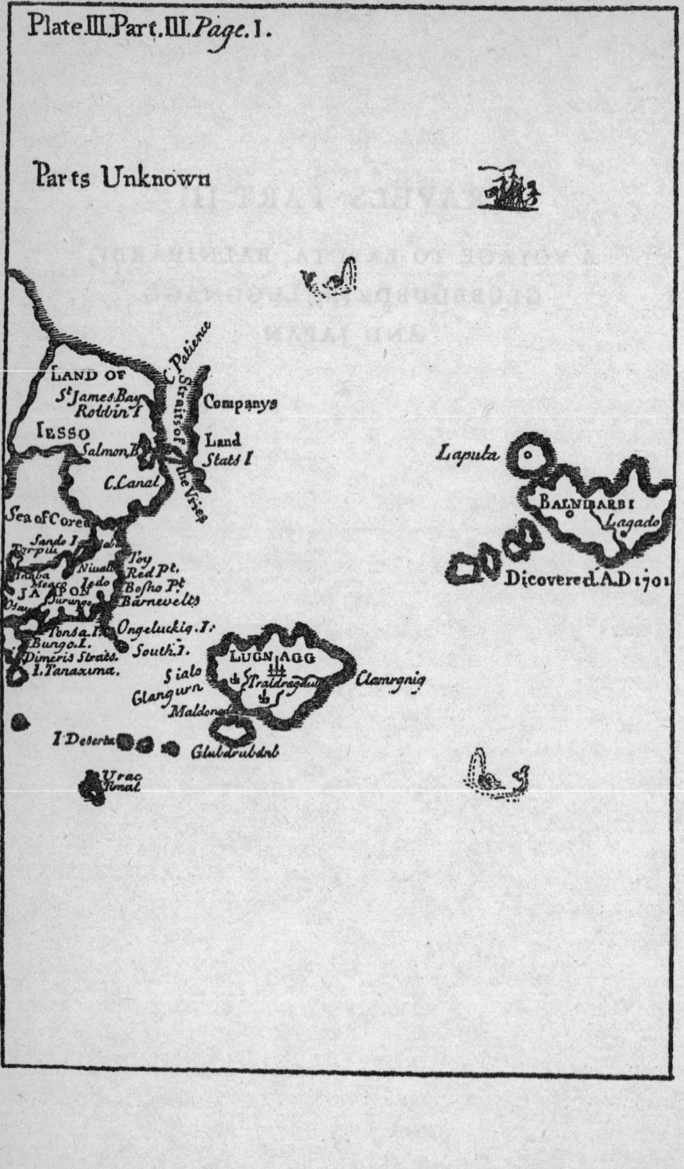

Plate.III.Part.III.*Page*.I.

Parts Unknown

LAND OF
St James Bay
Robbin T.
IESSO
Salmon B.
C.Canal

Patience
Straits of the Vries

Companys

Land
Stats I

Sea of Corea
Sando I.
Torpila
Inaba
Meaco do
JA doo
Olau Burungo
Tonsa.I.
Bungo.I.
Dimeris Straits
I.Tanaxuma.

Toy
Niuala Red Pt.
Bosho Pt.
Barnevelts

Ongeluckig.I.
South.I.

LUGNAGG
St Traldragdubh

Sialo
Glangurn
Maldonada

Clamegnig

I.Deserta

Glubdrubdrb

Urag
Ymal

Lapula

BALNIBARBI
Lagado

Dicovered.AD.1701

CHAPTER I

The author sets out on his third voyage, is taken by pirates. The malice of a Dutchman. His arrival at an island. He is received into Laputa.

I HAD not been at home above ten days, when Captain William Robinson, a Cornish man, commander of the *Hope-well*, a stout ship of three hundred tons, came to my house. I had formerly been surgeon of another ship where he was master, and a fourth part owner, in a voyage to the Levant; he had always treated me more like a brother than an inferior officer, and hearing of my arrival made me a visit, as I apprehended only out of friendship, for nothing passed more than what is usual after long absence. But repeating his visits often, expressing his joy to find me in good health, asking whether I were now settled for life, adding that he intended a voyage to the East Indies, in two months; at last he plainly invited me, though with some apologies, to be surgeon of the ship; that I should have another surgeon under me besides our two mates; that my salary should be double to the usual pay; and that having experienced my knowledge in sea-affairs to be at least equal to his, he would enter into any engagement to follow my advice, as much as if I had share in the command.

He said so many other obliging things, and I knew him to be so honest a man, that I could not reject his proposal; the thirst I had of seeing the world, notwithstanding my past misfortunes, continuing as violent as ever. The only difficulty that remained, was to persuade my wife, whose consent however I at last obtained, by the prospect of advantage she proposed to her children.

We set out the 5th day of August, 1706, and arrived at Fort St George,[1] the 11th of April, 1707, stayed there three weeks to refresh our crew, many of whom were sick. From thence we went to Tonquin, where the captain resolved to continue some time, because many of the goods he intended to buy were not ready, nor could he expect to be dispatched in several months. Therefore in hopes to defray some of the charges he must be at, he bought a sloop, loaded it with several sorts of goods, wherewith the Tonquinese usually trade to the neighbouring islands, and putting fourteen men on board, whereof three were of the country, he appointed me master of the sloop, and gave me power to traffic, while he transacted his affairs at Tonquin.

We had not sailed above three days, when, a great storm arising, we were driven five days to the north-north-east, and then to the east, after which we had fair weather, but still with a pretty strong gale from the west. Upon the tenth day we were chased by two pirates, who soon overtook us; for my sloop was so deep loaden, that she sailed very slow, neither were we in a condition to defend ourselves.

We were boarded about the same time by both the pirates, who entered furiously at the head of their men, but finding us all prostrate upon our faces (for so I gave order), they pinioned us with strong ropes, and setting a guard upon us, went to search the sloop.

I observed among them a Dutchman, who seemed to be of some authority, though he were not commander of either ship. He knew us by our countenances to be Englishmen, and jabbering to us in his own language, swore we should be tied back to back, and thrown into the sea. I spoke Dutch tolerably well; I told him who we were, and begged him in consideration of our being Christians and Protestants, of neighbouring countries, in strict alliance,[2] that he would move the captains to take some pity on us. This inflamed his rage, he repeated his threatenings, and turning to his companions, spoke with great vehemence, in the Japanese language, as I suppose, often using the word *Christianos*.

The largest of the two pirate ships was commanded by a Japanese captain, who spoke a little Dutch, but very imperfectly. He came up to me, and after several questions, which I answered in great humility, he said we should not die. I made the captain a very low bow, and then turning to the Dutchman, said, I was sorry to find more mercy in a heathen, than in a brother Christian. But I had soon reason to repent those foolish words; for that malicious reprobate, having often endeavoured in vain to persuade both the captains that I might be thrown into the sea (which they would not yield to after the promise made me, that I should not die), however prevailed so far as to have a punishment inflicted on me, worse in all human appearance than death itself. My men were sent by an equal division into both the pirate ships, and my sloop new manned. As to myself, it was determined that I should be set adrift, in a small canoe, with paddles and a sail, and four days' provisions, which last the Japanese captain was so kind to double out of his own stores, and would permit no man to search me. I got down into the canoe, while the Dutchman, standing upon the deck, loaded me with all the curses and injurious terms his language could afford.

About an hour before we saw the pirates, I had taken an observation, and found we were in the latitude of 46 N. and of longitude 183. When I was at some distance from the pirates, I discovered by my pocket-glass several islands to the southeast. I set up my sail, the wind being fair, with a design to reach the nearest of those islands, which I made a shift to do in about three hours. It was all rocky; however I got many birds' eggs, and striking fire I kindled some heath and dry seaweed, by which I roasted my eggs. I ate no other supper, being resolved to spare my provisions as much as I could. I passed the night under the shelter of a rock, strowing some heath under me, and slept pretty well.

The next day I sailed to another island, and thence to a third and fourth, sometimes using my sail, and sometimes my paddles. But not to trouble the reader with a particular account of my distresses; let it suffice, that on the 5th day I arrived at the last island in my sight, which lay south-south-east to the former.

This island was at a greater distance than I expected, and I did not reach it in less than five hours. I encompassed it almost round before I could find a convenient place to land in, which was a small creek, about three times the wideness of my canoe. I found the island to be all rocky, only a little intermingled with tufts of grass, and sweet-smelling herbs. I took out my small provisions, and after having refreshed myself, I secured the remainder in a cave, whereof there were great numbers. I gathered plenty of eggs upon the rocks, and got a quantity of dry seaweed, and parched grass, which I designed to kindle the next day, and roast my eggs as well as I could. (For I had about me my flint, steel, match, and burning-glass.) I lay all night in the cave where I had lodged my provisions. My bed was the same dry grass and seaweed which I intended for fuel. I slept very little, for the disquiets of my mind prevailed over my weariness, and kept me awake. I considered how impossible it was to preserve my life, in so desolate a place, and how miserable my end must be. Yet I found myself so listless and desponding, that I had not the heart to rise, and before I could get spirits enough to creep out of my cave, the day was far advanced. I walked a while among the rocks; the sky was perfectly clear, and the sun so hot, that I was forced to turn my face from it: when all on a sudden it became obscured, as I thought, in a manner very different from what happens by the interposition of a cloud. I turned back, and perceived a vast opaque body between me and the sun, moving forwards towards the island: it seemed to be about two miles high, and hid the sun six or seven minutes, but I did not observe the air to be much colder, or the sky more darkened, than if I had stood under the shade of a mountain. As it approached nearer over the place where I was, it appeared to be a firm substance, the bottom flat, smooth, and shining very bright from the reflection of the sea below. I stood upon a height about two hundred yards from the shore, and saw this vast body descending almost to a parallel with me, at less than an English mile distance. I took out my pocket-perspective, and could plainly discover numbers of people moving up and down the sides of it, which appeared to be sloping, but what those people were doing, I was not able to distinguish.

The natural love of life gave me some inward motions of joy, and I was ready to entertain a hope, that this adventure might some way or other help to deliver me from the desolate place and condition I was in. But at the same time the reader can hardly conceive my astonishment, to behold an island in the air, inhabited by men, who were able (as it should seem) to raise, or sink, or put it into a progressive motion, as they pleased. But not being at that time in a disposition to philosophize upon this phenomenon, I rather chose to observe what course the island would take, because it seemed for a while to stand still. Yet soon after it advanced nearer, and I could see the sides of it, encompassed with several gradations of galleries, and stairs, at certain intervals, to descend from one to the other. In the lowest gallery, I beheld some people fishing with long angling-rods, and others looking on. I waved my cap (for my hat was long since worn out) and my handkerchief towards the island; and upon its nearer approach, I called and shouted with the utmost strength of my voice; and then looking circumspectly, I beheld a crowd gathered to that side which was most in my view. I found by their pointing towards me and to each other, that they plainly discovered me, although they made no return to my shouting. But I could see four or five men running in great haste up the stairs to the top of the island, who then disappeared. I happened rightly to conjecture, that these were sent for orders to some person in authority upon this occasion.

The number of people increased, and in less than half an hour, the island was moved and raised in such a manner, that the lowest gallery appeared in a parallel of less than an hundred yards' distance from the height where I stood. I then put myself into the most supplicating postures, and spoke in the humblest accent, but received no answer. Those who stood nearest over-against me seemed to be persons of distinction, as I supposed by their habit. They conferred earnestly with each other, looking often upon me. At length one of them called out in a clear, polite, smooth dialect, not unlike in sound to the Italian; and therefore I returned an answer in that language, hoping at least that the cadence might be more agreeable to his ears. Although neither of us understood the other, yet my meaning was easily known, for the people saw the distress I was in.

They made signs for me to come down from the rock, and go towards the shore, which I accordingly did; and the flying island being raised to a convenient height, the verge directly over me, a chain was let down from the lowest gallery, with a seat fastened to the bottom, to which I fixed myself, and was drawn up by pulleys.

CHAPTER 2

The humours and dispositions of the Laputians described. An account of their learning. Of the King and his Court. The author's reception there. The inhabitants subject to fears and disquietudes. An account of the women.

AT my alighting I was surrounded by a crowd of people, but those who stood nearest seemed to be of better quality. They beheld me with all the marks and circumstances of wonder, neither indeed was I much in their debt, having never till then seen a race of mortals so singular in their shapes, habits, and countenances. Their heads were all reclined either to the right, or the left; one of their eyes turned inward, and the other directly up to the zenith. Their outward garments were

adorned with the figures of suns, moons, and stars,[3] interwoven with those of fiddles, flutes, harps, trumpets, guitars,
harpsichords, and many more instruments of music, unknown
to us in Europe. I observed here and there many in the habit of
servants, with a blown bladder fastened like a flail to the end
of a short stick, which they carried in their hands. In each
bladder was a small quantity of dried pease or little pebbles (as
I was afterwards informed). With these bladders they now and
then flapped the mouths and ears of those who stood near
them, of which practice I could not then conceive the meaning; it seems, the minds of these people are so taken up with
intense speculations, that they neither can speak, nor attend to
the discourses of others, without being roused by some
external taction[4] upon the organs of speech and hearing; for
which reason, those persons who are able to afford it always
keep a *flapper* (the original is *climenole*) in their family, as one of
their domestics, nor ever walk abroad or make visits without
him. And the business of this officer is, when two or more
persons are in company, gently to strike with his bladder the
mouth of him who is to speak, and the right ear of him or
them to whom the speaker addresseth himself. This *flapper* is
likewise employed diligently to attend his master in his walks,
and upon occasion to give him a soft flap on his eyes, because
he is always so wrapped up in cogitation, that he is in manifest
danger of falling down every precipice, and bouncing his head
against every post, and in the streets, of jostling others or
being jostled himself into the kennel.[5]

It was necessary to give the reader this information, without
which he would be at the same loss with me, to understand the
proceedings of these people, as they conducted me up the
stairs, to the top of the island, and from thence to the royal
palace. While we were ascending, they forgot several times
what they were about, and left me to myself, till their memories were again roused by their *flappers*; for they appeared
altogether unmoved by the sight of my foreign habit and

countenance, and by the shouts of the vulgar, whose thoughts and minds were more disengaged.

At last we entered the palace, and proceeded into the chamber of presence, where I saw the King seated on his throne, attended on each side by persons of prime quality. Before the throne, was a large table filled with globes and spheres, and mathematical instruments of all kinds. His Majesty took not the least notice of us, although our entrance were not without sufficient noise, by the concourse of all persons belonging to the Court. But, he was then deep in a problem, and we attended at least an hour, before he could solve it. There stood by him on each side, a young page, with flaps in their hands, and when they saw he was at leisure, one of them gently struck his mouth, and the other his right ear, at which he started like one awaked on the sudden, and looking towards me, and the company I was in, recollected the occasion of our coming, whereof he had been informed before. He spoke some words, whereupon immediately a young man with a flap came up to my side, and flapped me gently on the right ear; but I made signs as well as I could, that I had no occasion for such an instrument; which as I afterwards found gave his Majesty and the whole Court a very mean opinion of my understanding. The King, as far as I could conjecture, asked me several questions, and I addressed myself to him in all the languages I had. When it was found, that I could neither understand nor be understood, I was conducted by his order to an apartment in his palace (this Prince being distinguished above all his predecessors for his hospitality to strangers),[6] where two servants were appointed to attend me. My dinner was brought, and four persons of quality, whom I remembered to have seen very near the King's person, did me the honour to dine with me. We had two courses, of three dishes each. In the first course, there was a shoulder of mutton, cut into an equilateral triangle, a piece of beef into a rhomboides, and a pudding into a cycloid. The second course was two ducks, trussed up into the form of fiddles; sausages and puddings resembling flutes and hautboys,[7] and a breast of veal in the shape of a harp. The servants cut our bread into cones, cylinders, parallelograms, and several other mathematical figures.

While we were at dinner, I made bold to ask the names of several things in their language, and those noble persons, by the assistance of their *flappers*, delighted to give me answers, hoping to raise my admiration of their great abilities, if I could be brought to converse with them. I was soon able to call for bread and drink, or whatever else I wanted.

After dinner my company withdrew, and a person was sent to me by the King's order, attended by a *flapper*. He brought with him pen, ink, and paper, and three or four books, giving me to understand by signs, that he was sent to teach me the language. We sat together four hours, in which time I wrote down a great number of words in columns, with the translations over-against them. I likewise made a shift to learn several short sentences. For my tutor would order one of my servants to fetch something, to turn about, to make a bow, to sit, or stand, or walk, and the like. Then I took down the sentence in writing. He showed me also in one of his books, the figures of the sun, moon, and stars, the zodiac, the tropics, and polar circles, together with the denominations of many figures of planes and solids. He gave me the names and descriptions of all the musical instruments, and the general terms of art in playing on each of them. After he had left me, I placed all my words with their interpretations in alphabetical order. And thus in a few days, by the help of a very faithful memory, I got some insight into their language.

The word, which I interpret the *Flying* or *Floating Island*, is in the original *Laputa*, whereof I could never learn the true etymology.[8] *Lap* in the old obsolete language signifieth *high*, and *untuh* a *governor*, from which they say by corruption was derived *Laputa* from *Lapuntuh*. But I do not approve of this derivation, which seems to be a little strained. I ventured to offer to the learned among them a conjecture of my own, that *Laputa* was *quasi Lap outed*; *Lap* signifying properly the dancing of the sunbeams in the sea, and *outed* a wing, which however I shall not obtrude, but submit to the judicious reader.

Those to whom the King had entrusted me, observing how ill I was clad, ordered a tailor to come next morning, and take my measure for a suit of clothes. This operator did his office after a different manner from those of his trade in Europe. He first took my altitude by a quadrant, and then with rule and compasses, described the dimensions and outlines of my whole body, all which he entered upon paper, and in six days brought my clothes very ill made, and quite out of shape, by happening to mistake a figure in the calculation.[9] But my comfort was, that I observed such accidents very frequent and little regarded.

During my confinement for want of clothes, and by an indisposition that held me some days longer, I much enlarged my dictionary; and when I went next to Court, was able to understand many things the King spoke, and to return him some kind of answers. His Majesty had given orders that the island should move north-east and by east, to the vertical point over Lagado, the metropolis of the whole kingdom below upon the firm earth. It was about ninety leagues distant, and our voyage lasted four days and an half. I was not in the least sensible of the progressive motion made in the air by the island. On the second morning about eleven o'clock, the King himself in person, attended by his nobility, courtiers, and officers, having prepared all their musical instruments, played on them for three hours without intermission, so that I was quite stunned with the noise; neither could I possibly guess the meaning till my tutor informed me. He said that the people of their island had their ears adapted to hear the music of the spheres, which always played at certain periods, and the Court was now prepared to bear their part in whatever instrument they most excelled.

In our journey towards Lagado the capital city, his Majesty ordered that the island should stop over certain towns and villages, from whence he might receive the petitions of his subjects. And to this purpose several pack-threads were let down with small weights at the bottom. On these pack-threads the people strung their petitions, which mounted up directly like the scraps of paper fastened by schoolboys at the end of the string that holds their kite. Sometimes we received wine and victuals from below, which were drawn up by pulleys.

The knowledge I had in mathematics gave me great assistance in acquiring their phraseology, which depended much upon that science and music; and in the latter I was not unskilled. Their ideas are perpetually conversant in lines and figures. If they would, for example, praise the beauty of a woman or any other animal, they describe it by rhombs, circles, parallelograms, ellipses, and other geometrical terms, or else by words of art drawn from music, needless here to repeat. I observed in the King's kitchen all sorts of mathematical and musical instruments, after the figures of which they cut up the joints that were served to his Majesty's table.

Their houses are very ill built, the walls bevel, without one right angle in any apartment, and this defect ariseth from the contempt they bear for practical geometry, which they despise as vulgar and mechanic, those instructions they give being too refined for the intellectuals[10] of their workmen, which occasions perpetual mistakes. And although they are dexterous enough upon a piece of paper in the management of the rule, the pencil and the divider, yet in the common actions and behaviour of life, I have not seen a more clumsy, awkward, and unhandy people, nor so slow and perplexed in their conceptions upon all other subjects, except those of mathematics and music. They are very bad reasoners, and vehemently given to opposition, unless when they happen to be of the right opinion, which is seldom their case. Imagination, fancy, and invention, they are wholly strangers to, nor have any words in their language by which those ideas can be expressed; the whole compass of their thoughts and mind being shut up within the two forementioned sciences.

Most of them, and especially those who deal in the astronomical part, have great faith in judicial astrology,[11] although they are ashamed to own it publicly. But, what I chiefly admired, and thought altogether unaccountable, was the strong disposition I observed in them towards news and politics, perpetually enquiring into public affairs, giving their judgments in matters of state, and passionately disputing every inch of a party opinion. I have indeed observed the same disposition among most of the mathematicians I have known in Europe, although I could never discover the least analogy between the two sciences; unless those people suppose, that because the smallest circle hath as many degrees as the largest, therefore the regulation and management of the world require no more abilities than the handling and turning of a globe. But, I rather take this quality to spring from a very common infirmity of human nature, inclining us to be more curious and conceited in matters where we have least concern, and for which we are least adapted either by study or nature.

These people are under continual disquietudes, never enjoying a minute's peace of mind; and their disturbances proceed from causes which very little affect the rest of mortals. Their apprehensions arise from several changes they dread in the celestial bodies. For instance; that the earth by the continual approaches of the sun towards it, must in course of time be absorbed or swallowed up.[12] That the face of the sun will by degrees be encrusted with its own effluvia, and give no more light to the world. That the earth very narrowly escaped a brush from the tail of the last comet, which would have infallibly reduced it to ashes; and that the next, which they have calculated for one and thirty years hence, will probably destroy us. For, if in its perihelion it should approach within a certain degree of the sun (as by their calculations they have reason to dread), it will conceive a degree of heat ten thousand times more intense than that of red-hot glowing iron; and in its absence from the sun, carry a blazing tail ten hundred thousand and fourteen miles long; through which if the earth should pass at the distance of one hundred thousand miles from the nucleus or main body of the comet, it must in its passage be set on fire, and reduced to ashes. That the sun daily spending its rays without any nutriment to supply them, will at last be wholly consumed and annihilated; which must be attended with the destruction of this earth, and of all the planets that receive their light from it.

They are so perpetually alarmed with the apprehensions of these and the like impending dangers, that they can neither sleep quietly in their beds, nor have any relish for the common pleasures or amusements of life. When they meet an acquaintance in the morning, the first question is about the sun's health, how he looked at his setting and rising, and what hopes they have to avoid the stroke of the approaching comet. This conversation they are apt to run into with the same temper that boys discover, in delighting to hear terrible stories of sprites and hobgoblins, which they greedily listen to, and dare not go to bed for fear.

The women of the island have abundance of vivacity; they contemn their husbands, and are exceedingly fond of strangers, whereof there is always a considerable number from the continent below, attending at Court, either upon affairs of the several towns and corporations, or their own particular occasions, but are much despised, because they want the same endowments. Among these the ladies choose their gallants: but the vexation is, that they act with too much ease and security, for the husband is always so wrapped in speculation, that the mistress and lover may proceed to the greatest familiarities before his face, if he be but provided with paper and implements, and without his *flapper* at his side.

The wives and daughters lament their confinement to the island, although I think it the most delicious spot of ground in the world; and although they live here in the greatest plenty and magnificence, and are allowed to do whatever they please, they long to see the world, and take the diversions of the metropolis, which they are not allowed to do without a particular licence from the King; and this is not easy to be obtained, because the people of quality have found by frequent experience, how hard it is to persuade their women to return from below. I was told that a great Court lady, who had several children, is married to the prime Minister, the richest subject in the kingdom, a very graceful person, extremely fond of her, and lives in the finest palace of the island, went down to Lagado, on the pretence of health, there hid herself for several months, till the King sent a warrant to search for her, and she was found in an obscure eating-house all in rags, having pawned her clothes to maintain an old deformed foot-man, who beat her every day, and in whose company she was taken much against her will. And although her husband received her with all possible kindness, and without the least reproach, she soon after contrived to steal down again with all her jewels, to the same gallant, and hath not been heard of since.

This may perhaps pass with the reader rather for an European or English story, than for one of a country so remote. But he may please to consider, that the caprices of womankind are not limited by any climate or nation, and that they are much more uniform than can be easily imagined.

In about a month's time I had made a tolerable proficiency in their language, and was able to answer most of the King's questions, when I had the honour to attend him. His Majesty discovered not the least curiosity to enquire into the laws, government, history, religion, or manners of the countries where I had been, but confined his questions to the state of mathematics, and received the account I gave him with great contempt and indifference, though often roused by his *flapper* on each side.

CHAPTER 3

A phenomenon solved by modern philosophy and astronomy. The Laputians' great improvements in the latter. The King's method of suppressing insurrections.

I DESIRED leave of this Prince to see the curiosities of the island, which he was graciously pleased to grant, and ordered my tutor to attend me. I chiefly wanted to know to what cause in art or in nature it owed its several motions, whereof I will now give a philosophical account [13] to the reader.

The Flying or Floating Island is exactly circular, its diameter 7,837 yards, or about four miles and an half, and consequently contains ten thousand acres. It is three hundred yards thick. The bottom or under surface, which appears to those who view it from below, is one even regular plate of adamant, shooting up to the height of about two hundred yards. Above it lie the several minerals in their usual order, and over all is a coat of rich mould ten or twelve foot deep. The declivity of the upper surface, from the circumference to the centre, is the natural cause why all the dews and rains which fall upon the island, are conveyed in small rivulets towards the middle, where they are emptied into four large basins, each of about half a mile in circuit, and two hundred yards distant from the centre. From these basins the water is continually exhaled by the sun in the day-time, which effectually prevents their overflowing. Besides, as it is in the power of the monarch to raise the island above the region of clouds and vapours, he can prevent the falling of dews and rains whenever he pleases. For the highest clouds cannot rise above two miles, as

Plate III. Part.III.   Page.39.

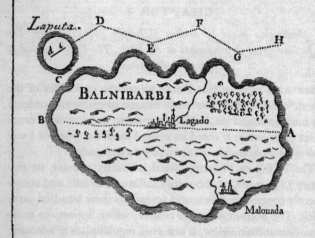

naturalists agree, at least they were never known to do so in that country.

At the centre of the island there is a chasm about fifty yards in diameter, from whence the astronomers descend into a large dome, which is therefore called *Flandona Gagnole*, or the *Astronomers' Cave*,[14] situated at the depth of an hundred yards beneath the upper surface of the adamant. In this cave are twenty lamps continually burning, which from the reflection of the adamant cast a strong light into every part. The place is stored with great variety of sextants, quadrants, telescopes, astrolabes, and other astronomical instruments. But the greatest curiosity, upon which the fate of the island depends, is a loadstone of a prodigious size, in shape resembling a weaver's shuttle. It is in length six yards, and in the thickest part at least three yards over.[15] This magnet is sustained by a very strong axle of adamant passing through its middle, upon which it plays, and is poised so exactly that the weakest hand can turn it. It is hooped round with an hollow cylinder of adamant, four foot deep, as many thick, and twelve yards in diameter, placed horizontally, and supported by eight adamantine feet, each six yards high. In the middle of the concave side there is a groove twelve inches deep, in which the extremities of the axle are lodged, and turned round as there is occasion.

The stone cannot be moved from its place by any force, because the hoop and its feet are one continued piece with that body of adamant which constitutes the bottom of the island.

By means of this loadstone,[16] the island is made to rise and fall, and move from one place to another. For, with respect to that part of the earth over which the monarch presides, the stone is endued at one of its sides with an attractive power, and at the other with a repulsive. Upon placing the magnet erect with its attracting end towards the earth, the island descends; but when the repelling extremity points downwards, the island mounts directly upwards. When the position of the stone is oblique, the motion of the island is so too. For in this magnet the forces always act in lines parallel to its direction.

By this oblique motion the island is conveyed to different parts of the Monarch's dominions. To explain the manner of its progress, let A B represent a line drawn cross the dominions of Balnibarbi, let the line c d represent the loadstone, of which let d be the repelling end, and c the attracting end, the island being over C; let the stone be placed in the position c d with its repelling end downwards; then the island will be driven upwards obliquely towards D. When it is arrived at D, let the stone be turned upon its axle till its attracting end points towards E, and then the island will be carried obliquely towards E; where if the stone be again turned upon its axle till it stands in the position E F, with its repelling point downwards, the island will rise obliquely towards F, where by directing the attracting end towards G, the island may be carried to G, and from G to H, by turning the stone, so as to make its repelling extremity point directly downwards. And thus by changing the situation of the stone as often as there is occasion, the island is made to rise and fall by turns in an oblique direction, and by those alternate risings and fallings (the obliquity being not considerable) is conveyed from one part of the dominions to the other.

But it must be observed, that this island cannot move beyond the extent of the dominions below, nor can it rise above the height of four miles. For which the astronomers (who have written large systems concerning the stone) assign the following reason: that the magnetic virtue does not extend beyond the distance of four miles, and that the mineral which acts upon the stone in the bowels of the earth, and in the sea about six leagues distant from the shore, is not diffused through the whole globe, but terminated with the limits of the King's dominions; and it was easy from the great advantage of such a superior situation, for a prince to bring under his obedience whatever country lay within the attraction of that magnet.

When the stone is put parallel to the plane of the horizon, the island standeth still; for in that case, the extremities of it being at equal distance from the earth, act with equal force, the one in drawing downwards, the other in pushing upwards; and consequently no motion can ensue.

This loadstone is under the care of certain astronomers, who from time to time give it such positions as the Monarch directs. They spend the greatest part of their lives in observing the celestial bodies, which they do by the assistance of glasses far excelling ours in goodness. For, although their largest telescopes do not exceed three feet, they magnify much more than those of a hundred with us, and show the stars with greater clearness. This advantage hath enabled them to extend their discoveries much farther than our astronomers in Europe; for they have made a catalogue of ten thousand fixed stars, whereas the largest of ours do not contain above one third part of that number. They have likewise discovered two lesser stars, or *satellites*, which revolve about Mars, whereof the innermost is distant from the centre of the primary planet exactly three of his diameters, and the outermost five; the former revolves in the space of ten hours, and the latter in twenty-one and an half; so that the squares of their periodical times are very near in the same proportion with the cubes of their distance from the centre of Mars, which evidently shows them to be governed by the same law of gravitation, that influences the other heavenly bodies.

They have observed ninety-three different comets, and settled their periods with great exactness. If this be true (and they affirm it with great confidence), it is much to be wished that their observations were made public, whereby the theory of comets, which at present is very lame and defective, might be brought to the same perfection with other parts of astronomy.

The King would be the most absolute prince in the universe, if he could but prevail on a Ministry to join with him; but these having their estates below on the continent, and considering that the office of a favourite hath a very uncertain tenure, would never consent to the enslaving their country.

If any town should engage in rebellion or mutiny, fall into violent factions, or refuse to pay the usual tribute, the King hath two methods of reducing them to obedience. The first and the mildest course is by keeping the island hovering [17] over such a town, and the lands about it, whereby he can deprive them of the benefit of the sun and the rain, and consequently afflict the inhabitants with dearth and diseases. And if the crime deserve it, they are at the same time pelted from above with great stones, against which they have no defence, but by creeping into cellars or caves, while the roofs of their houses are beaten to pieces. But if they still continue obstinate, or offer to raise insurrections, he proceeds to the last remedy, by letting the island drop directly upon their heads, which makes a universal destruction both of houses and men. However, this is an extremity to which the Prince is seldom driven, neither indeed is he willing to put it in execution, nor dare his Ministers advise him to an action, which as it would render them odious to the people, so it would be a great damage to their own estates, that lie all below, for the island is the King's demesne.

But there is still indeed a more weighty reason, why the Kings of this country have been always averse from executing so terrible an action, unless upon the utmost necessity. For if the town intended to be destroyed should have in it any tall rocks, as it generally falls out in the larger cities, a situation probably chosen at first with a view to prevent such a catastrophe; or if it abound in high spires or pillars of stone, a sudden fall might endanger the bottom or under surface of the island, which although it consist as I have said of one entire adamant two hundred yards thick, might happen to crack by too great a shock, or burst by approaching too near the fires from the houses below, as the backs both of iron and stone will often do in our chimneys. Of all this the people are well apprised, and understand how far to carry their obstinacy, where their liberty or property is concerned. And the King, when he is highest provoked, and most determined to press a city to rubbish, orders the island to descend with great gentleness, out of a pretence of tenderness to his people, but indeed for fear of breaking the adamantine bottom; in which case it is the opinion of all their philosophers, that the loadstone could no longer hold it up, and the whole mass would fall to the ground.

About three years before my arrival[18] among them, while the King was in his progress over his dominions, there happened an extraordinary accident which had like to have put a period to the fate of that monarchy, at least as it is now instituted. Lindalino, the second city in the kingdom, was the first his Majesty visited in his progress. Three days after his departure, the inhabitants, who had often complained of great oppressions, shut the town gates, seized on the Governor, and with incredible speed and labour erected four large towers, one at every corner of the city (which is an exact square), equal in height to a strong pointed rock that stands directly in the centre of the city. Upon the top of each tower, as well as upon the rock, they fixed a great loadstone, and in case their design should fail, they had provided a vast quantity of the most combustible fuel, hoping to burst therewith the adamantine bottom of the island, if the loadstone project should miscarry.

It was eight months before the King had perfect notice that the Lindalinians were in rebellion. He then commanded that the island should be wafted over the city. The people were unanimous, and had laid in store of provisions, and a great river runs through the middle of the town. The King hovered over them several days to deprive them of the sun and the rain.

He ordered many pack-threads to be let down, yet not a person offered to send up a petition, but instead thereof, very bold demands, the redress of all their grievances, great immunities, the choice of their own Governor, and other the like exorbitances. Upon which his Majesty commanded all the inhabitants of the island to cast great stones from the lower gallery into the town; but the citizens had provided against this mischief by conveying their persons and effects into the four towers, and other strong buildings, and vaults under ground.

The King being now determined to reduce this proud people, ordered that the island should descend gently within forty yards of the top of the towers and rock. This was accordingly done; but the officers employed in that work found the descent much speedier than usual, and by turning the loadstone could not without great difficulty keep it in a firm position, but found the island inclining to fall. They sent the King immediate intelligence of this astonishing event, and begged his Majesty's permission to raise the island higher; the King consented, a general council was called, and the officers of the loadstone ordered to attend. One of the oldest and expertest among them obtained leave to try an experiment. He took a strong line of an hundred yards, and the island being raised over the town above the attracting power they had felt, he fastened a piece of adamant to the end of his line which had in it a mixture of iron mineral, of the same nature with that whereof the bottom or lower surface of the island is composed, and from the lower gallery let it down slowly towards the top of the towers. The adamant was not descended four yards, before the officer felt it drawn so strongly downwards, that he could hardly pull it back. He then threw down several small pieces of adamant, and observed that they were all violently attracted by the top of the tower. The same experiment was made on the other three towers, and on the rock with the same effect.

This incident broke entirely the King's measures and (to dwell no longer on other circumstances) he was forced to give the town their own conditions.

I was assured by a great Minister, that if the island had descended so near the town, as not to be able to raise itself, the citizens were determined to fix it for ever, to kill the King and all his servants, and entirely change the government.

By a fundamental law of this realm, neither the King nor either of his two elder sons are permitted to leave the island,[10] nor the Queen till she is past child-bearing.

CHAPTER 4

The author leaves Laputa, is conveyed to Balnibarbi, arrives at the metropolis. A description of the metropolis and the country adjoining. The author hospitably received by a great Lord. His conversation with that Lord.

ALTHOUGH I cannot say that I was ill treated in this island, yet I must confess I thought myself too much neglected, not without some degree of contempt. For neither Prince nor people appeared to be curious in any part of knowledge, except mathematics and music, wherein I was far their inferior, and upon that account very little regarded.

On the other side, after having seen all the curiosities of the island, I was very desirous to leave it, being heartily weary of those people. They were indeed excellent in two sciences for which I have great esteem, and wherein I am not unversed, but at the same time so abstracted and involved in speculation that I never met with such disagreeable companions. I conversed only with women, tradesmen, *flappers*, and Court-pages, during two months of my abode there, by which at last I rendered myself extremely contemptible, yet these were the only people from whom I could ever receive a reasonable answer.

I had obtained by hard study a good degree of knowledge in their language: I was weary of being confined to an island where I received so little countenance, and resolved to leave it with the first opportunity.

There was a great Lord at Court, nearly related to the King, and for that reason alone used with respect. He was universally reckoned the most ignorant and stupid person among them. He had performed many eminent services for the Crown, had great natural and acquired parts, adorned with integrity and honour, but so ill an ear for music, that his detractors reported he had been often known to beat time in the wrong place; neither could his tutors without extreme difficulty teach him to demonstrate the most easy proposition in the mathematics. He was pleased to show me many marks of favour, often did me the honour of a visit, desired to be informed in the affairs of Europe, the laws and customs, the manners and learning of the several countries where I had travelled. He listened to me with great attention, and made very wise observations on all I spoke. He had two *flappers* attending him for state, but never made use of them except at Court, and in visits of ceremony, and would always command them to withdraw when we were alone together.

I entreated this illustrious person to intercede in my behalf with his Majesty for leave to depart, which he accordingly did, as he was pleased to tell me, with regret: for indeed he had made me several offers very advantageous, which however I refused with expressions of the highest acknowledgement.

On the 16th day of February, I took leave of his Majesty and the Court. The King made me a present to the value of about two hundred pounds English, and my protector his kinsman as much more, together with a letter of recommendation to a friend of his in Lagado, the metropolis; the island being then hovering over a mountain about two miles from it, I was let down from the lowest gallery, in the same manner as I had been taken up.

The continent, as far as it is subject to the Monarch of the Flying Island, passeth under the general name of Balnibarbi, and the metropolis, as I said before, is called Lagado. I felt some little satisfaction in finding myself on firm ground. I walked to the city without any concern, being clad like one of the natives, and sufficiently instructed to converse with them. I soon found out the person's house to whom I was recommended, presented my letter from his friend the grandee in the island, and was received with much kindness. This great Lord, whose name was Munodi,[20] ordered me an apartment in his own house, where I continued during my stay, and was entertained in a most hospitable manner.

The next morning after my arrival he took me in his chariot to see the town, which is about half the bigness of London, but the houses very strangely built, and most of them out of repair. The people in the streets walked fast, looked wild, their eyes fixed, and were generally in rags. We passed through one of the town gates, and went about three miles into the country, where I saw many labourers working with several sorts of tools in the ground, but was not able to conjecture what they were about, neither did I observe any expectation either of corn or grass, although the soil appeared to be excellent. I could not forbear admiring at these odd appearances both in town and country, and I made bold to desire my conductor, that he would be pleased to explain to me what could be meant by so many busy heads, hands and faces, both in the streets and the fields, because I did not discover any good effects they produced; but on the contrary, I never knew a soil so unhappily cultivated, houses so ill contrived and so ruinous, or a people whose countenances and habit expressed so much misery and want.

This Lord Munodi was a person of the first rank, and had been some years Governor of Lagado, but by a cabal of Ministers was discharged for insufficiency. However the King treated him with tenderness, as a well-meaning man, but of a low contemptible understanding.

When I gave that free censure of the country and its inhabitants, he made no further answer than by telling me, that I had not been long enough among them to form a judgement; and that the different nations of the world had different customs, with other common topics to the same purpose. But when we returned to his palace, he asked me how I liked the building, what absurdities I observed, and what quarrel I had with the dress or looks of his domestics. This he might safely do, because everything about him was magnificent, regular, and polite. I answered that his Excellency's prudence, quality, and fortune had exempted him from those defects which folly and beggary had produced in others. He said if I would go with him to his country house, about twenty miles distant, where his estate lay, there would be more leisure for this kind of conversation. I told his Excellency that I was entirely at his disposal, and accordingly we set out next morning.

During our journey, he made me observe the several methods used by farmers in managing their lands, which to me were wholly unaccountable, for except in some very few places, I could not discover one ear of corn or blade of grass. But, in three hours travelling, the scene was wholly altered; we came into a most beautiful country; farmers' houses at small distances, neatly built, the fields enclosed, containing vineyards, corn-grounds and meadows. Neither do I remember to have seen a more delightful prospect. His Excellency observed my countenance to clear up; he told me with a sigh, that there his estate began, and would continue the same till we should come to his house. That his countrymen ridiculed and despised him for managing his affairs no better, and for setting so ill an example to the kingdom, which however was followed by very few, such as were old and wilful, and weak like himself.

We came at length to the house, which was indeed a noble

structure, built according to the best rules of ancient architecture. The fountains, gardens, walks, avenues, and groves were all disposed with exact judgment and taste. I gave due praises to everything I saw, whereof his Excellency took not the least notice till after supper, when, there being no third companion, he told me with a very melancholy air, that he doubted he must throw down his houses in town and country, to rebuild them after the present mode, destroy all his plantations, and cast others into such a form as modern usage required, and give the same directions to all his tenants, unless he would submit to incur the censure of pride, singularity, affectation, ignorance, caprice, and perhaps increase his Majesty's displeasure.

That the admiration I appeared to be under would cease or diminish when he had informed me of some particulars, which probably I never heard of at Court, the people there being too much taken up in their own speculations, to have regard to what passed here below.

The sum of his discourse was to this effect. That about forty years ago, certain persons went up to Laputa either upon business or diversion, and after five months continuance came back with a very little smattering in mathematics, but full of volatile spirits acquired in that airy region. That these persons upon their return began to dislike the management of everything below, and fell into schemes of putting all arts, sciences, languages, and mechanics upon a new foot.[21] To this end they procured a royal patent for erecting an Academy of PROJECTORS in Lagado; and the humour prevailed so strongly among the people, that there is not a town of any consequence in the kingdom without such an Academy. In these colleges, the professors contrive new rules and methods of agriculture and building, and new instruments and tools for all trades and manufactures, whereby, as they undertake, one man shall do the work of ten; a palace may be built in a week, of materials so durable as to last for ever without repairing. All the fruits of the earth shall come to maturity at whatever season we think fit to choose, and increase an hundred fold more than they do at present, with innumerable other happy proposals. The only inconvenience is, that none of these projects are yet brought to perfection, and in the meantime the whole country lies miserably waste, the houses in ruins, and the people without food or clothes. By all which, instead of being discouraged, they are fifty times more violently bent upon prosecuting their schemes, driven equally on by hope and despair; that as for himself, being not of an enterprising spirit, he was content to go on in the old forms, to live in the houses his ancestors had built, and act as they did in every part of life without innovation. That, some few other persons of quality and gentry had done the same, but were looked on with an eye of contempt and ill-will, as enemies to art, ignorant, and ill commonwealth's-men, preferring their own ease and sloth before the general improvement of their country.

His Lordship added, that he would not by any further particulars prevent the pleasure I should certainly take in viewing the grand Academy, whither he was resolved I should go. He only desired me to observe a ruined building upon the side of a mountain about three miles distant, of which he gave me this account. That he had a very convenient mill within half a mile of his house, turned by a current from a large river, and sufficient for his own family as well as a great number of his tenants. That, about seven years ago, a club of those projectors came to him with proposals to destroy this mill, and build another on the side of that mountain, on the long ridge whereof a long canal must be cut for a repository of water, to be conveyed up by pipes and engines to supply the mill: because the wind and air upon a height agitated the water, and thereby made it fitter for motion: and because the water descending down a declivity would turn the mill with half the current of a river whose course is more upon a level. He said, that being then not very well with the Court, and pressed by many of his friends, he complied with the proposal; and after employing an hundred men for two years, the work miscarried, the projectors went off, laying the blame entirely upon him, railing at him ever since, and putting others upon the same experiment, with equal assurance of success, as well as equal disappointment.

In a few days we came back to town, and his Excellency, considering the bad character he had in the Academy, would not go with me himself, but recommended me to a friend of his to bear me company thither. My Lord was pleased to represent me as a great admirer of projects, and a person of much curiosity and easy belief, which indeed was not without truth, for I had myself been a sort of projector in my younger days.

CHAPTER 5

The author permitted to see the grand Academy of Lagado. The Academy largely[22] *described. The arts wherein the professors employ themselves.*

THIS Academy[23] is not an entire single building, but a continuation of several houses on both sides of a street, which growing waste was purchased and applied to that use.

I was received very kindly by the Warden, and went for many days to the Academy. Every room hath in it one or more projectors, and I believe I could not be in fewer than five hundred rooms.

The first man I saw was of a meagre aspect, with sooty hands and face, his hair and beard long, ragged and singed in several places. His clothes, shirt, and skin were all of the same colour. He had been eight years upon a project for extracting sunbeams out of cucumbers, which were to be put into vials hermetically sealed, and let out to warm the air in raw inclement summers. He told me, he did not doubt in eight years more, that he should be able to supply the Governor's gardens with sunshine at a reasonable rate; but he complained that his stock was low, and entreated me to give him something as an encouragement to ingenuity,[24] especially since this had been a very dear season for cucumbers. I made him a small present, for my Lord had furnished me with money on purpose, because he knew their practice of begging from all who go to see them.

I went into another chamber, but was ready to hasten back, being almost overcome with a horrible stink. My conductor pressed me forward, conjuring me in a whisper to give no offence, which would be highly resented, and therefore I durst not so much as stop my nose. The projector of this cell was the most ancient student of the Academy. His face and beard were of a pale yellow; his hands and clothes daubed over with filth. When I was presented to him, he gave me a very close embrace (a compliment I could well have excused). His employment from his first coming into the Academy was an operation to reduce human excrement to its original food, by separating the several parts, removing the tincture which it receives from the gall, making the odour exhale, and scumming off the saliva. He had a weekly allowance from the Society of a vessel filled with human ordure, about the bigness of a Bristol barrel.

I saw another at work to calcine ice into gunpowder, who likewise showed me a treatise he had written concerning the malleability of fire, which he intended to publish.

There was a most ingenious architect who had contrived a new method for building houses, by beginning at the roof and working downwards to the foundation, which he justified to me by the like practice of those two prudent insects, the bee and the spider.

There was a man born blind, who had several apprentices in his own condition: their employment was to mix colours for painters, which their master taught them to distinguish by feeling and smelling.[25] It was indeed my misfortune to find them at that time not very perfect in their lessons, and the professor himself happened to be generally mistaken: this artist is much encouraged and esteemed by the whole fraternity.

In another apartment I was highly pleased with a projector, who had found a device of ploughing the ground with hogs, to save the charges of ploughs, cattle, and labour. The method is this; in an acre of ground you bury, at six inches distance, and eight deep, a quantity of acorns, dates, chestnuts, and other mast [26] or vegetables whereof these animals are fondest: then you drive six hundred or more of them into the field, where in a few days they will root up the whole ground in search of their food, and make it fit for sowing, at the same time manuring it with their dung; it is true upon experiment they found the charge and trouble very great, and they had little or no crop. However, it is not doubted that this invention may be capable of great improvement.

I went into another room, where the walls and ceiling were all hung round with cobwebs, [27] except a narrow passage for the artist to go in and out. At my entrance he called aloud to me not to disturb his webs. He lamented the fatal mistake the world had been so long in of using silkworms, while we had such plenty of domestic insects, who infinitely excelled the former, because they understood how to weave as well as spin. And he proposed farther, that by employing spiders, the charge of dyeing silks would be wholly saved, whereof I was fully convinced when he showed me a vast number of flies most beautifully coloured, wherewith he fed his spiders, assuring us, that the webs would take a tincture from them; and as he had them of all hues, he hoped to fit everybody's fancy, as soon as he could find proper food for the flies, of certain gums, oils, and other glutinous matter to give a strength and consistence to the threads.

There was an astronomer who had undertaken to place a sundial upon the great weathercock on the town-house, by adjusting the annual and diurnal motions of the earth and sun, so as to answer and coincide with all accidental turnings of the wind.

I was complaining of a small fit of the colic, upon which my conductor led me into a room, where a great physician resided, who was famous for curing that disease by contrary operations from the same instrument. He had a large pair of bellows with a long slender muzzle of ivory. This he conveyed eight inches up the anus, and drawing in the wind, he affirmed he could make the guts as lank as a dried bladder. But when the disease was more stubborn and violent, he let in the muzzle while the bellows was full of wind, which he discharged into the body of the patient, then withdrew the instrument to replenish it, clapping his thumb strongly against the orifice of the fundament; and this being repeated three or four times, the adventitious wind would rush out, bringing the noxious along with it (like water put into a pump) and the patient recover. I saw him try both experiments upon a dog, but could not discern any effect from the former. After the latter, the animal was ready to burst, and made so violent a discharge, as was very offensive to me and my companions. The dog died on the spot, and we left the doctor endeavouring to recover him by the same operation.

I visited many other apartments, but shall not trouble my reader with all the curiosities I observed, being studious of brevity.

I had hitherto seen only one side of the Academy, the other being appropriated to the advancers of speculative learning, of whom I shall say something when I have mentioned one illustrious person more, who is called among them *the universal artist*. He told us he had been thirty years employing his thoughts for the improvement of human life. He had two large rooms full of wonderful curiosities, and fifty men at work. Some were condensing air into a dry tangible substance, by extracting the nitre,[28] and letting the aqueous or fluid particles percolate; others softening marble for pillows and pincushions; others petrifying the hoofs of a living horse to preserve them from foundering. The artist himself was at that time busy upon two great designs: the first, to sow land with chaff, wherein he affirmed the true seminal virtue to be contained, as he demonstrated by several experiments which I was not skilful enough to comprehend. The other was, by a certain composition of gums, minerals, and vegetables outwardly applied, to prevent the growth of wool upon two young lambs; and he hoped in a reasonable time to propagate the breed of naked sheep all over the kingdom.

We crossed a walk to the other part of the Academy, where, as I have already said, the projectors in speculative learning resided.

The first professor I saw was in a very large room, with forty pupils about him. After salutation, observing me to look earnestly upon a frame, which took up the greatest part of both the length and breadth of the room, he said perhaps I might wonder to see him employed in a project for improving speculative knowledge by practical and mechanical operations. But the world would soon be sensible of its usefulness, and he flattered himself that a more noble exalted thought never sprang in any other man's head. Every one knew how laborious the usual method[29] is of attaining to arts and sciences; whereas by his contrivance, the most ignorant person at a reasonable charge, and with a little bodily labour, may write books in philosophy, poetry, politics, law, mathematics and theology, without the least assistance from genius or study. He then led me to the frame, about the sides whereof all his pupils stood in ranks. It was twenty foot square, placed in the middle of the room. The superficies was composed of several bits of wood, about the bigness of a die,[30] but some larger than others. They were all linked together by slender wires. These bits of wood were covered on every square with papers pasted on them, and on these papers were written all

Plate.V.Part.III.

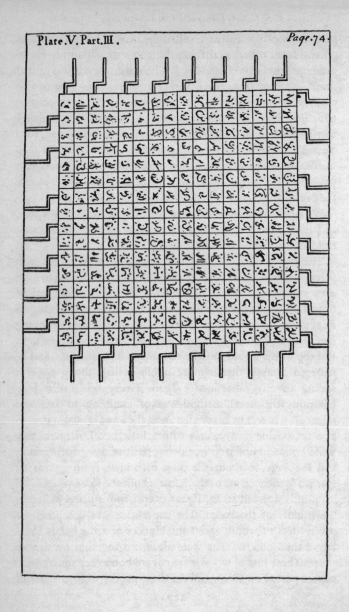

the words of their language in their several moods, tenses, and declensions, but without any order. The professor then desired me to observe, for he was going to set his engine at work. The pupils at his command took each of them hold of an iron handle, whereof there were forty fixed round the edges of the frame, and giving them a sudden turn, the whole disposition of the words was entirely changed. He then commanded six and thirty of the lads to read the several lines softly as they appeared upon the frame; and where they found three or four words together that might make part of a sentence, they dictated to the four remaining boys who were scribes. This work was repeated three or four times, and at every turn the engine was so contrived, that the words shifted into new places, as the square bits of wood moved upside down.

Six hours a day the young students were employed in this labour, and the professor showed me several volumes in large folio already collected, of broken sentences, which he intended to piece together, and out of those rich materials to give the world a complete body of all arts and sciences; which however might be still improved, and much expedited, if the public would raise a fund for making and employing five hundred such frames in Lagado, and oblige the managers to contribute in common their several collections.

He assured me, that this invention had employed all his thoughts from his youth, that he had emptied the whole vocabulary into his frame, and made the strictest computation of the general proportion there is in books between the numbers of particles, nouns, and verbs, and other parts of speech.

I made my humblest acknowledgements to this illustrious person for his great communicativeness, and promised if ever I had the good fortune to return to my native country, that I would do him justice, as the sole inventor of this wonderful machine; the form and contrivance of which I desired leave to delineate upon paper as in the figure here annexed. I told him, although it were the custom of our learned in Europe to steal inventions from each other, who had thereby at least this advantage, that it became a controversy which was the right owner, yet I would take such caution, that he should have the honour entire without a rival.

We next went to the school of languages, where three professors sat in consultation upon improving that of their own country.

The first project was to shorten discourse by cutting polysyllables into one, and leaving out verbs and participles, because in reality all things imaginable are but nouns.

The other project was a scheme for entirely abolishing all words whatsoever; and this was urged as a great advantage in point of health as well as brevity. For, it is plain, that every word we speak is in some degree a diminution of our lungs by corrosion, and consequently contributes to the shortening of our lives. An expedient was therefore offered, that since words are only names for *things*,[31] it would be more convenient for all men to carry about them such *things* as were necessary to express the particular business they are to discourse on. And this invention would certainly have taken place, to the great ease as well as health of the subject, if the women in conjunction with the vulgar and illiterate had not threatened to raise a rebellion, unless they might be allowed the liberty to speak with their tongues, after the manner of their forefathers; such constant irreconcilable enemies to science are the common people. However, many of the most learned and wise adhere to the new scheme of expressing themselves by *things*, which hath only this inconvenience attending it, that if a man's business be very great, and of various kinds, he must be obliged in proportion to carry a greater bundle of *things* upon his back, unless he can afford one or two strong servants to attend him. I have often beheld two of those sages almost sinking under the weight of their packs, like pedlars among us; who when they met in the streets would lay down their loads, open their sacks and hold conversation for an hour together; then put up their implements, help each other to resume their burthens, and take their leave.

But for short conversations a man may carry implements in his pockets and under his arms, enough to supply him, and in his house he cannot be at a loss; therefore the room where company meet who practise this art, is full of all *things* ready at hand, requisite to furnish matter for this kind of artificial converse.

Another great advantage proposed by this invention, was that it would serve as an universal language to be understood in all civilised nations, whose goods and utensils are generally of the same kind, or nearly resembling, so that their uses might easily be comprehended. And thus, ambassadors would be qualified to treat with foreign princes or ministers of state, to whose tongues they were utter strangers.

I was at the mathematical school, where the master taught his pupils after a method scarce imaginable to us in Europe. The proposition and demonstration were fairly written on a thin wafer, with ink composed of a cephalic[32] tincture. This the student was to swallow upon a fasting stomach, and for three days following eat nothing but bread and water. As the wafer digested, the tincture mounted to his brain, bearing the proposition along with it. But the success hath not hitherto been answerable, partly by some error in the *quantum* or composition, and partly by the perverseness of lads, to whom this bolus is so nauseous that they generally steal aside, and discharge it upwards before it can operate; neither have they been yet persuaded to use so long an abstinence as the prescription requires.

CHAPTER 6

A further account of the Academy. The author proposeth some improvements which are honourably received.

In the school of political projectors I was but ill entertained, the professors appearing in my judgment wholly out of their senses, which is a scene that never fails to make me melancholy. These unhappy people were proposing schemes for persuading monarchs to choose favourites upon the score of their wisdom, capacity and virtue; of teaching ministers to consult the public good; of rewarding merit, great abilities and eminent services; of instructing princes to know their true interest by placing it on the same foundation with that of their people: of choosing for employments persons qualified to exercise them; with many other wild impossible chimeras,[33] that never entered before into the heart of man to conceive, and confirmed in me the old observation, that there is nothing so extravagant and irrational which some philosophers have not maintained for truth.

But, however, I shall so far do justice to this part of the Academy, as to acknowledge that all of them were not so visionary. There was a most ingenious doctor who seemed to be perfectly versed in the whole nature and system of government. This illustrious person had very usefully employed his studies in finding out effectual remedies for all diseases and corruptions, to which the several kinds of public administration are subject by the vices or infirmities of those who govern, as well as by the licentiousness of those who are to obey. For instance; whereas all writers and reasoners have agreed, that there is a strict universal resemblance between the natural and the political body; can there be anything more evident, than that the health of both must be preserved, and the diseases cured by the same prescriptions? It is allowed, that senates and great councils are often troubled with re-

dundant, ebullient, and other peccant humours,[34] with many
diseases of the head, and more of the heart; with strong con-
vulsions, with grievous contractions of the nerves and
sinews in both hands, but especially the right; with spleen,
flatus, vertigos and deliriums; with scrofulous tumours full of
fetid purulent matter; with sour frothy ructations, with canine
appetites and crudeness of digestion, besides many others
needless to mention. This doctor therefore proposed, that
upon the meeting of a senate, certain physicians should attend
at the three first days of their sitting, and at the close of each
day's debate, feel the pulses of every senator; after which,
having maturely considered, and consulted upon the nature
of the several maladies, and the methods of cure, they should
on the fourth day return to the senate house, attended by
their apothecaries stored with proper medicines, and before
the members sat, administer to each of them lenitives,[35]
aperitives, abstersives, corrosives, restringents, palliatives,
laxatives, cephalalgics, icterics, apophlegmatics, acoustics, as
their several cases required; and according as these medicines
should operate, repeat, alter, or omit them at the next meeting.

This project could not be of any great expense to the public,
and might in my poor opinion, be of much use for the dispatch of business in those countries where senates have any
share in the legislative power, beget unanimity, shorten debates, open a few mouths which are now closed, and close
many more which are now open; curb the petulancy of the
young, and correct the positiveness of the old; rouse the
stupid, and damp the pert.

Again, because it is a general complaint that the favourites of
princes are troubled with short and weak memories, the same
doctors proposed, that whoever attended a first minister, after
having told his business with the utmost brevity, and in the
plainest words, should at his departure give the said minister a
tweak by the nose, or a kick in the belly, or tread on his corns,
or lug him thrice by both ears, or run a pin into his breech, or

pinch his arm black and blue, to prevent forgetfulness: and at every levee day repeat the same operation, till the business were done or absolutely refused.

He likewise directed, that every senator in the great council of a nation, after he had delivered his opinion, and argued in the defence of it, should be obliged to give his vote directly contrary; because if that were done, the result would infallibly terminate in the good of the public.

When parties in a state are violent, he offered a wonderful contrivance to reconcile them. The method is this. You take an hundred leaders of each party, you dispose them into couples of such whose heads are nearest of a size; then let two nice operators saw off the *occiput* 36 of each couple at the same time, in such a manner that the brain may be equally divided. Let the *occiputs* thus cut off be interchanged, applying each to the head of his opposite party-man. It seems indeed to be a work that requireth some exactness, but the professor assured us, that if it were dexterously performed, the cure would be infallible. For he argued thus; that the two half brains being left to debate the matter between themselves within the space of one skull, would soon come to a good understanding, and produce that moderation as well as regularity of thinking, so much to be wished for in the heads of those, who imagine they came into the world only to watch and govern its motion: and as to the difference of brains in quantity or quality, among those who are directors in faction, the doctor assured us from his own knowledge, that it was a perfect trifle.

I heard a very warm debate between two professors, about the most commodious 37 and effectual ways and means of raising money without grieving the subject. The first affirmed the justest method would be to lay a certain tax upon vices and folly, and the sum fixed upon every man to be rated after the fairest manner by a jury of his neighbours. The second was of an opinion directly contrary, to tax those qualities of body and mind for which men chiefly value themselves, the rate to be more or less, according to the degrees of excelling, the decision whereof should be left entirely to their own breast. The highest tax was upon men who are the greatest favourites of the other sex, and the assessments according to the number and natures of the favours they have received; for which they are allowed to be their own vouchers. Wit, valour, and politeness were likewise proposed to be largely taxed, and collected in the same manner, by every person's giving his own word for the quantum of what he possessed. But as to honour, justice, wisdom and learning, they should not be taxed at all, because they are qualifications of so singular a kind, that no man will either allow them in his neighbour, or value them in himself.

The women were proposed to be taxed according to their beauty and skill in dressing, wherein they had the same privilege with the men, to be determined by their own judgement. But constancy, chastity, good sense, and good nature were not rated, because they would not bear the charge of collecting.

To keep senators in the interest of the Crown, it was proposed that the members should raffle for employments, every man first taking an oath, and giving security that he would vote for the Court, whether he won or no, after which the losers had in their turn the liberty of raffling upon the next vacancy. Thus hope and expectation would be kept alive, none would complain of broken promises, but impute their disappointments wholly to Fortune, whose shoulders are broader and stronger than those of a ministry.

Another professor showed me a large paper of instructions for discovering plots and conspiracies against the government. He advised great statesmen to examine into the diet of all suspected persons; their times of eating; upon which side they lay in bed; with which hand they wiped their posteriors; to take a strict view of their excrements, and from the colour, the odour, the taste, the consistence, the crudeness or maturity of digestion, form a judgment of their thoughts and designs. Because men are never so serious, thoughtful, and intent, as when they are at stool,[38] which he found by frequent experiment: for in such conjunctures, when he used, merely as a trial, to consider which was the best way of murdering the King, his ordure would have a tincture of green, but quite different when he thought only of raising an insurrection or burning the metropolis.

The whole discourse was written with great acuteness, containing many observations both curious and useful for politicians, but as I conceived not altogether complete. This I ventured to tell the author, and offered if he pleased to supply him with some additions. He received my proposition with more compliance than is usual among writers, especially those of the projecting species, professing he would be glad to receive farther information.

I told him, that in the kingdom of Tribnia, by the natives called Langden,[39] where I had long sojourned, the bulk of the people consisted wholly of discoverers, witnesses, informers, accusers, prosecutors, evidences, swearers, together with their several subservient and subaltern instruments, all under the colours, the conduct, and pay of ministers and their deputies. The plots in that kingdom are usually the workmanship of those persons who desire to raise their own characters of profound politicians, to restore new vigour to a crazy administration, to stifle or divert general discontents, to fill their coffers with forfeitures, and raise or sink the opinion of public credit, as either shall best answer their private advantage. It is first agreed and settled among them what suspected persons shall be accused of a plot: then effectual care is taken to secure all their letters and other papers, and put the owners in chains. These papers are delivered to a set of artists very dexterous in finding out the mysterious meanings of words, syllables, and letters. For instance, they can decipher a close-stool to signify a Privy Council, a flock of geese a senate, a lame dog an invader, a cod's-head a —, the plague a standing army, a buzzard a prime minister, the gout a high priest, a gibbet a secretary of state, a chamber-pot a committee of grandees, a sieve a court lady, a broom a revolution, a mousetrap an employment, a bottomless pit the Treasury, a sink the Court, a cap and bells a favourite, a broken reed a court of justice, an empty tun a general, a running sore the administration.

When this method fails, they have two others more effectual, which the learned among them call acrostics and anagrams. First they can decipher all initial letters into political meanings. Thus *N.* shall signify a plot, *B.* a regiment of horse, *L.* a fleet at sea. Or secondly by transposing the letters of the alphabet in any suspected paper, they can lay open the deepest designs of a discontented party. So, for example, if I should say in a letter to a friend, *Our brother Tom has just got the piles*, a man of skill in this art would discover how the same letters which compose that sentence, may be analysed into the following words; *Resist; a plot is brought home, the tour*. And this is the anagrammatic method.

The professor made me great acknowledgements for communicating these observations, and promised to make honourable mention of me in his treatise.

I saw nothing in this country that could invite me to a longer continuance, and began to think of returning home to England.

CHAPTER 7

The author leaves Lagado, arrives at Maldonada. No ship ready. He takes a short voyage to Glubbdubdrib. His reception by the Governor.

THE continent of which this kingdom is a part, extends itself, as I have reason to believe, eastward to that unknown tract of America, westward of California, and north to the Pacific

Ocean, which is not above an hundred and fifty miles from Lagado, where there is a good port and much commerce with the great island of Luggnagg, situated to the north-west about 29 degrees north latitude, and 140 longitude. This island of Luggnagg stands south-eastwards of Japan, about an hundred leagues distant. There is a strict alliance between the Japanese Emperor and the King of Luggnagg, which affords frequent opportunities of sailing from one island to the other. I determined therefore to direct my course this way in order to my return to Europe. I hired two mules with a guide to show me the way, and carry my small baggage. I took leave of my noble protector, who had shown me so much favour, and made me a generous present at my departure.

My journey was without any accident or adventure worth relating. When I arrived at the port of Maldonada (for so it is called), there was no ship in the harbour bound for Luggnagg, nor like to be in some time. The town is about as large as Portsmouth. I soon fell into some acquaintance, and was very hospitably received. A gentleman of distinction said to me, that since the ships bound for Luggnagg could not be ready in less than a month, it might be no disagreeable amusement for me to take a trip to the little island of Glubbdubdrib, about five leagues off to the south-west. He offered himself and a friend to accompany me, and that I should be provided with a small convenient bark for the voyage.

Glubbdubdrib, as nearly as I can interpret the word, signifies the Island of *Sorcerers* or *Magicians*. It is about one third as large as the Isle of Wight, and extremely fruitful: it is governed by the head of a certain tribe, who are all magicians. This tribe marries only among each other, and the eldest in succession is Prince or Governor. He hath a noble palace and a park of about three thousand acres, surrounded by a wall of hewn stone twenty foot high. In this park are several smaller enclosures for cattle, corn, and gardening.

The Governor and his family are served and attended by

domestics of a kind somewhat unusual. By his skill in necromancy, he hath power of calling whom he pleaseth from the dead, and commanding their service for twenty-four hours, but no longer; nor can he call the same persons up again in less than three months, except upon very extraordinary occasions.

When we arrived at the island, which was about eleven in the morning, one of the gentlemen who accompanied me went to the Governor, and desired admittance for a stranger, who came on purpose to have the honour of attending on his Highness. This was immediately granted, and we all three entered the gate of the palace between two rows of guards, armed and dressed after a very antic [40] manner, and something in their countenances that made my flesh creep with a horror I cannot express. We passed through several apartments between servants of the same sort, ranked on each side as before, till we came to the chamber of presence, where after three profound obeisances, and a few general questions, we were permitted to sit on three stools near the lowest step of his Highness's throne. He understood the language of Balnibarbi, although it were different from that of his island. He desired me to give him some account of my travels; and to let me see that I should be treated without ceremony, he dismissed all his attendants with a turn of his finger, at which to my great astonishment they vanished in an instant, like visions in a dream, when we awake on a sudden. I could not recover myself in some time, till the Governor assured me that I should receive no hurt; and observing my two companions to be under no concern, who had been often entertained in the same manner, I began to take courage, and related to his Highness a short history of my several adventures, yet not without some hesitation, and frequently looking behind me to the place where I had seen those domestic spectres. I had the honour to dine with the Governor, where a new set of ghosts served up the meat, and waited at table. I now observed myself to be less terrified than I had been in the morning. I stayed till sunset, but humbly desired his Highness to excuse me for not accepting his invitation of lodging in the palace. My two friends and I lay at a private house in the town adjoining, which is the capital of this little island; and the next morning we returned to pay our duty to the Governor, as he was pleased to command us.

After this manner we continued in the island for ten days, most part of every day with the Governor, and at night in our lodging. I soon grew so familiarized to the sight of spirits, that after the third or fourth time they gave me no emotion at all; or if I had any apprehensions left, my curiosity prevailed over them. For his Highness the Governor ordered me to call up whatever persons I would choose to name, and in whatever numbers among all the dead from the beginning of the world to the present time, and command them to answer any questions I should think fit to ask; with this condition, that my questions must be confined within the compass of the times they lived in. And one thing I might depend upon, that they would certainly tell me truth, for lying was a talent of no use in the lower world.

I made my humble acknowledgements to his Highness for so great a favour. We were in a chamber, from whence there was a fair prospect into the park. And because my first inclination was to be entertained with scenes of pomp and magnificence, I desired to see Alexander the Great, at the head of his army just after the battle of Arbela,[41] which upon a motion of the Governor's finger immediately appeared in a large field under the window, where we stood. Alexander was called up into the room: it was with great difficulty that I understood his Greek, and had but little of my own. He assured me upon his honour that he was not poisoned,[42] but died of a fever by excessive drinking.

Next I saw Hannibal[43] passing the Alps, who told me he had not a drop of vinegar in his camp.

I saw Cæsar and Pompey at the head of their troops, just ready to engage. I saw the former in his last great triumph. I desired that the Senate of Rome might appear before me in one large chamber, and a modern representative, in counterview, in another. The first seemed to be an assembly of heroes and demigods; the other a knot of pedlars, pickpockets, highwaymen and bullies.

The Governor at my request gave the sign for Cæsar and Brutus to advance towards us. I was struck with a profound veneration at the sight of Brutus, and could easily discover the most consummate virtue, the greatest intrepidity, and firmness of mind, the truest love of his country, and general benevolence for mankind in every lineament of his countenance. I observed with much pleasure, that these two persons were in good intelligence[44] with each other, and Cæsar freely confessed to me, that the greatest actions of his own life were not equal by many degrees to the glory of taking it away. I had the honour to have much conversation with Brutus; and was told that his ancestor Junius,[45] Socrates, Epaminondas, Cato the younger, Sir Thomas More and himself, were perpetually together: a *sextumvirate* to which all the ages of the world cannot add a seventh.

It would be tedious to trouble the reader with relating what vast numbers of illustrious persons were called up, to gratify that insatiable desire I had to see the world in every period of antiquity placed before me. I chiefly fed mine eyes with beholding the destroyers of tyrants and usurpers, and the restorers of liberty to oppressed and injured nations. But it is impossible to express the satisfaction I received in my own mind, after such a manner as to make it a suitable entertainment to the reader.

CHAPTER 8

A further account of Glubbdubdrib. Ancient and modern history corrected.

HAVING a desire to see those ancients who were most renowned for wit and learning, I set apart one day on purpose. I proposed that Homer and Aristotle might appear at the head of all their commentators; but these were so numerous that some hundreds were forced to attend in the court and outward rooms of the palace. I knew and could distinguish those two heroes at first sight, not only from the crowd, but from each other. Homer was the taller and comelier person of the two, walked very erect for one of his age, and his eyes were the most quick and piercing I ever beheld. Aristotle stooped much, and made use of a staff. His visage was meagre, his hair lank and thin, and his voice hollow. I soon discovered that both of them were perfect strangers to the rest of the company, and had never seen or heard of them before. And I had a whisper from a ghost, who shall be nameless, that these commentators always kept in the most distant quarters from their principals in the lower world, through a consciousness of shame and guilt, because they had so horribly misrepresented the meaning of those authors to posterity. I introduced Didymus and Eustathius [46] to Homer, and prevailed on him to treat them better than perhaps they deserved, for he soon found they wanted a genius to enter into the spirit of a poet. But Aristotle was out of all patience with the account I gave him of Scotus [47] and Ramus, [48] as I presented them to him, and he asked them whether the rest of the tribe were as great dunces as themselves.

I then desired the Governor to call up Descartes [49] and Gassendi, [50] with whom I prevailed to explain their systems to Aristotle. This great philosopher freely acknowledged his own mistakes in natural philosophy, because he proceeded in many things upon conjecture, as all men must do; and he found, that Gassendi, who had made the doctrine of Epicurus as palatable as he could, and the *vortices* [51] of Descartes, were equally exploded. He predicted the same fate to *attraction*, [52] whereof the present learned are such zealous asserters. He said, that new systems of nature were but new fashions, which would vary in every age; and even those who pretended to demonstrate them from mathematical principles would flourish but a short period of time, and be out of vogue when that was determined. [53]

I spent five days in conversing with many others of the ancient learned. I saw most of the first Roman Emperors. I prevailed on the Governor to call up Eliogabalus's cooks [54] to dress us a dinner, but they could not show us much of their skill, for want of materials. A helot [55] of Agesilaus [56] made us a dish of Spartan broth, but I was not able to get down a second spoonful.

The two gentlemen who conducted me to the island were pressed by their private affairs to return in three days, which I employed in seeing some of the modern dead, who had made the greatest figure for two or three hundred years past in our own and other countries of Europe; and having been always a great admirer of old illustrious families, I desired the Governor would call up a dozen or two of kings with their ancestors in order for eight or nine generations. But my disappointment was grievous and unexpected. For, instead of a long train with royal diadems, I saw in one family two fiddlers, three spruce courtiers, and an Italian prelate. In another, a barber, an abbot, and two cardinals. I have too great a veneration for crowned heads to dwell any longer on so nice a subject. But as to counts, marquesses, dukes, earls, and the like, I was not so scrupulous. And I confess it was not without some pleasure that I found myself able to trace the particular features, by which certain families are distinguished, up to their originals. I could plainly discover from whence one family derives a long chin, why a second hath abounded with knaves for two generations, and fools for two more; why a third happened to be crack-brained, and a fourth to be sharpers. Whence it came, what Polydore Virgil[57] says of a certain great house, *Nec vir fortis, nec fæmina casta.*[58] How cruelty, falsehood, and cowardice grew to be characteristics by which certain families are distinguished as much as by their coat of arms. Who first brought the pox into a noble house, which hath lineally descended in scrofulous tumours to their posterity. Neither could I wonder at all this, when I saw such an interruption of lineages by pages, lackeys, valets, coachmen, gamesters, fiddlers, players, captains, and pickpockets.

I was chiefly disgusted with modern history. For having strictly examined all the persons of greatest name in the courts of princes for an hundred years past, I found how the world had been misled by prostitute writers, to ascribe the greatest exploits in war to cowards, the wisest counsel to fools, sincerity to flatterers, Roman virtue to betrayers of their country, piety to atheists, chastity to sodomites, truth to informers. How many innocent and excellent persons had been condemned to death or banishment, by the practising of great ministers upon the corruption of judges, and the malice of factions. How many villains had been exalted to the highest places of trust, power, dignity, and profit: how great a share in the motions and events of courts, councils, and senates might be challenged by bawds, whores, pimps, parasites, and buffoons: how low an opinion I had of human wisdom and integrity, when I was truly informed of the springs and motives of great enterprises and revolutions in the world, and of the contemptible accidents to which they owed their success.

Here I discovered the roguery and ignorance of those who pretend to write *anecdotes*,[59] or secret history; who send so many kings to their graves with a cup of poison; will repeat the discourse between a prince and chief minister, where no witness was by; unlock the thoughts and cabinets of ambassadors and secretaries of state; and have the perpetual misfortune to be mistaken. Here I discovered the true causes of many great events that have surprised the world, how a whore can govern the back-stairs, the back-stairs a council, and the council a senate. A general confessed in my presence, that he got a victory purely by the force of cowardice and ill conduct: and an admiral, that for want of proper intelligence, he beat the enemy to whom he intended to betray the fleet. Three kings protested to me, that in their whole reigns they did never once prefer any person of merit, unless by mistake or treachery of some minister in whom they confided: neither would they do it if they were to live again; and they showed with great strength of reason, that the royal throne could not be supported without corruption, because that positive, confident, restive temper, which virtue infused into man, was a perpetual clog to public business.

I had the curiosity to enquire in a particular manner, by what method great numbers had procured to themselves high titles of honour, and prodigious estates; and I confined my enquiry to a very modern period: however without grating upon present times, because I would be sure to give no offence even to foreigners (for I hope the reader need not be told that I do not in the least intend my own country in what I say upon this occasion), a great number of persons concerned were called up, and upon a very slight examination, discovered such a scene of infamy, that I cannot reflect upon it without some seriousness. Perjury, oppression, subornation, fraud, panderism, and the like *infirmities* were amongst the most excusable arts they had to mention, and for these I gave, as it was reasonable, due allowance. But when some confessed they owed their greatness and wealth to sodomy or incest, others to the prostituting of their own wives and daughters; others to the betraying their country or their prince; some to poisoning, more to the perverting of justice in order to destroy the innocent: I hope I may be pardoned if these discoveries inclined me a little to abate of that profound veneration which I am naturally apt to pay to persons of high rank, who ought to be treated with the utmost respect due to their sublime dignity, by us their inferiors.

I had often read of some great services done to princes and states, and desired to see the persons by whom those services were performed. Upon enquiry I was told that their names were to be found on no record, except a few of them whom history hath represented as the vilest rogues and traitors. As to the rest, I had never once heard of them. They all appeared with dejected looks, and in the meanest habit, most of them telling me they died in poverty and disgrace, and the rest on a scaffold or a gibbet.

Among others there was one person whose case appeared a little singular. He had a youth about eighteen years old standing by his side. He told me he had for many years been commander of a ship, and in the sea fight at Actium [60] had the good fortune to break through the enemy's great line of battle, sink three of their capital ships, and take a fourth, which was the sole cause of Antony's flight, and of the victory that ensued; that the youth standing by him, his only son, was killed in the action. He added, that upon the confidence of some merit, the war being at an end, he went to Rome, and solicited at the Court of Augustus to be preferred to a greater ship, whose commander had been killed; but without any regard to his pretensions, it was given to a boy who had never seen the sea, the son of a *libertina*, [61] who waited on one of the Emperor's mistresses. Returning back to his own vessel, he was charged with neglect of duty, and the ship given to a favourite page of Publicola [62] the Vice-Admiral; whereupon he retired to a poor farm, at a great distance from Rome, and there ended his life. I was so curious to know the truth of this story, that I desired Agrippa might be called, who was admiral in that fight. He appeared, and confirmed the whole account, but with much more advantage to the captain, whose modesty had extenuated or concealed a great part of his merit.

I was surprised to find corruption grown so high and so quick in that Empire, by the force of luxury so lately introduced, which made me less wonder at many parallel cases in other countries, where vices of all kinds have reigned so much longer, and where the whole praise as well as pillage hath been engrossed by the chief commander, who perhaps had the least title to either.

As every person called up made exactly the same appearance he had done in the world, it gave me melancholy reflections to observe how much the race of human kind was degenerate among us, within these hundred years past. How the pox [63] under all its consequences and denominations had altered every lineament of an English countenance, shortened the size of bodies, unbraced the nerves, relaxed the sinews and muscles, introduced a sallow complexion, and rendered the flesh loose and *rancid*.

I descended so low as to desire that some English yeomen of the old stamp might be summoned to appear, once so famous for the simplicity of their manners, diet and dress, for justice in their dealings, for their true spirit of liberty, for their valour and love of their country. Neither could I be wholly unmoved after comparing the living with the dead, when I considered how all these pure native virtues were prostituted for a piece of money by their grandchildren, who in selling their votes, and managing at elections, have acquired every vice and corruption that can possibly be learned in a Court.

CHAPTER 9

The author's return to Maldonada. Sails to the kingdom of Lugg-nagg. The author confined. He is sent for to Court. The manner of his admittance. The King's great lenity to his subjects.

THE day of our departure being come, I took leave of his Highness the Governor of Glubbdubdrib, and returned with my two companions to Maldonada, where after a fortnight's waiting, a ship was ready to sail for Luggnagg. The two gentlemen and some others were so generous and kind as to furnish me with provisions, and see me on board. I was a month in this voyage. We had one violent storm, and were under a necessity of steering westward to get into the trade wind, which holds for above sixty leagues. On the 21st of April, 1709, we sailed in the river of Clumegnig, which is a seaport town, at the south-east point of Luggnagg. We cast anchor within a league of the town, and made a signal for a pilot. Two of them came on board in less than half an hour, by whom we were guided between certain shoals and rocks, which are very dangerous in the passage, to a large basin, where a fleet may ride in safety within a cable's length of the town wall.

Some of our sailors, whether out of treachery or inadvertence, had informed the pilots that I was a stranger and a great traveller, whereof these gave notice to a custom-house officer, by whom I was examined very strictly upon my landing. This officer spoke to me in the language of Balnibarbi, which by the force of much commerce is generally understood in that town, especially by seamen, and those employed in the customs. I gave him a short account of some particulars, and made my story as plausible and consistent as I could; but I thought it necessary to disguise my country, and call myself a Hollander; because my intentions were for Japan, and I knew the Dutch were the only Europeans permitted to enter into that kingdom.[64] I therefore told the officer, that having been shipwrecked on the coast of Balnibarbi, and cast on a rock, I was received up into Laputa, or the Flying Island (of which he had often heard) and was now endeavouring to get to Japan, from whence I might find a convenience of returning to my own country. The officer said I must be confined till he could receive orders from Court, for which he would write immediately, and hoped to receive an answer in a fortnight. I was carried to a convenient lodging, with a sentry placed at the door; however I had the liberty of a large garden, and was treated with humanity enough, being maintained all the time at the King's charge. I was visited by several persons, chiefly out of curiosity, because it was reported I came from countries very remote, of which they had never heard.

I hired a young man who came in the same ship to be an interpreter; he was a native of Luggnagg, but had lived some years at Maldonada, and was a perfect master of both languages. By his assistance I was able to hold a conversation with those that came to visit me; but this consisted only of their questions, and my answers.

The dispatch came from Court about the time we expected. It contained a warrant for conducting me and my retinue to Traldragdubh or Trildrogdrib, for it is pronounced both ways as near as I can remember, by a party of ten horse. All my retinue was that poor lad for an interpreter, whom I persuaded into my service. At my humble request we had each of us a mule to ride on. A messenger was dispatched half a day's journey before us, to give the King notice of my approach, and to desire that his Majesty would please to appoint a day and hour, when it would be his gracious pleasure that I might have the honour to *lick the dust before his footstool*. This is the Court style, and I found it to be more than matter of form. For upon my admittance two days after my arrival, I was commanded to crawl upon my belly, and lick the floor as I advanced; but on account of my being a stranger, care was taken to have it so clean that the dust was not offensive. However, this was a peculiar grace, not allowed to any but persons of the highest rank, when they desire an admittance. Nay, sometimes the floor is strewed with dust on purpose, when the person to be admitted happens to have powerful enemies at Court. And I have seen a great Lord with his mouth so crammed, that when he had crept to the proper distance from the throne, he was not able to speak a word. Neither is there any remedy, because it is capital for those who receive an audience to spit or wipe their mouths in his Majesty's presence. There is indeed another custom, which I cannot altogether approve of. When the King hath a mind to put any of his nobles to death in a gentle indulgent manner, he commands to have the floor strowed with a certain brown powder, of a deadly composition, which being licked up infallibly kills him in twenty-four hours. But in justice to this Prince's great clemency, and the care he hath of his subjects' lives (wherein it were much to be wished that the monarchs of Europe would imitate him), it must be mentioned for his honour, that strict orders are given to have the infected parts of the floor well washed after every such execution, which if his domestics neglect, they are in danger of incurring his royal displeasure. I myself heard him give directions, that one of his pages should be whipped, whose turn it was to give notice about washing the floor after an execution, but maliciously had omitted it, by which neglect a young Lord of great hopes coming to an audience, was unfortunately poisoned, although the King at that time had no design against his life. But this good Prince was so gracious, as to forgive the page his whipping, upon promise that he would do so no more, without special orders.

To return from this digression; when I had crept within four yards of the throne, I raised myself gently upon my knees, and then striking my forehead seven times against the ground, I pronounced the following words, as they had been taught me the night before, *Ickpling gloffthrobb squutserumm blhiop mlash-nalt zwin tnodbalkguffh slhiophad gurdlubh asht*. This is the compliment established by the laws of the land for all persons admitted to the King's presence. It may be rendered into English thus: *May your Celestial Majesty outlive the sun, eleven moons and an half*. To this the King returned some answer, which although I could not understand, yet I replied as I had been directed; *Fluft drin yalerick dwuldum prastrad mirplush*, which properly signifies, *My tongue is in the mouth of my friend*, and by this expression was meant that I desired leave to bring my interpreter; whereupon the young man already mentioned was accordingly introduced, by whose intervention I answered as many questions as his Majesty could put in above an hour. I spoke in the Balnibarbian tongue, and my interpreter delivered my meaning in that of Luggnagg.

The King was much delighted with my company, and ordered his *Bliffmarklub* or High Chamberlain to appoint a lodging in the Court for me and my interpreter, with a daily allowance for my table, and a large purse of gold for my common expenses.

I stayed three months in this country out of perfect obedience to his Majesty, who was pleased highly to favour me, and made me very honourable offers. But, I thought it more consistent with prudence and justice to pass the remainder of my days with my wife and family.

CHAPTER 10

The Luggnaggians commended. A particular description of the Struldbruggs, with many conversations between the author and some eminent persons upon that subject.

THE Luggnaggians are a polite and generous people, and although they are not without some share of that pride which is peculiar to all Eastern countries, yet they show themselves courteous to strangers, especially such who are countenanced by the Court. I had many acquaintance among persons of the best fashion, and being always attended by my interpreter, the conversation we had was not disagreeable.

One day in much good company I was asked by a person of quality, whether I had seen any of their Struldbruggs or Immortals. I said I had not, and desired he would explain to me what he meant by such an appellation applied to a mortal creature. He told me, that sometimes, though very rarely, a child happened to be born in a family with a red circular spot in the forehead, directly over the left eyebrow, which was an infallible mark that it should never die. The spot, as he described it, was about the compass of a silver threepence, but in the course of time grew larger, and changed its colour; for at twelve years old it became green, so continued till five and twenty, then turned to a deep blue; at five and forty it grew coal black, and as large as an English shilling, but never admitted any farther alteration. He said these births were so rare, that he did not believe there could be above eleven hundred Struldbruggs of both sexes in the whole kingdom, of which he computed about fifty in the metropolis, and among the rest a young girl born about three years ago. That these productions were not peculiar to any family, but a mere effect of chance, and the children of the Struldbruggs themselves, were equally mortal with the rest of the people.

I freely own myself to have been struck with inexpressible delight upon hearing this account: and the person who gave it me happening to understand the Balnibarbian language, which I spoke very well, I could not forbear breaking out into expressions perhaps a little too extravagant. I cried out as in a rapture; Happy nation where every child hath at least a chance for being immortal! Happy people who enjoy so many living examples of ancient virtue, and have masters ready to instruct them in the wisdom of all former ages! But, happiest beyond all comparison are those excellent Struldbruggs, who being born exempt from that universal calamity of human nature, have their minds free and disengaged, without the weight and depression of spirits caused by the continual apprehension of death. I discovered my admiration that I had not observed any of these illustrious persons at Court, the black spot on the forehead being so remarkable a distinction, that I could not have easily overlooked it: and it was impossible that his Majesty, a most judicious Prince, should not provide himself with a good number of such wise and able counsellors. Yet perhaps the virtue of those reverend sages was too strict for the corrupt and libertine manners of a Court. And we often find by experience that young men are too opinionative and volatile to be guided by the sober dictates of their seniors. However, since the King was pleased to allow me access to his royal person, I was resolved upon the very first occasion to deliver my opinion to him on this matter freely, and at large, by the help of my interpreter; and whether he would please to take my advice or no, yet in one thing I was determined, that his Majesty having frequently offered me an establishment in this country, I would with great thankfulness accept the favour, and pass my life here in the conversation of those superior beings the Struldbruggs, if they would please to admit me.

The gentleman to whom I addressed my discourse, because (as I have already observed) he spoke the language of Balnibarbi, said to me with a sort of a smile, which usually ariseth from pity to the ignorant, that he was glad of any occasion to keep me among them, and desired my permission to explain to the company what I had spoke. He did so, and they talked together for some time in their own language, whereof I understood not a syllable, neither could I observe by their countenances what impression my discourse had made on them. After a short silence the same person told me, that his friends and mine (so he thought fit to express himself) were very much pleased with the judicious remarks I had made on the great happiness and advantages of immortal life, and they were desirous to know in a particular manner, what scheme of living I should have formed to myself, if it had fallen to my lot to have been born a Struldbrugg.

I answered, it was easy to be eloquent on so copious and delightful a subject, especially to me who have been often apt to amuse myself with visions of what I should do if I were a King, a General, or a great Lord: and upon this very case I had frequently run over the whole system how I should employ myself, and pass the time if I were sure to live for ever.

That, if it had been my good fortune to come into the world a Struldbrugg, as soon as I could discover my own happiness by understanding the difference between life and death, I would first resolve by all arts and methods whatsoever to procure myself riches. In the pursuit of which by thrift and management, I might reasonably expect in about two hundred years, to be the wealthiest man in the kingdom. In the second place, I would from my earliest youth apply myself to the study of arts and sciences, by which I should arrive in time to excel all others in learning. Lastly I would carefully record every action and event of consequence that happened in the public,[65] impartially draw the characters of the several successions of princes, and great ministers of state, with my own observations on every point. I would exactly set down the several changes in customs, language, fashions of dress, diet and diversions. By all which acquirements, I should be a living treasury of knowledge and wisdom, and certainly become the oracle of the nation.

I would never marry after threescore, but live in an hospitable manner, yet still on the saving side. I would entertain myself in forming and directing the minds of hopeful young men, by convincing them from my own remembrance, experience and observation, fortified by numerous examples, of the usefulness of virtue in public and private life. But, my choice and constant companions should be a set of my own immortal brotherhood, among whom I would elect a dozen from the most ancient down to my own contemporaries. Where any of these wanted fortunes, I would provide them with convenient lodges round my own estate, and have some of them always at my table, only mingling a few of the most valuable among you mortals, whom length of time would harden me to lose with little or no reluctance, and treat your posterity after the same manner, just as a man diverts himself with the annual succession of pinks and tulips in his garden, without regretting the loss of those which withered the preceding year.

These Struldbruggs and I would mutually communicate our observations and memorials through the course of time, remark the several gradations by which corruption steals into the world, and oppose it in every step, by giving perpetual warning and instruction to mankind; which, added to the strong influence of our own example, would probably prevent that continual degeneracy of human nature so justly complained of in all ages.

Add to all this, the pleasure of seeing the various revolutions of states and empires, the changes in the lower and upper world,[66] ancient cities in ruins, and obscure villages become the seats of kings. Famous rivers lessening into shallow brooks, the ocean leaving one coast dry, and overwhelming another: the discovery of many countries yet unknown. Barbarity overrunning the politest nations, and the most barbarous becoming civilized. I should then see the discovery of the *longitude*,[67] the *perpetual motion*, the *universal medicine*, and many other great inventions brought to the utmost perfection.

What wonderful discoveries should we make in astronomy, by outliving and confirming our own predictions, by observing the progress and returns of comets, with the changes of motion in the sun, moon and stars.

I enlarged upon many other topics which the natural desire

of endless life and sublunary happiness could easily furnish me with. When I had ended, and the sum of my discourse had been interpreted as before, to the rest of the company, there was a good deal of talk among them in the language of the country, not without some laughter at my expense. At last the same gentleman who had been my interpreter said, he was desired by the rest to set me right in a few mistakes, which I had fallen into through the common imbecility of human nature, and upon that allowance was less answerable for them. That, this breed of Struldbruggs was peculiar to their country, for there were no such people either in Balnibarbi or Japan, where he had the honour to be ambassador from his Majesty, and found the natives in both those kingdoms very hard to believe that the fact was possible, and it appeared from my astonishment when he first mentioned the matter to me, that I received it as a thing wholly new, and scarcely to be credited. That in the two kingdoms above-mentioned, where during his residence he had conversed very much, he observed long life to be the universal desire and wish of mankind. That whoever had one foot in the grave, was sure to hold back the other as strongly as he could. That the oldest had still hopes of living one day longer, and looked on death as the greatest evil, from which Nature always prompted him to retreat; only in this island of Luggnagg, the appetite for living was not so eager, from the continual example of the Struldbruggs before their eyes.

That the system of living contrived by me was unreasonable and unjust, because it supposed a perpetuity of youth, health, and vigour, which no man could be so foolish to hope, however extravagant he might be in his wishes. That the question therefore was not whether a man would choose to be always in the prime of youth, attended with prosperity and health, but how he would pass a perpetual life under all the usual disadvantages which old age brings along with it. For although few men will avow their desires of being immortal upon such hard conditions, yet in the two kingdoms before-mentioned of Balnibarbi and Japan, he observed that every man desired to put off death for some time longer, let it approach ever so late, and he rarely heard of any man who died willingly, except he were incited by the extremity of grief or torture. And he appealed to me whether in those countries I had travelled, as well as my own, I had not observed the same general disposition.

After this preface he gave me a particular account of the Struldbruggs among them. He said they commonly acted like mortals, till about thirty years old, after which by degrees they grew melancholy and dejected, increasing in both till they came to fourscore. This he learned from their own confession; for otherwise there not being above two or three of that species born in an age, they were too few to form a general observation by. When they came to fourscore years, which is reckoned the extremity of living in this country, they had not only all the follies and infirmities of other old men, but many more which arose from the dreadful prospect of never dying. They were not only opinionative, peevish, covetous, morose, vain, talkative, but uncapable of friendship, and dead to all natural affection, which never descended below their grandchildren. Envy and impotent desires are their prevailing passions. But those objects against which their envy seems principally directed, are the vices of the younger sort, and the deaths of the old. By reflecting on the former, they find themselves cut off from all possibility of pleasure; and whenever they see a funeral, they lament and repine that others are gone to an harbour of rest, to which they themselves never can hope to arrive. They have no remembrance of anything but what they learned and observed in their youth and middle age, and even that is very imperfect. And for the truth or particulars of any fact, it is safer to depend on common traditions than upon their best recollections. The least miserable among them appear to be those who turn to dotage, and entirely lose their memories; these meet with more pity and assistance, because they want many bad qualities which abound in others.

If a Struldbrugg happen to marry one of his own kind, the marriage is dissolved of course by the courtesy of the kingdom, as soon as the younger of the two comes to be fourscore. For the law thinks it a reasonable indulgence, that those who are condemned without any fault of their own to a perpetual continuance in the world, should not have their misery doubled by the load of a wife.

As soon as they have completed the term of eighty years, they are looked on as dead in law; their heirs immediately succeed to their estates, only a small pittance is reserved for their support, and the poor ones are maintained at the public charge. After that period they are held incapable of any employment of trust or profit, they cannot purchase lands or take leases, neither are they allowed to be witnesses in any cause, either civil or criminal, not even for the decision of meres [68] and bounds.

At ninety they lose their teeth and hair, they have at that age no distinction of taste, but eat and drink whatever they can get, without relish or appetite. The diseases they were subject to, still continue without increasing or diminishing. In talking they forget the common appellation of things, and the names of persons, even of those who are their nearest friends and relations. For the same reason they never can amuse themselves with reading, because their memory will not serve to carry them from the beginning of a sentence to the end; and by this defect they are deprived of the only entertainment whereof they might otherwise be capable.

The language of this country being always upon the flux, the Struldbruggs of one age do not understand those of another, neither are they able after two hundred years to hold any conversation (farther than by a few general words) with their neighbours the mortals, and thus they lie under the disadvantage of living like foreigners in their own country.

This was the account given me of the Struldbruggs, as near as I can remember. I afterwards saw five or six of different ages, the youngest not above two hundred years old, who were brought to me at several times by some of my friends; but although they were told that I was a great traveller, and had seen all the world, they had not the least curiosity to ask me a question; only desired I would give them *slumskudask*, or a token of remembrance, which is a modest way of begging, to avoid the law that strictly forbids it, because they are provided for by the public, although indeed with a very scanty allowance.

They are despised and hated by all sorts of people; when one of them is born, it is reckoned ominous, and their birth is recorded very particularly; so that you may know their age by consulting the registry, which however hath not been kept above a thousand years past, or at least hath been destroyed by time or public disturbances. But the usual way of computing how old they are, is, by asking them what kings or great persons they can remember, and then consulting history, for infallibly the last Prince in their mind did not begin his reign after they were fourscore years old.

They were the most mortifying sight I ever beheld, and the women more horrible than the men. Besides the usual deformities in extreme old age, they acquired an additional ghastliness in proportion to their number of years, which is not to be described, and among half a dozen I soon distinguished which was the eldest, although there were not above a century or two between them.

The reader will easily believe, that from what I had heard and seen, my keen appetite for perpetuity of life was much abated. I grew heartily ashamed of the pleasing visions I had formed, and thought no tyrant could invent a death into which I would not run with pleasure from such a life. The King heard of all that had passed between me and my friends upon this occasion, and rallied me very pleasantly, wishing I would send a couple of Struldbruggs to my own country, to arm our people against the fear of death; but this it seems is forbidden by the fundamental laws of the kingdom, or else I should have been well content with the trouble and expense of transporting them.

I could not but agree that the laws of this kingdom, relating to the Struldbruggs, were founded upon the strongest reasons, and such as any other country would be under the necessity of enacting in the like circumstances. Otherwise, as avarice is the necessary consequent [69] of old age, those Immortals would in time become proprietors of the whole nation, and engross the civil power, which, for want of abilities to manage, must end in the ruin of the public.

CHAPTER II

The author leaves Luggnagg and sails to Japan. From thence he returns in a Dutch ship to Amsterdam, and from Amsterdam to England.

I THOUGHT this account of the Struldbruggs might be some entertainment to the reader, because it seems to be a little out of the common way, at least, I do not remember to have met the like in any book of travels that hath come to my hands: and if I am deceived, my excuse must be, that it is necessary for travellers, who describe the same country, very often to agree in dwelling on the same particulars, without deserving the censure of having borrowed or transcribed from those who wrote before them.

There is indeed a perpetual commerce between this kingdom and the great Empire of Japan, and it is very probable that the Japanese authors may have given some account of the Struldbruggs; but my stay in Japan was so short, and I was so entirely a stranger to the language, that I was not qualified to make any enquiries. But I hope the Dutch upon this notice will be curious and able enough to supply my defects.

His Majesty having often pressed me to accept some employment in his Court, and finding me absolutely determined to return to my native country, was pleased to give me his licence to depart, and honoured me with a letter of recommendation under his own hand to the Emperor of Japan. He likewise presented me with four hundred forty-four large pieces of gold (this nation delighting in even numbers) and a red diamond which I sold in England for eleven hundred pounds.

On the sixth day of May, 1709, I took a solemn leave of his Majesty, and all my friends. This Prince was so gracious as to order a guard to conduct me to Glanguenstald, which is a royal port to the south-west part of the island. In six days I found a vessel ready to carry me to Japan, and spent fifteen days in the voyage. We landed at a small port-town called Xamoschi, situated on the south-east part of Japan; the town lies on the western point where there is a narrow strait, leading northward into a long arm of the sea, upon the north-west part of which, Yedo[70] the metropolis stands. At landing I showed the custom-house officers my letter from the King of Luggnagg to his Imperial Majesty. They knew the seal perfectly well; it was as broad as the palm of my hand. The impression was, *A king lifting up a lame beggar from the earth*. The magistrates of the town, hearing of my letter, received me as a public minister; they provided me with carriages and servants, and bore my charges to Yedo, where I was admitted to an audience, and delivered my letter, which was opened with great ceremony, and explained to the Emperor by an interpreter, who then gave me notice of his Majesty's order, that I should signify my request, and whatever it were, it should be granted for the sake of his royal brother of Luggnagg. This interpreter was a person employed to transact affairs with the Hollanders; he soon conjectured by my countenance that I was an European, and therefore repeated his Majesty's commands in Low Dutch, which he spoke perfectly well. I answered (as I had before determined), that I was a Dutch merchant, shipwrecked in a very remote country, from whence I travelled by sea and land to Luggnagg, and then took shipping for Japan, where I knew my countrymen often traded, and with some of these I hoped to get an opportunity of returning into Europe: I therefore most humbly entreated his royal favour to give order, that I should be conducted in safety to Nangasac:[71] to this I added another petition, that for the sake of my patron the King of Luggnagg, his Majesty would condescend to excuse my performing the ceremony imposed on my countrymen of *trampling upon the Crucifix*, because I had been thrown into his kingdom by my misfortunes, without any intention of trading. When this latter petition was interpreted to the Emperor, he seemed a little surprised, and said, he believed I was the first of my countrymen who ever made any scruple in this point, and that he began to doubt whether I were a real Hollander or no; but rather suspected I must be a CHRISTIAN. However, for the reasons I had offered, but chiefly to gratify the King of Luggnagg, by an uncommon mark of his favour, he would comply with the *singularity* of my humour, but the affair must be managed with dexterity, and his officers should be commanded to let me pass as it were by forgetfulness. For he assured me, that if the secret should be discovered by my countrymen, the Dutch, they would cut my throat in the voyage. I returned my thanks by the interpreter for so unusual a favour, and some troops being at that time on their march to Nangasac, the commanding officer had orders to convey me safe thither, with particular instructions about the business of the Crucifix.

On the 9th day of June, 1709, I arrived at Nangasac, after a very long and troublesome journey. I soon fell into company of some Dutch sailors belonging to the *Amboyna*[72] of Amsterdam, a stout ship of 450 tons. I had lived long in Holland, pursuing my studies at Leyden, and I spoke Dutch well. The seamen soon knew from whence I came last; they were curious to enquire into my voyages and course of life. I made up a story as short and probable as I could, but concealed the greatest part. I knew many persons in Holland, I was able to invent names for my parents, whom I pretended to be obscure people in the province of Guelderland. I would have given the captain (one Theodorus Vangrult) what he pleased to ask for my voyage to Holland; but understanding I was a surgeon, he was contented to take half the usual rate, on condition that I would serve him in the way of my calling. Before we took shipping, I was often asked by some of the crew, whether I had performed the ceremony above-mentioned? I evaded the question by general answers, that I had satisfied the Emperor and Court in all particulars. However, a malicious rogue of a skipper[73] went to an officer, and pointing to me, told him, I had not yet *trampled on the Crucifix*; but the other, who had received instructions to let me pass, gave the rascal twenty strokes on the shoulders with a bamboo, after which I was no more troubled with such questions.

Nothing happened worth mentioning in this voyage. We sailed with a fair wind to the Cape of Good Hope, where we stayed only to take in fresh water. On the 16th of April we arrived safe at Amsterdam, having lost only three men by sickness in the voyage, and a fourth who fell from the foremast into the sea, not far from the coast of Guinea. From Amsterdam I soon after set sail for England in a small vessel belonging to that city.

On the 20th of April, 1710, we put in at the Downs. I landed the next morning, and saw once more my native country after an absence of five years and six months complete. I went straight to Redriff, where I arrived the same day at two in the afternoon, and found my wife and family in good health.

THE END OF THE THIRD PART

TRAVELS · PART IV

A VOYAGE TO THE COUNTRY OF
THE HOUYHNHNMS

*

Plate.VI.Part.IIII.Page.1.

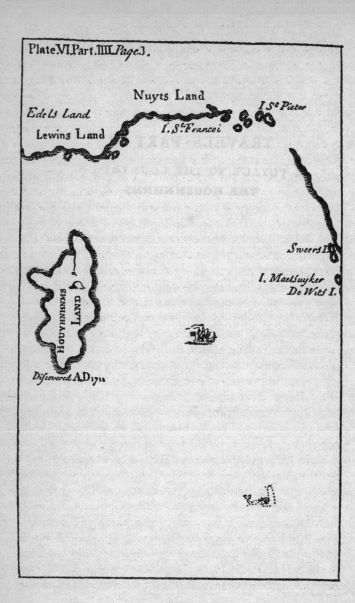

Edels Land

Lewins Land

Nuyts Land

I. St Francoi

I St Pieter

Sweers Il.

I. Maelsuyker
De Wits I.

HOUYHNHNMS LAND

Discovered AD 1711

CHAPTER I

The author sets out as Captain of a ship. His men conspire against him, confine him a long time to his cabin, set him on shore in an unknown land. He travels up into the country. The Yahoos, a strange sort of animal, described. The author meets two Houyhnhnms.

I CONTINUED at home with my wife and children about five months in a very happy condition, if I could have learned the lesson of knowing when I was well. I left my poor wife big with child, and accepted an advantageous offer made me to be Captain of the *Adventure*, a stout merchantman of 350 tons: for I understood navigation well, and being grown weary of a surgeon's employment at sea, which however I could exercise upon occasion, I took a skilful young man of that calling, one Robert Purefoy, into my ship. We set sail from Portsmouth upon the seventh day of September, 1710; on the fourteenth, we met with Captain Pocock of Bristol, at Teneriffe, who was going to the bay of Campechy,¹ to cut logwood. On the sixteenth, he was parted from us by a storm; I heard since my return, that his ship foundered, and none escaped, but one cabin-boy. He was an honest man, and a good sailor, but a little too positive in his own opinions, which was the cause of his destruction, as it hath been of several others. For if he had followed my advice, he might at this time have been safe at home with his family as well as myself.

I had several men died in my ship of calentures,² so that I was forced to get recruits out of Barbadoes, and the Leeward Islands, where I touched by the direction of the merchants who employed me, which I had soon too much cause to repent; for I found afterwards that most of them had been buccaneers. I had fifty hands on board, and my orders were, that I should trade with the Indians in the South Sea, and make what discoveries I could. These rogues whom I had picked up debauched my other men, and they all formed a conspiracy to seize the ship and secure me; which they did one morning, rushing into my cabin, and binding me hand and foot, threatening to throw me overboard, if I offered to stir. I told them, I was their prisoner, and would submit. This they made me swear to do, and then unbound me, only fastening one of my legs with a chain near my bed, and placed a sentry at my door with his piece charged, who was commanded to shoot me dead, if I attempted my liberty. They sent me down victuals and drink, and took the government of the ship to themselves. Their design was to turn pirates, and plunder the Spaniards, which they could not do till they got more men. But first they resolved to sell the goods in the ship, and then go to Madagascar for recruits, several among them having died since my confinement. They sailed many weeks, and traded with the Indians, but I knew not what course they took, being kept close prisoner in my cabin, and expecting nothing less than to be murdered, as they often threatened me.

Upon the ninth day of May, 1711, one James Welch came down to my cabin; and said he had orders from the Captain to set me ashore. I expostulated with him, but in vain; neither would he so much as tell me who their new captain was. They forced me into the long-boat, letting me put on my best suit of clothes, which were as good as new, and a small bundle of linen, but no arms except my hanger; and they were so civil as not to search my pockets, into which I conveyed what money I had, with some other little necessaries. They rowed about a league; and then set me down on a strand. I desired them to tell me what country it was. They all swore, they knew no more than myself, but said, that the Captain (as they called him) was resolved, after they had sold the lading, to get rid of me in the first place where they discovered land. They pushed off immediately, advising me to make haste, for fear of being overtaken by the tide, and bade me farewell.

In this desolate condition I advanced forward, and soon got upon firm ground, where I sat down on a bank to rest myself,

and consider what I had best to do. When I was a little refreshed, I went up into the country, resolving to deliver myself to the first savages I should meet, and purchase my life
from them by some bracelets, glass rings, and other toys,[3]
which sailors usually provide themselves with in those
voyages, and whereof I had some about me: the land was
divided by long rows of trees, not regularly planted, but
naturally growing; there was great plenty of grass, and several
fields of oats. I walked very circumspectly for fear of being
surprised, or suddenly shot with an arrow from behind or on
either side. I fell into a beaten road, where I saw many tracks
of human feet, and some of cows, but most of horses. At last
I beheld several animals in a field, and one or two of the same
kind sitting in trees. Their shape was very singular, and deformed, which a little discomposed me, so that I lay down
behind a thicket to observe them better. Some of them coming
forward near the place where I lay, gave me an opportunity of
distinctly marking their form. Their heads and breasts were
covered with a thick hair, some frizzled and others lank; they
had beards like goats, and a long ridge of hair down their
backs, and the foreparts of their legs and feet, but the rest of
their bodies were bare, so that I might see their skins, which
were of a brown buff colour. They had no tails, nor any hair
at all on their buttocks, except about the anus; which, I
presume, Nature had placed there to defend them as they sat
on the ground; for this posture they used, as well as lying
down, and often stood on their hind feet. They climbed high
trees, as nimbly as a squirrel, for they had strong extended
claws before and behind, terminating in sharp points, and
hooked. They would often spring, and bound, and leap with
prodigious agility. The females were not so large as the males;
they had long lank hair on their heads, and only a sort of
down on the rest of their bodies, except about the anus, and
pudenda. Their dugs hung between their fore-feet, and often
reached almost to the ground as they walked. The hair of

both sexes was of several colours, brown, red, black and yellow. Upon the whole, I never beheld in all my travels so disagreeable an animal, nor one against which I naturally conceived so strong an antipathy. So that thinking I had seen enough, full of contempt and aversion, I got up and pursued the beaten road, hoping it might direct me to the cabin of some Indian. I had not gone far when I met one of these creatures full in my way, and coming up directly to me. The ugly monster, when he saw me, distorted several ways every feature of his visage, and stared as at an object he had never seen before; then approaching nearer, lifted up his forepaw, whether out of curiosity or mischief, I could not tell. But I drew my hanger, and gave him a good blow with the flat side of it; for I durst not strike him with the edge, fearing the inhabitants might be provoked against me, if they should come to know, that I had killed or maimed any of their cattle. When the beast felt the smart, he drew back, and roared so loud, that a herd of at least forty came flocking about me from the next field, howling and making odious faces; but I ran to the body of a tree, and leaning my back against it, kept them off, by waving my hanger. Several of this cursed brood getting hold of the branches behind leaped up into the tree, from whence they began to discharge their excrements on my head: however, I escaped pretty well, by sticking close to the stem of the tree, but was almost stifled with the filth, which fell about me on every side.

In the midst of this distress, I observed them all to run away on a sudden as fast as they could, at which I ventured to leave the tree, and pursue the road, wondering what it was that could put them into this fright. But looking on my left hand, I saw a horse walking softly in the field, which my persecutors having sooner discovered, was the cause of their flight. The horse started a little when he came near me, but soon recovering himself, looked full in my face with manifest tokens of wonder: he viewed my hands and feet, walking round me several times. I would have pursued my journey, but he placed himself directly in the way, yet looking with a very mild aspect, never offering the least violence. We stood gazing at each other for some time; at last I took the boldness to reach my hand towards his neck, with a design to stroke it, using the common style and whistle of jockeys when they are going to handle a strange horse. But this animal, seeming to receive my civilities with disdain, shook his head, and bent his brows, softly raising up his left fore-foot to remove my hand. Then he neighed three or four times, but in so different a cadence, that I almost began to think he was speaking to himself in some language of his own.

While he and I were thus employed, another horse came up; who applying himself to the first in a very formal manner, they gently struck each other's right hoof before, neighing several times by turns, and varying the sound, which seemed to be almost articulate. They went some paces off, as if it were to confer together, walking side by side, backward and forward, like persons deliberating upon some affair of weight, but often turning their eyes towards me, as it were to watch that I might not escape. I was amazed to see such actions and behaviour in brute beasts, and concluded with myself, that if the inhabitants of this country were endued with a proportionable degree of reason, they must needs be the wisest people upon earth. This thought gave me so much comfort, that I resolved to go forward until I could discover some house or village, or meet with any of the natives, leaving the two horses to discourse together as they pleased. But the first, who was a dapple-grey, observing me to steal off, neighed after me in so expressive a tone, that I fancied myself to understand what he meant; whereupon I turned back, and came near him, to expect[4] his farther commands. But concealing my fear as much as I could, for I began to be in some pain, how this adventure might terminate; and the reader will easily believe I did not much like my present situation.

The two horses came up close to me, looking with great earnestness upon my face and hands. The grey steed rubbed my hat all round with his right fore-hoof, and discomposed it so much, that I was forced to adjust it better, by taking it off, and settling it again; whereat both he and his companion (who was a brown bay) appeared to be much surprised; the latter felt the lappet of my coat, and finding it to hang loose about me, they both looked with new signs of wonder. He stroked my right hand, seeming to admire the softness, and colour; but he squeezed it so hard between his hoof and his pastern, that I was forced to roar; after which they both touched me with all possible tenderness. They were under great perplexity about my shoes and stockings, which they felt very often, neighing to each other, and using various gestures, not unlike those of a philosopher, when he would attempt to solve some new and difficult phenomenon.

Upon the whole, the behaviour of these animals was so orderly and rational, so acute and judicious, that I at last concluded, they must needs be magicians, who had thus metamorphosed themselves upon some design, and seeing a stranger in the way, were resolved to divert themselves with him; or perhaps were really amazed at the sight of a man so very different in habit, feature, and complexion from those who might probably live in so remote a climate. Upon the strength of this reasoning, I ventured to address them in the following manner: Gentlemen, if you be conjurers, as I have good cause to believe, you can understand any language; therefore I make bold to let your Worships know, that I am a poor distressed Englishman, driven by his misfortunes upon your coast, and I entreat one of you, to let me ride upon his back, as if he were a real horse, to some house or village, where I can be relieved. In return of which favour, I will make you a present of this knife and bracelet (taking them out of my pocket). The two creatures stood silent while I spoke, seeming to listen with great attention; and when I had ended, they neighed frequently towards each other, as if they were engaged in serious conversation. I plainly observed that their language expressed the passions very well, and the words might with little pains be resolved into an alphabet more easily than the Chinese.

I could frequently distinguish the word *Yahoo,* which was repeated by each of them several times; and although it were impossible for me to conjecture what it meant, yet while the two horses were busy in conversation, I endeavoured to practise this word upon my tongue; and as soon as they were silent, I boldly pronounced *Yahoo* in a loud voice, imitating, at the same time, as near as I could, the neighing of a horse; at which they were both visibly surprised, and the grey repeated the same word twice, as if he meant to teach me the right accent, wherein I spoke after him as well as I could, and found myself perceivably to improve every time, although very far from any degree of perfection. Then the bay tried me with a second word, much harder to be pronounced; but reducing it to the English *orthography,* may be spelt thus, *Houyhnhnm.*[5] I did not succeed in this so well as the former, but after two or three farther trials, I had better fortune; and they both appeared amazed at my capacity.

After some farther discourse, which I then conjectured might relate to me, the two friends took their leaves, with the same compliment of striking each other's hoof; and the grey made me signs that I should walk before him; wherein I thought it prudent to comply, till I could find a better director. When I offered to slacken my pace, he would cry *Hhuun,* *Hhuun;* I guessed his meaning, and gave him to understand, as well as I could, that I was weary, and not able to walk faster; upon which, he would stand a while to let me rest.

CHAPTER 2

The author conducted by a Houyhnhnm to his house. The house des-
cribed. The author's reception. The food of the Houyhnhnms. The
author in distress for want of meat, is at last relieved. His manner of
feeding in that country.

HAVING travelled about three miles, we came to a long kind
of building, made of timber stuck in the ground, and wattled
across; the roof was low, and covered with straw. I now began
to be a little comforted, and took out some toys, which travellers usually carry for presents to the savage Indians of America
and other parts, in hopes the people of the house would be
thereby encouraged to receive me kindly. The horse made me
a sign to go in first; it was a large room with a smooth clay
floor, and a rack and manger extending the whole length on
one side. There were three nags, and two mares, not eating,
but some of them sitting down upon their hams, which I very
much wondered at; but wondered more to see the rest employed in domestic business. The last seemed but ordinary
cattle; however, this confirmed my first opinion, that a people
who could so far civilize brute animals, must needs excel in
wisdom all the nations of the world. The grey came in just
after, and thereby prevented any ill treatment, which the
others might have given me. He neighed to them several
times in a style of authority, and received answers.

Beyond this room there were three others, reaching the
length of the house, to which you passed through three doors,
opposite to each other, in the manner of a vista; we went
through the second room towards the third; here the grey
walked in first, beckoning me to attend: I waited in the second
room, and got ready my presents, for the master and mistress
of the house: they were two knives, three bracelets of false
pearl, a small looking-glass and a bead necklace. The horse
neighed three or four times, and I waited to hear some answers

in a human voice, but I heard no other returns than in the same dialect, only one or two a little shriller than his. I began to think that this house must belong to some person of great note among them, because there appeared so much ceremony before I could gain admittance. But, that a man of quality should be served all by horses, was beyond my comprehension. I feared my brain was disturbed by my sufferings and misfortunes: I roused myself, and looked about me in the room where I was left alone; this was furnished as the first, only after a more elegant manner. I rubbed mine eyes often, but the same objects still occurred. I pinched my arms and sides, to awake myself, hoping I might be in a dream. I then absolutely concluded, that all these appearances could be nothing else but necromancy and magic. But I had no time to pursue these reflections; for the grey horse came to the door, and made me a sign to follow him into the third room, where I saw a very comely mare, together with a colt and foal, sitting on their haunches, upon mats of straw, not unartfully made, and perfectly neat and clean.

The mare, soon after my entrance, rose from her mat, and coming up close, after having nicely observed my hands and face, gave me a most contemptuous look; then turning to the horse, I heard the word *Yahoo* often repeated betwixt them; the meaning of which word I could not then comprehend, although it were the first I had learned to pronounce; but I was soon better informed, to my everlasting mortification: for the horse beckoning to me with his head, and repeating the word *Hhuun, Hhuun*, as he did upon the road, which I understood was to attend him, led me out into a kind of court, where was another building at some distance from the house. Here we entered, and I saw three of those detestable creatures, which I first met after my landing, feeding upon roots, and the flesh of some animals, which I afterwards found to be that of asses and dogs, and now and then a cow dead by accident or disease. They were all tied by the neck with strong withes, fastened to a beam; they held their food between the claws of their fore-feet, and tore it with their teeth.

The master horse ordered a sorrel nag, one of his servants, to untie the largest of these animals, and take him into the yard. The beast and I were brought close together, and our countenances diligently compared, both by master and servant, who thereupon repeated several times the word *Yahoo*. My horror and astonishment are not to be described, when I observed, in this abominable animal, a perfect human figure; the face of it indeed was flat and broad, the nose depressed, the lips large, and the mouth wide. But these differences are common to all savage nations, where the lineaments of the countenance are distorted by the natives suffering their infants to lie grovelling on the earth, or by carrying them on their backs, nuzzling with their face against the mother's shoulders. The fore-feet of the Yahoo differed from my hands in nothing else but the length of the nails, the coarseness and brownness of the palms, and the hairiness on the backs. There was the same resemblance between our feet, with the same differences, which I knew very well, though the horses did not, because of my shoes and stockings; the same in every part of our bodies, except as to hairiness and colour, which I have already described.

The great difficulty that seemed to stick with the two horses, was, to see the rest of my body so very different from that of a Yahoo, for which I was obliged to my clothes, whereof they had no conception: the sorrel nag offered me a root, which he held (after their manner, as we shall describe in its proper place) between his hoof and pastern; I took it in my hand, and having smelt it, returned it to him as civilly as I could. He brought out of the Yahoo's kennel a piece of ass's flesh, but it smelt so offensively that I turned from it with loathing; he then threw it to the Yahoo, by whom it was greedily devoured. He afterwards showed me a wisp of hay, and a fetlock full of oats; but I shook my head, to signify, that neither of these were food for me. And indeed, I now apprehended, that I must absolutely starve, if I did not get to some of my own species: for as to those filthy Yahoos, although there were few greater lovers of mankind, at that time, than myself; yet I confess I never saw any sensitive being so detestable on all accounts; and the more I came near them, the more hateful they grew, while I stayed in that country. This the master horse observed by my behaviour, and therefore sent the Yahoo back to his kennel. He then put his fore-hoof to his mouth, at which I was much surprised, although he did it with ease, and with a motion that appeared perfectly natural, and made other signs to know what I would eat; but I could not return him such an answer as he was able to apprehend; and if he had understood me, I did not see how it was possible to contrive any way for finding myself nourishment. While we were thus engaged, I observed a cow passing by, whereupon I pointed to her, and expressed a desire to let me go and milk her. This had its effect; for he led me back into the house, and ordered a mare-servant to open a room, where a good store of milk lay in earthen and wooden vessels, after a very orderly and cleanly manner. She gave me a large bowl full, of which I drank very heartily, and found myself well refreshed.

About noon I saw coming towards the house a kind of vehicle drawn like a sledge by four Yahoos. There was in it an old steed, who seemed to be of quality; he alighted with his hind feet forward, having by accident got a hurt in his left fore-foot. He came to dine with our horse, who received him with great civility. They dined in the best room, and had oats boiled in milk for the second course, which the old horse ate warm, but the rest cold. Their mangers were placed circular in the middle of the room, and divided into several partitions, round which they sat on their haunches upon bosses of straw. In the middle was a large rack with angles answering to every partition of the manger. So that each horse and mare ate their own hay, and their own mash of oats and milk, with much decency and regularity. The behaviour of the young colt and foal appeared very modest, and that of the master and mistress extremely cheerful and complaisant [6] to their guest. The grey ordered me to stand by him, and much discourse passed between him and his friend concerning me, as I found by the stranger's often looking on me, and the frequent repetition of the word Yahoo.

I happened to wear my gloves, which the master grey observing, seemed perplexed, discovering signs of wonder what I had done to my fore-feet; he put his hoof three or four times to them, as if he would signify, that I should reduce them to their former shape, which I presently did, pulling off both my gloves, and putting them into my pocket. This occasioned farther talk, and I saw the company was pleased with my behaviour, whereof I soon found the good effects. I was ordered to speak the few words I understood, and while they were at dinner, the master taught me the names for oats, milk, fire, water, and some others; which I could readily pronounce after him, having from my youth a great facility in learning languages.

When dinner was done, the master horse took me aside, and by signs and words made me understand the concern he was in, that I had nothing to eat. Oats in their tongue are called *hlunnh*. This word I pronounced two or three times; for although I had refused them at first, yet upon second thoughts, I considered that I could contrive to make of them a kind of bread, which might be sufficient with milk to keep me alive, till I could make my escape to some other country, and to creatures of my own species. The horse immediately ordered a white mare-servant of his family to bring me a good quantity of oats in a sort of wooden tray. These I heated before the fire as well as I could, and rubbed them till the husks came off, which I made a shift to winnow from the grain; I ground and beat them between two stones, then took water, and made them into a paste or cake, which I toasted at the fire, and ate warm with milk. It was at first a very insipid diet, although common enough in many parts of Europe, but grew tolerable by time; and having been often reduced to hard fare in my life, this was not the first experiment I had made how easily nature is satisfied. And I cannot but observe, that I never had one hour's sickness, while I stayed in this island. 'Tis true, I sometimes made a shift to catch a rabbit, or bird, by springes made of Yahoos' hairs, and I often gathered wholesome herbs, which I boiled, or ate as salads with my bread, and now and then, for a rarity, I made a little butter, and drank the whey. I was at first at a great loss for salt; but custom soon reconciled the want of it; and I am confident that the frequent use of salt among us is an effect of luxury, and was first introduced only as a provocative to drink; except where it is necessary for preserving of flesh in long voyages, or in places remote from great markets. For we observe no animal to be fond of it but man: and as to myself, when I left this country, it was a great while before I could endure the taste of it in anything that I ate.

This is enough to say upon the subject of my diet, wherewith other travellers fill their books, as if the readers were personally concerned whether we fared well or ill. However, it was necessary to mention this matter, lest the world should think it impossible that I could find sustenance for three years in such a country, and among such inhabitants.

When it grew towards evening, the master horse ordered a place for me to lodge in; it was but six yards from the house, and separated from the stable of the Yahoos. Here I got some straw, and covering myself with my own clothes, slept very sound. But I was in a short time better accommodated, as the reader shall know hereafter, when I come to treat more particularly about my way of living.

CHAPTER 3

*The author studious to learn the language, the Houyhnhnm his master
assists in teaching him. The language described. Several Houyhnhnms
of quality come out of curiosity to see the author. He gives his master
a short account of his voyage.*

My principal endeavour was to learn the language, which my
master (for so I shall henceforth call him) and his children, and
every servant of his house were desirous to teach me. For they
looked upon it as a prodigy that a brute animal should discover
such marks of a rational creature. I pointed to everything, and
enquired the name of it, which I wrote down in my journal-
book when I was alone, and corrected my bad accent, by
desiring those of the family to pronounce it often. In this
employment, a sorrel nag, one of the under servants, was very
ready to assist me.

In speaking, they pronounce through the nose and throat,
and their language approaches nearest to the High Dutch or
German, of any I know in Europe; but is much more graceful
and significant. The Emperor Charles V[7] made almost the
same observation, when he said, that if he were to speak to
his horse, it should be in High Dutch.

The curiosity and impatience of my master were so great,
that he spent many hours of his leisure to instruct me. He was
convinced (as he afterwards told me) that I must be a Yahoo,
but my teachableness, civility and cleanliness astonished him;
which were qualities altogether so opposite to those animals.
He was most perplexed about my clothes, reasoning sometimes with himself, whether they were a part of my body; for
I never pulled them off till the family were asleep, and got
them on before they waked in the morning. My master was
eager to learn from whence I came, how I acquired those
appearances of reason, which I discovered in all my actions,
and to know my story from my own mouth, which he hoped

he should soon do by the great proficiency I made in learning and pronouncing their words and sentences. To help my memory, I formed all I learned into the English alphabet, and writ the words down with the translations. This last, after some time, I ventured to do in my master's presence. It cost me much trouble to explain to him what I was doing; for the inhabitants have not the least idea of books or literature.

In about ten weeks' time I was able to understand most of his questions, and in three months could give him some tolerable answers. He was extremely curious to know from what part of the country I came, and how I was taught to imitate a rational creature, because the Yahoos (whom he saw I exactly resembled in my head, hands and face, that were only visible), with some appearance of cunning, and the strongest disposition to mischief, were observed to be the most unteachable of all brutes. I answered, that I came over the sea, from a far place, with many others of my own kind, in a great hollow vessel made of the bodies of trees. That my companions forced me to land on this coast, and then left me to shift for myself. It was with some difficulty, and by the help of many signs, that I brought him to understand me. He replied, that I must needs be mistaken, or that I *said the thing which was not*. (For they have no word in their language to express lying or falsehood.) He knew it was impossible that there could be a country beyond the sea, or that a parcel of brutes could move a wooden vessel whither they pleased upon water. He was sure no Houyhnhnm alive could make such a vessel, or would trust Yahoos to manage it.

The word *Houyhnhnm*, in their tongue, signifies a *horse*, and in its etymology, *the Perfection of Nature*. I told my master, that I was at a loss for expression, but would improve as fast as I could; and hoped in a short time I should be able to tell him wonders: he was pleased to direct his own mare, his colt and foal, and the servants of the family to take all opportunities of instructing me, and every day for two or three hours, he was at the same pains himself: several horses and mares of quality in the neighbourhood came often to our house upon the report spread of a wonderful Yahoo, that could speak like a Houyhnhnm, and seemed in his words and actions to discover some glimmerings of Reason. These delighted to converse with me; they put many questions, and received such answers as I was able to return. By all which advantages, I made so great a progress, that in five months from my arrival, I understood whatever was spoke, and could express myself tolerably well.

The Houyhnhnms who came to visit my master, out of a design of seeing and talking with me, could hardly believe me to be a right Yahoo, because my body had a different covering from others of my kind. They were astonished to observe me without the usual hair or skin, except on my head, face, and hands; but I discovered that secret to my master, upon an accident, which happened about a fortnight before.

I have already told the reader, that every night when the family were gone to bed, it was my custom to strip and cover myself with my clothes: it happened one morning early, that my master sent for me, by the sorrel nag, who was his valet; when he came, I was fast asleep, my clothes fallen off on one side, and my shirt above my waist. I awaked at the noise he made, and observed him to deliver his message in some disorder; after which he went to my master, and in a great fright gave him a very confused account of what he had seen: this I presently discovered; for going as soon as I was dressed, to pay my attendance upon his Honour, he asked me the meaning of what his servant had reported, that I was not the same thing when I slept as I appeared to be at other times; that his valet assured him, some part of me was white, some yellow, at least not so white, and some brown.

I had hitherto concealed the secret of my dress, in order to distinguish myself as much as possible, from that cursed race of Yahoos; but now I found it in vain to do so any longer.

Besides, I considered that my clothes and shoes would soon wear out, which already were in a declining condition, and must be supplied by some contrivance from the hides of Yahoos or other brutes; whereby the whole secret would be known: I therefore told my master, that in the country from whence I came, those of my kind always covered their bodies with the hairs of certain animals prepared by art, as well for decency, as to avoid inclemencies of air both hot and cold; of which, as to my own person, I would give him immediate conviction, if he pleased to command me; only desiring his excuse, if I did not expose those parts that Nature taught us to conceal. He said my discourse was all very strange, but especially the last part; for he could not understand why Nature should teach us to conceal what Nature had given. That neither himself nor family were ashamed of any parts of their bodies; but however I might do as I pleased. Whereupon, I first unbuttoned my coat, and pulled it off. I did the same with my waistcoat; I drew off my shoes, stockings and breeches. I let my shirt down to my waist, and drew up the bottom, fastening it like a girdle about my middle to hide my nakedness.

My master observed the whole performance with great signs of curiosity and admiration. He took up all my clothes in his pastern, one piece after another, and examined them diligently; he then stroked my body very gently, and looked round me several times, after which he said, it was plain I must be a perfect Yahoo; but that I differed very much from the rest of my species, in the softness, and whiteness, and smoothness of my skin, my want of hair in several parts of my body, the shape and shortness of my claws behind and before, and my affectation of walking continually on my two hinder feet. He desired to see no more, and gave me leave to put on my clothes again, for I was shuddering with cold.

I expressed my uneasiness at his giving me so often the appellation of *Yahoo*, an odious animal, for which I had so utter an hatred and contempt; I begged he would forbear applying that word to me, and take the same order in his family, and among his friends whom he suffered to see me. I requested likewise, that the secret of my having a false covering to my body might be known to none but himself, at least as long as my present clothing should last; for, as to what the sorrel nag his valet had observed, his Honour might command him to conceal it.

All this my master very graciously consented to, and thus the secret was kept till my clothes began to wear out, which I was forced to supply by several contrivances, that shall hereafter be mentioned. In the meantime, he desired I would go on with my utmost diligence to learn their language, because he was more astonished at my capacity for speech and reason, than at the figure of my body, whether it were covered or no; adding, that he waited with some impatience to hear the wonders which I promised to tell him.

From thenceforward he doubled the pains he had been at to instruct me; he brought me into all company, and made them treat me with civility, because, as he told them privately, this would put me into good humour, and make me more diverting.

Every day when I waited on him, beside the trouble he was at in teaching, he would ask me several questions concerning myself, which I answered as well as I could; and by those means he had already received some general ideas, though very imperfect. It would be tedious to relate the several steps, by which I advanced to a more regular conversation: but the first account I gave of myself in any order and length, was to this purpose:

That, I came from a very far country, as I already had attempted to tell him, with about fifty more of my own species; that we travelled upon the seas, in a great hollow vessel made of wood, and larger than his Honour's house. I described the ship to him in the best terms I could, and explained by the help of my handkerchief displayed, how it was driven forward by the wind. That upon a quarrel among us, I was set on shore on this coast, where I walked forward without knowing whither, till he delivered me from the persecution of those execrable Yahoos. He asked me, who made the ship, and how it was possible that the Houyhnhnms of my country would leave it to the management of brutes? My answer was, that I durst proceed no farther in my relation, unless he would give me his word and honour that he would not be offended, and then I would tell him the wonders I had so often promised. He agreed; and I went on by assuring him, that the ship was made by creatures like myself, who in all the countries I had travelled, as well as in my own, were the only governing, rational animals; and that upon my arrival hither, I was as much astonished to see the Houyhnhnms act like rational beings, as he or his friends could be in finding some marks of reason in a creature he was pleased to call a Yahoo, to which I owned my resemblance in every part, but could not account for their degenerate and brutal nature. I said farther, that if good fortune ever restored me to my native country, to relate my travels hither, as I resolved to do, everybody would believe that I *said the thing which was not*; that I invented the story out of my own head; and with all possible respect to himself, his family, and friends, and under his promise of not being offended, our countrymen would hardly think it probable, that a Houyhnhnm should be the presiding creature of a nation, and a Yahoo the brute.

CHAPTER 4

The Houyhnhnms' notion of truth and falsehood. The author's discourse disapproved by his master. The author gives a more particular account of himself, and the accidents of his voyage.

MY master heard me with great appearances of uneasiness in his countenance, because *doubting* or *not believing*, are so little known in this country, that the inhabitants cannot tell how to behave themselves under such circumstances. And I remember in frequent discourses with my master concerning the nature of manhood,[8] in other parts of the world, having occasion to talk of *lying*, and *false representation*, it was with much difficulty that he comprehended what I meant, although he had otherwise a most acute judgement. For he argued thus; That the use of speech was to make us understand one another, and to receive information of facts; now if any one *said the thing which was not*, these ends were defeated; because I cannot properly be said to understand him, and I am so far from receiving information, that he leaves me worse than in ignorance, for I am led to believe a thing *black* when it is *white*, and *short* when it is *long*. And these were all the notions he had concerning that faculty of *lying*, so perfectly well understood, and so universally practised among human creatures.

To return from this digression; when I asserted that the Yahoos were the only governing animal in my country, which my master said was altogether past his conception, he desired to know, whether we had Houyhnhnms among us, and what was their employment: I told him, we had great numbers, that in summer they grazed in the fields, and in winter were kept in houses, with hay and oats, where Yahoo servants were employed to rub their skins smooth, comb their manes, pick their feet, serve them with food, and make their beds. I understand you well, said my master; it is now very plain, from all you have spoken, that whatever share of reason the

Yahoos pretend to, the Houyhnhnms are your masters; I heartily wish our Yahoos would be so tractable. I begged his Honour would please to excuse me from proceeding any farther, because I was very certain that the account he expected from me would be highly displeasing. But he insisted in commanding me to let him know the best and the worst: I told him, he should be obeyed. I owned, that the Houyhnhnms among us, whom we called *horses*, were the most generous and comely animal we had, that they excelled in strength and swiftness; and when they belonged to persons of quality, employed in travelling, racing, or drawing chariots, they were treated with much kindness and care, till they fell into diseases, or became foundered in the feet; but then they were sold, and used to all kind of drudgery till they died; after which their skins were stripped and sold for what they were worth, and their bodies left to be devoured by dogs and birds of prey. But the common race of horses had not so good fortune, being kept by farmers and carriers and other mean people, who put them to greater labour, and fed them worse. I described as well as I could, our way of riding, the shape and use of a bridle, a saddle, a spur, and a whip, of harness and wheels. I added, that we fastened plates of a certain hard substance called *iron* at the bottom of their feet, to preserve their hoofs from being broken by the stony ways on which we often travelled.

My master, after some expressions of great indignation, wondered how we dared to venture upon a Houyhnhnm's back, for he was sure that the weakest servant in his house would be able to shake off the strongest Yahoo, or by lying down, and rolling upon his back, squeeze the brute to death. I answered, that our horses were trained up from three or four years old to the several uses we intended them for; that if any of them proved intolerably vicious, they were employed for carriages; that they were severely beaten while they were young, for any mischievous tricks; that the males, designed for the common use of riding or draught, were generally *castrated* about two years after their birth, to take down their spirits, and make them more tame and gentle; that they were indeed sensible of rewards and punishments; but his Honour would please to consider, that they had not the least tincture of reason any more than the Yahoos in this country.

It put me to the pains of many circumlocutions to give my master a right idea of what I spoke; for their language doth not abound in variety of words, because their wants and passions are fewer than among us. But it is impossible to express his noble resentment at our savage treatment of the Houyhnhnm race, particularly after I had explained the manner and use of *castrating* horses among us, to hinder them from propagating their kind, and to render them more servile. He said, if it were possible there could be any country where Yahoos alone were endued with Reason, they certainly must be the governing animal, because Reason will in time always prevail against brutal strength. But, considering the frame of our bodies, and especially of mine, he thought no creature of equal bulk was so ill-contrived for employing that Reason in the common offices of life; whereupon he desired to know whether those among whom I lived, resembled me or the Yahoos of his country. I assured him, that I was as well shaped as most of my age: but the younger and the females were much more soft and tender, and the skins of the latter generally as white as milk. He said, I differed indeed from other Yahoos, being much more cleanly, and not altogether so deformed, but in point of real advantage, he thought I differed for the worse. That my nails were of no use either to my fore or hinder feet; as to my fore-feet, he could not properly call them by that name, for he never observed me to walk upon them; that they were too soft to bear the ground; that I generally went with them uncovered, neither was the covering I sometimes wore on them of the same shape, or so strong as that on my feet behind. That I could not walk with any security, for if either of my hinder feet slipped, I must inevitably fall. He then began to find fault with other parts of my body, the flatness of my face, the prominence of my nose, mine eyes placed directly in front, so that I could not look on either side without turning my head: that I was not able to feed myself, without lifting one of my fore-feet to my mouth: and therefore Nature had placed those joints to answer that necessity. He knew not what could be the use of those several clefts and divisions in my feet behind; that these were too soft to bear the hardness and sharpness of stones without a covering made from the skin of some other brute; that my whole body wanted a fence against heat and cold, which I was forced to put on and off every day with tediousness and trouble. And lastly, that he observed every animal in this country naturally to abhor the Yahoos, whom the weaker avoided, and the stronger drove from them. So that supposing us to have the gift of Reason, he could not see how it were possible to cure that natural antipathy which every creature discovered against us; nor consequently, how we could tame and render them serviceable. However, he would (as he said) debate that matter no farther, because he was more desirous to know my own story, the country where I was born, and the several actions and events of my life before I came hither.

I assured him, how extremely desirous I was that he should be satisfied in every point; but I doubted much, whether it would be possible for me to explain myself on several subjects whereof his Honour could have no conception, because I saw nothing in his country to which I could resemble them. That however, I would do my best, and strive to express myself by similitudes, humbly desiring his assistance when I wanted proper words; which he was pleased to promise me.

I said, my birth was of honest parents, in an island called England, which was remote from this country, as many days' journey as the strongest of his Honour's servants could travel in the annual course of the sun. That I was bred a surgeon, whose trade it is to cure wounds and hurts in the body, got by accident or violence; that my country was governed by a female man, whom we called a *Queen*. That I left it to get riches, whereby I might maintain myself and family when I should return. That in my last voyage, I was commander of the ship, and had about fifty Yahoos under me, many of which died at sea, and I was forced to supply them by others picked out from several nations. That our ship was twice in danger of being sunk; the first time by a great storm, and the second, by striking against a rock. Here my master interposed, by asking me, How I could persuade strangers out of different countries to venture with me, after the losses I had sustained, and the hazards I had run. I said, they were fellows of desperate fortunes, forced to fly from the places of their birth, on account of their poverty or their crimes. Some were undone by lawsuits; others spent all they had in drinking, whoring, and gaming; others fled for treason; many for murder, theft, poisoning, robbery, perjury, forgery, coining false money, for committing rapes or sodomy, for flying from their colours, or deserting to the enemy, and most of them had broken prison; none of these durst return to their native countries for fear of being hanged, or of starving in a jail; and therefore were under a necessity of seeking a livelihood in other places.

During this discourse, my master was pleased often to interrupt me. I had made use of many circumlocutions in describing to him the nature of the several crimes, for which most of our crew had been forced to fly their country. This labour took up several days' conversation before he was able to comprehend me. He was wholly at a loss to know what could be the use or necessity of practising those vices. To clear up which I endeavoured to give him some ideas of the desire of power and riches, of the terrible effects of lust, intemperance, malice and envy. All this I was forced to define and describe by putting of cases, and making suppositions.

After which, like one whose imagination was struck with something never seen or heard of before, he would lift up his eyes with amazement and indignation. Power, government, war, law, punishment, and a thousand other things had no terms, wherein that language could express them, which made the difficulty almost insuperable to give my master any conception of what I meant. But being of an excellent understanding, much improved by contemplation and converse, he at last arrived at a competent knowledge of what human nature in our parts of the world is capable to perform, and desired I would give him some particular account of that land, which we call Europe, but especially, of my own country.

CHAPTER 5

The author at his master's commands informs him of the state of England. The causes of war among the Princes of Europe. The author begins to explain the English Constitution.

THE reader may please to observe, that the following extract of many conversations I had with my master, contains a summary of the most material points, which were discoursed at several times for above two years; his Honour often desiring fuller satisfaction as I farther improved in the Houyhnhnm tongue. I laid before him, as well as I could, the whole state of Europe; I discoursed of trade and manufactures, of arts and sciences; and the answers I gave to all the questions he made, as they arose upon several subjects, were a fund of conversation not to be exhausted. But I shall here only set down the substance of what passed between us concerning my own country, reducing it into order as well as I can, without any regard to time or other circumstances, while I strictly adhere to truth. My only concern is, that I shall hardly be able to do justice to my master's arguments and expressions, which must needs suffer by my want of capacity, as well as by a translation into our barbarous English.

In obedience therefore to his Honour's commands, I related to him the Revolution[9] under the Prince of Orange, the long war with France entered into by the said Prince, and renewed by his successor the present Queen, wherein the greatest powers of Christendom were engaged, and which still continued: I computed, at his request, that about a million of Yahoos might have been killed in the whole progress of it, and perhaps a hundred or more cities taken, and five times as many ships burnt or sunk.

He asked me what were the usual causes or motives that made one country go to war with another. I answered they were innumerable, but I should only mention a few of the chief. Sometimes the ambition of princes, who never think they have land or people enough to govern: sometimes the corruption of ministers, who engage their master in a war in order to stifle or divert the clamour of the subjects against their evil administration. Difference in opinions[10] hath cost many millions of lives: for instance, whether *flesh* be *bread,* or *bread* be *flesh*; whether the juice of a certain *berry* be *blood* or *wine*; whether *whistling* be a vice or a virtue; whether it be better to *kiss a post,* or throw it into the fire; what is the best colour for a *coat,* whether *black, white, red* or *grey*; and whether it should be *long* or *short, narrow* or *wide, dirty* or *clean,* with many more. Neither are any wars so furious and bloody, or of so long continuance, as those occasioned by difference in opinion, especially if it be in things indifferent.

Sometimes the quarrel between two princes is to decide which of them shall dispossess a third of his dominions, where neither of them pretend to any right. Sometimes one prince quarrelleth with another, for fear the other should quarrel with him. Sometimes a war is entered upon, because the enemy is too *strong,* and sometimes because he is too *weak.* Sometimes our neighbours *want* the *things* which we *have,* or *have* the *things* which we *want*; and we both fight, till they take ours or give us theirs. It is a very justifiable cause of war to invade a country after the people have been wasted by famine, destroyed by pestilence, or embroiled by factions amongst themselves. It is justifiable to enter into a war against our nearest ally, when one of his towns lies convenient for us, or a territory of land, that would render our dominions round and compact. If a prince send forces into a nation where the people are poor and ignorant, he may lawfully put half of them to death, and make slaves of the rest, in order to civilize and reduce them from their barbarous way of living. It is a very kingly, honourable, and frequent practice, when one prince desires the assistance of another to secure him against an invasion, that the assistant, when he hath driven out the invader, should seize on the dominions himself, and kill, imprison or banish the prince he came to relieve. Alliance by blood or marriage is a sufficient cause of war between princes, and the nearer the kindred is, the greater is their disposition to quarrel: *poor* nations are *hungry*, and *rich* nations are *proud*, and pride and hunger will ever be at variance. For these reasons, the trade of a *soldier* is held the most honourable of all others: because a *soldier* is a Yahoo hired to kill in cold blood as many of his own species, who have never offended him, as possibly he can.

There is likewise a kind of beggarly princes in Europe, not able to make war by themselves, who hire out their troops [11] to richer nations, for so much a day to each man; of which they keep three fourths to themselves, and it is the best part of their maintenance; such are those in Germany and other northern parts of Europe.

What you have told me (said my master), upon the subject of war, doth indeed discover most admirably the effects of that Reason you pretend to: however, it is happy that the *shame* is greater than the *danger*; and that Nature hath left you utterly uncapable of doing much mischief. For your mouths lying flat with your faces, you can hardly bite each other to any purpose, unless by consent. Then as to the claws upon your feet before and behind, they are so short and tender, that one of our Yahoos would drive a dozen of yours before him. And therefore in recounting the numbers of those who have been killed in battle, I cannot but think that you have *said the thing which is not*.

I could not forbear shaking my head and smiling a little at his ignorance. And, being no stranger to the art of war, I gave him a description of cannons, culverins, muskets, carabines, pistols, bullets, powder, swords, bayonets, battles, sieges, retreats, attacks, undermines, countermines, bombardments, sea-fights; ships sunk with a thousand men, twenty thousand killed on each side; dying groans, limbs flying in the air, smoke, noise, confusion, trampling to death under horses' feet; flight, pursuit, victory; fields strewed with carcasses left for food to dogs, and wolves, and birds of prey; plundering, stripping, ravishing, burning, and destroying. And to set forth the valour of my own dear countrymen, I assured him, that I had seen them blow up a hundred enemies at once in a siege, and as many in a ship, and beheld the dead bodies drop down in pieces from the clouds, to the great diversion of all the spectators.

I was going on to more particulars, when my master commanded me silence. He said, whoever understood the nature of Yahoos might easily believe it possible for so vile an animal to be capable of every action I had named, if their strength and cunning equalled their malice. But as my discourse had increased his abhorrence of the whole species, so he found it gave him a disturbance in his mind, to which he was wholly a stranger before. He thought his ears being used to such abominable words, might by degrees admit them with less detestation. That although he hated the Yahoos of this country, yet he no more blamed them for their odious qualities, than he did a *gnnayh* (a bird of prey) for its cruelty, or a sharp stone for cutting his hoof. But when a creature pretending to Reason could be capable of such enormities, he dreaded lest the corruption of that faculty might be worse than brutality itself. He seemed therefore confident, that instead of Reason, we were only possessed of some quality fitted to increase our natural vices; as the reflection from a troubled stream returns the image of an ill-shapen body, not only *larger*, but more *distorted*.

He added, that he had heard too much upon the subject of war, both in this, and some former discourses. There was another point which a little perplexed him at present. I had said, that some of our crew left their country on account of being ruined by *law*; that I had already explained the meaning of the word; but he was at a loss how it should come to pass, that the *law* which was intended for *every* man's preservation, should be any man's ruin. Therefore he desired to be farther satisfied what I meant by *law*, and the dispensers thereof, according to the present practice in my own country; because he thought Nature and Reason were sufficient guides for a reasonable animal, as we pretended to be, in showing us what we ought to do, and what to avoid.

I assured his Honour, that law was a science wherein I had not much conversed, further than by employing advocates in vain, upon some injustices that had been done me; however, I would give him all the satisfaction I was able.

I said there was a society of men among us, bred up from their youth in the art of proving by words multiplied for the purpose, that white is black, and black is white, according as they are paid. To this society all the rest of the people are slaves. For example, if my neighbour hath a mind to my cow, he hires a lawyer to prove that he ought to have my cow from me. I must then hire another to defend my right, it being against all rules of law that any man should be allowed to speak for himself. Now in this case, I who am the true owner lie under two great disadvantages. First, my lawyer, being practised almost from his cradle in defending falsehood, is quite out of his element when he would be an advocate for justice, which as an office unnatural, he always attempts with great awkwardness, if not with ill-will. The second disadvantage is, that my lawyer must proceed with great caution, or else he will be reprimanded by the Judges, and abhorred by his brethren, as one who would lessen the practice of the law. And therefore I have but two methods to preserve my cow. The first is to gain over my adversary's lawyer with a double fee, who will then betray his client by insinuating that he hath justice on his side. The second way is for my lawyer to make my cause appear as unjust as he can, by allowing the cow to belong to my adversary; and this if it be skilfully done will certainly bespeak the favour of the Bench.

Now, your Honour is to know that these Judges are persons appointed to decide all controversies of property, as well as for the trial of criminals, and picked out from the most dexterous lawyers who are grown old or lazy, and having been biassed all their lives against truth and equity, lie under such a fatal necessity of favouring fraud, perjury, and oppression, that I have known several of them refuse a large bribe from the side where justice lay, rather than injure the *Faculty* [12] by doing anything unbecoming their nature or their office.

It is a maxim among these lawyers, that whatever hath been done before, may legally be done again: and therefore they take special care to record all the decisions formerly made against common justice and the general reason of mankind. These, under the name of *precedents*, they produce as authorities to justify the most iniquitous opinions; and the Judges never fail of directing accordingly.

In pleading, they studiously avoid entering into the *merits* of the cause; but are loud, violent and tedious in dwelling upon all *circumstances* which are not to the purpose. For instance, in the case already mentioned; they never desire to know what claim or title my adversary hath to my cow, but whether the said cow were red or black, her horns long or short; whether the field I graze her in be round or square, whether she were milked at home or abroad, what diseases she is subject to, and the like; after which they consult *precedents*, adjourn the cause from time to time, and in ten, twenty, or thirty years come to an issue.

It is likewise to be observed that this society hath a peculiar cant and jargon of their own, that no other mortal can understand, and wherein all their laws are written, which they take special care to multiply; whereby they have wholly confounded the very essence of truth and falsehood, of right and wrong; so that it will take thirty years to decide whether the field, left me by my ancestors for six generations, belong to me or to a stranger three hundred miles off.

In the trial of persons accused for crimes against the state the method is much more short and commendable: the Judge first sends to sound the disposition of those in power, after which he can easily hang or save the criminal, strictly preserving all the forms of law.

Here my master, interposing, said it was a pity, that creatures endowed with such prodigious abilities of mind as these lawyers, by the description I gave of them, must certainly be, were not rather encouraged to be instructors of others in wisdom and knowledge. In answer to which, I assured his Honour, that in all points out of their own trade they were usually the most ignorant and stupid generation among us, the most despicable in common conversation, avowed enemies to all knowledge and learning, and equally disposed to pervert the general reason of mankind in every other subject of discourse, as in that of their own profession.

CHAPTER 6

A continuation of the state of England. The character of a first Minister.

MY master was yet wholly at a loss to understand what motives could incite this race of lawyers to perplex, disquiet, and weary themselves by engaging in a confederacy of injustice, merely for the sake of injuring their fellow-animals; neither could he comprehend what I meant in saying they did it for *hire*. Whereupon I was at much pains to describe to him the use of *money*, the materials it was made of, and the value of the metals; that when a Yahoo had got a great store of this precious substance, he was able to purchase whatever he had a mind to, the finest clothing, the noblest houses, great tracts of land, the most costly meats and drinks, and have his choice of the most beautiful females. Therefore since *money* alone was able to perform all these feats, our Yahoos thought they could never have enough of it to spend or to save, as they found themselves inclined from their natural bent either to profusion or avarice. That the rich man enjoyed the fruit of the poor man's labour, and the latter were a thousand to one in proportion to the former. That the bulk of our people was forced to live miserably, by labouring every day for small wages to make a few live plentifully. I enlarged myself much on these and many other particulars to the same purpose: but his Honour was still to seek: for he went upon a supposition that all animals had a title to their share in the productions of the earth, and especially those who presided over the rest. Therefore he desired I would let him know, what these costly meats were, and how any of us happened to want them. Whereupon I enumerated as many sorts as came into my head, with the various methods of dressing them, which could not be done without sending vessels by sea to every part of the world, as well for liquors to drink, as for sauces, and innumerable other conveniencies. I assured him, that this whole globe of earth must be at least three times gone round, before one of our better female Yahoos could get her breakfast, or a cup to put it in. He said, That must needs be a miserable country which cannot furnish food for its own inhabitants. But what he chiefly wondered at was how such vast tracts of ground as I described should be wholly without *fresh water*, and the people put to the necessity of sending over the sea for drink. I replied, that England (the dear place of my nativity) was computed to produce three times the quantity of food more than its inhabitants are able to consume, as well as liquors extracted from grain, or pressed out of the fruit of certain trees, which made excellent drink, and the same proportion in every other convenience of life. But in order to feed the luxury and intemperance of the males, and the vanity of the females, we sent away the greatest part of our necessary things to other countries, from whence in return we brought the materials of diseases, folly, and vice, to spend among ourselves. Hence it follows of necessity, that vast numbers of our people are compelled to seek their livelihood by begging, robbing, stealing, cheating, pimping, forswearing, flattering, suborning, forging, gaming, lying, fawning, hectoring, voting, scribbling, star-gazing, poisoning, whoring, canting, libelling, free-thinking, and the like occupations: every one of which terms, I was at much pains to make him understand.

That *wine* was not imported among us from foreign countries to supply the want of water or other drinks, but because it was a sort of liquid which made us merry, by putting us out of our senses; diverted all melancholy thoughts, begat wild extravagant imaginations in the brain, raised our hopes, and banished our fears, suspended every office of reason for a time, and deprived us of the use of our limbs, till we fell into a profound sleep; although it must be confessed, that we always awaked sick and dispirited, and that the use of this liquor filled us with diseases, which made our lives uncomfortable and short.

But beside all this, the bulk of our people supported themselves by furnishing the necessities or conveniencies of life to the rich, and to each other. For instance, when I am at home and dressed as I ought to be, I carry on my body the workmanship of an hundred tradesmen; the building and furniture of my house employ as many more, and five times the number to adorn my wife.

I was going on to tell him of another sort of people, who get their livelihood by attending the sick, having upon some occasions informed his Honour that many of my crew had died of diseases. But here it was with the utmost difficulty that I brought him to apprehend what I meant. He could easily conceive, that a Houyhnhnm grew weak and heavy a few days before his death, or by some accident might hurt a limb. But that Nature, who worketh all things to perfection, should suffer any pains to breed in our bodies, he thought impossible, and desired to know the reason of so unaccountable an evil. I told him, we fed on a thousand things which operated contrary to each other; that we ate when we were not hungry, and drank without the provocation of thirst; that we sat whole nights drinking strong liquors without eating a bit, which disposed us to sloth, inflamed our bodies, and precipitated or prevented digestion. That prostitute female Yahoos acquired a certain malady, which bred rottenness in the bones of those who fell into their embraces; that this and many other diseases were propagated from father to son, so that great numbers come into the world with complicated maladies upon them; that it would be endless to give him a catalogue of all diseases incident to human bodies; for they could not be fewer than five or six hundred, spread over every limb, and joint; in short, every part, external and intestine, having diseases appropriated to each. To remedy which, there was a sort of people bred up among us, in the profession or

pretence of curing the sick. And because I had some skill in
the faculty, I would, in gratitude to his Honour, let him know
the whole mystery and method by which they proceed.

Their fundamental is, that all diseases arise from *repletion*,
from whence they conclude, that a great *evacuation* of the body
is necessary, either through the natural passage, or upwards at
the mouth. Their next business is, from herbs, minerals, gums,
oils, shells, salts, juices, seaweed, excrements, barks of trees,
serpents, toads, frogs, spiders, dead men's flesh and bones,
birds, beasts and fishes, to form a composition for smell and
taste the most abominable, nauseous and detestable that they
can possibly contrive, which the stomach immediately rejects
with loathing; and this they call a *vomit*; or else from the same
storehouse, with some other poisonous additions, they command us to take in at the orifice *above* or *below* (just as the
physician then happens to be disposed), a medicine equally
annoying and disgustful to the bowels, which, relaxing the
belly, drives down all before it; and this they call a *purge*, or a
clyster. For Nature (as the physicians allege) having intended
the superior anterior orifice only for the *intromission* of solids
and liquids, and the inferior posterior for ejection, these
artists ingeniously considering that in all diseases Nature is
forced out of her seat; therefore to replace her in it, the body
must be treated in a manner directly contrary, by interchang-
ing the use of each orifice, forcing solids and liquids in at the
anus, and making evacuations at the mouth.

But, besides real diseases, we are subject to many that are
only imaginary, for which the physicians have invented
imaginary cures; these have their several names, and so have
the drugs that are proper for them, and with these our female
Yahoos are always infested.

One great excellency in this tribe is their skill at *prognostics*,
wherein they seldom fail; their predictions in real diseases,
when they rise to any degree of malignity, generally portend-
ing *death*, which is always in their power, when recovery is not:

and therefore, upon any unexpected signs of amendment, after they have pronounced their sentence, rather than be accused as false prophets, they know how to approve their sagacity to the world by a seasonable dose.

They are likewise of special use to husbands and wives who are grown weary of their mates, to eldest sons, to great ministers of state, and often to princes.

I had formerly upon occasion discoursed with my master upon the nature of *government* in general, and particularly of our own *excellent Constitution,* deservedly the wonder and envy of the whole world. But having here accidentally mentioned a *Minister of State*, he commanded me some time after to inform him, what species of Yahoo I particularly meant by that appellation.

I told him, that a *First* or *Chief Minister of State,* whom I intended to describe, was a creature wholly exempt from joy and grief, love and hatred, pity and anger; at least made use of no other passions but a violent desire of wealth, power, and titles; that he applies his words to all uses, except to the indication of his mind; that he never tells a *truth,* but with an intent that you should take it for a *lie*; nor a *lie*, but with a design that you should take it for a *truth*; that those he speaks worst of behind their backs are in the surest way to preferment; and whenever he begins to praise you to others or to yourself, you are from that day forlorn.[13] The worst mark you can receive is a *promise*, especially when it is confirmed with an oath; after which every wise man retires, and gives over all hopes.

There are three methods by which a man may rise to be Chief Minister: the first is, by knowing how with prudence to dispose of a wife, a daughter, or a sister: the second, by betraying or undermining his predecessor: and the third is, by a *furious zeal* in public assemblies against the corruptions of the Court. But a wise prince would rather choose to employ those who practise the last of these methods; because such zealots prove always the most obsequious and subservient to the will and passions of their master. That the *Ministers* having all employments at their disposal, preserve themselves in power by bribing the majority of a senate or great council; and at last, by an expedient called an *Act of Indemnity* [14] (whereof I described the nature to him) they secure themselves from after-reckonings, and retire from the public, laden with the spoils of the nation.

The palace of a *Chief Minister* is a seminary to breed up others in his own trade: the pages, lackeys, and porter, by imitating their master, become *Ministers of State* in their several districts, and learn to excel in the three principal *ingredients*, of *insolence*, *lying*, and *bribery*. Accordingly, they have a *subaltern* court paid to them by persons of the best rank, and sometimes by the force of dexterity and impudence arrive through several gradations to be successors to their lord.

He is usually governed by a decayed wench or favourite footman, who are the tunnels through which all graces are conveyed, and may properly be called, *in the last resort*, the governors of the kingdom.

One day my master, having heard me mention the *nobility* of my country, was pleased to make me a compliment which I could not pretend to deserve: that he was sure I must have been born of some noble family, because I far exceeded in shape, colour, and cleanliness, all the Yahoos of his nation, although I seemed to fail in strength and agility, which must be imputed to my different way of living from those other brutes, and besides, I was not only endowed with a faculty of speech, but likewise with some rudiments of Reason, to a degree, that with all his acquaintance I passed for a prodigy.

He made me observe, that among the Houyhnhnms, the *white*, the *sorrel*, and the *iron-grey* were not so exactly shaped as the *bay*, the *dapple-grey*, and the *black*; nor born with equal talents of mind, or a capacity to improve them; and therefore continued always in the condition of servants, without ever aspiring to match out of their own race, which in that country would be reckoned monstrous and unnatural.

I made his Honour my most humble acknowledgements for the good opinion he was pleased to conceive of me; but assured him at the same time, that my birth was of the lower sort, having been born of plain honest parents, who were just able to give me a tolerable education: that *nobility* among us was altogether a different thing from the idea he had of it; that our young *noblemen* are bred from their childhood in idleness and luxury; that as soon as years will permit, they consume their vigour and contract odious diseases among lewd females; and when their fortunes are almost ruined, they marry some woman of mean birth, disagreeable person, and unsound constitution, merely for the sake of money, whom they hate and despise. That the productions of such marriages are generally scrofulous, rickety, or deformed children, by which means the family seldom continues above three generations, unless the wife take care to provide a healthy father among her neighbours or domestics, in order to improve and continue the breed. That a weak diseased body, a meagre countenance, and sallow complexion are the true marks of *noble blood*; and a healthy robust appearance is so disgraceful in a man of quality, that the world concludes his real father to have been a groom, or a coachman. The imperfections of his mind run parallel with those of his body, being a composition of spleen, dullness, ignorance, caprice, sensuality, and pride.

Without the consent of this *illustrious body* no law can be enacted, repealed, or altered, and these nobles have likewise the decision of all our possessions without appeal.

CHAPTER 7

The author's great love of his native country. His master's observations upon the Constitution and Administration of England, as described by the author, with parallel cases and comparisons. His master's observations upon human nature.

THE reader may be disposed to wonder how I could prevail on myself to give so free a representation of my own species, among a race of mortals who were already too apt to conceive the vilest opinion of human kind from that entire congruity betwixt me and their Yahoos. But I must freely confess, that the many virtues of those excellent *quadrupeds*, placed in opposite view to human corruptions, had so far opened mine eyes and enlarged my understanding, that I began to view the actions and passions of man in a very different light, and to think the honour of my own kind not worth managing;[15] which, besides, it was impossible for me to do before a person of so acute a judgement as my master, who daily convinced me of a thousand faults in myself, whereof I had not the least perception before, and which with us would never be numbered even among human infirmities. I had likewise learned from his example an utter detestation of all falsehood or disguise; and *truth* appeared so amiable to me, that I determined upon sacrificing everything to it.

Let me deal so candidly with the reader, as to confess, that there was yet a much stronger motive for the freedom I took in my representation of things. I had not been a year in this country before I contracted such a love and veneration for the inhabitants, that I entered on a firm resolution never to return to human kind, but to pass the rest of my life among these admirable Houyhnhnms in the contemplation and practice of every virtue; where I could have no example or incitement to vice. But it was decreed by Fortune, my perpetual enemy, that so great a felicity should not fall to my share. However, it is now some comfort to reflect, that in what I said of my country-men, I *extenuated* their faults as much as I durst before so strict an examiner, and upon every article gave as *favourable* a turn as the matter would bear. For, indeed, who is there alive that will not be swayed by his bias and partiality to the place of his birth?

I have related the substance of several conversations I had with my master, during the greatest part of the time I had the honour to be in his service, but have indeed for brevity sake omitted much more than is here set down.

When I had answered all his questions, and his curiosity seemed to be fully satisfied, he sent for me one morning early, and commanding me to sit down at some distance (an honour which he had never before conferred upon me), he said, he had been very seriously considering my whole story, as far as it related both to myself and my country: that he looked upon us as a sort of animals to whose share, by what accident he could not conjecture, some small pittance of *Reason* had fallen, whereof we made no other use than by its assistance to aggra-vate our *natural* corruptions, and to acquire new ones which Nature had not given us. That we disarmed ourselves of the few abilities she had bestowed, had been very successful in multiplying our original wants, and seemed to spend our whole lives in vain endeavours to supply them by our own inventions. That as to myself, it was manifest I had neither the strength or agility of a common Yahoo, that I walked infirmly on my hinder feet, had found out a contrivance to make my claws of no use or defence, and to remove the hair from my chin, which was intended as a shelter from the sun and the weather. Lastly, that I could neither run with speed, nor climb trees like my *brethren* (as he called them) the Yahoos in this country.

That our institutions of *Government* and *Law* were plainly owing to our gross defects in *Reason*, and by consequence, in *Virtue*; because *Reason* alone is sufficient to govern a *rational* creature; which was therefore a character we had no pretence to challenge, even from the account I had given of my own people, although he manifestly perceived, that in order to favour them I had concealed many particulars, and often *said the thing which was not*.

He was the more confirmed in this opinion, because he observed, that as I agreed in every feature of my body with other Yahoos, except where it was to my real disadvantage in point of strength, speed and activity, the shortness of my claws, and some other particulars where Nature had no part; so from the representation I had given him of our lives, our manners, and our actions, he found as near a resemblance in the disposition of our minds. He said the Yahoos were known to hate one another more than they did any different species of animals; and the reason usually assigned, was, the odiousness of their own shapes, which all could see in the rest, but not in themselves. He had therefore begun to think it not unwise in us to *cover* our bodies, and, by that invention, conceal many of our deformities from each other, which would else be hardly supportable. But, he now found he had been mistaken, and that the dissensions of those brutes in his country were owing to the same cause with ours, as I had described them. For if (said he) you throw among five Yahoos as much food as would be sufficient for fifty, they will, instead of eating peaceably, fall together by the ears, each single one impatient to *have all to itself*; and therefore a servant was usually employed to stand by while they were feeding abroad, and those kept at home were tied at a distance from each other; that if a cow died of age or accident, before a Houyhnhnm could secure it for his own Yahoos, those in the neighbourhood would come in herds to seize it, and then would ensue such a battle as I had described, with terrible wounds made by their claws on both sides, although they seldom were able to kill one another, for want of such convenient instruments of death as we had invented. At other times the like battles have been fought between the Yahoos of several neighbourhoods without any visible cause: those of one district watching all opportunities to surprise the next before they are prepared. But if they find their project hath miscarried, they return home, and for want of enemies, engage in what I call a *civil war* among themselves.

That in some fields of his country there are certain *shining stones* of several colours, whereof the Yahoos are violently fond, and when part of these *stones* are fixed in the earth, as it sometimes happeneth, they will dig with their claws for whole days to get them out, and carry them away, and hide them by heaps in their kennels; but still looking round with great caution, for fear their comrades should find out their treasure. My master said, he could never discover the reason of this unnatural appetite, or how these *stones* could be of any use to a Yahoo; but now he believed it might proceed from the same principle of *avarice* which I had ascribed to mankind; that he had once, by way of experiment, privately removed a heap of these *stones* from the place where one of his Yahoos had buried it: whereupon, the sordid animal, missing his treasure, by his loud lamenting brought the whole herd to the place, there miserably howled, then fell to biting and tearing the rest, began to pine away, would neither eat, nor sleep, nor work, till he ordered a servant privately to convey the *stones* into the same hole, and hide them as before; which when his Yahoo had found, he presently recovered his spirits and good humour, but took care to remove them to a better hiding-place, and hath ever since been a very serviceable brute.

My master farther assured me, which I also observed myself, That in the fields where these *shining stones* abound, the fiercest and most frequent battles are fought, occasioned by perpetual inroads of the neighbouring Yahoos.

He said, it was common, when two Yahoos discovered such a *stone* in a field, and were contending which of them should be the proprietor, a third would take the advantage, and carry it away from them both; which my master would needs contend to have some resemblance with our *suits at law*; wherein I thought it for our credit not to undeceive him; since the decision he mentioned was much more equitable than many decrees among us: because the plaintiff and defendant there lost nothing beside the *stone* they contended for, whereas our *courts of equity* would never have dismissed the cause while either of them had anything left.

My master, continuing his discourse, said, There was nothing that rendered the Yahoos more odious, than their undistinguished [16] appetite to devour everything that came in their way, whether herbs, roots, berries, the corrupted flesh of animals, or all mingled together: and it was peculiar in their temper, that they were fonder of what they could get by rapine or stealth at a greater distance, than much better food provided for them at home. If their prey held out, they would eat till they were ready to burst, after which Nature had pointed out to them a certain *root* that gave them a general evacuation.

There was also another kind of *root* very *juicy*, but something rare and difficult to be found, which the Yahoos sought for with much eagerness, and would suck it with great delight; and it produced in them the same effects that wine hath upon us. It would make them sometimes hug, and sometimes tear one another; they would howl and grin, and chatter, and reel, and tumble, and then fall asleep in the mud.

I did indeed observe, that the Yahoos were the only animals in this country subject to any diseases; which, however, were much fewer than horses have among us, and contracted not by any ill-treatment they meet with, but by the nastiness and greediness of that sordid brute. Neither has their language any more than a general appellation for those maladies, which is borrowed from the name of the beast, and called *hnea-Yahoo*, or the *Yahoo's-evil*, and the cure prescribed is a mixture of *their own dung* and *urine* forcibly put down the Yahoo's throat.

This I have since often known to have been taken with success, and do here freely recommend it to my countrymen, for the public good, as an admirable specific against all diseases produced by repletion.

As to learning, government, arts, manufactures, and the like, my master confessed he could find little or no resemblance between the Yahoos of that country and those in ours. For, he only meant to observe what parity there was in our natures. He had heard indeed some curious Houyhnhnms observe, that in most herds there was a sort of ruling Yahoo (as among us there is generally some leading or principal stag in a park), who was always more *deformed* in body, and *mischievous in disposition*, than any of the rest. That this *leader* had usually a favourite as *like himself* as he could get, whose employment was to *lick his master's feet and posteriors, and drive the female Yahoos to his kennel*; for which he was now and then rewarded with a piece of ass's flesh. This *favourite* is hated by the whole herd, and therefore to protect himself, keeps always *near the person of his leader*. He usually continues in office till a worse can be found; but the very moment he is discarded, his successor, at the head of all the Yahoos in that district, young and old, male and female, come in a body, and discharge their excrements upon him from head to foot. But how far this might be applicable to our *Courts* and *favourites*, and *Ministers of State*, my master said I could best determine.

I durst make no return to this malicious insinuation, which debased human understanding below the sagacity of a common *hound*, who hath judgement enough to distinguish and follow the cry of the *ablest dog in the pack*, without being ever mistaken.

My master told me, there were some qualities remarkable in the Yahoos, which he had not observed me to mention, or at least very slightly, in the accounts I had given him of human kind; he said, those animals, like other brutes, had their females in common; but in this they differed, that the she-

Yahoo would admit the male while she was pregnant, and that the he's would quarrel and fight with the females as fiercely as with each other. Both which practices were such degrees of infamous brutality, that no other sensitive creature ever arrived at.

Another thing he wondered at in the Yahoos, was their strange disposition to nastiness and dirt, whereas there appears to be a natural love of cleanliness in all other animals. As to the two former accusations, I was glad to let them pass without any reply, because I had not a word to offer upon them in defence of my species, which otherwise I certainly had done from my own inclinations. But I could have easily vindicated human kind from the imputation of singularity upon the last article, if there had been any *swine* in that country (as unluckily for me there were not), which although it may be a *sweeter quadruped* than a Yahoo, cannot, I humbly conceive, in justice pretend to more cleanliness; and so his Honour himself must have owned, if he had seen their filthy way of feeding, and their custom of wallowing and sleeping in the mud.

My master likewise mentioned another quality which his servants had discovered in several Yahoos, and to him was wholly unaccountable. He said, a fancy would sometimes take a Yahoo to retire into a corner, to lie down and howl, and groan, and spurn away all that came near him, although he were young and fat, and wanted neither food nor water; nor did the servants imagine what could possibly ail him. And the only remedy they found was to set him to hard work, after which he would infallibly come to himself. To this I was silent out of partiality to my own kind; yet here I could plainly discover the true seeds of *spleen*,[17] which only seizeth on the *lazy*, the *luxurious*, and the *rich*; who, if they were forced to undergo the *same regimen*, I would undertake for the cure.

His Honour had farther observed, that a female Yahoo would often stand behind a bank or a bush, to gaze on the young males passing by, and then appear, and hide, using many antic gestures and grimaces, at which time it was observed, that she had a most *offensive smell*; and when any of the males advanced, would slowly retire, looking often back, and with a counterfeit show of fear, run off into some convenient place where she knew the male would follow her.

At other times if a female stranger came among them, three or four of her own sex would get about her, and stare and chatter, and grin, and smell her all over, and then turn off with gestures that seemed to express contempt and disdain.

Perhaps my master might refine a little in these speculations, which he had drawn from what he observed himself, or had been told him by others: however, I could not reflect without some amazement, and much sorrow, that the rudiments of *lewdness*, *coquetry*, *censure*, and *scandal*, should have place by instinct in womankind.

I expected every moment that my master would accuse the Yahoos of those unnatural appetites in both sexes, so common among us. But Nature it seems hath not been so expert a schoolmistress; and these politer pleasures are entirely the productions of art and reason, on our side of the globe.

CHAPTER 8

The author relateth several particulars of the Yahoos. The great virtues of the Houyhnhnms. The education and exercise of their youth. Their general Assembly.

As I ought to have understood human nature much better than I supposed it possible for my master to do, so it was easy to apply the character he gave of the Yahoos to myself and my countrymen, and I believed I could yet make farther discoveries from my own observation. I therefore often begged his Honour to let me go among the herds of Yahoos in the neighbourhood, to which he always very graciously consented, being perfectly convinced that the hatred I bore those brutes would never suffer me to be corrupted by them; and his Honour ordered one of his servants, a strong sorrel nag, very honest and good-natured, to be my guard, without whose protection I durst not undertake such adventures. For I have already told the reader how much I was pestered by those odious animals upon my first arrival. I afterwards failed very narrowly three or four times of falling into their clutches, when I happened to stray at any distance without my hanger. And I have reason to believe they had some imagination that I was of their own species, which I often assisted myself, by stripping up my sleeves, and showing my naked arms and breast in their sight, when my protector was with me. At which times they would approach as near as they durst, and imitate my actions after the manner of monkeys, but ever with great signs of hatred, as a tame *jackdaw*, with cap and stockings, is always persecuted by the wild ones, when he happens to be got among them.

They are prodigiously nimble from their infancy; however, I once caught a young male of three years old, and endeavoured by all marks of tenderness to make it quiet; but the little imp fell a squalling, and scratching, and biting with such violence, that I was forced to let it go, and it was high time, for a whole troop of old ones came about us at the noise, but finding the cub was safe (for away it ran), and my sorrel nag being by, they durst not venture near us. I observed the young animal's flesh to smell very rank, and the stink was somewhat between a *weasel* and a *fox*, but much more disagreeable. I forgot another circumstance (and perhaps I might have the reader's pardon, if it were wholly omitted), that while I held the odious vermin in my hands, it voided its filthy excrements of a yellow liquid substance all over my clothes; but by good fortune there was a small brook hard by, where I washed myself as clean as I could, although I durst not come into my master's presence, until I were sufficiently aired.

By what I could discover, the Yahoos appear to be the most

unteachable of all animals, their capacities never reaching higher than to draw or carry burthens. Yet I am of opinion this defect ariseth chiefly from a perverse, restive disposition. For they are cunning, malicious, treacherous and revengeful. They are strong and hardy, but of a cowardly spirit, and by consequence insolent, abject, and cruel. It is observed, that the *red-haired* of both sexes are more libidinous and mischievous than the rest, whom yet they much exceed in strength and activity.

The Houyhnhnms keep the Yahoos for present use in huts not far from the house; but the rest are sent abroad to certain fields, where they dig up roots, eat several kinds of herbs, and search about for carrion, or sometimes catch weasels and *luhimuhs* (a sort of wild rat), which they greedily devour. Nature hath taught them to dig deep holes with their nails on the side of a rising ground, wherein they lie by themselves, only the kennels of the females are larger, sufficient to hold two or three cubs.

They swim from their infancy like frogs, and are able to continue long under water, where they often take fish, which the females carry home to their young. And upon this occasion, I hope the reader will pardon my relating an odd adventure.

Being one day abroad with my protector the sorrel nag, and the weather exceeding hot, I entreated him to let me bathe in a river that was near. He consented, and I immediately stripped myself stark naked, and went down softly into the stream. It happened that a young female Yahoo, standing behind a bank, saw the whole proceeding, and inflamed by desire, as the nag and I conjectured, came running with all speed, and leaped into the water within five yards of the place where I bathed. I was never in my life so terribly frighted; the nag was grazing at some distance, not suspecting any harm. She embraced me after a most fulsome manner; I roared as loud as I could, and the nag came galloping towards me, whereupon she quitted her grasp, with the utmost reluctancy, and leaped upon the opposite bank, where she stood gazing and howling all the time I was putting on my clothes.

This was matter of diversion to my master and his family, as well as of mortification to myself. For now I could no longer deny, that I was a real Yahoo in every limb and feature, since the females had a natural propensity to me as one of their own species: neither was the hair of this brute of a red colour (which might have been some excuse for an appetite a little irregular) but black as a sloe, and her countenance did not make an appearance altogether so hideous as the rest of the kind; for, I think, she could not be above eleven years old.

Having already lived three years in this country, the reader I suppose will expect that I should, like other travellers, give him some account of the manners and customs of its inhabitants, which it was indeed my principal study to learn.

As these noble Houyhnhnms are endowed by Nature with a general disposition to all virtues, and have no conceptions or ideas of what is evil in a rational creature, so their grand maxim is, to cultivate *Reason,* and to be wholly governed by it. Neither is *Reason* among them a point problematical as with us, where men can argue with plausibility on both sides of a question; but strikes you with immediate conviction; as it must needs do where it is not mingled, obscured, or discoloured by passion and interest. I remember it was with extreme difficulty that I could bring my master to understand the meaning of the word *opinion*, or how a point could be disputable; because *Reason* taught us to affirm or deny only where we are certain; and beyond our knowledge we cannot do either. So that controversies, wranglings, disputes, and positiveness in false or dubious propositions are evils unknown among the Houyhnhnms. In the like manner, when I used to explain to him our several systems of *natural philosophy*, he would laugh that a creature pretending to *Reason* should value itself upon the knowledge of other people's conjectures, and in things where that knowledge, if it were certain, could be of no use. Wherein he agreed entirely with the sentiments of Socrates, as Plato delivers them; which I mention as the highest honour I can do that prince of philosophers. I have often since reflected what destruction such a doctrine would make in the libraries of Europe, and how many paths to fame would be then shut up in the learned world.

Friendship and benevolence are the two principal virtues among the Houyhnhnms, and these not confined to particular objects, but universal to the whole race. For a stranger from the remotest part is equally treated with the nearest neighbour, and wherever he goes, looks upon himself as at home. They preserve *decency* and *civility* in the highest degrees, but are altogether ignorant of *ceremony*. They have no fondness[18] for their colts or foals, but the care they take in educating them proceedeth entirely from the dictates of *Reason*. And I observed my master to show the same affection to his neighbour's issue that he had for his own. They will have it that *Nature* teaches them to love the whole species, and it is *Reason* only that maketh a distinction of persons, where there is a superior degree of virtue.

When the matron Houyhnhnms have produced one of each sex, they no longer accompany with their consorts, except they lose one of their issue by some casualty, which very seldom happens: but in such a case they meet again. Or when the like accident befalls a person, whose wife is past bearing, some other couple bestow him one of their own colts, and then go together a second time, till the mother be pregnant. This caution is necessary to prevent the country from being overburthened with numbers. But the race of inferior Houyhnhnms bred up to be servants is not so strictly limited upon this article; these are allowed to produce three of each sex, to be domestics in the noble families.

In their marriages they are exactly careful to choose such colours as will not make any disagreeable mixture in the breed. *Strength* is chiefly valued in the male, and *comeliness* in the female, not upon the account of *love*, but to preserve the race from degenerating; for where a female happens to excel in *strength*, a consort is chosen with regard to *comeliness*. Courtship, love, presents, jointures, settlements, have no place in their thoughts, or terms whereby to express them in their language. The young couple meet and are joined, merely because it is the determination of their parents and friends: it is what they see done every day, and they look upon it as one of the necessary actions in a reasonable being. But the violation of marriage, or any other unchastity, was never heard of: and the married pair pass their lives with the same friendship, and mutual benevolence that they bear to others of the same species who come in their way; without jealousy, fondness, quarrelling, or discontent.

In educating the youth of both sexes, their method is admirable, and highly deserveth our imitation. These are not suffered to taste a grain of *oats*, except upon certain days, till eighteen years old; nor *milk*, but very rarely; and in summer they graze two hours in the morning, and as many in the evening, which their parents likewise observe, but the servants are not allowed above half that time, and a great part of their grass is brought home, which they eat at the most convenient hours, when they can be best spared from work.

Temperance, *industry*, *exercise* and *cleanliness*, are the lessons equally enjoined to the young ones of both sexes: and my master thought it monstrous in us to give the females a different kind of education from the males, except in some articles of domestic management; whereby as he truly observed, one half of our natives were good for nothing but bringing children into the world: and to trust the care of their children to such useless animals, he said, was yet a greater instance of brutality.

But the Houyhnhnms train up their youth to strength, speed, and hardiness, by exercising them in running races up and down steep hills, or over hard stony grounds, and when they are all in a sweat, they are ordered to leap over head and ears into a pond or a river. Four times a year the youth of certain districts meet to show their proficiency in running, and leaping, and other feats of strength or agility, where the victor is rewarded with a song made in his or her praise. On this festival the servants drive a herd of Yahoos into the field, laden with hay, and oats, and milk for a repast to the Houyhnhnms; after which, these brutes are immediately driven back again, for fear of being noisome to the assembly.

Every fourth year, at the *vernal equinox,* there is a Representative Council of the whole nation, which meets in a plain about twenty miles from our house, and continueth about five or six days. Here they enquire into the state and condition of the several districts, whether they abound or be deficient in hay or oats, or cows or Yahoos? And wherever there is any want (which is but seldom) it is immediately supplied by unanimous consent and contribution. Here likewise the regulation of children is settled: as for instance, if a Houyhnhnm hath two males, he changeth one of them with another who hath two females: and when a child hath been lost by any casualty, where the mother is past breeding, it is determined what family in the district shall breed another to supply the loss.

CHAPTER 9

A grand debate at the general Assembly of the Houyhnhnms, and how it was determined. The learning of the Houyhnhnms. Their buildings. Their manner of burials. The defectiveness of their language.

ONE of these grand Assemblies was held in my time, about three months before my departure, whither my master went as the Representative of our district. In this Council was resumed their old debate, and indeed, the only debate that ever happened in their country; whereof my master after his return gave me a very particular account.

The question to be debated, was, Whether the Yahoos

should be exterminated from the face of the earth. One of the *Members* for the affirmative offered several arguments of great strength and weight, alleging, that as the Yahoos were the most filthy, noisome, and deformed animal which Nature ever produced, so they were the most restive and indocile,[19] mischievous and malicious: they would privately suck the teats of the Houyhnhnms' cows, kill and devour their cats, trample down their oats and grass, if they were not continually watched, and commit a thousand other extravagancies. He took notice of a general tradition, That Yahoos had not been always in their country: but, that many ages ago, two of these brutes appeared together upon a mountain, whether produced by the heat of the sun upon corrupted mud and slime, or from the ooze and froth of the sea, was never known. That these Yahoos engendered, and their brood in a short time grew so numerous as to overrun and infest the whole nation. That the Houyhnhnms, to get rid of this evil, made a general hunting, and at last enclosed the whole herd; and destroying the elder, every Houyhnhnm kept two young ones in a kennel, and brought them to such a degree of tameness, as an animal so savage by nature can be capable of acquiring; using them for draught and carriage. That there seemed to be much truth in this tradition, and that those creatures could not be *ylnhniamshy* (or *aborigines* of the land) because of the violent hatred the Houyhnhnms, as well as all other animals, bore them; which although their evil disposition sufficiently deserved, could never have arrived at so high a degree, if they had been *aborigines*, or else they would have long since been rooted out. That the inhabitants taking a fancy to use the service of the Yahoos, had very imprudently neglected to cultivate the breed of *asses*, which were a comely animal, easily kept, more tame and orderly, without any offensive smell, strong enough for labour, although they yield to the other in agility of body; and if their braying be no agreeable sound, it is far preferable to the horrible howlings of the Yahoos.

Several others declared their sentiments to the same purpose, when my master proposed an expedient to the assembly, whereof he had indeed borrowed the hint from me. He approved of the tradition, mentioned by the *Honourable Member* who spoke before, and affirmed, that the two Yahoos said to be first seen among them had been driven thither over the sea; that coming to land, and being forsaken by their companions, they retired to the mountains, and degenerating by degrees, became in process of time, much more savage than those of their own species in the country from whence these two originals came. The reason of his assertion was, that he had now in his possession a certain wonderful Yahoo (meaning myself), which most of them had heard of, and many of them had seen. He then related to them, how he first found me, that my body was all covered with an artificial composure of the skins and hairs of other animals: that I spoke in a language of my own, and had thoroughly learned theirs: that I had related to him the accidents which brought me thither: that when he saw me without my covering, I was an exact Yahoo in every part, only of a whiter colour, less hairy, and with shorter claws. He added, how I had endeavoured to persuade him, that in my own and other countries the Yahoos acted as the governing, rational animal, and held the Houyhnhnms in servitude: that he observed in me [20] all the qualities of a Yahoo, only a little more civilized by some tincture of Reason, which however was in a degree as far inferior to the Houyhnhnm race, as the Yahoos of their country were to me: that, among other things, I mentioned a custom we had of *castrating* Houyhnhnms when they were young, in order to render them tame; that the operation was easy and safe; that it was no shame to learn wisdom from brutes, as industry is taught by the ant, and building by the swallow. (For so I translate the word *lyhannh*, although it be a much larger fowl.) That this invention might be practised upon the younger Yahoos here, which, besides rendering them tractable and fitter for use, would in an age put an end to the whole species without destroying life. That, in the meantime the Houyhnhnms should be *exhorted* to cultivate the breed of asses, which, as they are in all respects more valuable brutes, so they have this advantage, to be fit for service at five years old, which the others are not till twelve.

This was all my master thought fit to tell me at that time, of what passed in the grand Council. But he was pleased to conceal one particular, which related personally to myself, whereof I soon felt the unhappy effect, as the reader will know in its proper place, and from whence I date all the succeeding misfortunes of my life.

The Houyhnhnms have no letters, and consequently their knowledge is all traditional. But there happening few events of any moment among a people so well united, naturally disposed to every virtue, wholly governed by Reason, and cut off from all commerce with other nations, the historical part is easily preserved without burthening their memories. I have already observed, that they are subject to no diseases, and therefore can have no need of physicians. However, they have excellent medicines composed of herbs, to cure accidental bruises and cuts in the pastern or frog of the foot by sharp stones, as well as other maims and hurts in the several parts of the body.

They calculate the year by the revolution of the sun and the moon, but use no subdivisions into weeks. They are well enough acquainted with the motions of those two luminaries, and understand the nature of *eclipses*; and this is the utmost progress of their *astronomy*.

In *poetry* they must be allowed to excel all other mortals; wherein the justness of their similes, and the minuteness, as well as exactness of their descriptions, are indeed inimitable. Their verses abound very much in both of these, and usually contain either some exalted notions of friendship and benevolence, or the praises of those who were victors in races, and other bodily exercises. Their buildings, although very rude and simple, are not inconvenient, but well contrived to defend them from all injuries of cold and heat. They have a kind of tree, which at forty years old loosens in the root, and falls with the first storm; it grows very straight, and being pointed like stakes with a sharp stone (for the Houyhnhnms know not the use of iron), they stick them erect in the ground about ten inches asunder, and then weave in oat-straw, or sometimes wattles betwixt them. The roof is made after the same manner, and so are the doors.

The Houyhnhnms use the hollow part between the pastern and the hoof of their fore-feet as we do our hands, and this with greater dexterity than I could at first imagine. I have seen a white mare of our family thread a needle (which I lent her on purpose) with that joint. They milk their cows, reap their oats, and do all the work which requires hands, in the same manner. They have a kind of hard flints, which by grinding against other stones, they form into instruments, that serve instead of wedges, axes, and hammers. With tools made of these flints they likewise cut their hay, and reap their oats, which there groweth naturally in several fields: the Yahoos draw home the sheaves in carriages, and the servants tread them in certain covered huts, to get out the grain, which is kept in stores. They make a rude kind of earthen and wooden vessels, and bake the former in the sun.

If they can avoid casualties, they die only of old age, and are buried in the obscurest places that can be found, their friends and relations expressing neither joy nor grief at their departure; nor does the dying person discover the least regret that he is leaving the world, any more than if he were upon returning home from a visit to one of his neighbours; I remember, my master having once made an appointment with a friend and his family to come to his house upon some affair of importance, on the day fixed, the mistress and her two children came very late; she made two excuses, first for her husband, who, as she said, happened that very morning to *lhnuwnh*. The word is strongly expressive in their language, but not easily rendered into English; it signifies, *to retire to his first mother*. Her excuse for not coming sooner, was, that her husband dying late in the morning, she was a good while consulting her servants about a convenient place where his body should be laid; and I observed she behaved herself at our house as cheerfully as the rest: she died about three months after.

They live generally to seventy or seventy-five years, very seldom to fourscore: some weeks before their death they feel a gradual decay, but without pain. During this time they are much visited by their friends, because they cannot go abroad with their usual ease and satisfaction. However, about ten days before their death, which they seldom fail in computing, they return the visits that have been made them by those who are nearest in the neighbourhood, being carried in a convenient sledge drawn by Yahoos, which vehicle they use, not only upon this occasion, but when they grow old, upon long journeys, or when they are lamed by an accident. And therefore when the dying Houyhnhnms return those visits, they take a solemn leave of their friends, as if they were going to some remote part of the country, where they designed to pass the rest of their lives.

I know not whether it may be worth observing, that the Houyhnhnms have no word in their language to express anything that is *evil*, except what they borrow from the deformities or ill qualities of the Yahoos. Thus they denote the folly of a servant, an omission of a child, a stone that cuts their feet, a continuance of foul or unseasonable weather, and the like, by adding to each the epithet of *yahoo*. For instance, *hhnm yahoo*, *whnaholm yahoo*, *ynlhmnawihlma yahoo*, and an ill-contrived house, *ynholmhnmrohlnw yahoo*.

I could with great pleasure enlarge farther upon the manners and virtues of this excellent people; but intending in a short time to publish a volume by itself expressly upon that subject, I refer the reader thither. And in the meantime, proceed to relate my own sad catastrophe.

CHAPTER 10

The author's economy and happy life among the Houyhnhnms. His great improvement in virtue, by conversing with them. Their conversations. The author hath notice given him by his master that he must depart from the country. He falls into a swoon for grief, but submits. He contrives and finishes a canoe, by the help of a fellow-servant, and puts to sea at a venture.

I HAD settled my little economy to my own heart's content. My master had ordered a room to be made for me after their manner, about six yards from the house, the sides and floors of which I plastered with clay, and covered with rush mats of my own contriving; I had beaten hemp, which there grows wild, and made of it a sort of ticking: this I filled with the feathers of several birds I had taken with springes made of Yahoos' hairs, and were excellent food. I had worked two chairs with my knife, the sorrel nag helping me in the grosser and more laborious part. When my clothes were worn to rags, I made myself others with the skins of rabbits, and of a certain beautiful animal about the same size, called *nnuhnoh*, the skin of which is covered with a fine down. Of these I likewise made very tolerable stockings. I soled my shoes with wood which I cut from a tree, and fitted to the upper leather, and when this was worn out, I supplied it with the skins of Yahoos dried in the sun. I often got honey out of hollow trees, which I mingled with water, or ate it with my bread. No man could more verify the truth of these two maxims, *That nature is very easily satisfied*; and, *That necessity is the mother of invention*. I enjoyed perfect health of body and tranquillity of mind; I did not feel the treachery or inconstancy of a friend, nor the injuries of a secret or open enemy. I had no occasion of bribing, flattering or pimping, to procure the favour of any great man or of his minion. I wanted no fence against fraud or oppression; here was neither physician to destroy my body, nor lawyer to ruin my fortune; no informer to watch my words and actions, or forge accusations against me for hire: here were no gibers, censurers, backbiters, pickpockets, highwaymen, housebreakers, attorneys, bawds, buffoons, gamesters, politicians, wits, splenetics, tedious talkers, controvertists, ravishers, murderers, robbers, virtuosos; no leaders or followers of party and faction; no encouragers to vice, by seducement or examples: no dungeon, axes, gibbets, whipping-posts, or pillories; no cheating shopkeepers or mechanics: no pride, vanity, or affectation: no fops, bullies, drunkards, strolling whores, or poxes: no ranting, lewd, expensive wives: no stupid, proud pendants: no importunate, overbearing, quarrelsome, noisy, roaring, empty, conceited, swearing companions: no scoundrels, raised from the dust upon the merit of their vices, or nobility thrown into it on account of their virtues: no Lords, fiddlers, Judges or dancing-masters.

I had the favour of being admitted to several Houyhnhnms, who came to visit or dine with my master; where his Honour graciously suffered me to wait in the room, and listen to their discourse. Both he and his company would often descend to ask me questions, and receive my answers. I had also sometimes the honour of attending my master in his visits to others. I never presumed to speak, except in answer to a question, and then I did it with inward regret, because it was a loss of so much time for improving myself: but I was infinitely delighted with the station of an humble auditor in such conversations, where nothing passed but what was useful, expressed in the fewest and most significant words: where (as I have already said) the greatest *decency* was observed, without the least degree of ceremony; where no person spoke without being pleased himself, and pleasing his companions: where there was no interruption, tediousness, heat, or difference of sentiments. They have a notion, that when people are met together, a short silence doth much improve conversation: this I found to be true; for during those little intermissions of talk, new ideas would arise in their minds, which very much enlivened the discourse. Their subjects are generally on friendship and benevolence, or order and economy, sometimes upon the visible operations of Nature, or ancient traditions, upon the bounds and limits of virtue, upon the unerring rules of Reason, or upon some determinations to be taken at the next great Assembly, and often upon the various excellencies of *poetry*. I may add without vanity, that my presence often gave them sufficient matter for discourse, because it afforded my master an occasion of letting his friends into the history of me and my country, upon which they were all pleased to descant in a manner not very advantageous to human kind; and for that reason I shall not repeat what they said: only I may be allowed to observe, that his Honour, to my great admiration, appeared to understand the nature of Yahoos much better than myself. He went through all our vices and follies, and discovered many which I had never mentioned to him, by only supposing what qualities a Yahoo of their country, with a small proportion of Reason, might be capable of exerting; and concluded, with too much probability, how vile as well as miserable such a creature must be.

I freely confess, that all the little knowledge I have of any value, was acquired by the lectures I received from my master, and from hearing the discourses of him and his friends; to which I should be prouder to listen, than to dictate to the greatest and wisest assembly in Europe. I admired the strength, comeliness, and speed of the inhabitants; and such a constellation of virtues in such amiable persons produced in me the highest veneration. At first, indeed, I did not feel that natural awe which the Yahoos and all other animals bear towards them, but it grew upon me by degrees, much sooner than I imagined, and was mingled with a respectful love and gratitude, that they would condescend to distinguish me from the rest of my species.

When I thought of my family, my friends, my countrymen, or human race in general, I considered them as they really were, Yahoos in shape and disposition, perhaps a little more civilized, and qualified with the gift of speech, but making no other use of Reason, than to improve and multiply those vices, whereof their brethren in this country had only the share that Nature allotted them. When I happened to behold the reflection of my own form in a lake or a fountain, I turned away my face in horror and detestation of myself, and could better endure the sight of a common Yahoo, than of my own person. By conversing with the Houyhnhnms, and looking upon them with delight, I fell to imitate their gait and gesture, which is now grown into a habit, and my friends often tell me in a blunt way, that *I trot like a horse*; which, however, I take for a great compliment: neither shall I disown, that in speaking I am apt to fall into the voice and manner of the Houyhnhnms, and hear myself ridiculed on that account without the least mortification.

In the midst of all this happiness, when I looked upon myself to be fully settled for life, my master sent for me one morning a little earlier than his usual hour. I observed by his countenance that he was in some perplexity, and at a loss how to begin what he had to speak. After a short silence, he told me, He did not know how I would take what he was going to say; that in the last general Assembly, when the affair of the Yahoos was entered upon, the Representatives had taken offence at his keeping a Yahoo (meaning myself) in his family more like a Houyhnhnm, than a brute animal. That he was known frequently to converse with me, as if he could receive some advantage or pleasure in my company: that such a practice was not agreeable to Reason or Nature, or a thing ever heard of before among them. The Assembly did therefore *exhort* him, either to employ me like the rest of my species, or command me to swim back to the place from whence I came. That the first of these expedients was utterly rejected by all the Houyhnhnms who had ever seen me at his house or their own: for they alleged, that because I had some rudiments of Reason, added to the natural pravity of those animals, it was to be feared, I might be able to seduce them into the woody and mountainous parts of the country, and bring them in troops by night to destroy the Houyhnhnms' cattle, as being naturally of the ravenous kind, and averse from labour.

My master added, that he was daily pressed by the Houyhnhnms of the neighbourhood to have the Assembly's *exhortation* executed, which he could not put off much longer. He doubted it would be impossible for me to swim to another country, and therefore wished I would contrive some sort of vehicle resembling those I had described to him, that might carry me on the sea, in which work I should have the assistance of his own servants, as well as those of his neighbours. He concluded, that for his own part he could have been content to keep me in his service as long as I lived, because he found I had cured myself of some bad habits and dispositions, by endeavouring, as far as my inferior nature was capable, to imitate the Houyhnhnms.

I should here observe to the reader, that a decree of the general Assembly in this country is expressed by the word *hnhloayn*, which signifies an *exhortation*, as near as I can render it: for they have no conception how a rational creature can be *compelled*, but only advised, or *exhorted*, because no person can disobey Reason, without giving up his claim to be a rational creature.

I was struck with the utmost grief and despair at my master's discourse, and being unable to support the agonies I was under, I fell into a swoon at his feet; when I came to myself, he told me, that he concluded I had been dead. (For these people are subject to no such imbecilities of nature.) I answered, in a faint voice, that death would have been too great an happiness; that although I could not blame the Assembly's *exhortation*, or the urgency of his friends; yet in my weak and corrupt judgement, I thought it might consist with Reason to have been less rigorous. That I could not swim a league, and probably the nearest land to theirs might be distant above an hundred; that many materials, necessary for making a small vessel to carry me off, were wholly wanting in this country, which, however, I would attempt in obedience and gratitude to his Honour, although I concluded the thing to be impossible, and therefore looked on myself as already devoted to destruction. That the certain prospect of an unnatural death was the least of my evils: for, supposing I should escape with life by some strange adventure, how could I think with temper of passing my days among Yahoos, and relapsing into my old corruptions, for want of examples to lead and keep me within the paths of virtue? That I knew too well upon what solid reasons all the determinations of the wise Houyhnhnms were founded, not to be shaken by arguments of mine, a miserable Yahoo; and therefore after presenting him with my humble thanks for the offer of his servants' assistance in making a vessel, and desiring a reasonable time for so difficult a work, I told him I would endeavour to preserve a wretched being; and, if ever I returned to England, was not without hopes of being useful to my own species, by celebrating the praises of the renowned Houyhnhnms, and proposing their virtues to the imitation of mankind.

My master in a few words made me a very gracious reply, allowed me the space of two *months* to finish my boat; and ordered the sorrel nag, my fellow-servant (for so at this distance I may presume to call him) to follow my instructions, because I told my master, that his help would be sufficient, and I knew he had a tenderness for me.

In his company my first business was to go to that part of the coast, where my rebellious crew had ordered me to be set on shore. I got upon a height, and looking on every side into the sea, fancied I saw a small island, towards the north-east: I took out my pocket-glass, and could then clearly distinguish it about five leagues off, as I computed; but it appeared to the sorrel nag to be only a blue cloud: for, as he had no conception of any country beside his own, so he could not be as expert in distinguishing remote objects at sea, as we who so much converse in that element.

After I had discovered this island, I considered no farther; but resolved it should, if possible, be the first place of my banishment, leaving the consequence to Fortune.

I returned home, and consulting with the sorrel nag, we went into a copse at some distance, where I with my knife, and he with a sharp flint fastened very artificially,[21] after their manner, to a wooden handle, cut down several oak wattles about the thickness of a walking-staff, and some larger pieces. But I shall not trouble the reader with a particular description of my own mechanics; let it suffice to say, that in six weeks' time, with the help of the sorrel nag, who performed the parts that required most labour, I finished a sort of Indian canoe, but much larger, covering it with the skins of Yahoos well stitched together, with hempen threads of my own making. My sail was likewise composed of the skins of the same animal; but I made use of the youngest I could get, the older being too tough and thick, and I likewise provided myself with four paddles. I laid in a stock of boiled flesh, of rabbits and fowls, and took with me two vessels, one filled with milk, and the other with water.

I tried my canoe in a large pond near my master's house, and then corrected in it what was amiss; stopping all the chinks with Yahoos' tallow, till I found it staunch, and able to bear me and my freight. And when it was as complete as I could possibly make it, I had it drawn on a carriage very gently by Yahoos, to the sea-side, under the conduct of the sorrel nag, and another servant.

When all was ready, and the day came for my departure, I took leave of my master and lady, and the whole family, mine eyes flowing with tears, and my heart quite sunk with grief. But his Honour, out of curiosity, and perhaps (if I may speak it without vanity) partly out of kindness, was determined to see me in my canoe, and got several of his neighbouring friends to accompany him. I was forced to wait above an hour for the tide, and then observing the wind very fortunately bearing towards the island, to which I intended to steer my course, I took a second leave of my master: but as I was going to prostrate myself to kiss his hoof, he did me the honour to raise it gently to my mouth. I am not ignorant how much I have been censured for mentioning this last particular. For my detractors are pleased to think it improbable, that so illustrious a person should descend to give so great a mark of distinction to a creature so inferior as I. Neither have I forgot, how apt some travellers are to boast of extraordinary favours they have received. But if these censurers were better acquainted with the noble and courteous disposition of the Houyhnhnms, they would soon change their opinion.

I paid my respects to the rest of the Houyhnhnms in his Honour's company; then getting into my canoe, I pushed off from shore.

CHAPTER II

The author's dangerous voyage. He arrives at New Holland, hoping to settle there. Is wounded with an arrow by one of the natives. Is seized and carried by force into a Portuguese ship. The great civilities of the captain. The author arrives at England.

I BEGAN this desperate voyage on February 15, 1715, at 9 o'clock in the morning. The wind was very favourable; however, I made use at first only of my paddles, but considering I should soon be weary, and that the wind might probably chop about, I ventured to set up my little sail; and thus, with the help of the tide, I went at the rate of a league and a half an hour, as near as I could guess. My master and his friends continued on the shore, till I was almost out of sight; and I often heard the sorrel nag (who always loved me) crying out, *Hnuy illa nyha maiah Yahoo*, Take care of thyself, gentle Yahoo.

My design was, if possible, to discover some small island uninhabited, yet sufficient by my labour to furnish me with the necessaries of life, which I would have thought a greater happiness than to be first Minister in the politest Court of Europe; so horrible was the idea I conceived of returning to live in the society and under the government of Yahoos. For in such a solitude as I desired, I could at least enjoy my own thoughts, and reflect with delight on the virtues of those inimitable Houyhnhnms, without any opportunity of degenerating into the vices and corruptions of my own species.

The reader may remember what I related when my crew conspired against me, and confined me to my cabin. How I continued there several weeks, without knowing what course we took, and when I was put ashore in the long-boat, how the sailors told me with oaths, whether true or false, that they knew not in what part of the world we were. However, I did then believe us to be about ten degrees southward of the Cape of Good Hope, or about 45 degrees southern latitude, as I gathered from some general words I overheard among them, being I supposed to the south-east in their intended voyage to Madagascar. And although this were but little better than conjecture, yet I resolved to steer my course eastward, hoping to reach the south-west coast of New Holland, and perhaps some such island as I desired, lying westward of it. The wind was full west, and by six in the evening I computed I had gone eastward at least eighteen leagues, when I spied a very small island about half a league off, which I soon reached. It was nothing but a rock, with one creek, naturally arched by the force of tempests. Here I put in my canoe, and climbing a part of the rock, I could plainly discover land to the east, extending from south to north. I lay all night in my canoe, and repeating my voyage early in the morning, I arrived in seven hours to the south-west point of New Holland. This confirmed me in the opinion I have long entertained, that the maps and charts place this country at least three degrees more to the east than it really is; which thought I communicated many years ago to my worthy friend Mr Herman Moll,[22] and gave him my reasons for it, although he hath rather chosen to follow other authors.

I saw no inhabitants in the place where I landed, and being unarmed, I was afraid of venturing far into the country. I found some shellfish on the shore, and ate them raw, not daring to kindle a fire, for fear of being discovered by the natives. I continued three days feeding on oysters and limpets, to save my own provisions, and I fortunately found a brook of excellent water, which gave me great relief.

On the fourth day, venturing out early a little too far, I saw twenty or thirty natives upon a height, not above five hundred yards from me. They were stark naked, men, women, and children, round a fire, as I could discover by the smoke. One of them spied me, and gave notice to the rest; five of them advanced towards me, leaving the women and children at the fire. I made what haste I could to the shore, and getting into my canoe, shoved off: the savages observing me retreat, ran after me; and before I could get far enough into the sea, discharged an arrow, which wounded me deeply on the inside of my left knee (I shall carry the mark to my grave). I apprehended the arrow might be poisoned, and paddling out of the reach of their darts (being a calm day) I made a shift to suck the wound, and dress it as well as I could.

I was at a loss what to do, for I durst not return to the same landing-place, but stood to the north, and was forced to paddle; for the wind though very gentle was against me, blowing north-west. As I was looking about for a secure landing-place, I saw a sail to the north-north-east, which appearing every minute more visible, I was in some doubt, whether I should wait for them or no; but at last my detestation of the Yahoo race prevailed, and turning my canoe, I sailed and paddled together to the south, and got into the same creek from whence I set out in the morning, choosing rather to trust myself among these *barbarians*, than live with European Yahoos. I drew up my canoe as close as I could to the shore, and hid myself behind a stone by the little brook, which, as I have already said, was excellent water.

The ship came within a half a league of this creek, and sent out her long-boat with vessels to take in fresh water (for the place it seems was very well known) but I did not observe it till the boat was almost on shore, and it was too late to seek another hiding-place. The seamen at their landing observed my canoe, and rummaging it all over, easily conjectured that the owner could not be far off. Four of them well armed searched every cranny and lurking-hole, till at last they found me flat on my face behind the stone. They gazed a while in admiration at my strange uncouth dress, my coat made of skins, my wooden-soled shoes, and my furred stockings; from whence, however, they concluded I was not a native of the place, who all go naked. One of the seamen in Portuguese bid me rise, and asked who I was. I understood that language very well, and getting upon my feet, said, I was a poor Yahoo, banished from the Houyhnhnms, and desired they would please to let me depart. They admired to hear me answer them in their own tongue, and saw by my complexion I must be an European; but were at a loss to know what I meant by Yahoos and Houyhnhnms, and at the same time fell a laughing at my strange tone in speaking, which resembled the neighing of a horse. I trembled all the while betwixt fear and hatred: I again desired leave to depart, and was gently moving to my canoe; but they laid hold on me, desiring to know, What country I was of? whence I came? with many other questions.

I told them, I was born in England, from whence I came about five years ago, and then their country and ours were at peace. I therefore hoped they would not treat me as an enemy, since I meant them no harm, but was a poor Yahoo, seeking some desolate place where to pass the remainder of his unfortunate life.

When they began to talk, I thought I never heard or saw anything so unnatural; for it appeared to me as monstrous as if a dog or a cow should speak in England, or a Yahoo in Houyhnhnmland. The honest Portuguese were equally amazed at my strange dress, and the odd manner of delivering my words, which however they understood very well. They spoke to me with great humanity, and said they were sure their captain would carry me *gratis* to Lisbon, from whence I might return to my own country; that two of the seamen would go back to the ship, to inform the captain of what they had seen, and receive his orders; in the meantime, unless I would give my solemn oath not to fly, they would secure me by force. I thought it best to comply with their proposal. They were very curious to know my story, but I gave them very little satisfaction; and they all conjectured, that my misfortunes had impaired my reason. In two hours the boat, which went loaden with vessels of water, returned with the captain's commands to fetch me on board. I fell on my knees to preserve my liberty; but all was in vain, and the men having tied me with cords, heaved me into the boat, from whence I was taken into the ship, and from thence into the captain's cabin.

His name was Pedro de Mendez; he was a very courteous and generous person; he entreated me to give some account of myself, and desired to know what I would eat or drink; said, I should be used as well as himself, and spoke so many obliging things, that I wondered to find such civilities from a Yahoo. However, I remained silent and sullen; I was ready to faint at the very smell of him and his men. At last I desired something to eat out of my own canoe; but he ordered me a chicken and some excellent wine, and then directed that I should be put to bed in a very clean cabin. I would not undress myself, but lay on the bed-clothes, and in half an hour stole out, when I thought the crew was at dinner, and getting to the side of the ship was going to leap into the sea, and swim for my life, rather than continue among Yahoos. But one of the seamen prevented me, and having informed the captain, I was chained to my cabin.

After dinner Don Pedro came to me, and desired to know my reason for so desperate an attempt: assured me he only meant to do me all the service he was able, and spoke so very movingly, that at last I descended to treat him like an animal which had some little portion of Reason. I gave him a very short relation of my voyage, of the conspiracy against me by my own men, of the country where they set me on shore, and of my three years' residence there. All which he looked upon as if it were a dream or a vision; whereat I took great offence; for I had quite forgot the faculty of lying, so peculiar to Yahoos in all countries where they preside, and consequently the disposition of suspecting truth in others of their own species. I asked him, Whether it were the custom of his country to *say the thing that was not?* I assured him I had almost forgot what he meant by falsehood, and if I had lived a thousand years in Houyhnhnmland, I should never have heard a lie from the meanest servant; that I was altogether indifferent whether he believed me or no; but however, in return for his favours, I would give so much allowance to the corruption of his nature, as to answer any objection he would please to make, and then he might easily discover the truth.

The captain, a wise man, after many endeavours to catch me tripping in some part of my story, at last began to have a better opinion of my veracity. But he added, that since I professed so inviolable an attachment to truth, I must give him my word of honour to bear him company in this voyage without attempting anything against my life, or else he would continue me a prisoner till we arrived at Lisbon. I gave him the promise he required; but at the same time protested that I would suffer the greatest hardships rather than return to live among Yahoos.

Our voyage passed without any considerable accident. In gratitude to the captain I sometimes sat with him at his earnest request, and strove to conceal my antipathy against human kind, although it often broke out, which he suffered to pass without observation. But the greatest part of the day, I confined myself to my cabin, to avoid seeing any of the crew. The captain had often entreated me to strip myself of my savage dress, and offered to lend me the best suit of clothes he had. This I would not be prevailed on to accept, abhorring to cover myself with anything that had been on the back of a Yahoo. I only desired he would lend me two clean shirts, which having been washed since he wore them, I believed would not so much defile me. These I changed every second day, and washed them myself.

We arrived at Lisbon, Nov. 5, 1715. At our landing the captain forced me to cover myself with his cloak, to prevent the rabble from crowding about me. I was conveyed to his own house, and at my earnest request, he led me up to the highest room backwards. I conjured him to conceal from all persons what I had told him of the Houyhnhnms, because the least hint of such a story would not only draw numbers of people to see me, but probably put me in danger of being imprisoned, or burnt by the Inquisition. The captain persuaded me to accept a suit of clothes newly made, but I would not suffer the tailor to take my measure; however, Don Pedro being almost of my size, they fitted me well enough. He accoutred me with other necessaries all new, which I aired for twenty-four hours before I would use them.

The captain had no wife, nor above three servants, none of which were suffered to attend at meals, and his whole deportment was so obliging, added to very good *human* understanding, that I really began to tolerate his company. He gained so far upon me, that I ventured to look out of the back window. By degrees I was brought into another room, from whence I peeped into the street, but drew my head back in a fright. In a week's time he seduced me down to the door. I found my terror gradually lessened, but my hatred and contempt seemed to increase. I was at last bold enough to walk the street in his company, but kept my nose well stopped with rue, or sometimes with tobacco.

In ten days Don Pedro, to whom I had given some account of my domestic affairs, put it upon me as a point of honour and conscience, that I ought to return to my native country, and live at home with my wife and children. He told me, there was an English ship in the port just ready to sail, and he would furnish me with all things necessary. It would be tedious to repeat his arguments, and my contradictions. He said, it was altogether impossible to find such a solitary island as I had desired to live in; but I might command in my own house, and pass my time in a manner as recluse as I pleased.

I complied at last, finding I could not do better. I left Lisbon the 24th day of November, in an English merchantman, but who was the master I never inquired. Don Pedro accompanied me to the ship, and lent me twenty pounds. He took kind leave of me, and embraced me at parting, which I bore as well as I could. During this last voyage I had no commerce with the master or any of his men, but pretending I was sick kept close in my cabin. On the fifth of December, 1715, we cast anchor in the Downs about nine in the morning, and at three in the afternoon I got safe to my house at Redriff.

My wife and family received me with great surprise and joy, because they concluded me certainly dead; but I must freely confess the sight of them filled me only with hatred, disgust and contempt, and the more by reflecting on the near alliance I had to them. For, although since my unfortunate exile from the Houyhnhnm country, I had compelled myself to tolerate the sight of Yahoos, and to converse with Don Pedro de Mendez, yet my memory and imaginations were perpetually filled with the virtues and ideas of those exalted Houyhnhnms. And when I began to consider, that by copulating with one of the Yahoo species, I had become a parent of more, it struck me with the utmost shame, confusion and horror.

As soon as I entered the house, my wife took me in her arms, and kissed me, at which, having not been used to the touch of that odious animal for so many years, I fell in a swoon for almost an hour. At the time I am writing it is five years since my last return to England: during the first year I could not endure my wife or children in my presence, the very smell of them was intolerable, much less could I suffer them to eat in the same room. To this hour they dare not presume to touch my bread, or drink out of the same cup, neither was I ever able to let one of them take me by the hand. The first money I laid out was to buy two young stone-horses, which I keep in a good stable, and next to them the groom is my greatest favourite; for I feel my spirits revived by the smell he contracts in the stable. My horses understand me tolerably well; I converse with them at least four hours every day. They are strangers to bridle or saddle, they live in great amity with me, and friendship to each other.

CHAPTER 12

The author's veracity. His design in publishing this work. His censure of those travellers who swerve from the truth. The author clears himself from any sinister ends in writing. An objection answered. The method of planting Colonies. His native country commended. The right of the Crown to those countries described by the author is justified. The difficulty of conquering them. The author takes his last leave of the reader, proposeth his manner of living for the future, gives good advice, and concludeth.

THUS, gentle reader, I have given thee a faithful history of my travels for sixteen years, and above seven months, wherein I have not been so studious of ornament as of truth. I could perhaps like others have astonished thee with strange improbable tales; but I rather chose to relate plain matter of fact in the simplest manner and style, because my principal design was to inform, and not to amuse thee.

It is easy for us who travel into remote countries, which are seldom visited by Englishmen or other Europeans, to form descriptions of wonderful animals both at sea and land. Whereas a traveller's chief aim should be to make men wiser and better, and to improve their minds by the bad as well as good example of what they deliver concerning foreign places.

I could heartily wish a law were enacted, that every traveller, before he were permitted to publish his voyages, should be obliged to make oath before the Lord High Chancellor that all he intended to print was absolutely true to the best of his knowledge; for then the world would no longer be deceived as it usually is, while some writers, to make their works pass the better upon the public, impose the grossest falsities on the unwary reader. I have perused several books of travels with great delight in my younger days; but having since gone over most parts of the globe, and been able to contradict many fabulous accounts from my own observation, it hath given me a great disgust against this part of reading, and some indignation to see the credulity of mankind so impudently abused. Therefore since my acquaintance were pleased to think my poor endeavours might not be unacceptable to my country, I imposed on myself as a maxim, never to be swerved from, that I would *strictly adhere to truth*; neither indeed can I be ever under the least temptation to vary from it, while I retain in my mind the lectures and example of my noble master, and the other illustrious Houyhnhnms, of whom I had so long the honour to be an humble hearer.

— — *Nec si miserum Fortuna Sinonem
Finxit, vanum etiam mendacemque improba finget.*

I know very well how little reputation is to be got by writings which require neither genius nor learning, nor indeed any other talent, except a good memory or an exact journal. I know likewise, that writers of travels, like dictionary-makers, are sunk into oblivion by the weight and bulk of those who come last, and therefore lie uppermost. And it is highly probable, that such travellers who shall hereafter visit the countries described in this work of mine, may, by detecting my errors (if there be any), and adding many new discoveries of their own, jostle me out of vogue, and stand in my place, making the world forget that ever I was an author. This indeed would be too great a mortification if I wrote for fame: but, as my sole intention was the PUBLIC GOOD, I cannot be altogether disappointed. For who can read of the virtues I have mentioned in the glorious Houyhnhnms, without being ashamed of his own vices, when he considers himself as the reasoning, governing animal of his country? I shall say nothing of those remote nations where Yahoos preside, amongst which the least corrupted are the Brobdingnagians, whose wise maxims in morality and government it would be our happiness to observe. But I forbear descanting further, and rather leave the judicious reader to his own remarks and applications.

I am not a little pleased that this work of mine can possibly meet with no censurers: for what objections can be made against a writer who relates only plain facts that happened in such distant countries, where we have not the least interest with respect either to trade or negotiations? I have carefully avoided every fault with which common writers of travels are often too justly charged. Besides, I meddle not the least with any *party*, but write without passion, prejudice, or ill-will against any man or number of men whatsoever. I write for the noblest end, to inform and instruct mankind, over whom I may, without breach of modesty, pretend to some superiority from the advantages I received by conversing so long among the most accomplished Houyhnhnms. I write without any view towards profit or praise. I never suffer a word to pass that may look like reflection, or possibly give the least offence even to those who are most ready to take it. So that I hope I may with justice pronounce myself an author perfectly blameless, against whom the tribe of answerers, considerers, observers, reflecters, detecters, re-markers, will never be able to find matter for exercising their talents.

I confess, it was whispered to me, that I was bound in duty as a subject of England, to have given in a memorial to a Secretary of State, at my first coming over; because, whatever lands are discovered by a subject belong to the Crown. But I doubt whether our conquests in the countries I treat of, would be as easy as those of Ferdinando Cortez over the naked Americans. The Lilliputians, I think, are hardly worth the charge of a fleet and army to reduce them, and I question whether it might be prudent or safe to attempt the Brobding-nagians. Or whether an English army would be much at their ease with the Flying Island over their heads. The Houy-hnhnms, indeed, appear not to be so well prepared for war, a science to which they are perfect strangers, and especially against missive weapons. However, supposing myself to be a

Minister of State, I could never give my advice for invading them. Their prudence, unanimity, unacquaintedness with fear, and their love of their country would amply supply all defects in the military art. Imagine twenty thousand of them breaking into the midst of an European army, confounding the ranks, overturning the carriages, battering the warriors' faces into mummy, by terrible yerks from their hinder hoofs. For they would well deserve the character given to Augustus; *Recalcitrat undique tutus.* But instead of proposals for conquering that magnanimous nation, I rather wish they were in a capacity or disposition to send a sufficient number of their inhabitants for civilizing Europe, by teaching us the first principles of honour, justice, truth, temperance, public spirit, fortitude, chastity, friendship, benevolence, and fidelity. The *names* of all which virtues are still retained among us in most languages, and are to be met with in modern as well as ancient authors; which I am able to assert from my own small reading.

But I had another reason which made me less forward to enlarge his Majesty's dominions by my discoveries. To say the truth, I had conceived a few scruples with relation to the distributive justice of princes upon those occasions. For instance, a crew of pirates are driven by a storm they know not whither, at length a boy discovers land from the topmast, they go on shore to rob and plunder; they see an harmless people, are entertained with kindness, they give the country a new name, they take formal possession of it for the King, they set up a rotten plank or a stone for a memorial, they murder two or three dozen of the natives, bring away a couple more by force for a sample, return home, and get their pardon. Here commences a new dominion acquired with a title by *divine right.* Ships are sent with the first opportunity, the natives driven out or destroyed, their princes tortured to discover their gold; a free licence given to all acts of inhumanity and lust, the earth reeking with the blood of its inhabitants: and this execrable crew of butchers employed in so pious an expedition, is a *modern colony* sent to convert and civilize an idolatrous and barbarous people.

But this description, I confess, doth by no means affect the British nation, who may be an example to the whole world for their wisdom, care, and justice in planting colonies; their liberal endowments for the advancement of religion and learning; their choice of devout and able pastors to propagate Christianity; their caution in stocking their provinces with people of sober lives and conversations from this the mother kingdom; their strict regard to the distribution of justice, in supplying the civil administration through all their Colonies with officers of the greatest abilities, utter strangers to corruption; and to crown all, by sending the most vigilant and virtuous Governors, who have no other views than the happiness of the people over whom they preside, and the honour of the King their master.

But, as those countries which I have described do not appear to have any desire of being conquered, and enslaved, murdered or driven out by colonies, nor abound either in gold, silver, sugar or tobacco; I did humbly conceive they were by no means proper objects of our zeal, our valour, or our interest. However, if those whom it more concerns, think fit to be of another opinion, I am ready to depose, when I shall be lawfully called, That no European did ever visit those countries before me. I mean, if the inhabitants ought to be believed.

But as to the formality of taking possession in my Sovereign's name, it never came once into my thoughts; and if it had, yet as my affairs then stood, I should perhaps in point of prudence and self-preservation, have put it off to a better opportunity.

Having thus answered the *only* objection that can ever be raised against me as a traveller, I here take a final leave of my courteous readers, and return to enjoy my own speculations in my little garden at Redriff, to apply those excellent lessons of virtue which I learned among the Houyhnhnms, to instruct the Yahoos of my own family as far as I shall find them docible animals, to behold my figure often in a glass, and thus if possible habituate myself by time to tolerate the sight of a human creature: to lament the brutality of Houyhnhnms in my own country, but always treat their persons with respect, for the sake of my noble master, his family, his friends, and the whole Houyhnhnm race, whom these of ours have the honour to resemble in all their lineaments, however their intellectuals came to degenerate.

I began last week to permit my wife to sit at dinner with me, at the farthest end of a long table, and to answer (but with the utmost brevity) the few questions I ask her. Yet the smell of a Yahoo continuing very offensive, I always keep my nose well stopped with rue, lavender, or tobacco leaves. And although it be hard for a man late in life to remove old habits, I am not altogether out of hopes in some time to suffer a neighbour Yahoo in my company, without the apprehensions I am yet under of his teeth or his claws.

My reconcilement to the Yahoo-kind in general might not be so difficult if they would be content with those vices and follies only, which Nature hath entitled them to. I am not in the least provoked at the sight of a lawyer, a pickpocket, a colonel, a fool, a lord, a gamester, a politician, a whoremonger, a physician, an evidence, a suborner, an attorney, a traitor, or the like: this is all according to the due course of things: but when I behold a lump of deformity and diseases both in body and mind, smitten with *pride*, it immediately breaks all the measures of my patience; neither shall I be ever able to comprehend how such an animal and such a vice could tally together. The wise and virtuous Houyhnhnms, who abound in all excellencies that can adorn a rational creature, have no name for this vice in their language, which hath no terms to express anything that is evil, except those whereby they describe the detestable qualities of their Yahoos, among which they were not able to distinguish this of pride, for want of thoroughly understanding human nature, as it showeth itself in other countries, where that animal presides. But I, who had more experience, could plainly observe some rudiments of it among the wild Yahoos.

But the Houyhnhnms, who live under the government of Reason, are no more proud of the good qualities they possess, than I should be for not wanting a leg or an arm, which no man in his wits would boast of, although he must be miserable without them. I dwell the longer upon this subject from the desire I have to make the society of an English Yahoo by any means not insupportable, and therefore I here entreat those who have any tincture of this absurd vice, that they will not presume to appear in my sight.

FINIS.

Notes

Two limitations in the scope of the notes should be explained. First, no attempt is made to list Swift's possible literary sources. There are many passages in which he seems to be indebted to, among others, Lucian, Rabelais and Cyrano de Bergerac, but the parallels can only be established by extensive quotation and a mere list of references calls Swift's originality into question without showing what he has made of his source material. For a detailed discussion of the matter reference should be made to *Gulliver's Travels: A Critical Study,* by W. A. Eddy (1923). Secondly, it has been taken as a general principle that words which can be explained by reference to the *Concise Oxford Dictionary* should not be glossed here.

JOHN CHALKER

A LETTER FROM CAPT. GULLIVER
TO HIS COUSIN SYMPSON

1. (p. 37) *A Letter . . . :* Although the *Letter* is dated 1727 it was first published in Faulkner's edition of 1735. The name *Sympson* may allude to a William Symson who published *A New Voyage to the East-Indies* in 1715.

2. (p. 37) *Dampier:* William Dampier (1652–1715), a well-known mariner who published several volumes about his voyages. His chief work, *A New Voyage Round the World,* appeared in 1697.

3. (p. 37) *Queen Anne:* refers to a passage inserted in the first edition in Book IV, Chapter 6, which praised Anne for submitting 'the Behaviour and Acts of those She intrusts with the Administration of Her Affairs to the Examination of Her great Council'. Swift is being ironical about the steadily increasing power of Walpole.

4. (p. 37) *Godolphin:* Sidney Godolphin (1645–1712), who was created an earl in 1706, was Lord High Treasurer from 1702–10.

5. (p. 37) *Oxford:* Robert Harley (1661–1724) became Earl of Oxford and was appointed Lord High Treasurer in 1711.

6. (p. 37) *hardly know mine own work:* Swift complained that the first edition of his work was incorrectly printed. See page 31.

7. (p. 38) *Smithfield:* an area to the north-west of St Paul's, the site of a cattle market and the annual Bartholomew Fair from the twelfth century onwards. Many martyrs were burnt there in the sixteenth century.

8. (p. 38) *eat . . . their own cotton:* probably referring to a ball of cotton held in the hand, or else on a stick, for wiping type when it had become clogged

9. (p. 39) *Keys:* Commentaries on the political allusions in *Gulliver's Travels* began to appear as early as 1726. Examples include *Lemuel Gulliver's Travels Into Several Remote Regions of the World Compendiously Methodiz'd* (1726) and *Gulliver Decypher'd* (1727).

10. (p. 39) *to which I am wholly a stranger:* In the literary conditions of the early eighteenth century any famous author was likely to have works fathered upon him by unscrupulous publishers anxious to trade upon his name.

11. (p. 39) *confound the times:* The dates given by Gulliver for his various movements are sometimes difficult to reconcile with each other.

THE PUBLISHER TO THE READER

1. (p. 43) *Redriff:* Rotherhithe

PART I: A VOYAGE TO LILLIPUT

1. (p. 53) *fourteen years old:* In the seventeenth century students matriculated earlier than they do now and fourteen was a normal age.

2. (p. 53) *Leyden:* Students from all countries were attracted to the University of Leyden in Holland, and especially to the faculties of medicine and law.

3. (p. 53) *Physic:* medicine

4. (p. 53) *Old Jury:* now called Old Jewry. In the details of this paragraph Swift is parodying the circumstantial style of the mariners' tales.

5. (p. 53) *Mrs Mary Burton:* Adult women, whether married or single, were referred to as 'Mistress'.

6. (p. 54) *Van Diemen's Land:* Tasmania

7. (p. 56) *not six inches high:* By and large Swift keeps to an accurate scale: in Lilliput sizes are reduced to one twelfth and in Brobdingnag they are multiplied by twelve. But Swift sometimes tampers with the scale to reinforce a satirical point as, for example, when he makes the Lilliputian cavalry exercise on Gulliver's pocket handkerchief (p. 75). For a detailed study of this question see *Gulliver's Travels: A Critical Study* by W. A. Eddy (Peter Smith, 1923).

8. (p. 56) *admiration:* amazement

9. (p. 56) *Hekinah degul:* Many attempts have been made to decipher Swift's constructed languages, but the traditional view that they are playful nonsense seems to be correct. See, however, 'A *Gulliver* Dic-

tionary' by P. Odell Clark (*Studies in Philology*, 1953) and the 'Glossary of Terms' in *Gulliver's Travels*, edited by Herbert Davis (the Shakespeare Head Press, 1959).

10. (p. 59) *imaginations:* schemes

11. (p. 61) *engines:* mechanical contrivances

12. (p. 62) *an ancient temple:* From the earliest commentaries it has been suggested that this refers to Westminster Hall in which Charles I had been condemned to death, but the real explanation may be that Swift had to justify the existence of an empty building large enough to contain Gulliver.

13. (p. 63) *stang:* a rood, a quarter of an acre

14. (p. 64) *The Emperor:* In his political relations (e.g. his preference for low heels, or Whigs) the Emperor resembles George I, but in this character Swift is primarily concerned to satirize inflated regal pride and the tyranny of monarchs.

15. (p. 66) *High and Low Dutch:* German and Dutch

16. (p. 66) *Six hundred beds:* Eddy (op. cit.) notes that on a twelve times scale this figure is approximately correct, and also that the fourfold mattress would have been inadequate, as Gulliver complains, to a man who needed a twelvefold one.

17. (p. 67) *beeves:* oxen

18. (p. 68) *orders ... to search me:* In 1715 the Whigs, who had come to power on the accession of George I in 1714, formed a committee to investigate the conduct of the previous Government and especially of Oxford and Bolingbroke who were suspected of treasonable relationships with France and with the Old Pretender. Swift's sympathies were with the hard-pressed Tories (he was a personal friend of both Oxford and Bolingbroke), and the search of Gulliver's person is generally thought to satirize the activities of the Whig committee.

19. (p. 73) *perspective:* telescope

20. (p. 74) *Flimnap:* Generally agreed to represent Sir Robert Walpole, chief minister from 1715-17, and from 1721-42. C. H. Firth writes that the capering on a tightrope 'symbolizes Walpole's dexterity in parliamentary tactics and political intrigues' ('The Political Significance of *Gulliver's Travels*' in *Proceedings of the British Academy* 1919-20).

21. (p. 74) *summerset:* summersault

22. (p. 74) *Reldresal:* Various suggestions have been made as to the identity of Reldresal including Lord Carteret, Lord Townshend and the first Earl Stanhope. Carteret, who was a friend of Swift, seems the likeliest candidate. Firth (op. cit.) pointed out that in 1724 Walpole made Carteret Lord Lieutenant of Ireland and that in that capacity he was obliged to offer £300 as a reward for the discovery of the

author of *The Drapier's Letters* (see Part III, Note 18) just as Reldresal was forced to suggest a method of punishing Gulliver.

23. (p. 74) *one of the King's cushions*: It is agreed that this is a reference to the Duchess of Kendal, one of the King's mistresses who helped to restore Walpole to favour after his fall in 1717. Swift had a particular animus against her because it was she who sold William Wood a patent allowing him to mint a copper coinage for Ireland, a scheme against which Swift wrote *The Drapier's Letters*.

24. (p. 74) *three fine silken threads*: Swift is ridiculing the presentation of various orders to the King's favourites. Blue is the colour of the Order of the Garter (bestowed on Walpole in May 1726), red of the Order of the Bath (which had been revived by George I in 1725) and green of the Order of the Thistle. Cf. *Verses on the Revival of the Order of the Bath* (doubtfully attributed to Swift) which end:

> And he who will leap over a stick for the King
> Is qualified best for a Dog in a String.

25. (p. 76) *close chair*: sedan chair

26. (p. 77) *presently*: immediately

27. (p. 77) *colossus*: The Colossus at Rhodes, one of the Seven Wonders of the World, was a huge statue bestriding the harbour entrance.

28. (p. 78) *Skyresh Bolgolam*: usually identified as the Earl of Nottingham whom Swift had attacked because, though a Tory, he had withdrawn his support from the Harley Government

29. (p. 81) *sideling*: sideways

30. (p. 82) *cross*: across

31. (p. 84) *Tramecksan and Slamecksan*: the High and Low Church parties, or the Tories and the Whigs

32. (p. 84) *the heir to the Crown*: The Prince of Wales (afterwards George II) was opposed to his father and consequently offered some hope to the Tories, but when he became king he kept Walpole as chief minister.

33. (p. 84) *Blefuscu*: France

34. (p. 84) *obstinate war*: the War of the Spanish Succession which lasted from 1701–13

35. (p. 85) *the larger end*: The controversy between the Big Endians and Little Endians is both a commentary on the history of religous controversy in England and a characteristic example of Swift's ability to ridicule hair splitting theological disputation by discussing it in terms of concrete examples.

36. (p. 85) *his present Majesty's grandfather*: generally taken to be Henry VIII

37. (p. 85) *one Emperor ... crown*: Charles I and James II

38. (p. 85) *incapable by law:* By the Test Act of 1673 all those holding office under the Crown were obliged to take the sacrament according to the rites of the Anglican Church Catholics and nonconformists therefore suffered from serious civil disabilities.

39. (p. 89) *I would never . . . slavery:* The Whigs had wished to continue the war until they could impose harsher terms upon France, but the Tories worked for a negotiated settlement.

40. (p. 89) *a junto of Ministers:* At this point Gulliver seems to stand both for Bolingbroke, who was the chief negotiator for a settlement, and Swift who had supported his efforts. Both were hated by the Whigs.

41. (p. 89) *offers of a peace:* The war was ended by the Treaty of Utrecht which was signed on 11 April 1713. The treaty brought great benefits to the country, particularly as regards trade, but the Whigs remained dissatisfied.

42. (p. 92) *the fire was wholly extinguished:* This episode is usually said to refer to Queen Anne's disgust with Swift's *Tale of a Tub* (in part a satire against abuses in religion), and to her refusal to give him a bishopric, but Swift may be attacking royal ingratitude in general.

43. (p. 93) *clinched:* clenched

44. (p. 93) *vegetables:* plants

45. (p. 93) *Cascagians:* Swift may have invented this people, but in his account of writing methods he seems to be recollecting a passage in *Purchas, his Pilgrimage* (1614), Book VIII, Chapter 13.

46. (p. 94) *fence:* guard, defence

47. (p. 95) *never intended . . . mystery:* This is one of Swift's settled themes, cf. *An Enquiry into the Behaviour of the Queen's Last Ministry:* 'the art of government . . . requires no more, in reality, then diligence, honesty, and a moderate share of plain natural sense'.

48. (p. 97) *professors:* teachers

49 (p. 99) *domestic:* household arrangements

50. (p. 101) *white staff:* the symbol of office of the Lord Treasurer

51. (p. 101) *the reputation of an excellent Lady:* This episode has been given detailed interpretations by some commentators, Firth (op. cit.) suggesting, for example, that it 'may be an ironical hit at Walpole, whose first wife, Catherine Shorter, was not above suspicion', but its more important function is surely to ridicule the innuendos of Court scandal.

52. (p. 104) *Articles:* Swift satirizes the impeachment of four Tory ex-ministers – Bolingbroke, Oxford, Ormonde and Strafford – in 1715. Bolingbroke and Ormonde escaped to France (as Gulliver escapes to Blefuscu) and were declared traitors; the impeachment of Strafford was dropped, and Oxford was acquitted after being kept in the Tower for two years.

53. (p. 106) *only give order to put out both your eyes:* It had been suggested that Oxford and Bolingbroke should be accused of high misdemeanour instead of high treason which would have led to the forfeiture of their titles and estates instead of the death penalty.

54. (p. 108) *without the formal proofs:* Swift is obviously mocking at the state of English justice in general, but there may be a specific reference to the trial of Atterbury, Bishop of Rochester and one of the most formidable supporters of the Pretender, in 1722. The evidence against him was weak and his condemnation was defective in law although there was little doubt about his guilt.

55. (p. 109) *encomiums on his Majesty's mercy:* The execution of captured Jacobite leaders which followed the rising of 1715 was accompanied by a proclamation in praise of the King's clemency.

56. (p. 111) *discover:* make known

57. (p. 113) *a person of quality was dispatched:* The English Government remonstrated with the French for supporting the Pretender.

58. (p. 114) *glad of my resolution:* The Pretender found Bolingbroke inconveniently realistic in assessing political events and soon dismissed him in favour of more flattering advisers.

59. (p. 116) *ancient:* ensign, flag

60. (p. 116) *North and South Seas:* North and South Pacific· Gulliver returns via Cape Horn.

61. (p. 117) *towardly:* dutiful

PART II: A VOYAGE TO BROBDINGNAG

1. (p. 121) *gale:* 'a wind not tempestuous yet stronger than a breeze' (Johnson)

2. (p. 121) *to overblow:* No attempt is made to gloss the technical terms used in this paragraph: Swift is laughing at the exaggerations of nautical language and takes his phrasing almost word for word from Samuel Sturmy's *Mariner's Magazine.* The original passage is printed by Eddy (op. cit.).

3. (p. 122) *Great Tartary:* the region extending eastwards from the Caspian Sea

4. (p. 122) *frozen sea:* Arctic Ocean

5. (p. 122) *whether:* which of the two

6. (p. 125) *comparison:* George Berkeley's *New Theory of Vision* (1709) had emphasized the relativity of our judgements of size.

7. (p. 126) *hinds:* farm workers

8. (p. 133) *baby:* doll

9. (p. 134) *reverence:* bow

10. (p. 135) *public spectacle:* The treatment of Gulliver in Brobdingnag is a reflection of conditions in eighteenth-century England, when it was still a normal amusement to visit Bethlehem Hospital (Bedlam) to watch the lunatics, and when exhibitions of freaks were a commonplace.

11. (p. 137) *pumpion:* pumpkin

12. (p. 139) *Sanson's Atlas:* Nicolas Sanson was a seventeenth-century French cartographer whose work was used as a basis for many subsequent atlases.

13. (p. 141) *scrutore:* escritoire, writing table

14. (p. 141) *philosophy:* natural philosophy, science

15. (p. 142) *weekly waiting:* There seems to have been a rota of scholars.

16. (p. 143) *lusus naturae:* sport of nature

17. (p. 144) *artist:* skilled workman

18. (p. 146) *Royal Sovereign:* one of the largest ships of the English navy, completed in 1637

19. (p. 146) *birthday clothes:* On the royal birthday courtiers appeared in new and elaborate costumes.

20. (p. 148) *Dunstable lark:* Dunstable downs were celebrated for the number of larks caught there.

21. (p. 149) *Gresham College:* The Royal Society met at Gresham College in Bishopsgate from 1661 until the Fire of London in 1666 when it moved to Arundel House.

22. (p. 151) *a square of Westminster Hall:* a square with its sides the length of Westminster Hall

23. (p. 154) *battalia:* order of battle

24. (p. 155) *a Bristol barrel:* Barrels varied in size in different parts of the country.

25. (p. 156) *stoop:* swoop

26. (p. 158) *spectacles:* Executions were popular events in the eighteenth century and execution days at Tyburn were public holidays.

27. (p. 160) *officiously:* kindly

28. (p. 164) *levee:* a reception held on rising from bed, a morning assembly

29. (p. 165) *consorts:* concerts

30. (p. 167) *plantations:* colonies

31. (p. 169) *prostitute chaplains:* Swift frequently attacked the quality of the bishops, many of whom owed their appointment to political sycophancy.

32. (p. 170) *more than double:* Swift is here reflecting the Tories' strong opposition to the extension of the national debt.

33. (p. 171) *generals ... kings:* directed at Marlborough for whom Blenheim Palace was built at a cost of over half a million pounds.

Swift frequently commented on his riches and insinuated that he had prolonged the war against France for his own profit.

34. (p. 171) *a mercenary standing army:* The Tories were opposed to the maintenance of a standing army in peace time.

35. (p. 171) *no reason ... conceal them:* This reflects Swift's own position· cf. *Thoughts on Religion:* 'Every man, as a member of the Commonwealth, ought to be content with the possession of his own opinion in private, without perplexing his neighbours or disturbing the public.'

36. (p. 173) *Dionysius Halicarnassensis:* a Greek writer who lived in Rome in the days of Augustus. His *Archaeologia* presents a favourable account of Roman history.

37. (p. 176) *entities, abstractions and transcendentals:* Swift constantly attacked abstruse philosophical and theological jargon – cf. *A Tale of a Tub.*

38. (p. 177) *style is clear:* cf. *Letter to a Young Gentleman Lately Entered Into Holy Orders* in which Swift criticizes the florid style

39. (p. 178) *Nature was degenerated:* Traditional seventeenth-century thinkers saw nature as being in a state of continuous decay which had begun with the Fall, but in opposition to this scientific discoveries seemed to offer the hope of a progressive development in Man's power. Swift makes it clear that he finds the argument of little real importance.

40. (p. 178) *if that may be called an army:* The Brobdingnagians maintain a militia which is very different from the professional standing army that the Tories opposed.

41. (p. 190) *Phaethon:* Phaeton persuaded Apollo to allow him to drive the chariot of the sun, but when he drove too near the earth he was struck with a thunderbolt by Jupiter and hurled headlong from heaven into the River Eridanus.

42. (p. 190) *Tonquin:* Tongking, a port in North Vietnam

43. (p. 190) *New Holland:* the name given to Australia by the Dutch

PART III: A VOYAGE TO LAPUTA, BALNIBARBI,
GLUBBDUBDRIB, LUGGNAGG, AND JAPAN

1. (p. 195) *Fort St George:* a station of the East India Company which became Madras

2. (p. 196) *alliance:* At this date England and Holland were members of the Grand Alliance against France. Swift argued in *The Conduct of the Allies* that England had kept to the alliance far more faithfully than the Dutch.

3. (p. 201) *figures of suns, moons ...:* Marjorie Hope Nicolson's *Science*

and Imagination (Cornell University Press, 1956) contains an extremely valuable chapter, written in conjunction with Nora M. Mohler, on 'The Scientific Background of Swift's *Voyage to Laputa*'. A detailed study of contemporary attitudes to music and mathematics leads to the conclusion that 'Swift's main point is that the Laputans are concerned with the theory, not with the application' of both subjects.

4. (p. 201) *taction:* touch

5. (p. 201) *kennel:* gutter

6. (p. 202) *hospitality to strangers:* George I had been criticized for his hospitality to Hanoverians who had followed him to England.

7. (p. 203) *hautboys:* oboes

8. (p. 203) *etymology:* The mock solemnity of the derivation is a hit at the great editor Richard Bentley who was one of the butts of the Swift/Pope circle. Firth (op. cit.) suggested that the name 'Laputa' is taken from the Spanish for 'the harlot'.

9. (p. 204) *mistake a figure in the calculation:* probably a gibe at Newton whose printer had brought him into ridicule by adding a cipher to his calculations of the distance of the sun from the earth. Swift may have been annoyed with Newton because, as Comptroller of the Mint, he had made a favourable report on Wood's coinage.

10. (p. 205) *intellectuals:* minds

11. (p. 206) *judicial astrology:* the art of judging the influence of the stars on human affairs

12. (p. 206) *be absorbed or swallowed up:* Nicolson and Mohler (op. cit.) show that the Laputans' fears were all entertained by scientists in Swift's day. Newton's calculations in the *Principia* recognized the possibility that the earth would eventually fall into the sun; William Derham, among others, thought that sun spots were a sign of volcanic action, and, finally, it was thought that the return of Halley's comet, which had been forecast for 1758, was capable of destroying the earth by collision.

13. (p. 209) *a philosophical account:* The account parodies the *Transactions of the Royal Society*.

14. (p. 211) *Astronomers' Cave:* apparently suggested by the cave in the Royal Observatory in Paris

15. (p. 211) *over:* across

16. (p. 211) *By means of this loadstone:* Swift's account of the movement and navigation of the island is based on the theories of William Gilbert's *De Magnete* (1600).

17. (p. 214) *keeping the island hovering:* Firth (op. cit.) suggests that the hovering of the island represents the repressive 'laws in restraint of trade which England had enacted to keep Ireland in subjection'.

Ireland was thus robbed of the benefits of nature just as Balnibarbi was robbed of 'the benefit of the sun and the rain': consequently its land was barren and its capital ruinous.

18. (p. 215) *About three years before my arrival:* This episode, which was not published in any of the early editions of *Gulliver,* is an allegory of the successful resistance of Ireland to Wood's halfpence. In 1722 William Wood had paid the Duchess of Kendal £10,000 for a patent to mint copper halfpence and farthings for Ireland, but when the new coinage began to be distributed an outcry was aroused because of its poor quality and because the Irish had not been consulted over its introduction. Swift began to write *The Drapier's Letters,* the most successful of the many attacks on the coinage and the 'combustible fuel' of the allegory. Eventually, in August 1725, Wood's patent was withdrawn.

19. (p. 217) *to leave the island:* The Act of Settlement (1701) provided that the King could only leave the country with the consent of Parliament, but this clause was repealed at George I's request in 1715. His protracted visits to Hanover caused popular resentment.

20. (p. 219) *Munodi:* Various identifications have been suggested for this figure, including Viscount Middleton, Lord Chancellor of Ireland, who, although a Whig, was opposed to Wood's halfpence; Bolingbroke, who retired to Dawley after his exile, and Harley, who retired to the country after the charges against him had been dropped in 1717.

21. (p. 221) *putting all arts ... upon a new foot:* a reference to the many new agricultural methods in vogue at the beginning of the eighteenth century

22. (p. 223) *largely:* at large

23. (p. 223) *This Academy:* an allegorical account of the Royal Society which Swift himself had visited in 1710. Despite the elements of exaggeration and satiric manipulation the most surprising thing is that for the most part, as Nicolson and Mohler (op. cit.) have shown, Swift simply 'set down before his readers experiments actually performed by members of the Royal Society, more preposterous to the layman than anything imagination could invent and more devastating in their satire'.

24. (p. 224) *ingenuity:* power of invention

25. (p. 224) *colours ... by feeling and smelling:* Robert Boyle tells a story of a blind man who could distinguish colours in *Experiments and Observations Upon Colour.*

26. (p. 225) *mast:* fruit of beech, oak and other forest trees

27. (p. 225) *cobwebs:* Swift here combines two items from the *Transactions of the Royal Society.* In 1710 M. Bon, a Frenchman, had published an

essay on the possibility of making silk from spider-webs, and in 1708 Dr Wall had written on the colourings to be derived from East-Indian pismires.

28. (p. 226) *nitre:* a nitrous substance supposed to have been present in the air

29. (p. 227) *how laborious the usual method:* cf. *The Spectator* (No. 220) in which Steele ridiculed a pamphlet by John Peters called *Artificial Versifying: A New Way to Make Latin Verses* (1678): 'This virtuoso, being a mathematician, has, according to his taste, thrown the art of poetry into a short problem, and contrived tables by which anyone without knowing a word of grammar or sense, may, to his great comfort, be able to compose, or rather to erect, Latin verses.'

30. (p. 227) *die:* singular of dice

31. (p. 230) *names for things:* One aspect of the development of science had been a demand that language should be made less abstract and rhetorical: Thomas Spratt wrote, for example, in *The History of the Royal Society* (1667), that its members wished 'to return back to the primitive purity and shortness when men delivered so many things in an equal number of *words*'. Locke had also emphasized 'how great a dependence our words have on common sensible ideas', and had argued (*An Essay Concerning Human Understanding*, III, xi) that 'the shape of a horse or cassowary will be but rudely and imperfectly imprinted on the mind by words, but the sight of the animals doth it a thousand times better'. For a useful discussion of the background, see A. C. Howell '*Res et Verba:* Words and things' (*Journal of English Literary History*, 1946).

32. (p. 231) *cephalic:* pertaining to the head

33. (p. 232) *chimera:* fanciful idea

34. (p. 233) *peccant humours:* a reference to the old medical theory that health depended upon a correct balance between the four bodily fluids of blood, phlegm, choler, and melancholy

35. (p. 233) *lenitive:* soothing drug; *abstersive:* purge; *restringent:* astringent; *cephalalgic:* cure for the headache; *icteric:* cure for jaundice; *apophlegmatic:* purge for phlegm

36. (p. 234) *occiput:* back of the head

37. (p. 234) *commodious:* convenient

38. (p. 236) *at stool:* At Bishop Atterbury's trial for Jacobite intrigues in 1722 (see Part I, note 54) papers were presented that were said to have been found in his close-stool. The reference later to a lame dog, an invader, also alludes to the trial. Much of the evidence against Atterbury was based on intercepted letters which were supposed to refer to plots under feigned names, and references to a lame dog called Harlequin were made to appear particularly sinister. See Swift's poem *Upon the Horrid Plot Discovered by Harlequin, the Bishop of Rochester's French Dog.*

39. (p. 236) *Tribnia . . . Langden:* anagrams for Britain and England

40. (p. 239) *antic:* grotesque, bizarre

41. (p. 240) *Arbela:* In this battle, fought in 331 B.C., Alexander defeated Darius and won Mesopotamia and Babylon.

42. (p. 240) *he was not poisoned:* alludes to a tradition, which is denied in Plutarch's *Lives,* that Alexander the Great was poisoned by his cup-bearer

43. (p. 240) *Hannibal:* Livy (Book XXI, Chapter 37) tells how, when his path through the Alps was blocked by a rock, Hannibal heated it and soaked it with vinegar after which it could be easily cut. In this section it is the pointlessness of much historical inquiry that Swift wishes to satirize.

44. (p. 241) *in good intelligence:* on good terms

45. (p. 241) *Junius:* The group of men gathered together here are all celebrated for their public virtues. Lucius Junius Brutus was one of the first two Roman consuls, and on the occasion of the rape of Lucretia he led the rising against the Tarquins; Socrates is included here particularly perhaps because of his courage in refusing to comply with the political passions of the moment; Epaminondas (420–362 B.C.) for his love of truth as well as his great military accomplishments; Marcus Porcius Cato (95–46 B.C.) because he was a man of absolute integrity and a great defender of Republican liberties against Caesar and the triumvirate; Sir Thomas More (1475–1535) for his refusal to compromise his religious convictions in accordance with Henry VIII's political needs.

46. (p. 242) *Didymus and Eustathius:* Didymus (b. Alexandria, 63 B.C.) lived and taught in Rome. He was a voluminous commentator and part of his treatise on Homer survives. Eustathius, Archbishop of Thessalonica in the twelfth century, composed a commentary on Homer which preserved material from earlier writers.

47. (p. 242) *Scotus:* Duns Scotus (c. 1270–1308), a chief critic of the system of Thomas Aquinas and commentator on Aristotle. It is from his name that the word 'dunce' derives and Aristotle's question is therefore particularly pointed.

48. (p. 242) *Ramus:* Pierre de la Ramée or Petrus Ramus (1515–72), a noted opponent of the idea of Aristotelian infallibility.

49. (p. 242) *Descartes:* René Descartes (1596–1650), one of the most influential figures of his age in philosophy, physics and mathematics

50. (p. 242) *Gassendi:* Pierre Gassendi (1592–1655) opposed the idea of Aristotelian infallibility and argued the superiority of Epicurean over Aristotelian and Cartesian physics.

51. (p. 243) *vortices:* Descartes' theory of vortices explained the movement of the heavenly bodies and was only superseded by Newton's theory of gravitation.

52. (p. 243) *attraction:* gravitation

53. (p. 243) *determined:* ended

54. (p. 243) *Eliogabalus's cooks:* Heliogabalus was Emperor of Rome from 218–22 until his assassination at the age of eighteen and is remembered for his exceptional cruelty and licentiousness.

55. (p. 243) *helot:* one of a class of serfs in ancient Sparta

56. (p. 243) *Agesilaus:* King of Sparta from 397 to 360 B.C., known for his hardiness and frugality in old age

57. (p. 244) *Polydore Virgil:* Italian cleric who spent a large part of his life in England and wrote a *History of England* (1534)

58. (p. 244) *Nec vir fortis, nec faemina casta:* 'neither a brave man nor a chaste woman'

59. (p. 244) *anecdotes:* Swift may be thinking here of Gilbert Burnet's *History of My Own Time.*

60. (p. 246) *Actium:* the sea-battle in 31 B.C. in which Mark Antony and Cleopatra were defeated by Octavius Caesar

61. (p. 246) *a libertina:* a freedwoman

62. (p. 246) *Publicola:* not identified

63. (p. 247) *pox:* Syphilis appeared as a widespread disease in Europe in the late fifteenth century.

64. (p. 249) *the Dutch . . . kingdom:* After a century of missionary activity by the Spanish and the Portuguese, Japan was closed in 1638 to all Europeans except the Dutch who were subject to severe restrictions and forbidden to show any sign of professing Christianity.

65. (p. 254) *public:* state, republic

66. (p. 255) *lower and upper world:* the earth and the heavens

67. (p. 255) *discovery of the longitude:* From 1714 onwards the British Government offered a series of rewards ranging from £10,000 to £20,000 for any generally practicable method of finding the longitude at sea.

68. (p. 258) *meres:* boundaries

69. (p. 260) *consequent:* consequence

70. (p. 261) *Yedo:* Tokyo

71. (p. 262) *Nangasac:* Nagasaki, which contained a Dutch colony

72. (p. 262) *Amboyna:* It has been suggested that, in giving the ship this name, Swift intended to recall a massacre of Englishmen by the

Dutch which had taken place at Amboyna in the East Indies in 1623.

73. (p. 263) *skipper*: ship's boy.

PART IV: A VOYAGE TO THE COUNTRY OF THE HOUYHNHNMS

1. (p. 267) *Campechy*: Campeche in the west of Yucatan in Mexico
2. (p. 267) *calenture*: tropical fever in which sailors leap into the sea
3. (p. 269) *toys*: trifles
4. (p. 271) *expect*: wait for
5. (p. 273) *Houyhnhnm*: The word has been variously pronounced but may be taken to echo the whinny of a horse.
6. (p. 278) *complaisant*: polite
7. (p. 280) *Charles V*: Charles V is supposed to have said that he would address his God in Spanish, his mistress in Italian and his horse in German.
8. (p. 286) *manhood*: human nature
9. (p. 292) *the Revolution*: the revolution of 1688 in which William of Orange supplanted James II as King
10. (p. 292) *Difference in opinions*: The allusions are to the controversies over transubstantiation, church music, the use of images in worship, and the use of church vestments.
11. (p. 293) *beggarly princes ... troops*: George I employed German mercenaries, a practice which caused great indignation in England.
12. (p. 296) *the Faculty*: the profession
13. (p. 302) *forlorn*: lost, desperate
14. (p. 303) *Act of Indemnity*: an act passed by Parliament to indemnify a person against liability for penalties incurred for unlawful acts innocently committed in the course of their duties
15. (p. 305) *managing*: treating with consideration
16. (p. 309) *undistinguished*: undiscriminating
17. (p. 311) *spleen*: a fashionable eighteenth-century complaint involving depression and melancholy
18. (p. 316) *fondness*: foolish affection
19. (p. 319) *indocible*: unteachable
20. (p. 320) *observed in me ... to me*: Just as Gulliver stood half-way physically between the Lilliputians and the Brobdingnagians so he stands half-way morally between the Houyhnhnms and the Yahoos.
21. (p. 330) *artificially*: artfully
22. (p. 333) *Mr Herman Moll*: a Dutchman who settled in London about 1698 and published a series of maps and geographical works

MORE ABOUT PENGUINS
AND PELICANS

Penguinews, which appears every month, contains details of all the new books issued by Penguins as they are published. From time to time it is supplemented by *Penguins in Print,* which is our complete list of almost 5,000 titles.

A specimen copy of *Penguinews* will be sent to you free on request. Please write to Dept EP, Penguin Books Ltd, Harmondsworth, Middlesex, for your copy.

In the U.S.A.: For a complete list of books available from Penguins in the United States write to Dept CS, Penguin Books, 625 Madison Avenue, New York, New York 10022.

In Canada: For a complete list of books available from Penguins in Canada write to Penguin Books Canada Ltd, 2801 John Street, Markham, Ontario L3R 1B4.

The Penguin English Library

DANIEL DEFOE

A TOUR THROUGH THE
WHOLE ISLAND OF GREAT BRITAIN

EDITED BY PAT ROGERS

Defoe's *Tour* (1724–6) was described by G. M. Trevelyan as 'a treasure indeed' and by Dorothy George as 'far the best authority for early eighteenth-century England'. But the *Tour* is something more than an invaluable source of social and economic history: Defoe's unfailing sense of process and of the mutability of things raises the work to the level of imaginative literature. Along with his remarkable gift for observation and for the telling anecdote and his truly poetic vision, Defoe brought to the tradition of travel-writing a lifetime's experience as businessman, soldier, economic journalist and spy.

National consciousness has usually marched to the literary tune of the epic. It was, however, 'not in some strutting Brutiad' but in this modest picture of British commerce and industry, cities and villages, country seats and market towns, in their growth and their decay, that the Augustan age produced 'not just a mirror of Britain . . . but a vision of nationhood'.

The Penguin English Library

LAURENCE STERNE

A SENTIMENTAL JOURNEY

WITH AN INTRODUCTION BY
A. ALVAREZ

Owing, perhaps, to his Irish blood, Laurence Sterne is one of the most engaging buttonholers in literature. He launches into conversation with no story to tell, little plan of narration, and a habit of slipping down every side-turning ... but there is no getting away from him. *A Sentimental Journey* began as an account of a tour by coach through France and Italy: it ends as a treasury of dramatic sketches, pathetic and ironic incidents, philosophical musings, reminiscences, and anecdotes. 'It is perhaps the most bodiless novel ever written', as Mr Alvarez remarks in his introduction. Nevertheless the studied artlessness of a work which was written by the dying author of *Tristram Shandy* forestalled by nearly two centuries those modern writers who in some ways resemble him – Joyce, Beckett, and Virginia Woolf.

The Penguin English Library

THREE GOTHIC NOVELS

WALPOLE
THE CASTLE OF OTRANTO

BECKFORD
VATHEK

MARY SHELLEY
FRANKENSTEIN

WITH AN INTRODUCTION BY MARIO PRAZ

The Gothic novel, that curious literary genre which flourished from about 1765 until 1825, revels in the horrible and the supernatural, in suspense and exotic settings. This volume, with its erudite introduction by Mario Praz, presents three of the most celebrated Gothic novels: *The Castle of Otranto*, published pseudonymously in 1765, is one of the first of the genre and the most truly Gothic of the three; in its blending of two kinds of romanticism, ancient and modern, it is a precursor of Romanticism. *Vathek* (1786), an oriental tale by an eccentric millionaire, exotically combines Gothic romanticism with the vivacity of *The Arabian Nights*, and is a narrative *tour de force*. The story of *Frankenstein* (1818) and the monster he created is as spine-chilling today as it ever was; as in all Gothic novels, horror is the keynote.

The Penguin English Library

JOHN BUNYAN

THE PILGRIM'S PROGRESS

EDITED BY ROGER SHARROCK

Bunyan wrote the first part of *The Pilgrim's Progress* when he was in prison as a Baptist preacher. It was published in 1678. In Bunyan's hands a pious tract is transformed into a work of imaginative literature which has been more widely read than any book in English except the Bible. Its influence, both indirectly on the English consciousness and directly on the literature that followed, has been immeasurable. The rich countryman's phrases that Bunyan borrowed or invented have become enshrined in the language, and many of the characters he created to people his imaginary world have won for themselves an independent and unforgettable existence.

The Penguin English Library

CHRISTOPHER MARLOWE

COMPLETE PLAYS

EDITED BY J. B. STEANE

In recent years there has been a widening of opinion about Marlowe; at one extreme he is considered an atheist rebel and at the other a Christian traditionalist. There is as much divergence in Marlowe's seven plays and, as J. B. Steane says in his introduction, that a man's work should encompass the extremes of *Tamburlaine* and *Edward the Second* is one of the most absorbingly interesting facts of literature; the range of Marlowe's small body of work covers such amazingly unlike pieces as *Doctor Faustus* and *The Jew of Malta*. Controlled and purposeful, these plays contain a poetry which enchants and lodges in the mind.

ALSO BY JOSHUA HAMMER

The Bad-Ass Librarians of Timbuktu: And Their Race
to Save the World's Most Precious Manuscripts

Yokohama Burning: The Deadly 1923 Earthquake and
Fire That Helped Forge the Path to World War II

A Season in Bethlehem: Unholy War in a Sacred Place

Chosen by God: A Brother's Journey

A TRUE TALE

of

ADVENTURE,

TREACHERY,

and the

HUNT FOR THE

PERFECT BIRD

"Joshua Hammer has that rare eye for a thrilling story, and with *The Falcon Thief* he has found the perfect one—a tale brimming with eccentric characters, obsession, deception, and beauty. It has the grip of a novel, with the benefit of being all true."

—David Grann, *New York Times* bestselling author of
Killers of the Flower Moon and *The Lost City of Z*

"I love this book. Josh Hammer has an amazing ability to find truly great yarns, and he's done this again with *The Falcon Thief*. It is a tremendous relief to read a book that teleports you out of current politics into a wholly new world that is both magical and thrilling and weird and wholly unknown. Stop, sit, read, think, savor, enjoy."

—Janet Reitman, bestselling author of *Inside Scientology*

"Middle Eastern sheikhs. 180-mph apex predators. An agile and fearless globe-trotting obsessive dangling beneath helicopters and slipping through borders from Patagonia to the high Arctic. *The Falcon Thief* is more than just a ripping page-turner; it is a cautionary tale about what happens when our most precious wildlife becomes status symbol in our diminishing natural world."

—Carl Hoffman, *New York Times* bestselling author of
The Last Wild Men of Borneo and *Savage Harvest*

"You don't need to know, or care, about birds to enjoy *The Falcon Thief*. I couldn't tell a jaybird from a jaywalker, but I loved this book: an international, ornithological whodunit. By the final page, I had learned, and cared, more about the secret world of falcons and the people who love them than I ever thought possible."

—Eric Weiner, *New York Times* bestselling author of
The Geography of Genius

"This book moves like a falcon: sleek and fast. It's an absorbing story of a thief, an obsession, and an astounding bird."

—Russell Shorto, *New York Times* bestselling author of
Revolution Song and *The Island at the Center of the World*

"Hammer is one of our great nonfiction storytellers, and he's got a terrific one here: a true-crime saga about how love of nature can go very, very wrong."

—Bruce Handy, author of *Wild Things*

"[A] well-written, engaging detective story that underscores the continuing need for conservation of rare bird species . . . A sleek, winning nonfiction thriller."
—*Kirkus Reviews* (starred review)

"Hammer delivers a vivid tale of obsession and international derring-do . . . this swashbuckling account should hold its audience rapt until the very end."
—*Publishers Weekly*

"Hammer paints a vivid portrait . . . Ultimately, this book is a fine tribute to Mc-William and to others dedicated to conservation, and a compelling deep dive into the psyche of a very specific sort of criminal."   —*BookPage*

"This stranger-than-fiction story is as engrossing as a fast-paced action-adventure, and is sure to hold the attention of a variety of readers. Fans of Jennie Erin Smith's *Stolen World* or Craig Welch's *Shell Games* will be piqued."
—*Library Journal*

"Hammer's chronicle is a captivating and surprising read with just the right touch of suspense and mystery."   —*Booklist*

"Slipping as perfectly into the newly developing natural history–true-crime sub-genre as it does into a carry-on, *The Falcon Thief* both informs and thrills."
—*Open Letters Review*

"Startling from the first page to the last."   —*Air Mail*

"Entertaining and illuminating . . . How McWilliam finally nailed his man should be left for Hammer . . . to tell, which he does in high style." —*The Washington Post*

"Enthralling . . . This rollicking tale follows the exploits of an audacious thief who stole raptor eggs from all corners of the globe for decades."   —*Shelf Awareness*

"It's a compelling and remarkable tale, vibrant and authentic, rendered more resonant by author Joshua Hammer's impressive research."
—*Washington Independent Review of Books*

"Hammer's account is both riveting and eye-opening."

—*Undark*

"Combining adventure and true crime, this gripping narrative is a fascinating and infuriating story that reads more like a novel than nonfiction. *The Falcon Thief* will appeal to those who also were enthralled by *The Feather Thief* by Kirk Wallace Johnson and *The Orchid Thief* by Susan Orlean, and to anyone who enjoys reading about birds, nature, and travel."

—*Forbes*

"*The Falcon Thief* has come along at a good time. If you are looking for a 'good read' while you are sheltering in place, this is a very good choice—entertaining, part true-crime thriller, part journalistic puzzle, part educational."

—*10,000 BIRDS*

"*The Falcon Thief* is a fast-moving narrative, written to entertain, yet Hammer weaves into it enough hard-to-find literature to make it a valuable primer on oology, raptor biology, Rhodesia, oriental falconry, and the birth of wildlife law enforcement in Britain. The author retraces his subject's . . . ambitious trips . . . in breathless detail."

—*The Times Literary Supplement*

"Hammer's investigation of Lendrum's theft of the eggs from a cliffside and the underground market for rare raptors is thrilling."

—*The Los Angeles Times*

"A truly wacky story about rare egg theft. . . . If you love nonviolent true crime, this is a great one, full of fascinating tidbits about the history of falconry, wildlife conservation and crime, and oology."

—*Book Riot*

"Absorbing, entertaining, and well-written."

—*The Spectator*

The
FALCON
THIEF

Joshua Hammer

SIMON & SCHUSTER PAPERBACKS

NEW YORK   LONDON   TORONTO

SYDNEY   NEW DELHI

Simon & Schuster Paperbacks
An imprint of Simon & Schuster, Inc.
1230 Avenue of the Americas
New York, NY 10020

First Simon & Schuster trade paperback edition February 2021

SIMON & SCHUSTER PAPERBACKS and colophon are registered trademarks of Simon & Schuster, Inc.

For information about special discounts for bulk purchases, please contact Simon & Schuster Special Sales at 1-866-506-1949 or business@simonandschuster.com.

The Simon & Schuster Speakers Bureau can bring authors to your live event. For more information or to book an event, contact the Simon & Schuster Speakers Bureau at 1-866-248-3049 or visit our website at www.simonspeakers.com.

Interior design by Carly Loman

Manufactured in the United States of America

10   9   8   7   6   5   4   3   2   1

Library of Congress Cataloging-in-Publication Data

Names: Hammer, Joshua, 1957- author.
Title: The falcon thief : a true tale of adventure, treachery, and the hunt for the perfect bird / Joshua Hammer.
Description: New York : Simon & Schuster, 2020. | Includes bibliographical references and index.
Identifiers: LCCN 2019031607 (print) | LCCN 2019031608 (ebook) | ISBN 9781501191886 (hardcover) | ISBN 9781501191893 (ebook)
Subjects: LCSH: Wildlife crimes. | Falcons—Eggs. | Wild bird trade. | Rare birds.
Classification: LCC HV6410 .H36 2020 (print) | LCC HV6410 (ebook) | DDC 364.16/28598961468092—dc23
LC record available at https://lccn.loc.gov/2019031607
LC ebook record available at https://lccn.loc.gov/2019031608

ISBN 978-1-5011-9188-6
ISBN 978-1-5011-9189-3 (ebook)
ISBN 978-1-5011-9190-9 (pbk)

CONTENTS

AUTHOR'S NOTE

This book is based on dozens of first-person interviews plus trial transcripts, videotaped interrogations, contemporary media accounts, and secondary source materials. FOIA requests filed with the British government for transcripts of police interviews were not successful, as these transcripts are generally disposed of after five years. In such cases, I reconstructed the exchanges based on extensive interviews with participants. Some other dialogue has also been reconstructed from memory and notes, to the best of my ability.

PROLOGUE

Shortly after New Year's Day in 2017, I was on vacation with my family in England when I happened to pick up a copy of the *Times* of London. A short article buried inside the newspaper caught my eye. "Thief Who Preys on Falcon Eggs Is Back on the Wing," declared the headline. The report by the *Times*'s crime correspondent John Simpson described a notorious wild-bird trafficker who had jumped bail and disappeared in South America:

> He has dangled from helicopters and abseiled down cliffs in search of falcon eggs for wealthy Arab clients . . . Now, the international egg thief is on the wing again after the authorities in Brazil admitted that they had lost him. [Jeffrey] Lendrum, 55, slipped the net after being caught with four albino falcon eggs stolen from Patagonia and jailed for more than four years. He is said to pose a serious threat to falcons in Britain and beyond . . .

The story of the egg thief grabbed my attention. The notion that there was a lucrative black market for wild birds' eggs seemed faintly ridiculous to me, like some wacky quest out of Dr. Seuss's *Scrambled Eggs Super!*, which I'd read aloud many times over the course of a decade to my three boys. I'd never considered that obtaining the world's most valuable eggs would require dangerous, logistically complex missions to the most remote corners of the planet. What kind of character would make a living that way? Was Lendrum one oddball or part of a whole hidden industry? Always a little skeptical of tabloid hype, I also wondered how much of a threat to endangered raptors Lendrum really posed. I tore out the clipping and started making casual inquiries when I got home.

As I found myself falling deeper into the life of Jeffrey Lendrum, discovering his childhood fascination with falcons and his compulsive tree climbing and nest raiding, something not altogether unexpected happened: I began to notice birds. That spring I traveled to southern Wales with two officers from Great Britain's National Wildlife Crime Unit to search for peregrines and their aeries in the cliffs of the Rhondda Valley. Later that summer, on a magazine assignment in the marshes of southern Iraq, I threaded through canals in a motorboat, acutely attuned to the avian life around me. Pied kingfishers, little black-and-white birds with needle-sharp beaks, darted out of the reeds as our craft sped past; a sacred ibis, with enormous black-tipped white wings and a scythe-like black bill, skimmed the surface of the marsh. I reread "My Bird Problem," a 2005 *New Yorker* essay, in which Jonathan Franzen described how his early bird-watching forays had heightened his excitement about venturing into the wild and encountering nature's breathtaking diversity. "A glimpse of dense brush or a rocky shoreline gave me a crush-like feeling, a sense of the world's being full of possibility," he wrote. "There were new birds to look for everywhere."

It wasn't only the rare ones that caught my eye. In April 2018, I returned from one of my last field-research trips about the falcon thief to discover my five-year-old son in a state of high excitement. By a remarkable coincidence, a pair of common pigeons, *Columba livia*, had built a nest on the bathroom window ledge of our third-floor apartment. For a month, as I wrote about the breeding behavior of birds in the wild and excavated the story of Lendrum's transformation from an adolescent nest raider to an international outlaw, I found regular inspiration looking at that ledge, easily visible across the courtyard from our kitchen window. Watching the pigeon incubate her eggs, observing the tiny, down-covered chicks as they huddled beneath their mother and grew in two weeks into awkward fledglings, made Lendrum's crimes more vivid to me—and more outrageous.

The bird-watching urge was proving irresistible. On Martha's Vineyard, in Massachusetts, the next summer I followed by kayak a pair of regal, ruffle-headed ospreys circling high above their man-made nest at the Long Point Wildlife Refuge; lost myself in a canoe for an hour among honking, socializing Canadian geese on Chilmark Pond; admired a red-tailed hawk soaring above the dunes at Great Rock Bight; and called my family outside to watch when an American robin briefly alit in our garden.

And then, as I was writing this book in the fall, came the most serendipitous moment. Early one morning I caught a flash of color just outside my office window in Berlin. A parakeet—an *Australian* parakeet—had landed on the ledge. Its brilliant green body and yellow head, illuminated by the morning sun, matched the changing leaves of the linden tree behind it. The bird must have escaped from somebody's cage and would soon be devoured by the predatory crows that stalk our neighborhood. One year earlier, I would probably have paid no attention to the sight, but now I called my partner excitedly and we watched it together, exhilarated by the bird's vivid presence, aware of its near-certain fate. The parakeet sat on the ledge for a good two minutes. Then it flew off and, pursued by a sparrow, was swallowed up by the leaves of the linden tree.

ONE

THE AIRPORT

The man had been in there far too long, John Struczynski thought. Twenty minutes had elapsed since he had entered the shower facility in the Emirates Lounge for business and first-class passengers at Birmingham International Airport, in the West Midlands region of England, 113 miles north of London. Now Struczynski stood in the corridor outside the shower room, a stack of fresh towels in the cart beside him, a mop, a pail, and a pair of CAUTION WET FLOOR signs at his feet. The janitor was impatient to clean the place.

The man and a female companion had been the first ones that day to enter the lounge, a warmly decorated room with butterscotch armchairs, a powder-blue carpet, dark wood columns, glass coffee tables, and black-shaded Chinese porcelain lamps. It was Monday, May 3, 2010—a bank holiday in the United Kingdom—and the lounge had opened at noon to accommodate passengers booked on the 2:40 p.m. Emirates direct flight to Dubai. The couple had settled into an alcove with a television near the reception desk. Minutes later the man had stood up and headed for the shower, carrying a shoulder bag and two small suitcases. That had struck Struczynski as strange. Who brings all of his luggage into the business-and-first-class shower room? And now he had been in there two or three times longer than any normal passenger.

A tall, lean man in his forties with short-cropped graying hair and a brush mustache, Struczynski had spent a decade monitoring 130 closed-circuit television cameras on the night shift at a Birmingham shopping mall, a job that "gave me a background in watching people," he would later say. That February, after the security firm laid him off, a management company had hired him to clean the Emirates Lounge. The first week he was there, the contractor enrolled him in an on-site training course to identify potential terrorist threats. The course, he would later say, heightened his normal state of suspicion.

As Struczynski puttered around the hallway, the shower room door opened, and the passenger—a balding, slender, middle-aged white man of average height—stepped out. He slipped past Struczynski without looking at him.

The cleaner opened the shower facility door and looked around the room.

My goodness, he thought. *What do we have here?*

The shower floor and glass partition surrounding it were both bone-dry. All the towels remained stacked and neatly folded. The toilet for the disabled hadn't been used. The washbasin didn't have a drop of water in it. Though the man had been inside the room for twenty minutes, he didn't appear to have touched anything.

Struczynski recalled the terrorism workshop that he had taken three months earlier, the exhortations from the instructor to watch out for odd looks and unusual behavior. This passenger was up to something. He knew it. Not sure what he was looking for, he rifled through the towels and facecloths, rummaged beneath the complimentary toothpaste tubes and other toiletries, checked the rubbish bin. He mounted a footstool and dislodged two ceiling tiles, wedging his hand into the hollow space just above them. Nothing.

He shifted his attention to the baby-changing area. In the corner of the alcove stood a plastic waist-high diaper bin with a round flip lid. Struczynski removed the top and looked inside. He noticed something sitting on the bottom: a green cardboard egg carton.

In one of the middle slots sat a single egg, dyed blood-red.

He stared at it, touched it gently. What could it mean?

He recalled the recent arrest at Heathrow Airport outside London of a man trying to smuggle rare Indian box turtles in egg cartons. But that seemed so odd. More likely this passenger was moving narcotics—like the gangsters in Liverpool who wedged packets of heroin and cocaine inside plastic Kinder Egg containers. *That's it*, he thought. *It must have something to do with drugs*.

Struczynski approached the reception area, a few steps from where the man and his traveling companion were sitting, and spoke softly to the two women working at the front desk. We may have a problem, he murmured, describing what he had just observed. He suggested that they call airport security, then returned to the shower and locked the door so that no one could disturb the evidence. Soon two uniformed security men entered the lounge, interviewed Struczynski, and examined the shower. The facility couldn't be seen from the alcove in which the passengers were sitting, and so, absorbed in conversation, the couple failed to notice the sudden activity.

The security guards summoned a pair of airport-based plainclothes officers from the West Midlands Counter Terrorism Unit. Formed in 2007 in the wake of the London bus-and-underground bombings, the unit had grown from seventy to nearly five hundred

officers, and was chiefly concerned with combating Islamist extrem-
ism. Counterterrorism forces had recently arrested a gang that had
conspired to kidnap and behead a British officer and post the footage
online, and had helped foil a plot by a Birmingham-born terrorist to
blow up transatlantic airliners using liquid explosives. These men,
too, questioned Struczynski, examined the egg box in the diaper bin,
and asked the janitor to point out the passenger. They flashed the
badges attached to lanyards around their necks, and chatted with him
and his companion politely. Struczynski watched discreetly as the
pair stood up and, flanked by the police, exited the lounge.

=

As hundreds of people hurried past them to their gates, the Counter Terrorism agents turned the woman over to colleagues and led
the man into a small, windowless room near a security checkpoint.
Several other officers squeezed into the space. The police asked the
passenger to sit down at a table, and informed him that they would
be questioning him under schedule seven of the Terrorism Act 2000,
which allowed them to detain him for up to twenty-four hours without a lawyer.

"Are you carrying any sharp objects?"

"No," he said, turning his pockets inside out.

"May we see your airline ticket and travel documents?"

The passenger presented an Irish passport identifying him as Jeffrey Paul Lendrum, born in Northern Rhodesia, now Zambia, on
October 26, 1961. He was traveling economy gold class in seat 40F
on flight EK040 on his Emirates Skywards frequent flyer miles, arriving in Dubai at twelve-fifteen in the morning local time after a
nearly seven-hour flight. Then he had a fourteen-hour layover be-

fore catching a connecting Royal Emirates flight to Johannesburg at two-thirty in the afternoon. It seemed a roundabout way to travel to South Africa: a journey of more than thirty hours, as opposed to a twelve-hour direct flight from the United Kingdom. Stapled to his boarding pass were baggage-claim stubs for four pieces of luggage, including a mountain bicycle.

A search of his hand luggage turned up an assortment of unusual gear: insulated hot-cold thermal bags, a Leica viewing scope, a thermometer, binoculars, a GPS system, a walkie-talkie, and a golf ball retriever, which used telescopic extensions to stretch up to seventeen feet. Lendrum carried plenty of cash: £5,000, $3,500 in US dollars, and some South African rand. He also had two more egg cartons. The first was empty. The other was filled with ten quail eggs—tiny white orbs with black speckles, about one-quarter the size of a hen's. Lendrum presented a receipt from Waitrose, the British supermarket chain, and explained that he was carrying farm-fresh organic eggs back home, because they were hard to find in Johannesburg.

The police ordered Lendrum to strip to his underwear.

Lendrum unbuttoned his shirt and slipped out of it. He stood there, arms at his sides, a blank expression on his face.

The agents stared.

Ribbons of white surgical tape were wrapped around his abdomen. Tucked snugly beneath the tape were one green, one black, and one blue woolen sock. Plastic zip ties divided each sock into five segments, and inside each segment was an oval-shaped object. The police unwrapped the surgical tape, removed the socks, cut off the ties, and, one by one, extracted the contents. They laid fourteen eggs gently on a table.

They were slightly smaller than ordinary hens' eggs, ranging in hue from marbleized brown to dark red. One was pale, with chocolate speckles; another had a background of caramel, bruised with plum-colored blotches. Yet another, all brown archipelagoes and continental landmasses juxtaposed against bright red lakes, gulfs, and seas, resembled high-resolution telescopic images of the surface of Mars. None of the police had ever seen anything like them.

"What kind of eggs are these?" an officer asked Lendrum.

"They're duck eggs," he replied.

"What were you planning to do with them?"

"Well, actually," he said, "I was taking them down to Zimbabwe, where my father lives." He was going to play a trick on the old man, he explained, hard-boiling every egg but one, and then getting a good laugh when his unsuspecting father cracked them all open.

"Why were you hiding them on your body?"

He was suffering from spinal problems, he explained, and his physiotherapist had recommended that he carry raw eggs strapped to his abdomen. Wearing the fragile objects against his belly would force him to keep his stomach muscles taut, he said, and strengthen his lower back.

The police officers exchanged incredulous looks.

This one, they realized, was entirely out of their league.

TWO

THE INVESTIGATOR

Andy McWilliam was in the rear garden of his home in Liverpool, playing with his two-year-old granddaughter in the late-afternoon sun, and trying to keep the toddler from running through the flower beds, when his cell phone went off in his kitchen. An officer of the Counter Terrorism Unit at Birmingham International Airport was on the line. He apologized for disturbing McWilliam on a bank holiday, but the unit was dealing with an unusual case, and a policewoman from Staffordshire, the neighboring county, had recommended that they contact him for guidance.

McWilliam was a retired policeman who now served as a senior investigative support officer for the National Wildlife Crime Unit (NWCU), a twelve-person team created in 2006 and headquartered in Stirling, outside Edinburgh. The unit employed four former detectives with a comprehensive knowledge of wildlife legislation to travel across Great Britain, helping local police investigate a range of offenses—from the trading of endangered species to animal cruelty. Unlike active-duty policemen, these support officers had no powers of arrest and couldn't obtain search warrants. They were essentially consultants, providing close-at-hand expertise to law enforcement officers who lacked a background in wildlife law.

Before joining the National Wildlife Crime Unit at its 2006 birth, McWilliam had spent thirty years on the police force in Merseyside, the county covering Liverpool and five metropolitan boroughs on both banks of the Mersey Estuary, which flows into the Irish Sea. In his last four years on the Merseyside force, McWilliam had specialized in wildlife crime, pursuing rhino-horn and ivory smugglers, tracking down dodgy taxidermists, and building cases against "badger baiters"—criminals who use dogs fitted with transmitters to corner the short-legged omnivores in their burrows six feet below-ground, and then drag them outside to torture and kill them for sport. Now he was doing much the same thing in an advisory capacity, and his beat had expanded to cover half of England. At the moment, the officer was gathering evidence against a trader in endangered-animal skulls, as well as a man who illegally sold protected tortoises over the Internet, and a Chinese-medicine dealer who was clandestinely distributing plasters made from the ground bones of leopards.

McWilliam's particular area of expertise, however, was bird crime. A ferocious rugby player for an amateur police team until his mid-thirties, he had quit the sport after suffering a series of injuries, and, in an attempt to fill his leisure time, had taken up a pursuit that could not have been a greater departure from the world of blood bins and choke tackles: bird-watching. Since then he had spent many weekends ambling through a wetland reserve north of Liverpool, twelve square miles of marshes and fields that attracted tens of thousands of migrating pink geese, along with snipes, black-tailed godwits, dunlins, lapwings, redshanks, great crested grebes, ospreys, and dozens of other species that rotated in and out throughout the year.

The interest had carried over into his professional life. In the early 2000s, he made a name for himself arresting obsessives who raided eggs from the nests of endangered species, blew out the live embryos, and mounted the hollowed shells in personal collections. He also investigated numerous cases of "bird laundering"—stealing protected birds of prey from the wild and passing them off as the offspring of captive-bred raptors. McWilliam had developed a nearly unmatched expertise in the birds of Great Britain.

McWilliam was a burly man with arched eyebrows, deep-set blue eyes, a broad nose, a square jaw, and a thatch of tousled gray hair that was thinning on top. One unruly strand often dangled down the center of his forehead. His owlish features, accentuated by square-framed spectacles, suggested a keen intelligence and sense of humor, and his powerful physique gave him the appearance of a man not to be trifled with. He had the grace and the quickness of a former athlete, though a modest paunch had crept up on him since the end of his rugby-playing days. He listened intently as the Counter Terrorism officer characterized the case.

"We're not quite sure what we've got here," he said. They had stopped a passenger bound for South Africa with a fourteen-hour layover in Dubai, he explained, and then recounted the body search and discovery of what the passenger had claimed were duck eggs.

"Describe the eggs," McWilliam said.

As his colleague detailed their size, colors, and patterns, McWilliam knew that the passenger had been lying. The eggs, he was all but certain, were those of the peregrine falcon, the fastest animal on the planet, a denizen of all continents except Antarctica. The strong and solitary raptors—with an average wingspan of forty inches, sooty black feathers around the head and neck, blue-gray wings, a black-barred buff-white underside, bright orange-yellow eyes, and a sharply hooked beak—nest in rock quarries and on ledges in the cliffs of England, Wales, and Scotland, and are relatively easy for a backcountry bird-watcher to spot. But the species nearly died out in both Europe and North America during the 1950s and 1960s as their prey—chiefly wood pigeons and pheasants—became riddled with organochloride pesticides, most notably dichlorodiphenyltrichloroethane, or DDT.

First synthesized by an Austrian chemist in 1874, DDT came into widespread use during World War II as a lice-killer, after the compound was discovered to have pesticidal properties in 1939. Allied doctors successfully dusted thousands of soldiers, refugees, and prisoners with a powdered form of the chemical; none suffered ill effects. Buoyed by the conviction that the compound was harmless, governments and industries began promoting liquid DDT (dissolved in oil) as the perfect way to kill off agricultural pests and yellow-fever-carrying mosquitoes. But when inhaled, ingested, or absorbed by the skin, liquid DDT worked its way to organs that stored fat—such as the liver, testicles, and intestines—and built up with deadly effect. Even a tiny amount, three parts in a million, was capable of disintegrating healthy cells in humans. DDT also passed easily from mother to unborn child, and from species to species.

During surveys in the 1950s, English ornithologist Derek Ratcliffe began to notice dwindling peregrine populations and strange behavior among the remaining birds. Some mothers even seemed to be pecking apart their own eggs. When Ratcliffe, acting on a hunch, later compared newly laid eggs to those in a museum collection gathered before 1946, when DDT was introduced to the United Kingdom, he discovered that the new eggs weighed 19 percent less than the old. The mother peregrines, he realized, hadn't pecked their eggs to pieces. They were feeding on the remains of thin, brittle eggs that had collapsed beneath their weight during incubation.

Laboratory tests at Cornell University would show that DDT increased the size of peregrines' livers, stimulating production of an enzyme that defends the organ against foreign chemicals. This enzyme in turn caused a plunge in female peregrines' production of sex hormones, including estrogen, which regulates the amount of calcium stored in bones. Less calcium in the females' bodies resulted in thinner, more fragile eggs.

hormones in birds?

The result was, as Ratcliffe wrote in his book *The Peregrine Falcon*, "a spectacular crash of population with a speed and on a scale seldom found in the vertebrate kingdom." By the early 1970s, only 250 breeding pairs of peregrine falcons were left in Great Britain. The losses were even steeper in North America. There, the *New York Times* reported in 1970 that "all peregrine eyries in the East and in the Upper Mississippi Valley, where once the bird flourished, were empty. In the Rocky Mountains and Far West, less than 10 percent of the prepesticide breeding population remains . . . In all the US, excepting Alaska, perhaps a dozen, and certainly no more than two or three dozen, peregrine families mated, laid eggs and hatched and fledged their young this year . . . The birds are gone."

Rachel Carson's seminal 1962 book *Silent Spring* (originally titled *Man Against the Earth*) had already drawn international attention to the link between DDT and the destruction of bird populations across the United States. Calling insecticides "as crude a weapon as the caveman's club," Carson documented how the lethal chemicals worked their way up the food chain. In California, irrigation water laden with pesticides was recycled back into lakes, where it settled in the organs of fish. As herons, pelicans, gulls, and other birds frequented the lakes and ate there, their populations died off. In Wisconsin, the culprit was pesticides sprayed on trees to protect against Dutch elm disease; the pesticides poisoned the earthworms that ate the trees' leaves, which passed the toxins on to robins. American bald eagles vanished across coastal Florida, New Jersey, and Pennsylvania, swan grebes declined in the western states and Canada, and pheasants, ducks, and blackbirds disappeared from the rice-growing regions of California and the South. "This sudden silencing of the song of birds, this obliteration of the colour and beauty and interest they lend to our world," wrote Carson, "have come about swiftly, insidiously, and un-noticed by those whose communities are as yet unaffected." Carson's groundbreaking work, along with research papers by Ratcliffe and other ornithologists on the near-extinction of the peregrine, led to a North American ban on the use of DDT in 1972, and dieldrin, an-other devastating insecticide, in 1974. The United Kingdom and the rest of Europe followed with legislation a decade later.

Since then, Great Britain's peregrine population had climbed back to fourteen hundred pairs—about five hundred more pairs than there had been in the 1930s, before the DDT disaster struck. In recent years, a few hardy peregrines had also taken up residence in urban areas, including a pair roosting atop the clock tower of City Hall in the Welsh city of Cardiff, and a total of thirty pairs in London. But the birds were still considered at risk. The Convention on International Trade in Endangered Species of Wild Flora and Fauna (CITES), a global wildlife protection agreement signed by 183 countries, had designated the peregrine an Appendix I bird, meaning that it was threatened with extinction and subject to the highest level of commercial restrictions. Following guidelines established by CITES, the British government had enacted the Control of Trade in Endangered Species Enforcement Regulations in 1997, making both the peregrine's removal from the wild and trade in the bird punishable by lengthy prison terms. That legislation was enforced alongside the Customs and Excise Management Act from 1979, which made it a crime to "knowingly and fraudulently evad[e] regulations" on restricted goods, including narcotics, weapons, and protected wildlife.

Still, conservationists were not in complete agreement on the issue: some argued that the number of wild peregrines in the United Kingdom and elsewhere had stabilized, and that the laws should be modified. In 1999 the US government removed peregrines from its endangered species list. At a biannual CITES conference in October 2016, Canada would propose downgrading the peregrine's status from Appendix I to Appendix II, a category for animals considered to be in less immediate danger. But most member countries rejected the proposal, citing "concern over inadequate precautionary measures" to prevent the raptor's disappearance. "As an apex predator [the peregrine falcon] always will have a small population, and be vulnerable to persecution because it sits at the top of the food chain," said Guy Shorrock, the senior investigative officer of the UK's influential Royal Society for the Protection of Birds.

—

Without even seeing the eggs seized at Birmingham Airport, McWilliam had little doubt that they were fertile and close to hatching. Late April to early May was the period in which peregrine chicks would be breaking out of their shells across the northern hemisphere. That the passenger was carrying the eggs strapped to his body suggested he needed to keep them warm until their incubation period was complete.

Plus there was the fact that he was heading for Dubai.

McWilliam's work on bird-related cases with the Merseyside police had introduced him to a thriving international market for birds of prey. This legal trade linked wealthy Arab devotees of the ancient sport of falconry with licensed breeders in the United States, Great Britain, and other countries in Western Europe. The business was tightly regulated, using a system of government-issued metal or plastic rings fitted around the birds' legs and certificates to guarantee that the birds had been born and bred in captivity. No bird of prey could be sold legally in the United Kingdom unless it had an "Article 10"—a document issued by the country's Animal and Plant Health Agency, in accordance with regulations established by the Convention on International Trade in Endangered Species of Wild Flora and Fauna—testifying that it had not been snatched from the wild.

But McWilliam was also aware of a lucrative underground market for falcons. Investigative studies by conservation groups, along with information provided by commercial breeders, had disclosed that the richest Middle Eastern aficionados were spending huge sums, allegedly up to $400,000 for a single bird, to acquire raptors illegally from the wild. Believing that wild birds were faster, stronger, and healthier than those born and raised in captivity, these sheikhs employed "trappers" to snatch young birds from the most remote corners of the globe. The thieves used pigeons and other lures to take fledglings in mid-flight, or, on occasion, scaled cliffs and trees and seized chicks from nests.

Expensive paramilitary-style expeditions to the Kamchatka Peninsula in southeastern Russia, Siberia, Mongolia, the Indian subcontinent, Greenland, and other remote wilderness areas were said to be disturbing the delicate ecological balance of pristine regions by decimating bird populations, threatening the survival of some of the world's most endangered species. In the two decades since the collapse of the Soviet Union, raptor raiders had nearly wiped out saker falcons—a migratory species, larger and slower than the peregrine, that breeds from Central Europe eastward across Asia to Manchuria. It thrives especially in the desert environments of the Altai-Sayan region of Central Asia, a 386,000-square-mile area known for its remarkable biological diversity and home to a variety of threatened species, including the snow leopard and the Lake Baikal seal. The majestic gyrfalcon, the largest and most sought-after falcon of all, was in danger of eradication from huge swaths of the Russian wilderness, including the Chukotka Peninsula near the Bering Strait. Mark Jeter, a former assistant chief of the California Department of Fish and Wildlife, describes the black market trade succinctly: "I always say, if there is a $50,000 bill flying around, someone is going to try to catch it."

The trafficking of live wild falcon eggs was an ingenious variation on this scheme. Back in October 1986, a Welsh falcon breeder named Ceri Griffith had arrived at Manchester Airport, on a flight from Morocco, carrying twenty-seven lanner falcon eggs stitched into secret pockets in his shirt. In a bit of bad timing for Griffith, one egg hatched at the moment that he was passing through customs—and officials, hearing tweeting, ordered him to strip and seized the live contraband. Griffith avoided jail time but paid a £1,350 fine, close to the maximum penalty a wild-bird egg smuggler could receive at that time.

The egg trafficking went in both directions: In April 1990 customs officials at Dover, on the southeast coast of England, pulled over a Mercedes-Benz bound for mainland Europe and, acting on a tip, took the car apart and found a sophisticated incubation system hidden inside the dashboard, heated by the vehicle's engine and filled with a dozen live peregrine falcon eggs taken from cliffs in Wales and Scotland. The two Germans in the vehicle pleaded guilty to smuggling offenses and were sentenced to thirty months in prison.

Since the incident in 1990, however, nobody had been arrested in the United Kingdom for smuggling wild raptor eggs; most law enforcement officials regarded the two busts in Manchester and Dover as isolated incidents. Now the detention of this new suspect at Birmingham Airport en route to Dubai suggested not only that egg trafficking was still a problem, but also that the operation was more ambitious than anybody had believed. Smugglers could be running eggs between Europe and the Arab world in a far-reaching conspiracy to defy international wildlife laws and damage the environment, financed by some of the richest and most powerful men on earth.

It disgusted McWilliam to think about it. Human beings had an obligation, he believed, to protect the environment and to coexist with other species with as little fuss as possible. "All living things were not made for man," the biologist and co-originator of evolutionary theory Alfred Russel Wallace had written in 1869, expressing a philosophy that McWilliam embraced. "Their happiness and enjoyments, their loves and hates, their struggles for existence, their vigorous life and early death, would seem to be immediately related to their own well-being and perpetuation alone." What better reminder that humans were not the sole proprietors of the planet than the birds in your backyard? And as Rachel Carson pointed out in *Silent Spring*, it served man's interests to avoid rupturing the bonds between species—after all, the beauty, variety, and vitality of the planet depended on it. "To the bird watcher, the suburbanite who derives joy from birds in his garden, the hunter, the fisherman or the explorer of wild regions, anything that destroys the wildlife of an area . . . has deprived him of pleasure to which he has a legitimate right," she wrote. Lendrum's crime was a rebuke to the laws that Great Britain had carefully put into place over the decades to safeguard the future. Robbing nests for sport, or for greed, struck McWilliam as an egregious violation of the fragile, symbiotic relationship between man and the wild.

"Don't let the man go," McWilliam told the officer. He suggested that the Counter Terrorism Unit arrest the suspect on a preliminary charge of possessing endangered species, which constituted a violation of the Wildlife and Countryside Act, a 1981 law passed by Parliament that expanded the protections afforded wild birds and animals and increased penalties for those who harmed them.

"I'm dropping everything and coming down to meet you," McWilliam said, adding, "Whatever you do, keep the eggs warm."

Five minutes later, McWilliam grabbed a toothbrush and a knapsack full of notebooks, said goodbye to his wife, son, daughter-in-law, and granddaughter, and climbed into his leased Peugeot hatchback for the one-hundred-mile trip to Birmingham.

=

As McWilliam drove south from Liverpool on the M6 with the late-afternoon sunlight streaming through the passenger window, he felt a rising sense of anticipation. Since the Welsh lanner-egg smuggler Griffith had walked free after paying a modest fine in 1986, Great Britain's courts had hardened their attitudes toward wildlife crime. Environmental damage and profit motive had become key considerations in determining sentencing: a professional criminal making off with protected species to supply an underground market was a far bigger threat, law enforcement officials believed, than someone stealing birds for a small personal collection. If the eggs were indeed what McWilliam presumed they were, this offense would constitute one of the most serious crimes ever investigated by the National Wildlife Crime Unit in its four years of existence. Until now, McWilliam's cases mostly involved cruelty to animals or the illegal sale by taxidermists of the preserved parts of protected species—crimes considered the equivalent of misdemeanors and usually punishable by a fine. Live falcon smuggling carried a maximum punishment of seven years in prison.

McWilliam had reason to think that the case might be a game-changer. McWilliam had been aware of the role allegedly played by Middle Eastern royal families in the illicit trade of wild raptors, but had never come across hard evidence. Maybe the suspect could lead him to some sheikhs. The oddity of the crime was also likely to attract the interest of the media, giving the National Wildlife Crime Unit, a bare-bones outfit engaged in a permanent struggle with politicians and the police force to obtain enough funding to operate, a chance to prove that its money was being well spent. A headline-making conviction of a notorious wildlife criminal could protect the unit from closure—or even, if McWilliam was very, very lucky, get his budget significantly raised for the next year.

He called the unit's intelligence chief, a Scottish former drug investigator named Colin Pirie, to alert him to the arrest and to request that he begin digging into the suspect's background. Then he reached out to Lee Featherstone, a local raptor expert and a breeder of goshawks—large, red-eyed, white-browed raptors that frequent the forests of Europe and North America. Featherstone and McWilliam had crossed paths during a wild-bird laundering investigation the previous year. McWilliam asked Featherstone, who was on the way home from a birds-of-prey fair in the Midlands, to join him at the airport to verify what species the eggs belonged to, and whether they were viable.

Ninety minutes later, McWilliam parked his car at Birmingham International Airport and made his way to an operational office belonging to the Counter Terrorism Unit. Two of the arresting officers briefed him on Lendrum's detention, and then escorted him down a bland hallway to a cramped room used by the United Kingdom Border Agency, with three desks and an array of 1990s-era computers. The officers showed him the fourteen eggs that now rested, wrapped in their woolen socks, atop a computer monitor. Fluorescent lights and heated air blowing through the bulky machine's fan vents were keeping them warm. Beside them on the officers' desk lay the mysterious egg carton retrieved from the diaper bin inside the Emirates Lounge shower facility. The red-dyed egg that had piqued the janitor's interest—as it turned out, an ordinary chicken egg—was still sitting inside the carton. Next to the carton was the box full of tiny, black-speckled quail eggs that the police had found in Lendrum's luggage.

When Lee Featherstone arrived ten minutes later, he extracted from his backpack a blue digital monitor called an Egg Buddy, a device about the size of a butter tray used by breeders to detect the heartbeat of a chick inside its shell. The breeder untied the socks and carefully removed the eggs. Featherstone noted the size, marbling, and presence of protoporphyrin, a brownish red pigment found in the shells of many raptor eggs. The color could be useful, evolutionary scientists theorize, to protect against solar radiation and for camouflage on rock ledges.

Without a doubt, Featherstone said, these were the eggs of peregrine falcons.

Featherstone gently placed one egg inside the Egg Buddy and closed the lid. On the green rectangular LED screen he and McWilliam watched a black line rise and fall rapidly and rhythmically, registering six hundred beats per minute, the normal heart rate for a peregrine chick. "That's alive," Featherstone said. He placed another egg in the tray. "That's alive." Huddled inside its shell, a tiny creature was preparing to punch with its beak through the internal membrane that protected its body, take its first breaths from an air pocket that lay just beyond, and then peck its way through the shell and into the world. One after another, the eggs registered strong heartbeats. Only one of the fourteen showed a flat line.

To Featherstone, the fact that Lendrum had absconded with fourteen eggs, and that thirteen were still alive, proved that the thief was a professional. Even just locating so many peregrine eggs in the wilderness—at four eggs to a clutch, a minimum of four aeries—must have required patience, acute powers of observation, physical courage, and athletic skill. It took more expertise to ensure that the fragile creatures survived being ripped out of their nests, bounced around in a car for hours, and then strapped to a human body for a four-thousand-mile journey to the Middle East. If the thief snatched the eggs too early—within the first three weeks of the peregrine's thirty-four-day incubation period, when the ambient temperature must remain between 99.1 and 99.5 degrees Fahrenheit at all times—they would die. If he snatched them too late, he risked having them hatch in his pocket or his backpack while he was going through customs or waiting in the airport security line. The falcon thief's calculations had to be perfect.

The decoy quail eggs and the painted hen's egg were further signs of the criminal's attention to detail. It was a clever tactic, probably meant to persuade a customs agent that he was carrying ordinary farm eggs home to eat.

"He knew what he was doing," Featherstone told McWilliam. "You have to wonder how many times he's gotten away with it."

Featherstone placed the eggs back in the socks, secured them with the plastic ties, took off his woolen sweater, and carefully wrapped the socks up inside it. Then he tied the sweater and the socks around his chest, so that the eggs would absorb his body warmth. "They're fertile, they're alive, but they're getting chilled," Featherstone told the police. The raptor breeder drove to his home ten minutes from the airport, where he kept the eggs warm, manually rotating them every hour for the next several days and nights.

The thirteen eggs would hatch between five and eight days later, and ornithologists from the Royal Society for the Protection of Birds, the country's biggest environmental charity, would introduce the newborn chicks to active nest sites on cliff ledges in northern Scotland. Eleven of the thirteen would fledge in the wild.

In Birmingham, McWilliam checked into an airport hotel and prepared for the next morning, when he would meet the egg thief.

THREE

THE INTERVIEW

Shortly before eleven o'clock in the morning on Tuesday, May 4, Andy McWilliam parked his Peugeot at the rear of the police headquarters in Solihull, a town in the West Midlands region southeast of Birmingham. A police sergeant buzzed him through a security gate at the back of the three-story concrete slab, and escorted him and two plainclothes detectives from the local Counter Terrorism Unit to the "custody suites" on the ground floor.

McWilliam and his fellow investigators entered a small, windowless interview room, furnished with a metal table and six chairs bolted to the floor as a precaution against outbursts from unruly detainees. A cassette recorder on the table would record four tapes—for the court, the police, and the solicitor, plus one backup—using a microphone mounted on the wall.

Accompanied by a solicitor provided by the court, Jeffrey Lendrum walked into the chamber. He had been brought in handcuffs from Birmingham International Airport to the custody suites the previous evening. The woman who'd been with him in the Emirates Lounge, his domestic partner and a South African citizen, had claimed to know nothing about the eggs on Lendrum's body. After strip-searching her and finding no incriminating evidence, the police had permitted her to board her afternoon flight to Dubai. "She was in a terrible state," Lendrum would say years later. "I regret that."

McWilliam studied the man. Dressed in jeans and a polo shirt, Lendrum was trim and good-looking, with large, deep-set eyes, vestiges of gray hair around an otherwise bald head, and an open and friendly face. He seemed in good shape, yet he didn't fit the image of a swaggering stuntman or adventurer. McWilliam could as easily picture him in a business suit as rappelling down a cliff.

The lead Counter Terrorism officer read Lendrum his rights and informed him that his statements were being recorded. As they had agreed earlier, McWilliam would let his colleague begin the interrogation; McWilliam, the wildlife expert, would take over when the moment seemed right.

"Okay, you were arrested yesterday," the agent began. "Why were you carrying the eggs strapped to your body?"

Lendrum repeated the story that he had told the airport police: he suffered from a chronic lower backache and his physiotherapist had instructed him to wear raw eggs strapped around his abdomen. It was an unusual remedy, he acknowledged, but nothing else had helped, so he'd decided to give it a try.

McWilliam, scribbling silently in a notepad, let Lendrum ramble on for several minutes. Then he jumped in.

"This is ridiculous," he said. "It's a cock-and-bull story. You and I both know exactly what kind of eggs you were carrying."

"They're duck eggs," Lendrum said. The solicitor sat beside Lendrum silently, jotting occasional notes, whispering into Lendrum's ear, but making no attempts to interrupt the questioning.

"They're peregrine falcon eggs," said McWilliam.

"Duck eggs," Lendrum insisted.

"They're peregrine falcon eggs," McWilliam repeated. Identifying himself as an investigative support officer with the National Wildlife Crime Unit, McWilliam described the marbleized browns and reds, the dark pigments produced by natural selection over the millennia to protect eggs from direct sunlight on the cliff ledges where peregrines nest.

Lendrum leaned back in his chair and went silent. McWilliam sensed what the suspect was probably thinking: the investigator across the table knew far more about birds of prey than he had expected.

"All right," Lendrum conceded. "They're peregrine falcon eggs. I've got an egg collection at home, and I was taking them back there."

"So they were for a collection, then?"

"Yes," Lendrum replied. Under McWilliam's gentle prodding, Lendrum talked of a boyhood spent climbing trees and rock faces near his Rhodesian home, of his longtime fascination with peregrines, eagles, and hawks. He described the weavers, rollers, and other passerines, or perching birds, that frequented the African bush. He had lived on and off for a decade in Towcester, a town in Northamptonshire in the Midlands, where his former wife and two stepdaughters still resided, but he always returned to Southern Africa, partly because of his love of the birds and other wildlife of the region.

"Hang on a minute," McWilliam said. "So you've lived in the United Kingdom, on and off, for many years?"

"That's right," Lendrum replied.

"But you can't live in this country and not know the legislation. It's inconceivable that you wouldn't know about the protections afforded these birds."

"I—I know that there are some laws," Lendrum said, appearing to sense a trap, "but I'm not familiar with the specifics." Besides, he went on, "I'm not quite sure what harm there is in what I did. The eggs that I collected were all dead."

"We had them all tested yesterday," McWilliam said. "They're alive."

"No," Lendrum replied.

"You know exactly what you were doing," the investigator said, exasperated by the smug denials. Lendrum had to have realized by now that McWilliam understood exactly what he'd done. "You strapped them to your body to get them through security because you didn't want them to be found, and you wanted to keep them warm."

"No, no," Lendrum protested.

"Let's cut the rubbish," McWilliam said. "You were taking these falcon eggs out live because they are destined for the falcon trade in Dubai."

"Dubai was just a stopover," Lendrum insisted. He preferred to travel from London to Johannesburg on Emirates using frequent-flyer miles, he explained, which made it far cheaper than a direct flight to South Africa.

McWilliam tried a new tack.

"So," he asked, "where did these eggs come from, Jeff?"

Lendrum said that he had taken them from four aeries in and around the Rhondda Valley, a rugged former coal mining region in the south of Wales. He had driven there on holiday in his car, he said, and had stumbled by chance across a dozen peregrine nests while hiking in the hills. His initial thought was that he might hatch them and breed them when he returned to Africa, but when he took them out of the vehicle at Birmingham Airport, he realized that they were dead.

So he wrapped them in socks to protect the shells, with the intention of "blowing" the dead embryos when he got home and mounting the eggs in his collection. He insisted that he hadn't realized he was breaking any laws.

"You parked your car at the airport?" McWilliam asked.

When Lendrum answered in the affirmative, McWilliam stopped the interview, ushered the two Counter Terrorism agents out of the building, and climbed back into his Peugeot.

"Let's go find that car," he said.

=

At Birmingham Airport, Counter Terrorism investigators typed Lendrum's name into a police database to obtain his registration information. The car in question was a 2008 gray Vauxhall Vectra Estate registered to his ex-wife's address in Towcester, with license plate number Y262KPP.

McWilliam and his two colleagues drove to long-term parking, a sprawling outdoor lot with a capacity of seven hundred vehicles. Dividing the lot, McWilliam and a second carload of agents drove up and down their allotted rows, seeking out the gray car. After twenty minutes, the other car radioed that they'd found the Vauxhall in spot C10. McWilliam had retrieved the key from Lendrum's personal effects before leaving the station. Now he inserted it in the door. It didn't turn.

"Smash open the window," McWilliam said.

An agent punched through the front passenger window with a tire jack. McWilliam opened the door, brushed the glass off the seat, and peered inside. Old folded maps of Wales and the Midlands and used coffee cups littered the musty interior. McWilliam opened the glove compartment. Inside, he discovered a handheld satellite navigation device. Then he walked to the rear. An officer popped the rear door using a lever beneath the steering column.

"Bloody hell," McWilliam said.

A large metal-and-yellow-plastic box bearing a label from British hatcher manufacturer Brinsea lay inside. McWilliam recognized it immediately as an egg incubator. An electric cable joined to a two-foot extension cord ran from the incubator through the space between the two backseats to the cigarette lighter on the dashboard. Beside the incubator was a three-foot-high blue canvas backpack filled with coiled climbing ropes, carabiners, and steel stakes. McWilliam photographed the evidence and returned to the interview room at police headquarters, where Lendrum was still waiting.

McWilliam laid the incubator, the ropes, and the other gear on the table.

"If you're just an egg collector, then how do you explain this?" McWilliam asked. "Why the hell do you have an incubator in your car?"

Lendrum shrugged. The incubator was intended for "hens in Zimbabwe." The eggs, he repeated, were for his collection in South Africa. Again he insisted that the embryos inside were no longer alive. He had worn them on his body to self-treat a bad back. He denied that the dyed red egg left behind in the Emirates shower room was a decoy.

McWilliam was used to dealing with liars, but this was a new level of willful deceit. Did Lendrum really expect him to believe such blatant prevarication? Was this some kind of casually sociopathic detachment from reality? Or had he gotten away with his crimes for so long that he'd come to believe he could talk his way out of anything?

"Bollocks," McWilliam said. "You know that peregrines are a protected species. You know you cannot legally export them without a permit."

"I didn't know that," Lendrum said.

"If you thought it was okay, then why did you conceal them? Why did you strap them to your body? All of your actions, the fact that you didn't declare them at any time to security, the fact that you were hiding them on your body, the evidence in the boot [the car's trunk], all of the evidence shows planning and preparation. Is there anything you want to say?"

Lendrum shook his head, and McWilliam terminated the interview. He saw nothing more to be gained from it.

=

The Crown Prosecution Service ordinarily has twenty-four hours following an arrest to charge a suspect with a crime, although the custody period can be extended for twelve more hours at the discretion of the police officer responsible for the prisoner. If the prosecution declines to charge the suspect by that deadline, he must be released immediately. If it decides to file charges, then it is up to a judge to set bail or to keep him in jail until trial. In this case, the police superintendent at Solihull had extended Lendrum's detention to thirty-six hours, and about eight hours remained on the "custody clock." McWilliam knew that most prosecutors in the United Kingdom had no familiarity with wildlife legislation, and it was impossible to predict what they would say about a batch of stolen eggs. If Lendrum walked out the door, McWilliam was certain that he would flee the country. Beneath the nonchalant demeanor, he sensed a career criminal who'd been undertaking this kind of operation for years—and would for decades more, despite this tussle with the law.

How had he financed his expedition to South Wales? Who had sent him there? How often had he made these trips? McWilliam wanted answers, and he knew he was running out of time.

FOUR

THE ART OF FALCONRY

In 1839, a twenty-two-year-old aspiring diplomat and amateur archaeologist named Austen Henry Layard quit his job as a clerk in his uncle's London law office and set out on what would become a decade-long journey across the Middle East. Arriving six years later at the Tigris River near Mosul in what is now Iraq, Layard excavated the ruins of Dur-Sharrukin, an Assyrian capital built between 720 and 700 B.C. There—amid temples emblazoned with cuneiform writings celebrating King Sargon II, the conqueror of Babylon, and giant statues of lamassus (winged creatures with the head of a man and body of a lion or a bull)—Layard unearthed a bas-relief that showed, he wrote, "a falconer bearing a hawk on his wrist." The bearded hunter holds thin straps made of leather, known as jesses, or *sbuq* in Arabic, between his thumb and index finger, with the ends tied around the raptor's feet. Layard's discovery, the earliest known representation of falconry, made a strong case that the sport had originated in the Arab world at least twenty-five hundred years before.

In its early days, long before the arrival of Islam in the Middle East, falconry served as a means of survival. Bedouins in the Arabian Desert trapped peregrines during the raptors' autumn migration from Europe or Central Asia to Africa. The nomads trained the birds to kill and return to the gauntlet worn on their human's fist, and to hunt hares or houbara bustards (large terrestrial birds) to supplement the Bedouins' meager diet of milk and dates and rice. It was an efficient way of putting food on the table, and it established a unique relationship between man and bird. "For the Bedouin the [falcon's] victory over its quarry was a feat of courage and strength in which they felt able to share," wrote Mark Allen, a noted Arabist and the onetime director of MI6's counterterrorism unit, in his 1980 book *Falconry in Arabia*. "In the [falcon's] graceful restraint at rest and her grim hardness in the field, the Bedouin saw qualities which were for him among the criteria for honor in a tribal society."

Arab traders likely introduced falconry to the West before the fall of the Roman Empire: in *Eucharisticos*, a confessional meditation written by the Macedonian Christian poet Paulinus of Pella in A.D. 458, the author recalls his adolescent wish to possess "a swift dog and a splendid hawk." But in medieval Europe, falconry was practiced differently than in the early Bedouin hunts: training and housing birds of prey was beyond the means of most manor-bound peasants, and forests were the protected domains of the nobility, so "hawking," as the sport also was known, became a leisure pursuit of monarchs and nobles, who organized lavish hunting parties on their estates. The aristocracy even established a pecking order, laid out in the *Book of Saint Albans* in 1486, for who could hunt with what. Only the king was entitled to a gyrfalcon, the world's most exotic raptor, brought by traders from frozen Nordic cliffs. A prince could use a "falcon gentle," or female peregrine, while a knight would have to make do with the slower but often equally agile saker. To a lady went a merlin, a small and sturdy falcon with a blocklike head. Lesser birds were designated for those common folk who did have the resources to hunt; these included the sparrow hawk for a priest, and the lowly kestrel for the "knave or servant" of a lord. Kings built elaborate mews on palace grounds, and lavished privileges on master falconers. The Laws of the Court under Hywel the Good, a tenth-century Welsh prince, stipulated that the royal falconer "is to have his horse in attendance, and his clothing three times in the year, his woolen clothing from the king, and his linen clothing from the queen, and his land free."

During falconry's boom times in the Middle Ages, relationships between Eastern and Western falconers flourished. In 1228 Frederick II of Hohenstaufen, the Holy Roman Emperor, hunted in the desert with Malik al-Kamil, the fourth Ayyubid sultan of Egypt, for three months during a lull in the Sixth Crusade. Twenty years later Emperor Frederick relied on the knowledge imparted to him by Syrian falconers whom he had brought back to Europe to write his classic work *De Arte Venandi cum Avibus* (*On the Art of Hunting with Birds*). By the seventeenth century, however, the proliferation of guns and, in England, the enclosure of land, rendered falconers an anachronism. No more than a few hundred falconers were left on the entire continent after the French Revolution and the Napoleonic Wars swept away the aristocracy.

And yet, as Austen Henry Layard made his way through the Tigris and Euphrates Valleys in 1845, he found that there, falconry was still appreciated as a form of art. In a caravansary (roadside inn) by the Euphrates, the archaeologist encountered Timour Mirza, an exiled Persian prince and the region's most famed falconer. Reclining on carpets spread on a platform, Mirza "was surrounded by hawks of various kinds standing on perches fixed into the ground," Layard would write in his 1853 memoir *Discoveries Among the Ruins of Nineveh and Babylon*, "and by numerous attendants, each bearing a falcon on his wrist." Layard noted the pageantry surrounding falconry and the esteem accorded the finest participants—and their birds. He admired such accoutrements as the raptor's hood, which temporarily blinded the bird, protecting its delicate optic nerves from a blitz of sensations and soothing its high-strung disposition. The hood "is generally made of colored leather, with . . . gold and variegated thread," Layard observed. "Tassels and ornaments are added, and the great chiefs frequently adorn a favourite bird with pearls and precious stones."

The bird that had come to command the greatest respect among falconers was the *shahin*, or peregrine falcon, a term derived from the Middle Persian word *šāhēn* (literally majestic or kingly). "Although the smallest in size," Layard explained to his readers, "it is esteemed for its courage and daring, and is constantly the theme of Persian verse." This raptor "strikes its quarry in the air and may be taught to attack even the largest eagle, which it will boldly seize, and, checking its flight, fall with it to the ground."

=

No consensus has ever been reached about the maximum speed of a peregrine as it stoops, or plummets, toward its prey. A BBC documentary pitted a peregrine named Lady against a free-falling skydiver equipped with a speedometer and a lure. The skydiver clocked in at 158 miles per hour. Lady, who hurtled past him, may have surpassed 180.

Perhaps the best accounts of falcons' hunting behavior come from

British writer J. A. Baker in his classic work *The Peregrine*. Baker, a nearsighted and arthritic clerk from Essex, tracked peregrines in the winter landscapes of his native East Anglia between 1954 and 1962. His observations are infused with a sense of the fragility of nature (the DDT poisonings were at their height), the beauty of the English countryside, and appreciation for the raptor's grace in flight. But over and over he returns in his writings to the stoop and the kill. "The peregrine swoops down toward his prey," he writes in *The Peregrine*. "As he descends, his legs are extended forward till the feet are underneath his breast . . . His extended toe . . . gashes into the back or breast of the bird, like a knife—If the prey is cleanly hit—and it's usually hit hard or missed altogether—it dies at once, either from shock or from the perforation of some vital organ." He describes with grisly admiration the raptor's "tomial tooth"—a sharp projection on the upper mandible that lets the bird snap the vertebrae of any prey that isn't killed instantly on the stoop. "The hawk breaks its neck with his bill, either while he is carrying it or immediately [when] he alights," he observed. "No flesh-eating creature is more efficient, or more merciful, than the peregrine."

To accomplish that—to target and then dive-bomb a wood pigeon or a grouse from five thousand feet at nearly two hundred miles an hour, and strike it dead with a single swipe of the foot—requires extraordinary physical abilities. The bird's large, well-developed chest muscles, connected to a broad breastbone and nourished by oxygen drawn in continuously by nine air sacs throughout the body, power its wings through high-speed flight. This hyperefficient respiratory and circulatory system also keeps the air flowing and the blood pumping as the peregrine descends at velocities that would render any other species unconscious. Light and hollow bones, long and stiff flight feathers, and streamlined wings keep air resistance to a minimum, while the extra-wide tail base supports powerful musculature to turn and brake while in hot pursuit. All this allows the bird to maximize its speed and flexibility. The bird's optic nerves, meanwhile, relay images to its brain ten times faster than those of a human, "so events in time that we perceive as a blur," Helen Macdonald, best known for her memoir *H Is for Hawk,* noted in an earlier study, *Falcon,* "like a dragonfly zipping past our eyes, are much slower to them."

Above all, peregrine falcons perceive the world with a vividness and depth that human beings can hardly appreciate. Photoreceptor cells cram into the falcon's fovea, the tiny pit located in the retina that handles the most important visual tasks. A human has about thirty thousand color-sensitive cones in the retina; a falcon has *one million.* With two foveae in each eye, one for depth and one for lateral perception, the falcon's eye functions simultaneously as both a macro lens and a zoom lens. Falcons can also perceive ultraviolet light, making colors stand out even more vividly and enabling the falcon to identify the shape and texture of plumage from as far as a mile away. Macdonald quoted Andy Bennett, a researcher in the field of avian vision, as saying that the difference between the eyesight of a human and that of a falcon is like the difference "between black-and-white and color television."

=

On October 16, 1931, south of the desert mountain known as Jebel Dukhan (Mountain of Smoke) in the island kingdom of Bahrain, the first oil spouted from a well drilled by the Bahrain Petroleum Company, a firm established two years earlier by Standard Oil of California. The well, which was soon pumping ninety-six hundred barrels a day, was the first to produce oil on the Arabian side of the Persian Gulf. Others quickly followed—in Qatar in 1935, Saudi Arabia and Kuwait in 1938, Abu Dhabi in 1958, and Oman in 1964.

The flood of petrodollars over the next decades turned Gulf societies upside down. The oil industry covered vast swaths of desert with wells, pipelines, refineries, access roads, and other infrastructure, creating a new urban population and erasing much of Bedouin society. Yet despite the upheaval, falconry remains fundamental to the culture of that part of the world. Falcons appear on corporate logos, banknotes, and the national emblem of the United Arab Emirates, a federation of seven Gulf sheikhdoms, the largest of which are Abu Dhabi and Dubai. The most extravagant new real estate project in Dubai is "Falconcity of Wonders," a 107-square-mile conglomeration of opulent hotels and residences, all laid out in the shape of a peregrine. And the sheikhs there have managed to retain fragments of a mostly vanished way of life. Wealthy falconers stock private reserves with prey such as captive-bred houbara bustards—having hunted the wild ones out of existence decades ago—and pack their falcons onto 747s and fly to leased hunting grounds in Central Asia and North Africa.

In 2002, Sheikh Hamdan bin Mohammed bin Rashid Al Maktoum, son and heir of Sheikh Mohammed bin Rashid Al Maktoum, the billionaire ruler of Dubai, introduced a new sport to the Arab world: falcon racing. While the crown prince had the luxury of hawking in his own private hunting grounds and on royal expeditions, he recognized that such opportunities were out of reach for the average Gulf citizen. Racing was Sheikh Hamdan's ambitious attempt to keep Emiratis connected to their heritage. The populist move also turned falconry into a multimillion-dollar global enterprise.

At the first falcon race organized by the crown prince in January 2002, several thousand participants—ranging from royal family members with an aviary full of falcons to ordinary citizens with a single bird—gathered beside a field of sand in Dubai to time their birds with stopwatches over a four-hundred-meter course. The falcons flew sequentially, to avoid catastrophic midair collisions, coaxed into action by a man positioned at the far end of the field swinging a *telwah*—a lure fashioned from a pair of bustard wings. A younger brother of Dubai's ruler trounced all other competitors with a peregrine that flew the course in sixteen seconds, or fifty miles an hour.

The races quickly caught on—and spawned a cottage industry. Royal families dispatched high-paid agents to purchase promising racers from breeders domestically and abroad, and set up desert training grounds where elite coaches could teach their falcons to fly in straight lines and stay low to the ground, even using light aircraft to drag feathered lures ahead of the birds at high speeds. Dieticians maintained the birds at racing weight, while veterinarians kept their feathers in perfect condition; a frayed or broken quill could be a significant disadvantage in a sport where a few tenths of a second can separate the top contestants in a heat. A champion falcon can compete for only three or four years before losing its edge, at which point the best are often retired to stud. (Rumors have persisted, but have never been proven, that older falcons are destroyed once they've passed their racing prime.) One of the greatest studs in racing history, Fast Lad, a sixteen-year-old gyrfalcon owned by Bryn Close—a breeder in Northern England for various Emirati royal families—has sired hundreds of winners in a dozen years.

Five years after bringing racing to Dubai, Crown Prince Hamdan introduced the Fazza ("Victory") Championships, a two-week competition with $8 million in prizes provided by his family. An Italian-designed system of laser beams that sensed exactly when a peregrine crossed the starting and finish lines ensured precision timing to the hundredth of a second. The crown prince created separate racing categories for sheikhs, professional falconers, and the public, with distinct heats for juvenile and adult birds, hybrids and purebreds, and males and females. In 2014 Sheikh Khalifa bin Zayed Al Nahyan, the ruler of Abu Dhabi and the fourth wealthiest monarch in the world, with a fortune estimated at $15 billion, created a tournament with even greater rewards. The President Cup, held each January at the Abu Dhabi Falconers Club and paid for by the Al Nahyan clan, offers a purse of $11 million. The prizes include sixty Nissan Patrol SUVs, dozens of cash awards of up to twenty-five thousand dirhams ($6,800), and—most important to status-obsessed royals—engraved golden trophies for the winners in the six championship events.

The President Cup is an exquisitely organized affair. In the huge spectators' tent at the edge of the desert racecourse, sheikhs and their entourages, draped in white gowns and keffiyehs, relax on ornate sofas and wing chairs, plucking grapes, apples, and oranges from porcelain bowls while observing the races through floor-to-ceiling windows or on closed-circuit television screens. Boys in white turbans circulate among the guests—mostly Emiratis, but also breeders from across the globe—pouring shots of bitter Arabic coffee from brass urns into white ceramic cups. Dozens of hooded falcons of different hues and sizes wait on wooden perches to be carried down a red carpet one by one to the starting gate, where an announcer whips up excitement with vehement exhortations and pleas to God. Dehooded and released from the trainer's wrist at a signal, most falcons hug the ground and fly on a straight trajectory across the four-hundred-meter-long field, but a few rise up as if preparing for the stoop, and, when I visited the President Cup in January 2018, one gyrfalcon belonging to Sheikh Mohammed, the ruler of Dubai, veered off toward a distant line of sand dunes, to the dismay of her supporters, before finding her way back to the course. She crossed the finish line with a time four seconds slower than the next-to-last bird.

The competition between the Al Maktoum and the Al Nahyan families, and to a lesser extent the ruling clans of other Gulf States, has fueled a quest for the fastest, hardiest, and most beautiful falcons in the world. The falcon market was "on a downward spiral before the races— breeders all around the world were struggling," Zimbabwean breeder Howard Waller told *Arabian Business* for a 2015 article entitled "Sheikh Hamdan's Bid to Revive the Glorious Arab Sport of Falconry." Now, he said, "it's become an international business opportunity—everybody's trying to get in." Waller quoted the top price for a captive-bred female peregrine from the United Kingdom as £70,000, up from just £1,500 a few years earlier. In 2013 a pure white gyrfalcon, the largest and most powerful species of the Falconidae family, had been sold to a royal in Doha, the capital of Qatar, for one million dirhams, or $272,000, "drawing gasps from breeders," according to the magazine. Crown Prince Hamdan matched that price four years later, a well-placed source in Abu Dhabi told me, for a captive-bred gyrfalcon-peregrine hybrid that had just swept to victory in four consecutive races in the President Cup. "Any strong falcon the Crown Prince hears about he buys," the source said. "For him, it is all about prestige."

=

By the twentieth century, Europeans had come to revile peregrines as pests and vermin. In June 1940 Great Britain's Air Ministry declared the peregrine a menace to the carrier pigeons that Royal Air Force pilots were releasing from cockpits to dispatch messages to contacts in Nazi-occupied Europe. The government authorized the shooting of hundreds of adult and juvenile birds and the killing of thousands of chicks and eggs in the nests.

The environmental consciousness that spread across Europe and the United States in the 1960s and 1970s helped revive an appreciation for birds of prey. These days some five thousand Americans and twenty-five thousand Britons participate in falconry, triple the number from five decades ago. The birders range from urban enthusiasts like Helen Macdonald, who trained a goshawk named Mabel in her home in Cambridge, to wealthy landowners who stage hunts on horseback each summer in the Northumberland countryside. One English writer called the revival a "back-to-nature quest," stemming from "a postindustrial society's hunger to reconnect with ancient traditions."

Near the Welsh village of Carmarthen, an English biologist, sportsman, and entrepreneur named Nick Fox has bred falcons for thirty years for Sheikh Mohammed bin Rashid Al Maktoum, the ruler of Dubai, an Anglophile who first traveled to the United Kingdom in 1966 to study English in Cambridge. In recent years he's been joined by other registered breeders in the United Kingdom, Ireland, France, Spain, Germany, the United States, and South Africa who now compete for shares of the fantastically lucrative Arab market; today, the majority of the twelve thousand captive-bred raptors exported from the West are destined for the United Arab Emirates. Fox also sells the richest Arabs a falconry flight-training device called the Robara, a remote-controlled machine, shaped like a houbara bustard, that can match the cruising speeds of falcons and act as the bait. In Dubai a venture partly owned by the Al Maktoum family takes Western tourists in hot-air balloons over the Arabian Desert to watch trained falcons fly and dive at five thousand feet.

This money-fueled globalization also has an underside: a thriving black market for wild birds of prey, driven by wealthy enthusiasts who believe that falcons stolen from nests are innately superior to those bred in captivity, and who are willing to break the law to get them. It's a shadowy world that would draw in a skilled climber, obsessive egg collector, footloose adventurer, and cunning manipulator, who had been heading for trouble since his boyhood in the Southern African bush half a century ago.

FIVE

RHODESIA

The boy was up to something, Pat Lorber was sure of it. From the moment she'd first noticed him carrying a fishing rod around the Hillside Dams, she could tell that he hadn't come there to fish. He was deep in the woods, nowhere near the water. And he was looking toward the treetops, where the nests were.

Lorber visited the Hillside Dams—a pair of man-made lakes in Bulawayo, the second largest city of Rhodesia (the Southern African country today known as Zimbabwe)—a couple of days a week to survey the birds during breeding season. The amateur ornithologist would leave her infant daughter with her mother or a caretaker to roam the footpaths for hours through forests and fields with a notebook and binoculars, compiling observations on nest building, breeding behavior, feeding methods, and birdcalls for articles she published frequently in a local journal or a South African bird-watchers' magazine. There were splendid sights at nearly every turn. African jacanas—chestnut-colored waders with black wingtips and a long black stripe sweeping across their white heads—probed for insects atop water lilies, using their enormous feet and claws to balance on the floating vegetation. Crimson-breasted shrikes, white-bellied sunbirds, scarlet-chested sunbirds, black-headed orioles, and fiery-necked nightjars, as brilliantly colorful as their names suggest, nested in the thick cover of acacias and leadwood trees. On that day, in late 1972, she had been studying the fork of a massive acacia where a spotted eagle owl, with prominent ear tufts and bright yellow eyes, laid its eggs each year. She was "hyperactive and aware," she remembers, when she noticed the boy peering into the trees.

Lorber ducked behind a rocky hill that rose over the forest. From her perch she watched the boy, a slightly built adolescent, expertly scale a leadwood tree and disappear amid the foliage. After fifteen minutes of probing the branches, he began his descent. As soon as his feet touched the ground, Lorber clambered down from the rocks.

"Hello," she said. "I'm Pat Lorber. Who are you?"

"I'm Jeffrey," he replied.

"What are you doing, Jeff?"

"Going to go fishing up at the dam," he said.

"You're not nest or egg collecting, are you?" she asked. Many local boys liked to clamber into trees and raid birds' nests after school, but this was the first time Lorber had ever encountered anyone threatening her work at the Hillside Dams, a government sanctuary where egg foraging was strictly forbidden.

"No," he said, "I just like to see what's in the nests."

"Now, here is the thing, Jeff," Lorber said. "I'm doing a survey where I'm trying to establish how many birds breed in this particular area. You're not going to be taking eggs, are you?"

"No, I don't collect eggs."

"Because a small and determined egg collector is going to muck up my figures."

"I'm not doing anything," the boy insisted. Then he scampered off.

That evening, the phone rang at Lorber's home.

"Jeffrey said you accused him of egg collecting while he was down at the Hillside Dams," said Peggy Lendrum, Jeffrey Lendrum's mother. Lorber knew her in passing as a teacher at the local high school, but they had never spoken and she was surprised the woman had managed to obtain her phone number. Peggy sounded defensive and aggressive. "I want you to know that Jeffrey is a very truthful boy," she said, "and if he says he's not egg collecting, he's not egg collecting."

"Okay, Peggy," Lorber said. "All right, then. 'Bye." She was certain that Jeffrey Lendrum had been lying, but she didn't want to make too much of it. The Lendrums were a respectable family. Hopefully the boy had learned his lesson.

=

It was Jeffrey Lendrum's father, Adrian, he would always say, who had sparked his interest in egg collecting. "My father was passionate about wildlife," the younger Lendrum would recall decades later, "not just birds, but beetles, butterflies, moths. He collected everything." When Jeffrey was eight years old, Adrian enlisted him to raid the nest of a groundscraper thrush, a small, black-and-white-speckled songbird that lays its tiny blue eggs in clutches of two to four, high in trees in cup-shaped nests often woven from spiders' webs. After Jeffrey had taken the eggs, Adrian taught him how to insert a pipette and "blow" the contents—expelling the live embryo so that it wouldn't rot inside the eggshell—and mount the empty shell in Adrian's modest egg collection, which contained about twenty specimens.

With his father's encouragement, Jeffrey Lendrum became a prolific nest raider, clambering perilously from tree limb to tree limb dozens of feet off the ground, combing through the foliage and grabbing colorful treasures. Lendrum had an instinctive sense of how to "read" a tree—calculating his route by the pattern of the branching, the brittleness of the wood, the width of the trunk and branches, even the quality of the bark. He prided himself on his intimate knowledge of the forest. "I've climbed to more nests than you probably had hot breakfasts," he would later say. And because most collecting was against the law, it required stealth and, sometimes, an ability to lie with a straight face. That day he was spotted by Lorber, Lendrum had been searching for the distinctive blue eggs of the redheaded weaver, a perching bird that builds nests out of leaf stalks, twigs, and tendrils in baobabs and other trees throughout Southern Africa.

Rhodesia had some of the strictest conservation legislation on the continent. The eggs of most small birds and common raptors could be taken from private land, but only if one had the landowner's written permission. The government banned collecting eggs in national parks, except with a hard-to-obtain permit for scientific research. It was illegal everywhere to take the eggs of several dozen "Specially Protected Species," including secretary birds, black pelicans, cranes, flamingos, and most raptors. African black eagles, martial eagles, bateleur eagles, brown snake eagles, black breasted snake eagles, Ovambo sparrow hawks, yellow-billed kites, black-shouldered kites, giant eagle owls, spotted eagle owls, tawny eagles, peregrine falcons, lanner falcons, and a dozen more birds of prey were very much sought-after by unscrupulous sportsmen, collectors, and traders; several of these species were unique to Southern Africa. The hunting, removal, and sale of these endangered animals was punishable by up to several years in prison. A handful of researchers and top falconers could get an exemption, but for everyone else, it was taboo.

Jeffrey Lendrum ignored all the prohibitions. He rode through the bush for miles each day on his bicycle, carrying a throw line with a heavy weight on one end to wrap around high branches and facilitate his ascent. He'd scan trees for bunches of sticks and developed a keen eye for following birds to their nests. And he came up with ingenious tricks for procuring eggs. Vernon Tarr, a neighbor in Bulawayo, remembers Lendrum's determination to sneak an egg away from a crowned eagle—one of Southern Africa's rarest raptors, a large and powerful bird with a russet-brown crest that has been known to seize small children in its huge talons. (In 1924, anthropologists in South Africa unearthed the skeleton of a toddler known as the "Taung Child," a humanoid that lived two million years ago; scientists would determine that a crowned eagle had swept up the child and taken it to its nest, where the raptor ripped out its eyes.) Lendrum would find a suitable tree, carry up "tons of sticks, and build a rudimentary nest there," Tarr says. "The next year the crowned eagles moved in." Lendrum would wait until the female laid her eggs in the aerie he had built, and then would climb into her nest and snatch them.

Howard Waller, one of Lendrum's closest boyhood friends, says that Lendrum was driven by an obsession that went far beyond that of a schoolboy hobbyist. Even then, stealing eggs was about more than just collecting; he had a real competitive streak. Waller remembers clambering into nests as an adolescent to take the live eggs of the common sparrow hawk. "I'd climb a tree and there would be a chicken egg in the nest with a sign on it saying, 'Too late sucker,'" he recalls.

=

The Lendrum family's route to Rhodesia had been a long one. Adrian Lendrum, a third-generation African with roots in Cork, Ireland, had been born in Kenya in the 1930s. (The word "Lendrum" is Celtic for "moor of the ridge.") His mother died just after his birth, leaving Adrian's father devastated, and with three young children to raise on his own. When Adrian was about three months old, he and his two older siblings left Kenya to live with their paternal grandparents in South Africa. Several years later, they were summoned back by their father, now remarried with stepchildren in Northern Rhodesia, a copper-rich and landlocked British protectorate in Southern Africa, just south of the Belgian Congo. Adrian attended school there, worked as a manager for the Rhokana Copper Mine, and met his wife, Peggy, also a third-generation African. Jeffrey, their oldest child, was born in October 1961 in Kitwe, the colony's second-largest city. It wouldn't be long, however, before Adrian Lendrum was moving on again.

In February 1960, British Prime Minister Harold Macmillan acknowledged, standing before the South African Parliament, that a black "national consciousness" was rising across the continent. Over the next four years, one British colony after another—Nigeria, Sierra Leone, Uganda, Tanganyika (modern-day Tanzania), Kenya—declared independence, along with the Belgian Congo and France's colonies in North, West, and Central Africa. Northern Rhodesia's turn came in 1964. Following nearly a decade of protest marches, strikes, and other civil disobedience, Britain's Colonial Office allowed an election early that year, with universal suffrage. A party led by a popular teacher and freedom fighter named Kenneth Kaunda won by a landslide, and what was once Northern Rhodesia became the independent black-ruled nation of Zambia.

Kaunda, who became Zambia's first president, soon declared his country a one-party state, and launched a massive scheme to nationalize land and private enterprises, which was when Adrian Lendrum started thinking about leaving the country. "He saw the way things were going in Zambia," says his younger son Richard, who was born in 1966. "He wanted something else." According to younger sister Paula, who was born in 1969, the immediate catalyst for the move was a robbery in Kitwe during which Peggy Lendrum was held at knifepoint.

In 1969, Adrian and his wife, Peggy, drove south from Kitwe with their children, across the massive Lake Kariba dam on the Zambezi River, to Southern Rhodesia, now known simply as Rhodesia, one of Africa's last holdouts of white-minority rule. Many of Rhodesia's 270,000 whites owned farms that had been in the family for two or three generations, and were terrified by what they saw happening around them. In 1965, the Rhodesian cabinet had unilaterally broken free of Great Britain and, in defiance of the international community, declared Rhodesia a sovereign state.

Situated on the Rhodesian Highveld, a vast stretch of savanna and bush-covered hills between the Zambezi and Limpopo Rivers, Bulawayo was a bustling colonial outpost, a factory town known for its furniture, clothing, and wooden construction parts, and the railhead for Southern Africa. About sixty thousand whites and several hundred thousand blacks lived in the city, their interactions limited by the white-supremacist politics of the era. The black population lived in crowded townships, while middle-class whites were all but guaranteed a big house, a garden, and servants. (Poorer whites, most of whom had come to Bulawayo to work for the railway, lived far more modestly.) White boys and girls learned British history and geography and played cricket, rugby, and field hockey on idyllic campuses carved out of the bush. For white adults, one's social life revolved around an academy of music, a theater club, a ballet society, a choral society, the Rotary Club, and the Bulawayo Club, a billiards-and-drinking establishment founded in the 1890s exclusively for men. The annual highlight was a parade down Abercorn Street, Bulawayo's main avenue, commemorating the Pioneer Column: a force of five hundred colonists and soldiers recruited by the mining magnate Cecil John Rhodes, that marched from South Africa through Matabeleland and Mashonaland in 1890 and established the first white settlements in what would become Southern Rhodesia. Just twenty miles down the road lay the Matobo National Park, carved in part from Rhodes's former cattle ranch, a sprawling reserve filled with big game and birds of prey.

The Lendrums moved into a handsome house in the leafy Hillside neighborhood on the eastern side of town, with a large garden filled with flowering trees and a live-in husband-and-wife team that worked as the family's gardener and domestic servant. After arriving in Bulawayo, Adrian landed a position as a human resources manager at Dunlop Tyres Africa, while Peggy taught at Girls' College, a private high school. Jeffrey attended a private elementary school, where he was well behaved but bored and easily distracted in class, preferring to roam the bush in search of birds and other wildlife with a handful of like-minded friends. The family was close, Richard says, but it was the older son, Jeffrey, with whom Adrian formed the deepest bond.

In early 1973, Adrian showed up with eleven-year-old Jeffrey at the monthly meeting of the Rhodesian Ornithological Society. Bird-watching was a popular pursuit in the young country, reflecting the pride that many of its privileged white citizens took in its game parks and rich wildlife. About thirty members were present the evening the Lendrums walked into the cozy basement lecture room of Bulawayo's Natural History Museum of Zimbabwe, opened in 1964 and considered one of the best in Southern Africa. The Lendrums, younger than almost all of the rest, exuded an energy and enthusiasm that drew a crowd as Adrian Lendrum recounted how an Ayres's hawk eagle, a fierce-looking bird mottled black and white, had roosted in his garden a year before. It was a thrilling sight, he said, and had sparked a fascination for birds of prey.

The father and son "were likable, smooth, gregarious, and chatty," says Pat Lorber, who was there that evening. She'd chalked up her encounter with the younger Lendrum the previous year to typical boyhood mischief and hadn't given him another thought. The Lendrums were asked to join a Saturday survey of waterbirds at the Aiselby Dam outside town, a reservoir rich with African pipits, sacred ibises, red-capped larks, African wattled lapwings, African purple swamp hens, ospreys, Temminck's coursers, and dozens of other species. The birders also encouraged the pair to come back to the museum for evening ornithological documentaries. Soon the group invited them to participate in its longest-running and most prestigious project: the African Black Eagle Survey, launched by a warden at Matobo National Park in the early 1960s. It was an invitation that all would come to regret.

—

Matobo is one of the African continent's geological oddities: a 165-square-mile field of granite domes, huge rolling rock slabs known as whalebacks, and blocks of broken granite piled one on top of the other as if some gargantuan toddler had used the boulders as playthings. The cooling and erosion of buried magma some two billion years ago formed the stony landscape. In between the striking rock formations, some of which rise to thirty-five hundred feet, lie swampy valleys, or *vleis*, fed by rainwater runoff and rich in acacias, mopanis, figs, euphorbias, and other vegetation. Thirty-two species of raptors—four hundred breeding pairs—nest in tall trees or on rock ledges, largely protected from baboons and other predators, subsisting on rock hyraxes and yellow-spotted hyraxes—small, furry mammals both known in Rhodesia as "dassies."

The black eagle has been one of the park's star attractions since tourists began visiting Matobo in the 1920s. Otherwise known as Verreaux's eagle, after French ornithologist Jules Verreaux, who brought back specimens to the National Academy of Sciences in Paris in the early nineteenth century, this coal-black raptor has fierce yellow eyes, a massive wingspan, and a telltale white V on its back. "They can fly in a gale of [one hundred miles] per hour," the South African raptor expert Rob Davies observed, "draw their wings in slightly and make progress into the eye of the wind, while other birds are being flung across the sky." Watching them fly alongside lesser eagle species was, he said, "like watching jet fighters escort a bomber." The raptors build massive stick nests on the ledges of cliff faces, often hundreds of feet above the ground, and frequently occupy them for decades. Some nests, augmented with twigs, grass, and other materials over the years, grow to twenty feet deep and ten feet wide. Survey participants had counted sixty pairs of black eagles in Matobo National Park—the highest concentration of the raptors in the world.

At the time that the Lendrums became involved, the survey leader was Valerie Gargett, a Quaker and former high school math teacher who had quit her job in 1969 to devote herself full-time to ornithology. Her many admirers had come to view her as a sort of Jane Goodall of the raptor world. A teetotaling vegetarian, whose years in the field had left her lean, suntanned, and supremely fit, Gargett spent many hours each week clambering up rock faces and perching on ledges to observe the life cycle of her beloved black eagles. Several of these wild raptors came to trust her and granted her extraordinary access. "Val could go put her hand gently under one particular eagle, feel how many eggs she had, then take the egg and weigh it," Lorber remembers. Vernon Tarr, the Lendrums' neighbor, once watched Gargett slip a thermometer between the eagle's breast feathers and her brood patch—a bare patch of skin filled with blood vessels that provides insulation for her chicks—to measure the incubation temperature. "The eagle didn't flinch," he says.

Gargett had assembled several dozen volunteers to help her follow the courtship of eagle pairs, their nest building and egg laying, and the incubation, hatching, and fledging of their young. "Do not stay at or near the nest for longer than five minutes to obtain the information," she instructed her assistants, who paired off and monitored two or three aeries per team during nesting season between January and April. "We are visitors to their world and respect their right to live undisturbed and uninfluenced by us." She urged volunteers, most of whom were not young, to keep in top condition. "It paid to be physically fit and if possible a little underweight, [as] it was sometimes necessary to pass through narrow cracks in the rocks, and even down short rock tunnels," Gargett wrote in her 1990 book *The Black Eagle*. "One member on the portly side became wedged in a crack and laughed at his own predicament, until he became so firmly fixed that nobody could move him. In those circumstances one simply had to wait for the victim to relax; struggling was useless."

When Jeffrey and Adrian Lendrum joined the group, Valerie and her husband, Eric, were delighted to have a vigorous, agile father and son to monitor some of the least accessible nest sites. Eric Gargett, a member of the Bulawayo city council and an experienced technical climber, taught Jeffrey the basics of rappelling, or abseiling, as it was called in Rhodesia: how to fix a secure belay at the top of a cliff, thread the line through the caribiners on his harness, tie the complex knots upon which his life depended, and maintain the proper stance as he launched from the top of the cliff and moved down and across the face. The younger Lendrum, a natural athlete, became a fearless rappeller, descending six-hundred-foot rock faces to perch on a narrow ledge beside an aerie. Sometimes his *shamwari* ("friend" in Shona, the dominant tribal language of Rhodesia) Howard Waller, an avid falconer, would join him. "Jeff was cocky, macho, and athletic, like his father," Lorber remembers. "Howard was the quiet, geeky one."

After two years Val Gargett entrusted Adrian and his son with a spin-off survey of the augur buzzard, a black raptor with a rust-colored tail that builds nests on ledges at the base of vertical cracks in cliffs, or at the intersection of trees and cliffs. Gargett had an endless appetite for data and often created new surveys to be carried out by other members of the society. "The Lendrums are so active, and so useful, and so nice," Gargett enthused to Lorber. "Adrian and Jeffrey will be perfect." Thirteen-year-old Jeffrey Lendrum was now struggling at the Christian Brothers College in Bulawayo, an all-boys day school staffed by lay teachers. Discipline was lax, Paula remembers, and her brother's difficulties focusing on classes and homework worsened. But his enthusiasm for the outdoors balanced out his lack of concentration in the classroom. Working on weekends and on holidays, the Lendrums located thirty aeries and surveyed the buzzards for hundreds of hours between 1975 and 1977. Hiking side by side for hours through the bush, climbing trees and cliffs, and sharing observations about the birds' behavior strengthened the father-son relationship. They noted the raptors' "kow-kow" courtship call and the "bombing-diving-and-stooping" and "spiraling-twisting-and-talon grasping" of the male's mating dance, as Adrian Lendrum described it in one report. They observed the bird's swoop from a perch and its plunge from a hover "that resembled a fast parachute drop" in pursuit of a rodent or an insect.

Three years later Adrian and Jeffrey took over a survey of the African hawk eagle, the park's second-most-prevalent bird of prey, which constructs large, heavy stick nests in tree forks. Gargett passed on to her protégés dozens of nest locations. Back in his element, Jeffrey—now lithe, strong, and brimming with a self-confidence in the outdoors that verged on brashness—scrambled to nests at the tops of euphorbias, ficuses, and brown ironwood, or *Homalium dentatum* trees, and though his father wasn't nearly the climber that Jeffrey was, he sometimes joined his son. "They would throw up a claw, and climb up the tree as high as they could," Lorber remembers. "It required a lot of skill, and involved some risk. This was derring-do stuff."

Adrian and his son didn't confine their contributions to the field. In their nine years working with Gargett and her team of volunteers, the Lendrums published a total of eighteen academic studies of hawk eagles, augur buzzards, crowned eagles, and other birds of prey, chiefly for *Ostrich*, a quarterly produced by the South African Ornithological Society. The pair also contributed to *Bokmakierie*, another South African magazine for bird-watchers. These were serious-minded and technical articles filled with exhaustive descriptions of clutch and egg sizes, the types of green foliage used in nests, the establishment of hunting territory, and, on a lurid note, examples of what Gargett called "Cain-and-Abel conflict"—the killing of one raptor sibling by the other shortly after hatching, usually by pecking it to death. Adrian Lendrum was the brains of the team, colleagues understood, while his son provided the derring-do.

Delighted by his development as an ornithologist, Gargett invited the elder Lendrum to join the Rhodesian Ornithological Society's steering committee, a select set of half a dozen individuals who met once a month to organize the bird-watching and film program for the next half year. She also took the Lendrums on field trips across Matobo, sharing the society's most closely guarded secrets: the exact locations of hundreds of nests.

=

In the late 1970s, as the Lendrums were surveying birds in Matobo, the Rhodesian Bush War crept up on Bulawayo. Rhodesia didn't have the brutal apartheid system of neighboring South Africa, but the country was riddled with injustices. The 1961 Constitution guaranteed that whites would hold fifty of the sixty-five seats in Parliament, even though they made up only 8 percent of the population. Other laws forced two-thirds of the country's black population to live in communally held Tribal Trust lands, which quickly became overpopulated and overgrazed; banned black-opposition groups; and forbade speech and writing critical of Prime Minister Ian Smith. In 1972 the Zimbabwe People's Revolutionary Army, an Ndebele force in the south led by the trade union leader, politician, and activist Joshua

Nkomo, joined with Robert Mugabe's Zimbabwe African National Union guerrillas, most of whom belonged to Rhodesia's majority Shona tribe, to try to bring down the country's racist white-minority regime.

By 1978, 12,500 insurgents were fighting in Rhodesia. About 10,800 Rhodesian Army regulars and 40,000 white reservists opposed them. All white males between eighteen and sixty were obligated to train and serve part of the year in the reserve. Lorber's husband, a German national who wasn't even a Rhodesian citizen, volunteered to be a police reservist. Adrian Lendrum was drafted into service, too. "My dad used to go up on call-ups every six weeks to serve in the bush," Richard Lendrum recalled. "The war affected everyone."

At sixteen, in 1977, Jeffrey Lendrum transferred from Christian Brothers to Gifford High School, a boys-only, government-run institution with a reputation for strict discipline. But he failed most of his O levels—nationwide qualification exams in a variety of subjects—and left school in 1978, with no hope of continuing to college. That same year, as warfare intensified, he applied, at the age of seventeen, to join the Rhodesian Special Air Service (SAS) C Squadron, an elite unit originally formed during the Second World War. Lendrum has said that he spent about six months going through the unit's arduous selection process but was then felled by a hernia and never completed the training. His sister, Paula, remembers it differently. "Being a non-conformist [he] gave up," she says. He transferred to Internal Affairs, a unit responsible for guarding villages in the Rhodesian bush, a less-than-heroic posting that usually meant hunkering down with a rifle behind a pile of sandbags. Still, Lendrum claims that he saw some action, conducting "hot extractions" of troops under fire by military helicopter. "He saw some terrible things," says his friend Michelle

Conway, who grew up with the Lendrums in Bulawayo and later attended university in South Africa with Jeffrey's brother, Richard.

Today Lendrum's name adorns a "Wall of Shame" on the SAS C Squadron website, comprised of individuals who falsely claim to have served with the unit. "Some of these impostors are coming out with such ludicrous stories about their time spent in [C Squadron] that we have to expose them for the sad cases they are," the website says. "One thing you get to know about Jeff," says a friend of twenty years, "is that he likes to think that he's done everything and seen everything, and he has done a lot of things, but you got to take some of it with a pinch of salt."

In the last year of the war, Joshua Nkomo's guerrillas sought sanctuary in the rocky redoubts of the Matobo Hills just outside the national park. They buried land mines on roads, sabotaged water pumps, ambushed cars, and laid explosives on tracks. The Rhodesian Ornithological Society struggled to keep its projects going. Some volunteers dropped out. At her husband's insistence, Lorber never ventured into the field without stashing her nine-millimeter pistol under her seat. Gargett, who refused to carry a gun, made the twenty-mile journey to Matobo alone until her husband demanded that she either ride with him or find another armed escort.

As the war heated up, the Ornithological Society became an escape, a bit of normality in terrible times. Society members' opinions on the war ran across the spectrum, from hard-liners who backed Ian Smith and his Rhodesian Front and feared that black rule would lead to catastrophe, to liberals like Val and Eric Gargett, who wished for power-sharing and a more just society. Val Gargett had taught at a black high school before becoming a full-time ornithologist, and her husband had fought to improve health and education for black

Rhodesians while serving on Bulawayo's city council. But no matter their differences, all bird lovers flocked to the monthly meetings at the national museum to forget, briefly, the threat of being blown up by a land mine, ambushed by guerrillas—or jumpy government troops—or shot by a surface-to-air missile from out of the sky, as had happened to a mother and daughter the Lendrums knew.

It was around this time that Gargett began to notice disturbing things happening to her surveys in Matobo. The irregularities were small at first: a lanner falcon or snake eagle nest being monitored would suddenly turn up empty. Monkeys or other predators, people assumed, had eaten the eggs. Then the survey turned up an alarming rise in the number of "incomplete breeding cycles" among Gargett's black eagles. Breeding pairs built nests with sticks and lined them with greenery—the standard pre-laying ritual—but no eggs were ever seen by researchers. It could have been that the birds couldn't find enough to eat, which would have affected productivity. But scientists had determined that the park's dassie population had grown by 20 percent in recent years. The evidence pointed to sabotage or theft. And it seemed to be an inside job. "This had never happened before," Lorber remembers. "This was a small, tight community, threatened by a bush war, and you don't want internal strife. You are holding people together."

In the last weeks of 1979, with the war at a stalemate, Rhodesian Prime Minister Ian Smith entered into negotiations with the insurgents. The British government, led by Margaret Thatcher, brokered the talks in London. On December 12, the sides announced a ceasefire, and the following March, Robert Mugabe was elected the first president of Zimbabwe. Most blacks were jubilant. White reactions ranged from exhilaration to restrained optimism to a conviction that the country was about to descend into chaos. Pat Lorber tried to persuade her father and her husband, both of whom were strong Rhodesian Front supporters, that Mugabe intended to rule inclusively and transparently. But, unlike her friend and mentor Val Gargett, she also harbored doubts about the new state's viability.

Even as the fate of the new nation dominated thoughts and conversations, the inexplicable little troubles in Matobo continued. One day Adrian Lendrum joined Gargett to photograph a breeding pair of the rare Mackinder's eagle owl (*Bubo mackinderi*), one of the largest owls in Africa, a tawny brown bug-and-lizard-eater with massive talons and startlingly bright pumpkin-colored eyes. Only a single pair had ever been sighted in the park. Gargett carefully guarded the nest location, telling only Lendrum and a few other confidants. The nest had a clutch of two eggs inside it when Gargett and Lendrum visited. When Gargett returned alone to inspect the nest a week later, she was shocked to discover that the clutch was gone.

The Lendrums, meanwhile, were gaining more official responsibilities. In May 1982, the Department of National Parks and Wildlife Management issued the Lendrums a permit to place tracking tags on birds of prey in Matobo and in Hwange National Park, a fifty-six-hundred-square-mile reserve, two hundred miles northwest of Bulawayo, that was home to one of Southern Africa's largest populations of elephants. Jeffrey Lendrum, still living with his parents, was working as the manager of a local cannery, and he and his father now had carte blanche to roam both parks.

Later that same year Steve Edwards, a senior warden at Matobo, came across a spectacular find: a crowned eagle nest with a single egg—large, creamy white, with dark brown specks and blotches—perched in a high fork of a 120-foot-tall tree off one of the park roads.

The crowned eagle was, like the Mackinder's eagle owl, one of the rarest Southern African raptors; only three mating pairs had been counted in the park. Edwards, exhilarated by the discovery, headed back for another look two days later, the usual time it took for a crowned eagle to lay the second egg in its two-egg clutch. This time Edwards encountered Jeffrey Lendrum heading in the other direction.

"Have you just been to the crowned eagle nest?" Edwards asked him.

"Yes, and there are two eggs in there," Lendrum replied, adding, oddly, that the ranger now had no reason to check. Edwards clambered up the tree anyway and discovered that the nest was empty.

What the hell is going on here? he wondered. All but certain that Lendrum had stolen them, he would soon report to Val Gargett what he had seen.

Gargett had been wrestling with conflicted feelings about her protégés. She found it hard to imagine that the father and son she had watched grow into self-assured ornithologists might be engaged in anything unethical. She and her husband had mentored the Lendrums, spent many hours with them in the field, and come to view them almost as family; the possibility that they had betrayed the Gargetts' trust, lied to them, and corrupted their surveys was emotionally wrenching for her even to consider. Still, she began quietly increasing her visits to the aeries that the Lendrums had surveyed. At one African hawk eagle nest—where the Lendrums had reported that the eaglet had fledged—the surrounding rocks were missing the telltale "whitewash," or bird feces, that always accumulates as the chick grows older. She saw no indication that the eggs had ever hatched.

Gargett shared her suspicions about the Lendrums with Steve Edwards, and he agreed to initiate an investigation.

SIX

LIVERPOOL

Andy McWilliam fell into police work by a process of elimination. McWilliam's father had left school at fourteen following the death of his own father in his thirties from the lingering effects of a poison-gas attack in the trenches during World War I. After dropping out, the elder McWilliam had joined the British Merchant Navy, the national commercial fleet, and worked until retirement as a shipboard electrician. Growing up in the 1960s in Litherland, a working-class town in the Metropolitan Borough of Sefton, just north of Liverpool, and later in nearby Crosby, the young McWilliam had shown similar restlessness and no great enthusiasm for study. He couldn't wait to escape the classroom and join his friends on the rugby field or cricket ground. The only facts and figures that grabbed his attention were the wins and losses of the Everton Football Club, his family's favorite team for three generations.

Everton's archrival, Liverpool FC, had begun its rise to the championship of English football in the early 1960s, and matches between the two clubs were charged with tension. McWilliam watched them play from the standing-room-only tier at Goodison Park, Everton's home ground. On occasion he ventured into enemy territory, walking half a mile across Stanley Park, a 110-acre spread of lawns, flower gardens and lakes, to Liverpool's Anfield stadium. After every Liverpool goal, thousands of fans would break into spirited renditions of "She Loves You" and other hits by the hometown Beatles. The crowd would surge, and McWilliam would be right in the thick of it.

As a boy and into his adolescence, McWilliam watched two popular police procedurals each week on the BBC. *Z Cars*, a half-hour midweek drama set in the fictional town of Newton in northwest England, featured a rotating pair of patrolmen and a rousing theme song that Everton adopted as its anthem in 1963. On Saturdays came *Dixon of Dock Green*, centering around the relationship between a grizzled desk sergeant, Constable George Dixon, and a young detective, Andy Crawford, at a fictional station in London's East End. Each week the policemen cracked crimes ranging from missing persons cases to bank robberies to gangland killings. McWilliam loved everything about the dramas: the investigations, interrogations, banter between the police, and even Dixon's famous catchphrases that started and ended the program each Saturday night: "Evening all" and "Night all." Later, at Waterloo secondary school, McWilliam began searching regularly through the index card file at the Career Office for an occupation that matched his poor academic credentials. Great Britain's police forces in those years were desperate to fill their ranks, and paid little attention to test scores or grades. "I thought, *I can do this*," he recalls. The only other option, as he saw it, was joining the Merchant Navy like his father, which, considering his proclivity for seasickness, held little appeal.

In the summer of 1973, while waiting for the results of his O levels, he sat for the police exam to become a cadet in the Liverpool and Bootle Constabulary. It turned out to be more challenging than he had anticipated. "What is the Ku Klux Klan?" was one multiple-choice question. Flummoxed, he answered, "A Chinese political party." He failed the test. Then, as he pondered what possible career options he had left, his mother found an advertisement in the local newspaper, seeking recruits for the police in Surrey, a county in southeast England. The glossy brochure that the force sent him when he requested more information stressed "the active side of the job," he recalled, promising a heavy emphasis on sports and physical fitness. McWilliam decided to take the county's test. "They must have been really struggling to find recruits," he says, "because the questions were along the lines of, 'What is wet and puts out fires? And here's another clue: Ducks swim in it.'" This time, he passed.

Shortly after that, McWilliam received his O level results: he had failed six out of his eight exams, eking out passing grades in only mathematics and English. It was a dismal performance, but he consoled himself with the knowledge that he was already on his way to a career. In the fall, he took a part-time job in the toy section of Owen Owens, a Liverpool department store, waiting for his police training to begin at the start of the new year.

On the third of January, 1974, McWilliam's parents drove him down to the Hendon Police Cadet College in north London and dropped him and his single suitcase at the front gate of the urban complex. He was sixteen, the same age as most of his fellow students, facing his first extended period away from home, and he was terrified. A cadet in full regalia met McWilliam at the entrance and escorted him across the parade ground to a room with eight bunks in one of three concrete dormitories. Cadets rose at dawn, put on their uniforms, made their bedrolls, ate a quick breakfast, and then assembled on the field at seven-thirty. Inspection officers moved up and down the rows, searching for signs of sloppiness—"You, boots!"—and sentencing those who failed to "fourteen days' default" or "twenty-eight days' default"—two weeks or a month of extra predawn dress parades alongside other transgressors. McWilliam felt alone, friendless, and overwhelmed by regimented life. *What the hell am I doing here?* he thought. By the end of the second week, half the four hundred recruits had dropped out.

But McWilliam grew used to the military discipline and he came to feel at home in the academy. The course load was light. McWilliam spent a couple of hours each day learning about British common law—derived from tradition and precedent rather than from statutes—and took training in police tactics and martial arts. Since the era of Sir Robert Peel, a Conservative Party politician (and future prime minister) who founded London's Metropolitan Police in the 1820s, British law enforcement officers followed a policy of "policing by consent," in recognition that the power of the police rested on public approval of their behavior, not on force. McWilliam was regularly reminded that the key to good policing was public outreach, and learning how "to talk down a situation." British law enforcement officers proudly went about their duties unarmed, a policy that had earned the force respect around the world.

When he wasn't in class or marching on the parade ground, McWilliam was free to explore London's West End and other lively neighborhoods, and do what he enjoyed most—playing sports. He competed in rugby, football, and cricket. He race-walked and ran track. He developed a passion for weight lifting, impressing and amusing his peers with his intense competitive streak. Desperate to slim down to his weight class before one match, he donned two judo suits and ran dozens of laps around the gym. Then, bathed in sweat and in danger of overheating, he tore off his clothes and performed twenty sets of jumping jacks nude. As he swung his arms and legs feverishly to shed the final ounces, his eyes were drawn to a large picture window that looked out over the campus. A dozen cadets in a driver's education class had gathered on the pavement below, gaping and laughing at the naked, flailing figure. McWilliam nodded at them, grinned, and kept going.

McWilliam graduated from police college after one year, and then took a ten-week intensive training course in Kent. On the first of September, 1975, the British government, intent on increasing the number of police officers, lowered the minimum age from nineteen to eighteen and a half. McWilliam reached that age on the third of September, and joined the Surrey Police Force the same day—becoming the youngest policeman, by his reckoning, in the British Isles.

=

The Surrey command dispatched McWilliam to a precinct in Woking, a drab commuter town south of London, with a population of about sixty thousand. His first week, he learned the ropes with a veteran. Then he was told, "That's it, mate. You're on your own." Soon he was both walking the beat and patrolling the streets by car: a teenage cop, proudly wearing a blue uniform with shiny brass buttons and, while on foot, a tall rounded custodian helmet. He carried a pair of handcuffs and a twelve-inch wooden truncheon for protection. One evening a friend introduced him to an attractive and spirited eighteen-year-old named Linda Gilbart, who grimaced when he told her he worked as a cop.

"Don't you like the police?" he asked.

"No," she replied, explaining that she'd been arrested and fined at sixteen for riding a motorcycle with learner plates. Undaunted, he popped up the courage and asked her on a date. They spent the evening at a pub in Staines, an old market town alongside the River Thames.

McWilliam enjoyed being a constable in Surrey. But after three years of trying to afford housing in the London suburbs on £40 a month (£600 today, or about $780), he realized that he would never escape from financial worries as long as he lived there. McWilliam transferred back to Liverpool, to the Merseyside Police Force. He married Lin a few months later. He was happy to be back home among his fellow "Scousers," or born-and-bred Liverpudlians—a name deriving from "lobscouse," a cheap salted-lamb-onion-and-pepper stew that Liverpool seamen first ate about three hundred years ago.

In the late nineteenth century, when McWilliam's great-grandparents were growing up in Liverpool, the city had been one of the world's richest ports, described in an 1851 issue of *The Bankers' Magazine* as "the New York of Europe." McWilliam's maternal grandfather had been a merchant seaman in the early twentieth century; his paternal grandfather had joined the flood of young men who proudly left the port during the Great War for Continental Europe, where he inhaled the poison gas that would ultimately take his life. McWilliam's family was also present for the city's most traumatic chapter: a relentless eight-day aerial bombardment in May 1941 that became known as the Liverpool blitz. McWilliam's father, then an apprentice electrician, served fire-watch duty near the docks, dodging rats in total darkness, and was sheltering in a bomb-proof bunker in his front garden when the house across the street took a direct hit.

He was called up to serve the following year, and joined the Fleet Air Arm of the Royal Navy. McWilliam's mother, the daughter of the seaman, also survived the blitz, then entered the Women's Royal Naval Service in 1942 and left for a base in Scotland. (They would meet in Liverpool soon after the war.)

All told, the Luftwaffe bombed the docks and other parts of Merseyside eighty-eight times between August 1940 and January 1942, killing four thousand people, destroying ten thousand houses, and damaging a hundred eighty thousand more—the worst aerial bombardment suffered by any British city outside of London. Liverpool never recovered. Factories closed, trade moved to other ports, and the unemployment rate soared to among the highest in the country. The postwar government threw up shoddy council housing in the bombed-out districts but by the late 1970s, when McWilliam returned there from Surrey, an average of twelve thousand people each year fled the city, and a fifth of its land stood abandoned.

It wasn't long before McWilliam came face-to-face with his city's desperation in a once-grand neighborhood called Toxteth. During its commercial heyday, merchants and sea captains had built brick-and-stucco Georgian mansions along the portside quarter's boulevards and side streets. But most were subdivided or boarded up after the war. The houses "faced stretches of waste ground, where uncleared rubble from the war mixed with fly-tippings and dog shit," wrote Andy Beckett in *Promised You a Miracle*, a history of Britain in the early eighties. "Inhabited streets ended abruptly or degenerated into roofless shells . . . After dark, prostitutes used the shadows." Liverpool had long been one of the most racially diverse cities in England, with a large black population that dated to the 1730s, and a recent wave of Afro-Carribean and African immigrants. But largely black communities like Toxteth had suffered most from the city's post-war decline, and the police practice of stopping and searching black youths—known as the "sus" laws—had generated ill will. McWilliam rarely entered Toxteth, but from speaking to other policemen who patrolled there and simply living in Liverpool he knew that it was a neighborhood on the brink of an explosion.

In July 1981, three years after McWilliam's return, an unmarked police car was chasing a young motorbike-riding black man on Selbourne Street in the heart of Toxteth. The man lost his balance and fell. As the police moved in, apparently to arrest him, an angry crowd gathered and began throwing bricks and stones. The confrontation escalated into what would become a week of bloody street battles between the police and local residents, some of the worst riots in England's history.

McWilliam, a twenty-four-year-old who worked out of a station house eight miles north along the Mersey, was bused down to man the police line on Upper Parliament Street, ground zero in the urban war zone. He had a shield and a nightstick to defend himself; the rioters threw stones, chunks of pavement, and firebombs. The bobby helmets, made of molded cork, offered no protection from the barrage. A well-placed rock could drive the sharp metal badge straight through the cork, causing deep lacerations. A colleague beside McWilliam collapsed after he was hit in the head. Another suffered a fractured skull.

When they weren't hurling projectiles, the rioters stole cars and weighed the accelerators with rocks, so they could send them racing downhill at the police. They charged the lines with spear-like pieces of scaffolding, attacked fire engines, and hacked police vans with axes. McWilliam took a painful whack on the hip and had his helmet nearly

torn off by a well-placed stone, but otherwise he escaped the riot-
ing unscathed. Hundreds of officers, however, were injured. At the
time, McWilliam had no sympathy for the rioters—"It was us against
them," he would say—and after the violence subsided he mostly felt
grateful for the extra pay. He and Lin were hard up, and the overtime
meant that they could replace some windows in their home.

Soon after the Toxteth riots, McWilliam was called out to police another violent dispute. Prime Minister Margaret Thatcher had
ordered the shutdown of dozens of unproductive coal mines across
Great Britain, and the National Union of Mineworkers declared a
countrywide strike. Thatcher tried to reduce the unions' power by
protecting workers who chose to remain on the job, and McWilliam
was bused to bleak mining towns in Nottinghamshire and South
Yorkshire to stand between strikers and strikebreakers and prevent
the conflict from escalating into a bloody melee. He knew almost
nothing about the reasons for the strife. He was simply told, "You're
going to the Linby Colliery for a week." Thatcher made almost no
concessions, and after a yearlong standoff, the strike ended with
many coal mines shut for good, and Great Britain's once-powerful
unions badly weakened. Families in the old mining regions were
permanently divided. "There are fathers and sons who never spoke
again," McWilliam said.

=

But most of McWilliam's work was closer to home. Based at the
Crosby Police Station in Sefton, a fourteen-mile stretch of towns
along the Mersey Estuary near Liverpool, McWilliam arrested bur-
glars, thieves, and drug dealers, and executed search warrants against
the organized crime gangs that had seized control of the heroin trade.

By the mid-1980s they had flooded the streets with so much junk that Liverpool had become known as "Smack City." One drug baron, Colin "Smigger" Smith, amassed a fortune of £200 million; another, Curtis Warren, was reportedly even wealthier, earning a spot on the *Sunday Times*'s Rich List. Nearby Manchester Airport had become a transit point for drugs from Asia and North Africa, and McWilliam regularly provided relevant intelligence that he had gathered on the street.

One evening his colleagues in customs invited him to witness a multiple arrest based on information that he had supplied: three drug runners were about to land, carrying high-quality cannabis oil from Morocco. McWilliam watched real-time footage of the three stepping off the plane and going their separate ways, and he was waiting inside the customs office when one suspect was brought in for a search. The drug mule was grinning and laughing, playing pals with the agents. *He's a cocky little sod, acting like he's one step ahead of us*, McWilliam thought. The man looked McWilliam's uniform up and down and smirked. "All right, blue?" he said. "How you doin', blue?" Minutes later the customs men cut away the false sides of his suitcase, and pulled out dozens of pouches of cannabis oil. As the trafficker was handcuffed and led to a holding cell, McWilliam caught his eye and grinned. "How you doin', blue?" he asked, in a near-perfect imitation of the mule.

He worked night shifts and day shifts, in uniform and in street clothes, on the drug squad and the special crime unit. He cleaned up after suicides and investigated murders. He led a three-man team that broke up a ring responsible for an epidemic of bike thefts in Merseyside, arresting sixty-six people. He cultivated informants, and came to know almost all the local hoodlums, known in the lingo as "scrotes" and "scallies." The thugs got violent from time to time, but McWilliam, a rugby standout known on the pitch for both meting out and taking punishment, wasn't averse to—even welcomed—the occasional scrap.

Then, in 1984, he got into a scuffle that almost cost him his life. Serving on the plainclothes unit, driving "an old shat of a car" around Sefton, he received a radio dispatch about two men who had fled a stolen vehicle on foot and were reportedly armed. McWilliam and his partner spotted the suspects, who took off in two directions. McWilliam chased one to the end of a cul-de-sac, and pulled out his radio to call for assistance. The man hurled himself at McWilliam, knocking the radio from his hands and pinning him against a gate. One of his arms became trapped between rails. Immobilized, McWilliam thrashed as the assailant squeezed his forearm against his throat. He couldn't breathe, and realized with terror that he was blacking out. As he slipped into unconsciousness, McWilliam thought of the Scotland Yard investigator who'd been stabbed ten times, fatally, the year before, while staking out a suspect in a £26 million gold bullion and jewel heist. *John Fordham, John Fordham, John Fordham*, ran the voice in his head. *What must have been going through his mind?* A moment later, two constables arrived and pulled off the assailant. They stuck him in their van and drove away. McWilliam was left gasping on the ground.

McWilliam could have come in from the streets after a few years as a patrolman and settled into a comfortable desk job, but he had no desire to advance in his career. "You become detached" when you leave the beat, he would explain to friends, when asked why he never pressed to become a sergeant. "I've always provided for me family and paid the mortgage. I've never been that driven." His bosses questioned his absence of ambition at his annual job appraisal. "You've been at this station for fifteen years," they would say. "Why?" McWilliam would shrug. "I like it here," he replied. "I know everybody, and everybody knows me." Living in the area where he worked meant he was never far from the people who needed his help, or those who meant to do harm.

The proximity worked both ways. Sound asleep at home at two a.m. after an evening shift, he once awoke to furious banging on his front door. The assistant headmaster of a local school, an ex-neighbor whom he'd arrested years earlier for being drunk and disorderly, had decided to confront him. The schoolmaster, obviously intoxicated, grabbed McWilliam. "Listen here, you bastard," he began, before McWilliam sternly ordered him to leave the property. There were gratifying moments, too. Summoned to a wrecked car that had smashed into a tree, he discovered the driver unconscious, a hose leading from the exhaust pipe into the vehicle and an overdose of barbiturates in the man's system. McWilliam dragged the would-be suicide from the wreckage, roused him, and kept talking to him as he was rushed to the hospital. Three years later, when he answered a call about a burglary, he thought the victim looked familiar. "Do you remember me?" the caller asked. It was the man who'd attempted suicide, who wept as he thanked McWilliam for saving his life.

Still, the misery wore him down: Once, McWilliam broke into the house of a physician who'd been reported missing. The doctor's corpse was sprawled on his bed, soaked in blood. "Christ! This is murder," McWilliam exclaimed to his partner. Then he found a suicide note addressed to the doctor's son: the man had taken a knife, surgically cut a main artery, and lay down until he bled out. On another occasion, he inspected the corpse of a young hoodlum who'd been clubbed to death by a chain binder—a mace-like tool used to secure loads on trucks. The victim's skull was smashed in like a rotten fruit.

Then there was the woman strangled in her flat by a perennial sex offender nicknamed "Dirty Bertie." Dirty Bertie, whom McWilliam had often arrested and come to know well, lay in the next room, unconscious from an overdose he'd taken after killing her, and died a short time later. Beyond these quotidian horrors, there was the decomposed body in the trash, the mangled jumper on the railroad tracks. The worst were the crib deaths. He dealt with a few, the parents waking up and finding their baby motionless, unresponsive, for no understandable reason. For a man with a family, that was as bad as it got.

The athletic field provided McWilliam with a regular escape. Throughout the early eighties he ran track at the National Police Athletics Championships, one year winning silver medals in both the one-hundred- and two-hundred-meter dashes. For a decade and a half he competed every Saturday for the Merseyside Police Rugby Union team, which played an eighteen-match season in the North West Division 1 League, one of the top amateur associations in England. McWilliam starred as the team's inside center, a position that required both hard, head-on tackles and acrobatic passing. But in the mid-1990s, he started feeling his age. A painful tear in a stomach muscle needed surgery. Then it was a torn patellar tendon. He had a second operation to stitch it back together, returned to the field, and soon afterward took a hard hit to the face. He stayed in the match, with blood oozing from his nose, but when he stopped to clear his sinuses, something peculiar happened to his vision. "Suddenly," he recalled, "the opposition had twice as many players as they should have had." McWilliam had broken his cheekbone in four places, and blowing through his nose had dislodged his eye from its socket. After a third surgery, he packed it in for good. "This didn't pay the mortgage," he had to acknowledge. "Keeping at it didn't make any sense."

That's when he began to rediscover the local wildlife. McWilliam hadn't had a real brush with nature since he was six years old, when his grandmother had given him a copy of *The Observer's Book of British Birds*, a pocket guide by S. Vere Benson to the 236 species that inhabit the United Kingdom. The black-and-white photographs made it difficult to tell many species apart, and McWilliam had soon lost interest. But three decades later he began making weekend trips with his three young sons—ages ten, eight, and two—and six-year-old daughter to an adventure playground at the Martin Mere Wetland Centre in Lancashire County, a low-lying depression of open water, marsh, and grassland, gouged out by receding glaciers at the end of the last Ice Age. It wasn't long before McWilliam was venturing deeper into the reserve to watch birds. The children didn't join in that, although McWilliam sometimes brought his wife, Lin—or, as he liked to refer to her, "Mrs. McW."

He hiked along nature trails bordered by whorled caraway, golden dock, tubular water dropwort, early marsh orchids, purple ramping fumitory, and large-flowered hemp-nettle, peering through binoculars at the remarkable variety of avian life that gathered in the marshes and fields. He came to know several rangers who shared their expertise with him, and who would prove helpful in the next phase of his career. Weekend by weekend, McWilliam became a regular. In springtime, the wildflowers bloomed, and lapwings, redshanks, and other waders dove for fish in the marshes. Summer brought out the harrier hawks, merlins, buzzards, peregrine falcons, and other raptors, gliding on upward currents of warm air known as thermals and stooping in pursuit of their prey. In autumn, tens of thousands of pink-footed geese returned from Iceland, long, wavering V formations soaring inland from the coastal mudflats, filling the air with their cacophonous honks. During the winter, migrating families of whooper swans and widgeons engaged in boisterous, clamorous displays in the sky. McWilliam loved to plant himself in a blind beside two adjoining fields that were flooded with pumped-in water every September, attracting huge numbers of teals, pintails, shovelers, and mallards. By April, the fields began to dry, bringing in new populations of migrating snipes, black-tailed godwits, and dunlins.

McWilliam also discovered a sanctuary closer to home: the Seaforth Nature Reserve by the Liverpool docks at the mouth of the Mersey. He had played in the area as a schoolboy, when it was a no-man's-land of dunes, train tracks, and vacant lots at the end of the bus line. An ambitious harborside redevelopment project had transformed it into seventy-four acres of freshwater and saltwater lagoons, reedbeds, and rabbit-grazed grassland.

Many mornings and afternoons before his shift began, McWilliam would drive through the industrial-waste dump that bordered the reserve and quickly find himself in a different world. Walking along the water's edge, he took in the pleasant din of cackling gulls, whistling waders, and babbling ducks, amazed that such an Eden could be thriving at the edge of Liverpool. He cast his eye on oystercatchers, Canadian geese, ringed plovers, and more subspecies of gulls than he had ever known existed: black-headed, common, herring, lesser, great black-backed, Ross's, and Bonaparte's. Cormorants arrived by the hundreds, seeking shelter from storms on the Irish Sea. During the annual spring passage, from the final week of March to the first week of May, thousands of lesser gulls gathered in the lagoons en route to their breeding grounds in Finland. He came to know his fellow bird-watchers, and learned to recognize dozens of species and identify birdcalls.

It was around this time, shortly after McWilliam turned forty, that colleagues aware of his growing interest in ornithology asked McWilliam to look into some unusual cases relating to that field. Before long these investigations would come to redirect his police career—and lead to his encounter with the greatest falcon thief of all time.

SEVEN

THE TRIAL

At three o'clock in the afternoon on October 5, 1983, Christopher "Kit" Hustler, a young environmentalist at Hwange National Park, received a radio call at Main Camp from the Parks and Wildlife Management Authority headquarters in Harare, the capital of the new nation of Zimbabwe. (The country's name was derived from the term for "house of stones" in the language of the largest tribe, the Shona, referring to a complex of granite ruins dating to the eleventh century and situated in the hills near the southern town of Masvingo.) After a months-long probe of Adrian and Jeffrey Lendrum on suspicion of illegally taking the eggs of endangered species from national parks, officers were preparing to raid their house in Bulawayo. Investigators had secretly interviewed the Lendrums' housekeeper, who had described "a pair of live birds eggs" being kept inside the family's refrigerator. Headquarters in Harare believed that the suspects were "clever and devious enough to hide evidence from our people." The superintendent wanted a bird expert to accompany them.

"Leave as fast as you can," the superintendent instructed Hustler. "The raid won't happen until you get there."

It was dark by the time Hustler arrived in his ancient diesel-powered Land Rover in Hillside, the neighborhood of large homes and lush gardens on the city's eastern edge. Austin Ndlovu, the provincial warden of Matabeleland, was waiting with two field assistants. All three wore the parks department uniform of khaki shorts and a khaki shirt adorned with green and yellow epaulets. Hustler hung back while Ndlovu (the surname means "elephant" in the Ndebele language) climbed to the veranda and knocked on the front door.

The door opened a crack.

"Are you Adrian Lendrum?" Ndlovu asked.

"I am," a man replied.

Ndlovu held up a sheet of paper.

"We have a warrant to search your house."

Lendrum, a handsome, fit man in his late forties, opened the door wider and stood in the threshold, reading the document under the porch light. He handed it back to Ndlovu.

"Better come in, then," he said.

"We're here to inspect your eggs," Ndlovu explained.

Lendrum led the officers down an entrance hall. The family was in the middle of dinner. Peggy Lendrum and her two younger children observed the intrusion from the dining room in confusion, while Jeffrey got up to join his father. Decades later, Jeffrey Lendrum would claim that he and his father had been unaware that they had done anything wrong and that the raid had caught them by surprise. "We had no warning," he would say. "We were in disbelief, we were shocked, looking for words, wondering 'What the hell is going on?'"

Expecting to be taken to the refrigerator in the kitchen, Ndlovu was surprised when Adrian Lendrum instead escorted him and his team into a bedroom. While the younger Lendrum looked on,

Adrian pointed to a green wooden cabinet, five feet high, four feet across, and two feet deep. Ndlovu pulled open the drawers, one by one, revealing wooden display trays divided into compartments and covered by glass. Eggs, arranged like jewels on beds of cotton, filled each slot. There were opalescent green weaver eggs the size of marbles; the larger, custard-and-chocolate-blotched eggs of the nightjar; the purple-speckled eggs of the common bulbul, Zimbabwe's most widespread songbird; a clutch of crimson-breasted shrike eggs, with brown speckles on a cream background; and hundreds and hundreds of others. Several deeper drawers contained the eggs of the most endangered birds in Zimbabwe: African black eagles, peregrine falcons, tawny eagles, and white-backed vultures. Astonished by the find, Ndlovu counted three hundred clutches in all, or nearly a thousand eggs. Hustler walked into the room as the inspection was going on and identified himself as a Parks and Wildlife ornithologist. Adrian Lendrum looked at Hustler with relief.

"Thank God you're here," Lendrum said. "There seems to be a terrible mistake." Hustler sensed that they were attempting to "butter me up," he would say decades later, as though they expected him to be flattered that they didn't trust his colleagues. Lendrum explained that he and his son were trained ornithologists with good reputations. The eggs on display, he insisted, were "just a schoolboy collection."

It hardly looked that way to Hustler. The collection was the most extensive private one that he had ever seen. It confirmed the rumors he'd been hearing from people like park ranger Steve Edwards that the Lendrums were secretly amassing a large stash of eggs. Written on every egg in black Indian ink with a fine draftsman's pen was a "set mark"—a series of tiny numbers and letters, barely readable without a magnifying glass, that assigned codes to individual eggs and clutches ("c. 236") and sometimes identified the year they'd been taken. These codes could in turn be correlated with data cards to obtain more details.

"Have you got the standard?" Hustler asked Lendrum, using the hobbyist's lingo for the information index that always accompanied a collection.

Lendrum fetched boxes full of index cards. "All the information is in here," he said. "We're happy to provide that."

"In order to clear this up, I'm going to have to take the collection," Hustler told Lendrum. "And I'm going to have to take your data cards."

Hustler continued exploring the home. In the kitchen refrigerator—sitting inside a lidless Tupperware container on a shelf beside milk, cheese, and leftovers—were the objects that had catalyzed the raid on the Lendrums' house: two mottled brown and red eggs, slightly smaller than a chicken's. These eggs, unlike those in the bedroom, had neither set marks nor the telltale puncture mark made to push out the embryo before mounting the prize in a display case. Adrian Lendrum claimed these were eggs of a gymnogene, or African harrier hawk, an omnivorous gray raptor with double-jointed legs. They, too, were heading for his egg collection. "We just got them today, so we put them in the fridge to cool them down, while we ate dinner," he said. But Hustler was skeptical. They looked to him like peregrine falcon eggs, which were greatly sought-after by sportsmen around the world. Placing them in the refrigerator would keep them in a state of suspended animation (freshly laid fertile eggs can survive for more than a week in frigid conditions) until the Lendrums could sell them live on the underground market, a crime punishable under Rhodesia's 1975 Parks and Wildlife Act by a steep fine and sometimes a stretch in prison.

The Lendrums watched calmly as Hustler and the Parks and Wildlife officers carried the trays and the refrigerated eggs to their truck. Then the officers placed Jeffrey Lendrum under arrest and drove him to the Hillside Police Station, where he was booked on charges of possessing wildlife trophies without a license, and released on bail. Adrian would soon be charged as well.

=

The news of the Lendrums' arrests spread quickly through Bulawayo's bird-watching community. Pat Lorber had begun working five mornings a week as an administrator in the ornithology department at the Natural History Museum of Zimbabwe while her daughter and son attended school. She was sitting behind her desk in the "Bird Room" the next morning when Hustler walked in carrying a tray filled with eggs.

"What do you think this is?" he asked.

"An egg collection?" Lorber said.

"It belongs to the Lendrums," Hustler told her. Behind him trooped half a dozen uniformed Parks and Wildlife officers bearing twenty more trays of eggs. Lorber watched the procession with amazement. She had been been well aware that Jeffrey Lendrum had accumulated eggs in his youth, but had assumed he'd grown out of it. She and Hustler began to identify, one by one, the eight hundred shells mounted in the trays. Adrian Lendrum had made it easy for them. The collector had meticulously documented every one of his egg raids, noting the species, date, peculiar characteristics ("one single red blotch at sharp end"), and, if the egg had been taken inside Matobo National Park, the number of the nest, according to a map of the park that Val Gargett had distributed to her field teams. They found seven clutches of black eagle eggs, one crowned eagle egg, one brown snake eagle egg, three clutches of martial eagle eggs, as well as clutches of the eggs from fish eagles, peregrines, lanner falcons, black storks, white-backed vultures, buzzards, and tawny eagles. In all, the Lendrums had thirty-four clutches of Specially Protected Species—many, it appeared, seized from Matobo. It was an impressive collection, though the Natural History Museum's own—eight thousand clutches acquired over six decades from dozens of donors—dwarfed it.

Lorber compared the information with the nest record cards that the Lendrums had filled out for Gargett's surveys—all kept on file at the museum. Here Lendrum had meticulously described the chicks' supposed development: "chicks growing well," "flapping wings on edge of nest," "nest empty, left."

Every word was a lie.

Hustler called Gargett and broke the news. Gargett, always discreet, had at first kept her suspicions about the Lendrums largely to herself. But as her concerns had grown in recent months, she had confided in a few members of the Rhodesian Ornithological Society, now called BirdLife Zimbabwe. Several had reacted with skepticism. "Val is being over-the-top," one elderly falconer had complained to Hustler. Now, as she sifted through dozens of protected species in the Lendrums' collection, dismay and fury combined with a sense of vindication.

Gargett held up the egg of a Mackinder's eagle owl, one of the rarest birds in the world. She clearly remembered showing a Mackinder's nest with a clutch of two eggs to Adrian Lendrum in early August 1978. Both eggs had vanished without explanation, a lingering mystery that would now appear to be solved. According to his note card, Lendrum had taken the owl eggs from that nest on August 13, 1978.

= *trial*

The trial of Adrian and Jeffrey Lendrum opened in August 1984, nearly one year after their arrests, at the Magistrates Court, a four-story colonnaded and whitewashed edifice built in the 1930s on Fort Street in downtown Bulawayo. In the year since their arrest, the Lendrums had gone about their business as usual—Adrian working at Dunlop, his son in the cannery. The fifty-odd members of BirdLife Zimbabwe shunned them, but few others in Bulawayo knew about the case. To anyone who did inquire, Jeffrey would blame the trouble on a personal feud between his father and Gargett. Now that the trial was beginning, however, the *Chronicle*, Bulawayo's most popular daily newspaper, brought the story to a wider audience. A colleague at Girls' College, where Peggy Lendrum taught, recalled that fellow teachers were bemused but sympathetic. Most blamed the family's troubles on a "misunderstanding." It was a fantastical notion, they argued, that Peggy's husband could be stealing eggs from a research project that he served with such devotion and loyalty.

The state had charged the Lendrums with the illegal collection of seventy-nine clutches of eggs from a national park, the illegal possession of thirty-four clutches of eggs of Specially Protected Species, and submission of fraudulent records. "Adrian had thought he would bullshit his way out of it, and that it would all go away," Pat Lorber remembers. A few weeks into the trial, during a week-long recess, he would even prematurely celebrate his acquittal with a tea-and-cake party for his colleagues at Dunlop.

Clad in the business attire that he wore to his office job, Adrian

Lendrum sat beside his casually dressed twenty-two-year-old son in the first row of the gallery. Benches were filled with dozens of members of BirdLife Zimbabwe. Sunlight streamed through the north-facing windows and fans suspended from the high ceiling stirred the air. A framed photo of Robert Mugabe hung on a scuffed white wall.

The evidence that the Lendrums had committed a crime against endangered species was overwhelming. Lorber, Gargett, Hustler, and other experts explained the double sets of record cards and the phony data. Acquaintances described watching Jeffrey Lendrum ascending to the tops of trees in pursuit of protected species, and then trying to hide the eggs by stashing them in his clothing or in a bag. An acquaintance of Adrian Lendrum testified that, after his arrest, Lendrum had begged him to provide a phony statement to police that he had given Lendrum a large collection of eggs; he had refused.

Unlike the prosecutor, who was privately perplexed by the experts' equating egg theft wth elephant or rhino poaching, the magistrate—typically a judge who presides over a trial involving a less serious criminal offense than a murder, assault, or armed robbery—Giles Romilly, a respected holdover from the days of white-ruled Rhodesia and an avid outdoorsman, viewed the Lendrums' alleged offenses as serious crimes. At one point Romilly organized a field trip to inspect a black eagle aerie that the Lendrums were accused of robbing. The Matobo Hills were filled with Ndebele dissidents who had declared war on Mugabe the prior year following a series of politically motivated massacres and had vowed to kill government officials. Surrounded by armed guards, the magistrate inspected the nest, determined that the chicks had never hatched and so had likely been stolen—then got out of the park as quickly as he could.

On the witness stand, Adrian and Jeffrey Lendrum denied everything in self-assured but nonconfrontational tones. Jeffrey Lendrum swore that the few eggs he had taken from the national parks were dead, and demonstrated how he ran tests to determine if they were rotten by shaking them vigorously and listening for a particular sound, or by rolling them to see if they moved in an "irregular" manner. But Lorber and Hustler testified that such techniques were useless; shaking an egg as Lendrum described would kill the embryo. The Lendrums also attributed the false data on the nest record cards to their lack of scientific training, and not from any intention to commit fraud.

On October 1, six weeks after the trial began, the magistrate announced that he had reached a verdict. In a hushed courtroom, Romilly found both men guilty of theft and illegal possession. Adrian Lendrum was also convicted of fraud. "By their actions the accused have prejudiced an extensive research programme conducted by authorities over many years," Romilly said, according to the official transcript. "There was a trust placed in you by the Department of National Parks and Wildlife, your colleagues in the Ornithological Society and the museum staff [and] you abused this position."

The scale of the crime demanded the "maximum penalty," the magistrate said. Romilly imposed a $2,500 fine on the father and an equal amount on the son, confiscated their pickup truck, incubators, and egg collection, and sentenced each to four months in prison at hard labor, suspended for five years. If they managed to stay out of trouble during that period, they would serve no time at all. Parks and Wildlife had already barred them from Zimbabwe's national parks, a humiliation that, said Romilly, "will obviously bear very hard on you."

Pat Lorber was in the courtroom when the magistrate read aloud the judgment. Upon hearing the sentence, Adrian Lendrum's "face just fell," she said.

=

A year earlier the father and son had been Val Gargett's most accomplished protégés. Now they were pariahs. "People didn't want to have anything to do with them," Lorber says. Yet the verdict left conservationists dissatisfied. Kit Hustler was certain that the Lendrums were smuggling live eggs and chicks out of the country to buyers in Western Europe. The fresh peregrine eggs in the refrigerator had first raised his suspicions. Parks and Wildlife investigators had also found before the trial a five-egg incubator at the Lendrums' home and a belt with pouches that seemed custom-made for keeping eggs warm as they were being transported on foot—perhaps through airports. The most powerful evidence came from a statement provided in confidence by the family's maid, who had seen the younger Lendrum packing eggs into the pouch and taking them to the airport. "He would be gone for three days," she told the police, according to Hustler, who was closely involved in the investigation. Just before the trial, however, the maid recanted, afraid that she would lose her job if she testified in public against the Lendrums and perhaps remain unemployable. Romilly was left with only circumstantial evidence of the Lendrums' guilt—the incubator, the egg belt—neither of which was presented at their trial. It was not enough, he said, to convict them of trafficking and send them to prison.

Hustler's suspicions gained credibility a few days after the trial, when British police raided a farmhouse near Birmingham and arrested a man who had illegally imported both chicks and the fertile eggs of four martial eagles, three crowned eagles, and two black eagles from Zimbabwe, valued together at £10,000. Evidence that the police would never make public pointed to Adrian Lendrum as the source. (His son was apparently not implicated.) "British police asserted that they had enough evidence to arrest Lendrum should he set foot in Britain," reported the *Chronicle*.

In the end, Zimbabwean authorities again believed they lacked the proof—bank deposits or sworn testimony from buyers—that the Lendrums were profiting from their egg thefts. They never charged Adrian Lendrum, but the rumors of the Lendrums' involvement in a black market lingered. The March 1985 newsletter of the World Working Group on Birds of Prey and Owls, a pan-European network of enthusiasts and bird protectors, described the Lendrums as active bird-egg smugglers and explained that the trade "is organized internationally in a manner similar to international traffic in drugs." With ingenious new methods of keeping eggs protected in transit, and new tactics to hatch well-advanced embryos, unscrupulous elements in the tight-knit community of rare-bird collectors had begun spreading the word that raptors-in-the-shell could be had for the right price. The article estimated that the trade grossed a modest $3 million a year, with the most expensive raptor egg, that of a gyrfalcon, fetching $80,000 on the black market. For connoisseurs of birds of prey in search of the most beautiful and exotic specimens in the world, there would be no greater mark of prestige than flying an African black eagle—or even better, a rare crowned eagle—thousands of miles from the birds' native habitat.

Looking back two decades later, Peter Mundy, an ornithology professor at Bulawayo's National University of Science and Technology and a confidante of Val Gargett, would view the father and son as mutual enablers. Mundy had been friendly with Jeffrey and

Adrian Lendrum for years—attending evening gatherings with the father at the Ornithological Society, chatting with both of them amiably at the airport, a tire shop, and other spots around the city. But the trial and conviction of the Lendrums exposed a dark side that he had never seen. The younger Lendrum was "a very personable and likable young man, and terribly energetic," Mundy would write years later in *Honeyguide*, the quarterly magazine published by BirdLife Zimbabwe. "If only he had gone down the right path of scientific curiosity and endeavour, he could have contributed significantly . . . to ornithology at large. What went wrong? Perhaps the father's behavior influenced the son."

Over the course of the trial, Kit Hustler says, Jeffrey Lendrum demonstrated a "sense of entitlement" that might, he thought, have derived in part from growing up white and privileged in colonial Rhodesia. "He believed that it was his right to go into the game reserves and help himself," Hustler says. What Hustler didn't know at the time was that Jeffrey claimed to have been encouraged in these activities by corrupt Parks and Wildlife officials. From the time he was a teenager, Lendrum would say decades later, he was paid handsomely to snatch the chicks of black eagles, African hawk eagles, lanner falcons, and other Specially Protected Species. "They couldn't climb, so they came to me," he would say. The officials, he would claim, would then smuggle them to destinations overseas. Jeffrey Lendrum had never mentioned any of this on the witness stand; he would later explain that he had thought nobody would believe him.

=

Jeffrey Lendrum lit out for South Africa a few months after the trial, fleeing a criminal record and intent on starting a new life. Still deep in the apartheid era, led by the hard-line Afrikaner Prime Minister P. W. Botha, nicknamed "the Big Crocodile," the country was an easy place for a young white male who had flunked most of his O levels to find steady and well-paying work. He left behind bad feelings and at least one broken heart. Gargett never again spoke to the Lendrums, and never forgave them. Burdened with guilt for having trusted them, she left behind her beloved black eagle survey and moved to Australia, where her two children and grandchildren had settled.

Aggrieved conservationists in Bulawayo, still frustrated over their failure to convict the Lendrums on smuggling charges, were intent on dragging the younger Lendrum back to court. Eventually, Peter Mundy says, the South African police made a deal with Zimbabwean authorities to arrest Lendrum and swap him at the border for a couple of South African poachers in Zimbabwe's jails. A colleague of Mundy's even traveled to South Africa to search for the egg thief on behalf of the police, eventually tracking him to his boyhood friend Howard Waller's farmhouse in the veldt outside Johannesburg. But Lendrum caught wind of the plan, and, Mundy wrote in *Honeyguide*, "he slipped away in the gloom" and disappeared. Decades later, Lendrum would claim that the supposed extradition plan was a fiction. "The guy has been reading too many Tom Clancy novels," he would say.

Whatever happened, Zimbabwe's wildlife authorities soon lost interest in Lendrum. His ban from the parks expired after one year, and he began venturing back into the country. Soon he would have a new shopping list of Specially Protected Species and new clients—in the deserts of the Middle East.

EIGHT

THE COLLECTORS

Andy McWilliam's transformation into Great Britain's most prominent wildlife cop was hatched during a stage of profound restlessness. He was forty-one years old, working the night shift and fielding radio calls. While he still enjoyed being out on the streets and keeping connections to the community, he was tired of drug busts, burglaries, and violence, and impatient to try something new. One day, a fellow officer familiar with McWilliam's love of bird-watching passed to him the name of a thirty-year-old man in Merseyside who was secretly keeping a collection of bird eggs stolen from the wild. McWilliam obtained a search warrant from a West Midlands judge, entered the man's house, climbed to his attic, and seized three wooden boxes lined with cotton wool and filled with two hundred eggs—many of them from endangered species. The man claimed that he had inherited the collection from his dead brother, and got his mother to vouch for him. McWilliam arrested him anyway. He busted a second egg collector, thanks to a tip from a fellow birder, a few weeks later.

Shortly after the arrests, McWilliam reached out to Guy Shorrock, the senior investigations officer at the Royal Society for the

Protection of Birds (RSPB). Founded by the animal-rights activist Emily Williamson in Manchester in 1889, the society had begun in protest against the exotic feather trade. The hunt for colorful plumage to meet a new desire for feathered hats among fashion-conscious women in the United States and Europe had devastated the world's populations of ostriches, parrots, and great crested grebes. Since then, the RSPB had grown into the country's largest conservation group. It had two million members, owned two hundred nature reserves across Great Britain, and operated from a manor house on a forty-acre estate in the town of Sandy, north of London, that had once belonged to the Peel family—kin of the founder of London's Metropolitan Police. Shorrock was a member of a small team of full-time bird detectives at the private charity who kept a database on wildlife-crime offenders, and often joined forces with British police to solve bird-related crimes.

Shorrock was a wiry man with piercing blue eyes and sprinklings of gray-white hair. A biochemistry graduate and former Manchester police officer, he had a passion for chasing down wild-bird launderers; "pigeon fanciers" who poisoned or shot falcons, to stop them from preying on their flying pets; gamekeepers on hunting estates, who also viewed falcons as a threat; and, above all, egg collectors. "Their pointless pursuit of egg shells, for their own personal gratification, made them universally unpopular," Shorrock wrote in a blog post about a nationwide sweep he'd orchestrated to great public approval. "Each spring it seemed the phone was ringing every weekend with calls from around the country, particularly Scotland, about the sightings of possible suspects and their vehicles or the sad news that yet another nest had been raided." McWilliam asked Shorrock to keep his eye out for cases involving egg collectors in Merseyside.

As it happened, Shorrock had just opened a file on Dennis Green, a fifty-seven-year-old nature photographer, bird portraitist, and RSPB member, who lived quietly with his elderly mother in Liverpool. Green's name had turned up in the diary of another collector, and Shorrock suspected that he was hiding a large cache of eggs in his house. In April 1999, McWilliam obtained a search warrant, and he and Shorrock raided Green's small semi-detached home. A handsome man with bushy eyebrows and long strands of hair flowing from the back of his balding pate, Green first appeared shocked, then stood silently by as the investigators climbed up a narrow flight of stairs into a cramped loft jammed with the trophies of a lifetime of hoarding.

They sifted through stacks of football programs; moths mounted in display cases; autographs of British football players, television stars, and other celebrities; and taxidermied birds, including such rare species as hen harriers and short-eared owls. Then they began opening dozens of two-by-three-foot plywood boxes, each one screwed shut. Inside, McWilliam and Shorrock discovered hundreds of eggs. Hundreds more lay tucked inside plastic food containers, tins, and a forty-drawer display cabinet in Green's second-floor bedroom, half obscured behind many more stuffed birds. All told, Green had ninety-nine taxidermied specimens in the two rooms. McWilliam and Shorrock counted more than four thousand eggs— one of the biggest collections ever seized in Great Britain at the time. There were eggs of golden eagles, peregrine falcons, ospreys, and other species listed as "Schedule 1" under the 1981 Wildlife and Countryside Act—birds granted such a high level of protection that even "disturbing" them by approaching their nests is considered a crime. There were only 250 breeding pairs of golden eagles left in the United Kingdom, and McWilliam had found a dozen golden eagle eggs in Green's home.

Green insisted that it had all been "a misunderstanding." The eggs, he assured Shorrock and McWilliam, had been gathered by others before 1954, the year that Great Britain's Protection of Birds Act first made egg collecting a crime. He presented one thousand data record cards, all dating to the 1920s and 1930s, to support his claim. Analyses in a police lab, however, determined that the cards were forgeries, written by Green in ballpoint and felt-tipped pens, which hadn't gone on the market until decades later. Scribblings on two osprey eggs in Green's collection indicated that he had received them "as a gift" in 1991. Suspecting they had been snatched from the wild, Shorrock pored through hundreds of photographs of osprey nests in Scotland snapped that year by volunteer field monitors who kept tabs on eggs and recorded their characteristics in case they should be stolen. Two eggs bore the same unique red markings as the pair in Green's collection.

In Liverpool Magistrates Court later that year, Green accused Shorrock and McWilliam of behaving like "Nazi storm troopers" during the raid on his house. Shorrock presented to the magistrate a photo he had taken showing Green, McWilliam, and another police officer laughing over a joke in Green's living room.

"They don't look like Nazis," said the judge.

"But that was my nervous laugh," Green replied.

Green was found guilty of a dozen offenses, including illegal egg possession and possession of stuffed protected birds without a license. Then, citing Green's desperate finances—he survived on social welfare payments of £119 a week—the judge waived a fine, sentenced the photographer to a twelve-month conditional discharge—meaning he could avoid a guilty verdict unless he committed another offense within that time period—and confiscated both his egg collection and a handful of taxidermied birds. (Green claimed he had burned the rest of the birds in his garden; four years later he was discovered to have hidden the specimens in the home of a friend.) McWilliam had a T-shirt made up with the photo that Shorrock had taken and Green's "nervous laugh" quote, and sent the shirt to Shorrock as a souvenir.

=

Egg collectors hadn't always had such a dodgy reputation. In 1671, the writer John Evelyn, a contemporary of the famed Restoration-era diarist Samuel Pepys, visited Sir Thomas Browne, a distinguished physician, writer, and antiquary, at his home in Norwich, England. Evelyn remarked with wonder upon "a Cabinet of rarities, & that of the best collection, especially Medails, books, Plants, [and] natural things." Among Browne's "curiousities" was one of the world's first documented egg collections, a display "of the eggs of all foul and birds he could procure, that country (especially the promontorys of Norfolck) being . . . frequented with—cranes, storkes, eagles etc. and a variety of water-foule."

During the Victorian era, oology, as the study of eggs was known, became a distinct branch of ornithology. Wealthy sponsors such as Walter Rothschild, an heir to the Rothschild banking fortune and founder of a natural history museum at Tring, near London, dispatched collectors to sweep up specimens from the Amazon jungle, the Hawaiian Islands, Central Africa, Borneo, and other remote corners of the globe. "Acquisition in the name of national pride, meant that eggs and birds (in the form of study skins and skeletons), were accumulated on an unimaginable scale," wrote the British ornithologist Tim Birkhead in *The Most Perfect Thing* (the most perfect thing being, naturally, a bird's egg).

Oologists were often celebrated for their feats of bravery in the cause of scientific exploration. Charles Bendire, a German-born US Army officer, who collected eggs while based in a series of western forts after the Civil War, was snatching the egg of a zone-tailed hawk from a cottonwood tree in the Arizona desert in 1872 when Apache warriors on horseback attacked him. He placed the speckled orb between his teeth, shinnied down the tree, and made his escape. "As he rode headlong into camp, gasping and gagging, Bendire discovered that he couldn't spit the egg out," according to an admiring biographer. Soldiers pried open his mouth and removed the egg intact, in the process ripping out one of Bendire's teeth.

Other collectors lost more than denticulation: John C. Calhoon, from Taunton, Massachusetts, drew breathless newspaper coverage for his pursuit of ravens' eggs in the cliffs near St. John's, Newfoundland. "Daring Act of American Ornithologist at Birds Island," an 1889 headline proclaimed. "He scales Perpendicular Cliff Three Hundred Feet High. Shuddering Fishermen Lean on Their Oars and Witness the Dangerous Ascent." Two years later, Calhoon's strength gave out during a climb up from a raven's nest on those same cliffs, and he fell two hundred feet to his death. Gathering eggs during his Sierra Nevada honeymoon in 1901, Francis J. Britwell was blown from his perch atop a sixty-foot pine tree by a gust of wind, caught his neck in the loop of his safety rope, and strangled to death while his bride watched. Richardson P. Smithwick, the twenty-two-year-old scion of a family of North Carolina egg collectors, was smothered in a sand dune cave-in in southeastern Virginia in 1909 while raiding the nest of a belted kingfisher. The *Oologist*, a popular magazine for egg collectors in the United States, reported "the sad ending of an active, useful life. Mr. Smithwick was an active young worker in his chosen field of science."

A few oologists were, in fact, dedicated scientists: Edgar Chance, a Edwardian-era collector, devoted his life to observing the breeding habits of the common cuckoo and was the first ornithologist to document "brood parasitism"—laying eggs in the nest of another species and tricking the host bird into incubating them as her own. In 1911, three members of Robert Scott's doomed Antarctica expedition trekked seventy miles through blizzards and minus-eighty-degree-Fahrenheit temperatures to collect eggs from an emperor penguin colony. The explorers were out to prove a theory advanced by the nineteenth-century biologist Ernst Haeckel, that the development of an embryo from fertilization to gestation or hatching replicates the evolutionary stages of the same species. (Haeckel believed that grooves in the back of the human embryo's neck resembled gills, proving that man had a fishlike ancestor.) The Antarctic trio suspected that the penguin embryo would demonstrate that the bird had descended from reptiles. The eggs, alas, proved nothing. Most collectors, however, seemed driven by little more than what one Victorian observer called "a passion for beauty and a lust for curiousities."

The British curiosity seekers were by far the most prodigious. John Arthington Walpole-Bond, an Edwardian-era collector from Sussex, claimed to have seen in situ, or in their original place, the eggs of every species in the British Isles, and amassed a collection well into the thousands. "I have vivid memories of him striding along on the very brink of the Sussex cliffs," wrote one friend in his 1956 obituary, "and, in a high wind, stopping . . . to perch himself on the tip of a promontory in order to lean right over and clap his hands in an effort to put out a Peregrine"—that is, frighten the raptor away from the nest in order to seize her eggs. Francis Charles Robert Jourdain, an Oxford-educated minister, had a scar on his forehead from plunging off a cliff in pursuit of an eagle nest. He amassed 17,500 clutches, thought to be the largest collection of eggs in Western Europe. Tim Birkhead, in *The Most Perfect Thing*, speculates that many of these collectors felt an erotic attraction to their specimens. Cambridge University professor Alfred Newton, according to one contemporary, spent hours "ogling his eggs" and barred women from setting eyes on them. "Perhaps their wonderful curves trigger deep-rooted visual and tactile sensations among men," wrote Birkhead. "That may also be one reason Fabergé's eggs are so popular: an expensive nuptial gift that fuses sensuality of form with the ultimate symbol of fertility."

Newton and his fellow collectors eventually fell out of favor with other ornithologists and the British public. In the years after World War I a consensus was building that egg collecting had negligible scientific value and was threatening to drive some species to extinction. In 1922 the Royal Society for the Protection of Birds condemned egg collecting as a "distinct menace" to birds, and the British Ornithological Union, to which Rothschild, Chance, and Jourdain belonged, denounced the practice. The three oologists angrily split from the group and formed the British Oological Association, renamed the Jourdain Society after Jourdain's death in 1940. Its members gathered over dinners, often in evening dress, to show one another specimens and swap anecdotes about their adventures.

But the collectors were growing increasingly ostracized. "Are we English people so indifferent to the glorious heritage of birds that we will allow the selfish greed of individuals to denude our country of its rare birds?" wrote one enthusiast to *The Field*, a British ornithological journal, in 1935, reflecting the turning tide of public opinion. In 1952, the *Guardian*'s country diarist Harry Griffin scorned collectors as "the cloak-and-dagger men of the fells." Two years later the Protection of Birds Act made oology illegal. Undercover investigators from the Royal Society for the Protection of Birds bugged Jourdain members' hotel rooms and raided their dinners. Chris Mead, senior officer at the British Trust for Ornithology, claimed that the Jourdain Society provided a network for illegal collectors and had become the "pariah of the bird-watching world."

As a boy in Liverpool in the 1960s, Andy McWilliam had a few schoolmates whose fathers kept egg collections, and some of his friends made forays into the countryside to forage for themselves. But as an understanding of the dangers the hobby posed to nature spread, most collectors found other ways of passing the time. Still, some fanatics refused. After the Jourdain's secretary, James Whitaker, was found guilty of offenses under the 1981 Wildlife and Countryside Act—and had 148 illegally taken eggs seized (out of a collection numbering 2,895)—one Jourdain member likened the Royal Society for the Protection of Birds, which had gathered evidence for the arrest, to "little Hitlers."

——

Into the new millennium, hundreds of egg collectors across the British Isles continued to gather specimens on the sly. And Andy McWilliam was becoming one of their principal nemeses. In 2000 he was invited to participate in Operation Easter, a nationwide crackdown launched three years earlier by Guy Shorrock of the RSPB, and the Scottish police, that named 130 egg collectors as top-priority targets.

"It's very rare in the UK to have a national police operation of this kind," Alan Stewart, the police officer who started Operation Easter with Shorrock in the face of rampant nest robbing, and a man once described by the nature magazine *Scottish Field* as "Britain's foremost wildlife detective," told *The New Yorker* in 2012. "The others are for drug trafficking, human trafficking, and football hooliganism."

McWilliam began with a network of a dozen miscreants in Merseyside, many of whom ventured together on clandestine egg-hunting expeditions. The first target on his list was Carlton Julian D'Cruze, an unemployed cabinetmaker and longtime acquaintance of Dennis Green's, who had allegedly raided nests across the United Kingdom for years but had never been caught. Shorrock suspected that D'Cruze was keeping a huge stash of eggs hidden in a safe house somewhere in Liverpool. McWilliam shadowed D'Cruze, a moon-faced man with a shaved head and thin mustache and goatee. One evening he spotted the pickup truck of another Operation Easter suspect in D'Cruze's driveway. An inflatable dinghy lay in the truck bed. McWilliam was certain that they were preparing to drive to northern Scotland, one of D'Cruze's favorite nest-raiding spots. McWilliam accosted the men as they emerged from the house, but he had no evidence of a crime. The men grinned tauntingly as they drove off—but McWilliam may have had the last laugh. "I heard that when they reached wherever they were going, they couldn't blow up the dinghy because somebody had punctured it," McWilliam says coyly. "You can read into that whatever you want."

Soon after the driveway encounter, an informant told McWilliam that D'Cruze had moved—and had probably transferred his egg collection to his new residence. McWilliam obtained the address, secured a search warrant, and knocked on the front door. He waited, then knocked again. When a neighbor told McWilliam that D'Cruze was at home, the policeman kicked the door down and charged inside. McWilliam found D'Cruze on his knees in the second-floor bathroom, clad only in his underwear. He was frantically crushing eggs, tearing up data cards, and trying to flush the pieces down the toilet.

When Shorrock arrived from D'Cruze's mother's house—a second search warrant hadn't turned up anything—he shut off the water supply, took apart the toilet, and recovered the shredded note cards and egg fragments, which he laid out to dry. In the Royal Society for the Protection of Birds' laboratory outside London, Shorrock and other experts reassembled 138 eggs of peregrines, sea eagles, and ospreys. "We laid them out like a macabre jigsaw puzzle," he says.

They also had other evidence: McWilliam had seized 355 intact eggs that D'Cruze hadn't had time to crush and flush. D'Cruze pleaded guilty and was sentenced to six months in jail, making him only the second egg collector ever to serve time for his crime. In 2000 Parliament had amended the Wildlife and Countryside Act with the Countryside and Rights of Way Act, making egg collection punishable by a six-month jail term. Up until then, egg collectors could receive only a fine of £5,000 per egg, or about $7,500 at the time of the amendment. The highest penalty ever assessed had been £90,000, approximately $120,000, levied against Jamie and Lee McLaren, two brothers known to investigators as the "Abbott and Costello" of egg collecting, who had videotaped each other stealing seabird eggs in northern England.

=

After the D'Cruze conviction in 2002, the World Wildlife Fund honored McWilliam as its UK Law Enforcer of the Year. By now, with his supervisor's approval, McWilliam had scaled back his normal po-lice duties and was taking on more and more wildlife-crime-related cases—investigations that nobody else in the department seemed to want and that often took him to far-flung corners of Merseyside. He cultivated informants in the underworld of badger baiters, who use dogs to corner and kill the burrowing omnivores for sport. He raided farms, served search warrants, seized graphic videos, and collected badger-blood splatter on clothing and in cars. The evidence he gath-ered helped to convict several notorious "terrier men," as the bad-ger baiters call themselves, of animal cruelty under the Protection of Badgers Act of 1992. Some of the investigations he found hard to forget. McWilliam and his partner Steve Harris once raided the home of a suspected badger baiter near Liverpool, and found back-yard kennels filled with dogs that had suffered terrible injuries—one with no nose, another missing its lower jaw—from savagely fighting the sharp-toothed burrowers.

Further searching turned up stacks of brochures in the backseat of the suspect's four-by-four, advertising free pest-extermination services. "I pass the brochures out in the countryside to people who have a fox problem," the man told the officers after his arrest. Foxes in rural areas often carry off poultry, piglets, lambs, and household pets, and can spread rabies, prompting farmers to hire pest control services to shoot them.

"Why don't you charge your clients a fee?" asked Harris.

"Because," the man replied calmly, "I fucking love killing ani-mals."

Responding to complaints from animal welfare groups, McWilliam investigated the Southport Zoo, a decrepit Merseyside facility located beside the Pleasureland amusement park. He found wild cats—ocelots, servals, and snow leopards—pacing agitatedly in their enclosures next to a rickety wooden roller coaster, with carriages that clattered along the track every four minutes for ten hours a day during the summer. A solitary lioness spent most of her days confined in an indoor cell, while a pair of chimpanzee brothers lived separated and alone in barren, filthy cages. Disturbed by what he'd seen, McWilliam looked for a way to shut down the facility. In the end, he busted the owners for thirteen violations of Convention on International Trade in Endangered Species import regulations. The owners pled guilty, and authorities closed the zoo. To his discomfort, however, McWilliam "became a bit of a hero" to the animal rights protesters who'd demonstrated outside the zoo on weekends and bank holidays. "I wanted to distance myself from them," he recalls. He was a police officer, not an activist.

He investigated two real estate developers who had secretly dug up the riverside burrows of the water vole, a semi-aquatic rodent regarded as one of England's most endangered animals, to construct a drainage ditch for a housing complex. Relying on the account of a ninety-five-year-old witness who lived beside the reserve, McWilliam threatened the developers with arrest if they didn't come clean. In the end, McWilliam had them prosecuted for the reckless disturbance of a protected species, and they paid a significant fine. He carried out a sting operation on a local taxidermist who advertised stuffed rare birds and mammals in the classifieds of a Merseyside paper. Posing as a customer, he called the man. "Don't you need a CITES permit for that?" he asked, referring to the export and import documents issued by the Convention on International Trade in Endangered Species of Wild Flora and Fauna. "Nobody ever checks," the taxidermist replied. McWilliam made an appointment, brought along a search warrant, and arrested the man for import violations.

But it was the egg collectors who dominated his caseload. Working closely with Guy Shorrock from the Royal Society for the Protection of Birds, he deciphered encrypted notes and matched handwritten records to the bird charity's database of nest robberies, discrediting collectors' claims that they had acquired their collection at a garage sale or inherited it from family members. "The collectors couldn't bullshit him," says Steve Harris, who worked with McWilliam on many bird crime cases. McWilliam pored through eBay and other websites looking for suspicious purchases. One Liverpudlian had ordered large quantities of Bubble Wrap, plastic containers, egg box foam, and specialty books off the Internet; McWilliam got a search warrant while the suspect was out of the country, and found an egg-blowing kit—tiny files, drills, and pipettes—in his desk drawer and a thousand eggs in a specimen cabinet. He arrested him as soon as he returned to England.

He developed a network of tipsters, often cultivating the collectors' ex-girlfriends or collectors who had quarreled with their rivals. "Andy was a no-nonsense, old-fashioned bobby," said Shorrock. "He understood police work, he understood people." And he was discovering a web of hidden relationships. McWilliam turned up handwritten notes in D'Cruze's house that contained coded references to one Anthony Higham, a thirty-nine-year-old printing firm manager who had apparently been raiding nests across Great Britain. A source directed McWilliam to the likely location of Higham's collection: the home of an elderly woman who was a neighbor of Higham's ex-girlfriend. McWilliam obtained another search warrant, and knocked on the woman's door.

"Has Mr. Higham asked you to hide anything in your loft?" he asked.

"No," she replied, nervously.

She has "Yes" on her face, McWilliam thought.

McWilliam entered the house and, in a now-familiar routine, climbed to the attic and found boxes containing one thousand eggs, along with diaries and photographs documenting Higham's exploits. Higham had befriended the woman over several months and had asked her politely to store his cartons while being hazy on the details; she'd had no idea what was concealed inside them. After McWilliam arrested him, Higham, a broad-shouldered, clean-shaven man with trimmed blond hair and the slightly sagging physique of a former athlete, surrendered hundreds more eggs from another stash, including many from peregrines, ospreys, and golden eagles. As he handed them over, Higham looked at McWilliam wistfully. "They're beautiful, aren't they?" he said.

——

McWilliam struggled to understand the obsession. "It's the sixty-four-thousand-dollar question," he would tell Timothy Wheeler for the 2015 documentary *Poached*, which followed the lives of several egg collectors targeted by Operation Easter. "They blow the contents of the egg out and they keep a small piece of calcium which they can't put on display anywhere. They hide it away, and it's a mystery to me what they get out of it."

Some collectors had even narrowed their obsessions to a single species. D'Cruze focused compulsively on the chough, a crow-like bird found in Wales and Cornwall that lays cream-colored eggs with red markings, five to a clutch, on cliff ledges often hundreds of feet off the ground. Enticed by the nest sites' inaccessibility, D'Cruze had stolen twenty-eight chough clutches in his career. He had even written a lengthy manuscript about the eggs for a caliologists' series published by Oriel Stringer books, produced mostly by egg collectors for the benefit of other collectors and filled with clues about where to find nest sites. (Caliology is the study of bird's nests.) One book in the series, *The Osprey* by W. Pearson, guides collectors to eighty nesting sites in Great Britain, providing grid references and markers such as dead pine trees, Victorian-era monuments, and lochs. Pearson notes in his introduction that "the pseudo-protectionists were up in arms" after the publication of the series' first book, and "one society for the protection of birds tried to get a High Court injunction to get the book banned." The attempt failed.

Another collector McWilliam arrested had made his life's quest the tree pipit, a small songbird that lays its four to eight eggs in a ground nest, concealed in deep woodland or scrub. The man looked down on collectors who raided the nests of eagles and other raptors, he told McWilliam, because they were so large and conspicuous and, in his view, didn't present much of a challenge.

Anthony Higham admitted that he was "obsessed with the peregrine," while Derek Lee, a Manchester man whom McWilliam arrested in 2004, started at age sixteen and was led to increasingly rare specimens. Beginning with blackbirds and song thrushes, "I traveled elsewhere to pick up a kestrel or sparrowhawk egg," he told the *Guardian* in 2006. "Then the next challenge was the buzzard. Eventually I came across peregrines and red kites." The most tantalizing prize for many collectors, according to Guy Shorrock, is the egg of the greenshank, a large sandpiper with long green legs and gray plumage that inhabits the remote wetlands of northern Scotland. Laid in clutches of four in a depression in the ground and usually concealed among lichen, dwarf shrubs, and pine needles, the green-shank egg is almost impossible to find and represents, Shorrock says, "the pinnacle of egg collecting."

McWilliam noticed other common traits among the collectors. Several men styled themselves after their forerunners of a bygone age, back when oology was a respected pursuit. McWilliam found a handwritten thesaurus in D'Cruze's bedroom filled with turn-of-the-century terms that he used to make his diaries sound more like those of his Jourdain Society heroes. Higham fitted his home office with Victorian furniture, and, using John Walpole-Bond's diaries, retraced the famed collector's routes through the remote glens of northern Scotland. Higham undertook thirty-six treks, discovering sixty nests in many of the same spots where Walpole-Bond had found his. Matthew Gonshaw, among the most notorious egg collectors in British history, kept a photograph in his bedroom of Walpole-Bond. "In memory of Jock—The Man," Gonshaw had written on it, referring to Walpole-Bond by his nickname. In his long career, Gonshaw stole thousands of eggs, went to jail repeatedly, and was banned from Scotland for life.

All of the collectors relished the physical risks: the dangerous rappels down rock faces, the scrambles up trees, the crossings of turbulent waters. Climbing for peregrine eggs in a rock quarry in northern Wales in 1991, Higham had watched his partner, Dennis Hughes, slip and fall dozens of feet to his death. Instead of being traumatized by the accident, he wrote in his diary, "I was well and truly hooked." Higham came close to dying, too, after capsizing his dinghy while rowing to an island in a frigid loch. D'Cruze nearly froze to death one winter, he told McWilliam, while hunting for nests in northern Scotland and losing his way in the wilderness. Colin Watson, a maintenance man described in the media as "Britain's most ruthless egg collector," tumbled off a forty-foot larch tree in Yorkshire one May morning in 2006 while trying to raid a sparrow hawk nest. He suffered massive injuries and died at the scene. "Nest in Peace," declared the headline in the London *Daily Mirror*.

For many collectors, the cat-and-mouse game with the authorities was equally thrilling. Derek Lee posed as a bird-watcher and gleefully duped unsuspecting park rangers into leading him to nests. D'Cruze wrote field notes and letters filled with coded references to accomplices—one was "86," another "15"—and kept them in an envelope labeled "top secret." Several collectors whom McWilliam arrested had developed clever subterfuges, burying their caches in the ground or stashing them in the hollows of trees, then returning in the off-season to retrieve them, after the rangers and RSPB nest watchers had left. One of McWilliam's wildlife police colleagues arrested a master carpenter in Norfolk who had constructed secret compartments throughout his mobile home—hollow storage areas built inside seats and sofas, in which he had secreted thousands of eggs. Matthew Gonshaw hid the most prized eggs in his collection inside a hollowed-out bed frame.

The most exciting moment invariably came when the collector at last approached the object of desire. "The sight which met my eyes is one I shall treasure," wrote Higham about his first climb to a nest of osprey eggs, in 1992. As the female osprey flew off, "shouting" in agitation, Higham moved in. "Three richly marked eggs bedded in a cup of damp moss were visible in the twilight," he wrote. "I packed them into my gloves, then into my hat, carrying my haul in my teeth." In 1997 D'Cruze attempted to rob the nest of a white-tailed sea eagle, a large raptor that had been wiped out in Great Britain by hunters in the early twentieth century. An RSPB program had recently reintroduced a dozen breeding pairs to Scotland. D'Cruze traveled with an accomplice to the remote Isle of Mull in the Inner Hebrides, where a few pairs had taken up residence. "My body felt cold as there was quite a chill, so W and myself set a steady pace along the track towards the loch," began the harrowing account in his diary:

> A hell of a walk in the dark and I slipped many times, but eventually we reached the wood around midnight—as quietly as possible W climbed the tree. When he was only half way, [the eagle] started screeching and clapping her wings up and down on the edge of the eyrie . . . W shouted to me that he could not get her off. I called up to him to remove a branch from the eyrie and ease her off. After a few minutes she decamped and W was able to reach in, only to find the eagle had broken the second egg and so we left it, hoping she would continue to incubate it. Both disappointed, we had a long walk back along the loch.

Such accounts reinforced McWilliam's view that egg collecting was an act of pure selfishness, an attack on the sanctity of the wild. As Holly Cale, the chief curator at Jemima Parry-Jones's International Centre for Birds of Prey, put it: "The [mother] bird's whole purpose of being is to procreate, to rear her young. She will be terribly distressed, traumatized by the loss, will vocalize about the fact that the eggs have gone, and sometimes she will come back to the nest, looking for the eggs." Birds can sometimes lay another clutch during the same breeding season if their first one fails, but producing calcium consumes a tremendous amount of the female's energy; usually the opportunity is lost until the next year.

effect on mother bird

But McWilliam wasn't incapable of feeling compassion for those he arrested. Many whom he came across were "loners and social misfits" in his eyes, who seemed to live for little else but their eggs. Dennis Green had resided with his mother in poverty until she died, then Scotch-taped a life-sized photo of her to the settee where she used to sit. Matthew Gonshaw was a recluse surviving on public assistance. He traveled to nest sites by public transport, and calculated down to the last pence the cost of every supply he would need in the field, according to *The New Yorker*, "from butter to packets of instant custard made by a company called Bird's."

Anthony Higham was a different sort. He had a solid job as the manager of a printing firm, a decent house, a long-term partner, and friends, and he was mortified that he had jeopardized everything to satisfy what he recognized as an addiction. "I can't believe that I'm going to prison, all for taking birds' eggs," he lamented to McWilliam in 2004, when the policeman visited him at his home in Merseyside, shortly before he began a four-month sentence. McWilliam, touched by Higham's genuine distress over what he had done, shared the perception of Timothy Wheeler, who likened the behavior of the egg collector to that of an alcohol or drug abuser. "They are somehow able to rationalize their behavior because the lust for the egg becomes more important to them than seeing that they're actually harming the very thing they love," Wheeler told the Audubon Society. Scientific research into what compels men like Anthony Higham has been thin, but a study of collectors of fossilized dinosaur eggs, published in the *Journal of Economic Psychology* in June 2011, hypothesized that the pursuit of eggs is a modern residue of a "signalling" strategy used by our ancestors to attract a mate through the acquisition of "rare and difficult to obtain . . . resources." Although such behavior has "low reproductive value today," it became hardwired into our genetic code through natural selection, the author suggests, and, for some anyway, is impossible to resist. The Anxiety and Depression Association of America drew a distinction between hoarding—which it linked to obsessive-compulsive disorder, attention-deficit/hyperactivity disorder, and depression—and the more refined and organized pursuit of collecting. For some egg collectors such as Dennis Green, however, who lived surrounded by useless mementos and seemed unable to throw anything away, the differences were clearly blurred.

McWilliam stayed in contact with Higham following his release on parole. Higham managed to get his old job back at the printing firm and had engaged a craftsman to make replicas of some eggs in his confiscated collection. "They're good, aren't they?" he told McWilliam, proudly showing him a peregrine egg made of plexiglass. *Oh my God*, McWilliam thought, saying nothing, but disturbed by the depth of Higham's obsession. Higham still loved walking in the wilderness, but he worried that his criminal record made him vulnerable to arrest. One day he went hiking on a mountain trail in North Wales and spotted a dead chough on the ground. The bird had half a dozen leg rings from scientific studies and a succession of owners, and Higham, fascinated by such arcania, could hardly resist retrieving the chough to study its history. He phoned McWilliam from the mountain. "If I pick this bloody thing up and get stopped, I'll be in trouble," he said. "What should I do?" McWilliam advised him not to lay his hands on it. Then he contacted a wildlife police colleague nearby, who met Higham on the trail, and took away the tiny corpse.

For other collectors, the stigma of incarceration did nothing to break the mesmerizing power of the egg. Gregory Peter Wheal, a roofer from Coventry in the West Midlands, was arrested ten times in a decade; he "just didn't seem to be able to stop," McWilliam said, even after serving a six-month prison sentence. After D'Cruze served five months in jail, McWilliam asked, "Is this going to be it? You going to quit?"

"You can never say never," D'Cruze replied.

=

Between 1999 and 2005 magistrates in the United Kingdom jailed eight egg collectors for their crimes; McWilliam arrested five of them. Anthony Higham served four months in prison and Carlton D'Cruze five. Dennis Green went to jail for four months in 2002 for "perversion of justice," after hiding dozens of illegal taxidermic trophies in D'Cruze's house and then lying to authorities about it. In 2004 McWilliam arrested John Latham, a cabinetmaker who had amassed 282 eggs in a three-month spree, including 14 from the rare kingfisher. That same year he apprehended Manicunian Derek Lee, who specialized in hard-to-find specimens. Then, thanks to Operation Easter's success and the imposition of jail sentences rather than fines, "egg collecting just fell off completely," says Guy Shorrock. "The major collectors stopped or died." While there are surely some big collections still hidden away in England, periodic amnesty programs have been successful at encouraging owners to turn them over to the police.

Yet despite a string of arrests and successful prosecutions, many of McWilliam's colleagues saw what he did as a bit of a joke. McWilliam and Harris would bring to the Crosby station a suspect they had just arrested for stealing rare birds or collecting endangered eggs, and other police officers would poke fun at them. "Put him before the beak," they would tell McWilliam—a British slang term for magistrate. Wildlife crime "was regarded as trivial," Harris says. But McWilliam shrugged off the mockery. After years of investigating egg enthusiasts—observing their idiosyncracies, familiarizing himself with their subterfuges, and grasping their obsessions—McWilliam understood the stakes of bird-related crime. And he would soon turn his skills to taking down the most formidable egg thief that he would ever encounter.

NINE

AFRICAXTREME

In the summer of 1998, Jeffrey Lendrum was thirty-six years old, recently divorced, and residing in Jukskei Park, a leafy middle-class neighborhood in northwest Johannesburg. Thirteen years had gone by since he'd left Bulawayo in disgrace, and he had built a new life for himself. He'd married a South African woman, who had a son with a previous partner, and though the relationship hadn't lasted and they'd had no children of their own, the two had stayed on good terms. She would still drop by Lendrum's house with her son for an occasional meal.

Lendrum now ran a one-man business called Wallace Distributors, procuring auto parts, mining equipment, and aircraft components and then driving them in his Toyota pickup truck to customers across the border in Zimbabwe. Strict limits imposed by the Mugabe regime on the flow of foreign currency in and out of Zimbabwe, along with high taxes and quotas on imports, had made it increasingly difficult to obtain spare parts through official channels. And Lendrum could get his hands on nearly anything: braided ropes for mine elevator shafts, engine blocks, chrome door-edge moldings. He seemed to be always on the road, driving as far north as the copper, tungsten, and nickel mines near Zambia, a fifteen-hundred-mile round trip.

Some years, during droughts, if he wasn't running other hustles, Lendrum would return to Zimbabwe to carry out mercy killings of elephants and other species on behalf of Parks and Wildlife. But he had, he would insist, abandoned his nest-raiding ways completely. "I had nothing to do with birds at all," he said. (Later, on a witness stand, he would modify that claim, admitting that he had continued to dabble in cliff climbing and nest raiding, legally "collecting black sparrowhawks for the Transvaal Falconry Club for their breeding program.")

Paul Mullin, a British businessman, met Lendrum that July after settling in Johannesburg as a senior manager for an American firm helping to roll out Internet access across southern Africa and the Middle East. Mullin's job was to advise state-owned telecommunications firms on installing servers and other hardware. Mullin was an army brat who claimed that his father had guarded Spandau Prison in Berlin when the Nazi war criminal Rudolf Hess was its sole inmate. He was a nomad who had traveled across Africa half a dozen times, a racing car enthusiast who self-published guidebooks each year to the Formula 1 Grand Prix season, and a spycraft aficionado who drove a Mitsubishi Pajero with the vanity license plate PCM 007.

Mullin's girlfriend, a former stripper at a nightclub called the House of Lords, who'd met Lendrum at work and sometimes paid him to be her driver, made the introduction. Lendrum invited Mullin to drop by his bungalow, a modest home that overlooked a garden bisected by the Jukskei River, a narrow, shallow stream that coursed over a bed of rocks. Over a round of beers, the men discovered that they shared an interest in fast cars and African safaris. Mullin found

Lendrum personable, garrulous, and passionate about his red Mini Cooper S. Before long they were getting together regularly for coffee or to take Lendrum's Mini Cooper out for 140-mile-per-hour spins at a Grand Prix–style racecourse outside Johannesburg. During their excursions, Lendrum bragged several times about his exploits as a member of the Special Air Service during the Rhodesian Bush War. Mullin says he knew it was "bollocks," but didn't let it get in the way of their developing friendship. A few months later Lendrum enlisted Mullin for a favor: to carry back from England a coil of walnut wood for the dashboard of a Jaguar E-type sports car that a friend was customizing in Bulawayo.

Lendrum was always looking for the next opportunity, and in early 1999 he made his friend a pitch. He had been struck by the curio shops he saw across South Africa, selling everything from novelty T-shirts to carved rhinos. There was even a large one at Johannesburg's international airport. "Wouldn't it be a good idea," he told Mullin, while eating oysters at an Ocean Basket seafood franchise in a Johannesburg shopping mall, "if we could bring African handicrafts into the UK and sell them?" Mullin thought that Lendrum might be on to something. "Let's give it a go," he said.

Mullin and Lendrum pooled their resources and came up with £15,000. They made a trial run to Zimbabwe, where they found reliable vendors and a company to clear everything with customs and ship the goods. Then they opened their first shop in Southampton, seventy miles south of London, where Mullin owned a house and where a former girlfriend and their five-year-old daughter still lived. Mullin hired his ex to work behind the counter, and decorated the store in African-bush-style, stringing a tented canopy from the ceiling, painting the walls in a zebra-skin pattern, and covering the countertops with thatch. Mullin and Lendrum called their venture AfricaXtreme.

The partners began traveling to Zimbabwe every month, on the hunt for handicrafts. Mullin could make his own hours, and none of his clients complained if he vanished for a week. He and Lendrum would drive from Bulawayo north to Victoria Falls, and then back south through Hwange National Park—a thousand-mile journey that typically took them five days. After their first binge-buy to fill the Southampton shop, an entrepreneur with a few dozen artisans in her employ struck a deal with the partners to produce wooden safari animals in bulk. Mullin and Lendrum paid cash and also gave the carvers soap, sugar, mealy meal (a coarse flour made from maize), clothing, and other necessities. Other dealers provided them with ebony walking sticks, hippos and rhinos carved from soapstone, leopards fashioned from the mottled dark green mineral serpentine, herons and storks made of polished mukwa wood, teakwood side tables and fruit baskets, traditional drums, and carved giraffes of all sizes, from two-inch miniatures to nearly life-sized sculptures.

They packed their purchases into a trailer attached to Lendrum's pickup truck and, back in Bulawayo, loaded everything into a container at the Southern Comfort Lodge—a thatched-roof retreat with a pool filled with the skulls of culled elephants, owned by one of Lendrum's boyhood friends, a professional leopard hunter named Craig Hunt. A shipping company fumigated the goods, transported them to Durban, a South African port on the Indian Ocean, and put them on a boat to London. Mullin collected the crafts and delivered them to the store in Southampton. Mullin and Lendrum tried to avoid buying mass-produced kitsch and sought out hand-carved works by skillful artisans: in Cameroon Mullin found antique tribal masks in a street market that he bought for a pittance and sold in England for several hundred pounds apiece.

Lendrum was still bringing spare parts to his clients in Zimbabwe for Wallace Distributors, and Mullin often came along for the ride. To avoid the hours-long traffic jams at the Beit Bridge, the main crossing point between South Africa and Zimbabwe, Lendrum would pay someone at the front of the line two hundred rand (about $20) or give him case of Coke to trade places with him. Then he would chat up the Zimbabwean customs agents and slip them small gifts to wave him through the checkpoint. "If you're a border controller, and you're paid the equivalent of a month's salary to turn a blind eye, that will do it," Mullin says. Lendrum would make his deliveries, receive payment in cash, and play Zimbabwe's wildly fluctuating currency markets, trading rand, Zimbabwe dollars, and US dollars. Lendrum impressed Mullin as a relentless wheeler-dealer, willing, he said, "to do anything to make a quick buck."

The business spun off in new directions. A Harare craftsman sold them African heron and egret sculptures made of welded steel, three to four feet tall, which did so well in Southampton that they decided to manufacture their own. They imported welding machines from South Africa, set up a metalwork shop in Bulawayo, hired local craftsmen, and struck a deal with two chains of garden centers in the United Kingdom to export the steel birds in bulk. In Nairobi, they discovered an open-air crafts market and soon had a procession of carvers of ebony and kisii stone (an easily shaped, peach-colored soapstone found only near Lake Victoria) bringing their wares to their hotel room. They bought woven reed baskets in the wetlands of Botswana and wooden masks in Zambia. Lendrum knew how to

bargain, had an eye for African arts, and chatted easily with the traders. As a boy, he'd picked up some isiNdebele, the Zulu-based language of southern Zimbabwe, and could converse in Fanagolo, a mix
of Zulu, English, and Afrikaans that had become the lingua franca
of Southern Africa's miners and other workers, who came from a
collage of ethnic and linguistic groups. (Many white Rhodesians of
a certain age learned to speak Fanagolo to communicate with their
servants.)

When Lendrum claimed to be short on funds, Mullin assumed
more and more of the financial risk. Mullin knew his business partner would probably never contribute his fair share, but he also understood that if he didn't keep providing the money the handicrafts
would stop flowing and the venture would collapse. "There's something wrong with that guy," Mullin's ex—while still working behind
the counter—warned him. "You can't trust him." By that point Mullin was in way too deep.

Their frantic pace led, on one occasion, to near-disaster. Mullin had
bought a four-wheel-drive Mitsubishi Pajero, ideal for driving in the
bush, and souped it up with a three-liter engine and a supercharger—
an air compressor that feeds extra oxygen into the engine, greatly improving the car's performance. Racing up to Bulawayo from the Beit
Bridge one scorching afternoon, he and Lendrum saw black smoke
billowing out the side of the four-by-four, and a trail of black oil on
the road. As they would later discover, one of the pistons had burned
through, building up pressure in the crankcase and sending oil cascad-
ing over the engine manifold. When Mullin opened the hood to have
a look, the influx of air ignited the oil. The pair managed to pull out
their valuables just before flames destroyed the vehicle. They hitched
a ride and left the Pajero smoldering on the road. Mullin bought a

new Toyota Prado three-liter diesel four-by-four with the insurance money; this time he customized the license plate to read BOND.

=

As they traveled through the bush, Mullin began to see a different side of Lendrum. Often they would drive together into Matobo National Park and climb a sloping, lichen-covered rock face whose summit provided panoramic views of mist-shrouded pinnacles receding into distant hills. Hippos lolled in the reserve's rivers far below, their tiny ears and eyes protruding just above the waterline, while twelve-foot-long crocodiles basked in the sun on the sandbanks. Antelopes, zebras, warthogs, klipspringers, and baboons sometimes leapt across the roads as they approached. Scanning the sky over the craggy rock faces where African black eagles nested, Lendrum impressed his partner with his expertise about ornithology. He knew the scientific name of every bird, from the short-toed snake eagle (*Circaetus gallicus*) to the black stork (*Ciconia nigra*), from the white-necked raven (*Corvus albicollis*) to the mocking cliff chat (*Thamnolaea cinnamomeiventris*). He could glance at a raptor and instantly identify the creature's species and gender. "You could blindfold him and let him touch a dozen falcons and he could tell you which was which," Mullin says.

Lendrum took Mullin to the Chipangali Wildlife Orphanage outside Bulawayo, established in the early 1970s to rehabilitate creatures that had been abandoned or injured in the wild. Lendrum had often delivered wounded wildlife there and had become familiar with some of the animals' personalities. "Throw some meat in there and show my mate what he does," he instructed the caretaker of a male lion. The beast picked up the bloody slab and dunked it in a trough filled with water, daintily cleaning it with his paws as Lendrum and Mullin watched in amusement. Moving to a nearby cage holding a leopard, Lendrum urged his partner to "go up to the fence." As Mullin approached, the giant cat hurled himself against the barrier with a snarl, terrifying Mullin and sending Lendrum into paroxysms of laughter. When Lendrum beckoned to a vulture that he had rescued from the bush, the vulture, to Mullin's surprise, flew straight to him. "I've always rescued animals," Lendrum would say years later. "When I see a cow lying dead on the road in Africa, I will drag the cow off the road to save the vultures from being hit by trucks."

He showed equal compassion for other unloved species. During the Southern African winter, when temperatures can plummet to near-freezing and snakes slither across Zimbabwe's asphalt roads to absorb the warmth, Lendrum and Mullin would venture out in Lendrum's truck after dark. Headlights illuminating the way ahead, Lendrum might spot a puff adder—an aggressive snake whose cytotoxic bite can kill an adult human in twenty-four hours—screech to a stop, leap out of the truck, pin its head with a stick, and then pick it up by the neck and drop it safely into a cooler box. After accumulating a few snakes, Lendrum would release them all into a field. A YouTube video that Lendrum uploaded around this time shows him toying with an eight-foot-long Egyptian cobra: he dangles the snake by the tail, forces open its jaws, and displays its fangs before tossing it gently aside.

On another occasion, Lendrum rescued from the road a rhombic egg eater, a favorite of his: a slender nonpoisonous snake that climbs trees to raid birds' nests and feeds exclusively on eggs. Lendrum phoned Mullin in England.

"Do you want it?" he asked.

"Sure," Mullin said. Lendrum smuggled it in his pocket on a plane to Heathrow. Mullin gave it to his daughter, who named it Twinkle.

=

Despite all the energy that Mullin and Lendrum put into their project, AfricaXtreme struggled to turn a profit. The Southampton shop, situated on a main street, attracted a steady stream of curious passersby, but many came to browse, not to buy. The partners spent lavishly on print and radio advertising to get the word out. Throughout 2001 and into 2002, short spots would run ten times a day during rush hours on two local radio stations. Accompanied by elephant trumpets, monkey screeches, birdcalls, and beating drums, a sonorous-voiced announcer invited locals to come check out the exotic carvings and to "turn your garden into a tropical paradise with unique, handcrafted metal birds made from recycled metal from Southern Africa." But the blitz of publicity failed to whip up sales.

Still, the partners forged ahead. They opened a second shop in Towcester, an affluent town of twenty thousand in the East Midlands, where Mullin had several friends. They started a mail-order business. Mullin took advantage of his travels for the telecommunications firm to make solo buying excursions in Uganda, Zambia, Cameroon, and the Democratic Republic of Congo. Lendrum divided his time between the crafts business and Wallace Distributors. He continued to complain about money, but he had a new distraction: he had begun a relationship with a Frenchwoman of Algerian descent, who was married but separated from her English husband. She'd met Lendrum at a dance party in Towcester, and shared his enthusiasm for auto racing. Lendrum sold his house in South Africa, and moved to a one-bedroom apartment in Towcester—and then into the house where his girlfriend lived with her two young daughters. He also hired her to run his shop. During his trips to Zimbabwe he could talk about little else.

"I'm so in love," he would tell Mullin while lying in his bed in the chalet they shared at the Southern Comfort Lodge during their handicraft-buying trips in the bush. Mullin would roll his eyes.

"For fuck's sake, shut up," he would say.

=

Lendrum would always publicly insist that he had given up illegal nest robbing after leaving Zimbabwe in 1985. But in late 1999, Mullin began noticing something odd: cartons of hard-boiled eggs, dyed yellow, green, and brown, were turning up in the Bulawayo chalet. When Mullin asked Lendrum what he'd been up to, Lendrum replied that he had been driving into Matobo and snatching live raptor eggs for clients whom he wouldn't identify. He then filled the nests he robbed with hard-boiled replacements in the hope that the birds would reject the eggs as rotten and lay another clutch.

Lendrum loosened up and confided to Mullin that he also had more ambitious plans: he wanted to steal the eggs of exotic birds of prey from around the world and deliver them to wealthy falconers in the Middle East. Several months later, Lendrum left the handicraft business in Mullin's hands and traveled to northern Canada on what he called a "proof of concept" mission. His aim was to study the feasibility of bringing back the eggs of Arab falconers' favorite raptor, the gyrfalcon.

Financing the operation by himself, Lendrum flew for several days over cliffs and uninhabited tundra with a pilot in a chartered helicopter. "It's the most beautiful place in the world," he told Mullin when he got back. "In a week it changed from a place where you could land your helicopter on the frozen lakes to greenness and bears and all the rest of it. If you had come with me, you would have had such good fun." But, he reported with chagrin, he'd managed to spot just a single gyrfalcon and only one aerie. The guidebook that Lendrum had consulted claimed that gyrfalcons build south-facing nests; in fact, as he learned only toward the end of the trip, the aeries always face north, to avoid the prolonged exposure to sunlight that would melt the snow on cliff ledges and cause the eggs to rot from the moisture. He vowed to try again.

Lendrum talked of traveling to South America to raid the nest of a harpy eagle, named by the eighteenth-century naturalist Carl Linnaeus after the mythical harpy beast, the half-human, half-avian personification of storm-force winds in Greek mythology. The largest, strongest raptor in the rain forest and one of the world's most threatened birds, the harpy has slate-black upper feathers, a white breast, and a pale gray, double-crested head, and can grow to three feet tall and weigh as much as twenty-five pounds. Also high on his wish list were the eggs of the Eurasian eagle owl, a fast and powerful raptor with pumpkin-orange eyes and feathery ear tufts, which nests in rock crevices throughout much of Europe, Asia, and North Africa. But this was all just talk.

Then, one morning in early 2001, following another handicrafts-buying trip to Victoria Falls, Lendrum disappeared for several hours from the chalet at the Southern Comfort Lodge. When he returned he reached inside his backpack and set down three baby birds on his bed. The chicks had mottled black-and-white feathers, hooked beaks, and large yellow legs and black talons. They appeared to be one or two days old, and they were chirping and screeching at ear-piercing volume. They were lanner falcons, Lendrum told Mullin over the racket, a migratory raptor that is slightly smaller than the peregrine, with a propensity for hunting game by pursuing it horizontally, a technique known as the "chase and grab."

He told Mullin he planned to smuggle the babies to Dubai.

"What the fuck are you talking about?" Mullin asked.

"Don't worry," Lendrum assured him. He had a client—and a plan.

The next morning at dawn, Lendrum fashioned a nest made of towels and placed it at the bottom of his rucksack, then laid the three chicks inside. He placed the rucksack on the floor behind the driver's seat of his pickup truck, where it was cool and dark. The two men set forth on the thirteen-hour drive from Bulawayo to Johannesburg. Mullin wanted to see for himself if Lendrum could pull off the stunt and had invited himself along as far as London. On the road trip south Lendrum fed the birds every two hours with a blend of minced calf liver and raw egg yolk, placing the food into their beaks with a pair of tweezers. At the airport, Lendrum removed the birds from the rucksack to avoid the baggage scan machine, where their bones would be visible. Instead he put them carefully in the pockets of his fleece, and walked them through the metal detector. Lendrum fed them again in the shower room of the Virgin Atlantic business-class lounge, transferred them back to the rucksack, and, with Mullin, boarded a Virgin Atlantic flight to the UK. He stored the birds in the overhead compartment, and Lendrum and Mullin settled back in their business-class seats.

Then, in the middle of the night, Mullin awoke to a piercing noise emanating from directly above him.

Cheeep cheeep cheep. Cheeep cheeep cheeeep.

"Jeff," he said, shaking Lendrum awake. "I can hear the children crying."

Lendrum listened. Then he burst out laughing.

"Go feed the fuckers," Mullin said.

Lendrum brought down the rucksack and a small plastic container filled with the yolk-and-liver mix, and carried all into the toilet. When he returned, the chicks had gone back to sleep. Soon Mullin fell asleep, too.

Then, two hours later, Mullin was jolted awake again:

Cheeeep. Cheeep. Cheeeep.

Lendrum again scooped up the birds and the mix and retreated to the lavatory.

The chicks woke up four more times in the course of the flight to London, but the white noise of the jet engine masked their hunger-driven screeches from the other passengers and crew, and Lendrum and his live contraband made it safely off the plane.

The two parted ways at Heathrow. "Make sure you look after the children," Mullin called, as Lendrum rushed to catch his flight to Dubai. Mullin soon heard from Lendrum that he had safely delivered all the chicks to his mystery client. (Years later, Lendrum would insist that Mullin's story was "a complete flight of fiction. Have you heard how noisy those birds are?" Mullin would stand by what he said.)

This sort of escapade, Mullin would come to realize, was Lendrum's oxygen. He wasn't doing it for the money—Mullin saw no evidence that Lendrum was cashing in, at least not yet. "He lived a very basic lifestyle," Mullin would remember, two decades later. "If he was making sixty thousand dollars out of each egg that hatched and became an adult, where was the big house, the big car? He did buy himself a new Toyota double-cab four-by-four, but he didn't make a lot." Perhaps, Mullin speculated, Lendrum was content to work for a relative pittance in return for the promise of adventure. He needed challenges, loved living on the edge—whether playing with deadly snakes, scaling the tallest cliffs and trees, or stealing the world's most endangered species. "It's always been about the thrill for Jeff," his boyhood friend Howard Waller would say. "He likes to beat the system. That's been his thing since he was a kid."

Now Lendrum's appetite for risk and his willingness to skirt the rules had pulled him into a global enterprise.

TEN

DUBAI

Centuries before Jeffrey Lendrum began raiding nests for wealthy Arab clients, trappers were shinnying up trees and scaling cliffs in avid pursuit of falcons. In 1247, Frederick II of Hohenstaufen, the Holy Roman Emperor, offered instructions to falconers on how to obtain chicks from the wild. "If the nest is in a tree, a man can climb up and, having put the young ones in a basket, carry them home," he advised in *On the Art of Hunting with Birds*, his classic work on falconry. If the aerie was built into the fissure of a high rock face, however, "a man is secured to the end of a rope and descends or is lowered from the rim of the mountain or cliff to the level of the hollow, and, entering, lifts the bird from the nest."

Adelard of Bath, a twelfth-century English natural philosopher, recommended capturing chicks "seven days after hatching" in the morning when their stomachs were empty and it was cool. Frederick II thought it better to leave the chicks in the nest as long as possible, "because the longer they are fed by their parents the better and stronger will be their limbs and pinions," he wrote, "and they are less likely to become screechers or gapers."

While Europeans raided nests, Arabs of the era (and for centuries afterward) trapped "passage" falcons: young birds that had left the nest for good. During the September-to-November migration of millions of birds from Eastern Europe and Central Asia to Africa, the trappers waited for the falcons (mostly peregrines, but also some sakers) in the Syrian Desert, the Tigris and Euphrates Valleys, and farther down the Arabian Peninsula. They would strap a pigeon to a *shabichet hehmama*, a lightweight wooden frame covered with a dozen nooses made from woven strands of camel hair, and then, as the falcon passed overhead, send the bird aloft. The raptor would zero in for the kill, ensnare a toe or two in a noose, and flutter down to earth.

Other trappers employed a lugger falcon, a sluggish raptor known as a *bizzuar* in Arabic. Partially blinded from a thread passed through each eyelid, the bird would be sent into the air clutching a decoy bundle of feathers called a *nigil*. The passage bird would attack the bundle, intent on wresting it from the weaker falcon, and, its foot caught in a hidden noose, fall to the ground.

The passage falcons, eighteen months old or younger, were ideal birds for falconry, wrote diplomat and Arabist Mark Allen in *Falconry in Arabia*, being far superior to both chicks snatched from their nests and mature raptors that had been trapped after their first migration. The juvenile passage falcon, with fully developed musculature and feathers and an ability to hunt inculcated by its parents, combines, Allen declared, "the [malleability] of youth with its capacity for adventure and carelessness of danger."

—

By the 1970s the trapping of wild falcons was dying out in much of the world. In 1973 the United States, which had lost about 90 percent of its peregrine population to DDT and other pesticides, passed the Endangered Species Act, making it illegal to acquire, deliver, hold, sell, or market falcons except for scientific purposes. That same year, eighty countries ratified the Convention on International Trade in Endangered Species of Wild Flora and Fauna (CITES). The treaty, which was eventually signed by 183 nations, designated twelve hundred species, including many birds of prey, as Appendix I—"threatened with extinction"—and prohibited trade of wild raptors except with hard-to-obtain licenses for research. In the decades since, the United Kingdom, Canada, Germany, Russia, Pakistan, the United Arab Emirates, and other countries in Europe, Asia, and South America have made illegal the trapping of almost all birds of prey.

The new restrictions forced falconers to seek alternatives to taking birds from the wilderness. There had already been experiments with captive breeding, or mating falcons in a controlled environment. Renz Waller, a German falconer and artist best known for his portrait of a white gyrfalcon owned by General Field Marshall Hermann Göring, Hitler's supreme commander of the Luftwaffe, had tried repeatedly, although with very limited success, to induce peregrines to breed in an aviary in the Nazis' falcon center in Riddagshausen in north-central Germany. Nazi leaders admired falconry in part because of its ties to medieval Teutonic knights, and Hermann Göring and SS chief Heinrich Himmler, both avid falconers, supported an expansive program of training raptors and teaching Nazis to hunt with the birds.

Waller's experiment ended abruptly in 1944 when an Allied bombardment burned his facility to the ground. Three decades later, the Midwest-based Raptor Research Foundation, the Canadian Fish and Wildlife Service, and Cornell University's Peregrine Fund relied on

Waller's notes in their attempts to breed peregrines in captivity for the purpose of repopulating the wild.

problems w/ eggs in captivity

As Renz Waller had discovered, captive breeding turned out to be anything but easy. Raptors proved far more temperamental and sensitive to being cooped up than domestic fowl. Deprived of the acrobatic courtship flights, marked by loops, tight turns, and swooping dives, that served as an essential mating ritual in the wild, the birds usually refused to copulate. If they did, females would not sit on their fertilized eggs. Hatching falcon eggs in incubators was problematic, too. They often overheated, or weren't rotated at the proper intervals, preventing the embryo-nourishing albumen, or egg white, from spreading inside the shell. Moving an early embryo risked breaking the chalaza, the cord that anchors the yolk to the albumen, killing the chick-to-be; even tilting the egg at an incorrect angle could twist the cord and kill the embryo. Misjudging the humidity in the incubator could also prove fatal. High humidity would cause the egg to lose too much water between laying and hatching, leaving the chick too small and weak because of dehydration to break through the shell. Low humidity would result in a chick too large to maneuver inside the shell, and so it would be unable to peck its way out of its tiny enclosure.

Ornithological researcher Heinz K. Meng at the State University of New York at New Paltz succeeded in breeding the first pair of peregrines in North American captivity in 1971. He lent the birds to Tom Cade, the founder of the Peregrine Fund, who helped the couple—and two other pairs—produce twenty falcon chicks in 1973. Across the world, breeders were learning how to select compatible pairs, construct congenial nests, induce the birds to mate, perfect artificial incubation, get parents or surrogates to rear the incubator-hatched chicks, and encourage birds to lay a second clutch of eggs to increase the number of young. As the handful of breeding programs became more successful, "the whole thing snowballed," says Jemima Parry-Jones, who'd started breeding birds of prey in the early 1970s at her raptor center in rural Gloucestershire. Arab devotees of falconry, flush with oil wealth and prohibited by international law from obtaining wild birds, began buying captive-bred birds in the United States and Europe, creating a commercial market. By the early 1980s breeding programs had produced thousands of raptors of a dozen species, including two thousand peregrine falcons.

=

In 1968, Great Britain, after 150 years of controlling the armies and foreign policy of seven coastal sheikhdoms at the southeast end of the Arabian Peninsula, announced that it was granting them complete independence. Weeks later, at a desert oasis, Sheikh Zayed bin Sultan Al Nahyan, the ruler of Abu Dhabi, met with the leader of Dubai, Sheikh Rashid bin Mohammed Al Maktoum, and agreed to try to unite the sheikhdoms into a new federation. On December 2, 1971, Abu Dhabi and Dubai joined Sharjah, Ajman, Umm Al Quwain, and Fujairah in creating the United Arab Emirates. (The seventh sheikhdom, Ras Al Khaimah, joined a year later.) The UAE would be a constitutional monarchy, with laws enacted by a Federal Supreme Council made up of the seven dynastic rulers of the individual emirates. Whoever was the sheikh of Abu Dhabi would serve as president; the sheikh of Dubai would be prime minister.

Sheikh Zayed, a powerfully built figure with a lean and weatherbeaten face and a sternly charismatic presence, became the United Arab Emirates' first ruler. An ardent falconer, he considered the sport an essential part of the new nation's cultural identity, and set out to introduce captive breeding to the Arabian Peninsula by luring Western experts to run the programs. In the mid-1970s, Sheikh Zayed invited a prominent English falconer named Roger Upton to join him on a hunt in the Arabian Desert. The pair rode camels in a wilderness area about an hour from Abu Dhabi, then a small town on an island in the Persian Gulf; with half a dozen falcons, they brought down bustards throughout the day. Upton and Sheikh Zayed became close friends, and Upton stayed on to breed falcons for him.

Then, in the late 1980s, in a turn of events that would prove fateful for Jeffrey Lendrum, Howard Waller, Lendrum's boyhood companion (no relation to Renz Waller), who was then breeding falcons commercially in South Africa, heard through friends about potentially lucrative falcon-related opportunities in the United Arab Emirates. Waller had begun hunting with falcons and hawks as a boy in Bulawayo. "I remember being nine years old and walking down a dirt road when a sparrow hawk came up and caught a small bird right in front of me," Waller would recall. "I thought, 'Wow,' and that's where it started." (Falcons, belonging to the *falco* genus, are long-winged birds that hunt in open areas and kill their prey with their curved, notched beaks; hawks, which belong to the *accipiter* genus, have shorter, rounded wings and hunt in woodlands, seizing their quarry with their talons.) Lendrum would say years later that his initial encounters with Waller, who had been a part of the same adolescent gang of wildlife enthusiasts, had not been auspicious. "We actually hated each other at first," Lendrum would recall. "I thought he was a bit of a know-it-all, and I suppose I was a know-it-all, but eventually we became friends."

Around 1988, Waller was invited to visit a new breeding program that a Canadian former colleague had started in Dubai. When

Waller arrived, captive breeding programs were still trying to get off the ground, and wealthy Arabs remained dependent on wild falcons for hunting. Smugglers brought birds overland through Pakistan or Iran, and then ferried them across the Strait of Hormuz to the Arabian Peninsula. Waller ventured into the Arabian Desert during the annual bird migration, and encountered trappers hiding among the dunes. But bird populations in Europe had thinned over the past decades, largely because of rampant poaching in the Balkans and other countries directly on the southern migration route; fewer raptors were flying over the desert. And the Emirates had become a signatory to the Convention on International Trade in Endangered Species of Wild Flora and Fauna. The government announced its intention to crack down on wild taking, and many falconers agreed to play by the new rules.

In Dubai, Waller was later introduced to Sheikh Butti bin Juma Al Maktoum, an insurance and construction magnate then in his thirties, and a dedicated falconer and conservationist. An intense, energetic, and deeply knowledgeable figure with an aquiline nose, arched brows, and a trim mustache, Sheikh Butti was also the first cousin of Sheikh Mohammed bin Rashid Al Maktoum, Dubai's crown prince. Impressed by the Al Maktoum family's wealth, and by their devotion to falconry, Waller recognized a unique opportunity. "I said that I'd like to come out and start breeding for [Butti]," Waller says, "and he said yes."

Soon Waller, who was married, with two young children, opened falcon pens at Sheikh Butti's desert palace, on the edge of an eighty-seven-square mile camel farm that Butti's cousin, Sheikh Mohammed, would later purchase and turn into a wildlife refuge called the Dubai Desert Conservation Reserve. Waller was on his way to becoming one of the most successful breeders in the Emirates—and the world.

=

Waller's move to Dubai came at a time when falconry on the Arabian Peninsula was running up against the consequences of environmental recklessness. For centuries falconers had hunted, without limit, the Arabian Desert's population of houbara bustards (*Chlamydotis undulata*), ungainly turkey-sized birds known for flamboyantly flaring their white chest feathers, running around in circles at high speed, and emitting booming calls to impress a potential mate. When under attack, they vomit a slimy secretion that can paralyze a bird of prey. British travel writer Wilfred Thesiger had seen bustards everywhere during a hunting trip he took with Sheikh Zayed, already the ruler of Abu Dhabi, in the desert dunes of the Empty Quarter during the winter of 1949. In his book *Arabian Sands*, Thesiger captured the excitement of that hunt and of the battle to the death between pursuer and quarry that had transfixed Bedouin for millennia. "Suddenly an Arab on the left of the line signaled to us that he had found fresh tracks," he wrote:

> A falconer unhooded his bird and raised it in the air, then it was off flying a few feet above the ground; the bustard was climbing now but the peregrine was fast overhauling it . . . then someone shouted, "it's down!" and we were racing across the sands . . . We came upon the peregrine in a hollow, plucking at the lifeless bustard—Zayid pointed to some oily splashes on the ground and said, "Do you see that muck? The hubara squirts it at its attacker. If it gets into the *shahin*'s eyes it blinds it temporarily. Anyway if it

gets on to its feathers it makes a filthy mess of them, and you cannot use the bird again that day."

A decade or so later, Sheikh Butti, his father, and other members of the royal family of Dubai would take four-wheel-drive vehicles down sand tracks in the Arabian Desert and use falcons and salukis (hunting dogs also known as African greyhounds) to hunt for hares, bustards, kairowans (mid-sized birds), wolves, and rheem gazelles (miniature antelopes that stand only two and a half feet tall). "What I remember most is the fact that other than our vehicles there were no other car tracks in the desert. It was pristine," Sheikh Butti said in a 2011 interview with *Wildlife Middle East.* In this world of harsh sunlight and heavy silences, he recalled collecting truffles in the desert in February following drenching autumnal rains, and getting lost at night "and being navigated by an old Bedouin who took us safely out using only his knowledge of the vegetation and the wind direction pattern of the dunes."

But the landscape of Dubai was already changing. Sheikh Butti's uncle, Sheikh Rashid bin Mohammed Al Maktoum, a semiliterate visionary who spoke only Arabic and displayed the ascetic habits of his Bedouin ancestors, ordered Dubai's creek dredged in 1961, making the city the most accessible port in the Middle East. He brought electricity, running water, and telephones, built the first luxury hotels and dry docks, and turned Dubai into an international shipping center. The Al Maktoum family continued to build over the next four decades, expanding the airport and transforming Dubai into a giant shopping arcade and tourist magnet. They financed ambitious construction projects such as Dubai Internet City, a sleek campus of low-slung glass-and-concrete buildings and palm-fringed lawns with 1.5 million square feet of commercial office space designated for high-tech companies such as Microsoft and Oracle, and the Burj Al Arab, a 590-foot-high, sail-shaped hotel on an artificial island in the Persian Gulf. The building boom ripped up the desert and depleted the bustards' habitat. Thousands of workers "would go out onto the huge gravel plains, collect rocks, clean them, and load them onto trucks," remembered Howard Waller, who had watched the desert be torn up to supply building materials for the expanding municipality. "Amongst the rocks were the beetles, lizards, and other prey which the bustards had fed on." Four-wheel-drive vehicles had already replaced camels, allowing hunters to travel longer distances, and now the Arabs used shotguns as well as falcons to hunt down bustards in their increasingly constricted territory. Before long, hunters would wipe out the bustard on the Arabian Peninsula.

The billionaire sheikhs of the Emirates, Qatar, and other Arab countries, faced with the disappearance of their favorite prey, began to look for hunting opportunities overseas. The Al Nahyans, the Al Maktoums, and other wealthy Arabs leased vast tracts of desert in Uzbekistan, Kazakhstan, Afghanistan, Pakistan, Algeria, Morocco, Iraq, and other countries that still had healthy houbara bustard populations. Every fall they packed hundreds of falcons onto private jets and then spent a week or more hunting from mobile tent camps in the bush, preparing feasts each night with the prey that their falcons had killed. These lavish seven- or even ten-day expeditions, usually involving a caravan of four-by-fours and dozens of falconers, veterinarians, drivers, cooks, and other support staff, fueled a sense of competition as well as camaraderie among the sheikhs. It helped feed the demand for ever bigger, faster, and more powerful falcons.

By the new millennium, these trips would become shadowed by

legitimate concerns from conservation groups that argued they were
threatening the houbara bustard with global extinction. One Saudi
prince's party reportedly killed twelve hundred bustards during a
weeklong falcon hunt in Pakistan—where the birds migrate during
the late fall and winter breeding season—despite having a permit
to kill just one hundred. (In 2015, Pakistan's Supreme Court would
rule that no further hunting licenses for bustards could be issued.)
For the most part, however, "They don't care in these places," I was
told by one trainer who hunts in Uzbekistan every October and in
Algeria in November with Dubai's crown prince, Hamdan bin Mohammed bin Rashid Al Maktoum, and his father, Sheikh Mohammed, who became Dubai's ruler in 2006. The hunts also channel
millions of dollars into unstable areas, something that would have
calamitous consequences in November 2015, when a heavily armed,
Iran-backed Shia militia would seize twenty-six members of a Qa-
tari royal hunting party in Iraq's southern desert. Only after sixteen
months of negotiations and a ransom payment of $1 billion were the
royals released.

The increasing sensitivity to environmental protection, along
with fears of a scenario like the Iraq kidnapping, were among the
reasons that Crown Prince Hamdan would introduce falcon racing
to the Emirates.

=

In the early 1980s, in his search for bigger, more powerful, and more
beautiful birds, Sheikh Butti became one of the first Arabs to import a
gyrfalcon to the Middle East. The world's largest species of falcon—
and "a killing machine without equal," as the British falconer Emma
Ford wrote in a 1999 book on the birds—gyrfalcons almost exclu-

sively inhabit zones of ice floes and frozen tundra, stretching from Alaska and northern Canada through Greenland, Norway, and Lapland, to Siberia. Viking settlers in northern Scotland called them "geirfugel," from the epithet *geir*, meaning "spear." The scientific name is *Falco rusticolus*, or "country dweller." Roosting in rock crevices sheltered from blizzards and gale-force winds, they can survive for weeks on icebergs in the open ocean and circle the skies for hours in search of prey—including lemmings, voles, seabirds, and ptarmigans (game birds of the grouse family). Powerful musculature and circulatory and respiratory systems as hyperefficient as those of the peregrine falcon allow the raptors to outlast their quarry in exhausting horizontal pursuits or dive-bomb them like a missile. T. Edward Nickens described the gyrfalcon in *Audubon* magazine as "a predatorial mash-up of Muhammad Ali and Floyd Mayweather, speedy and large enough to kill a fleeing Pin-tailed Duck in midair but agile enough to snatch a Lapland Longspur off a tundra tussock."

Beginning in the medieval era, trappers embarked on expeditions to the Arctic to bring back gyrfalcons for European and Mongolian monarchs. These journeys, writes Ford, "required such courage and single-mindedness that they beggar belief." Many trappers froze to death, while others disappeared forever into glacial crevasses or tumbled fatally off cliffs. For the nobility, gyrfalcons—and white gyrfalcons in particular—became unsurpassed symbols of wealth and prestige. In 1396, Turkish soldiers captured Jean de Nevers, the future Duke of Burgundy, during the Battle of Nicopolis in Greece; the Ottoman Sultan refused increasing offers of ransom, setting de Nevers free only after he agreed to hand over the ultimate prize: twelve white gyrs. Ivan the Terrible, the Russian czar, dispatched his first envoy to England in 1550 with "a large and faire white Jewrfawcan" as a gift to Henry VIII's daughter, the future Elizabeth I. And in the mid–nineteenth century, Husan-Dawlah Mirza, a claimant to the Persian throne, wrote about a white gyrfalcon that had been brought from Russia and presented to his father, the Shah. Kept on a damp bed of pebbles and sand near Tehran, "she feels the heat greatly," Mirza observed, "so that she has to be well supplied with ice and snow." He watched with awe each time the gyrfalcon was sent out to hunt and dived headlong to earth in pursuit of her prey. "All I know," he declared, "is that neither I, nor has the oldest falconer of Persia, ever seen a falcon like it."

Butti's pure white gyrfalcon dazzled everyone in the sheikh's circle. But almost all feared that the bird—which he had obtained from a breeder in Germany—would drop dead of exhaustion in the desert heat, or succumb to local pathogens. Not to mention that no one had the skills to train it. But under Sheikh Butti's intuitive and attentive care, the gyrfalcon, named Hasheem ("Generosity"), became a skilled hunter—its talents easily visible during the sheikh's early-morning training sessions in the desert and on his annual fall hunts overseas. Emma Ford's *Gyrfalcon*, the classic text about the raptor, contains a photo of Sheikh Butti proudly holding a huge gyr on his *manqalah*, a muff-like cylinder of canvas or carpet, worn on the falconer's wrist instead of a glove. Members of Sheikh Butti's circle, as well as other enthusiasts on the Arabian Peninsula, began to import gyrfalcons, too.

=

Howard Waller's setup in Dubai exceeded anything he could have imagined back in South Africa. He established his base on the palace's expansive grounds, a serene retreat one hour east of central Dubai that offered views of the urban skyline on clear mornings. He'd venture into the desert before dawn to observe the training of the birds, sharing observations with Sheikh Butti about falcon lineages, injuries, past performances, and horizontal and vertical speeds. His employer would become a confidant and a soul mate. "Almost like a long-married couple, they eagerly anticipate each other's answers and communicate using a shorthand inscrutable to nearly everyone else," wrote Peter Gwin in an October 2018 profile of the two falconers in *National Geographic*: "'The gray whose father was the one we hunted with two years ago. . . . The gyr with the broken tail feather that we fixed.'" Waller could often be found on the palace grounds alone or with the sheikh, inspecting the aviaries that were home to several hundred falcons or visiting the kitchens where butchers prepared hundreds of quail and pigeons for daily feedings.

Encouraged by the sheikh, Waller introduced gyrfalcons to his breeding pens—purchased, he says, legally in the United States. From them he bred both pure gyrs and hybrids that, it was hoped, would combine the strongest qualities of different species. He crossed gyrfalcons with saker falcons (*Falco cherrug*), hardy flyers that are born and fledge in the arid zones of Mongolia and Central Asia, to create "turbo sakers"—big, fast-diving birds that thrive in a desert climate and are more aggressive than pure sakers. He also crossbred gyrfalcons and peregrines, which proved equally popular with Arab hunters. Over time Waller and Sheikh Butti would put together what the *National Geographic* described as "arguably . . . one of the most exquisite collections of falcons ever assembled."

To get their birds to build up wing strength, Waller and Sheikh Butti introduced "hack pens" to Dubai—enormous indoor bird gymnasiums—and equipped them with multimillion-dollar air-conditioning systems so that the birds wouldn't be exposed to the 130-degree summer heat. To keep his gyrfalcons healthy during the molting season that typically lasts from March until the end of September, when the Arctic birds shed their forty-four wing and twelve tail feathers and grow new ones, and are especially sensitive to desert temperatures, Waller introduced air-conditioned "moulting chambers," which led to higher survival rates and became a standard for raising gyrs in the Middle East.

When the birds got sick, they were taken to a falcon hospital in Dubai built by one of Sheikh Butti's uncles. The facility had dozens of air-conditioned rooms, an intensive care unit and an opthalmology department, the latest model X-ray machines, heart monitors and endoscopy instruments, a full range of antibiotics and other drugs, and a team of international veterinarians who treated everything from aspergillosis (a lung infection caused by a fungus) to bumblefoot (a bacterial disease causing lesions of the spurs of the feet) to damaged feathers.

Back in Sheikh Butti's desert palace, Waller was also conducting research into artifical insemination. From the time the chicks were just a few days old, he spent hours each day with his baby males in their breeding pens, talking to them, singing to them, playing with them, and eventually inducing them to regard him as a sexual partner. (Birds don't instinctively identify with their own species upon hatching, and can be taught to bond sexually with a human—a process known as "imprinting"—rather than another bird.) Waller would wear a tight-fitting hat resembling a honeycomb that the copulating male—known as a "hat bird"—would leap on top of, ejaculating into a hole. Waller would then collect the semen in a capillary tube and drop the liquid into a female.

During the breeding season that runs from March to May, when lengthening days and warmer temperatures trigger the hormonal changes that initiate the reproductive cycle, egg cells grow, and pass down to the mouth of the female's oviduct, awaiting fertilization. "I put my hands on her back, she lifts her back up, I bend her tail to the side, and I slip the semen into her cloaca," the bird's reproductive orifice, Waller explained to me. Waller and I were speaking in Inverness, Scotland, where Sheikh Butti had moved the bulk of his breeding operations in 2013; raptors breed more easily in a cold and windy climate. Waller now spends most of the year on the windswept, rocky moor with his second wife and their two children. "If the female is sucking [the semen] in well, chances are very good that it will fertilize the egg." The egg then condenses into a protective but permeable layer of calcium surrounding a yolk, which will develop into a chick in about a month. Most breeders have one or two reliable semen producers; Waller always had more than a dozen—and dozens of breeding females.

As Waller had discovered, artificial insemination was the only way to create hybrids because, as with almost all birds, interspecies mating among peregrines, sakers, and gyrfalcons is extremely rare in the wild. (One 1963 study estimated that only one in fifty thousand wild birds is a hybrid.) Insemination was also the only effective method to bring together the sperm and ova of desirable birds of the same species that didn't get along. "You can't just put a male and female together and say they're going to breed," Waller explained. "Falcons are like humans, they fall in love." Incubating the eggs proved to be another challenge. Natural hatching is impossible for falcons in the desert, because the females refuse to sit on their eggs in an inhospitable and unfamiliar environment. But incubating artificially requires constant monitoring: tracking weight reduction due to water loss, maintaining the exact ambient temperature to keep the developing embryo warm . . . Waller estimated his hatch rate from incubators in the early days was far below 50 percent, although that improved over the years.

Waller and Sheikh Butti boasted that their prolific production of captive-bred falcons was benefiting global conservation by eliminating the need for wild taking. "I am a falconer, but my desire is to protect the wild populations of falcons," Butti declared in a 2011 interview. He gave away falcons to family members and close friends, and maintained a loyal clientele of affluent Emirati enthusiasts. "The local falconers are very happy with the hunting quality of the birds I produce," he said.

Sheikh Butti's reputation as a wildlife conservationist preceded him. In the 1990s he'd opened the Sheikh Butti bin Juma Al Maktoum Wildlife Centre, a thirty-seven-acre walled zoo in the center of Dubai where he bred endangered animals. The project was the consummation of a fascination with animal husbandry that had begun when he was five years old and his father brought home baby hares, hedgehogs, and gazelles to live in the family compound in Jumeirah, a wealthy seaside neighborhood in Dubai. "There was one mountain gazelle I remember in particular that had been hand-reared and would follow us around the garden," Butti recalled.

In his zoo, he resuscitated species that had nearly vanished from the Arabian Peninsula—the Arabian oryx, the sand gazelle, the Rüppell's fox—as well as threatened African species, such as the black hippotragus, Cape giraffe, gerenuk (a long-necked antelope found in Somalia and other arid zones of the Horn of Africa), Speke's gazelle, bontebok (a medium-sized, brown antelope indigenous to Southern Africa), and Grant's gazelle. Butti's desert palace had a large aviary with doves, Somali guinea fowl, gray-crowned cranes, 250 flamingos, and (Butti's special pride) northern bald ibises—magnificently ungainly specimens listed by conservation groups as "critically endangered," with ruffled black feathers, a bare red face, and a long, curved red bill. Sheikh Butti even reared a female cheetah that he mated with a male from a wildlife center in the Emirate of Sharjah. The pair produced six cubs, the first cheetahs born in the Arabian Peninsula in decades.

But his main passion was falcons.

=

In the late 1990s, just as AfricaXtreme was getting off the ground, Waller invited Jeffrey Lendrum to come visit him at Sheikh Butti's desert palace. The friends had remained close in Lendrum's early years in South Africa, but had fallen out of touch during the mid-1990s. Lendrum was busy with his spare-parts trafficking schemes and Waller was dealing with some personal trouble. "Howard and his wife were going through a divorce, and I had kept out of the way," Lendrum would say. Now Waller missed his old *shamwari*.

Lendrum was impressed by the opulence of the palace, the attention lavished on the falcons, and his friend's success. Waller introduced Lendrum to Sheikh Butti—whom Lendrum would describe blandly as "a very nice guy"—and took him to see the Al Maktoums' veterinary hospital. But he laid down one strict rule: Lendrum could not accompany him as he collected semen in the breeding pens. "The birds would get stressed if they saw a stranger," Lendrum would recall. "Howard was the only one allowed in." When Lendrum returned to South Africa, he gushed to Mullin that "you wouldn't believe the job that Howard has." The medical care for falcons in Dubai was better than that available to humans, he said, and the hack pens on Sheikh Butti's property were "the size of three football fields."

One day, Lendrum alleges, Waller took him aside and made a stunning proposal: he asked Lendrum to work for him as a trapper in the wilderness. With his skill as a climber and his experience moving goods across borders, Lendrum would be the ideal partner in a covert plan to strengthen his stable with feral birds. Waller wanted Lendrum to provide wild falcon eggs, rather than live birds, Lendrum says, because they could be carried across borders undetected.

Lendrum claims he told Waller that it wasn't a promising idea. "It's ninety-nine percent unlikely that it would work," is the way that Lendrum says he put it. The length of time the eggs would be out of the nest—dozens of hours from door to door—"was just too long." He would have to keep the eggs warm, probably by wearing them strapped to his body, which just wasn't practical. And he questioned why Waller would need wild raptor eggs anyway, given the number of captive-bred chicks he was producing each season. "The time I went there, there were about one hundred babies," he would say. "What the hell was he going to do with one hundred babies?" After this discussion, Lendrum says Waller dropped the subject.

Years later Waller would not deny that such a conversation took place, but he described it as idle chatter. "Lendrum and I may have discussed the idea, or Lendrum may have come to me with it, but nothing ever happened," Waller would insist. Lendrum returned to South Africa, and they remained in periodic touch.

=

Lendrum and Waller would hardly have been the first Western birders to contemplate conducting sketchy business in the Middle East. In 1981, a few years after new regulations in the United States and Canada banned trapping and trading birds of prey, the US Fish and Wildlife Service recruited John Jeffrey McPartlin, a hunter, falconer, and convicted wild bird dealer from Great Falls, Montana, to assist them in a sting called Operation Falcon. It was the first attempt by law enforcement authorities to prove that a raptor underground linked Western smugglers with wealthy clients in the Middle East. After a three-year investigation, three hundred federal, state, and provincial agents swooped down on falconers and breeders in fourteen states and four Canadian provinces who had purchased wild gyrfalcons from McPartlin. Thirty people were arrested, dozens more interrogated, and one hundred birds seized. Fish and Wildlife Service agents claimed that the royal family of Saudi Arabia had acquired wild birds of prey illegally from some of these individuals, and might have used diplomatic privileges to sneak the birds past customs.

But although Operation Falcon officers described a "worldwide, multi-million dollar illegal black market in birds of prey," the sting failed to pin down anything concrete. (The only organization conclusively determined to have been involved in the trapping and selling of wild falcons was the Fish and Wildlife Service, which had permitted the seizure of fifty gyrfalcons from the wild to use in the sting operation.) The Saudi Arabian suspects hired a Washington, DC, lawyer who vigorously denied all the allegations. In the end, no Saudis were convicted of crimes, most buyers pleaded guilty only to misdemeanors, and Operation Falcon was widely attacked as a waste of government resources. One defense attorney claimed that McPartlin's sting was a classic case of entrapment. Offering to sell breeders pure white gyrfalcons was "like having someone bring Marilyn Monroe by and asking if she can spend the night," he said.

Nearly a decade after Operation Falcon, an investigative series on the British ITV nework aired "The Bird Bandits," a half-hour exposé of the Arab connection. The host, Roger Cook, promised to provide "evidence of an organized and vastly profitable trade in endangered birds of prey." Guided by an investigator from the Royal Society for the Protection of Birds, Cook's producer staked out a peregrine nest in northern Scotland, and caught on camera an egg thief, Steven McDonald, rappelling down a rock face and making off with a clutch. Cook dressed up as an Arab sheikh, with fake beard and mustache, keffiyeh, and robes, and—using a hidden camera—filmed himself meeting with a European smuggler who promised to deliver to him peregrines stolen from Scottish nests. "Many Arabs still believe that wild birds have superior speed and killing power, and Scotland . . . is the source of the most highly prized," Cook claimed in his narration. "The young birds are then passed into the system, and a variety of middlemen, in [Great Britain], France, Belgium, and Germany," arrange for their passage to the Middle East. The average price paid by Arabs for a wild peregrine, Cook claimed, was £15,000, then equal to about $25,000.

The falconry community vehemently disputed the program's contentions. The Hawk Board, an association of British falconers, charged that the producers had spent weeks in the Gulf "trying desperately" to locate a sheikh interested in buying a Scottish peregrine—and failed. The board insisted that the prices presented in the show were wildly exaggerated, that no market existed in the Middle East for British peregrines, either wild or captive-bred, and that eggs, chicks, and nestlings that had not yet developed into mature flyers had no value to the Arab falconer.

Perhaps it was true that sheikhs weren't purchasing many falcons stolen from Scotland, but, following the collapse of the Soviet Union, a huge black market trade sprang up in sakers and peregrines from the Kamchatka Peninsula and the Altai Mountains. In 2006, the World Wildlife Fund office in Vladivostok reported a "catastrophic drop" in the number of saker falcons in Russia, from sixty thousand to two thousand pairs in twenty years. The Middle East Falcon Research Group, an Abu Dhabi–based veterinary and ornithological institute, identified the perpetrators as Syrian and Lebanese students studying at Russian universities, including one Syrian gang that had captured fifty sakers before its leader was arrested, convicted, and sentenced to three and a half years in prison. A network of Russian coconspirators, from railway personnel to airline baggage handlers, moved the birds through the Russian interior, placing them on flights to Moscow, Novosibirsk, Yekaterinburg, and Irkutsk, before transferring them to Azerbaijan, Armenia, and other neighboring countries. From there, according to an article in the journal *Contemporary Justice Review*, they were smuggled into the Middle East. Traffickers wrapped the falcons in cloth and squeezed them into tubes, hiding them in sports bags, under fruit, and in diplomatic packages. "Eyes can be sewn shut, supposedly to reduce nervousness, and once swaddled they can be packed into rigid suitcases with holes drilled in them," the article reported. Many of the birds suffocated en route. Others died from high temperatures, stress, and lack of food and water.

Other investigations seconded that captured falcons were headed to the Middle East. The British newspaper the *Telegraph* reported that in October 2004, police had intercepted a commercial aircraft carrying 127 sakers shortly before it left a military air base in Kyrgyzstan. The falcons, estimated to have a black market value of £2.6 million,

DUBAI

then worth approximately $4.7 million, were heading for Syria. In
the same *Telegraph* article, a zoologist in the Mongolian capital Ulan
Bator described how falcons were trapped using pigeons fitted with
plastic noose traps as bait. "There were several Arabs and their Mongolian trappers careering all over the steppe in a Land Cruiser," the
zoologist said. "Every time they spotted a falcon, they leapt out and
released about twenty pigeons in different directions. It was crazy." In
October 2013, the *Express Tribune*, a Pakistani newspaper, reported
that the wildlife authorities had raided a falcon-hunting camp near
the Khyber Pass and confiscated pigeons intended as bait to catch
sakers and peregrines. A forest officer told the newspaper that most
of the sakers "are netted in Afghanistan, China and Russia," and then
transported to Peshawar for sale to visiting Arab sheikhs.

One licensed breeder in Europe who does frequent business with
royal families in the Middle East confirmed to me that the trade is
flourishing, although talking about it is taboo. "There's huge, huge
money in wild falcons," the breeder told me, with the most sought-
after bird, the "ultra-white" gyrfalcon, fetching $270,000 to $400,000
in the Arab world. During a recent trip to a sheikh's palace, his meeting was interrupted by the arrival of trapper-smugglers carrying gyrfalcons from eastern Russia. "They'd been hooded, and they were
in a horrible state. [The smugglers] had driven them three thousand
miles," he said. The breeder confirmed that the underground involves royals in such falconry-obsessed countries as the United Arab
Emirates, Bahrain, Qatar, Kuwait, and, increasingly, Saudi Arabia,
which remains one of the last countries in the region to permit wild
falcon trapping within its borders.

In 2012, after years of illegal smuggling of saker falcons from
Central Asia, the bird was declared "globally endangered" by the

Switzerland-based International Union for Conservation of Nature. Six years later the Convention on Migratory Species established a Saker Falcon Task Force, comprising forty specialists from twenty countries, to monitor the raptor and save it from extinction. By many accounts, the Emirates has successfully cracked down on bird smuggling. According to a 2017 report by the nonprofit Center for Advanced Defense Studies, the country had the highest number of bird-trafficking seizures in the world between 2009 and 2016. (The majority of the raptors were heading for Dubai.) But it is vastly more difficult to stop a skilled smuggler from sneaking eggs across a border than to prevent the smuggling of chicks or adolescent birds—and, once wild falcons or eggs have entered the Emirates, Convention on Endangered Species rules are still so loosely enforced that, as the European breeder put it, "laundering illegal birds into the system is easy."

=

The genetic superiority of falcons procured from the wild has been an article of faith among many Arab hunters since captive-breeding programs took hold decades ago. Only the toughest, strongest, and fastest birds survive in nature, the argument goes, and these genes are passed down through the generations. Yet Jemima Parry-Jones, who breeds raptors in Gloucestershire, insists that "anyone who believes that a peregrine egg from a wild nest is more viable, stronger, and healthier than a good bird bred in a captive situation is mistaken. You might as well say, 'Wild horses are better than specially bred race horses,' which is rubbish."

Nick Fox, the longtime breeder of falcons for the ruler of Dubai, says that Arab falconers want wild eggs primarily for a different reason: because they introduce new bloodlines into captive breeding programs. It is a widely held assumption that small populations of captive raptor species become vulnerable to "genetic decay" and need periodic reinvigoration from the wild. "Inbreeding has reduced survivability," says Fox, who started a breeding program thirty-five years ago with six New Zealand falcons and, unable to import more due to trade restrictions, watched the quality of the descendants gradually deteriorate over the decades. Toby Bradshaw, the chairman of the biology department at the University of Washington in Seattle, and an avid falconer, argued in a 2009 academic paper published on his departmental website that the "regular infusion of genes from wild populations [is] necessary" to keep captive-bred falcons from losing the "wild qualities"—speed, power, and hunting instinct—that expert falconers seek. "This is a strong argument for maintaining a modest wild take for propagation purposes even in countries where a falconry take is not allowed," Bradshaw maintained.

Jeffrey Lendrum had his own opinions about Arabs' affinity for wild birds. "The thing they would worry about is that so many birds are being interbred, they don't know what they've got anymore," he would explain. "A gyrfalcon could be one-quarter peregrine. A lot of these guys think, 'It's better to get something from the wild [so] we'll know what we've got.'" That may well have been the thinking of Lendrum's Emirates-based contacts when they sent him off for what would be the most ambitious wild take of his lifetime. He had a blank check, the full confidence of his sponsors, and a plan to capture the most prized falcon of them all.

ELEVEN

OPERATION CHILLY

On the early evening of June 10, 2001, Jeffrey Lendrum sat in the front passenger seat of a Bell JetRanger 406 helicopter, gazing through the window at the vast wilderness of northeastern Quebec. The sun was still high in the subarctic sky, and the temperature hovered just above freezing. As the helicopter traveled north, marshy valleys filled with forests of black spruce and larch gave way to near-treeless tundra still dappled with snow. Black bears and wolves loped along the boggy terrain. The chopper descended toward Kuujjuaq, an Inuit community of 2,500 that had served as a fur-trading post for the Hudson's Bay Company in the mid–nineteenth century. A few hundred bungalows lay in neat rows beside a boulder-strewn beach facing the Koksoak River, the longest waterway in Quebec's Nunavik territory, comprising the northern third of the province, an area larger than California. Ungava Bay, an icy basin at the mouth of the Koksoak just below Baffin Island and the Hudson Strait, lay about thirty-five miles to the north.

The pilot set down the helicopter gently at Kuujjuaq Airport, a single rutted tarmac runway. Then the pilot, Lendrum, and a third passenger, Paul Mullin, presented their passports to an official in a turquoise-painted corrugated-metal shed. They caught a waiting taxi to the Auberge Kuujjuaq Inn, a rustic two-story structure overlooking the river.

The men had booked rooms for a week. If anyone asked, they would say they were documentary filmmakers for *National Geographic* who had come to northern Canada to gather nature footage for the society's archives. But they were there for a different purpose: to steal the eggs of wild birds of prey. Four months earlier, in England, Lendrum had approached his business partner with a proposition. He was organizing his second trip to the Canadian subarctic, one of the prime habitats of the gyrfalcon. It'd been two years since he and Mullin had flown together from Johannesburg to London with the lanner falcon chicks concealed in Lendrum's carry-on bag. Now he invited his friend to tag along again.

"It's going to be the adventure of a lifetime," Lendrum promised. And all of their expenses would be covered.

Lendrum would later insist that the mission was just a sightseeing trip—"a dream on my bucket list"—financed by the sale of a house he owned in England. But Lendrum, who was sharing his girlfriend's home in Towcester, didn't own a house, Mullin maintains. Months earlier, Mullin says, Lendrum had met with Howard Waller in Dubai, and asked him to put up expenses for what he presented as the ultimate wild take. "The gyrfalcons are like bluebottle flies up there. They're all over the place," Lendrum assured Waller, according to Mullin—though his mission in 2000 had been something of a bust.

In Dubai Lendrum received $100,000 in hundred-dollar bills. Lendrum hid the cash on his body to avoid currency-reporting requirements, and then headed to Dubai International Airport for the flight home. Waller insists that Mullin's story is a fabrication. "Because we grew up together it's always assumed that it's me" who financed Lendrum's schemes, Waller said with a sigh when I pressed him on his role in Lendrum's egg-thieving adventures. He claimed that after each one of Lendrum's arrests he had tried to discourage his longtime friend from raiding nests and smuggling eggs. "I told him, 'Stop what you're doing, every time you do this it falls back on me,'" he said. "I told him this a long time ago." Lendrum, like Waller, denies Mullin's assertion that Waller commissioned him to obtain gyrfalcons in Canada. But when confronted with Waller's claims, Lendrum would call his old friend "a complete liar," insist that "he never rebuked me," and accuse him of acquiring rare wild birds, including gyrs, from all over the world. "He's trying to cover his own ass," says Lendrum, who claims he stole black sparrow hawk eggs from nests for Waller in South Africa in the 1980s. "When Howard finds himself backed into a corner, he shouts and he gets abusive." Waller denies that he ever asked Lendrum to steal wild raptors for him in South Africa or anywhere else.

=

Canada outlawed the wild harvesting of gyrfalcons in 1976—not that this stopped men like Lendrum. David Anderson, the director of the Gyrfalcon Conservation Project, says that pure white gyrs attract so much black market money that if he or his researchers spied one in the field, they kept the sighting a secret. The birds' hues run from black to brown to gray, but it's always the whites that disappear from their nests. "They are the biggest, baddest, meanest, prettiest falcons," he says. "It's not surprising at all that this mystique exists."

The black market trade isn't the only threat to the gyr's survival.

Scientists are finding increasing doses of mercury, DDE, aldrin, chlorinated hydrocarbons, polychlorinated biphenyls, and other toxic substances in birds and eggs as far north as Greenland and northern Norway, putting birds that eat other birds at a particular risk. And the warming of the Arctic's summers is causing migratory peregrines to expand their territory—seizing the nests of gyrfalcons and competing with them for scarce food and territory. Kurt Burnham, a raptor expert at the High Arctic Institute in Orion, Illinois, predicted in a 2016 article in the *Atlantic* that the intensifying battle between gyrs and peregrines would likely cause "one of them to go extinct in the area" by 2030.

The birds' difficult lives in the wild provided Lendrum with an argument for why removing eggs from their nests didn't present an ethical problem. He described to Mullin the satisfaction he'd feel knowing that he had "rescued" birds from increasingly uninhabitable environments and delivered them to a pampered life in the care of devoted Arab falconers—a life of generous feedings, plenty of room to fly, and state-of-the-art medical care.

Lendrum recruited a friend from his childhood to serve as his pilot in the far north. The son of a Special Forces operative in the Rhodesian Bush War, the pilot had flown helicopters for logging and power companies in Alaska and Canada, laying down pylons in the wilderness, and now conducted rescues for a sheriff's department in Northern California. "[I am a] utility bush pilot with over 16,000 hours spent freezing in Alaska to cooking in the [Papua New Guinea] jungle and everywhere in between," he wrote on his LinkedIn profile, "Africa, Australia, Venezuela, Hawaii and all over the Pacific—settling in California for the privilege to fly a Huey." Working for the sheriff's department, he had flown injured hikers and their rescuers on the end of a one-hundred-foot fixed line, a feat that required extraordinary concentration and precision maneuvering. These were the same skills the pilot would require on his clandestine new mission.

Lendrum chartered the Bell JetRanger 406, a robust, versatile machine on which the pilot had done much of his training, from Cherokee Helicopter Services in Pennsylvania. He arranged for the chopper to be delivered to Montréal-Dorval International Airport. In Montreal, Mullin, Lendrum, and the pilot loaded the helicopter with equipment that they had picked up mostly on a shopping spree in London, financed, according to Mullin, by the cash advance. They had titanium-threaded Arctic jackets, snow pants, and liners, ropes, generators, three GPS devices, harnesses, survival kits (containing knives, snares, a compass, a saw, waterproof matches, candles, fishing lines and hooks), mobile incubators, lights, boots, and dozens of jerricans filled with jet fuel. They also had a professional-quality Canon XL 10 video camera with multiple lenses, which they would use to support their *National Geographic* cover story; Mullin planned to shoot footage of gyrfalcons and peddle the video to nature-documentary companies when he got back home. The spycraft aficionado was still driving his Toyota Prada with BOND license plates, and he invented a code name for their mission: Operation Chilly. They hadn't told their wives, partners, friends, business associates, or anyone else about their plans.

The men were in a boisterous mood as they prepared to set off in the early morning of June 10 on the long journey north to Kuujjuaq, a nine-hundred mile, twelve-hour flight, with scheduled refueling stops in Quebec City and a series of old French trading posts, mining towns, and lumber settlements: Saguenay, Baie-Comeau, Labrador City, Schefferville . . . Gyrfalcon egg-hatching season runs from mid-May to mid-June. They were heading to the subarctic right on time.

Mullin broke out the video camera and filmed the pilot and Lendrum placing the last gear inside the JetRanger's cargo hold.

In the video, the pilot, a strapping blond-haired man wearing a pair of Ray-Bans, looks directly at the camera and grins.

"Look at us," he says. "We're fucking criminals."

Lendrum gives the thumbs-up.

=

The morning of June 11 dawned cold and clear in Kuujjuaq. The pilot guided the fully loaded helicopter west out of the Inuit village, leaving all traces of a human presence behind. They flew for half an hour over pale green and russet hills dotted with patches of ice and snow, and rivers choked with ice floes. Mullin, in the backseat, followed the route on a NATO topographical map that he had procured in London, and pointed excitedly to a pod of white beluga whales frolicking in an icy river. At last they arrived at a palisade that plunged at a near-ninety-degree angle to a body of water labeled Basalt Lake. The helicopter soared over sheets of ice, small breaks providing glimpses of the crystalline blue water underneath.

Lendrum, in the front, peered out the window, searching the sky. After several passes over the lake, the pilot set the chopper down on firm ground high above the water and the three men climbed out of the craft. The tundra abounded with lichens, tussock sedge, Arctic poppies, dwarf heath shrubs, scrub birch, and willows. It was the most unspoiled corner of the world that Mullin had ever seen. Then, suddenly came a screech through the silence. A pair of peregrines soared overhead, emitting high-pitched warning cries. An aerie was nearby.

"They're beautiful," Lendrum said. Mullin had his video camera out again. "Look at this male."

Even at a distance of several hundred feet, Lendrum could discern the difference in size between the two birds. Female peregrine falcons are about one-third larger than their mates, a phenomenon known as "reversed-size sexual dimorphism" and unique to owls, eagles, hawks, and falcons. Some evolutionary scientists theorize that because male raptors engage in territorial duels in midair, natural selection favors the smallest, lightest, and most agile of them. Others have posited that females need to be stronger because they are responsible for guarding the nest and protecting the eggs against predators, while males can remain focused on hunting prey.

"*That* is a fucking noise," the pilot said in the video, laughing. "See Lendrum fucking smiling now."

"It's fucking nice," Lendrum replied.

Then he picked out a speck of white on the horizon and knew—instantly, from half a mile away—that it was the raptor he had come to the end of the earth for: the elusive gyrfalcon, the bird of kings. Above the lake, the trio watched, enthralled, as the bird approached its aerie. "Here it comes on the right," the pilot could be heard exclaiming on the video. "She's coming in, coming in, staying on the ridgeline," he narrated like a sports announcer. "Here she comes, over the ridge now, traversing." The gyrfalcon settled on a ledge. "Beautiful," the pilot said, continuing to observe the gyrfalcon. "We're on."

It was a white gyr—meaning that if its breeding partner was also white, the chances were excellent that the chicks would be that color as well. Still, you could never be sure: a scientific study in the Koryak Mountains of far eastern Siberia had turned up a nest in which a pair of white gyrfalcons had produced gray chicks. And if a white gyrfalcon mated with a gray, black, orange, or other morph, there was no telling what the pair would produce. Sometimes one clutch could contain birds of three or four different hues. But Lendrum was optimistic.

The pilot and Lendrum fastened a one-hundred-foot static line to the helicopter skids, with the free end of the rope hanging down. Wearing leather boots, snow pants, gloves, and a green parka against the subarctic chill, Lendrum slipped a nylon safety harness around his legs and waist. He threaded the rope through a caribiner on his belt and secured it with a single figure-eight knot and a safety knot. The pilot lifted off slowly, making sure that the downwash from the rotors didn't tangle the rope. The slack tightened and Lendrum began to rise in a seated position into the azure sky.

Soon he was dangling seven hundred feet over the water. A video that Mullin shot of the moment would be seized by Great Britain's National Wildlife Crime Unit nine years later and broadcast around the world: Lendrum swayed calmly in the breeze, framed against water and sky both dazzlingly blue. One hand grasped a padded green cooler bag, large enough to fit four cans of beer, while the other held the rope. Nothing but two well-tied knots stood between him and oblivion, yet he seemed utterly self-assured. (Mullin didn't know how many times, if any, Lendrum had pulled off this stunt before, but he was so adept at climbing trees and scaling cliffs that "dangling from a helicopter would have been a piece of piss" for him, Mullin says.)

The Bell JetRanger hovered close to the rock wall, almost stationary, rotors spinning. The pilot masterfully manipulated the cyclic stick, collective lever, and anti-torque pedals to keep the machine virtually still. One tiny slip would have sheared off the blades and sent both pilot and thief plummeting to their deaths.

Lendrum turned toward the ledge. The female gyrfalcon circled overhead, distressed, as Lendrum inched closer to the aerie, an odoriferous heap splattered with whitewash, or bird feces, ptarmigan feathers, and other remains. "The nest was . . . the most filthy mess . . . covered with a thick layer of old wings and other debris, mostly of puffins and black guillemots, and simply hopping with little black flea-like creatures," a one-eyed, one-armed naturalist named Ernest Vesey wrote in his 1938 memoir *In Search of the Gyr-Falcon*, about his own aerie raid in northwestern Iceland. More than a century before Vesey's expedition, American ornithologist John James Audubon left a similar account of finding the nest of white gyrfalcons on the southern coast of Labrador, not far from Kuujjuaq. "The nest of these hawks was placed on the rocks, about fifty feet from their summit, and more than a hundred feet from their base," he wrote. "It was composed of sticks, sea-weeds, and mosses, about two feet in diameter, and almost flat. About its edges were strewed the remains of their food, and beneath, on the margin of the stream, lay a quantity of wings of the *Uria Troile*, *Mormon arcticus*, and *Tetrao Saliceti*, together with large pellets comprised of fur, bones, and various substances."

Inches from the aerie, Lendrum reached out and grabbed his prize: four large cream-colored eggs, with reddish brown freckles. Charles Bendire, the American oologist who escaped death at the hands of Apache Indians while snatching the eggs of a zone-tailed hawk, described gyrfalcon eggs vividly in an 1892 report from the field:

> The ground color, when distinctly visible . . . is creamy white. This is usually hidden by a pale cinnamon rufous suffusion . . . The eggs are closely spotted and blotched with small, irregular markings of dark reddish brown, brick red, ochraceous rufous, and tawny. Some specimens show scarcely any trace of markings, the egg being of near uniform color throughout . . . In shape they vary from ovate to rounded ovate. The shells of these eggs feel rough to the touch, are irregularly granulated, and without luster.

Lendrum placed the eggs in the cooler bag, and gave a hand signal. The pilot pulled away from the cliff, lifted into the sky, and deposited Lendrum gently on the tundra, before touching down nearby.

Later that day Mullin would slip into the harness and dangle from the helicopter just for the experience. He realized, terrified, that he had no control over his movements. "You're dependent on air flow, downwash, you're spinning left, and you're spinning right," he recalled. Hanging from the line made him appreciate Lendrum's athleticism even more.

Over the next few hours the pilot, Lendrum, and Mullin covered hundreds of square miles of gyrfalcon-rich territory, becoming steadily more proficient at spotting gyrs and their nests. The pilot circled high above the cliffs, zeroing in on a soaring bird and following it along the rock wall until its whitewash-splattered aerie came into view. Then he'd set down the helicopter in a meadow atop the cliff. If Lendrum thought the rock face was scalable, he fixed a rope, rappelled to the aerie, snatched the eggs, and climbed back up, with the cooler bag dangling from his belt. Sometimes the pilot managed to find flat ground at the base of the cliff where he could land his helicopter, and picked up Lendrum at the bottom, sparing him the arduous ascent back to the summit. Usually, however, the water reached to the very edge of the cliffs, making landing impossible. Three times that day, the rock face proved too steep to manage, and Lendrum approached the nest at the end of the fixed line suspended from the helicopter.

After each heist they flew on for another four or five miles—the limits of each gyr's territory—and renewed their search. Mullin observed the hunt from the backseat of the JetRanger, marveling at the birds' elegance and at the dramatic landscapes. "A lake, a mountain and the sea beyond," wrote Ronald Stevens in his 1956 book *The Taming of Genghis*, in which he traps a gyrfalcon chick in Iceland and teaches it to hunt. "The sky so blue in the transient smiles of an Arctic summer, so leaden and lowering at most other times. Against this background Genghis had his home."

Remarkably the trio made no attempt to hide their activities, apparently assuming that authorities would never obtain the visual and audio record. "Are you down?" shouted the pilot from the top of a cliff in one video sequence. A male gyrfalcon circled above, calling out in agitation. "Are you in the right spot?"

"Yeah, I'm here," Lendrum replied. "I may not have enough rope."

"I'll belay you down, keep going," his partner said. "We'll meet you at the bottom."

"I'll be fine," Lendrum said, as he clambered out of sight to snatch the eggs from the aerie.

The men showed no particular sensitivity to other species they encountered on their felonious romp. Halfway through the day, the pilot spotted a herd of caribou and chased it by helicopter across the tundra. Mullin filmed the beasts as they stampeded in terror, some of them slipping on the slick ground or toppling over into pools of water. They pursued a herd of musk oxen next—great shaggy beasts that look like a cross between a buffalo and a yak. Then the pilot and Lendrum headed off for some more aerial reconnaissance, leaving Mullin to explore the cliffs on his own. Unarmed and wary of encountering polar bears, he cautiously clambered up the rocks to an aerie where four unattended, pure-white gyrfalcon chicks, days old, chirped helplessly at him and huddled in fear.

Many years later, Mullin would try to rationalize his role in what he would forever refer to as a "black op." He pointed out that he had never raided a nest nor touched a gyrfalcon egg; that was all "Lendrum's business," not his. "He was always protective of the eggs," Mullin remembered. "I wasn't even allowed to hold one to feel what it was like." He repeated Lendrum's argument that stealing eggs was an unorthodox conservation method—"rescuing" the raptors from probable death. (There's some truth to Lendrum's reasoning. About 60 percent of gyrfalcons in the wild don't survive past their first year.) And he emphasized that the trip had been motivated by a lust for adventure, not greed. All he was getting was a vacation, all expenses paid. The real payoff—between $70,000 and $100,000 per white gyrfalcon egg, he had been told—would come long after Mullin had moved on.

Yet the phony identities, the secrecy (Mullin had kept his South African girlfriend in the dark about the trip), and the possibility of arrest had a powerful appeal. Like Lendrum, there were days he enjoyed being an outlaw.

=

On that first full day in northern Canada, Mullin says Lendrum climbed into six nests and took eight gyrfalcon eggs. Back at the hotel, he placed the trophies inside two incubators stored in a suitcase. The next morning the accomplices went up in the helicopter again. Over four days Lendrum invaded nineteen nests, found clutches in twelve, and stole twenty-seven eggs, a far greater haul, says Mullin, than any one of them had dreamed possible. Although Lendrum had announced to Mullin a plan to replace the live eggs with hard-boiled chicken eggs—with the hope that the breeding pair would reject them as rotten and lay a new clutch—Mullin admitted, "We never bothered to do that."

Lendrum wrapped the eggs in woolen socks and stored them in his hand luggage for the twelve-hour helicopter flight back to Montreal. At every refueling stop he took them out and shone a flashlight on them—a process known as "candling"—to make certain, through the glow of the light against the thin eggshell, that the embryos' hearts were still pumping. From Montreal, the pilot flew back to Northern California and returned to his job in the sheriff's department, telling nobody about what he had been up to in Nunavik. Mullin and Lendrum caught a British Airways flight to Heathrow with the twenty-seven eggs concealed in Lendrum's carry-on bag. There they parted ways. Mullin headed to Johannesburg, Lendrum to Dubai. Lendrum reported that he had delivered all the eggs alive to his sponsor.

"It was a total success," he announced.

It was such a triumph that Lendrum was already thinking ahead to the next year's trip. They would leave for Kuujjuaq a few weeks earlier, he told Mullin, when not as many chicks would have hatched and there would be even more eggs for them to steal. Lendrum had decided that he would hire a pilot and helicopter from a company in Kuujjuaq, rather than bring his boyhood friend back from California. He was financing this next venture himself, and he wanted to keep costs to a minimum. Mullin felt uneasy about inviting outsiders into their scheme, but Lendrum brushed off his concerns. It was the prelude to a disastrous series of events that would come to haunt Mullin for the next two decades.

TWELVE

BUSTED

They couldn't see a goddamned thing.

Paul Mullin trudged through knee-deep snow on a ridgeline high above a frozen lake, lugging his video camera, his face hidden behind a woolen ski mask. He wore a heavy down parka, fur-lined boots, and fur-lined gloves, the best he could find in London, but his fingers were so cold that he could barely feel them. When he went to urinate, the stream froze on impact. Every breath he took felt like a knife thrust in his lungs.

He was perched atop a cliff forty miles west of Kuujjuaq, the tiny Inuit settlement on the Koksoak River that he was visiting for the second time in a year; the tumbling snow had diminished visibility to a few yards. He and his partner, Jeffrey Lendrum, had instructed the helicopter pilot to leave them there, in the middle of the wilderness, with a promise that he would come back to fetch them in ninety minutes. They were shooting a documentary for *National Geographic*, they had told him, lying. If the helicopter stayed at the scene, the pilot would have to keep the engine running to avoid ice buildup, and the rotor noise would scare off the birds.

Mullin hadn't been keen on the plan. What if the pilot got way-laid somehow? They had no way of reaching him, no satellite phone, no cell phone signal, no emergency kit, a single Mars bar apiece if they got hungry, and no weapon for protection against polar bears or other predators, except for a twenty-two-inch Buck knife that Mullin had strapped to his leg.

What the hell had Lendrum been thinking?

It had been Lendrum's idea to arrive in Canada in early May, cal-culating that fewer eggs would have hatched but those would be far enough along to survive a journey to Dubai. He hadn't anticipated that four weeks might make all the difference in the subarctic between spring thaw and whiteout, between forty degrees Fahrenheit and ten below. The weather had been so bad they'd managed just a single flight during their first three days in Kuujjuaq, raiding three nests and stealing five eggs. They'd spent the rest of the time tooling around the frozen Koksoak River on snowmobiles.

While immersed in these thoughts, Mullin heard the *whup whup whup* of a rotor. Through the fog and the snow, he could just make out the ghostly outlines of the helicopter. The AStar 350 touched down on the frozen ground fifty yards from them, and Lendrum and Mullin climbed aboard. But rather than order the pilot to return to Kuujjuaq, Lendrum instructed him to drop them off at another lookout point farther west. The pilot, an Inuit from Kuujjuaq named Pete Duncan, steered the chopper through the snowstorm with fierce concentration. Mullin, in the front seat, would remember being mes-merized by "the *Star Wars* effect" of the flakes hurtling against the windshield.

"This is getting too much, man," Duncan muttered, looking for a place to land.

=

Duncan was the cofounder, vice president, and chief pilot of Nunavik Rotors, an all-Aboriginal-owned division of Air Inuit, the biggest commercial airline in Quebec's far north. He'd flown hundreds of sightseeing expeditions deep into the Nunavik outback—and conducted a fair share of search-and-rescue missions. The Kuujjuaq native had saved a tourist whose snowmobile had run out of fuel and who had wandered on foot, disoriented, deeper into the wilderness and pulled out five people stranded on an ice floe after a boating accident. He'd also taken hunters, fishermen, adventure tourists, and photographers into the Torngat Range—3,750 square miles of polar-bear-infested tundra and glaciated mountains stretching north from Saglek Fjord to the northern tip of Labrador.

But in his twenty years of running the airline Duncan had never encountered any clients like the two he was flying with today. He'd recognized the shorter one with the South African accent immediately: the man had hired a helicopter and pilot from Nunavik Rotors back in 2000, flying over rock walls for what he had claimed was a reconnaissance trip for a nature film. At the end of the mission, the South African had surprised Duncan by asking whether he could buy the helicopter. "I'm planning to come back for a few years in a row," he'd explained. "I'll just need it for May and June, and for the rest of the year you can do what you want with it." The fellow had even offered a large sum of cash, but Duncan, suspicious, had turned him down.

He'd seen the South African again the following June, although they hadn't spoken at all. On that trip the man had brought his own helicopter from the States, and a pilot and an English friend had joined him. Now, eleven months later, the South African and the

Englishman had returned to Kuujjuaq, claiming to be gathering more documentary footage. Duncan didn't believe them for a minute. The Englishman behaved as if he'd never shot video before; Duncan wondered whether the camera even held a battery. And when the "film crew" repeatedly had him drop them on a ridge and pick them up an hour later to take them to a new location, he was sure they were up to something shady. "Any wildlife photographer who's serious would ask to be dropped off at sunrise and picked up at sunset," Duncan would say years later. "Who in the hell sits around on a mountain and asks me to go back in town and return in a couple of hours? These guys had something to hide."

After his first day in the field with the suspect documentarians, Duncan stopped by the Kuujjuaq headquarters of Quebec's wildlife protection agency, to look up his old friend Dave Watt.

"There's something fishy about these two," he told Watt, a veteran law enforcement officer. "I'll be finished with them on May 11." He asked his friend to wait until they'd paid him for his last day of work before he closed in.

Early the next morning, during a break in the weather, while Mullin and Lendrum were charging around on snowmobiles, Watt and Vallée Saunders, another wildlife protection officer, retraced the route that the two alleged filmmakers had taken with Duncan the day before. As they flew low in a police helicopter over the frozen tundra, they could spot the men's footprints in the virgin snow along the ridgeline, clearly leading to ledges where gyrfalcons and peregrines nested. Circling in for a closer look, Watt and Saunders saw that several clutches at fresh aeries appeared to be missing.

"These guys are stealing eggs," Watt told Saunders, and Saunders agreed.

The officers contacted their superiors at the head office in Chibougamau, a logging and mining town in central Quebec, and requested a search warrant. Late in the afternoon of May 11, Watt, Saunders, and two officers from the Quebec Provincial Police drove across town to the Auberge Kuujjuaq Inn, where Mullin and Lendrum were settling down after a brutal day of egg snatching in a blizzard.

=

Stretched out on their backs on twin beds, too tired to remove their boots and gaiters, the two egg thieves luxuriated in the warmth of their hotel room. Twenty minutes earlier, Duncan had dropped off the pair in front of the inn and received his $5,000 payment, in cash, for eight hours of flying plus fuel costs. Duncan had known the police were planning a raid that evening, but hadn't given anything away. Now, as Watt and his fellow officers closed in, the men talked obliviously about the subzero temperatures, the sealskin gloves Duncan had lent Mullin to prevent frostbite, and their plans to leave the following day.

Conditions had been so awful today that Lendrum had rappelled down to only a single gyrfalcon nest in the snow and retrieved two eggs, giving them a total of seven for a week's work. Though just a quarter of the previous year's haul, "it was enough to turn a decent profit," Mullin would later say. (Mullin understood that he wouldn't be sharing in the profits; he had simply been hungry for another adventure.) Those eggs were now keeping warm in a portable incubator plugged into a wall socket. Ropes, carabiners, climbing harnesses, and egg boxes lay scattered about the room.

At five o'clock, someone knocked on the door. Mullin and Lendrum looked at each other.

It must be the police, Mullin thought, his heartbeat quickening. "This is it, Jeff," he said.

"Okay," Lendrum replied with resignation.

Mullin swung his legs around, stood up, and opened the door. Saunders, Watt, and the two Quebecois police officers burst into the room.

"Are you Paul Mullin and Jeffrey Lendrum?" asked Watt.

The men nodded.

"Stand to one side," he said.

Lendrum and Mullin watched silently as the officers removed the film from Mullin's video camera and seized the climbing equipment, GPS devices, and mobile telephones. They opened carry-on bags, unplugged and removed the incubators, and peered at the creamy white-and-yellow eggs being kept warm inside.

"Have you been stealing eggs?" asked Watt.

"No, no, I've been filming," insisted Mullin, gamely explaining that he was gathering "exclusive footage" about gyrfalcons for *National Geographic*. The four officers ordered Lendrum and Mullin outside, led each to the back of a separate four-by-four, and drove them across Kuujjuaq toward wildlife protection agency headquarters.

Lendrum and Mullin stared out the windows as they passed long rows of single- and two-story bungalows encrusted with snow and ice. They had agreed that if they were caught, they would stick to their cover story. The officers escorted them into the Wildlife Protection Services building and down a fluorescent-lit corridor, into separate rooms. Asked what he and his partner were doing with seven gyrfalcon eggs in a heated incubator in their hotel room, Mullin, who was still carrying the twenty-two-inch Buck knife strapped to his leg, professed ignorance.

Lendrum was a bit more voluble. He had taken a break from gathering *National Geographic* footage, he explained, to retrieve a few "addled" specimens from nest sites to perform postmortems to investigate possible pesticide poisoning. He planned to weigh and measure the eggs, just as the British ornithologist Derek Ratcliffe had done to examine the effects of DDT in rural England in the 1960s. He also intended, he insisted, to put the clutch back on the ledges the following day.

Watt, however, had found a laptop containing a record of expenses from the pair's trip the year before—including a $30,000 helicopter rental and thousands of dollars for plane tickets between London and Philadelphia, and Philadelphia and Montreal. Lendrum and Mullin were, he was sure, well-financed international wildlife smugglers, who intended to profit from selling the live eggs of one of Quebec's most endangered species. If it were his decision, Watt would have had them tried on wildlife trafficking charges, an offense that potentially carried a $1 million fine and a five-year jail term in Canada. But Watt knew that he lacked indisputable evidence—boarding a flight with the contraband, for example—that the two men intended to smuggle the gyrfalcon eggs abroad. Instead he conferred with the provincial prosecutor in Chibougamau, then came back to Lendrum and Mullin with an offer:

"You can either plead guilty and pay a fine, or we'll lock you up and Monday you'll go to court," Watt told them.

"How much?" Mullin asked.

"Seven thousand two hundred and fifty dollars," said Watt. It was the highest penalty possible under Canadian wildlife legislation.

"I need to speak to my partner," said Mullin.

Half an hour later Mullin and Lendrum pleaded guilty to twelve charges of illegal hunting and wild egg possession. The men paid their fine with US dollars. After the money changed hands, the police drove them through the darkened streets and deposited them in front of their hotel.

"Be on the first plane out of here tomorrow," Watt advised, "and don't come back to Canada."

Wildlife authorities transported the eggs to a birds-of-prey recovery center near Montreal, where only one hatched; the others had apparently died of shock from being ripped out of their nests and jostled by either the thieves or the police. Dave Watt would claim that Lendrum had turned up the heat in the incubator either in the hotel room or during a brief period when he was close to the hatcher at headquarters after his arrest. "He wanted to destroy the evidence," Watt would say. But Mullin insists that Lendrum would never deliberately kill a bird of prey under any circumstance. "He would risk his own life to save them," Mullin says.

Mullin and Lendrum, shaken by the arrest, speculated about who had turned them in. On the flight back to Montreal, Mullin hypothesized that a room cleaner might have rummaged through their equipment while they were out. But the most likely culprit, he believed, was the pilot. "He was the weakest link in this whole damned thing," he told Lendrum. "We shouldn't have done it this way." For his part, Lendrum suggested that his old friend Howard Waller might well have betrayed them "out of jealousy." Up to that point, Mullin had assumed that Waller may have been on the receiving end of the eggs. Lendrum, who had been guarded with Mullin about his clientele this time, now implied that he was freelancing for wealthy backers in the United Arab Emirates.

The first article about the pair appeared four days later on the front page of the *Nunatsiaq News*, a northeastern Quebec weekly. The antics of the globe-trotting criminals stood out amid the vocational school graduations, airport renovations, and other small-town events that typically filled the paper. "Poachers Fined for Illegal Possession of Falcon Eggs," the article was headlined: "Two men masquerading as nature photographers, one from South Africa and the other from Britain, were caught red-handed in Kuujjuaq last week with a cache of falcon eggs worth thousands of dollars on the international black market." In the article Guy Tremblay of the Quebec wildlife protection agency noted, "Kuujjuaq isn't a big place and word traveled fast. People found their activity strange." He estimated the black market value of each gyrfalcon egg at $30,000, theorized that the thieves "were linked to some organization," and said that the Quebec government planned "to alert federal officials to the men's identity so they can't try to enter Canada at some later date."

Toronto's *National Post* picked up the story on May 18. "Poached Eggs Seized from Fake Film Crew," the headline declared. "Wildlife Officials Confiscate Incubator to Thwart Falcon Trade." A spokesman for Canada's Ministry of the Environment and Fauna told the paper, "Nobody goes to Kuujjuaq to collect eggs to make an omelette. Clearly, they had another goal in mind." Canadian TV news ran a brief report about the arrests. Mullin and Lendrum later appeared at number fifty-seven in the rankings of the world's one hundred top birds-of-prey smugglers on the website of savethefalcons.org, an obscure conservation group run by an American raptor biologist. But after this flurry of attention, the story disappeared. The public shaming that Mullin had feared never happened. None of his friends or relatives ever learned about what had occurred during that bizarre week in Kuujjuaq.

Still, Mullin's brush with the authorities chastened him. He legally changed his name and received a fresh passport under his new identity. He had occasional business in Canada and took Tremblay's warning seriously; the last thing he wanted was to find himself turned back at the Canadian border. And he vowed never to accompany Lendrum on another egg stealing mission. It had been fun, but he should have known there would be consequences. Lendrum was too much of a risk-taker.

Lendrum, too, seemed spooked by the arrest. "That was it," he told Mullin when they returned to England. "The show's over." He would scale down his global wanderings for a while, mostly staying put in England with his French-Algerian girlfriend, and focus on running AfricaXtreme. But Lendrum was not a person who could sit still for long—especially when so many wild falcons were nesting just a short drive away.

THIRTEEN

THE UNIT

By 2002, the year Jeffrey Lendrum was arrested in northern Canada for stealing wild gyrfalcon eggs, British lawmakers were starting to become serious about fighting wildlife crime. Just fifteen years earlier, the only institutions investigating such offenses were private animal-welfare charities like the Royal Society for the Protection of Birds. Guy Shorrock at the RSPB had even mounted private criminal prosecutions against falcon poisoners and other animal abusers—applying for summonses, taking evidence, and hiring attorneys—because no law enforcement agency seemed willing to take them on. Only a few police forces had a dedicated wildlife officer, and the stiffest penalty one could receive for poaching, smuggling, or harming animals was a small fine. *Before*

Now about half of the forty-three police forces in England and Wales employed full-time wildlife cops. Some had two. The 2000 *Now* Countryside and Rights of Way Act had imposed jail sentences for wildlife offenses, including two years for the taking, sale, or killing of protected birds. (In 2005 Parliament would raise the maximum penalty to five years.) And Richard Brunstrom, the chief constable of North Wales and one of Britain's most high-profile law enforcement figures, had proposed creating an intelligence team dedicated to tracking down wildlife criminals.

Brunstrom, a longtime colleague of Andy McWilliam's—they had met at a conference when Brunstrom was the national police "lead," or specialist in a chiefs' committee, on wildlife crime—took an aggressive and often controversial approach to police work. He had once cracked down on public urination by having officers haul buckets and mops on patrol and order offenders to clean up their messes or face arrest. In his zeal to stop speeders, he'd proposed tripling roadside cameras and hiding traffic cops behind billboards and bushes, leading British tabloids to dub him the "Mad Mullah of the Traffic Taliban." He filmed himself being stunned by a fifty-thousand-volt taser to prove that it wasn't lethal. (Footage on the department's website showed him crying out as his legs buckled.) He climbed scaffolding and broke into his own office late one night to expose security lapses within the police department.

Brunstrom was also a conservationist with a degree in zoology from Bangor University in North Wales; he'd advanced half-way through a Ph.D. in the subject before joining the police. So he grasped the growing threat of wildlife crime and the sophistication of some of its perpetrators. The trade went far beyond the familiar smuggling of elephant ivory and rhino horn from African game parks to the Far East. It involved hundreds of protected species, global networks, and often-violent perpetrators. It extended from East Java, where smugglers were wiping out the island's population of yellow-crested cockatoos; to the Brazilian Amazon, where a British pet shop owner would be caught with one thousand rare spiders (including tarantulas) hidden in his suitcases; to Guyana, where traffickers sedated chestnut-bellied seed finches with rum, stuffed them inside hair curlers, and shipped them illegally to New York City, where local impresarios staged contests pitting caged finches against each other to see which one could reach fifty whistles the fastest.

The National Wildlife Crime Intelligence Unit, as the National Wildlife Crime Unit's precursor was called, started operations in London in 2002. The *Independent* reported that the new unit would "use investigative tactics similar to those deployed against drug barons, such as undercover operations and bugging suspects," to combat what was estimated as a "£5 billion a year illegal business." But Brunstrom's vision was ahead of its time: the unit had a minuscule budget and just three detectives, whom local forces largely ignored. By McWilliam's estimate, the unit sent out 250 requests for action in three years; police responded to just 30. McWilliam, who was still specializing in wildlife crime for the Merseyside Police Force, was involved in a handful, including a case that concerned Liverpool shops that sold Chinese "health tonics" manufactured from the bones of leopards, tigers, and other endangered mammals. But he was the exception. "Most officers would say, 'We've got drugs, we've got serious crimes, what are they going on about?'" McWilliam says. In 2005, the unit's parent organization, the National Criminal Intelligence Service, merged with a new group, the Serious Organised Crime Agency, and the National Wildlife Crime Intelligence Unit, never seen as particularly effective, was phased out of existence.

=

McWilliam often felt like he was fighting for a cause few cared about, but occasionally he received a reminder that some people were taking notice. In 2004 the BBC came to Merseyside to capture a day in the life of Great Britain's most prominent wildlife cop. McWilliam warned the producer that his daily routine was often uneventful, and suggested they restage some of his more dramatic arrests. While riding in a bus with his wife a few weeks before, McWilliam had witnessed a youth kicking to death a small songbird called a mistle thrush, as the bird tried to protect her young. McWilliam had leapt off the bus and arrested the killer, carried the corpse to a vet to verify the cause of death, and then stashed the thrush in a freezer at the police station to use as evidence.

Minutes before the BBC crew arrived to stage the reenactment, McWilliam remembered that he had forgotten to remove the bird from the freezer the night before. He quietly carried the rock-solid corpse upstairs to the deserted canteen, placed it on a plate, slid it into the microwave, and turned the setting to defrost.

Midway through the seven-minute thawing, a policewoman entered the kitchen to heat a bowl of oatmeal. McWilliam stood beside her, nervously making small talk. When the microwave pinged, McWilliam reached in and removed the plate. The policewoman stared at the dead thrush.

"Don't knock it until you've tried one," he told her. "Have you seen the salt and pepper?"

After that, McWilliam recalled, the colleague gave him a wide berth.

＝

The failure of the National Wildlife Crime Intelligence Unit to find support from local police only hardened Richard Brunstrom's resolve to create an effective environmental crime force. In 2005 he lobbied the Home Office—the British equivalent of some combination of the US Departments of Justice and Homeland Security, responsible for immigration, domestic security, and law and order— to fund a more hands-on outfit comprised of specialists who would roam the country, providing guidance and support to local forces. As Brunstrom envisioned it, the new National Wildlife Crime Unit ("Intelligence" had been dropped from the name) would have a staff of seven: two field investigators, a senior intelligence officer, two analysts, an administrator, and the unit's head. To avoid ruffling the feathers of turf-conscious police, all field investigators would be re- tired wildlife officers and would have no authority to make arrests. In 2006, the Home Office and the Department for Environment, Food & Rural Affairs allocated £450,000 for the NWCU's first year of operations.

McWilliam got a phone call from Chris Kerr, the first head of unit, that summer. Kerr was a longtime wildlife cop whom McWil- liam had come to know through the National Conference of Wildlife Enforcers, an annual gathering of police investigators and conserva- tion groups where he'd also encountered Brunstrom.

"Have you thought about applying?" Kerr asked him.

McWilliam hadn't, but after thirty-one years with the police he was again ready for a change. The Merseyside force was in the middle of reorganization. McWilliam had been reassigned against his wishes from the Crosby Police Station, where he had worked for the past three decades, to a new station filled with officers he didn't know. He cringed at the posters emblazoned with soaring eagles and motiva- tional slogans that papered the station's sterile walls. McWilliam had nurtured friendships with many people in and around Crosby, pass- ing out his phone number to hundreds and becoming a real member of the community. "Suddenly I was moved to a station with senior officers who didn't have a clue," he would say. "All the experience that people had built up, they didn't seem to give a toss about."

McWilliam had some reservations about the new position. He was not especially fond of traveling, and working for the National Wildlife Crime Unit would require being on the road for three, sometimes four days a week. The unit's very existence was precarious, dependent on a renewal of its funding every year. But his wife, Lin, was encouraging. "Give it a go," she said. McWilliam had a pro forma interview, and Kerr offered him the job. In July 2006, he retired from the police force and a month later signed a twelve-month contract as a field investigator.

On October 5, Biodiversity Minister Barry Gardiner inaugurated the National Wildlife Crime Unit at Dynamic Earth, an environmental education-and-entertainment center in Edinburgh. Gardiner railed against "people who think it is acceptable to kill endangered animals because their fur is a fashion statement, or steal a rare bird's egg because it's one that they don't yet have in their collection." He declared, as McWilliam looked on, "We are talking about something on a par with drug trafficking and people trafficking, with the same nasty people involved."

=

The National Wildlife Crime Unit commenced operations from a backwater: North Berwick, a picturesque Scottish fishing village of four thousand people on the southern shore of the Firth of Forth. The hamlet was perhaps best known for having the world's largest colony of northern gannets, white seabirds related to boobies. The deputy constable of the local Lothian and Borders Police Force had donated for the squad the top floor of a small police station. "The

[Home Office] didn't want the unit to be London-centric," explained Alan Roberts, a retired detective and bird expert from East Anglia who had worked on Operation Easter and joined the NWCU as an investigative support officer at the same time as McWilliam. "There was always that suggestion that if it's based in London that's all they care about."

Soon the NWCU relocated to a more convenient headquarters in two large adjoining rooms on the third floor of a police station in Stirling, just outside Edinburgh, where the unit head, his administrators, and his intelligence team based themselves. McWilliam and Roberts worked from home but traveled throughout the country, joining cops on investigations and sharing their expertise in complex wildlife legislation. Both men had studied the Control of Trade in Endangered Species (Enforcement) Regulations of 1997, for example, legislation enacted by the European Union that categorized thirty-six thousand species according to three levels of protection and gave the police the power to take punitive action against wildlife smugglers and traders. The regulations covered everything from the proper labeling of crocodile skins and caviar containers to the eight species of pangolins (spiny anteaters found in Africa and Southeast Asia) and nine species of howler and spider monkeys that could not be traded for any purpose but scientific research. The regulations were essential tools for the wildlife cop, telling him what activities were worth investigating, what permits were required for which animal, and what crimes, if any, had been committed. McWilliam took the north of Britain, Roberts the south, though they sometimes overlapped. The unit soon added two more investigators responsible for policing Wales and Scotland.

It wasn't long before raw intelligence came flowing in—300 to

350 reports a month from local police departments, wildlife protection agencies, and concerned citizens. McWilliam chased poaching gangs that roamed the countryside in four-by-fours, armed with guns, crossbows, night-vision goggles, dogs, snares, and poisons, killing deer, hares, and other mammals for thrill or for profit. He investigated raptor persecutions: the shooting, poisoning, and trapping of peregrine falcons and other protected birds of prey by disgruntled farmers or by gamekeepers on hunting estates in Scotland and northern England. "Those killing birds of prey are typically serial offenders, just like egg thieves," wrote Guy Shorrock in his blog for the Royal Society for the Protection of Birds. "We have received detailed reports of gamekeepers that have apparently killed hundreds of raptors during their career" to prevent the birds from eating their pheasants and grouse and so threatening their livelihood. McWilliam helped put several of the more prolific falcon killers behind bars.

Occasionally he was drawn into more esoteric offenses. One of Richard Brunstrom's signature initiatives had been Operation Bat, launched in 2004 to protect the nocturnal mammals from lumberjacks and developers. Following Brunstrom's lead, McWilliam arrested a commercial builder who had deliberately destroyed the roosts of a brown long-eared bat (*Plecotus auritus*), which often secretes itself in roof spaces and chimneys, and is listed as threatened under the Endangered Species Act. And he busted a farmer who had dredged up a riverbed filled with freshwater pearl mussels—another high-priority endangered species.

McWilliam did some of his most important work sitting in front of his home computer. After a stuffed orangutan sold on the British black market for £16,000 in 1993, prices for taxidermied rare animals—Philippine eagles, Siberian tigers, stuffed Palawan peacock-pheasants, blue-naped parrots, ring-tailed lemurs, golden lion tamarins—had soared. McWilliam scoured eBay, Alibaba, Bird-trader, Preloved, and other e-commerce websites that allowed users to trade live and stuffed animals and animal parts. He identified suspicious sales, obtained court orders forcing the websites to turn over trading records, and then, armed with a search warrant, joined the police in arresting suspected traffickers and buyers.

There was the curio dealer selling "antique ivory carvings" on eBay, which carbon dating proved had been made from an elephant killed illegally in the 1980s. This was a decade after the Convention on International Trade in Endangered Species banned the trafficking of ivory taken from Asian elephants after 1975 and from African elephants after 1976. There was the collector with a degenerative eye disease who had created a bucket list of wildlife trophies to acquire before he lost his sight. First on the list: the skull of a mountain gorilla from central Africa, one of the most endangered animals in the world. The man contacted a Cameroonian trader through Alibaba, obtained a photo of an ape's newly severed head, and was sent the trophy in the mail. When police searched the man's garage, they discovered the skull, still covered with bits of flesh. "It still smelled bad," remembers McWilliam's colleague Alan Roberts. The Cameroon dealer had pulled a bait and switch, delivering a chimpanzee head instead, but the species is also listed as Appendix I, accorded the highest level of protection, and the buyer was arrested for CITES violations.

The National Wildlife Crime Unit followed the activities of a dodgy couple who ran a pet shop in West Yorkshire, buying and selling exotic animal skulls from Indonesia, South Africa, and other countries on the side. One of the couple's major buyers was a man named Alan Dudley, a father of three who inspected Jaguar Land

Rovers for a living. When the investigators entered Dudley's storage room in his house in Coventry, they found two thousand skulls—including that of a howler monkey from Ecuador, a penguin, a loggerhead turtle, a chimpanzee, a giraffe, a hippo, a Goeldi's marmoset from Bolivia, and even a Great Dane. In addition to buying the grisly mementos online, some of them illegally, Dudley made use of contracts he had with zoos and academic institutions to "clean up" the carcasses of dead animals and return the skeletons for research and display. (He evidently held back some of the skulls for his personal collection.) Convicted of seven counts of violating CITES regulations, Dudley was given a fifty-week suspended sentence, a three-month dusk-to-dawn curfew, and a £1,000 fine, on top of £3,000 in court costs. The judge spoke of an "academic zeal" that had "crossed the line into unlawful obsession."

Soon the evidence room at the Stirling headquarters spilled over with ocelot and leopard skins, monkey skulls, elephant tusks, rare butterflies, stuffed badgers, taxidermied birds of prey, and other contraband. McWilliam dubbed the odoriferous chamber the Room of Death. But the animals that crossed his path in the line of duty weren't all deceased. Wildlife charities across the United Kingdom began writing to McWilliam with requests for assistance in keeping at-risk species alive. Froglife UK sought his help protecting Britain's endangered amphibians and reptiles. Buglife wanted support for the Ladybird Spider Project, the Narrow-Headed Ant Project, the Shrill Carder Bee Project, and other campaigns to bring threatened insects "back from the brink" by introducing new populations into carefully managed habitats. Plantlife UK sought to save from extinction the pasqueflower, the sand lizard, the Duke of Burgundy butterfly, and other fragile flora and fauna. McWilliam was a sympathetic listener, but he could offer little concrete assistance since such problems lay well outside his portfolio. "There's not a lot of bug crime or frog crime," he said dryly.

=

In 1984, Alec Jeffreys, a geneticist at Great Britain's Leicester University, produced the world's first DNA profile, revolutionizing crime scene analysis. Jeffreys extracted DNA from cells, used an enzyme to slice up the strands, mounted the fragments in gel, and then introduced radioactive "tracers" that attached to specific sequences of proteins and other genetic material. When Jeffreys exposed the irradiated DNA fragments to X-ray film, the exposure produced a unique pattern of more than thirty stripes, resembling a universal bar code. Two years later, DNA collected from semen stains on the bodies of two teenagers who had been raped and murdered in a small village in Leicestershire secured the first conviction using genetic profiling, and exonerated an innocent man implicated in the killings. Soon the RSPB's Guy Shorrock began promoting it as a tool to combat falcon laundering.

Because captive breeding had a successful hatching rate of just 33 percent, unscrupulous breeders often found it far more cost-effective to illegally snatch nearly hatched eggs or chicks from the wilderness and then pass them off as having been hatched legally in their breeding centers. The Wildlife and Countryside Act of 1981 required that nine species of birds of prey bred in captivity, known as Schedule 4 birds—honey buzzards, golden eagles, white-tailed eagles, peregrines, ospreys, merlins, Montagu's harriers, marsh harriers, and goshawks—be fitted with permanent identification rings on their legs when they were two weeks old or younger. Captive-bred birds of prey also had to have a registration certificate approved by the

Convention on International Trade in Endangered Species, known as an Article 10. But breeders found it easy to launder wild birds into the system, usually by mixing in very young, pre-banded chicks with those produced by captive parents. Sources told Shorrock that 30 percent of peregrines declared captive-bred were actually robbed from nests. It was easy money, and less risky than trying to sell wild birds or wild eggs directly into the black market.

In October 1992, prosecutors employed crude genetic profiling to prove that Joseph Seiga, an unemployed birdkeeper in Liverpool, had passed off four baby goshawk siblings stolen from the wild as the offspring of a captive-bred female. The babies shared multiple genetic markers but had none in common with the purported mother. Seiga was convicted and fined. Three years later DNA evidence helped send Derek Canning, a peregrine breeder in Northumbria who kept maps of aeries across Scotland and Wales, to prison for eighteen months for laundering dozens of wild-trapped falcons.

Some of McWilliam's former colleagues belittled that kind of work, but McWilliam loved the challenge of the investigations—and, like so many of the men he was tracking, he enjoyed the thrill of the chase. He also believed that each sketchy breeder that he put out of business served as a warning to others—and as an incremental victory for the cause of environmental protection. In 2009, he zeroed in on John Keith Simcox, a breeder in eastern England, who claimed that the ring on his twenty-three-year-old female goshawk, which he had obtained in the 1980s from a breeder in Hungary, had fallen off the bird's leg. An animal health inspector refitted the goshawk with the ring, but an informant told McWilliam that the inspector had unwittingly ringed a wild impostor; the elderly bird had died and Simcox had pulled a switch.

McWilliam swooped in with a search warrant and took a blood sample from the goshawk. Then, using a family tree attached to the bird's Article 10 certificate, he tracked down the Hungarian goshawk's offspring, obtained additional blood samples, and sent them all to a DNA lab. The results were indisputable: the newly ringed female could not be the birds' mother. Simcox pleaded guilty to possession of a wild bird—McWilliam suspected he had stolen it from an aerie in north Wales—and to making a false declaration to obtain a registration. He received a three-month prison sentence. Simcox had allegedly engaged in such fraud for years, but this conviction "finished him off," said McWilliam, forbidding him from ever again breeding Schedule 4 birds, including goshawks.

=

The rare-bird underground was far more extensive than a handful of launderers in England sneaking into aeries in Scotland and Wales. Criminals roamed from Southeast Asia to the former Yugoslavia to the Amazon jungle, plundering birds of prey, flouting export and import regulations, smuggling chicks and mature birds abroad in often horrific conditions, and feeding a voracious market for exotic fauna. In Bangkok in 2000, Raymond Leslie Humphrey, the owner of a British birds of prey center called Clouds Falconry, squeezed twenty-three live raptors—including Thai crested serpent eagles and Blyth's hawk eagles, both previously unknown in Europe—into plastic tubes. Humphrey hid the tubes inside two large suitcases, and then checked the baggage into the unpressurized and unheated hold of an airplane to London.

Customs officers at Heathrow got a tip, pulled Humphrey aside, and seized his luggage. Inside the bags they made a terrible discovery: six of the twenty-three birds were dead (another died shortly afterward), and the other seventeen had sustained massive pressure injuries, asphyxia, and hypothermia. A search of Humphrey's residence turned up dozens more endangered birds, as well as a golden-cheeked gibbon, one of the rarest apes in the world. Humphrey was sentenced to six and a half years in prison for illegally importing protected species—an act of "extreme and sickening cruelty," in the words of the appeals court judge who upheld Humphrey's conviction in 2003. The judge reduced the sentence by one year, but it was still the longest jail term ever given out in the United Kingdom for a wildlife crime.

Another rare-bird trader, Harry Sissen, used plastic tubes to smuggle birds from black market dealers in Eastern Europe overland to France and then by ferry across the English Channel to Dover. At Sissen's breeding center in North Yorkshire, Alan Roberts seized one hundred forty protected birds, including three Lear's macaws from the Brazilian Amazon (only one hundred fifty of the all-blue parrots remain in the wild) and three blue-headed macaws from the Peruvian jungle. Sentenced to thirty months in prison for violating the regulations of the Convention on International Trade in Endangered Species, Sissen "was prepared to go to any lengths to obtain endangered species from which to breed," the presiding judge declared. The black market value of a pair of Lear's macaws, according to *PsittaScene*, a conservation journal published by the World Parrot Trust, was £50,000.

The worst of these smugglers reminded McWilliam of the "terrier men" he'd arrested in rural England, who used dogs to drive badgers from their burrows and tear them apart. Some people seemed to get pleasure out of subjecting animals to pain, he thought, or were so consumed by greed that they didn't stop to consider the suffering they were inflicting on other creatures. McWilliam struggled to maintain his equanimity in the face of such brutality. "One of the things with being a police wildlife officer," he would tell Timothy Wheeler for the 2015 documentary *Poached*, "is you've got to leave your emotions out of it, even if you are an animal lover [or] a bird lover . . . You've got to be quite clinical . . . and know if you get emotionally involved in these things, you never sleep at night."

McWilliam knew that the greatest demand for illicit rare birds was coming from the Arab world. He had read intelligence about the Siberian raptor smuggling route to the Middle East, and his colleague Alan Roberts had helped Belgian authorities bust a zookeeper who ran a bird-laundering operation across the European Union: stealing peregrine eggs from their nests in southern Spain, forging Article 10s at Belgium's Merlin Zoo in Sint-Jan-in-Eremo, and then allegedly selling the birds for nearly one million euros to rich Arab clients, as well as wealthy Chinese. "We began to pick up intelligence about wild birds going to Dubai, Qatar, and Saudi Arabia," McWilliam would say a decade later, still careful about disseminating information from an active investigation. "Dubai was the one we got most about, because of the racing" that had been growing in popularity since its introduction to the Persian Gulf in the early 2000s. "We noticed people coming in who had no history of falcon breeding, or falconry, because of the new money."

In the mid-2000s Guy Shorrock heard about two wildlife criminals who had recently been convicted in northern Canada for stealing gyrfalcon eggs, possibly for sale to clients in the Middle East. One of these men, Jeffrey Lendrum, was already in the Royal Society database for a conviction in Zimbabwe in 1984. The other, Paul

Mullin, had no previous record. Shorrock wrote to the Canadian authorities, seeking more information, but citing privacy laws, the Canadians refused to share details with the charity. Then Shorrock attended a Convention on International Trade in Endangered Species lecture in London that happened to be hosted by Canadian wildlife officials. As they narrated the story of the notorious 2002 gyrfalcon heist, Paul Mullin's name flashed on the screen, along with a home address in Southampton. *Is Mullin still stealing eggs from the wilderness?* Shorrock wondered.

Shorrock never shared the information with McWilliam. Despite their fruitful collaboration busting egg collectors in the early 2000s, jealousies and resentments had been building between the National Wildlife Crime Unit and the Royal Society for the Protection of Birds, and the two men in particular. "It's all to do with the fact that a non-government agency [gets] frustrated . . . the police can't share information [or] intelligence with them," McWilliam would tell Timothy Wheeler in his interview for *Poached*. A series of email exchanges, made public via Britain's Freedom of Information Act, would expose the wildlife unit's growing resistance to working with, and even disdain for, the charity. "I do think on occasions they have something to offer," McWilliam wrote to his colleagues in 2013, "but their expertise would have to be required and . . . the Police must keep control." He seemed to waver. "Or then again we could just say 'F*** them.'" It was an attitude the Royal Society for the Protection of Birds apparently reciprocated.

As it turned out, the National Wildlife Crime Unit had the story of Mullin and Lendrum's Canadian heist, conviction, and subsequent movements in its files as well—though nobody had checked through the piles of records at the unit's Stirling headquarters. The documents dated back to the founding of the original National Wildlife Crime Intelligence Unit in 2002, the same year that Mullin and Lendrum were arrested in Quebec, and had been transferred to Scotland after the unit shut down in 2005, where they had been all but forgotten. A perusal of the records might have revealed not only that Mullin had changed his name and was back in England, but another tantalizing development: after years of globe-trotting, Lendrum had settled with his now-wife in a suburban town in the West Midlands, within striking distance of the peregrine falcons of Scotland and Wales.

FOURTEEN

THE RHONDDA VALLEY

In the years that followed his guilty plea for stealing gyrfalcon eggs in Canada's Nunavik territory, Jeffrey Lendrum tried to settle into a normal life. In the summer of 2002, just weeks after his arrest, he married his girlfriend in Sospel, a medieval mountain village in the Department of Alpes-Maritimes, north of the French Riviera. Paul Mullin, now living under a new name in the hope of burying his conviction for wildlife crime, served as the best man. After the ceremony in the village registrar's office, 150 guests gathered outside to celebrate. Almost all were members of the bride's Algerian-immigrant family, although a handful of Lendrum's mates from southern Africa and England also made an appearance. Three days of Arabic-inflected singing, dancing, and fraternizing in and around the ancient alleys and plazas of Sospel followed. When the festivities ended, Lendrum returned to the house that his bride owned in Towcester, where together they continued to co-run AfricaXtreme. Lendrum made regular trips back to South Africa and Zimbabwe, both for business and to see friends and family. He was also serving as stepfather to his wife's two preadolescent daughters from her previous marriage. His egg snatching days seemed behind him.

But the business took a turn for the worse in 2003. The sale of African handicrafts in England had reached a saturation point, and income fell off dramatically. With losses growing, Mullin closed the shop in Southampton and transferred his remaining stake in the venture to Lendrum; he had invested many tens of thousands of British pounds, and lost the entire amount. Lendrum renamed the Towcester shop African Art & Curios and struggled to keep it going, at one point borrowing money from his sister, Paula's, husband so that he could refill his inventory in Zimbabwe. But he was forced to shut the business for good in 2008 and dispose of the unsold merchandise. That same year, Lendrum's marriage broke up and his friendship with Mullin ended. The trouble began after Mullin's South African girlfriend, who had followed her boyfriend to England, flew to Johannesburg with their infant daughter on holiday. During the visit she began a relationship with Lendrum, who by that point had drifted apart from his wife. Mullin's now-ex-girlfriend decided to remain in South Africa with Lendrum and the child. The move sparked a bitter custody fight, and Lendrum took her side.

After the collapse of his marriage, the loss of his business, and the fallout with his closest friend, Lendrum returned to a nomadic existence, dividing his time between his ex-wife's near-empty house in Towcester—which she'd stripped of furniture and was trying to sell—and a temporary place in Johannesburg. He was unmoored and looking for a new way to earn a living. And, as would happen whenever Lendrum found himself adrift, the evidence suggests that he resumed his exploits for his clients in the Middle East.

=

Mike Thomas first noticed disturbing things happening during the peregrine falcon breeding season of 2007. The leader of the South Wales Peregrine Monitoring Group, a volunteer organization with about a dozen members, Thomas spent weekends between March and May rappelling to aeries in the Garw (*Ga-ROO*) Valley and neighboring glens and gorges in the country's former coal-mining heartland, a region with one of the densest concentrations of peregrine falcons in Great Britain, about fifty breeding pairs. On a gray morning in early May, Thomas, a thickset man then in his fifties with thin wire spectacles and a lantern jaw, hiked from his home in Blaengarw through a Japanese larch forest to an abandoned rock quarry. He followed a steep trail to the summit of a sandstone cliff, fixed a rope, and climbed down the rock face to a nesting site on a ledge that he'd been monitoring since March. Approaching the "scrape," a shallow depression filled with gravel and flat pebbles to hold in heat and prevent the clutch from rolling off the ledge, Thomas made a dismaying discovery: the four eggs were gone.

Thomas's first thought was they had been snatched by one of the peregrine falcon's mortal enemies: a pigeon fancier, or a devotee of the ten-thousand-year-old practice of breeding or racing domestic pigeons, the falcon's most common prey. But this nest would have been impossible to access without rappelling equipment, and pigeon men, in Thomas's experience, tended to go after aeries that were not difficult to reach. In addition, they often left beer cans strewn about nesting sites and crushed eggs rather than make off with them. Besides, Thomas and his fellow volunteers knew almost every pigeon fancier in the Garw. The peregrine monitors had let them know, he says, "If you steal the eggs, we'll come after your pigeons."

Days after the Blaengarw eggs went missing, two other clutches disappeared nearby. The next breeding season, a peregrine clutch vanished from a high ledge across the mountains in the Rhondda Fawr Valley. The ledge was reachable only by a rappel so dangerous that Thomas believed the thief had to be a professional. "Whoever is climbing this is nobody we know," he told a fellow volunteer. The group recorded half a dozen disappearances the next year, 2009. And who knew how many more they hadn't found? Working at their own expense, the volunteers were forced to leave many remote aeries unattended.

Thomas was obsessed by the mystery of the missing clutches. Who had stolen them? And why? The thief was clearly a skilled climber and an experienced peregrine spotter, yet he must also have had help from a local. "You can spend days trying to locate these sites," he explained. He found it disturbing to speculate about how much damage the egg thief might have caused. "Some years twenty-six peregrine clutches were in the area," he said. If the nest raider had been systematically attacking peregrine aeries since 2007, Thomas reasoned, he could have stolen well over one hundred eggs.

—

On the morning of April 28, 2010—a Wednesday—Jeffrey Lendrum placed his climbing equipment into the trunk of his Vauxhall Vectra sedan in Towcester and drove alone two hours to the southwest to rural Wales. He checked into the Heritage Park Hotel in Pontypridd, a town of ancient stone bridges where the River Rhondda flows into the River Taff, and set out shortly after dawn the next morning for the thinly populated upper reaches of the Rhondda Fawr Valley. Years later, he would admit that this was one of many trips to Wales he had made between 2002 and 2010—but this one, he would swear, was his first and only egg snatching mission.

Seven years later, I made arrangements to meet Andy McWilliam and Ian Guildford, the Wales-based investigator with the National Wildlife Crime Unit, to retrace Lendrum's steps that day. On an unseasonably chilly May morning, Guildford—a bespectacled, rangy Londoner, who'd lived in Wales for four decades—picked me up at Cardiff's central rail station. We drove north through verdant hills, past the old coal-mining town of Aberfan, to where McWilliam was waiting at a McDonald's in the town of Merthyr Tydfil. The burly, gray-haired investigator had driven down from Liverpool that morning. He had the GPS points of the four aeries that Lendrum had looted in April 2010, which would enable us to follow his tracks. McWilliam wasn't sure, though, that we'd be able to catch sight of any peregrines. His bird-spotting skills, he admitted, had grown rusty through lack of practice. "A couple of years ago," he told me, "I'd walk through woodlands and say, 'There's a lesser yellow legs.' Now I go out and I say, 'What the hell is that?'"

We began a switchback climb through denuded sandstone hills, blanketed in lichens and pale green grass and rising several thousand feet above the Rhondda Fawr. Gouged by slow-moving glaciers during the last Ice Age between eighteen thousand and ten thousand years ago, the Rhondda Fawr (the Great Rhondda) and a smaller valley just to the east, the Rhondda Fach (the Little Rhondda), had once been covered with dense woodlands. Then, in the mid–nineteenth century, geologists discovered a rich seam of coal running beneath the surface of the two valleys, anywhere from a few dozen feet to half a mile down.

Soon tens of thousands of men had swapped subsistence farming for the steady cash wages of a life underground, and the forests were razed to make "pit props," beams that support the roofs of coal mines. "The hills have been stripped of all their woodland beauty, and there they stand, rugged and bare, with immense rubbish heaps covering their surface," wrote Arthur Morris in the 1908 book *Glamorgan*. "The river Rhondda is a dark, turgid, and contaminated gutter, into which is poured the refuse of the host of collieries which skirt the thirteen miles of its course." Then, in the 1970s, the anthracite began to run out, and the collieries closed, the last in 2008. Today the two Rhondda Valleys have among the highest unemployment rates in the British Isles.

The road climbed higher, the pale green slopes covered in places by netting to prevent landslides, and darkened here and there by stands of pine recently planted by the British Forestry Commission to stop the erosion. Brecon Beacons National Park, a dramatic range of red sandstone peaks dotted with the burial cairns of Bronze Age tribes, rose a few miles to the north. A sign noting the distances to nearby villages—Abergwynfi, Blaengwynfi, Nantymoel—captured the linguistic oddity of this remote corner of the United Kingdom. The language derives from ancient Celtic, brought over to the British Isles from continental Europe more than 2,500 years ago. As late as 1800, the majority of Wales' population spoke Welsh as their first language, but it fell out of the school curriculum in the late nineteenth century, and English soon came to dominate the region. Today, though something of a revival of Welsh is going on, barely one in five people in Wales can speak it.

When I stepped out of the vehicle at the top of the escarpment, I was nearly blown off my feet by a gust of wind. Steadying myself, I followed the two officers across a meadow speckled with purple and yellow wildflowers and low-growing fruit shrubs called bilberry bushes. Bleating sheep, bells around their necks chiming, darted across our path through spongy tufts of grass. Bent against the gale, we arrived at the edge of the cliffs.

The ground fell away sharply, exposing dozens of steplike gray-black ledges sheltered from the wind—perfect spots for peregrines to lay their eggs. "We're at the end of the bloody world," shouted Guildford.

We walked around the edge of the cliffs to another lookout, this one providing a panoramic view of the escarpment. A smooth, curving ampitheater of black and tan sandstone, mottled with patches of grass, swept upward at a near-perpendicular angle from the Rhondda Valley floor. McWilliam and Guildford scanned the cloud-dappled sky with their binoculars, searching for peregrine falcons. They weren't able to spot one.

Lendrum had enjoyed much better luck. The egg thief waited patiently atop this escarpment, also peering through binoculars, looking for male falcons returning to their aeries with food for their incubating partners. At eight a.m. on Thursday, April 29, Lendrum laid a fixed rope at the top of the cliff and rappelled twenty feet down to a ledge, scooping up the clutch as the peregrine parents flew off in fright. He placed the four eggs in his thermal bag. He took a second clutch at four p.m., retired to the Heritage Park Hotel, and then returned the next morning at eight-thirty for two more rappels down the cliffs. That day, he seized seven more eggs—including one clutch at the abandoned quarry near Mike Thomas's village of Blaengarw in the adjacent Garw Valley. Back in Towcester, he wrapped the eggs snugly in woolen socks to keep them warm and well cushioned, and placed them in a carton in his carry-on bag. With his unsuspecting girlfriend—Paul Mullin's ex-partner, who was now sharing a life with Lendrum in South Africa—in the passenger seat beside him, he set out for Birmingham Airport.

"I've got a lucky ability," Lendrum would say years later when asked to explain his success at finding nests in the most remote and forbidding terrain. "I will always ask myself, 'If I were a peregrine, what would I do? Where would I breed?' I go to an area that looks good, I look carefully and I see them."

=

On Monday afternoon, May 3, responding to a tip from the vigilant janitor in the Emirates Lounge, Counter Terrorism agents detained Lendrum and seized the fourteen peregrine eggs that he had snatched from cliffsides in and around the Rhondda Valley. Thirty hours after Lendrum's arrest, on the early evening of Tuesday, May 4, Andy McWilliam and a colleague from the Counter Terrorism Unit (who cannot be named for reasons of security) sat in a borrowed office at the Solihull Police Headquarters, evaluating their notes from the afternoon's interrogations. The commanding officer at Solihull had extended Lendrum's detention period from twenty-four to thirty-six hours—a standard move in complicated cases. At the end of that period, the Crown Prosecution Service would assess the arrest report presented by the police and determine whether or not to file charges. If McWilliam and his partner failed to persuade prosecutors that Lendrum had committed a serious crime, the police would have no choice but to release him. Should Lendrum walk out of jail, McWilliam had no doubt that the suspect would "do a runner" and flee England as quickly as possible.

McWilliam and his partner in the Counter Terrorism force spent the evening going over their notes and typing a case summary. Then, at nine p.m., four hours before the deadline, they faxed the document to CPS Direct, a national 24/7 hotline that connects a duty prosecutor with police seeking to charge a suspect with a crime. The Counter Terrorism man got on the phone with the assigned prosecutor.

"We've got a man in custody who was attempting to smuggle fourteen peregrine falcon eggs out of the United Kingdom," he said.

The agent explained that the peregrine was an Appendix I bird, granted the highest level of protection by the Convention on International Trade in Endangered Species. Smuggling its eggs was a breach of the Customs and Excise Management Act of 1979, as well as the Control of Trade in Endangered Species Regulations of 1997. The suspect's acts were also violations of many other pieces of legislation: the European Union Wildlife Trade Regulations of 1996, the Endangered Species Act of 1976, the Wildlife and Countryside Act of 1981, the Theft Act of 1968, the Birds Directive of 1979, and the EU Habitats Directive of 1992. The suspect had been caught with incubators, a satnav, and climbing equipment. The circumstances of the arrest pointed to a "sophisticated one-man operation." What's more, he was not a British citizen, had no fixed address in the United Kingdom, and was traveling on a foreign passport.

"If we bail him," he said, "the guy is going on his toes."

The prosecutor listened mostly without comment.

"I just don't know the legislation," she said. "I think I need to do some research on this and get back to you."

McWilliam and his partner paced the halls, checking their watches for one hour, two, three . . . The minutes ticked by, and McWilliam's frustration grew. At the front desk of the custody suites, the night clerk gathered Lendrum's personal effects in preparation for his release. Finally, just before one a.m., with two minutes to go before the deadline, the duty inspector at the Solihull station, the highest-ranking officer in the building that night, stepped in to make an executive decision. (Though Crown prosecutors ordinarily have the final call on whether to charge a suspect, senior police officers can take on that role in emergencies.)

"Charge him," he said, overriding the usual procedure. He ordered Lendrum held overnight.

Early the next morning, at the Solihull Magistrates Court, a judge denied Lendrum's bail application, citing the gravity of his alleged offenses and the risk of flight. Court officers escorted Lendrum in handcuffs to pretrial detention in Hewell Prison, a twelve-hundred-bed maximum- and minimum-security facility on the grounds of a Victorian manor house in Worcestershire, southwest of Birmingham, to await a plea hearing in August—three months away.

===

As Lendrum remained locked up in a cellblock filled with prisoners who had likewise been denied bail, McWilliam began methodically to build the case against him. At this point, just two days after the egg thief's arrest, McWilliam had only circumstantial evidence that he was dealing with an experienced criminal—until he sat down to watch an unmarked DVD the Counter Terrorism police had discovered in one of Lendrum's carry-on bags. As the images rolled by—a Ray-Ban-wearing helicopter pilot smirking and announcing that he and Lendrum were "going on a tour," Lendrum dangling from a line seven hundred feet above a frozen lake, a Bell JetRanger hovering inches from a cliff, gyrfalcons circling overhead—McWilliam stared in amazement. Here was a video of Lendrum's pilot boasting about their being "fucking criminals," and it had fallen into the hands of the police. While it was still technically possible that Lendrum had, as he claimed, stumbled upon the Welsh peregrine eggs by chance, it was clear from the video that the risks, costs, and planning involved in this other operation must have been enormous.

McWilliam would soon learn that Lendrum's felonious missions had apparently extended to every corner of the globe—as free-ranging as the peregrine itself. On the suspect's laptop computer (which wasn't password protected), he pored through a Microsoft Word document that described a trip made to Sri Lanka in February 2010 to search for the aeries of the black shaheen falcon (*Falco peregrinus peregrinator*)—a powerful, nonmigratory peregrine subspecies that roosts on rock faces from Pakistan to northern Myanmar. Only forty breeding pairs are known to inhabit the island. "One [falcon] seen flying off rock . . . good site with large overhang, several places with droppings," read an account of a scouting mission to the jungled cliffs near Wellawaya. A nearby site proved to be less promising. "Military guarding elephants in area and every time [you] step [from] the car, they come out of the trees to ask what you are doing. Hard access to rock and military make this a no-go."

Lendrum—or whoever had written the report—then visited Sigiriya, a massive, six-hundred-sixty-foot column of congealed magma from an extinct volcano, with a stone palace at the summit carved by the fifth-century King Kasyapa. Neither this archaeological masterpiece nor the delicate sixteen-hundred-year-old frescoes of the women of the royal harem were of interest to the writer. "Good rock face not able to observe due to sun coming right into lens in morning," he wrote. "Mature male on rock face, very nice color with very small white bib." The author of the document also cased the security at Bandaranaike International Airport in Colombo. "On drive into airport there is security check and they open boots and doors of many vehicles to check inside," he noted. "A few meters inside doors to departure area there is a security checkpoint consisting of a row of standard baggage X-ray units, walk-through metal detector and just about everybody was patted down. The guy who patted me down was very good at it."

The notes left no doubt about where the author had flown to after leaving the jungled island. "Dubai customs were very iffy about the night vision glasses we had in our hand luggage," he warned, leaving the "we" unidentified. Lendrum would deny writing the report and, when asked if he had ever visited Sri Lanka, began to ramble. "I don't remember that, no," he would say a few years later, before adding, "We went to go and look at peregrines there. I can't remember when . . . I think it was probably just before Wales. They are beautiful birds. It's just a different subspecies of the peregrine. But I wasn't going out there to get them, no."

Days later, a key found in Lendrum's carry-on luggage, along with a receipt for the rental of a storage facility, led McWilliam to a Lok'nStore in Northamptonshire. Amid suitcases, duffel bags, and Sainsbury's shopping bags jammed inside a locker six feet high and five feet deep, he discovered more evidence of his quarry's outlaw life: an incubator purchased on eBay days before his mission to southern Wales, police records and a *Nunatsiaq News* account of his arrest in Canada back in 2002, and a copy of a letter Lendrum had written to the reporter behind the *Nunatsiaq News* article, in which he claimed to have been on a research project to determine "the effects of global warming" on gyrfalcons and insisted that he had planned to return the eggs to the nests. Lendrum's mischief went back decades, and, like some of the English egg collectors McWilliam had pursued, he had collected a trove of mementos documenting his bad behavior: there was correspondence from the early 1980s laying out a scheme apparently concocted by Jeffrey and Adrian Lendrum to smuggle African black eagle eggs and chicks to a breeder in Birmingham—just as Kit Hustler, the Zimbabwean ornithologist and prosecution witness at the Lendrums' 1984 trial, had long suspected. The breeder they'd been in contact with, Philip Dugmore, had been convicted and fined two years later for illegally keeping six black eagles. The raptors "in all probability, came from the supply of eggs from this defendant to him," Lendrum's new prosecutor would soon declare in court.

=

Then McWilliam secured another compelling piece of evidence. Paul Mullin, now living in southern England, learned from news reports that summer that his former friend had been arrested with falcon eggs at Birmingham Airport. Still bearing a grudge against Lendrum— "Karma's a bitch," he would say—he phoned the airport police. "If you want to know anything about Jeffrey Lendrum, I can help," he told the officer who answered the call. The policeman relayed the message to McWilliam, who called Mullin back within minutes. They met at a police station in Newbury, a market town south of Oxford, but the initial encounter didn't go well. "I was with Lendrum when he was caught in Canada," Mullin told McWilliam, as two Newbury officers hovered in the background. The constables interrupted the interview, and cautioned Mullin that anything he said could be used against him. "What I'm about to tell you is outside of your jurisdiction," Mullin snapped. "If you're not happy, I'm walking." Mullin called an early end to the encounter.

McWilliam arranged a second, private meeting at a highway rest stop in Oxfordshire. Wearing a baseball cap and sunglasses this time, and claiming to be worried that he was being followed, Mullin sat at a table across from the investigator and didn't stop talking for an hour. He brought photographs, plane tickets, receipts, field notes, maps, the business cards of the arresting officers in Kuujjuaq, and other evidence of his escapades with Lendrum and the helicopter pilot. He recounted his falling-out with his former best friend after Lendrum had taken up with his girlfriend and then written a letter to a judge in support of her application for full custody of her and Mullin's young daughter. He also showed McWilliam a photograph taken at Heathrow Airport of Lendrum and Howard Waller, whom Mullin maintained had sponsored the mission to Canada. McWilliam graded Mullin an "E41" according to police-intelligence lingo, meaning an "untested source"; there was no way to be certain that he was telling the truth. But McWilliam found him personable and credible, and the documents he presented supported his account. "I couldn't see a motivation to lie," he said.

Soon after that, Pat Lorber, formerly of the Rhodesian Ornithological Society, reached out to McWilliam from King's Lynn, in East Anglia, where she had settled after leaving Zimbabwe two decades earlier. She, too, had read newspaper accounts of Lendrum's arrest. Lorber filled in another critical part of Lendrum's bizarre life story: the scandal and trial in Bulawayo in 1984.

In the meantime, McWilliam had obtained persuasive evidence that Lendrum had not been acting alone in Wales. Colin Pirie, the National Wildlife Crime Unit's chief of intelligence, tracked Lendrum's vehicle through a police system that uses a countrywide network of license-plate recognition cameras. Pirie determined that

Lendrum had been to the Rhondda Valley in early April, three weeks before robbing the nests. He'd exchanged two hundred phone calls and text messages with a local breeder, to pinpoint the exact locations of the aeries. "If you've got somebody local who's keeping an eye on them, it makes the job easier," McWilliam would later say.

Police specialists traced the calls to a man named Robert Griffiths in the village of Ton Pentre at the upper end of the Rhondda Fawr, a few miles from Lendrum's primary nest-robbing zone. Law enforcement officers knew him as a career raptor snatcher. Guildford had arrested him in Scotland in the 1980s for stealing peregrines, and again in the 1990s for laundering merlins—small, powerfully built falcons—at his breeding facility. He was still selling birds of dubious provenance, and was said to be familiar with every ledge and crag in the Rhondda and its adjacent glens. "He knows more about the wild birds than those out there protecting them," Guildford said. "He knows their breeding habits, and he knows exactly where to look." When Guildford confronted Griffith in Ton Pentre with evidence that he had provided grid points to Lendrum, the breeder denied knowing the egg thief. The National Wildlife Crime Unit decided not to pursue criminal charges against him, but the discovery of the phone messages provided insight into Lendrum's modus operandi.

There were aspects of the case that McWilliam never could figure out—like why the janitor in the Emirates Lounge had found that one red-dyed egg in the diaper bin—but that Lendrum would later explain. Before arriving at the airport, he would say, he had placed the fourteen live peregrine eggs in a nine-egg carton and a six-egg carton, and he needed to fill the last slot with a similar-looking egg. He wanted it to look as if he had just bought ordinary farm-fresh eggs at the supermarket: "If [security] opened an egg box, they would just look like a whole bunch of spotted eggs. And I would say, 'Okay, take them.'"

Despite a few unanswered questions, McWilliam's summerlong investigation had exposed the patterns of a master criminal: an adventurer, athlete, and logistician who had operated confidently for decades. He had conspired to pillage the environment with unnamed "senior members of UAE society" for "significant" financial gain, acccording to a PowerPoint display that McWilliam would put together that year for the media and fellow officers. McWilliam had a pretty good idea of who some of Lendrum's clients were, but he couldn't reveal so publicly until they had been formally charged with a crime: that would be a violation of Great Britain's privacy laws.

The investigator was developing complicated feelings for the thief. "He's well traveled, he's fearless, he's resourceful, and his preparation is superb," said McWilliam. "I respected him without wanting to condone what he did." Nevin Hunter, who would command the National Wildlife Crime Unit from 2012 to 2014, shared his colleague's respect for Lendrum's gifts. Both of them had dealt with hundreds of wildlife criminals in their careers, but neither had encountered one who had covered so much ground, employed such flamboyant methods to carry out his thefts, and been so apparently successful at moving living, fragile creatures across vast distances. "I sat down with Andy, Ian Guildford, and Alan Roberts, one hundred fifty years of experience among us, and we couldn't come up with any other individual who works like Lendrum does," Hunter would say. "He identified a marketplace that hadn't been exploited by any criminal, and he was ideally suited for it."

Perhaps it was possible to appreciate Lendrum's accomplishments without too much guilt because the thief hadn't threatened any species with extinction. "Peregrines and gyrfalcons are not going to die out because one guy takes their eggs to sell to the Arab market," McWilliam's colleague Alan Roberts said, although he did sadly concede that "the principle is there. If the sheikhs decide that a more vulnerable species is going to be what they want, Lendrum made sure that all the mechanisms are in place."

In any event, begrudging respect didn't stop McWilliam from building a strong case. To round out his picture of Lendrum for the prosecution, McWilliam asked Nick Fox, the Wales-based falcon breeder to Sheikh Mohammed bin Rashid Al Maktoum, the ruler of Dubai, to estimate the value of the thirteen live peregrine eggs found on Lendrum's person. Fox projected that ten would have survived the journey to Dubai, and half would have been female. At £10,000 for a wild female, and £5,000 for a wild male, which is two-thirds the female's size and generally a slower racer, he placed a market value, in a sworn affidavit that would be presented in court, of £75,000 on the lot, then worth about $117,000. Officials of the Convention on International Trade in Endangered Species based in the United Arab Emirates corroborated the figure. Though far more conservative than other estimates of wild falcon prices over the years, the sum would hardly have been a bad income for a single month's work.

——

At the Warwick Crown Court in Royal Leamington Spa outside Birmingham, a media-heavy crowd began forming in the hour before Lendrum's mid-morning plea hearing on August 19, 2010. Alerted by McWilliam, reporters from the BBC, Sky News, the *Independent*, the *Sun*, the *Daily Mail*, and the *Times*, as well as local TV, radio, and print journalists, converged on the eighteenth-century colonnaded courthouse, one of the oldest still in use in Great Britain. The tale of the globe-trotting thief who had rappelled down cliffs to steal live falcon eggs on behalf of Arab sheikhs was irresistible to the tabloids and the evening news. McWilliam noted the satellite trucks as he walked up the courthouse steps, pleasantly surprised by the turnout. The outcome of the appearance was not in doubt: prosecutor Nigel Williams had let it be known that Lendrum, facing a compendium of powerful evidence against him, would acknowledge his guilt on one count of theft of an endangered species and one count of smuggling in violation of the regulations of the Convention on International Trade in Endangered Species. He hoped for a lighter sentence, possibly just a fine, in return.

McWilliam walked past the gallery in the small, wood-paneled courtroom—from which eighteenth-century thieves and murderers had been delivered in irons to the hangman. A few feet away, Lendrum sat in the dock. Not a single friend or family member was present. The falcon thief nodded at the investigator in recognition. McWilliam nodded back. McWilliam had faced plenty of defendants who'd hurled obscenities at him or threatened him in the courtroom. "I've been to court where I wouldn't piss on a defendant if he was on fire," McWilliam would say. He had once arrested and brought to trial a goshawk launderer named Leonard O'Connor, "a grade-one asshole," he says, who had flashed him his middle finger from the witness box every time the magistrate wasn't looking. McWilliam responded to each insult by repeating the obscene gesture. "We were like a pair of children," he would say with a laugh. Lendrum—polite and soft-spoken—was a pleasant change from such surly characters.

"You all right?" McWilliam asked.

Lendrum shrugged. "I've been keeping okay," he replied.

"You're pleading guilty," McWilliam said.

"Well," Lendrum replied, "you caught me bang to rights."

Judge Christopher Hodson entered the courtroom. He asked Lendrum to rise.

"How do you plead?"

"I'm guilty, Your Honor."

Lendrum's advocate, Nicola Purches, told the judge that her client had been "a model prisoner" in the remand block at Hewell. He was remorseful and ashamed, and the crime was completely out of character. What was more, Lendrum's father, Adrian, a lifetime heavy smoker now in his seventies, had developed emphysema, and had only a few months to live. His son hoped to fly to Zimbabwe and see him, Purches said, before he died.

Hodson asked Lendrum to rise again and to listen while he quoted from *Costing the Earth*, a document that Lord Justice Stephen Sedley, a distinguished appeals-court jurist, had prepared the previous year as a guide for sentencing wildlife criminals. "The environmental crime strikes not only at a locality and its population but at the planet and its future," Sedley had declared. "Nobody should be allowed to doubt its seriousness." Lendrum, Hodson said, had been motivated by the basest of reasons, "commercial profit . . . The amount that you would have needed to expend, on equipment, on travel, and in preparation, in my judgment proves that," he continued. "You have had two previous warnings of the consequences of dealing in protected wild birds and their eggs; convicted in 1984 in Zimbabwe; and in 2002 in Canada."

Then Hodson pronounced his judgment. "At the end of the day, a substantial sentence . . . needs to be imposed to punish you and deter others," he said. "The sentence on the indictment will be one of thirty months' imprisonment."

"Bloody hell," muttered McWilliam from a side bench. Two and a half years. The sentence was tougher than he had been expecting. He was happy enough to take the falcon thief out of circulation for a while, but he felt unexpected ambivalence about this punishment. Like a master jewel thief or other skilled practioner of the felonious arts, the man commanded appreciation of his talents, however twisted they might be. McWilliam regarded him as an accomplished adversary. He had even come to like him, in a way. He glanced at Lendrum, who looked back, stunned.

—

Over the next days, British newspapers devoted pages of coverage to Lendrum's exploits. "Caged: The £70K Egg Snatcher," the *Daily Mirror* declared. "A Bird in the Hand, a Smuggler in Jail," ran the front-page headline in the *Times* of London. "Jailed, Former Soldier Caught Smuggling £70,000 of Falcon Eggs," the *Daily Mail* proclaimed, reporting, inaccurately, that Lendrum had served in the Rhodesian SAS. The *Independent*, also embellishing a tale that needed no exaggeration, repeated the misreporting that Lendrum was "a former member of the Rhodesian SAS." Lendrum, the paper reported, "becomes the first person in 19 years to be prosecuted in the UK for attempting to smuggle peregrine falcon eggs out of the country," a reference to the two German citizens who had pleaded guilty in 1991 to smuggling twelve live eggs hidden in the dashboard of their Mercedes. The *Daily Express* ran a photo spread of "The Rare Falcon Chicks Saved from Clutches of Daring Egg Smuggler," while spinning a sensational yarn that bore little relation to the truth.

"Police feared a terrorist attack on a British airport was underway," the piece began. "The ingredients were all there—a shady character acting in a suspicious manner who was once a special forces soldier for a foreign power. Among his possessions were thousand of pounds in cash. But it wasn't explosives he was trying to sneak onto an international airliner—it was rare bird eggs."

McWilliam gave television producers permission to use the confiscated video from northern Canada, and dramatic excerpts played and played on British TV. Back in Bulawayo, members of BirdLife Zimbabwe and others who had felt betrayed by Lendrum in the 1980s expressed satisfaction that justice had been served. "At last the fellow is in prison, though a spell in a Zimbabwean jail might be a more effective deterrent," wrote Peter Mundy, the ornithology professor and friend of Val Gargett, who had once tried to arrange Lendrum's extradition to Zimbabwe, in the magazine *Honeyguide*. Mundy acknowledged that much of the case was likely to remain a mystery. "Few of the end users of illegally obtained wildlife ever seem to get convicted," he wrote. Lendrum "has proven himself to be an unrepentant reprobate and will presumably remain tight-lipped so we may never know his contacts."

Both the media and McWilliam had left another important question unanswered: What had happened to the money? Under the provisions of the Wildlife and Countryside Act, the police had confiscated everything that Lendrum had been traveling with: his Vauxhall Vectra Estate car, laptops, incubators, a spotting scope, cameras, lenses, and climbing equipment, as well as an expensive mountain bike that he was shipping back to South Africa, and a few thousand British pounds and US dollars. The total value of the forfeiture was placed at £20,000. Lendrum had a part interest with South African friends in a Cessna aircraft and owned a four-by-four in Johannes-burg, both of which were outside the jurisdiction of the British au-thorities. But a search for other assets under the 2002 Proceeds of Crime Act would turn up little else. A close friend in Zimbabwe had once jokingly called Lendrum "the world's poorest thief." The mys-tery lingered, and Lendrum wasn't talking.

McWilliam had a bite with the Counter Terorrism agent who'd worked on the case with him from the beginning and then made the 130-mile drive home to Liverpool, answering a dozen more report-ers' calls along the way. After brewing coffee and watching the late-evening news on the BBC, featuring images of Lendrum dangling from a helicopter, McWilliam and his wife went to bed.

One hundred ten miles away at Hewell, Jeffrey Lendrum settled into his first night in his cell as a convicted endangered-species smug-gler, still insisting that he was misunderstood, and still holding se-crets that McWilliam was determined to shake loose.

FIFTEEN

PRISON

After his sentencing, Jeffrey Lendrum moved into a wing for convicted felons at the high-security "B" block of Her Majesty's Prison Hewell. During his three months awaiting trial, his cellmate had been Jonathan Palmer, a white-haired former businessman accused (and later convicted) of bludgeoning his wife to death in the hallway of their home after she discovered his multiple affairs. Now he had a new cellmate and a new prison routine that stressed rehabilitation and vocational workshops. Cells opened at seven forty-five. Then came showers, breakfast, job training, lunch, cell cleaning, menial work, classes, dinner, gym, and a lockup at six-fifteen p.m. The staff offered prisoners a choice among courses in construction, double-glazing manufacture, industrial cleaning, waste management, and laundry services. Lendrum, who was forty-nine years old and had never held a nine-to-five job since managing the cannery in Bulawayo in his early twenties, wasn't interested.

Yet Lendrum discovered certain satisfactions in his life behind bars. As he moved through the exercise yard, cafeteria, and other communal areas of the cellblock, he was often treated like a celebrity.

Hardened felons wanted to hear about his adventures and expressed surprise, amusement, and sympathy that Lendrum was doing two and a half years for stealing eggs. "You got hit for taking birds?" they would ask. "My God, this country is nuts." Some prisoners, amazed by the reports that peregrine eggs could be sold in the Arab world for £5,000 or £10,000 apiece, begged him for tips on finding aeries. Lendrum assured them that the stories were "grossly exaggerated" and that the market price of a peregrine egg was barely one-tenth of that.

Two months into Lendrum's sentence, Andy McWilliam made an appointment to see him. Now that Lendrum had pleaded guilty to trafficking in wild peregrine eggs, the investigator hoped that he might be more forthcoming about his Middle Eastern sponsors. McWilliam had become increasingly aware of the role of wealthy Arabs in the underground falcon market. With Lendrum's admission of culpability, he saw an opportunity to implicate specific sheikhs—and pressure the Emirates or other Gulf states to take action. Lendrum was "a guy at the top of his game," recalled McWilliam, who a few days earlier had attended a ceremony in Birmingham presided over by Great Britain's Environmental Minister, honoring the sharp-eyed Emirates Lounge janitor, John Struczynski, for his contribution to Lendrum's May 2010 arrest. "We wanted him to spill the beans." And perhaps, McWilliam acknowledges, he hoped for more than that. From his encounters with repeat offenders such as Carlton D'Cruze, who had admitted he might never be able to control the impulse to raid aeries, and Gregory Peter Wheal, who had been arrested for stealing eggs ten times in a decade, McWilliam knew how difficult it was for a recidivist egg snatcher to break from lifelong criminalty. Still, he thought that maybe—just maybe—Lendrum would find a path out of the outlaw life.

McWilliam and his colleague from the West Midlands Counter Terrorism Unit drove through the gates to the old country estate one fall afternoon and followed a road past the manor house to the high-security block. They parked the vehicle, passed on foot through several more gates, and waited for Lendrum in a private interview room just off a sprawling prisoners' lounge. The falcon thief cast them a broad smile when he appeared. He shook their hands and sat opposite them at a scuffed table, chatting amiably about conditions inside the prison. After the shock of receiving a two-and-a-half-year jail sentence, he was surprisingly relaxed and seemed to be coming to terms with his loss of liberty. He was looking to the future, he told McWilliam. He had signed up for a photo-editing course, and was learning Adobe Lightroom and Photoshop.

Lendrum also seemed willing to cooperate with the police. He turned over to McWilliam the GPS points of all four aeries that he had robbed in the Rhondda and Garw Valleys. He dropped inside information about the birds-of-prey trade in Southern Africa, mentioning species that he knew were being systematically taken from Matobo and other Zimbabwe reserves and smuggled abroad. (A decade later, McWilliam still wouldn't say whether Lendrum had identified individual trappers and smugglers by name. Such material remained "restricted intelligence" under British law, and he could be criminally prosecuted for divulging it.) He spoke emotionally about his father, Adrian, who had died on September 2, two weeks after Lendrum's guilty plea, following a long struggle with emphysema. Great Britain's Prison and Probation Service had turned down his request to attend his father's funeral in South Africa.

But when pressed for intelligence about his clients in the Arab world, Lendrum claimed not to know what McWilliam was talking about. He didn't have any business in the Middle East, he insisted. McWilliam asked about his relationship with Howard Waller, mentioning a photo he had seen of Lendrum and Waller sitting together in a bar at Heathrow. Lendrum admitted that he had known Waller growing up in Rhodesia, but denied ever smuggling eggs for him. He insisted that he had stolen the live peregrine eggs in southern Wales to save them from being destroyed by pigeon fanciers. "It was spur of the moment," he said. "If you had seen me in Africa, and seen how I rescue things, then I think you would understand me. I catch snakes. I'm nuts." He was still covering for his Arab patrons, McWilliam assumed, perhaps fearful of retribution, perhaps eager to return to business with them once he was released from prison.

Despite his continuing evasiveness, the Hewell administration considered Lendrum a model prisoner who stood a good chance of successful reintegration into society. In late autumn, shortly after the visit from McWilliam, the governess rewarded him for his good behavior by moving him across the grounds to Hewell's Grange Resettlement Unit, a manor house that had once belonged to the Earls of Plymouth. The Grange had no formal lights-out, no lockdowns, and practically no supervision; prisoners lived together in a dormitory. The governess's only caution was a half-joking warning to Lendrum that "your pilot friend" refrain from "attempting a rescue" in his helicopter. Prisoners had relaxed phone privileges as well, and one of the first people Lendrum reached out to was McWilliam. He chatted about his progress in his photo course and mounted his usual defense of his actions in the Rhondda Valley, without any prompting from McWilliam this time, rambling on about pigeon fanciers and the shootings and poisonings of peregrines. "If I hadn't saved those birds nobody would have," he told the officer. Surprised by the call,

McWilliam wondered whether any of his friends or family had been by to visit.

=

Soon Lendrum received more good news. On February 1, England's Court of Appeals ruled that his punishment was "manifestly excessive and out of step with the sentences imposed in earlier cases" of bird smuggling, including that of Harry Sissen, the North Yorkshire rare-parrot trafficker whose two-and-a-half-year sentence had been reduced to eighteen months on appeal. Citing Lendrum's willingness to plead guilty and his "family circumstances in South Africa," the court reduced his sentence to eighteen months, including time served. Providing that he could present a proper residential address and find employment, the prisoner was free to leave Hewell immediately on parole. He would, however, have to remain in the United Kingdom for another nine months, until the end of his reduced sentence, and report weekly to a court officer.

Lendrum, as it turned out, did still have friends—one of whom put him in touch with an acquaintance named Charles Graham, an entrepreneur who owned four go-kart tracks in southern England. Graham agreed to take on the parolee as a rehabilitation project, and got him a job greeting customers, giving safety demonstrations, helping with catering, and serving as a "race marshal" on the nine-hundred-meter track at his Daytona Sandown Park. Soon Lendrum, his girlfriend, and her toddler daughter, Paul Mullin's child, moved into a wing of Graham's house on the North Downs, a ridge of chalk hills running west from the White Cliffs of Dover. The three settled into a comfortable life in limbo—making ample use of Graham's swimming pool and hot tub all summer long. "He had no bills to pay, he had food on the table every night," says Graham. Lendrum entertained employees at the track with stories about his nine months in prison and even bragged about his jailhouse nickname, the Birdman. "Jeff had this South African bonhomie," remembers Graham. "He was a swashbuckling adventurer." Over beers in the hot tub with Graham, Lendrum dropped his guard and admitted that he had stolen the falcon eggs for the money, estimating that the last operation in Wales could have brought a sum "in the high five figures" if he hadn't been caught at Birmingham Airport. Yet he assured other friends that he had put that phase of his life behind him. "He told me he was finished with it," says Craig Hunt, the boyhood mate who owned the Southern Comfort Lodge in Bulawayo. "He would never do it again."

=

At the end of 2011, his parole over, Lendrum returned to South Africa and moved in with his younger sister, Paula, and her husband in Johannesburg. Lendrum's brother, Richard—who'd had little contact with his brother during his months in prison—decided to join in helping his wayward sibling get back on his feet. As the publisher and editor in chief of *African Hunting Gazette*, a glossy quarterly with a print run of sixteen thousand, Richard hired his brother to replace a departing staff member who worked on Visited & Verified, an online customer guide to lodges, camps, and safari outfitters in Southern Africa. Jeffrey Lendrum "is excited to travel and meet prospective clients and friends in the hunting fraternity," the magazine's website declared in early 2012, introducing the new employee to readers of *African Hunting Gazette*, which mostly combined reviews of the latest weaponry and ammo with personal accounts of big game shooting safaris. "He's a wildlife enthusiast with an immense love for

Africa's flora and fauna and has spent many of his fifty years in the bush. His interest and knowledge is diverse, from the Big Five" game animals—lions, leopards, rhinos, elephants, and Cape buffalo—"to birds and insects."

For the second time since leaving prison, Lendrum had been offered a fresh start—and he seemed grateful for the opportunity to turn his life around. He traveled the hunting circuit, meeting safari lodge owners, touring their properties, authenticating their claims about the big game and terrain they offered hunters, and then passing on the information to the editorial staff. He was earning a decent salary, staying out of trouble, and spending his time in the environments where he had always been most content: the mopane woodlands, riverine bush, and thornveld savanna of Southern Africa.

One day McWilliam got a call from Johannesburg. "Hey, Andy, it's Jeffrey," the caller said. It took McWilliam a moment to register that the falcon thief was on the line. McWilliam hadn't expected to hear from him again, but Lendrum laid on an odd request: he needed help resolving a dispute about a parking ticket that he'd received before leaving England. "I wasn't even driving the bloody car," he told McWilliam.

"I thought to myself, *This is strange. If he's in Johannesburg, what the hell does it matter?*" McWilliam recalled. "Whether it was just an excuse to ring me up, I don't know." McWilliam told him there was nothing he could do.

Soon Lendrum was calling him every two or three weeks. He talked enthusiastically about the wildlife he'd seen and how grateful he was for this second chance. He shared his views on wildlife conservation, criticizing a program being introduced in Zimbabwe, Namibia, and South Africa to remove the horns from live rhinos to discourage poaching. "People will still follow the trail and shoot the animal. How are they going to know?" he said, dismissing the idea as ridiculous. He blamed the Convention on International Trade in Endangered Species in part for the rhino poaching epidemic, arguing that it had forced the rhino-horn trade underground, driven up prices, and created a black market. "If there was total transparency, rhino, as well as any endangered species, could be farmed like cattle," he said. McWilliam found Lendrum knowledgable and thoughtful, and he had to admit that much of what he said sounded reasonable. Eventually Lendrum came around to discussing raptors; the laws made no sense, he maintained. Lendrum tried to get McWilliam to agree that CITES should recategorize the peregrine falcon as a less endangered species and allow a certain amount of harvesting and exporting of wild birds of prey. "Whatever," McWilliam replied. His job was to enforce the law; he was happy to let the scientists and politicians make policy.

On another call, Lendrum surprised McWilliam with an invitation to come to South Africa for a safari. "You can stay with me," he even said. He'd moved out of his sister's and was renting his own place. McWilliam declined, knowing that fraternizing with a convicted wildlife criminal, even a reformed one, was hardly appropriate for a wildlife crime investigator. But he was touched—if a little puzzled—that Lendrum was intent on maintaining a relationship with him. Lendrum would extend the offer to McWilliam several more times.

=

While Lendrum was roving the bush for *African Hunting Gazette*, McWilliam was becoming enmeshed in office politics. In early 2010, a new boss had taken command of the National Wildlife Crime Unit. A former homicide detective with no wildlife experience, the man came across to some of his employees as a remote and clueless self-promoter. He disappeared from headquarters for days at a time, attending conferences in far-flung locations like China and India, burning through the unit's limited budget, and rarely explaining his absences. The staff took to calling him "the Walking Eagle" behind his back, because, McWilliam explained, "He's filled with so much shit that he can't get off the ground."

In February 2012, the *Scottish Sun* ran a puff piece about the crime unit boss called "Cop's Work on the Wild Side." The article compared him to the hero of a popular Hollywood comedy. "Unlike Jim Carrey's wacky character in *Ace Ventura: Pet Detective*, he is deadly serious about his role," the profile began. He bragged about the achievements of the unit since he had taken over, including "his greatest collar . . . an infamous smuggler who stole rare bird eggs to order." McWilliam couldn't believe that the man was taking credit for bagging Jeffrey Lendrum. McWilliam hadn't even informed him until after the arrest had gone down.

But the most insulting part of the profile was the chief's characterization of the NWCU. "Before I took over, the unit was seen as 'fluffy bunny,'" he told the reporter, "but things have changed since then." McWilliam was infuriated by the insinuation that he and the other seasoned investigators were sentimental animal huggers. He fired off several angry emails, accusing him of denigrating and demoralizing the staff. The chief claimed that the *Scottish Sun* reporter had made up the quote; McWilliam contacted the journalist, who stood by his reporting. When the chief found out, he berated McWilliam for speaking to the press without permission, and threatened to discipline him. "Bring it on," McWilliam dared. For weeks, it was unclear whether McWilliam would be fired from the unit. The dispute eventually subsided, but McWilliam and his superior never spoke to each other again.

==

In the spring of 2013, Jeffrey Lendrum passed his first anniversary working for his brother's magazine. He had, his brother, Richard, believed, finally put his days as an egg thief behind him. Then, that April, Jerome Philippe, a hunting concessionaire in Namibia and the founder of a popular website called AfricanHunting.com, posted an alert on the members' forum. "Jeffrey Lendrum of African Hunting Gazette: convicted wildlife smuggler," it declared, going on to inform the forum's twenty-thousand participants of his three convictions over twenty-six years.

Angry comments appeared on the AfricaHunting.com forum within hours. "Is *African Hunting Gazette* letting [safari camp owners] know that a convicted criminal is being sent to stay at their house with their family for the purpose of 'verifying' their outfits?" wrote one longtime subscriber. "If I was an outfitter knowing what I know now, I would not let this guy anywhere near my property!" Some readers canceled their subscriptions. Advertisers began to pull out.

Richard Lendrum had feared this day would come. Since putting out his first issue of *African Hunting Gazette* (originally called *African Sporting Gazette*) in 2000, Lendrum had successfully positioned the quarterly as a pro-conservation magazine, arguing that trophy hunting benefits wildlife by providing revenue for game management, anti-poaching patrols, and national park operations. Many big game hunters who subscribed to the *Gazette* liked to see themselves as wildlife conservationists at heart, and the revelation that a convicted thief and smuggler held a prominent position on the magazine's staff was, Lendrum understood, unlikely to go down well. "I knew I was running a risk having [Jeffrey's] association with my business," Richard would later admit, "but . . . he had served his time . . . His range of services for a division of the magazine was very restricted and limited, and to be honest, very useful. And he was my brother."

Jeffrey Lendrum begged for forgiveness. "What I did was stupid and believe me I paid for it," he posted on AfricaHunting.com, "or do I have to keep paying?" He profusely apologized, writing later in his post, "I am sincerely sorry . . . I did my time and am commited to my job." As the irate comments continued to pour in, he posted his cell number, his Skype address, and his email address, urging those who condemned him to make contact. "Please call me and after we have spoken and I have explained myself, we will be friends," he wrote. These awkward pleas for understanding failed to win over many hunters.

In early 2014, with Jeffrey Lendrum's presence at the magazine still eliciting threats of boycotts from advertisers and subscribers, Richard Lendrum informed his brother that he would have to let him go. It was a "horrific" moment for both of them, he would later acknowledge. Jeffrey felt abandoned, Richard mortified and angry that he had been given no choice but to cut his brother loose. But the survival of his business had to come first. Months later, still trying to put the controversy to rest, Richard Lendrum posted on AfricaHunting .com to reassure his readers that his generosity toward his sibling by no means implied sympathy for his crimes: Jeffrey Lendrum was a "wildlife trafficker," he acknowledged, and a "smuggler of falcon eggs." He insisted that he had nothing to do with his behavior and did not "support it in any way."

Losing his job at *African Hunting Gazette* was devastating for Jeffrey Lendrum. He sought steady employment, but his younger brother says that few opportunities were available in post-apartheid South Africa for a middle-aged white man, especially one with a felony conviction. For a while he tried a variation of his old hustle from before the days of AfricaXtreme. Reaching out to dealers in the United States and Europe, he procured spare parts for four-seat Cessna 172 Skyhawks and other single-engine planes and distributed them to aircraft-maintenance companies in South Africa. But the work was irregular, and provided him only a meager living. On an affidavit that he would later file with the police, he reported a monthly income of between $1,000 and $2,000, $500 of which went toward rent.

Bleak as things were, he found ways of keeping his connection to the natural world. He managed, somehow, to obtain an Honorary Ranger Certificate from South Africa's department of national parks, allowing him to participate in a volunteer program to place identification rings on owls, hawks, and other wild birds to study their life cycles, habits, and movements.

Richard Lendrum says that he lost track of his brother soon after his forced departure from *African Hunting Gazette*. Jeffrey Lendrum's calls to Andy McWilliam stopped, too. And so Richard Lendrum, Andy McWilliam, and everyone else in Jeffrey Lendrum's orbit were surprised some months later by the news reports from the other side of the world. Lendrum, it seemed, was in trouble again.

SIXTEEN

PATAGONIA

Early one morning in October 2015, at the start of spring in the southern hemisphere, a rented four-by-four departed the Chilean outpost of Punta Arenas and headed north across the bleak, windswept prairie known as the Patagonian Steppe. The vehicle followed La Ruta del Fin del Mundo, the Highway at the End of the World, a two-lane asphalt strip bordered to the west by fenced cattle and sheep ranches, and to the east by the icy blue waters of the Strait of Magellan. It passed the ghostly remains of an estancia abandoned a century ago, and a rusting freighter that had run aground in the 1930s. Lesser rheas—gray, flightless birds resembling ostriches—scurried away amid clouds of dust. Guanacos—alpaca-like wild grazers with brown fur and pale bellies—placidly munched the hardy yellow grass known as *coirón*. After two hours the asphalt ran out, and a gravel track wound through bush-covered hills. Then, just south of Chile's border with Argentina, Jeffrey Lendrum arrived at his destination: Pali Aike National Park, marked by a solitary green ranger hut with a sign welcoming visitors.

The indigenous Tehuelche tribe, hunter-gatherers who migrated to southern Patagonia after the glaciers receded ten thousand years ago, called Pali Aike both "the desolate place of bad spirits" and "the devil's country." The terrain is studded with volcanoes formed during the Jurassic era 100 million years ago by the collision of the Chile Rise and the Peru-Chile oceanic trench. A series of eruptions—the first taking place 3.8 million years ago, the most recent 15,000 years ago—covered the steppe with spills of black lava and parapets of basalt, which glow yellow, red, and greenish gray in the harsh desert sunlight. Half a dozen collapsed craters loom over the yellow plain like broken teeth.

Despite the otherworldly bleakness, the thirty-one-square-mile reserve teems with wildlife: hares, armadillos, gray foxes, pumas, guanacos, skunks, mole-like rodents known as tuco-tucos, and birds unique to Patagonia. Chilean flamingos, splashes of pink and orange in a charred landscape, gather in the park's salt lagoons. Colonies of buff-necked ibises, large rodent eaters with cream-and-russet throats and long, curving gray bills, build nests high in trees or inside the extinct volcanoes—sharing the ledges with peregrine falcons, in a relationship of mutual coexistence rare among birds of prey.

The raptors were what Lendrum had come for. After the loss of his job at the *African Hunting Gazette* eighteen months before, Lendrum had tried his hand at selling airplane parts. It had not worked out as he'd hoped, and now he had returned to the enterprise that he knew best. He had arrived in Chile at the height of the southern hemisphere's breeding season in pursuit of the eggs of one of the world's rarest birds of prey: the pallid peregrine, a snowy-white-breasted raptor found only in the wilds of the Patagonian mainland, the Falkland Islands, and Tierra del Fuego, an archipelago of hundreds of islands, many covered with volcanoes, mountains, and glaciers, at the southernmost tip of South America. Scientists had not even set eyes on the bird until 1925, when a *pallido* captured by Patagonian otter hunters near the Strait of Magellan ended up in a zoo in Münster, Germany. Otto Kleinschmidt, Germany's best-known ornithologist, triumphantly proclaimed that he had identified a hitherto unknown species, and gave it the scientific name *Falco kreyenborgi*, after Hermann Kreyenborg, the falconer who had first brought it to his attention. But field researchers in Patagonia later found the white-breasted raptors sharing nests with southern peregrine falcons, most of which have black-barred, light gray breast feathers. In 1981, scientists confirmed that the pallid falcon was a genetic fluke—a rare pale morph of the southern peregrine, the *Falco peregrinus cassini*.

=

As Lendrum slipped back into a life of crime, he had no idea that someone was watching him. Two weeks before Lendrum's arrival at the southern tip of Patagonia, the night watchman at the Hotel Plaza in Punta Arenas, Chile's southernmost city and a gateway to the Antarctic, had approached Nicolas Fernández, a young mountaineer and wilderness guide who was working part-time at the reception desk. A large black backpack had been gathering dust for a year in the storage room of the hotel, a 1920s French-neoclassical mansion built by a cattle ranching baron and overlooking the leafy Plaza de Armas. Nobody had claimed the luggage, and the guard wondered whether they could see if anything inside was worth taking. Fernández agreed that the pack had been abandoned, and said he thought that it would be fine to open it.

On their hands and knees in the storage room, the two hotel employees searched through the contents with growing curiosity: a pair of cargo pants, a pair of jeans, a six-hundred-foot-long coiled climbing rope, a two-pronged steel hook for grasping tree branches, and a black-and-yellow, shoe-box-sized device with a transparent door and an electrical cord, manufactured by Brinsea in the United Kingdom. After bringing the rope home with him to use on his next glacier expedition, Fernández searched the Internet and discovered that the piece of equipment from Brinsea was an incubator. The owner, Fernández surmised, must have come to Patagonia the previous year to steal the eggs of wild birds. But who was he? The backpack had no identification tag, and nobody in the Hotel Plaza could remember the owner's name.

Two days later, a man called from South Africa to make a reservation.

He needed a room for eight nights, he told Fernández, who was again working behind the reception desk. Then the man informed the clerk that he had left a black backpack behind during the week that he had stayed at the hotel in October 2014, with the expectation of retrieving it on his next visit.

"Is it still there?"

"Yes, we're holding it for you," Fernández replied, astonished by the timing of the call. After the caller hung up, Fernández typed his name, "Jeffrey Lendrum," into Google.

Fernández's first hit was a YouTube video of Lendrum toying with an Egyptian cobra in the bush. Next came Lendrum dangling from a helicopter in Quebec. *What kind of guy is this?* he wondered. Fernández typed in "Jeffrey Lendrum egg smuggler" and came up with five thousand hits. His concern mounting, the clerk read about the arrest at Birmingham Airport, the conviction and jail sentence, the gyrfalcon-egg-stealing escapade in Canada, and the 1984 trial for theft in Zimbabwe. The Internet had destroyed whatever anonymity Lendrum had once enjoyed on his egg-plundering capers. There on the first page of hits was Andy McWilliam of Britain's National Wildlife Crime Unit calling his quarry an international wildlife smuggler who worked "at the highest global level of wildlife crime." Guy Shorrock of the Royal Society for the Protection of Birds had told the BBC that Lendrum was "the highest level of wildlife criminal." Half a dozen newspapers, Fernández noted with alarm, had described the Irish national and South African resident as a "former member of the Rhodesian SAS."

Lendrum's reservation at the hotel began on October 13, one week away. Unsure what to do, Fernández returned the climbing rope to Lendrum's black backpack and consulted a longtime friend and former policeman, who urged him to reach out to Chile's Agriculture and Livestock Service (SAG), the government agency responsible for protecting the country's wildlife. The hotel clerk explained what he had uncovered to SAG representatives in Punta Arenas and Santiago. He mentioned that Lendrum appeared to have an elite military background. "I'm uneasy about this and hope that you could be discreet in your actions," he wrote in an email, concerned for his own safety. His contacts at the Agriculture and Livestock Service and, later, the police, advised him to watch Lendrum, remain calm, and avoid revealing to the egg thief what he knew. Maybe they could catch him in the act.

—

At the entrance to Pali Aike National Park, Lendrum paid the gatekeeper three thousand Chilean pesos (about $4.50), drove on for a couple of miles, and parked at the trailhead leading to an extinct volcano called Morada del Diablo, "the Devil's Dwelling." Carrying a backpack filled with rope, spikes, a harness, and carabiners, he set out on foot on a dirt trail that cut through a fifteen-thousand-year-old field of congealed black lava. The collapsed crater, otherwise known as a caldera, loomed directly ahead of him. Small black lizards covered with white speckles skittered over the rocks; when I retraced Lendrum's steps three years later, the skeletal remains of guanacos killed by pumas baked beneath the morning sun. He passed nobody—hardly surprising, considering that the park attracts an average of only eight visitors a day.

After a mile's hike he began a steep climb over loose gray stones, and emerged at the top of the caldera. Perched behind a guardrail at the edge of the drop-off, with pillars of basaltic lava behind him, Lendrum looked across the maw of the dead volcano. A curving wall of basaltic rock—tinted green, splattered with whitewash, and riven with fissures—formed the remnant of the volcano's lip. Steep slopes of gray scree and soil laden with red-tinted hematite fell away into the abyss, and the cries of buff-necked ibises echoed off the wall. Moments after I made the same climb, a peregrine rose, plummeted into the crater, circled back up, and disappeared inside a crevice.

Lendrum spotted an aerie, fastened a rope, and rappelled down the wall. He worked his way toward the nest, his excitement rising. But as he landed on the ledge, Lendrum identified the raptor as an ordinary cassini, not the rare pallid morph that he was seeking. He left the Morada del Diablo, one of most spectacular places he had ever climbed, exhilarated but empty-handed.

Even so, there were many more places for aeries in the rugged Patagonian landscape. He followed a dirt road through the pampas to a line of sixty-foot cliffs overlooking Posession Bay, an inlet between the mainland and the Isla Grande, the largest island of the Tierra del Fuego archipelago. The gray-sand beach below was deserted, except for a few plywood shanties inhabited by fishermen. (When I visited the area in 2018, one informed me that he had often seen a pair of the legendary *peregrino pallido* nesting on the rock face.) Lendrum hiked along a beach strewn with mussel shells, scanning the sky and the cliffs—some of them bare, some blanketed in scrub and dwarf pine. "Basically you've got to know what you're looking for, or you won't see them, because there are so many sea birds there," Lendrum would later say. "Someone who's never seen a peregrine could find a couple of nests in a day or two in the Rhondda Valley. Here it was a lot harder." A 2002 study by the Raptor Research Foundation noted that the pallid peregrines are especially difficult to spot, "being less conspicuous and gull-like when seen beneath gray, overcast skies."

Waves lapped gently over the shoal just offshore, and the sky abounded with southern giant petrels, oystercatchers, southern lapwings, cinnamon-bellied ground tyrants, austral negritos, and upland geese. It seemed like a proverbial needle-in-a-haystack search, but Lendrum soon spotted a pair of *pallidos* and they led him to what he was looking for: their clutch of four mottled brown eggs, nestled on a ledge halfway up the rock face. He carefully wrapped the prizes and carried them back to the Hotel Plaza in Punta Arenas, a two-hour drive south.

=

From behind the desk in the wood-paneled hotel lobby, up a steep flight of stairs from the street, Nicolas Fernández quietly observed Lendrum's comings and goings. He watched Lendrum leave with his large black backpack in the early mornings and return in the evenings, his clothing soiled and sweaty. He'd helped him move into a spacious room on the top floor of the hotel, hauling a second piece of luggage, a duffel bag, up two flights of stairs and feeling the hard, square edges of what he was certain was another incubator inside. Because Fernández spoke fluent English, Lendrum approached him regularly for advice. What restaurants would he recommend? Where in Punta Arenas could he get a down jacket repaired? Where could he hire a helicopter and fly to Rio Grande on the Isla Grande, in the far south of Argentina? "He was a nice, friendly guy, always wandering around the hotel," Fernández would later say. Yet despite his easygoing demeanor, the staff was on edge, having been informed of Lendrum's history by Fernández. "Every employee knew that he was up to no good, but we didn't want to say anything," Fernández recalled. "We were scared."

After a few days, Lendrum was relaxed enough to invite Fernández into his room, a sunlit chamber with French windows overlooking a Renaissance-style cathedral. Ropes and incubators lay strewn across the floor. Fernández pretended not to notice. Later, Lendrum emailed Fernández his travel itinerary and asked him to print out a hard copy. Fernández did so—and immediately forwarded the itinerary to SAG headquarters in Santiago, and the police.

SAG Director Rafael Asenjo saw that the convicted wildlife criminal was planning to fly on LATAM Airlines from Punta Arenas to Santiago in the early morning of October 21. In Santiago he would connect to São Paulo, Brazil, arriving at five-thirty p.m. From there he would continue on to Dubai. Detaining Lendrum in Santiago, Asenjo knew, would be problematic: SAG agents had no experience arresting smugglers of wild bird eggs. At worst, their actions could tip off Lendrum and give him time to dispose of his contraband—or the officers might inadvertently manhandle and kill the unhatched chicks. So Asenjo came up with another solution.

On the morning of Lendrum's departure, Asenjo contacted the Management Authority of the Convention on International Trade in Endangered Species in Brasília, the Brazilian capital. "We received the following communication about a probable case of wild egg trafficking on the part of a foreigner who is about to enter your country," he wrote in the email. "I'm sending you the accusation so that you can take all the necessary actions." Asenjo attached Nicolas Fernández's original message and Lendrum's itinerary. The authority passed the alert to the Brazilian Institute of the Environment and Renewable Natural Resources (IBAMA), the wildlife protection police. IBAMA dispatched two experienced officers to Guarulhos International Airport to await Lendrum's arrival.

Lendrum, completely unaware of the trap being set for him, checked out of the Hotel Plaza at dawn on October 21 and caught the flight to Santiago. He carried the four eggs in socks tied off with cords and concealed in the pockets of his fleece. In Santiago, Lendrum walked through the metal detector at the security checkpoint separating the domestic arrivals wing and international departures without setting off an alarm. He boarded the flight to São Paulo, landed at Guarulhos in the early evening, and entered the Emirates Lounge to await his flight to Dubai. Inside the shower room, Lendrum transferred the eggs, still wrapped in socks, to a battery-powered yellow Brinsea incubator that he kept in a carry-on bag. Then, around 8:30, as he prepared to board his flight, he hit a snag: security agents diverted him before the gate and ran his bags through an X-ray scanner. The four eggs were clearly visible. Two green-uniformed wildlife policemen descended on him. The IBAMA agents examined the incubator and removed the four mottled brown eggs from their socks.

"They're chicken eggs," Lendrum insisted. The wildlife officers summoned the federal police, who placed Lendrum under arrest.

Then, for the first time in his entanglements with authorities around the world, the falcon thief lost his composure. Almost as soon as he arrived in his airport holding cell, he complained of heart palpitations. Perhaps the realization of the criminal proceedings that lay ahead had had a physiological effect. Rushed to a nearby hospital, Lendrum was given an electrocardiogram, an examination by a heart specialist, and medication for chest pains. Then he was turned back over to police custody.

Experts would positively identify the eggs and transport them to a birds-of-prey center outside São Paulo. From there they would be hand-carried back to Patagonia and reintroduced to the wild, where only one would survive.

Meanwhile, a federal court judge in Guarulhos confiscated Lendrum's passport, set a trial date for late November, and released the multiple offender on eight thousand reais ($2,100) bail.

—

As he stepped into the crowded streets of Guarulhos in the tropical heat, Lendrum found himself in a predicament. Alone and unable to speak a word of Portuguese, he was stranded in Brazil's thirteenth-largest city, an unlovely sprawl of highway overpasses, shantytown favelas, factories, and traffic-choked boulevards. He was a multiple offender with the threat of a long incarceration in a foreign prison hanging over him. After all the ups and downs of Lendrum's last few years, nothing had prepared him for this.

He took a room at the Hotel Sables—a seven-story, $80-a-night hotel on the Avenida Salgado Filho, a busy thoroughfare—to wait out the month until his trial. The Guarulhos Federal Court had offered Lendrum a public defender, but the attorney spoke only Portuguese, so Lendrum had declined his services. As luck would have it, the young receptionist at the Sables mentioned that his father had a law practice a few blocks away, and spoke English. Lendrum went to see him that afternoon.

Rodrigo Tomei was a friendly, bearded attorney in his early forties with an easygoing manner and a command of idiomatic English. In 1990 Tomei's father, an airline pilot and union activist, had moved his family to Calgary, Alberta, to escape persecution by Brazil's military dictatorship. Tomei, who was then seventeen, had stayed in Canada for seven years—including a two-year stint in the army—before returning to Brazil after the end of military rule.

"They caught me with chicken eggs," Lendrum told the attorney.

"Look, man," replied Tomei, who had read the arrest report. "If I'm going to represent you I need to know the truth."

At their third meeting, Lendrum admitted that he'd been smuggling peregrine eggs, but refused to answer Tomei's questions about their intended recipients in the Middle East. When Tomei pressed him about his 2010 arrest at Birmingham Airport, Lendrum fell back on his standard explanation: "I wasn't trafficking the birds, I was rescuing them." The falcon eggs he had taken in southern Wales had been "dying because of pesticides," he said. "But the British authorities didn't believe me."

"The Brazilians are not going to believe you, either," Tomei replied. Plead guilty, he advised his client, and take a shorter sentence.

But Lendrum was certain, recalls Tomei, that "he could convince the judge that he was innocent." Under oath in a courtroom in Guarulhos, Lendrum insisted, through an interpreter, that he was just a bird-watcher. He claimed that he had taken the four eggs to save them after finding the corpse of their mother lying near the nest, and explained that the three incubators seized from his luggage by the police belonged to an American photographer friend who had used them to keep his cameras warm in the frosty Patagonian climate. He swore that he had visited Dubai just once in his life—a sightseeing trip to the Burj Khalifa skyscraper, the world's tallest building. Judge Paulo Marcos Rodrigues de Almeida called his testimony "laughable" and handed down the harshest possible sentence for violating Brazil's Environmental Crimes Act: four years and six months in prison. The defendant could remain free on bail pending his appeal, but he would have to appear before the court secretary every two months to register his address and account for his activities. He was also ordered to pay a fine of forty thousand reais, or $10,500.

=

Tomei received the twenty-six-page judgment in December via an alert sent to the online mailbox he maintained as a member of the Brazilian Order of Attorneys. (Under Brazilian law, neither a defendant nor his counsel is required to be present for the verdict or the sentencing.) The lawyer informed Lendrum on WhatsApp that he had "some news" about his case. "Let's have coffee and talk about it," he suggested.

When Tomei translated the court decision, Lendrum blinked a few times and seemed about to cry.

"Look, we knew you would get convicted. It was a question of how much jail time you would get," Tomei said. The next step, he told Lendrum, trying to give him some hope, was filing an appeal. "We're not going to reverse the verdict, but we can try to reduce the sentence."

Where would he serve his time? Lendrum asked.

The Penitenciária Cabo PM Marcelo Pires da Silva, Tomei replied, in the remote town of Itaí, about 190 miles west of São Paulo. Nicknamed the "Tower of Babel," Marcelo Pires da Silva had opened in 2000 exclusively for foreigners, after disgruntled Brazilian prisoners in other jails had threatened to kill international inmates in an effort to embarrass the government. A total of 1,443 detainees of eighty-nine nationalities were incarcerated there by 2011, according to the Brazilian magazine *Veja*. "During [downtime] in Itaí, it is possible to see kipa-wearing Jews conversing in Hebrew," *Veja* reported, "Lithuanian and Dutch doing sit-ups, Peruvians playing dominoes surrounded by other Latinos and a Muslim kneeling toward Mecca to do one of his five daily prayers." Eighty percent of the inmates were reportedly doing time for drug trafficking. Marcelo Pires da Silva was not the worst prison in Brazil's notoriously violent and overcrowded penal system, but it was hardly an easy place. "Sometimes not even a mattress is available to you . . . You should also be aware that the conditions of toilets and showers are extremely poor," the British Consular Network in Brazil wrote in an information pack for British prisoners. Serious illnesses often went untreated: "The system is relatively overwhelmed [so] people can wait up to 12 months for a doctor's appointment."

Lendrum told Tomei that he was considering fleeing the country.

"If you're going to do something like that, I don't want to know about it," Tomei says he told him.

—

And then, just when it seemed that things could not possibly get any worse for Jeffrey Lendrum, they did.

One morning in January, shortly after learning the verdict, Lendrum awoke in the Sables Hotel in excruciating pain. A gaping wound the size of an eight ball had appeared overnight on his thigh. Alarmed, a hotel employee rushed Lendrum to a public hospital in Guarulhos. Finding nobody who spoke English, Lendrum handed Tomei's business card to a hospital social worker, and she summoned the attorney to serve as an interpreter. Physicians determined that the wound was probably the bite of a poisonous spider that had crept into his bed and attacked him while he slept.

Doctors and nurses administered painkillers and a powerful antibiotic intravenously, and advised Lendrum to remain at the hospital under supervision for one week. "There was a danger that the toxin would infect his nervous system," said Tomei, who stayed by his bedside. "He was having heart failure. He almost died." But Lendrum ignored the doctors' advice. After three days, he hobbled back to the hotel, and started self-medicating with antibiotic tablets from a pharmacy. Still, the infection was so severe that he remained weak and in frequent pain, and his wound would not heal.

"I had nothing but shit in Brazil," Lendrum would later say.

When Michelle Conway, a longtime friend from the United Kingdom, reached out to ask where Lendrum had been for so many months, he said only that a sightseeing trip in Brazil had gone awry. A rare tropical spider had bitten him, he explained, and the airline, fearing that the infection was "contagious," had refused to allow him to board a plane home to Johannesburg. Howard Waller, who had broken off contact with Lendrum after his arrest at Birmingham Airport, received an email from him around this time, asking if he could borrow $20,000. "Then I saw an article on the Internet about this guy who had been caught with eggs in Brazil," he said, "and then I thought, 'You're asking me for *money*?'"

Soon afterward, Lendrum disappeared again.

=

Lendrum knew what he had to do. He prepared a backpack, checked out of the hotel, and traveled hundreds of miles south to the edge of the country, near Iguaçu Falls. "I knew that I was going to die in that prison," he would later explain, "so I got resourceful." Carrying a GPS and a day's supply of food and water, he slipped past border police and walked "a couple of kilometers through the jungle" into Argentina. The journey, he said, took him "most of a day." That, anyway, is Lendrum's version of how he eluded Brazilian justice. Tomei says that Lendrum was too weak to escape on foot, and theorizes that the egg thief might have taken advantage of lax immigration controls between the two economically integrated neighbors, and crossed the official border without presenting a passport. "Nobody was looking for him, so there was no need for him to sneak anywhere," Tomei said. "He could have just taken a bus."

Once safely in Argentina, Lendrum traveled 780 miles south to Buenos Aires. In the Argentine capital he appeared at the Embassy of Ireland, claiming that he had lost his passport, and was issued a new one. (He had obtained Irish citizenship some years earlier through his great-grandfather.) Then, from Ministro Pistarini Airport, Lendrum flew home to Johannesburg.

Half a year after Lendrum's disappearance, Tomei received a

WhatsApp message from his missing client. "Hey Rodrigo, I'm in South Africa seeing my doctor," Lendrum announced. "My wound is slowly getting better. How's the appeal going?" Tomei replied that he still hadn't gotten an answer.

On October 24, 2016, the Brazilian Superior Tribunal rejected the appeal and ordered Lendrum to surrender immediately. "There's nothing else we can do," Tomei messaged Lendrum. But Lendrum didn't return. Brazilian authorities soon announced that Lendrum had jumped bail, and the British media picked up the news. "Ex-SAS Rare Egg Thief Who Tried to Smuggle Birds Through Birmingham Airport on the Run," the *Birmingham Mail* declared, still buying into the fiction about Lendrum's elite Rhodesian army career. "Britain's Most Protected Bird Under Threat From SAS-Trained Wildlife Hunter," proclaimed the *Daily Mirror*.

If he tried to return to Brazil, Tomei told him, he would be arrested the moment he stepped off the plane. Lendrum decided to lie low.

SEVENTEEN

GAUTENG

In May 2017, shortly after my trip to Wales, I reached out to Paul Mullin for help tracking Jeffrey Lendrum down. Friends had told him that Lendrum was holed up at a rented home in the Johannesburg area. Rumors were circulating that Brazilian authorities had requested that Interpol, the international organization that links the police forces of 190 countries, issue a Red Notice requesting his extradition. That would place Lendrum in a select club of fugitives including Roman Polanski, Julian Assange, and Vorayuth "Boss" Yoovidhya, the thirty-two-year-old heir to the Red Bull fortune who is on the run from Thai authorities after fatally running over a Bangkok policeman with his Ferrari. But South Africa has no extradition treaty with Brazil for wildlife smuggling, and nobody appeared to be hunting for Lendrum. Mullin gave me a cell phone number, and I reached Lendrum on the first try.

I introduced myself as a journalist who had just spent a day with Andy McWilliam in the Rhondda Valley. I had hoped that dropping the investigator's name would make him more receptive to my intrusion, but whatever affection Lendrum once had for the wildlife cop had curdled into resentment. "Andy McWilliam is telling people that I was selling birds for a fortune, and that I had become a multi-millionaire," he told me. "The whole press has portrayed me as the Pablo Escobar of the falcon egg trade. Everybody writes absolute rubbish about me."

McWilliam had blown the case out of proportion, he insisted, to exaggerate the importance of the National Wildlife Crime Unit. In their meeting at Hewell Prison, Lendrum claimed, McWilliam had offered his condolences for his father's death—and then confessed that Lendrum's arrest and conviction had been like "manna from heaven" for the unit. (McWilliam would call Lendrum's accusation "complete and utter rubbish.") Lendrum brought up Michael Upson, a Suffolk constable convicted in 2012 of amassing 649 rare birds' eggs and given a fourteen-week suspended sentence and 150 hours of community service. "I got two and a half years in prison. How unfair is that?" he said. McWilliam had apparently become a scape-goat for all of the disastrous turns his life had taken since his arrest at Birmingham Airport in May 2010.

I asked Lendrum if I could visit him, and he told me that he would consider it. But when I called him back a few days later, he told me that he had just been diagnosed with prostate cancer and was about to begin radiation treatment. He didn't feel up for talking further.

Seven months later, I flew to Southern Africa, with a plan to retrace Lendrum's footsteps and make one more attempt to talk to him face-to-face. I wanted to understand the roots of his obsession with birds of prey and see whether the falcon thief would finally take responsibility for what he had done. I wanted to ask him about the appeal of the outlaw life, and why he kept raiding nests around the world despite his growing profile and the increasing likelihood that he would be caught. And, yes, I hoped to persuade him to talk about the Arab connection.

My first stop on the journey was Bulawayo, Lendrum's hometown. Most of the white community had fled the lush, now-down-at-the-heels city, driven out by Robert Mugabe's destructive policies—the forceful seizures of white-owned farms by war veterans and ruling party cronies in the early 2000s, the collapse of agriculture and then the whole economy, the rampant corruption, the uncontrolled printing of money that in 2008 sent inflation soaring to 80 billion percent in a single month, wiping out the value of pensions . . . But Peggy Lendrum was still there, living in a retirement village not far from the house in Hillside where Jeffrey had grown up. She was mortified, I was told, by her son's crimes and global notoriety. "She is very stressed, brought on by Jeffrey's lack of transparency, not to mention his lifestyle," Julia Dupree, a family friend, emailed me before my arrival, informing me that Peggy had cautiously agreed to, then turned down, my request to meet with her. "How she remains sane I have no idea."

Lendrum had been through months earlier, Dupree told me, weakened by his treatments for prostate cancer and professing remorse. He'd announced his intention to build a memorial to Val Gargett for all the trouble he'd caused her. Yet during the same visit he had tried, without success, to obtain a list of nest locations from the curator of the bird egg collections at Bulawayo's Natural History Museum, and had asked to join a raptor survey in Matobo National Park—a request the ornithological society had rejected. "What f****** audacity!" Pat Lorber emailed me when I told her about Lendrum's entreaty. "Doesn't he realize how discredited he is?"

The African Black Eagle Survey was still going, nearly sixty years after the study's start, though its participants had dwindled to a handful of elderly volunteers. John Brebner, the current head of the project, agreed to take me on a search for nests inside Matobo. Beforehand, he had me sign an agreement pledging not to give away the locations of the black eagle aeries. "You're sworn to secrecy," said Brebner, a genial onetime cattle rancher turned pesticide sales-man. The precaution was the most obvious legacy of the Lendrums' betrayals.

Early one morning in December, the height of the warm, dry season, we set off with Brebner's wife, Jen, in his four-by-four and headed down a potholed tarmac highway through the bush. The Zimbabwe Defence Forces had driven Mugabe from office two weeks earlier following months of escalating tensions between the ninety-three-year-old president's power-hungry wife, Grace, and the vice president, Emmerson Mnangagwa. Now Mugabe was sidelined with his wife at his villa in Harare, and some of the indignities of life under an increasingly incompetent dictator were already being ad-dressed. For the last two years of Mugabe's rule, police checkpoints had lined this road—manned by hungry cops owed back wages who cited drivers for fake violations and extorted small fees. The day after Mugabe's forced resignation, the new president, Mnangagwa, had ordered all such roadblocks in the country removed.

John and Jen Brebner and I entered Matobo through the main gate, and bounced over a rough dirt track. Scanning a fissure-ridden cliff one hundred feet high, my guide pointed to a huge spherical bundle of twigs and branches inside a horizontal crevice seventy feet up. "That's a fairly new black eagle nest, only six or seven years old," Brebner told me. "There's one in the park that's been here for thirty-eight years." I tried to imagine young Jeffrey Lendrum rappelling down to a rock fissure like this one, disappearing into the giant stick nest, and fishing out the precious eagle eggs, excited by the adventure, the strangeness, the illicitness, and the secrecy of it all. Brebner pointed to a regal creature nearby, perched at eye level on the branch of a thorn tree. Its sharply hooked black beak, orange body, barred plumage, ruffled reddish crown, massive black-feathered legs, and fearsome talons identified it as a crowned eagle, one of the rarest raptors in the park. "They hunt in the canopy and they will take anything—black vervet monkeys, dassies, even a baby klippie [antelope]," he said. I wondered how many crowned-eagle eggs snatched by Lendrum here had ended up in the hands of birds-of-prey enthusiasts in Europe and the Middle East—and how many more eagles might have populated the park had it not been for him.

═

Through friends of Lendrum's family, I learned that the falcon thief's life had continued to disintegrate. He had broken up with his longtime girlfriend (Mullin's ex-partner) several years earlier, had no job, and was living in a rented bungalow near Pretoria, an hour north of Johannesburg. His treatments for his cancer had weakened him, and in mid-2017 someone had broadsided his vehicle at an intersection after dark, leaving him badly injured. Whatever money he had made from his falcon smuggling—and Mullin and others insist that it wasn't much—had apparently been spent long ago. Lendrum had gone from being a swaggering outlaw to suffering as the victim of a self-destructive obsession. "He's got a very tough life," Richard Lendrum told me when I met him at a coffee shop in an affluent neighborhood in northern Johannesburg. "Nothing great at all."

I asked the younger Lendrum, a trim man in his early fifties with chiseled features and fine lines around his eyes, to speculate about what had driven his brother into a life of crime. "We both love wildlife, it's just that he's gone down a slightly different path," he said with a pained smile. "It's a high adventure, high adrenaline way of eking out a living. It's just gone a little wrong." Richard had learned much over the years about his brother's egg-thieving business, but he was parsimonious with the details. "Obviously, there are breeders that . . . get intermediaries to do their dirty work for them. That's the reality. They will do anything to get birds around the world," he told me. When I prodded him, he named Howard Waller and Arab royals as his brother's clients, and warned me about approaching them: "What would you think if your world was going to be exposed and it may affect you, your family, your livelihood, and your potential future earnings?"

Richard said that he was trying to provide some direction to his brother's life and wean him off his criminal behavior. Jeffrey Lendrum was part owner of an old Cessna single-engine airplane, and had been attempting, so far unsuccessfully, to raise enough money to repair the plane and hire it out for charter flights. "I try to help him out, offering guidance and a brotherly perspective," Richard said. "But the main thing is that he's trying to come back from his cancer, and that's the focus, getting healthy." Lendrum doubted his brother would talk to me. He had ambitions to write a memoir and he didn't want to give away trade secrets. And, Richard said, his brother knew that if he revealed anything about his Middle Eastern royal partners, he could be endangering himself. "He's not going to go and squeal," he told me. "He's aware of how powerful these people are."

"And you think that Jeff is afraid of them?" I asked.

"I know that he is," he said.

=

Two hours after meeting Richard Lendrum, I reached Jeffrey Lendrum on the phone. I was flying out of South Africa that evening, I told him. This would be my last opportunity to hear his side of the story. Could he meet me for an hour?

Lendrum hesitated, and then, to my surprise, he said yes. He directed me to meet him at the Featherbrooke Shopping Centre in Roodepoort, a city a bit north of Johannesburg in Gauteng, formerly known as Transvaal, the smallest, richest, and most densely populated province in South Africa. I should look for an Ocean Basket seafood restaurant, next to an indoor ice-skating rink. (Lendrum had a particular fondness for the seafood chain: it was in another Ocean Basket in the late 1990s that he had proposed to Mullin that they go into business together selling African handicrafts.) He would be waiting for me at the entrance.

An Uber driver picked me up at my guesthouse in Johannesburg and took me across the parched plains and low rolling hills of the Highveld, past farms, tin-roofed shacks, and bus stops. It was a hazy summer day, and the temperature had climbed into the high eighties. He dropped me off outside a sprawling commercial complex, and I found an Ocean Basket. But I saw no sign of a skating rink—or of Lendrum.

Lendrum was apologetic when I called him minutes later. He had sent me to the wrong shopping mall. "My short-term memory is failing," he said. He blamed the mistake on the side effects of his cancer treatment—and, indirectly, on South Africa's growing middle class. "They're putting up so many of these malls all over Gauteng, with 'feathers' and 'brooks' and 'meadows' in the names. I can't keep them all straight," he told me. He had meant to send me to the Forest Hill City Mall in Centurion, a town formerly known as Verwoerdburg, after Hendrik Verwoerd, the architect of apartheid. I called for another Uber. The driver headed north for forty more minutes and let me out at the entrance to a massive structure near a highway interchange. Just inside I caught sight of the skating rink—and beside it, an Ocean Basket.

Lendrum walked up to me and stuck out his hand. "You probably recognized me from my photos," he said. His receding hairline, black-framed glasses, and orange-white-and-blue striped button-down shirt hanging loosely over a pair of khaki shorts made him look more like a clerk in a sporting-goods store than a daredevil adventurer. But after months of fighting prostate cancer, he was tanner and healthier-looking than I'd expected. "I haven't been doing anything, just trying to get better," he told me, sliding into a coffee-shop booth. "I haven't been well at all."

Lendrum took me through his exploits in Zimbabwe, Canada, Great Britain, Chile, and Brazil. When I pressed him to explain his crimes, he presented each egg heist as a well-meaning if overzealous rescue mission or a scientific expedition gone wrong. He told me his story persuasively, looking me in the eye. If I weren't already familiar with his pattern of falsehoods—if I hadn't seen Mullin's video from Canada and watched Lendrum tell lie after lie before a judge in his videotaped testimony in Brazil—I might have believed parts of it. Lendrum had ready explanations for all of his misfortunes, a long story of bad luck, miscarriages of justice, and victimhood. But so much still didn't add up. And one thing was clear: Lendrum had gotten sloppier. His last mission in South America had been almost comically inept: deliberately leaving a backpack filled with incriminating evidence for a year at his hotel, allowing the receptionist to see the ropes and incubators in his room, sharing his flight itinerary, and doing nothing to mask his identity. "He seems to be successful at stealing the birds' eggs, but not very successful in smuggling them out," Bob Elliot, head of investigations for the Royal Society for the Protection of Birds, had told the BBC following Lendrum's flight from Brazil. Lendrum himself admitted his planning had sometimes been less than meticulous. "The devil is in the details," he said with a shrug, when I asked him about the twenty minutes that he had stayed in the Emirates Lounge shower room in Birmingham without bothering to turn on the water, and the red-dyed egg he had discarded in the diaper bin.

But then again, there could be dozens of egg trafficking trips he'd made over the years that have gone undetected. Lendrum had traveled to Patagonia six times "as a tourist," he told me, in the decade before his South American misadventure, drawn, he said, by the region's majestic landscapes and the most bountiful and varied bird life on the planet. How many eggs might he have smuggled out with him?

"Weren't you taking a big risk by stealing eggs again?" I asked.

"I never thought that the hotel clerk in Chile would rummage through my stuff or that he'd Google me." It was, I thought, a remarkable display of cluelessness.

"And the prospect of jail didn't make you hesitate?"

"I honestly didn't think that there would be a problem if I were caught," he said, "maybe just a fine." That seemed disingenuous, or delusional, considering his recent imprisonment.

The discussion shifted to the memoir he wanted to write. I asked whether he planned to expose the wild falcon trade in the Middle East. "I can write about it," he said—acknowledging, for the first time, that the black market exists—"but I'd end up in a tunnel somewhere—killed."

I asked if he really believed his former clients were that dangerous.

"Things happen," he said darkly. "I don't know the ramifications, I could say this and they could take out my sister." He also didn't trust that Britain's National Wildlife Crime Unit or Middle Eastern governments would do anything with the information. "What do I gain out of it by besmirching a royal figure?" he asked. "All I will do is get my fifteen minutes of fame, and it will be forgotten about." Nothing significant, he was certain, would come from his naming names.

I wondered whether Lendrum was deliberately exaggerating the threat he faced in order to pump up the drama of his life, but Andy McWilliam wouldn't dismiss the danger out of hand. Lendrum had never shared such fears with McWilliam, the investigator told me, "but there could be something in what he says."

I felt sorry for Lendrum in some ways. Charming, energetic, resourceful, intelligent, and passionate about birds of prey, he could, as the Zimbabwean professor Peter Mundy had observed in the ornithological magazine *Honeyguide*, have probably made a noteworthy career in academics, field research, or wildlife conservation. But he was conflicted between his love for animals and his need to possess them. Driven by the thrill of the chase, by a juvenile need to break the rules, and by his ambition to be seen as a globe-trotting daredevil—and by financial incentives as well—he had followed a twisted path into this South African cul-de-sac. Now, despised by conservationists, fearful of his handlers, broke, and sick, he had lost almost everything.

=

"Do you imagine that there will be a time when you will get back to egg collecting?" I asked. We had been talking at the Forest Hill City Mall for nearly two hours, and Lendrum was growing restless. He had an appointment to speak to a friend about the charter airline company he was trying to get off the ground. I knew it was time to end the meeting.

He said he doubted that he would return to the field. He was on the run from Brazil, had been banned from Dubai, wasn't welcome in Canada, couldn't travel to the United States (for reasons he never explained), and was under scrutiny in the United Kingdom. Besides, he wasn't the formidable outdoorsman that he'd once been. "I'm getting too old for it," he said. "Look at me." Prostate cancer had depleted his energy, and the car wreck had damaged the nerves in his neck and limbs.

We said our goodbyes. Lendrum shook my hand and moved slowly off. Then, before disappearing around the corner, he turned and hit me with a proposition. "Do you want to steal some eggs sometime?" he asked, grinning. "We'll go into the Rhondda Valley and see how many peregrines we can get—right under Andy McWilliam's nose. You do the climbing. We'll make millions."

It was, I thought, all bluster and self-mockery. Lendrum's egg snatching days were finally behind him. But I turned out to be wrong.

EPILOGUE

On June 21, 2018, I was sitting in a stifling auditorium, watching my oldest son's graduation ceremony at the John F. Kennedy International School in Berlin, when my iPhone went off in my pocket. The caller's ID had been blocked, and, over the valedictorian's amplified speech I heard a muffled voice with a South African accent speaking my name. I didn't register who it was. "I'm at my son's graduation," I told the caller. "I'll have to call you back."

Only after hanging up did I realize that it must have been Lendrum, calling to chat, as he had done periodically in recent months, about peregrine falcons and pigeon fanciers, a proposed trip with me to Matobo National Park, my impending visit to South America, or some questions I had about his childhood. Minutes later I found a message in my in-box:

"Call if you want. Cheers jeff."

"Sorry Jeff!" I typed back. "I just couldn't make out who it was. Will call when I get home." In spite of Lendrum's long history of environmental pillaging, and his many attempts to bamboozle me, I, like McWilliam, had found it hard not to like him. He was cheerful, garrulous, and full of energy. His lying was so transparent that it made it easier to shrug off. His haplessness in recent years also made him seem less toxic: he was the thief who couldn't steal straight. Talking to Lendrum at length had made me realize something else, too: he was always dancing on the edge of a confession, as if prevaricating so consistently for so long had worn him out.

Distractions came up, and it wasn't until four days later that I finally got around to ringing Lendrum's cell.

The phone was off.

I tried the next day, and couldn't get through. That was unusual: Lendrum hadn't let his phone go unanswered for so long before. Three more attempts over the next several days went directly to voice mail.

It didn't take me long to discover where Lendrum was.

On June 29, the British Home Office issued a press release: "Rare Bird Eggs Importation Prevented by Border Force at Heathrow." Three days earlier a passenger from South Africa identified as a "56-year-old Irish national" had aroused the suspicion of Border Force agents. They had stopped him, searched him, and discovered seventeen eggs from endangered birds of prey—African fish eagles, black sparrow hawks, Cape vultures, and African hawk eagles, similar to crowned eagles but more common—as well as two fish eagle chicks that had hatched in transit, in a customized belt hidden beneath his clothing. The Convention on International Trade in Endangered Species lists the fish eagle as an Appendix I bird, threatened with extinction; the other three species are Appendix II. The suspect had no documentation for any of them. British law doesn't allow a suspect to be identified until he is charged in court, but I had little doubt about who it was.

Sure enough, in late July, British newspapers reported that Jeffrey Lendrum had been charged with four counts of fraudulently evading prohibition—i.e., importing protected wildlife—and that he had been packed off to the Dickensian-sounding Wormwood Scrubs Prison in London to await a plea hearing in August. The National Crime Agency, founded in 2013 to combat "serious and organized crime," has a close relationship with Heathrow's Border Force and had immediately taken control of the investigation, relegating McWilliam, who probably knew more about Lendrum than any other law enforcement officer in England, to the sidelines. The details from the court appearance were skimpy—Lendrum's lawyer had argued that his client was on his way to declare the eggs and chicks before he was intercepted—and I had a wealth of questions that, for the moment, couldn't be answered. How had he procured the eggs? Who was he delivering them to? Why had the Border Force stopped him? And, most of all, what the hell had he been thinking?

I flew to London for Lendrum's pretrial hearing on August 23. His solicitor, Keith Astbury, had told me that his client intended to plead not guilty. But risking a jury trial could result in a tougher jail sentence than a plea bargain would—up to the maximum penalty of seven years. Had Lendrum rejected his solicitor's advice, as he had in Brazil? Astbury wouldn't comment.

At Isleworth Crown Court, in a drab London suburb directly beneath the flight path of jets landing at Heathrow Airport, I sat in the empty public gallery of a tiny second-floor courtroom, waiting for Lendrum to appear. I knew from Astbury that Lendrum had no interest in talking to me, but I hoped to make eye contact, at least. It wasn't to be. Court officers escorted Lendrum from a holding cell to a bulletproof booth at the rear of the courtroom, out of sight of the gallery. I heard his disembodied voice—faint, downcast—say, "I'm not guilty." When I stood in an attempt to get a look at him, a court officer motioned furiously for me to sit back down. Tony Bell, Lendrum's in-court lawyer, or barrister, promised to provide the judge with records about his client's ongoing cancer treatment to expedite a request for bail—a request that would be denied. Then his trial was set for January 7, 2019.

=

Four and a half months later, on a cold, drizzly morning, I traveled by tube to Snaresbrook Crown Court, a mid-nineteenth-century Gothic-revival manor house on eighteen acres of manicured grounds at the eastern edge of London. Barristers wearing white wigs and black robes walked along paths past stone turrets and arched entryways, looking like extras on a Georgian-era movie set. The third and climactic day of *The Queen v. Jeffrey Lendrum* was scheduled to unfold in Courtroom 15, a modern chamber with coral-colored upholstered chairs, blond-wood desks, gray carpeting, and soft track lighting on a white-paneled ceiling. I sat in the gallery a few feet from the glass-partitioned section reserved for defendants, and had a close-hand view of Lendrum as the bailiff escorted him into the courtroom. Dressed in sneakers, jeans, and a shapeless gray sweatshirt over a white cotton polo, he sat down, expressionless.

Craig Hunt, Lendrum's childhood friend who owned the Southern Comfort Lodge, would later speculate that Lendrum, floundering in the outside world, had deliberately engineered his own arrest at Heathrow, trading away his liberty for "free medical care, three meals a day, and a television set." If so, Lendrum had badly miscalculated the conditions of his incarceration. Wormwood Scrubs had become notorious for filth, narcotics, and gang warfare. After half a year awaiting trial, working as an orderly, or trusted assistant to the staff, in the segregation unit, which was reserved for disruptive prisoners or for those who faced a threat from other inmates, Lendrum looked paler, thinner, and more disheveled than the last time I had seen him. Still, when he had caught my eye the first morning of the trial, he flashed a smile. I smiled back.

At ten o'clock the usher rapped three times on the door separating the courtroom from the judge's chambers and called the session to order for the trial's third and penultimate day. All the attendees—Lendrum; his barrister, Tony Bell; the prosecutor, Sean Sullivan; four journalists; and Michelle Conway, a friend from his Rhodesian childhood who lived in England and had visited him frequently at Wormwood Scrubs ("Jeff is gentle as a lamb," she would tell me)—rose for the judge's entrance.

"God save the Queen," the usher intoned.

Judge Neil Saunders, a silver-haired jurist in his sixties, swept in with a bow. The previous afternoon, during a discussion of procedural issues, Saunders had derailed Lendrum's barrister's plans to try the case before a jury, which was still waiting in another room to be empanelled. Lendrum was not acting criminally, Bell had planned to argue to the jury, because his intention all along had been to hand the eggs over to British authorities upon arrival. The judge had ruled that what mattered in establishing culpability was not the defendant's alleged "intention," but the simple act of bringing prohibited goods into the country and not immediately declaring them. (To my surprise, this issue hadn't been dealt with before the proceedings began.) With his defense thrown out of court, Lendrum had been forced to plead guilty on the spot, uttering the plea to the judge from behind

the glass barrier. The jury pool was dismissed without even setting foot in the courtroom. Now, on day three, the trial would head
straight to the sentencing phase; prosecutor and barrister would each
call witnesses and present their arguments for and against a lengthy
incarceration directly to the judge.

Birds-of-prey expert Jemima Parry-Jones, the first prosecution
witness to be called, told the court that the birds Lendrum had stolen
came from a wide range of South African habitats—cliffs, mountain
peaks, old-growth forests, and riparian woodlands (forests near rivers or lakes)—indicating that his latest project had covered significant territory and had probably lasted days or even weeks, quite an
achievement for a man who claimed to suffer from nerve damage in
his arms and neck. Parry-Jones placed a street value on the eggs at
between £80,000 and £100,000, or between $104,000 and $130,000.

Lendrum had raised the suspicions of Heathrow's Border Force
the moment he stepped up to the immigration counter, a customs of-
fical testified in an affidavit read aloud in court. He had worn a heavy
winter coat during a brutal summer heat wave (better to conceal his
belt filled with eggs), held a return ticket to Johannesburg for six
o'clock that same evening, and offered a flimsy story about coming
to purchase airplane parts in Luton, a London suburb. He may also
have been on a watch list, though border officials would neither confirm nor deny this. Lendrum certainly thought so—although, trou-
blingly, Lendrum claimed that this hadn't stopped customs officials
from letting him through in the past. "A couple of times coming into
the UK, I joked with the guys, and they let me go," Lendrum told the
court when summoned to the stand in the afternoon. "'I know what
you're here for,' they said."

Lendrum again cast himself as a misunderstood animal savior.

He had rescued the eggs from forests because "South Africa was cutting down all the trees," he testified, "destroying their habitat." He had told customs officers at Heathrow that his intention all along had been to turn the eggs over to them and to request that they deliver them to Parry-Jones's birds-of-prey center in Gloucestershire, where they would be hatched under close supervision and protected. There were rumors, however, that the intended recipient was an unscrupulous Welsh breeder and longtime friend of Lendrum's, who'd been waiting just outside Heathrow that morning, and who had fled when he realized that Lendrum had been arrested. Lendrum's unpersuasive performance on the stand reminded me of the classic definition of insanity: doing the same thing over and over and expecting different results.

"You are a convicted smuggler of rare birds around the globe for profit, are you not?" Sullivan, a young, sandy-haired Oxford graduate, challenged Lendrum as the cross-examination phase got under way. "In Brazil you are convicted of those offenses, and you run. You flee jurisdiction, is that right?"

"On—on the advice of my lawyer, yes," Lendrum stammered.

"You are an absconded smuggler of birds eggs, and that's what you were when you arrived at Heathrow, weren't you? You were on the run, as a convicted smuggler."

"I spoke to my lawyer and I thought I had won the appeal."

"It's not the case, is it?"

"Now I know."

When it came time to pronounce his sentence, at ten o'clock the following morning, Saunders, echoing several judges before him, called Lendrum's testimony "completely implausible." The judge asked him to rise. He had weighed the gravity of Lendrum's offense, he said, against his age, precarious health, last-minute change of plea to guilty, and the character references submitted by Michelle Conway and Craig Hunt. Conway had compared Lendrum admiringly to "Crocodile Dundee," while Hunt had described his gentle, fun-loving, but "impulsive" nature, ever since his school days.

"The sentence I pass," Saunders said, "is one of thirty-seven months' imprisonment on each count, to run concurrently." Lendrum would serve his sentence at Pentonville Prison in North London, a hulking, high-walled fortress erected during the early Victorian era, where the Irish poet and playwright Oscar Wilde had spent two months of his two-year sentence at hard labor for homosexuality. A 2018 report by the Independent Monitoring Board declared the penitentiary crumbling and "rife" with vermin and complained that inmates went weeks without getting exercise in fresh air.

Lendrum rose without expression and left the courtroom, holding the best-selling nonfiction book that Conway had given him during her most recent jailhouse visit: *Factfulness: Ten Reasons We're Wrong About the World—and Why Things Are Better Than You Think.* Lendrum's own prospects offered little reason for optimism. With his five convictions on four continents, two terms in prison, a flight from a felony conviction in Brazil, and an Interpol Red Notice, it was hard to imagine that any prospective employer would be willing to give the hapless thief another chance once he got out. He faced the threat of extradition to Brazil, though the authorities had yet to file a request at the Westminster Magistrates Court in London, the clearinghouse for all such petitions. He was on immigration watch lists around the world, and his criminal record was all over the Internet. "There's more hits on my name than the Yorkshire Ripper," he had complained, near tears, once again the self-proclaimed victim, at one point in his testimony. Lendrum had made an attempt to cover his tracks, yet it demonstrated the same degree of ineptitude and half-heartedness as his latest egg smuggling escapade. In 2017, it had emerged in court that morning, the falcon thief had officially changed his name to "John Smith." Lendrum was a man trapped in an endless loop of criminality, unable to outrun his past.

=

Andy McWilliam had followed the Lendrum proceedings from Liverpool, sidelined from the investigation by the National Crime Agency. For a brief time in the run-up to the trial, McWilliam had thought that the prosecutor might summon him to court to provide evidence of Lendrum's "bad character." But by autumn his hopes of playing a useful role had faded. The day after Lendrum's sentencing, I caught a train from London Euston to Liverpool Lime Street to get his take on the trial.

McWilliam was waiting for me at the end of the platform. I almost didn't recognize him: He was thirty pounds lighter than the last time I had seen him, having embarked on an extreme bicycling regimen after a health scare. He was not surprised by Lendrum's relatively modest punishment, which all but guaranteed that he would walk out of prison, on parole, in thirteen months. "The prisons are so damned bloody crowded," he told me, as we ambled through the Victorian heart of Liverpool, a time capsule of the port's glory days. "As long as you're not considered a 'threat to society' the judge will grant you some leeway." Unlike Craig Hunt, who believed that Lendrum had intended to get caught at Heathrow Airport that June morning, the investigator was convinced that Lendrum had made the smuggling journey from Johannesburg to London several times—until his luck had run out that June. This time, McWilliam didn't offer any optimism that Lendrum would stay out of trouble after his release on parole in the winter of 2020. (In the late spring of 2019 Lendrum would be transferred from the grim purgatory of Pentonville to the category "D," or minimum security, Ayelesbury Prison, in Buckinghamshire, north of London.)

We walked past St. George's Hall, a colonnaded concert venue built of sandstone. McWilliam had stood on its steps on December 9, 1980, keeping watch over the thousands of Liverpudlians grieving for John Lennon, who'd been murdered in New York City the night before. As McWilliam spoke, I wondered, not for the first time, whether intertwining his story so closely with Lendrum's diminished his accomplishments. He'd been around long before Lendrum— and would keep investigating crimes now that his quarry was locked away.

The National Wildlife Crime Unit was entering its thirteenth year, having survived a series of bruising funding battles. In the winter of 2014, only a last-minute plea by Head of Unit Nevin Hunter to the Home Ministry and the Department for Environment, Food & Rural Affairs (DEFRA) had saved the unit from dissolution and McWilliam and his colleagues from unemployment. Nearly the same scenario had occurred when funding lapsed two years later. This time the government had, in the final hours, committed to keeping the unit active until 2020.

McWilliam seemed confident that the existential struggles were over. The unit had achieved headline-making successes in recent years. An international investigation had resulted in the convictions and jailing of members of the Rathkeale Rovers, an Irish organized crime gang that had carried out a series of brazen rhino-horn robberies in museums across England, selling the artifacts to China. Some of the thieves got eight years. McWilliam had also become ever more skilled at scrutinizing the Internet for evidence of wildlife crime; two weeks earlier, photos that he'd spotted on Facebook had led to a raid and an arrest in Merseyside for that peculiar British scourge, badger baiting. He and his colleagues had expanded their investigation into the illegal falcon trade, too. McWilliam hinted that he'd gotten intelligence on some of the biggest financiers in Dubai and other Emirates; once again, though, he wasn't allowed to name names. Efforts to persuade Arab governments to act on the intelligence collected by the National Wildlife Crime Unit had so far led nowhere. "It's out of our control," McWilliam said with resignation.

McWilliam's appearance in *Poached* had made him something of a law-enforcement celebrity—much like the heroes of his favorite police drama from his childhood, *Dixon of Dock Green*. The documentary focused in part on the relationship between the wildlife officer and John Kinsley, a prolific Merseyside egg collector turned bird photographer. In 2002, McWilliam had blocked Kinsley's application for a license to photograph birds' nests, skeptical about his claim that he had reformed; four years later, police in South Wales arrested Kinsley for disturbing goshawks while climbing a tree to take pictures without a permit. "I got twelve months' probation and was banned from every national park and reserve . . . because of Andy McWilliam," Kinsley told the director bitterly early in the film.

After that setback, Kinsley had self-published a book, *Scourge of the Birdman*, a long attack on McWilliam that contained a doctored photograph of his nemesis with a Hitler mustache. The book, according to the jacket copy, "reveals the issues of corruption and dishonesty [of] some of those with positions of authority." But in recent years, McWilliam and Kinsley had set aside their animosity, and the officer had evolved into something of a confidant for the egg thief. At the film's conclusion, Kinsley, a haunted-looking figure who struggled for years with depression and unemployment, seeks to take advantage of an offer of amnesty and break from his criminal past. He summons McWilliam to his home and voluntarily turns over to him on camera his entire collection of thousands of eggs.

=

Several egg collections that McWilliam confiscated from Merseyside criminals in the 1990s and 2000s are held under lock and key in a storage room at the Liverpool World Museum, a bounty of archaeological and natural history wonders opened in 1860, at the height of the British Empire. I asked McWilliam if he could give me a tour, and, after a scramble on the phone to obtain permission, we rendezvoused with a curator in the museum's cavernous central gallery.

The curator led McWilliam and me down a corridor, past administrators' offices and storage rooms, to a door marked NO ENTRY. We followed him into a refrigerated chamber where the museum stores nearly ten thousand clutches. Almost all the specimens are kept in Tupperware-type plastic containers or glass-topped wooden trays on shelves in long rows of steel cabinets, which are compressed together and slide open with a turn of a handle, like a bank vault.

McWilliam opened drawers filled with trays of eggs belonging to Dennis Hughes, a daring peregrine egg collector who had been killed in a fall in a rock quarry in 1991. The collection had remained hidden for a decade after his death. In 2000, an informant told McWilliam that Hughes's mother had kept her son's bedroom locked since the day he died. "I went round and gently persuaded his mum, 'Let's have a look,'" McWilliam recalled. Inside a false bottom in Hughes's bed, McWilliam found hundreds of eggs. A magistrate ordered their forfeiture, and McWilliam turned them over to the museum.

Here, too, were the collections of Anthony Higham and Carlton D'Cruze, the two Merseyside miscreants who'd been among the first significant collars of McWilliam's wildlife-crime-fighting career. But the most impressive cache had belonged to Dennis Green, the destitute bird portraitist and onetime member of the Royal Society for the Protection of Birds who'd amassed four thousand eggs, one of the largest collections ever seized in Great Britain.

We cast our eyes over Green's artfully arranged clutches of oystercatchers, stone curlews, peregrine falcons, and other endangered species: gem-like orbs resting on beds of cotton, fragile spheres of white, cream, and violet spotted and speckled with dark pigment. For a year I had been speaking to McWilliam about the compulsiveness and self-destructiveness of the collectors, had interviewed Lendrum about his relentless pursuit of live raptor eggs, at the risk of his freedom and sometimes his life, and viewed the famous oological collection at the British Natural History Museum in Tring, packed with the trophies gathered by eighteenth- and nineteenth-century obsessives. There, in Hertfordshire, I'd seen the peregrine eggs that Derek Ratcliffe had used to document the lethal effects of DDT, one example of egg collecting serving, however inadvertently, the cause of science. I had also inspected perhaps the collection's greatest treasures: six freckled, pale yellow, pyriform or pear-shaped eggs of the great auk, a flightless seabird that had lived across the upper latitudes and been driven into extinction by excessive hunting in the mid-nineteenth century. These eggs included an eighteenth-century specimen once owned by the famed Italian biologist Lazzaro Spallanzani, which

Walter Rothschild, the museum's founder, had purchased for a substantial sum in 1901.

I had dived deep into the esoteric world of the oologist, and begun to understand the eggs' remarkable power: the beauty of their many shapes, textures, colors, and patterns, each the product of natural selection, the better to perpetuate the species . . . The complex metabolic system wrapped in a delicate casing, from the protein-rich albumen that cushions and nourishes the developing embryo to the microscopic pores on the surface of the shell that draw in oxygen and expel carbon dioxide . . . The egg, a symbol of new life and fertility, a self-contained miracle of genesis and development, requiring only heat and air to thrive, was "incorporated as a sacred sign in the cosmogony of every people on the earth," wrote Helena Blavatsky, a nineteenth-century Russian occultist and philosopher, "and was revered on account of its form and inner mystery." McWilliam sometimes ridiculed the collectors for their bizarre attachment to "a piece of calcium," but I was coming to see that he, too, grasped their mysterious allure. "I think that if required on pain of death to name instantly the most perfect thing in the universe, I should risk my fate on a bird's egg," declared the clergyman and political activist Thomas Wentworth Higginson in 1862.

Next to the rows of cabinets, McWilliam recognized an antique wooden display case with forty thin drawers that he had seized from Green's bedroom on a spring day in 1999, almost exactly twenty years earlier. "It's like meeting an old friend," McWilliam said. He opened the drawers to reveal the speckled buff-colored eggs of black-legged kittiwakes; the marble-like, lily-white eggs of Dartford warblers; and the black-and-purple-splattered eggs of red-backed shrikes, whose disappearance from Britain in the 1970s had turned public opinion decisively against the oologists. Each clutch had a story behind it—of human obsession and nature's fragility, of man's perpetual insistence on imposing his will upon the wildness of our world, and of the tiny handful of investigators, most unrecognized, working to safeguard the environment's bounty and wonder.

The curator closed the cabinets and sealed the vault, and McWilliam led me back to the museum's main gallery and out into the world.

Rafael Asenjo and Nicolas Soto Volkart of Chile's Agriculture and Livestock Service provided key information about the trap they'd laid for Lendrum, while Nicolas's son, Alvaro Soto, served as my guide in the wilds of Chilean Patagonia—imparting his knowledge about the resident birdlife and giving my Spanish a three-day workout. Nicolas Fernández at the Hotel Plaza recounted Lendrum's sojourn there and gave me a personal tour of Punta Arenas. Dorothea Cist, a resident of Santiago, was instrumental in making the Chile trip happen. In Dubai, the estimable Pranay Gupte provided introductions to key contacts. Linda El Sayed Ahmed and Suad Ibrahim Darwish of the Hamdan bin Mohammed Heritage Center arranged visits to falcon breeders and trainers working for the Al Maktoum family; in Abu Dhabi, Bryn Close and his daughter Natalie allowed me to shadow them for three days at the President Cup, and Angelique Engels, an official at the Abu Dhabi Falconer's Club, answered all my questions about the sport.

I'm grateful to Timothy Wheeler, the director of *Poached*, who shared the raw transcript of his long interview with Andy McWilliam; and to Paula Lendrum Maughan and Richard Lendrum, who filled in details about their brother's early years. Jeffrey Lendrum met with me near Pretoria for three hours and continued conversing with me by phone for six months, making me understand his genuine passion for birds of prey and even turning over the GPS coordinates of the nests he plundered in the Rhondda Valley and Patagonia.

Kevin Cote was involved in this project from its early days, serving as an enthusiastic listener, problem solver, and sounding board over dozens of hours of bike riding along the Havelchaussee and through the Grunewald in Berlin. Philip and Terrie Stoltzfus hosted me at their home during my frequent visits to London, serving me fantastic dinners, putting me up in a guest room, and listening to my tales of egg collectors, bird smugglers, and falcon racers. Their daughter, Ellie Chamberlain Stolztfus, and her husband, Dan Chamberlain, often joined us and also lent an ear to my ramblings. Kathleen Burke, Janet Reitman, Lee Smith, Yudhijit Bhattacharjee, Diane Edelman, David Dobrin, and Melissa Eddy helped to assuage anxieties and self-doubt. Alex Perry provided keen advice and, with his family, hosted me at his lovely home in Hampshire. David Van Biema, a fellow bird enthusiast, kept me excited about the project; Terry McCarthy was a pal and soul mate during his too-brief sojourn in Berlin. Geoffrey Gagnon in New York and Claudio Edinger in São Paulo also offered friendship and support.

Jon Sawyer and Tom Hundley at the Pulitzer Center, Ian Buruma, formerly of the *New York Review of Books*, and Suzanne MacNeille of the *New York Times* underwrote my trip to Southern Africa in December 2017; Suzanne also assigned me pieces from Chile and Dubai, further helping me defray the costs of my global odyssey. The gang at *Outside*—Chris Keyes, Alex Heard, Reid Singer, Luke Whelan, and my longtime editor Elizabeth Hightower Allen—commissioned, edited, and published my article "The Egg Thief," which became the basis for *The Falcon Thief*.

I'm deeply indebted to my editor, Priscilla Painton at Simon & Schuster, who believed in this project from its inception and pushed me onward. Megan Hogan edited the manuscript line by line, vastly ramping up the quality of the narrative, shepherded it along from start to finish, and took care of countless production-related details. Emily Simonson also contributed valuable comments and questions, as did production editors Samantha Hoback and Yvette Grant. Flip Brophy, my longtime agent, was an eager listener over breakfasts at

Barney Greengrass and other eateries in New York City. Nell Pierce, Flip's assistant, cheerfully and efficiently dealt with contract issues and other details.

Finally, great thanks to my mother, Nina Hammer, my father, Richard Hammer, my stepmother, Arlene Hammer, and my sister, Emily Hammer, for being there for me on the other side of the pond. In Berlin, my sons, Max, Nico, and Tom abided my frequent absences, and understood—even shared a bit—my growing fascination for birds. Above all, Cordula Kraemer believed in me, stood by me, kept me focused when I was seized by structural problems and anxieties, and gave endlessly to me. Without her love, generosity, and patience, this story would never have taken flight.

NOTES

Prologue

xi *"Thief Who Preys on Falcon Eggs"*: John Simpson, the *Times*, January 5, 2017.

xii *"A glimpse of dense brush"*: Jonathan Franzen, "My Bird Problem," *The New Yorker*, August 8, 2005.

Chapter One: The Airport

2 *"gave me a background"*: John Struczynski, interview by author, April 14, 2018.

4 *"Are you carrying"*: Mark Owen, Midlands-Birmingham Police, interview by author, October 4, 2017; Andy McWilliam, interview by author, Liverpool, August 22, 2017.

6 *"What kind of eggs"*: Owen, interview, October 4; McWilliam, interview, August 22.

Chapter Two: The Investigator

9 *"We're not quite sure"*: Andy McWilliam, interview by author, Liverpool, January 21, 2017.

11 *"a spectacular crash"*: Derek Ratcliffe, *The Peregrine Falcon* (London: A&C Black, 1993), 66.

11 *"all peregrine eyries"*: David R. Zemmerman, "Death Comes to the Peregrine Falcon," the *New York Times*, August 9, 1970, p. 161.

11 *"as crude a weapon"*: Rachel Carson, *Silent Spring* (New York: Houghton Mifflin, 1962), 297.

12 *"This sudden silencing"*: Carson, *Silent Spring*, 103.

13 *"As an apex predator"*: Guy Shorrock, interview by author, Sandy, England, August 26, 2017.

15 *"I always say"*: Mark Jeter, quoted in "The Egg Thief" by Joshua Hammer, *Outside*, January 7, 2019.

16 *"All living things"*: Alfred Russel Wallace, *The Malay Archipelago: the Land of the Orang-utan and the Bird of Paradise: A Narrative of Travel with Studies of Man and Nature* (London: Macmillan, 1890).

16 *"To the bird watcher"*: Carson, *Silent Spring*, 86.

17 *"Don't let the man go"*: Andy McWilliam, interview by author, August 23, 2017.

20 *"That's alive"*: Lee Featherstone, phone interview by author, March 3, 2018.

21 *"He knew what he was doing"*: Featherstone, interview, March 3.

21 *"They're fertile, they're alive"*: Featherstone, interview, March 3.

Chapter Three: The Interview

24 *"She was in a terrible state"*: Jeffrey Lendrum, phone interview by author, March 16, 2018.

24 *"Okay, you were arrested"*: Andy McWilliam, interview by author, Liverpool, January 21, 2018.

24 *"This is ridiculous"*: McWilliam, interview, January 21.

24 *"They're duck eggs"*: McWilliam, interview, January 21.

27 *"Let's go find that car"*: McWilliam, interview, January 21.

27 *"Smash open the window"*: McWilliam, interview, January 21.

28 *"If you're just an egg collector"*: McWilliam, interview, January 21.

Chapter Four: The Art of Falconry

31 *"a falconer bearing a hawk"*: Austen Henry Layard, *Discoveries Among the Ruins of Ninevah and Babylon* (London: Harper, 1853), 112.

32 *"For the Bedouin"*: Mark Allen, *Falconry in Arabia*, with a foreword by Wilfred Thesiger (London: Orbis, 1980), 15.

32 *"a swift dog and a splendid hawk"*: Robin S. Oggins, *The Kings and Their Hawks: Falconry in Medieval England* (New Haven, CT: Yale University Press, 2004), 38.

32 *"falcon gentle"*: Oggins, 38.

33 *"is to have his horse"*: Oggins, 38.

33 *"was surrounded by hawks"*: Layard, *Discoveries*, 409.

34 *"is generally made"*: Layard, 412.

34 *"Although the smallest"*: Layard, 410.

35 *"The peregrine swoops"*: J. A. Baker, *The Peregrine* (London: HarperCollins, 1967), 40.

35   *"The hawk breaks"*: Baker, 40.

36   *"so events in time"*: Helen Macdonald, *Falcon* (London: Reaktion Books, 2006), 31.

36   *"between black-and-white"*: Macdonald, 32.

40   *"on a downward spiral"*: Sarah Townsend, "Sheik Hamdan's Bid to Revive the Glorious Arab Sport of Falconry," *Arabian Business*, June 13, 2015.

40   *"drawing gasps from breeders"*: Townsend.

40   *"Any strong falcon"*: Anonymous falconry expert, interview by author, Abu Dhabi, United Arab Emirates, January 9, 2018.

41   *"back-to-nature quest"*: Fernanda Eberstadt, "Falconry's Popularity Soars in England and Scotland," *Condé Nast Traveler*, January 15, 2013.

Chapter Five: Rhodesia

44   *"hyperactive and aware"*: Pat Lorber, interview by author, King's Lynn, England, August 23, 2017.

44   *"I'm Pat Lorber. Who are you?"*: Lorber, interview, August 23.

45   *"My father was passionate"*: Jeffrey Lendrum, interview by author, Centurion, South Africa, December 18, 2017.

46   *"I've climbed to more nests"*: Jeffrey Lendrum, phone interview by author, March 16, 2018.

47   *"tons of sticks, and build a rudimentary nest"*: Vernon Tarr, interview by author, Bulawayo, Zimbabwe, December 10, 2017.

47   *"I'd climb a tree"*: Howard Waller, interview by author, Inverness, Scotland, January 22, 2018.

49   *"He saw the way things were going"*: Richard Lendrum, interview by author, Rosebank, South Africa, December 18, 2017.

51   *"were likable, smooth, gregarious, and chatty"*: Lorber, interview, August 23.

52   *"They can fly in a gale"*: Rob Davies, "The Verreaux's Eagle—An Interview with Dr. Rob Davies," *African Raptors: The Online Home of African Raptor Interests*, August 12, 2010, http://www.africanraptors.org/the-verreauxs-eagle-an-interview-with-dr-rob-davies/.

52   *"like watching jet fighters"*: Davies.

53   *"Val could go put her hand gently"*: Lorber, interview, August 23.

53   *"The eagle didn't flinch"*: Tarr, interview, December 10.

53   *"Do not stay"*: Valerie Gargett, *The Black Eagle: A Study* (Randburg: Acorn Books, 1990), 22.

53   *"We are visitors"*: Gargett, 22.

53   *"It paid to be physically fit"*: Gargett, 22.

54   *"Jeff was cocky"*: Lorber, interview, August 23.

54   *"The Lendrums are so active"*: Lorber, interview, August 23.

55 *"kow-kow"* . . . *"bombing-diving-and-stooping"*: A. Lendrum and J. Lendrum, *Augur Buzzard Study*, Ornithological Association of Zimbabwe, ninth annual report, 1982.

55 *"They would throw up a claw"*: Lorber, interview, August 23.

57 *"My dad used to go up on call-ups"*: Richard Lendrum, interview, Rosebank, South Africa, December 18.

57 *"Being a nonconformist"*: Paula Lendrum Maughan, Facebook Messenger interview with author, April 17, 2019.

57 *"hot extractions"*: Jeffrey Lendrum, testimony, *The Queen v. Jeffrey Lendrum*, Snaresbrook Crown Court London, January 9, 2019.

57 *"He saw some terrible things"*: Michelle Conway, interview by author, London, January 9, 2019.

58 *"Some of these impostors"*: "Wall of Shame," The C Squadron 22 Special Air Service web page, http://www.csqnsas.com/dishonour.html.

58 *"One thing you get to know"*: Paul Mullin, phone interview by author, May 9, 2018.

59 *"incomplete breeding cycles"*: Lorber, interview, August 23.

59 *"This had never happened before"*: Lorber, interview, August 23.

61 *"Have you just been to the crowned eagle nest?"*: Christopher "Kit" Hustler, phone interview by author, September 12, 2017.

Chapter Six: Liverpool

64 *"I thought,* I can do this*"*: Andy McWilliam, interview by author, Liverpool, August 22, 2017.

65 *"What is the Ku Klux Klan?"*: McWilliam, interview, August 22.

65 *"the active side"*: Andy McWilliam, phone interview by author, May 17, 2018.

65 *"They must have been"*: McWilliam, interview, August 22.

66 *"You, boots!"*: Andy McWilliam, interview by author, Liverpool, January 11, 2019.

66 *"policing by consent"*: British Home Office, "Definition of Policing by Consent," December 10, 2012, https://www.gov.uk/government/publications/policing-by-consent/definition-of-policing-by-consent.

66 *"to talk down"*: McWilliam, interview, January 11.

67 *"That's it, mate"*: McWilliam, interview, August 22.

67 *"Don't you like the police?"*: McWilliam, interview, August 22.

68 *"the New York of Europe"*: *The Bankers' Magazine*, vol. 11 (London: Groombridge & Sons, 1851).

69 *" faced stretches of waste ground"*: Andy Beckett, *Promised You a Miracle: Why 1980–82 Made Modern Britain* (London: Penguin, 2016).

71 *"It was us against them"*: McWilliam, phone interview, May 17.

71   *"You're going to the Linby Colliery"*: McWilliam, interview, August 22.

71   *"There are fathers"*: Andy McWilliam, interview by author, Liverpool, October 2, 2017.

73   *"an old shat of a car"*: McWilliam, interview, August 22.

73   *"You become detached"*: McWilliam, interview, August 22.

74   *"Listen here, you bastard"*: McWilliam, interview, October 2.

74   *"Do you remember me?"*: McWilliam, interview, October 2.

74   *"Christ! This is murder"*: McWilliam, interview, October 2.

75   *"the opposition"*: McWilliam, interview, August 22.

Chapter Seven: The Trial

79   *"a pair of live bird eggs"*: Christopher "Kit" Hustler, phone interview by author, May 7, 2018.

79   *"Leave as fast as you can"*: Hustler, phone interview, May 7.

80   *"Are you Adrian Lendrum?"*: Hustler, phone interview, May 7.

80   *"We had no warning"*: Jeffrey Lendrum, interview by author, Centurion, South Africa, December 18, 2017.

81   *"Thank God you're here"*: Hustler, phone interview, May 7.

82   *"Have you got the standard?"*: Hustler, phone interview, May 7.

82   *"We just got them today"*: Hustler, phone interview, May 7.

83   *"What do you think this is?"*: Pat Lorber, interview by author, King's Lynn, England, August 23, 2017.

83   *"one single red blotch"*: Lorber, interview, August 23.

84   *"chicks growing well"*: Lorber, interview, August 23.

84   *"Val is being over-the-top"*: Hustler, phone interview, May 7.

85   *"misunderstanding"*: Anonymous former colleague of Peggy Lendrum at Girls' College, Bulawayo, email to Pat Lorber, April 10, 2019, sent to author.

85   *"Adrian had thought"*: Lorber, interview, August 23.

87   *"irregular"*: Prosecutor, *State v. Adrian Lloyd Lendrum and Jeffrey Paul Lendrum*, case number 7904-5/6, transcript, October 1, 1984.

87   *"There was a trust placed in you"*: Giles Romilly, *State v. Adrian Lloyd Lendrum and Jeffrey Paul Lendrum*, case number 7904-5/6, transcript, October 1, 1984.

88   *"face just fell"*: Lorber, interview, August 23.

88   *"People didn't want"*: Lorber, interview, August 23.

88   *"He would be gone"*: Hustler, phone interview, May 7.

89   *"British police asserted"*: "A Matter of Trust," *Honeyguide: Journal of Zimbabwean and Regional Ornithology* 31, no. 2 (September 1985).

89   *"is organized internationally"*: "A Matter of Trust."

90   *"a very personable"*: P. C. Mundy, "The Lendrum Case: Retrospective 2," *Honeyguide: Journal of Zimbabwean and Regional Ornithology* 56, no. 2 (September 2010).

90 *"sense of entitlement"*: Christopher "Kit" Hustler, phone interview by author, April 10, 2019.

90 *"They couldn't climb, so they came to me"*: Jeffrey Lendrum, phone interview by author, May 18, 2018.

91 *"he slipped away in the gloom"*: Mundy, "The Lendrum Case: Retrospective 2."

91 *"The guy has been reading"*: Jeffrey Lendrum, interview, December 18.

Chapter Eight: The Collectors

94 *"Their pointless pursuit"*: Guy Shorrock, "Operation Easter: The Beginnings," *Royal Society for the Protection of Birds Blog*, May 9, 2018, https://community .rspb.org.uk/ourwork/b/investigations/posts/operation-easter-the -beginnings.

96 *"a misunderstanding"*: Andy McWilliam, interview by author, Liverpool, January 21, 2018.

96 *"as a gift"*: Guy Shorrock, phone interview by author, May 23, 2018.

96 *"Nazi storm troopers"*: McWilliam, interview, January 21.

97 *"a Cabinet of rarities"*: Tim Birkhead, *The Most Perfect Thing: Inside (and Outside) a Bird's Egg* (London: Bloomsbury, 2017), 10.

97 *"Acquisition in the name"*: Birkhead, 12.

98 *"As he rode headlong"*: Carrol L. Henderson, *Oology and Ralph's Talking Eggs: Bird Conservation Comes Out of Its Shell* (Austin: University of Texas Press, 2009), 30.

98 *"Daring Act of American Ornithologist"*: Mark Barrow, *A Passion for Birds: American Ornithology After Audubon* (Princeton, NJ: Princeton University Press, 1998), 42.

99 *"the sad ending of an active"*: Frank Haak Lattin, et al., *The Oologist* 26 (1908): 92.

99 *"a passion for beauty"*: Birkhead, *Most Perfect Thing*, 13.

99 *"I have vivid memories"*: *British Birds: An Illustrated Monthly Magazine*, vol. 51, 1958, pp. 237–38.

100 *"ogling his eggs"*: Birkhead, *Most Perfect Thing*, 15.

100 *"Perhaps their wonderful curves"*: Birkhead, 15.

100 *"distinct menace"*: Julian Rubinstein, "Operation Easter," *The New Yorker*, July 22, 2013.

100 *"Are we English people"*: Eric Parker, "Ethics of Egg Collecting," *The Field* (London), 1935.

101 *"the cloak-and-dagger"*: Patrick Barkham, "The Egg Snatchers," *The Guardian*, December 11, 2006.

101 *"pariah of the bird-watching world"*: Mary Braid, "Birds Egg Society Faces Inquiry," *The Independent*, January 15, 1995.

101   *"little Hitlers"*: Stephen Moss, ed., *The Hedgerows Heaped with May: The Telegraph Book of the Countryside* (London: Aurum Press, 2012).

102   *"It's very rare"*: Rubinstein, "Operation Easter."

102   *"Britain's foremost wildlife detective"*: *The Field* magazine, cited on back cover of Alan Stewart, *Wildlife Detective: A Life Fighting Wildlife Crime* (Edinburgh: Argyll Publishing, 2008).

102   *"I heard that when they reached wherever they were going"*: Andy McWilliam, interview by author, Liverpool, October 2, 2017.

103   *"We laid them out like a macabre jigsaw puzzle"*: Guy Shorrock, phone interview, May 23.

103   *"Abbott and Costello"*: Barkham, "The Egg Snatchers."

104   *"I pass the brochures out in the countryside"*: Steve Harris, phone interview by author, September 13, 2017.

105   *"became a bit of a hero"*: McWilliam, interview, January 21.

105   *"Don't you need a CITES"*: Andy McWilliam, interview by author, Liverpool, August 22, 2017.

106   *"The collectors couldn't bullshit"*: Harris, phone interview, September 13.

106   *"Andy was a no-nonsense"*: Guy Shorrock, interview by author, Sandy, England, August 26, 2017.

106   *"Has Mr. Higham asked"*: McWilliam, interview, January 21.

107   *"They're beautiful, aren't they"*: McWilliam, interview, January 21.

107   *"It's the sixty-four-thousand-dollar"*: *Poached*, directed by Timothy Wheeler (Ignite Channel, 2015), transcript of interview with Andy McWilliam.

108   *"the pseudo-protectionists"*: W. Pearson, *The Osprey: Nesting Sites in the British Isles*, (Brighton, England: Oriel Stringer, 1987), 11.

108   *"obsessed with the peregrine"*: Shorrock, interview, August 26.

108   *"I traveled elsewhere"*: Barkham, "Egg Snatchers."

109   *"the pinnacle of egg collecting"*: Shorrock, interview, August 26.

109   *"In memory of Jock—The Man"*: Rubinstein, "Operation Easter."

109   *"I was well and truly hooked"*: Rachel Newton, "Jailed Egg Thief 'A Threat to Wildlife,'" *Daily Post* (Liverpool), April 11, 2003.

110   *"Britain's most ruthless"*: Rubinstein, "Operation Easter."

110   *"Nest in Peace"*: Rubinstein.

110   *"top secret"*: McWilliam, interview, January 21.

110   *"The sight which met"*: Rachel Newton, "Jailed egg thief 'a threat to wildlife,'" *Liverpool Daily Press*, April 11, 2003, p. 11.

111   *"My body felt cold"*: "Jail For Prolific Collector of Eggs," extract from field notes, *Legal Eagle: The RSPB's Investigations Newsletter*, January 2003, no. 35.

111 *"The [mother] bird's"*: Holly Cale, interview by author, Newent, Gloucester-shire, England, August 22, 2017.

112 *"loners and social misfits"*: McWilliam, interview, October 2.

112 *"from butter to packets of instant custard"*: Rubinstein, "Operation Easter."

112 *"I can't believe"*: McWilliam, interview, October 2.

112 *"They are somehow"*: Emma Bryce, "Inside the Bizarre, Secretive World of Ob-sessive Egg Thieves," *Audubon*, January 6, 2016.

112 *"rare and difficult"*: Menelaos Apostolou, "Why Men Collect Things? A Case Study of Fossilized Dinosaur Eggs," *Journal of Economic Psychology* 32, no. 3 (June 2011): 410–17.

113 *"They're good, aren't they?"*: McWilliam, interview, October 2.

113 *"If I pick this bloody"*: McWilliam, interview, October 2.

114 *"just didn't seem"*: McWilliam, interview, October 2.

114 *"Is this going to be it?"*: McWilliam, interview, October 2.

114 *"egg collecting just fell"*: Shorrock, interview, August 26.

114 *"Put him before the beak"*: Harris, phone interview, September 13.

115 *"was regarded as trivial"*: Harris, phone interview, September 13.

Chapter Nine: AfricaXtreme

118 *"I had nothing to do"*: Jeffrey Lendrum, phone interview by author, February 23, 2018.

118 *"collecting black sparrowhawks"*: Lendrum, testimony, *The Queen v. Jeffrey Lendrum*, Snaresbrook Crown Court London, January 9, 2019.

119 *"Wouldn't it be"*: Paul Mullin, interview by author, Hampshire, England, Au-gust 27, 2017.

121 *"If you're a border controller"*: Mullin, interview, August 27.

122 *"There's something wrong"*: Mullin, interview, August 27.

123 *"You could blindfold"*: Mullin, interview, August 27.

123 *"Throw some meat"*: Mullin, interview, August 27.

124 *"I've always rescued animals"*: Lendrum, phone interview by author, March 16, 2018.

124 *"Do you want it?"*: Mullin, interview, August 27.

125 *"turn your garden"*: Radio commercial, recorded by Paul Mullin and Jeffrey Lendrum, played for author by Mullin.

126 *"I'm so in love"*: Mullin, interview, August 27.

126 *"proof of concept"*: Mullin, interview, August 27.

126 *"It's the most beautiful"*: Jeffrey Lendrum, interview by author, Centurion, South Africa, December 18, 2017.

128 *"What the fuck"*: Mullin, interview, August 27.

128   *"I can hear"*: Mullin, interview, August 27.

129   *"a complete flight"*: Lendrum, phone interview, February 23.

129   *"He lived a very basic"*: Mullin, interview, August 27.

Chapter Ten: Dubai

131   *"If the nest is"*: Frederick II, *The Art of Falconry* [De arte venandi cum avibus], trans. and ed. Casey A. Wood and F. Marjorie Fyfe (Palo Alto: Stanford University Press, 1943), 129.

131   *"seven days after hatching"*: Robin S. Oggins, *The Kings and Their Hawks: Falconry in Medieval England* (New Haven, CT: Yale University Press, 2004), 21.

131   *"because the longer"*: Frederick II, *Art of Falconry*, 129.

132   *"the [malleability] of youth"*: Mark Allen, *Falconry in Arabia*, with a Foreword by *Wilfred Thesiger* (London: Orbis, 1980), 47.

135   *"the whole thing snowballed"*: Jemima Parry-Jones, interview by author, Newent, Gloucestershire, England, August 21, 2017.

136   *"I remember being nine"*: Howard Waller, interview by author, Inverness, Scotland, January 22, 2018.

136   *"We actually hated each other at first"*: Jeffrey Lendrum, interview by author, Centurion, South Africa, December 18, 2017.

137   *"I said that I'd like"*: Waller, interview, January 22.

138   *"Suddenly an Arab"*: Wilfred Thesiger, *Arabian Sands* (New York: Penguin Digital Editions, 2007), chapter 14.

139   *"What I remember most"*: Tom Bailey and Declan O'Donovan, "Interview with His Excellency Sheikh Butti bin Maktoum bin Juma Al Maktoum," *Wildlife Middle East News* 5, no. 4 (March 2011).

140   *"would go out onto"*: Waller, interview, January 22.

141   *"They don't care"*: Anonymous falcon breeder for Crown Prince Hamdan, interview by author, Dubai, October 31, 2017.

141   *"a killing machine"*: Emma Ford, *Gyrfalcon* (London: John Murray, 1999), 13.

142   *"a predatorial mash-up"*: T. Edward Nickens, "What One Magnificent Predator Can Show Us about the Arctic's Future," *Audubon*, January-February 2016.

142   *"a large and faire"*: Thomas T. Allsen, "Falconry and the Exchange Networks of Medieval Eurasia," *Pre-Modern Russia and Its World: Essays in Honor of Thomas S. Noonan* (Wiesbaden, Germany: Otto Harrassowitz Verlag, 2006), 39.

143   *"she feels the heat"*: Husam Al-Dawlah Taymur Mirza, *The Baz-Nama-Yi Nasiri, a Persian Treatise on Falconry*, trans. D. C. Philliott (London: Bernard Quaritch, 1908), 36.

144 *"Almost like a long-married"*: Peter Gwin, "Inside a Sheikh's Plan to Protect the World's Fastest Animal," *National Geographic*, October 2018.

144 *"arguably . . . one of the most"*: Gwin.

146 *"I put my hands"*: Waller, interview, January 22.

146 *"If the female is sucking"*: Waller, interview, January 22.

146 *"You can't just put"*: Waller, interview, January 22.

147 *"I am a falconer"*: Bailey and O'Donovan, "Interview with His Excellency."

147 *"There was one mountain gazelle"*: Bailey and O'Donovan.

148 *"Howard and his wife"*: Jeffrey Lendrum, phone interview by author, February 2018.

148 *"a very nice guy"*: Lendrum, interview, December 18.

148 *"The birds would get stressed"*: Lendrum, interview, December 18.

149 *"It's ninety-nine percent"*: Lendrum, interview, December 18.

149 *"Lendrum and I may have"*: Waller, interview, January 22.

150 *"worldwide, multi-million dollar"*: George Reiger, "Operation Falcon: The Anatomy of a Sting," *Field & Stream*, January 1985, p. 23.

151 *"like having someone"*: Ford, *Gyrfalcon*, 144.

151 *"Many Arabs still believe"*: Roger Cook, "The Bird Bandits," *The Cook Report*, ITV, February 1996.

151 *"trying desperately"*: The Hawk Board, press release, "Summary of Events Leading Up to and Following the Cook Report," February 10, 1996.

152 *"Eyes can be sewn shut"*: Tanya Wyatt, "The Illegal Trade of Raptors in the Russian Federation," *Contemporary Justice Review: Issues in Criminal, Social, and Restorative Justice* 14, no. 2 (2011).

153 *"There were several Arabs"*: Tom Parfitt, "Smuggling Trade Threatens Falcons with Extinction," *The Telegraph*, March 27, 2005.

153 *"There's huge, huge money"*: Anonymous falcon breeder, interview by author, undisclosed location, August 2017.

154 *"laundering illegal birds"*: Anonymous falcon breeder, interview by author, August 2017.

154 *"anyone who believes"*: Jemima Parry-Jones, interview by author, Newent, England, May, 2017.

155 *"Inbreeding has reduced survivability"*: Nick Fox, interview by author, Carmarthen, Wales, May 2, 2018.

155 *"regular infusion of genes"*: Toby Bradshaw, "Genetic Improvement of Captive Bred Raptors," University of Washington faculty website, October 2009, http://faculty.washington.edu/toby/baywingdb/Genetics%20of%20captive-bred%20raptors.pdf.

155 *"The thing they would worry about"*: Jeffrey Lendrum, phone interview by author, March 16, 2018.

Chapter Eleven: Operation Chilly

158 *"It's going to be the adventure"*: Paul Mullin, phone interview by author, October 31, 2018.

158 *"a dream on my bucket list"*: Jeffrey Lendrum, interview by author, Centurion, South Africa, December 18, 2017.

158 *"The gyrfalcons are like bluebottle flies"*: Paul Mullin, phone interview by author, June 4, 2018.

159 *"Because we grew up together"*: Howard Waller, interview by author, Inverness, Scotland, January 22, 2018.

159 *"I told him"*: Waller, interview, January 22.

159 *"a complete liar"*: Jeffrey Lendrum, phone interview by author, February 23, 2018.

159 *"They are the biggest"*: David Anderson, interview with Luke Whelan for author's article, "The Egg Thief," *Outside*, January 2019.

160 *"one of them to go extinct"*: Robinson Meyer, "The Battle over 2,500-Year-Old Shelters Made of Poop," *The Atlantic*, July 24, 2017, https://www.theatlantic.com/science/archive/2017/07/falcon-battle-over-nests-of-bird-poop/534510/.

160 *"[I am a] utility bush pilot"*: LinkedIn profile of "bush pilot."

162 *"Look at us"*: Video of "Operation Chilly," shot by Paul Mullin, June 2001, https://www.youtube.com/watch?v=lWce39190B0.

163 *"They're beautiful"*: Lendrum, video of "Operation Chilly," shot by Mullin, June 2001.

163 *"That is a fucking noise"*: Lendrum, video of "Operation Chilly," shot by Mullin, June 2001.

164 *"dangling from a helicopter"*: Paul Mullin, phone interview by author, May 3, 2019.

165 *"The nest was . . . the most filthy"*: Ernest Blakeman Vesey, *In Search of the Gyrfalcon: An Account of a Trip to Northwest Iceland* (London: Constable, 1938), 69.

165 *"The nest of these hawks"*: John James Audubon, *Birds of America* (New York: Welcome Rain Publishers, 2001; first edition published 1828).

166 *"The ground color"*: Arthur Cleveland Bent, *Life Histories of American Birds of Prey Part II*, Smithsonian Institution Bulletin 170 (Washington, DC: Government Printing Office, 1938), 12.

166 *"You're dependent on air flow"*: Paul Mullin, interview by author, Hampshire, England, August 27, 2017.

167 *"A lake, a mountain"*: Ronald Stevens, *The Taming of Genghis* (London: Hancock House, 2010; first edition published 1956).

167 *"Are you down?"*: Video of "Operation Chilly," shot by Paul Mullin.

168 *"He was always protective"*: Mullin, phone interview, June 4.

169 *"We never bothered"*: Mullin, phone interview, June 4.

169 *"It was a total success"*: Mullin, interview, August 27.

Chapter Twelve: Busted

172 *"the* Star Wars *effect"*: Paul Mullin, interview by author, Hampshire, England, August 27, 2017.

172 *"This is getting too much"*: Pete Duncan, phone interview by author, October 29, 2017.

173 *"I'm planning to come back"*: Duncan, phone interview, October 29.

174 *"Any wildlife photographer"*: Duncan, phone interview, October 29.

174 *"There's something fishy"*: Duncan, phone interview, October 29.

174 *"These guys are stealing eggs"*: Dave Watt, phone interview by author, October 27, 2017.

175 *"it was enough"*: Mullin, interview, August 27.

176 *"This is it, Jeff"*: Mullin, interview, August 27.

176 *"Have you been stealing"*: Mullin, interview, August 27.

177 *"You can either plead"*: Watt, phone interview, October 27.

178 *"He wanted to destroy the evidence"*: Watt, phone interview, October 27.

178 *"He would risk his own life to save them"*: Paul Mullin, interview by author, Hampshire, England, May 3, 2018.

178 *"He was the weakest"*: Mullin, interview, May 3.

178 *"out of jealousy"*: Mullin, interview, May 3.

179 *"Poachers Fined for Illegal Possession"*: Jane George, *Nunatsiaq News*, May 15, 2002.

179 *"Poached Eggs Seized from Fake Film Crew"*: *National Post*, May 18, 2002.

180 *"That was it"*: Mullin, interview, May 3.

Chapter Thirteen: The Unit

182 *"Mad Mullah of the Traffic Taliban"*: "Mad Mullah of the Traffic Taliban Breaks into His OWN Police Station in Bizarre Security Stunt," *Evening Standard*, December 17, 2007.

183 *"use investigative tactics"*: Jason Bennetto, "Police Set Up Wildlife Crime Squad to Hunt Down Gangs Muscling in Lucrative Trade," *The Independent*, April 22, 2002.

183 *"Most officers would say"*: Andy McWilliam, interview by author, Liverpool, August 22, 2017.

184 *"Don't knock it"*: Andy McWilliam, email to author, October 20, 2017.

185 *"Have you thought"*: McWilliam, interview, August 22.

185 *"Suddenly I was moved"*: McWilliam, interview, August 22.

186 *"Give it a go"*: McWilliam, interview, August 22.

186 *"people who think"*: "UK Wildlife Crime Centre Launched," BBC News, October 18, 2006.

187 *"The [Home Office] didn't"*: Alan Roberts, phone interview by author, September 7, 2017.

188 *"Those killing birds"*: Guy Shorrock, *Royal Society for the Protection of Birds* blog, May 23, 2018, https://community.rspb.org.uk/ourwork/b/investigations /posts/op-easter-3-of-3-nearly-cracked.

189 *"antique ivory carvings"*: Andy McWilliam, interview by author, Liverpool, October 2, 2017.

189 *"It still smelled bad"*: Roberts, phone interview, September 7.

190 *"academic zeal"*: Simon Winchester, "The Bone Man: A Skull Collector Reveals His Extraordinary Private Collection," *The Independent*, October 12, 2012.

190 *"back from the brink"*: "Back from the Brink: Together We Can Bring Our Threatened Species Back from the Brink," website of Buglife, https://www .buglife.org.uk/back-from-the-brink.

191 *"There's not a lot"*: McWilliam, interview, October 2.

193 *"finished him off"*: McWilliam, interview, October 2.

194 *"extreme and sickening cruelty"*: Lord Justice Laws, Mr. Justice Gray, and Judge Rivlin QC, *Regina v. Raymond Leslie Humphrey*, Court of Appeal, June 23, 2003.

194 *"was prepared to go to any lengths"*: "Bird Smuggling Racket Netted £160,000," *Yorkshire Post*, August 2, 2001.

195 *"One of the things with being a police wildlife officer"*: *Poached*, directed by Timothy Wheeler (Ignite Channel, 2015), transcript of interview with Andy McWilliam.

195 *"We began to pick up"*: McWilliam, interview, October 2.

196 *"It's all to do with the fact"*: *Poached*.

196 *"I do think on occasions they have something to offer"*: Andy McWilliam, email to Alan Roberts and other NWCS personnel, February 26, 2013, obtained and originally published in the British press through the Freedom of Information Act.

Chapter Fourteen: The Rhondda Valley

201 *"If you steal the eggs"*: Mike Thomas, interview by author, Garw Valley, Wales, May 1, 2018.

202 *"Whoever is climbing this"*: Thomas, interview, May 1.

202 *"You can spend days"*: Thomas, interview, May 1.

203 *"A couple of years"*: Andy McWilliam, interview by author, Rhondda Valley, Wales, May 3, 2017.

204 *"The hills have been stripped"*: Arthur Morris, Glamorgan, cited in the *GENUKI Gazetteer, UK and Ireland Geneology*, GENUKI charitable trust, https://www.genuki.org.uk/big/wal/GLA/Rhondda/HistSnips.

205 *"We're at the end"*: Ian Guildford, interview by author, Rhondda Valley, Wales, May 3, 2017.

206 *"I've got a lucky ability"*: Jeffrey Lendrum, phone interview by author, March 16, 2018.

207 *"We've got a man in custody"*: Andy McWilliam, interview by author, Liverpool, August 22, 2017.

207 *"If we bail him"*: McWilliam, interview, August 22.

208 *"Charge him"*: McWilliam, interview, August 22.

208 *"going on a tour"*: Video of "Operation Chilly," shot by Paul Mullin, June 2001, https://www.youtube.com/watch?v=lWce39190B0.

209 *"One [falcon] seen flying"*: Jeffrey Lendrum, account of February 2010 Sri Lanka journey, found by Andy McWilliam on Lendrum's computer, shared with author.

209 *"Good rock face"*: Lendrum, account of February 2010 Sri Lanka journey.

210 *"Dubai customs were very iffy"*: Lendrum, account of February 2010 Sri Lanka journey.

210 *"I don't remember that"*: Lendrum, interview by author, Centurion, South Africa, December 18, 2017.

210 *"the effects of global warming"*: McWilliam, interview by author, Liverpool, January 21, 2018.

211 *"in all probability, came from the supply of eggs"*: Prosecutor, *Regina v. Jeffrey Paul Lendrum*, before His Honour Judge Hudson, Crown Court Warwick, August 19, 2010.

211 *"Karma's a bitch"*: Mullin, phone interview by author, May 3, 2019.

211 *"I was with Lendrum"*: Mullin, interview, May 3.

212 *"untested source"*: McWilliam, interview, January 21.

213 *"If you've got somebody local"*: McWilliam, interview, May 3.

213 *"He knows more about the wild birds"*: Ian Guildford, interview by author, Garw Valley, Wales, May 1, 2018.

213 *"If [security] opened"*: Jeffrey Lendrum, phone interview by author, February 23, 2018.

214 *"senior members of UAE society"*: McWilliam, PowerPoint display, NWCU, shared with author.

214 *"He's well traveled"*: Nevin Hunter, phone interview by author, October 25, 2017.

214 *"I sat down with Andy"*: Hunter, phone interview, October 25.

215 *"Peregrines and gyrfalcons"*: Alan Roberts, phone interview by author, September 7, 2017.

216 *"I've been to court"*: McWilliam, interview, January 21.

216 *"You all right?"*: McWilliam, interview, January 21.

217 *"The environmental crime"*: Judge Christopher Hodson, *Regina v. Jeffrey Paul Lendrum*, Crown Court Warwick, August 19, 2010.

217 *"At the end of the day"*: Hodson, *Regina v. Jeffrey Paul Lendrum*.

218 *"Bloody hell"*: Andy McWilliam, phone interview by author, May 2018.

218 *"Caged: The £70K Egg Snatcher"*: *Daily Mirror*, August 20, 2010, p. 3.

218 *"A Bird in the Hand, a Smuggler in Jail"*: the *Times*, August 20, 2010, p. 1.

218 *"Jailed, Former Soldier Caught"*: *Daily Mail*, August 20, 2010, p. 30.

218 *"a former member"*: Mark Hughes, "Ex-Soldier Jailed for Theft of Rare Falcon Eggs," *The Independent*, August 20, 2010, p. 7.

218 *"The Rare Falcon Chicks Saved"*: *Daily Express*, August 20, 2010, p. 3.

219 *"Few of the end users"*: P. C. Mundy, "The Lendrum Case: Retrospective 2," *Honeyguide* 56, no. 2 (September 2010).

220 *"the world's poorest thief"*: Michelle Conway, interview by author, London, January 9, 2019.

Chapter Fifteen: Prison

222 *"You got hit for taking birds?"*: Jeffrey Lendrum, phone interview by author, March 16, 2018.

222 *"a guy at the top of his game"*: Andy McWilliam, interview by author, Liverpool, August 22, 2017.

224 *"It was spur of the moment"*: Lendrum, phone interview, March 16.

224 *"your pilot friend"*: Lendrum, phone interview, March 16.

224 *"If I hadn't saved those birds"*: Andy McWilliam, interview by author, Liverpool, January 21, 2018.

225 *"manifestly excessive and out of step"*: Lord Justice Moore-Bick, Mrs. Justice Cox, and Sir Christopher Holland, *Regina v. Jeffrey Paul Lendrum*, Court of Appeal (Criminal Division), February 1, 2011.

225 *"He had no bills"*: Charles Graham, phone interview by author, January 14, 2019.

226 *"Jeff had this South African"*: Graham, phone interview, January 14.

226 *"He told me he was finished"*: Craig Hunt, phone interview by author, January 20, 2019.

226 *"is excited to travel"*: *African Hunting Gazette*, notice posted on AfricaHunting .com, April 8, 2013, https://www.africahunting.com/threads/jeffrey -lendrum-of-african-hunting-gazette-convicted-wildlife-smuggler.10615/.

227 *"Hey Andy, it's Jeffrey"*: McWilliam, interview, August 22.

227 *"I thought to myself"*: McWilliam, interview, August 22.

228 *"People will still follow"*: McWilliam, interview, August 22.

228 *"You can stay with me"*: Lendrum, phone interview, March 16.

229 *"He's filled with so much shit"*: Andy McWilliam, interview by author, Martin Mere Wetlands Reserve, England, October 2, 2017.

229 *"Cop's Work on the Wild Side"*: Douglas Walker, "Cop's Work on the Wild Side," *The Sun*, February 11, 2012.

229 *"Before I took over"*: Walker, "Cop's Work."

230 *"Bring it on"*: McWilliam, interview, October 2.

230 *"Jeffrey Lendrum of African Hunting Gazette"*: Jerome Philippe, post on message board, AfricaHunting.com, April 8, 2013, https://www.africahunting.com/threads/jeffrey-lendrum-of-african-hunting-gazette-convicted-wildlife-smuggler.10615/.

230 *"Is African Hunting Gazette letting"*: "africauntamed," post on AfricaHunting.com, April 8, 2013.

231 *"I knew I was running"*: Richard Lendrum, post on AfricaHunting.com, July 5, 2017, https://www.africahunting.com/threads/jeffrey-lendrum-of-african-hunting-gazette-convicted-wildlife-smuggler.10615/.

231 *"What I did was stupid"*: Jeffrey Lendrum, as "Bell407," post on AfricaHunting.com, April 10, 2013.

231 *"horrific"*: Richard Lendrum, interview by author, Rosebank, Johannesburg, South Africa, December 18, 2017.

231 *"wildlife trafficker"*: Richard Lendrum, post on AfricaHunting.com, July 5.

Chapter Sixteen: Patagonia

234 *"the desolate place of bad spirits"*: *The Rough Guide to Chile* (London: Rough Guides UK, September 2015), https://www.roughguides.com/destinations/south-america/chile/southern-patagonia/parque-nacional-pali-aike/.

236 *"Is it still there?"*: Nicolas Fernández, interview by author, Punta Arenas, Chile, October 19, 2018.

237 *"at the highest global"*: Andy McWilliam, quoted in "Award for Birmingham Cleaner Who Caught Egg Smuggler," BBC News, October 6, 2010.

237 *"the highest level"*: Guy Shorrock, quoted by Claire Marshall, "Egg Smuggler Was Wildlife Criminal," BBC News, August 19, 2010.

237 *"I'm uneasy about this"*: Nicolas Fernández, email provided to author, October 19, 2018.

239 *"Basically you've got to know"*: Jeffrey Lendrum, phone interview by author, February 23, 2018.

239　*"being less conspicuous"*: David Ellis, Beth Ann Sabo, James F. Fackler, and Brian A. Millsap, "Prey of the Peregrine Falcon (*Falco Peregrinus Cassini*) in Southern Argentina and Brazil," *Journal of the Raptor Research Foundation*, 2002, Vol. 36, no. 4: 318.

240　*"He was a nice, friendly"*: Fernández, interview, October 19.

241　*"We received the following"*: Rafael Asenjo, email provided to author by Rodrigo Tomei (Lendrum's attorney), October 14, 2018.

242　*"They're chicken eggs"*: Rodrigo Tomei, interview by author, Guarulhos, Brazil, October 14, 2018.

243　*"They caught me"*: Tomei, interview, October 14.

243　*"he could convince"*: Tomei, interview, October 14.

244　*"laughable"*: Judge Paulo Marcos Rodrigues de Almeida, Federal Justice Court, judgment and sentence, Guarulhos, Brazil, December 14, 2015.

244　*"Let's have coffee"*: Tomei, interview, October 14.

245　*"During [downtime] in Itaí"*: João Batista, Jr., "Os presos que vêm de fora: Torre de Babel carcerária guarda 1,443 detentos de 89 nacionalidades. Populacão nunca foi tão grande e não para de aumentar," *Veja* (Brazil), August 6, 2011.

245　*"Sometimes not even"*: "Information Pack for British Prisoners in Brazil," British Embassy Brazil, July 21, 2015.

246　*"There was a danger"*: Tomei, interview, October 14.

246　*"I had nothing but shit in Brazil"*: Jeffrey Lendrum, phone interview by author, March 16, 2018.

246　*"contagious"*: Michelle Conway, interview by author, London, January 9, 2019.

247　*"Then I saw an article"*: Howard Waller, interview by author, Inverness, Scotland, January 23, 2018.

247　*"I knew that I was going to die"*: Lendrum, phone interview, March 16.

247　*"Nobody was looking"*: Tomei, interview, October 14.

248　*"Hey Rodrigo, I'm in"*: Tomei, interview, October 14.

248　*"Ex-SAS Rare Egg"*: Ben Hurst, "Ex-SAS Rare Egg Thief Who Tried to Smuggle Birds Through Birmingham Airport on the Run," *Birmingham News*, January 6, 2017.

248　*"Britain's Most Protected"*: Abigail O'Leary, "Britain's Most Protected Bird Under Threat From SAS-Trained Wildlife Hunter," *Daily Mirror*, January 5, 2017.

Chapter Seventeen: Gauteng

250　*"Andy McWilliam is telling"*: Jeffrey Lendrum, phone interview by author, May 10, 2017.

250 *"manna from heaven"*: Jeffery Lendrum, phone interview, May 10.

250 *"complete and utter rubbish"*: Andy McWilliam, email to author, April 3, 2018.

251 *"She is very stressed"*: Julia Dupree, email to author, December 3, 2017.

251 *"What f****** audacity!"*: Pat Lorber, email to author, November 16, 2017.

252 *"You're sworn to secrecy"*: John Brebner, Black Eagle Project, interview by author, Bulawayo, Zimbabwe, December 11, 2017.

252 *"That's a fairly new"*: Brebner, interview, December 11.

253 *"He's got a very tough life"*: Richard Lendrum, interview by author, Rosebank, South Africa, December 18, 2017.

254 *"We both love wildlife"*: Richard Lendrum, interview, December 18.

254 *"Obviously, there are breeders"*: Richard Lendrum, interview, December 18.

255 *"My short-term memory is failing"*: Jeffrey Lendrum, phone interview by author, December 18, 2017.

256 *"You probably recognized"*: Jeffrey Lendrum, interview by author, December 18, 2017.

257 *"He seems to be successful"*: Bob Elliot, RSPB, interview, "Notorious Bird Egg Thief on the Run in Brazil," BBC Today radio program, January 6, 2017.

257 *"The devil is in the details"*: Jeffrey Lendrum, interview, December 18.

258 *"Things happen"*: Jeffrey Lendrum, interview, December 18.

259 *"Do you want to steal"*: Jeffrey Lendrum, interview, December 18.

Epilogue

261 *"I'm at my son's graduation"*: Author's notebook, June 24, 2018.

261 *"Call if you want"*: Jeffrey Lendrum, email to author, June 24, 2018.

262 *"Rare Bird Eggs Importation"*: "Rare Bird Eggs Importation Prevented by Border Force at Heathrow," National Wildlife Crime Unit press release, June 28, 2018.

264 *"free medical care"*: Craig Hunt, phone interview by author, January 20, 2019.

265 *"Jeff is gentle as a lamb"*: Michelle Conway, interview by author, London, January 9, 2019.

266 *"A couple of times"*: Jeffrey Lendrum, testimony, *The Queen v. Jeffrey Lendrum*, Snaresbrook Crown Court, January 10, 2019.

267 *"South Africa was cutting"*: Jeffrey Lendrum, testimony, *The Queen v. Jeffrey Lendrum*, January 10.

267 *"You are a convicted smuggler"*: Sean Sullivan, prosecutor, cross-examination of Jeffrey Lendrum, *The Queen v. Jeffrey Lendrum*, January 9, 2019.

267 *"completely implausible"*: Judge Neil Saunders, judgment, *The Queen v. Jeffrey Lendrum*, January 10, 2019.

268 *"rife"*: "Pentonville Is 'Crumbling and Rife with Vermin,'" BBC News, August 22, 2018.

NOTES

268 *"There's more hits"*: Jeffrey Lendrum, testimony, *The Queen v. Jeffrey Lendrum*, January 9, 2019.

269 *"bad character"*: Andy McWilliam, interview by author, Liverpool, January 11, 2019.

269 *"As long as you're"*: McWilliam, interview, January 11.

271 *"It's out of our control"*: McWilliam, interview, January 11.

271 *"I got twelve months' probation"*: *Poached*, directed by Timothy Wheeler (Ignite Channel, 2015), on-camera interview with John Kinsley.

271 *"reveals the issues"*: *Poached*, on-camera interview with Kinsley.

272 *"I went round"*: McWilliam, interview, January 11.

274 *"incorporated as a sacred sign"*: H. P. Blavatsky, *The Secret Doctrine* (New York: Penguin, 2016; original edition published 1888), 265.

274 *"I think that if required"*: Tim Birkhead, *The Most Perfect Thing: Inside (and Outside) a Bird's Egg* (London: Bloomsbury, 2017), 15.

274 *"It's like meeting"*: McWilliam, interview, January 11.

INDEX